FOOL'S PROMISE

ETEREAN EMPIRE

BOOK II

ANGELA BOORD

Impossible Books

For all the storytellers
Thank you for being generous and brave enough to share your worlds with us.

AUTHOR'S NOTE

If you're still with me after *Fortune's Fool*, you probably know that this story will go some dark and heavy places. In addition to scenes of graphic violence, there are also mentions of pregnancy loss, past trauma, past abuse, addiction and recovery, suicidal ideation, depression, and PTSD. But I promise that there will also be light in the darkness. (The romantic scenes are also a little steamier.) My greatest hope is that Kyrra and Arsenault's story will be somewhere you can escape to the way I escaped into so many other authors' stories when I needed a break from my own life. But if you need to sit this one out, I understand.

If you're ready, though—buckle up and here we go!

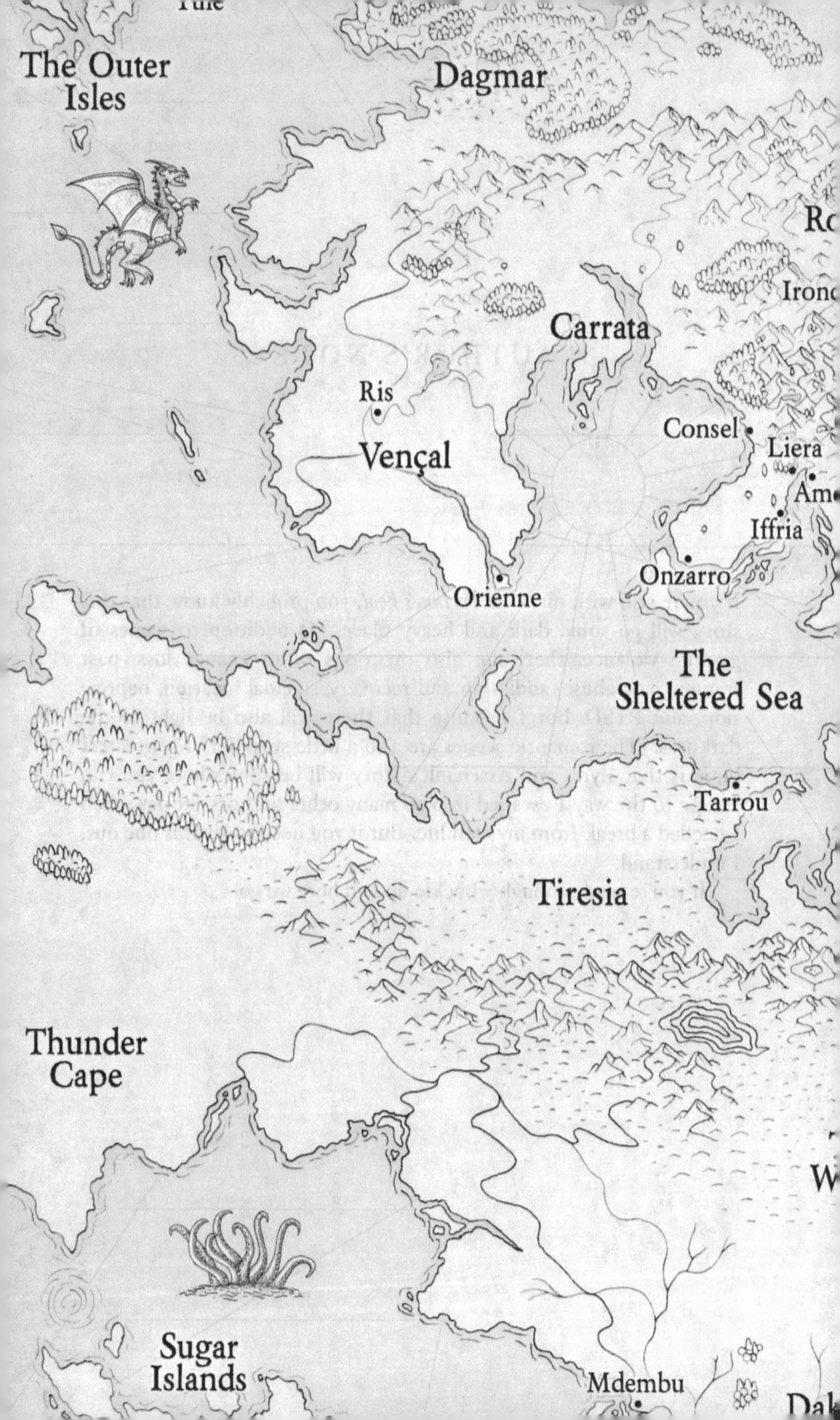
Thule
The Outer Isles
Dagmar
Ro
Irono
Carrata
Ris
Consel
Liera
Am
Vençal
Iffria
Onzarro
Orienne
The Sheltered Sea
Tarrou
Tiresia
Thunder Cape
W
Sugar Islands
Mdembu
Da
Da

ETEREA
Gorodnii
Kavo
Greater
Qalfa
N
W
E
S
Joffra
The
Nefeth
The Great
Salt Desert

PREVIOUSLY

For the past five years, the city of Liera has been ravaged by a war waged between two rival merchant families—the Prinze and the Caprine—and their allies. The rivalry between the families is an old one, but the war is blamed on a single woman...

Kyrra d'Aliente.

As a teenager, Kyrra was seduced and betrayed by Cassis di Prinze, the son of the most powerful man in Liera. After she became pregnant, her mother pressured her into ending the pregnancy so the Prinze would have no legal claims to the lands of the Aliente—famous throughout the world for their silk production.

When Kyrra's crime was discovered, she was stripped of her House name, affiliation, and privileges, her right arm amputated as an eternal mark of her transgression. Permitted to live on her father's land only as a serf, she retained few rights and possessed no future beyond her work in the boiling rooms.

There, a gavaro named Arsenault befriended her, helping her heal emotionally and physically. Over the course of their years together on the Aliente silk farm, Kyrra and Arsenault slowly chipped away at the isolating wounds of their pasts and fell in love. But Arsenault was also working undercover as a spy for Kyrra's father, collecting information about Geoffre di Prinze's plans to attack the Aliente. To protect Arsenault, Kyrra killed a woman who threatened to reveal his identity, and her own father sentenced her to hang in a sacrifice meant to convince the Prinze that the Aliente had bowed to their superiority.

Unwilling to stand by while Kyrra offered herself as a sacrifice,

Arsenault rescued her with magic, though magic was forbidden to him by the gods. He gave her a new magical arm made of metal, then extracted a promise from her that she would flee to the relative safety of bordering Rojornick while he remained to captain her father's army as it battled the Prinze. The Prinze eventually decimated the Aliente in a massacre at the battle of Kafrin Gorge, leaving Kyrra as the last remaining member of her House and Arsenault reportedly dead.

As a tenuous peace now reigns, Kyrra returns to Liera to look for Arsenault. Nine years after her ill-fated tryst with Cassis di Prinze, Kyrra d'Aliente is a changed woman. She disguises herself as a man and fights as a gavaro. After searching fruitlessly for Arsenault for months, she's offered a job she can't refuse—to kill her old lover, Cassis di Prinze.

Kyrra takes the job, not only for revenge but also to interrogate Cassis about Arsenault's whereabouts.

Rumors that Arsenault betrayed the Aliente have been swirling since war's end. Besides working as a spy among the Prinze, Arsenault also had a close association with Jon Barra, an erstwhile Dakkaran merchant who is in reality a prince of the Dakkaran royal family, conquered by the Prinze in their quest to monopolize the gun trade. Kyrra refuses to believe Arsenault would betray her, having faith that his love for her superseded all these murky associations.

But her attempts to buy a black-market pistol are constantly thwarted by a mysterious pursuer who murders her landlord and shoots her friend Razi, injuring his arm so badly that it must be amputated. When Jon Barra betrays Kyrra to the Prinze, she discovers her mysterious pursuer is actually Arsenault. Erelf, the god of magic, cursed him long ago for the accidental murder of his daughter, Arsenault's wife. The god exacts his revenge by refusing to allow Arsenault to die, stealing and twisting Arsenault's memories according to his whim with every resurrection. Not only is Arsenault far older than Kyrra imagined, he also retains none of his memories of Kyrra; Erelf stole them all when Arsenault "died" at Kafrin Gorge.

Kyrra escapes the Prinze by taking a prison guard hostage, only to discover the guard is Geoffre's di Prinze's nephew Mikelo, whom Geoffre is grooming to be his heir. Mikelo reveals his magical abilities only when a shepherd-turned-courtesan named Silva stabs Arsenault in revenge for what he swears was Arsenault's betrayal of the Aliente before Kafrin.

But Mikelo's magical healing returns Arsenault's memories of Kyrra and of Kafrin Gorge. Arsenault never betrayed Kyrra or the

Aliente; the Aliente were defeated by Kyrra's father's stubborn adherence to the letter of the law and his assumption that Geoffre di Prinze would also obey it.

Before Arsenault can fully recover, Kyrra, Arsenault, and Mikelo ride into an ambush laid by Cassis and captained by an old rival of Arsenault's, a gavaro named Lobardin, who takes them captive and brings them to Cassis at the Aliente hunting lodge, where Kyrra received her new arm five years before. There she learns that Arsenault and Jon have planned all along to play Cassis and Geoffre against each other and that Geoffre has been using her to get rid of Cassis for him. She also discovers that Cassis's lover, whom she was supposed to rescue, has already escaped to safety, pregnant with his heir. All that will happen at the lodge is a battle between father and son. The key to their destruction is Arsenault, who passes Geoffre's plans to Cassis but won't use his magic to destroy Geoffre as Cassis hopes. Instead, Arsenault gives himself up to Erelf to prevent him from taking Kyrra as a bride.

Just as Arsenault refused to stand by while her father hanged her, Kyrra refuses to allow Arsenault to sacrifice himself for her. With the help of the two gods who watch over her and Mikelo's magic shaping the metal in her character, Kyrra challenges Erelf to a duel for Arsenault's life.

But victory comes with a price. Grievously wounded, even after Mikelo's magical healing, her survival depends on the goddess of fortune for whom she's named. Fortune sends her back into a Liera balanced on the precipice of chaos, its most powerful citizen dead, his sons now embroiled in a battle for the Householder's Chair...

A NEW BEGINNING

KYRRA

I BEGAN MY THIRD LIFE AS I BEGAN MY SECOND—HIDING FROM THE
Prinze on the road to Rojornick.

This time I wasn't alone in the wilderness, my only reminder of
Arsenault a new arm made of cold metal. I had a bed, a roof over my
head...and Arsenault himself. It sometimes felt as if his presence itself
was magic, so much more unbelievable than my arm, which had
become commonplace to me over the past five years.

It should have been the kind of beginning that comes after the end
of a fairy story. The part where the lovers begin their new lives
together and live to a ripe old age in boring peace and happiness.

But in some ways, this new beginning reminded me of the past,
and the time I'd spent recovering from my amputation. I wasn't
tucked, forgotten, into the back room of a mediocre chirurgeon's
practice, but healing from the wounds Erelf had dealt me was slow
and fraught with setbacks. My arm hung mangled and useless at my
side, almost as if it had been severed again.

As I drifted through fevers and dreams, time ceased to have meaning. I saw through the eyes of other people and spoke to gods. In this
vast, turbulent sea of magic, there was no *me* or *you*. I was like a shipwrecked sailor who'd lost his craft, fighting to catch driftwood washed
past me by angry waves.

The magic was always restless, always moving. There was no
moment when it calmed and I could rest. People talked about magic
like it was a force Fixers harnessed and used. To me it had always
seemed like an aspect of nature that struck without warning, wreaking

havoc like a flood or earthquake. But what if it was something else entirely, an entity beyond men and gods—a giant soul of which we were all a part?

Magic patched me together.

And once it was invited, it didn't want to leave.

⚜

A MEMORY, PERHAPS MY STRONGEST.

Arsenault's voice. "Kyrra, stay with me. *Kyrra!*"

When I was fevered and dreaming, I felt like I was underwater. All the world happened above me—warped, refracted faces peering down, voices muffled and distorted, words ringing hollowly inside my head.

Then Arsenault would plunge into this blurry, watery world, crashing it apart, to haul me out before I drowned completely.

When I surfaced this time, he was holding me upright on a bed. His collarbone pressed into my cheek, my head tucked into the hollow of his throat. I leaned into his chest, and his warmth enveloped me. He had become the signpost of my reality, the only way I knew whether I was awake or dreaming anymore.

"Jon!" he called. "Bring me a knife, some wrapping—"

My left arm throbbed as if it harbored a smoldering fire. Memories of my amputation assaulted me, the claustrophobic darkness of the chirurgeon's back room. I clutched at Arsenault's sleeve.

"Don't cut my arm off," I begged. "Please, do whatever you have to, but—*Arsenault*."

He exhaled in a relieved rush that ruffled my hair. "The knife isn't for you, Kyrra; it's for me. Jon!"

Jon's mouth formed a grim line as he handed Arsenault the knife. My mind catalogued details in a topsy-turvy way—Jon's rumpled clothes, his locs bound in a scarf instead of tied back, Arsenault's unlaced shirt... I was also wearing a man's shirt, its hem bunched up above my knees.

Had they been asleep? Why did Arsenault need a knife? What in all the hells was going on?

Arsenault bent to catch my gaze. "Do you know me, Kyrra?"

His voice was gentle, but his words and the way he watched me shook me.

I touched the metallic silver-white streak that shot through his black hair. Brushed my thumb past the jagged scar near his eye, the scar that had newly reappeared after Erelf had been forced to give him back both his memories and his magic. The faint green remnants of a bruise lay along his cheekbone and his nose looked more like it used to. Had Geoffre broken it?

"What kind of question is that?" I asked shakily. "Arsenault."

Arsenault brought my fingers to his lips. I wanted to touch him with my metal hand, but my arm would only lie in my lap, dead and cold as the hilt of a sword, the only thing alive about it the brilliant reflections of light from its surface.

"Kyrra. Keep your eyes on me. Not the arm. Can you do that?"

When I nodded, his expression eased. "In my country, a man might pledge himself to a woman, make himself blood of her blood, and it would be her decision to accept or not. Do you understand?"

"You mean as a protector? A knight, like in stories?"

"Not exactly. He'll live as if he belongs to her. Even if they can't wed."

"Why would she be so cruel? To accept such a vow, then refuse to wed him?"

"Maybe she's sick. Or maybe she can't consent to wed because of her family. It happens."

His gaze felt like it was boring into me, though his words were as calm and measured as always. But our *always* had been a long time ago. Maybe he was different now. Maybe there was something about this situation I didn't understand.

"Why are you telling me this?" I asked.

"Jon, Mikelo, and Silva will witness my vow. If you're in your right mind enough to accept or reject it."

"Are you asking me to *marry* you?"

I felt as if I had stepped off a ledge. My mind was chasing my body as it hurtled through the air, unable to catch up.

What would I need for a wedding? Why would he do such a thing in the middle of the night? Why did my left arm hurt so much? Gods, I couldn't be in danger of losing it, could I?

I couldn't marry Arsenault like this. "I have no name, Arsenault. All I could give you is a love oath—"

He ran his fingers over mine, the calluses of his fingertips comforting and rough. "It's my pledge to you. You don't have to do anything but accept...or reject it." The smile he had attempted faltered, leaving his expression weary and earnest. "Kyrra. I made so many mistakes. I need to make them up to you."

"Right now?"

Arsenault brought his head up and I followed his gaze to Jon,

Mikelo, and Silva standing there dressed only in shirts and trousers, their worried faces illuminated by candlelight. Mikelo's curls were a wild mess. They looked as if they had all been awakened suddenly.

"Arsenault?" I asked, alarmed.

"*Kyrra.*" My name came out as a ragged, pleading breath this time. "Let me make you blood of my blood. I should have made this vow years ago. I don't want to lose my chance now."

"I'll spend the rest of my life with you, don't you know that?"

Silva, standing beside Mikelo, choked as if he were swallowing tears.

I stared at him, feeling increasingly wild, then back at Arsenault. I knew that look.

"You all think I'm dying, don't you! Ekyra wouldn't have sent me back just to die of fever. It doesn't make sense!"

Arsenault's tight expression softened along with his voice. "I don't think you're dying. But the magic wants you."

"Arsenault," Jon interrupted. "This is a bad idea. She's in no shape to decide—"

As if I wasn't sitting right there? As if I were a child?

"I know my own mind!" I shouted at him.

Jon put a hand on my shoulder in apology, more gently than I expected. Desperately, I searched for memories of what had happened after I woke from Ekyra's dream, but I had no idea how long I'd spent in this state.

"Arsenault," Mikelo said hoarsely. "Jon is right. Save it for later."

"There might not *be* a later," Arsenault answered through his teeth. Then he took a deep breath and spoke in a determined voice.

"Kyrra d'Aliente, daughter of Pallo, I, Ari, son of Gunnar, make this vow, that your honor shall be my honor, your health my health, your life my life, your blood my blood. Before all the gods, I vow to be true to my oath until my last breath, or may the gods strike me down in my betrayal."

It took a moment for his words to sink in.

"Arsenault! *Your* last breath? You'll live far, far longer than I ever will!"

"I offer you my honor, my breath, my life, my heart. Do you accept it?"

I searched his eyes for...I don't know what. Some hint that this wasn't as serious as it seemed. But all I saw was honesty and a desperate kind of hope. I knew he was doing a foolish thing, and maybe he did, too, but here he was, throwing himself over the chasm of the last five years like a lifeline. How could I reject him? He was giving me everything and more.

I let out all my fears in a long rush of breath. "*Yes.*"

He caught his own breath and slashed the knife across his palm. Blood welled up behind the blade, gleaming crimson. His fingers curled in reflex and the blood leaked out beneath them in a thin stream.

"Give me your hand," he said, his voice rough with pain.

Mikelo startled forward. "But the fever's in that arm!"

"She's not strong enough to close the gates on her magic. That's the problem, not the fever. I've burned the wound twice with silver; it will heal." Arsenault turned back to me. "Kyrra."

I opened my palm and held it up for him. "Let me make you a vow, too."

He gave me a painful smile. "When you're well."

"Arsenault," Jon murmured worriedly. "How many promises can you keep?"

I had never been able to tell what Jon really thought of me. I didn't know now if he thought the vow would be bad for Arsenault, bad for me, or wrong for both of us.

"I've no other vows like this one," Arsenault replied, his mouth a tight line, almost a grimace.

"But you made one once, didn't you?"

Arsenault whipped around to face him, his fist clenched so blood dripped down his wrist. I had never seen him look so angry. And hurt.

His wife. The vow he'd broken when the knife meant for his brother had found her instead. The vow that had set him on the road to his ruin.

Did Jon think I would refuse Arsenault's promise and shatter him like that? It was more than words and blood, or even all the years that would spin on for him after my death, whenever it came. It was more than an apology. It was the gift of commitment, the promise of honesty, the trust to make a new beginning.

I tried to grab the knife myself, but my right hand still wouldn't move. "Hurry, before the blood clots."

Arsenault took my hand and slashed it, firm and sure, straight across the palm.

The pain welled up suddenly, along with the blood, and the murkiness in my head burned away like clouds revealing a blue, sunlit sky.

"Blood of my blood," I whispered as Arsenault took my hand in his own. "I hereby pledge to be faithful to you in good times and in bad, in sickness and in health, to love you and to honor you all the days of my life."

Arsenault looked up in mute shock.

"I do so consent," I continued. "I consent and pledge of my own free will."

Once I had hoped to say these words at my own wedding, standing before the other members of my House. Before my titles had been stripped, my arm severed, and my family stolen from me. Once I'd wanted the fancy silk wedding dress, the dancing, the tea cakes. But now I knew the words themselves were enough. The words and the man sitting next to me.

Silva wrapped our hands together in a bandage. Arsenault's hand shook almost as much as mine, but we clung to each other anyway.

"Kiss her, Arsenault," Silva whispered.

For a moment, Arsenault stared at me as if he were stunned. Then I leaned toward him and he toward me. His lips were cool and sweet, as if he'd been drinking tea with honey.

My other memories are a tumble of fire and pain. Of the magic coaxing me to do and say things I never would have on my own. Of Ires wanting me to listen to his mad schemes.

But that kiss stood out like a shining island in a great expanse of angry sea.

AFTER THE BATTLE
CASSIS AND LOBARDIN

THE CORPSEFIRES HAD BEEN BURNING FOR A WEEK, SHROUDING THE valley with their foul black smoke.

Cassis didn't like being so exposed down here on the flat. Not with marauding bands of Geoffre's gavaros plundering the countryside, and a tight core of gavaros in control of his father's guns huddling behind Geoffre's earthworks. Cassis had allowed Geoffre's men to clear off their dead, but he didn't for a moment trust Devid to allow him the same. If Geoffre had taught him anything, it was that rules in warfare were more like guidelines. When it came down to life or death, *winning* was always most important.

He would have left the dead to the vultures if Geoffre hadn't lain somewhere on this field. All he needed was for his father's ghost to haunt him because his body hadn't been properly burned or interred.

Murder markers already littered the valley, stone reminders of generations of violent death. It had been a land of blood and fire long before this battle had fed the earth more corpses. The most recent markers were haphazard limestone monoliths, dedicated to the troops who'd battled and died to control the Aliente hunting lodge in the war of the Houses. Its strategic location at the bottleneck of a valley and the Eterean road made it a treasure even if the fabled Eterean riches buried on its grounds were only a myth. The lodge had once belonged to Attrasca, just like the Villa d'Aliente, or so it was said, but now...

It was a cold stone building, full of strange passageways and stolen furniture, and at night, the wind sounded like the wailing ghosts of the Aliente women who had died within its walls. Cassis was *sure* he'd seen the shade of Kyrra's mother patrolling the upper hall where she'd died, her dress still soaked in blood spilled by her own hand.

Gods, the flurry of sheer, frenetic revenge Geoffre had descended into after he'd watched Carolla die. And where had it led but to the horrible treachery at Kafrin, to empty pits dug to discover non-existent Eterean treasure, and now, these big bonfires of bodies that took for fucking ever to burn in the sleety drizzle that had been falling for the past week. But no sign of Geoffre's body anywhere.

Maybe his gavaros took him. Maybe they didn't count on me not to desecrate the corpse or to just let him lie.

But why would anyone have picked up his corpse after the gods had touched him like they had?

He needed to bury his father. And he needed the sword Geoffre had carried, too, if he was going to claim the Householder's Chair before Devid could.

Kinstealer. Its name seemed both ironic and appropriate.

"Mestere Prinze?" the man standing next to him asked hesitantly, voice muffled by the scarf he wore as a mask. He displayed his white messenger tunic prominently over his coat so nobody could miss it. "I've told you all we've been able to discover. The remains of the horses and the ropes used to quarter Andris have been burned, their ashes boxed. To which temple shall we send them?"

Cassis dug an embroidered handkerchief out of his pocket and wiped uselessly at his forehead. All the wool and leather he was wearing kept him too warm and the smoky fires reminded him too damn much of that day when they'd fought their way past the hopelessly strung-out Aliente forces only to realize the price of victory was to watch a room full of women commit suicide. Nausea twisted his stomach, the sudden visceral memory of that day overlaid with the battle he'd fought days ago on this ground, which had also ended in victory—for him, not his father—but not because of anything he'd done.

The Aliente had finally gotten their revenge. Kyrra and Arsenault had won that battle, not him. He'd heard the stories—Kyrra, half clad in metal like a valkyr, and Geoffre, still alive with a lead ball buried in his forehead, as if he'd been animated by the sheer force of his personality.

To which god did you give thanks when your forces defeated one of the gods' own? Should he send the ashes to Erelf as appeasement? *Oh, so sorry, didn't mean to upset you, but my father was driving our city to the brink of disaster.* Or should he send the ashes to a different god? *Look, I may have made a mistake in waging this war and making my allies, can I count on you if your brother takes his revenge on me?*

Gods. Damn. It.

But which fucking gods?

"Mestere?"

"Ekyra," Cassis said suddenly. "Send them to Ekyra's temple and let her sort it out. In a way it's Ekyra's fault, isn't it?"

"I'm—I'm sure I don't know, mestere," the messenger stammered, looking terrified. "I'm sure whatever you think is proper. The Silver Warrior—"

Cassis took a deep breath without thinking, sucked in lint from the scarf wrapped around his face, not to mention the *stench,* and started coughing. The man looked even more terrified. Eyes watering, Cassis pounded himself on the chest to clear his throat, driving the buckles of his leather jerkin into his breastbone.

Best leave Kyrra's involvement a legend for now; it was better for him that no one knew who she was. But it felt odd. Knowing it was *Kyrra* who had finally rid the world of his father. Knowing she had fought that battle for Arsenault and the goddess of fortune had been on her side.

It always comes back to Arsenault.

All the old feelings of jealousy and anger and betrayal smoldered in him like the smoke from the corpsefires he couldn't escape. Whenever he thought there would be peace, there were always more corpses to burn.

"The Silver Warrior is a legend," Cassis snapped. "Probably a lie spread by Jon Barra."

"Mestere, I saw myself—"

"I don't care what you saw! I just need to know where my father's body is, so I can bury him and erect a marker in his name. I don't need commentary!"

The man bowed low, hand crossed over his heart. "Forgive me, mestere. I do have one other piece of news if you'd care to hear it."

"Out with it, so I can get back to the lodge and out of this sodding rain."

The man hesitantly straightened and pulled an envelope from his tunic. "We received this from the enemy camp, mestere. It appears to be an invitation to dine with Mestere Devid di Prinze this evening."

Cassis snatched the letter and unfolded it quickly. In Devid's ungraceful handwriting, he read:

Dear brother: Congratulations on defeating our father. Please do me the great honor of negotiating a truce at four of the clock today in the Prinze camp.

   —Your loving brother, Devid

"The Prinze camp," Cassis growled. "Now that our father is out of the way, of course he assumes he'll be Householder. As if I fought that battle to do him a favor and now I'll just say, *yes, mestere*, and put my knee in the dirt to swear him fealty like a fucking Amoran. Just like he's always wanted."

Cassis ground his teeth and crumpled the soggy letter in his fist. He felt like he was steaming in his damp and dirty clothes, suffocating in the stench of sour, charred meat he carried with him wherever he went.

"If Devid thinks I'm going to stroll into his camp like a lamb to slaughter, he's insane. Do you have a writing kit so I can pen a reply?"

"Of-of course, mestere."

"Fine, hand it here. Now, so you can take it back to him."

"Yes, mestere." The messenger fumbled a small case out of his tunic. "But the ink will blot in the rain—"

"I don't care about the ink or the blasted rain. Tell Devid he can meet me on the battlefield if he wants to see me. And bring his own damn tent and dinner, since he's the one sending the invitation."

Only after stomping away did he realize letting Devid provide the food meant Devid could poison him. But if Devid *had* food, that was good to know...because Cassis was running out of it and running out of money to buy more.

The problem with being your own captain was that you were in charge of every damn thing. He splashed through the ashy, shit-littered muck and went to find Lobardin.

❦

LOBARDIN

KYRRA, I WISH I'D NEVER MET YOU. I WISH I HAD WALKED AWAY FROM Jon that day on the Talos when he offered me a job that paid in kacin. What in all the hells was I thinking?

Lobardin retched into the metal chamberpot at his feet again. He'd eaten so little in the past few days almost nothing came up, but his stomach felt like it was trying to turn itself inside out anyway. The dry heaves went on and on, and when they stopped, he was shaking and covered in a cold sweat. A rag appeared as if out of nowhere and he wiped his mouth with trembling hands.

The woman sitting across from him sighed. She wore Tiresian-style split skirts embroidered in raucous crimson and azure. Her black braids, threaded through with blue silk ribbons and glass beads, flashed and clacked when she moved. The colors and sounds were duller and less fascinating than when he was smoking kacin, but at the same time intense and unbearable. Every sensation in his body seemed painfully, grotesquely magnified. The colors of her skirts chewed their way under his skin like worms of pain. The light sparkling off the beads were tiny shards of glass grinding into his eyes. He wished she would go away and stay in equal measures, which was where he was with everything right now.

His stomach threatened to heave again.

Junei grimaced as she took the rag and struggled onto her knees to grab the chamberpot. "I thought you'd be done puking by now."

"Well, I'm not," he croaked. "It seems to last longer every time."

"How many times have you tried to stop smoking kacin?"

"A lot. Three. Eight. I can't remember. Oh, gods." His stomach cramped. He lay on his side and brought his knees toward his chest, hugging his midsection as if he could squeeze all the misery from his body. It didn't seem right that the absence of a thing could make you feel like this—too full and too empty at the same time. Maybe it would be smarter to ease his way into giving it up. He could trade his dinner ration for a sliver. Even a few tiny grains. He wouldn't have to go through this torture if he gave the kacin up a little at a time.

Why was smoking kacin so bad anyway? He wasn't one of those kinless addicts in Liera who forgot to eat and died in their sleep, covered in piss—

The mere thought of food and piss made his stomach revolt again. He barely struggled upright before retching this time. Only a string of saliva slithered over his chin, but gods, his ribs hurt. His nose—still healing from the blow Kyrra had dealt him with her metal fist—burned and throbbed. Surely he could use kacin for the pain.

The rag dabbed at his mouth again and a cup pressed against his lips. "Lobardin. Drink."

"I'll just throw it up," he said miserably.

"Try."

"You're good to me, Junei."

"I don't know why this sudden change of heart. You didn't seem to care to stop before."

"That was before." He pushed the cup away weakly after he drank. The lukewarm tea tasted vaguely of ginger and honey, something his stomach didn't resist outright, thank the gods. He waited to see if it would settle. When it did, he sighed in relief and sank slowly and carefully into the pallet of blankets spread on the cold, damp ground. Sleet pattered against the stretched wool cloth of the tent, but the brazier and the closeness of their bodies in the small space kept it reasonably snug. If the bloody weather ever let up and he stopped vomiting, he would need to treat the fabric with lanolin to keep it waterproof. The thought of grease made him nauseous again and he closed his eyes. If he only had some kacin.

Fabric rustled and a cold draft blew inside, followed by the low ring of metal as the chamberpot knocked against something; Junei must be dumping it outside. The sound of ringing metal reminded him too much of Kyrra's arm. He squeezed his eyes shut tighter to block out the memory of Kyrra lying mangled in the churned-up mud of the battlefield, Arsenault—white-faced—gripping her flesh hand so tightly it looked as if he would crush her bones. And dear gods, the blood—

This is ridiculous. I can't do it.

"Lobardin." Junei again. He could smell her, the scent of the oil she used in her hair. What was it? Almond? "Why did it matter, before and after? Before the battle? Or before that woman Cassis took prisoner, do you mean?"

He didn't know why Junei stayed with him; maybe Cassis had ordered her to, or maybe Jon wanted to squeeze something else out of him, damn the man. Lobardin shivered and burrowed into the blankets. "Both, maybe. When Kyr—when she—well, it was just—oh, gods, I don't know, it seemed like a good idea at the time. I spent all those years so fucking angry, pushed down by hatred. Like it was grinding me into the dirt."

But something had changed between him and Kyrra in those bedchambers in the lodge. He'd stood face to face with the demon Geoffre had made of him. He'd loathed that man, but that self had taken up more and more space until he'd wondered if he hadn't had their positions reversed all along. Maybe the world in the mirror was the real world and that horrible man was really who he was. Maybe the man he'd always thought of as his real self was only a reflection, a better version that existed only in his dreams.

He didn't know why he'd always wanted Kyrra so much. She was a pain in the arse. A beautiful pain in the arse and fucking dangerous and an idiot for thinking Arsenault was a hero. But it had sometimes felt, all those years ago, that maybe she understood. What it was like to fall so low, to be cast out of your House and exiled from everything you'd known, trampled on by Geoffre di Prinze—to have Ires in your head, always whispering at you, egging you on.

And yet, in spite of her downfall, she'd always been the stronger one. In that room, before she'd killed Geoffre, she'd been strong enough to help him see that he was standing *outside* the mirror, not inside it. When Lobardin had hired on with Cassis, he'd taken the first step toward wiping the mirror clean, but in that room with Kyrra and then on the battlefield with Geoffre, he'd stepped out of it completely, to stand on the right side of the silvered glass.

This was a harder road, but it was better. Was *going* to be better. Maybe. Except he couldn't do it. He wasn't strong enough.

"Lobardin, are you going to finish the story?"

"It's not much of a story," he murmured. He wished he could tell Junei—or anybody—about Kyrra, but he owed Kyrra that much, not to spread knowledge of her existence around. "Geoffre was dead," he said simply. "It seemed like I could be a better person. But she broke my godsdamned nose and now everything hurts. Surely just one pipe—"

"You told me to tell you no, so I am. You'll be through this in a few days. I've seen people go through it before."

"Surely not like this, Junei. I feel like I'm dying."

"That's what they all say, but eventually it stops."

"Maybe if you distracted me somehow."

Junei laughed. "Oh, you think you're so handsome, lying there in your own puke?"

"I think I'm vulnerable and in need of comfort. Surely, you'd spare a suffering man some comfort?"

"Are you sure you're trying to reform yourself?"

"I'm afraid I only have so much potential for reform. It doesn't extend to having enough pride not to beg."

"You'd get down on your knees, tell me how wonderful I am, ask *please* with all your pretty noble manners, like I was a lady and you were my—"

"Junei," he all but growled. He'd been joking, but the more she talked about it, the more his cock was convinced it was a good idea. How long had it been since he'd shared a bed with anyone? There had been the camp girl, but they'd both been smoking so much, maybe he'd dreamed it. Or maybe it hadn't been any good, a quick jerk of a hand in the dark, and she'd fallen in the mud and laughed—no, surely that was a dream—*shit*.

He opened his eyes and looked up at Junei. She was sitting cross-legged and leaning toward him, giving him an excellent view of her breasts, curved over the top of the leather stays that cinched her linen shirt like armor.

He wanted to reach for her, but that took too much effort, and anyway, she could hardly be serious. He didn't know what he looked like, but he knew what he *felt* like.

"Oh, please, Junei," he said, "let me make you squirm."

"You're an easy mark, Lobardin. But that's not exactly begging."

She crawled forward, her shoulder blades moving under her shirt in a sinuous way that reminded him of a big cat. The Empress of Gorodnii had gifted a tiger to his father long ago. He and his older brother Trefan had watched it pace its gilded cage, and Trefan had said, *What in all the hells do we do with this animal?* It had been glorious and murderous, and it had ripped a goat limb from limb right in front of them, blood had spattered everywhere.

Junei stared down at him with her big dark eyes. The firelight glinted in them wickedly.

Why were dangerous women so godsdamned attractive? It didn't seem fair.

He groaned. He wasn't sure why exactly. Maybe it was everything. The ache in his muscles and his godsdamned cock stiffening despite his misery, and the memory of his younger days when he'd thieved almond cookies from the kitchen and brought the kitchen girls up to his room, wrapped them in silk coverlets, and drunk fine Imisi wines from crystal goblets. And now he was puking and shivering on the frozen ground, dressed in dirty wool, dying like he was kinless. Gods only knew when last he'd washed or spoken to his family, and Junei wasn't fooling him.

"I would be happy to let you do whatever you want, Junei, but I think you're just tormenting me."

"Maybe I like my men vulnerable."

"Ah, I see the attraction. The dirt, the bruising... I can open my eyes now. That's a plus."

A soft touch at the bridge of his nose made him flinch; the bone was still tender. Probably crooked as all hells, though the chirurgeon had tried to set it straight. Why had he decided to give up kacin *now*? It didn't make sense.

"She really hit you, didn't she?"

"She was never the sort of woman to pull a punch," he mumbled. And then because he felt guilty grumbling about his nose when he had given Kyrra much worse, he added, "To be fair, it was war."

Junei stroked his cheek. He was sure he didn't deserve that, but he sank into the touch anyway. "Sounds as if it was a long war."

"Ten years? Gods, has it been that long?" Lobardin shivered again and clutched his stomach. "Wasn't always like this, though, between me and—between us. On another path, we might have been friends. Or at least not enemies."

"Is this penance, then? You're offering a sacrifice to... I don't know how all your Eterean gods work. Is it Adalus that accepts sacrifices?"

"I'd probably have to offer my penance to Ekyra," he said matter-of-factly. "If she'd take it." Another convulsion wracked him. "This was a shit idea. I don't believe in penance. Just get me a sliver of kacin. You can trade the bread—"

"No. Take another drink of tea."

Her hand slid under his head. "I don't need tea!" he cried out and jerked away, and then, before he could stop himself, he did beg. "Junei, *please.*"

The fabric of the tent rustled while his gaze was locked with hers and he willed her to ignore everything he'd said when he was in his right mind, three days ago. *I will do my best to talk you into giving me more kacin, but don't do it.* A wind blew in, cold and miserable, and he wished desperately for it to be one of Geoffre's marauding gavaros. *Please kill me now and get this over with.*

"Is he any better?"

Dammit. It was Cassis. Probably bringing him *more* misery. Junei moved away and he struggled to sit. "Mestere. I set a guard on the food stores, rotating shifts of four men—"

"They're doing a good job. I came to see you." The tent wasn't big enough for all of them; Cassis had to hunch inside the doorflap. Ice crystals spangled his hair, melted onto his shoulders, and dripped onto Lobardin's blankets. He looked gray. For a moment, Lobardin wondered if they were having a run of fever or dysentery in the camp, which would be the capping experience on what was supposed to be a victory but didn't feel like one. Then he realized the gray coloring was ash from the corpsefires dissolved in the sleet and rain.

"I thought I had leave, mestere."

"You did, and I wanted to give it to you," Cassis replied in a clipped, vexed voice. He flicked a quick glance at Lobardin's face, his body, the chamberpot. Lobardin laughed wearily and pushed his hair out of his face with a shaking hand.

"I look that bad, do I?"

"I just understand why you would need to take the time. For this." Cassis waved his hand—a piece of soggy parchment crunched in his fingers—and hastily looked at the puddle forming on the ground as if he were embarrassed. Then he cleared his throat. "You had my permission, and I see you have an attendant?"

Junei bristled. Lobardin tried not to smile, but his mouth twitched in amusement anyway. "Pardon, mestere, but I think that's like saying a lion is attending a wolf."

"A wolf, are you?" Junei retorted.

"I'm but a poor, sick puppy." Lobardin reached for the cup of tea. "She works for Jon. I talked her into staying with me."

"What's in it for you?" Cassis asked her bluntly.

She looked Lobardin up and down. "Not much."

"I appreciate the adulation." Lobardin grinned weakly and took another sip of tea. It seemed to be staying down. Maybe he was about to turn a corner. "You know there's a network of information in your camp, mestere."

Cassis's scowl deepened. "I'm sure Jon likes to keep tabs on everything. Devid's already moving to take what Geoffre left if that's what Jon wanted out of all of this. Lobardin, I'm cutting your casualty leave short. Get up and get moving. Come to the lodge and let someone make you look human again. I need you to accompany me to dinner with Devid."

⚬❧⚬

CASSIS

"I'M STILL NOT SURE WHY YOU NEED ME, MESTERE," LOBARDIN murmured as he stood next to Cassis in the stables while the grooms saddled their horses.

Cassis had hand-picked a group of men to accompany him, men he considered both skilled and loyal, Lobardin included if he could stay on his horse. He looked marginally better now that he'd bathed and changed his clothes, kept down more ginger tea and even some soup, at Cassis's behest. He still looked to Cassis like a specter in a uniform, especially with the weight he'd lost and the purple bruises underscoring both eyes, which were beginning to yellow and green at the edges.

"Because you're a Cozin," Cassis replied. "You know how House games are played. Presumably you also know your poisons."

Lobardin's brows flew upward in surprise, but then he laughed. "Mestere, you know not every citizen of Amora is a poisoner. It's like saying every Lieran is good at business."

"Of course I know that. But *you*...you're a Cozin, and not just any Cozin either. I imagine you had a chance to learn poisons at your father's knee. Didn't you?"

Lobardin shifted uncomfortably. "And what if I did, mestere? You know, the Grand Duke of Kavo really did die from eating bad fish. My father had nothing to do with that."

"I'm sure. And the Camerani Householder? The one who was maneuvering to edge the Cozin out of the silk contracts? I'm sure I heard my father talking about that before I'd even reached my age of majority."

Lobardin rubbed his brow. "All right. You've made your point. The Cozin have always operated for the good of the Amoran throne, no matter what it takes. Or at least that's how my father justified his actions."

"Sounds familiar," Cassis murmured.

"My father is nothing like Geoffre."

Cassis raised an eyebrow at him.

"Maybe a little like Geoffre," he muttered. "But for a better cause."

"Do you know about poisons?"

"Yes. Though I was never the assassin type. My father would have used me as an assassin; when you're the youngest of seven boys, you're rather useless unless you have some valuable skills or you can be married off to seal an alliance. But assassinating powerful people sounded like a dangerous occupation. It was easier to fleece ships and sell the cargo. At least, until my father found out. You're not planning on poisoning Devid, are you, mestere?"

Could he? He probably wouldn't have a chance to get closer to Devid, and perhaps Lobardin could drop something in Devid's food... But this meal was happening under a flag of truce, and if that damn flag was ever going to *mean* anything, one of them would have to stand up for it.

The way Pallo d'Aliente did in Kafrin Gorge?

He flinched. The difference between him and Pallo was that Pallo had trusted Geoffre to honor the same ideals in which Pallo had placed unshakeable faith, and Cassis did not trust Devid to honor a flag of truce. Not one whit.

"Let's just say I'm not planning on it, but I won't rule it out if the opportunity arises. I was hoping you'd be able to tell if Devid was using poisons and—"

"You want me to taste your food, mestere?" Lobardin said in disbelief. "I don't think that's in my contract." He tried to run a hand through his hair, but his hair was neatly bound in a queue and tied off with a smart Prinze blue ribbon because Cassis refused to change his colors. "Although maybe I should thank you for putting me out of my misery."

"I just want you there to be an extra pair of eyes and ears."

Lobardin nodded skeptically but then paled as if he was going to vomit again. He sank his fingernails into the timber post beside him like claws. For a brief, anxious moment, Cassis was unsure whether to grab the man, but fortunately his shaky breathing evened out and some color returned to his cheeks.

"Mestere, I think this is a mistake. Unless..."

Lobardin's voice trailed away.

"Unless what? Just say it. Is there something that will help?"

"No, never mind. I think it's a mistake, that's all."

"It's the kacin, isn't it? If we were going into battle, I'd get you a smoke to keep you fighting. I'm not that benevolent, Lobardin."

"Obviously," Lobardin replied dryly. His face paled again and he clutched at his midsection, bunching up his cloak in his gauntleted fist. "Are you sure this isn't battle?"

The naked, haunted longing in the other man's eyes stabbed too close to Cassis's own heart. *I could do with a smoke, too.*

It hadn't been that long since he'd locked himself in his chambers to hide his own shaking and vomiting. Told Camile he was sick, but he knew he hadn't fooled her; she just hadn't cared. She would have rammed a fistful of kacin slivers down his throat if it had served her. At least they'd both have been happy for once in this eternal marriage.

But if he'd died, Driese would have been alone, a woman bearing the bastard child of her enemy. Geoffre would have had them both killed. There was no reason to leave *her* alive, with or without her right arm.

Dammit, stop worrying. Geoffre's dead and Kyrra killed him.

At least there was no need to play the wastrel anymore. He *hated* parties. The only satisfaction he'd ever taken from those nights lay in wringing out all his frustration, helplessness, and hatred on Arsenault.

But even that had begun to seem tawdry and cruel after a time. You couldn't torment a man who'd given up. It was like kicking a dog that expected to be beaten.

He *refused* to become his father. Regardless of how Devid pushed him.

Cassis cleared his throat. "All I need you to do is stand in the tent and pay attention, Lobardin."

"Yes, and I think that will be difficult, mestere, don't you?"

"Some of my other gavaros were once householders, but you're unique. You knew Kyrra. You experienced my father. And you're part of the *information network* in my camp. Even a sliver of your attention is more valuable than anyone else's."

Lobardin's mouth quirked. A good sign even if it meant the man was returning to his damnably irritating self. Though Cassis supposed he didn't know what Lobardin was like when he wasn't smoking kacin; the kacin hadn't seemed to be an obstacle to Ires, and Lobardin was a terror with a sword when the god took him, so why would Cassis have made him stop?

"I didn't know you had such feelings for me, mestere," Lobardin said.

"Shall I just bark orders at you?" Cassis replied crossly. "I'm trying to explain why I'm not going to be that godsdamned ruthless. Not now anyway."

Lobardin looked chastised and straightened slowly. "The body responds when the mind balks." He pushed open the stall door and stepped in to untie the reins of the horse that had been saddled for him—one of the sturdy chestnut mountain horses they'd traded for when they'd arrived at the lodge. The gelding whickered, its hide rippling under Lobardin's remarkably gentle hand. He murmured quietly as he went about checking the tack, and something about it all —the smells, the sounds of horses, the contrast between Lobardin under Ires's control versus this Lobardin with the horse—made him remember Kyrra and the stables, a long time ago.

No, no, I am not going to think about that.

But the memory returned anyway. The slap of the riding crop against Pallo's thigh as he'd twitched it viciously against his own leg. Kyrra running down the center aisle of the stables, holding her flopping, unlaced bodice together. Just a girl. A girl who had turned into a mythical metal creature all because *he* had let a word slip to his father and *Arsenault* had remade her in the image of... Was it the goddess of fortune or the god of war?

Cassis took a deep breath.

It probably was a mistake, bringing Lobardin with him to face Devid, but maybe he just needed to not be alone when he faced his family.

❧

THE FITFUL SLEET AND ICY RAIN DIDN'T LET UP AS THEY RODE down the slope to the battlefield. A tent was barely visible through the late afternoon mist. Cassis stopped his men behind a screen of pine saplings on the edge of the forest. A lot of gavaros seemed to be milling about down there, but it was impossible to tell Devid's from his own; they wore the same Prinze blue. Lobardin handed him a spyglass, but the lens kept fogging up. He rubbed it on his sleeve to clear it.

"Perhaps you should consider starting your own House, mestere," Lobardin murmured. "So we can tell who's who in a fight. You could claim a color nobody else has. Peuce, perhaps."

Cassis shot Lobardin a sharp look. Lobardin hunched over his mount's neck, wrapped up in his black cloak with his hood hiding his face so Cassis couldn't see if he was poking on purpose. Cassis had to admit, seeing Devid's gavaros also wearing Prinze blue irrationally annoyed him.

"Peuce?" he muttered, looking through the glass again.

"I'm sorry, mestere, it was the first thing that came to mind. Perhaps burgundy. Kyrra's the only Aliente left to argue with you."

"The last time she argued with me, she hit me in the face with a bowl of hot stew. Since she killed Geoffre, I should probably leave her the colors. I don't want them anyway."

"Burgundy silk would be profitable. Why let the Forza have it? Do you think Devid will lift the ban?"

Cassis put down the glass. "Assuming Devid's Householder, you mean?"

"That's why he's inviting you to parley with him, isn't it? Because he wants assurances of your fealty?"

"That or he's trying to kill me." Cassis paused, squinting through the mist as he tried to sort the gavaros into lines. His men were keeping an eye on Devid. He trusted they were a higher quality of men, focused on reputation over coin. Not being able to tell the difference from here made him nervous though.

"Do you really think Devid ought to lead our House?" he asked in frustration.

"Are you asking my opinion, mestere, or is that a rhetorical question? Because I think it would be safer if I assume it's rhetorical."

Lobardin threw a weary leg over his horse and dropped to the slushy ground in a splash of mud and ice. Cassis watched curiously as he squelched through the muck to a clutch of boulders, where he dropped to a crouch and swept away a patch of sleet with one gloved hand.

"What are you doing?" he asked.

"You said you brought me because I know my poisons." Lobardin grimaced as he snapped off a stalk from a small, unassuming evergreen plant. "This won't kill a man, but he might wish he was dead. If you needed the assurance, mestere."

Cassis swallowed dryly. How had it all come to this? Poisoning his brother? Killing his father?

Gods damn everything.

He nodded curtly at Lobardin as he mounted, then ordered his men to move. *No turning back now. Men have died. Driese and the baby need to be protected. Our father is no longer here to hold everything together; it's the perfect moment for change.*

But as they rode down off the slope, the wind rattled the icy branches above them and blew the rancid smell of the corpsefires directly into their faces. Lobardin groaned softly and retched into the sleet-ridden sedges lining the path, then wiped his mouth on his sleeve and pulled his scarf up over his nose and mouth, shivering. The shadow of his hood revealed only the dull glint of his black eyes. The shiny, spiky strands of his wet black hair gleamed against his pasty forehead. He looked like a vulture hunching its shoulders to shed the rain.

Cassis *felt* like a vulture, swooping in to take the leavings. Once upon a time, he'd envisioned himself a young lion coming into his own. How could things going *right* seem as if they had still gone *wrong?*

Devid's gavaros tried to take his weapons and his horse when they clattered into the small camp. He brushed them off and handed his sword and guns to his own men. Lobardin did the same, although Cassis noted Lobardin didn't remove the small knife strapped to his wrist. Devid's gavaros were either lazy or loyal only to coin, so they didn't pat Lobardin down—a stroke of luck.

Cassis ducked into Devid's tent, only to stop in shock. Beside him, Lobardin let out a soft cry.

Geoffre's dead body lay on a table in the center of the tent.

Oh gods, it's him. It's really him.

On the other side of the tent, laughter bubbled up—familiar, despised.

Devid.

Cassis walked, stunned, to the table where their father's corpse lay. Geoffre still wore the tattered clothing in which he'd been killed, singed black with powder and stained with blood and mud.

It was impossible not to stare at the hole in Geoffre's head. *Fascinating* didn't seem like the right word because it was revolting and repugnant and he didn't want to look, but he couldn't stop. He had seen men literally blown to pieces by the fucking fougasses Arsenault had constructed all along their front—big pits full of bricks and stones he blew to hell with powder. But Geoffre's face was too familiar.

Complicated feelings old and new rushed in on him—hatred, sorrow, grief. Fear. Cassis suddenly had the urge to push his fingers into all the rips and tears in the bloodstained tunic to see if they were really the places Kyrra's sword had entered his father's flesh. If he could force his fingers into the holes in Geoffre's body, he could prove to himself this thing lying on the table had once been his father and that he was really dead.

It had been ten days, and yet the corpse wasn't blackened or bloated, didn't smell, hadn't begun to rot. Despite the hole in Geoffre's forehead that revealed his splintered yellow skull and the dull pewter sheen of the lead shot lodged inside, Geoffre looked like he might simply rise from the table and walk away.

Except, his body was full of holes.

This is what Kyrra did.

A chair creaked. Cassis tore his gaze from his father's corpse. Devid was unfolding himself from the chair. Lobardin had pressed his arm over his mouth and his back against the canvas side of the tent as if he were facing something more horrible than battle.

"The embalmer did a good job, didn't he?" Devid said as he came to stand beside Cassis.

"Embalmer?" Cassis repeated in horror. "Devid, how long have you had his body?"

"Oh, some of his men pulled him off the battlefield immediately. I got the message by bird and was able to bring in a scholar who knew the practice. He wanted to sew up the wounds to make Father look better—he thought he could disguise the hole in his forehead—but I told him to leave it. I said, *he thought he could be a god, but in the end, he was just as human as the rest of us.* He should cross over with the gods-damned hole in his head. Then everyone he encounters in the afterlife will know he reached too high and this was what he got. Nothing but holes, abandoned by the god who used him."

Startled at the viciousness in his brother's tone, Cassis stared at Devid. "Have you been drinking?"

"He's dead, Cassis. I don't have to be the good son anymore."

"You *have* been drinking."

"Don't tell me you don't want to join me." Devid paced around the table and picked up a bottle of imya and an empty glass, which he poured full and handed to Cassis.

Cassis took the glass, frowning vaguely. He wanted nothing more than a stiff drink, but he didn't trust it. He sniffed at it hesitantly.

Devid rolled his eyes. "Poisoning you would be the easy guess, wouldn't it? Why would I try if I knew you'd suspect me of it?"

"If it's all the same, I think I'd like a clear head."

Devid made an obvious point of drinking straight from the bottle. "I thought perhaps we could have a wake. Do some bonding. You know, discover our brotherly love. Now that our father's dead, maybe we won't have to *compete* so much, will we?"

"There was never any competition, Devid. You were the heir, I was the extra."

"Oh, poor Cassis. Forced to become his father's captain and lead troops to glory. So awful to have a family fortune to smoke away." Devid took another swig of imya and put on a fake mournful expression that made Cassis want to punch him.

"Well, we were both extra when he discovered Mikelo, may the gods bless the poor gentle soul. It was so *convenient* our dead uncle would be next in line for the Chair if only he were still alive, so why not pick up Renzo's bastard? Do you know there are rumors Renzo has been hiding in Dakkaran waters all this time? We failed our father in so many ways, Cassis. Just constantly...failing. You must tell me what it feels like to finally succeed."

Gods damn him. Devid was so much older, he could have been Cassis's mentor, his protector. Instead, Devid constantly made him feel even smaller, feeding his own ego by grinding Cassis into the dirt.

Lobardin's gaze settled on Cassis's back like a weight. Cassis wondered how watching him interact with Devid would affect the way Lobardin saw his authority. What Cassis wanted right now was not a drink but a smoke. That was what kacin wiped away, this feeling of always being *tested*.

He forced a smile. "It doesn't feel as satisfying as I thought it would. You called me here for a reason, Devid, and it wasn't to mourn over our father's body."

"I thought perhaps we could be honest with each other for a brief time."

Cassis looked around the tent. "There are too many men here for that."

Devid poured another glass of imya and handed it to a man sitting beside him. He accepted the glass from Devid and swirled the imya before he drank, watching Cassis with a quirk of one neat black eyebrow. Neat summed him up, from his eyebrows to his close-trimmed black beard, the unwrinkled blue tunic and crisp white sleeves of his shirt, his perfectly knotted neckcloth and shined black leather boots. He looked familiar.

Dammit, of course. Alozh Vokavik. The Kavol captain the Forza brought in at the end of the war. The man who had finally managed to capture Arsenault for Geoffre. He'd decimated a Rojornicki army before coming south to ply his trade in Liera, if the news Cassis had heard was true. Had Devid hired him already? The thought rattled him.

Devid continued to pace around the table. "You don't have to bare your heart to me. Though I did think you might want to pay your last respects to our father."

Cassis turned his attention away from Vokavik. "Were those respects?"

"Admit it, Cassis. If your champion hadn't run him through—and how that person must have hated him, to gouge him *so* many times—you would have done it yourself. He wasn't much of a father, was he? But if we'd killed him ourselves, we'd face the gods with the crime of patricide on our souls. Do you think it will taint yours by association?"

Cassis didn't like where this conversation was headed. "You know how unhinged Father was at the end. It was only a matter of time before he drove us all to ruin."

"He was lucky he had me to keep us afloat. But, how he dismissed everything I did. I was weak. Only good for counting out the coin. Well, Cassis, excellent luck for me. Now I have sole access to the Prinze fortune. And you... Well. I'd like to believe you were just fighting our father. Not the natural order of things."

Cassis tugged the hem of his tunic neat, trying to remain calm.

The natural order of things, was it? "I want what I wanted when I started this rebellion. The freedom to decide my own future. To marry the woman I want to marry, lift all the bans on trade, and make alliances with the other Houses instead of trying to rule them by fear. To lay these wars permanently to rest."

"And you believe if I were Householder, I'd achieve none of your aims? Or you don't believe I'd accede to your demands?"

"You should have burned Geoffre's body on a pyre."

"You think I'm treating him too well?"

Cassis's calm snapped suddenly, like a frayed rope finally giving way.

"I think you're out of your fucking mind! Geoffre was possessed by a god, by all accounts, and here you have him lying on a table ten days after his death! Have you read him the rites? Done anything to put his soul to rest?"

"Does he deserve to be put to rest? You know he considered us both failures because we had no magic. I used to make up visions just so I wouldn't have to spend hours staring into his godsdamned mirrors. When he found out, he shut me in a cell with a kinless man who'd been arrested for impersonating a Prinze, made me watch the man hang so I would know *exactly* what would happen if I tried to fool him again by reaching above my fucking station."

Lobardin darted a troubled glance between him and Devid. Cassis didn't know what it meant; surely Lobardin wasn't surprised that Geoffre had been capable of punishing children in such a way, especially his own. Had Lobardin's upbringing as a Cozin been so much better? All the Houses treated their children like wood and steel to hammer into place. He couldn't let Devid distract him with his grievances; they could both keep going far into the night.

"None of that matters now, Devid. It's his ghost we should worry about."

"*Fuck* his ghost, Cassis. Fuck him and every time he abandoned me because I wasn't good enough. You want to know why I called you here? The first thing I believe you can guess. I want you to kneel to the legitimate heir to the Chair of House di Prinze—*me*. And afterward, you can tell me where Father's godsdamned sword is, so I can wear it in the Circle and declare myself Head of House. Make everything *official* before I need to go to war with the Caprine to keep them in line."

"That's what I'm trying to avoid, dammit. If the Caprine go, this time we're not guaranteed to keep the Forza or the Garonze with us.

Liera is already in ruins because of the last war! The people can't take more."

"So, you won't kneel? You won't hand over the sword?"

"I don't have the godsdamned sword. But I'm not going to pledge fealty to you without getting something out of it first. If you want to rest on formalities, I'll deliver a list of written demands, but for the gods' sake—for *our* sake, Devid—bury Geoffre or burn his body, have the rites said over him instead of relying on these *embalming* techniques—"

The canvas door flap rustled. Cassis half-whirled before he realized the tall, bespectacled man entering the tent was no threat. The man's lenses fogged immediately, and he took them off and rubbed them on his wool coat, squinting as he dried them. He seemed familiar with his careless tail of dark cinnamon-colored curls and sharp nose, but he wore a deep brown coat with no House colors to indicate if he was in Devid's employ or a householder at all. And yet, he carried a certain presence Cassis couldn't explain. Then again, the whole tent was full of *presence* already. Lobardin shifted into Cassis, making room for the man who seemed to be all elbows.

"You wanted to see me about the body, mestere?" the man asked.

"You're a little late, Ser Lupa," Devid replied. "I'd like you to assure my brother our dear father has been adequately cared for."

"You're the embalmer?" Cassis asked in surprise. "I was expecting a Qalfan chirurgeon or—"

The man—Ser Lupa—perked up.

"Oh no, the embalming techniques are ancient. The Etereans were very skilled at this sort of thing. The techniques were already well known in the time of Attrasca. There are Eterean tombs everywhere with perfectly preserved bodies in them. The key is to remove the organs first—"

"His organs?" Cassis repeated in horror. "You've been rooting around in his body? You're a vivisectionist?"

The man turned innocent eyes on him, magnified by the lenses in their circular bronze wire frames. They were a murky color that seemed to blend into the rest of him, but his gaze carried a strange weight that made Cassis want to back away. Then he blinked and Cassis wondered what he'd been thinking; the man was obviously just a bumbling scholar.

"Vivisectionism is a crime, mestere. I'm sure I wasn't planning to *dissect* the Mestere di Prinze in any dishonorable fashion. Although the Etereans gained so much of their knowledge of anatomy because they did cut into the human body like the Qalfans do. We could learn much from—"

"I've seen enough of the insides of bodies on the battlefield, Ser Lupa," Cassis snapped.

The man pushed his glasses up his nose again. "I was pleased with the results in any case, and I think your father would have been pleased as well. I understand he was interested in preserving old Eterean knowledge?"

"He was interested in thinking of himself as a modern-day Attrasca. Which is different. I don't have your godsdamned sword, Devid, but I'm willing to negotiate as long as you put Geoffre in the ground. Or burn him on a pyre like a hero from one of those fucking Tulan epics he used to scour, looking for gods knew what."

"Oh, I'm sure I'll dispose of his body somehow. Can't keep him laid out on this table forever, though he's been rolled in salt. But if you don't have his sword, who does?"

Cassis traded a glance with Lobardin before he could help it.

Devid sat next to Vokavik and crossed his legs casually. Vokavik was watching the proceedings with nothing more than polite interest, like any good gavaro captain. "You know what I heard, Cassis," Devid said. "I heard your champion wasn't one of your gavaros at all. People are saying our father was killed by some fantastical Silver Warrior made partly from metal. You know what I think?"

"What, Devid."

"I ran into someone interesting in Liera recently. A gavaro. Took Mikelo hostage and refused to negotiate with our father. Geoffre said he'd take care of it, but I thought I'd do it myself before it got out of hand. Thought maybe that would make him happy, me finally showing some initiative. And if Mikelo and Andris just happened to partake, too...well, I was prepared to shift all the blame to Madame Triente. Everyone knew she was a double agent. Unfortunately, we ended up with a lot of dead pigeons, some dead courtesans, and Vanni di Forza with a lead ball in his thigh. And now there's no Mikelo, no sword, and our father lies here, full of holes."

Cassis eyed him nervously. "You'll have to connect the lines for me, Devid," he lied. "I'm not sure what you're saying."

"I imagine you heard the same buzz from the Aliente sympathizer networks I did: That Kyrra d'Aliente had risen from the dead to revenge her House. The gavaro who killed Geoffre was Kyrra, wasn't it? Who else would hate Geoffre enough to spend that kind of effort making sure he was dead? Who else who would also need a metal right arm?"

"Enough men lost limbs in the war," Cassis forced himself to say dryly.

"I met her. In that bathhouse in Liera. Or at least, it certainly could have been Kyrra d'Aliente dressed as a man. Blue eyes, blond curls, that shrewish temper. We never *saw* what happened to her body after Arsenault took her down from the noose. All we had was Arsenault's word."

"A metal arm," Lupa murmured, cleaning his glasses again. "How extraordinary."

"Captain Arsenault was a wily man," Vokavik interjected, contributing to the conversation for the first time. He had a heavy Kavol accent, all the vowels and r's rich and dark. "I had great respect for his methods. Many of them were quite ruthless, but of course the Aliente were losing and he knew it. I always wondered why their gavaros kept fighting. If it was for a woman..." He shrugged, as if to say he understood. "But I don't know about the metal arm. Markus Seroditch was rumored to have such a soldier fighting for him—a demon gavaro, some men said—but we took care of Seroditch's army easily at Vargis Pass. One man doesn't make much difference, even with a metal arm."

Lobardin cursed quietly under his breath. *One man did make a difference when the man was Kyrra*, Cassis thought nonsensically, staring at the hole in Geoffre's forehead. Aloud, he rephrased it. "One man made a difference when it was Arsenault."

Vokavik shrugged again—that infuriating Kavol habit. "Some men are more important than others. They don't need metal limbs."

"Some men don't need to spread rumors and myths," Devid said, looking pointedly at Cassis. "Where is the sword, Cassis? You can tell me now or I can march into your camp and find it."

"I'd like to see you try. I still have the lodge. All I need to do is sit there on the high ground and wait until everything falls apart while you try to hold Liera." He forced a smile. "Come on, Lobardin. I've said all I need to say."

He ducked out the door flap only to pull up quickly when a group of men blocked his way with guns and swords. Cassis raised his hands slowly. Behind him, Lobardin drew in his breath with a sharp hiss.

"You didn't really think I'd be stupid enough to let you out, did you, brother? I am sorry we couldn't get along. I had honestly hoped that perhaps without Geoffre—"

"Geoffre's poisoned everything, hasn't he? But you can't think I'd be stupid enough to trust you either."

There was a moment, a brief pause, when the world hitched in preparation for action. But Lobardin was already in whirling motion, hidden knives suddenly in his palms. Two clicks as the blades popped free of the hilts, and he plunged them into gavaros on either side of him—a neck, an exposed armpit.

Cassis lunged for the man in front of him, grabbing for his pistol.

The man grunted, tried to pull away; Cassis elbowed him in the face and rammed his knee into the man's stomach. The man let go of the gun and every instinct in Cassis's body screamed to shoot him. Instead, Cassis wrenched back the dog on the gun and fired a shot into the air, high enough for the men he'd hidden in the trees to see the brilliant orange flare and the rain of sparks.

They reacted immediately—thank the gods for his strategy of hiring men who cared about reputation! Pounding hooves drowned out the clatter of sleet on the icy ground; the noise mingled with the men's shouts and the gurgling, gasping scream of the gavaro Lobardin had stabbed in the neck as he wrenched out his knife. Suddenly it wasn't a diplomatic meeting or a quiet matter of poison, it was battle, in a war that had just begun or had been going on for years.

Cassis belted the man in front of him with the butt of the dikkarro, and blood splattered hot over his fist. He grabbed for the man's sword as another gavaro brought a heavy hilt down on his opposite shoulder. His hand spasmed open and he lost the gun, but he'd managed to take the sword with his left. The man clutched at his hair. Cassis slammed the sword's pommel up into the man's jaw and then a hand planted in his back shoved him forward.

"Move, mestere, move, *move*!"

Cassis jumped over the man he'd hit and ran for the line of horses just as his own horsemen swept the camp, swords out, covered by a volley of fire from arquebusiers stationed on their flank. A crashing boom sounded from the lodge wall as one of the big guns launched a whistling cannonball that reduced a nearby wagon to splinters.

Cassis made it to the horses and began freeing one with trembling hands when Lobardin let out a yell behind him. He darted a frantic glance over his shoulder to see Lobardin meeting the blows of one of Devid's gavaros with a stolen sword. Lobardin threw the man on the ground and ran him through. Over it all, Alozh Vokavik and Devid screamed out orders and Cassis's body took over the way it always did in battle. He was mounting the horse before he realized it.

Lobardin jammed the sword into the scabbard at his side and lunged for the horse beside his. Cassis looked up once he was in the saddle, into a mass of men who couldn't tell one side from the other because they were all wearing the same colors, and—

There was Lupa, the embalmer, standing in the middle of the chaos. He stared at the ground with a perplexed expression, as if he were perfectly calm in the center of a whirlwind. Then he crouched down and picked something up.

Metal glinted in the angry flare of light from the setting sun and torches and gunfire.

Kyrra's silver wolf.

Lupa slid it into his pocket, and then Lobardin leaned over to smack Cassis's horse, and they rode like all hells for the safety of their own high ground.

PART I

The Tulan saga of Ari the Smith is one of the great tragedies of the ancient world.
—Oji la Kaif
Revisiting the Old Epics

CHAPTER 1

ARSENAULT

KYRRA,

Sometimes, when I'm sitting with you in the dark, I keep my hand on your back because I'm afraid you'll stop breathing. It's an honest fear, not like the others—the fear of what you would say if you knew who I really was, the lives I've lived. The fear of what you *will* say when you're better.

The god picked over my memories like he was buying fruit at the market, plucking the ones that would hurt me most to lose. I can't pretend I didn't deserve the punishment, so I'm not surprised that getting my memories back should also cause pain. It's like being caught in a flood, grabbing at images to save myself from drowning.

Sometimes I put two time periods together out of context. I've been thinking about my first years of exile but also remembering what it was like after I sent you away, before I died at Kafrin, which felt like a different kind of exile. I remember how the magic used to swirl us together unpredictably. The glimpses of the hell you threw yourself into. The anguish of being unable to stop or save you. Perhaps if I'd retained more memories from my own past lives, I could have prepared you better for life as a gavaro. But we both know how sudden our last days together were.

Now I remember the cold, hard ride I made back to the villa alone. I couldn't bear to watch you go, so I left while you were sleeping, like a coward. I felt like I had taken a great wound in battle, a thrust that killed my soul but left my heart beating.

Perhaps you'll think this sounds melodramatic. I'm not sure, actually, but I think practicing trust means I should tell you what I'm feeling. Or at least, that's what Jon tells me. Though Jon kept most of his life secret from Jemma for years, so I'm not sure he's an authority on the matter.

But I recall feeling as if you understood, at least as much as anyone could. You didn't have all the facts and there were times when I felt as if you'd been put on earth just to nettle me, but you understood something no one else did—that I needed to be nettled. I needed someone who wouldn't take no for an answer, who would pry their way under my skin.

Trust feels a little like taking off your swordbelt, doesn't it?

I knew I had seen you as safe as I could. I told myself that I would die keeping my promises to you and Jon, and eventually you'd get over me. I felt like I was driving a spear point into my own flesh with every thought. I argued angrily with myself that I should have gone with you instead. Why in all the hells should I honor my promises to the man who tried to kill you—his own daughter? Why fight the battle when it was sure to be lost no matter what I did? I could turn the horse around, catch up with you, and we could both go to Orienne, together. I could live out a whole life with you, growing older at the same pace you did, and when I finally died and forgot you, at least I'd have stolen all those sweet moments from the gods.

But I kept riding south because I knew you would want me to. My dread grew more encompassing with every mile. Back at the villa, there were casualties. Not as many as I'd feared, but more than I'd hoped. A prison cell in your caves also awaited me, which was exactly what I'd expected. Pallo's rule of law was unforgiving.

It was so quiet. So dark. I thought of you sitting in the same cell, waiting on your father to send you to the hanging rope, and my anger felt as if it burned up all the air until I could barely breathe. The gods weren't happy with all the magic I had used to save you, but I was beyond caring. At least you were free, far from the scheming of your wretched Houses.

To pass the time, I told myself stories about your future. Perhaps you'd find a decent outpost in the Peaks, where there wasn't much fighting. Or maybe you'd hire on as a messenger, see the world on the caravans, visit places where your name and story wouldn't matter to anyone.

And then, you'd go to Orienne. You'd find out the truth about me, even if I never made it back, and you'd make a good life with Enri and his sons. Eventually, you'd move on, find someone else to love, settle down—run your own silk farm, maybe, and compete with the House that abandoned you.

You'd laugh at me if you were awake, and how I wish you would. The first time I heard you laugh was a revelation, though I'm sure you were laughing at me then, too. Sitting in your father's prison cell, I stuffed lies into my wounded heart like bandages to keep from bleeding to death. I did *not* want you to ride caravans to the ends of the earth, so far away; I did *not* want you to see the world—at least, not without me. And wishing for you to settle down with another man made me feel as if I was sawing off one of my own limbs. But I said the things I thought I should think, because my deepest desire, more important than anything else, was for you to be safe.

If I'd remembered my own first years of outlawry better, I wouldn't have fooled myself so easily about the safety of your exile. Now that you know my secret, I feel driven to confess all the terrible details to you. Honesty is like a fever, isn't it? This infection has lasted long enough, so I might as well get it all out even if it does hurt like hell.

After I committed my crime, the smart thing would have been to steal a boat and sail away, but I didn't run far at first. I couldn't bear for my children to know the monster I'd become, but I couldn't bear to be away from them either.

I used to creep behind my parents' house to watch my mother put them to bed. Pippa cried for me and for Sella every night; Brant wanted to look for us and was angry at being told no; Grim was the oldest, and maybe he suspected more than the others. But then, he'd always been the quiet, sensitive one. Seeing him so small and silent broke whatever was left of my heart. I thought about lying, trying to make them believe Sella had run off. Maybe they would have believed it, but I couldn't be that kind of monster, even worse than I already was. I wouldn't have been able to face my own reflection in their eyes.

Kyrra. I can't count how many years have passed and still...

There's more wine in the bottle, thank whatever gods wouldn't scoff if they heard me. I'm drinking too much again, but how else am I supposed to tell you this?

Late spring in the far north is far too bright for a man to hide. I was dragged up to the Ice to face the gods, tried, and convicted, branded an outlaw, the very land cursed against me. My own father had been forced to vote on my fate. The look on his face as he was made to choose between his sons yet lose us both... Erelf left that for me to remember. It's been like shrapnel lodged in my bones all these years.

I only realized how much I'd lost when I was sitting in the rowboat watching my home, my family, my children disappear into the mist. It felt like I should have been able to stop myself before I walked up the stairs into my brother's room—like turning back time was within my power to command. But I was adrift in a future that stretched out before me as limitless and savage as the sea.

There was a moment when Tavi and I had once again been brothers, united helplessly in a common tragedy as Sella threw herself between us. It was only an instant, just long enough to remind me that even when he lashed out in a wild fury with his magic—when I met it with my own violent anger—no matter how many crimes he committed, he would always be my brother.

I didn't know what to do when it was done. I had never killed a man before. I wasn't an adventurer or a warrior. To me, swords were problems to solve, objects of art and beauty. I felt as if my own blade had betrayed me.

Calling it an accident doesn't absolve me of the guilt. It *was* an accident, but I brought the knife and pulled it on my own brother in anger. It had never occurred to me that Sella would put herself in the way of it or that the magic woven into the blade could steal her mortality. I'd never realized what she'd sacrificed to move in the realm of mortals. I'd never realized it was the most important thing.

Maybe I wasn't cowardly enough to lie to my children, but I still responded like any common murderer. I wrapped their bodies in bed linens and loaded them into a cart, hitched Tavi's pony to it, and carried them to the beach to give them to the sea, the way we did. But the sea was angry that night. I worried their bodies would wash back up, so I dragged them into the cave where I'd gathered the metal for my sword.

I don't think I could properly be called a man at that point. I was just a ball of feelings that didn't make sense. Sella and Tavi had both betrayed me, but the fury I felt at their stupidity was only equal to my fury at myself. Dammit, if we had all just stopped to take a gods-damned *breath*...

What in all the hells did I think was going to happen? The dread that gripped me as I walked to that house, certain of what I would find but praying to all the gods I was wrong... Holding onto a *knife*, for the gods' sake! How could I think it would end any differently? Now it seems so obvious, after all these years of earning my coin by killing men, but I was so naïve and self-righteous then. I didn't realize *wanting* to do violence to my brother might result in *actual* violence. Violence that could never be reversed.

I couldn't stop weeping. My hands shook so badly I could barely use them. Every feeling felt like it alone consumed me, and yet there were so many different ones...

Forgive me, Kyrra. I've had a great deal of wine to get this far and I think it's beginning to show. The sky outside looks less like charcoal and more like ash; it seems I've burned most of the night, like I ought to burn this letter.

There have been times when I thought I spent most of my emotion in my first life. Some was left over for my second, mostly guilt and fear. By my third life, that had been whittled down to desperation—*surely Erelf can't be serious about this*—and in my fourth, only despair. After that, there wasn't any point to feeling at all.

But what feelings should I have had when your father incarcerated me for saving *his own daughter*, whom he had tried to murder publicly, brazenly, as if you were only a godsdamned sheep for sacrifice at his wedding banquet? I wanted him to kill me. *Prayed* for him to kill me. I knew I would forget you if he did, but how else would I be able to fight for such a man? The promise I'd made to you was too hard to keep, though I knew I had to, because how else could I fight against Erelf, except by fighting against Geoffre?

In the end, Pallo's gavaros helped me keep the promise. They refused to fight if Pallo didn't release me. They voted on it, like a real company, and decided they would only fight under my captaincy, in your memory. And that was how it went, Kyrra. You promised to return to me, so you ended up a soldier fighting your own war instead of going to Orienne the way I wanted you to. And the only reason the Aliente held out against the Prinze as long as they did was because your father's gavaros, the men you had lived among, were faithful to you, not him. Once I learned that, I knew I would fight, and fight hard.

Those are things you didn't know because I couldn't tell you. Now I have, and maybe I can get some sleep before Mikelo comes to check on you at dawn.

I don't want to disturb you. I'll make my bed on the floor, where I'll lie counting your breaths, trying to make sure I don't let you slip away from me again...

CHAPTER 2

ARSENAULT

THE SOUND OF PAPER SHUFFLING WOKE HIM.

The dim, silver light in the room glowed with gold overtones. Had someone stoked the fire? He was sure he'd banked it last night. He was careful about fires since Kafrin; that death was too fresh. He blinked stupidly, trying to figure out what time of day it was, but his eyelids sank closed again. His hand lay curled around someone's body, a warm, solid hip bone under his thumb, a thin linen shirt bunched in his fingers.

Triente? he thought in confusion. Had he made another trip to the bathhouse for information?

His eyes snapped open and he jerked up on his elbow. Found himself staring straight into Kyrra's eyes.

He remembered that blue. The dark ring around the outside, the frosty gray like a bright winter day speckling the iris, punctuated by feathery dark brows always ready to hitch in irony, just like her mouth. The little nick on her forehead. The sun freckles dusting her nose that reminded him of a brighter, warmer season.

But there were differences, too. Her eyes were both dull and too bright, still a little feverish. A flush lined her cheekbones, making them seem more prominent, and her skin was wan and pasty, nothing like the sun-touched gold he remembered. She looked hollow, harder than she had when he'd left her all those years ago. Everything was topsy-turvy. He felt as if he might be dreaming of Kyrra the way he sometimes had without remembering who she was.

But a solid core of metal wedged against his ribs.

It took a moment for his groggy mind to absorb the fact that she *was* real, and he was real, and they were here, together.

Triente. Gods, man, what in all the hells were you thinking?

His cheeks heated and that dark gold brow crept upward slowly in question. She was lucid, then—not lost in a Sight dream or under Ires's control. She held a sheaf of papers in her left hand, which was still wrapped in a bandage like his right.

"Are you reading?" he mumbled.

"It had my name on it."

He groaned and sank back into the mattress. "Shit."

More paper shuffling. He couldn't bear to watch her reading the letter he only half remembered writing. He closed his eyes again as he tried to put down the sick, nervous feeling in his gut. The sour remnants of the wine didn't help.

"It had my name on it, but you didn't mean it for me?" A dangerously ironic note lurked beneath the amusement in her voice, which he also remembered. Being able to remember was like rappelling down a cliffside: exhilarating and terrifying at the same time.

He cracked an eye open. His head still ached, but more dully now. "I meant it for you. But...in the future. Sometime. Not while I was in the same room."

Both brows rose. "I see."

"I had a lot of wine," he said hurriedly. "Everything is true, but maybe it's all illegible. And probably overly dramatic."

She frowned thoughtfully as she continued to shift the pages. The silence was excruciating. Finally, she moistened her bottom lip with her tongue in a gesture so definitively Kyrra he felt as if he must be back in the old Aliente gavaro barracks with her. One godsdamned month they'd had as lovers. *One godsdamned month.*

"Lobardin showed me one of your books. From after Kafrin, not before. It looked as if you tried to burn it, but someone rescued it and it ended up in the wrong hands. You wrote a letter to your brother."

"I must have been drunk then, too. Tavi never listens to me. He surely wouldn't read a godsdamned letter."

Silence for a heartbeat. Kyrra turned toward him on the pillow.

"Does Tavi haunt you?"

Arsenault pushed himself up on his elbow again, suddenly uneasy.

"Why are you asking? You haven't seen him, have you?"

Kyrra stared back at him flatly. "You haven't changed at all, have you? You still answer questions with more questions."

"It's complicated." He shifted, unsure if he wanted to move farther away or closer to her. Or whether he wanted to move, period. She hadn't answered his question either, he noted, but maybe it was all right to let it lie for the moment. Nothing hurt, the blankets were warm, the mattress was soft. *Stuffed with goose down, probably. I wonder if Jon's woman stitched all the quilts herself.*

"Arsenault."

"Did you finish reading the letter? The one I wrote last night?"

She let the sheaf of papers fall to her chest. "I feel as if I lost parts of it," she admitted. "My eyes hurt, I can't focus. Surely it can't still be that head wound."

"Mikelo didn't say anything about a head wound..." Arsenault lifted his hand to her forehead. The bandage wrapped around his promise cut fluttered against her skin. A draft was seeping in at the window; he should seal that. "You're still warm."

There was a pause, so heavy it felt like it sat down between them. Putting his hand to her head was a simple gesture, one he'd made many times over the past twelve days, but it was different when she was lucid...like his touch meant something more. He lifted his hand slowly, unsure what to do with it. Finally, he folded his arm around her and drew her closer.

Her hair scrubbed the pillowcase as she settled her head on his bad shoulder. It twinged and he fought not to stiffen. He wanted to feel her breath against him, the rise and fall of her body under his hand. But dammit, his shoulder.

"Am I hurting you?" she asked.

"No, I—" He winced. "Maybe a little. The injury from the horses. And the stripes on my back. Mikelo couldn't—you needed—"

She lifted her head. "I can move."

"No, stay. It's not—"

"I don't want to hurt you—"

"If neither of us move, we'll be fine."

She rested her head on his chest again. "Is awkwardness a symptom of fevers?"

"If only it were, we could find some cure for it. Send Mikelo out into the woods for an herb to put in our tea."

"Maybe we should start over. Formally. With introductions." It sounded like a joke, but a shadow passed through her words. She looked so vulnerable lying there, strangely familiar yet also alien with her longer hair, the golden ringlets spread out on the pillow, her hollow cheekbones, the fading bruises...

It was too early to parse this many emotions; he hadn't even had coffee.

"Do you want me to call you Ari?" she asked suddenly.

"Do you want me to call you Kyris?"

Her eyes grew round, like she hadn't considered it—of course she hadn't. She'd been lying in bed almost dead for nearly two weeks. But she also looked like she was trying to make room inside for all the people they'd become: Kyrra and Kyris, Ari and Arsenault. The way they used to be together, the way they were now, all the years they'd spent apart. There were many more years on his side than hers.

"Are you asking if I want you to treat me like Kyris?" she asked. "Like a man in truth?"

He turned his nose into her hair. "I'm not sure what I'm asking. Ari was a self-righteous prick, and I've been paying for the evil he did ever since. You know me as Arsenault, and that's who I hope I've become. He's a little broken, but hopefully he's learning. He's had long enough."

Kyrra snorted a little, unsure laugh. "You can't imagine how much I wanted someone to call me Kyrra all those years. To acknowledge me as a person instead of speaking to the disguise. Even Jon called me Kyris."

"I thought maybe—"

"I asked you once if sharing your bed meant you'd want me to stop wearing trousers, and you acted as if I'd spoken a language you didn't understand. Kyris is part of me, but not all of me."

Hearing her talk about sharing his bed sent a shot of heat through him. It was morning, it didn't take much. He squeezed her closer, gently, trying not to dwell on the fact they *were* sharing a bed, how he'd loved to watch her wake, regardless of what she was wearing.

"That's not what I meant," he murmured. "I just wondered if you liked being a man better."

"I was forced to be Kyris. I didn't choose him." She raised her hand like she was going to touch his face, stopped, then slowly, hesitantly, rested her fingers on his beard. "Maybe I should take a completely new name."

He gave in to the urge to push his fingers into her hair. It was snarled hopelessly from days spent in bed, though he'd tried to help her keep it neat. But he wanted to feel the pulse of her, to rub the soft place at the base of her skull, to stroke the delicate skin behind her ear with his thumb. She tilted her head back into his hand and idly brushed his new beard with her fingertips. Funny how such a light, comfortable touch could ignite his desire like it did. After all these years, everything that had happened between. It had never been like this with anyone else.

"Something impressive like Tekollonious, perhaps?"

She chuckled. He liked how it caught in her throat. It reminded him of velvet. "I'm flattered you think I could pull off Tekollonious."

"You'd wear that name well. Or perhaps Cythiomyestenes."

The chuckle became a snort, then a laugh, and then she was wheezing and wincing. "Ow, ow. Balls. Don't make me laugh, Arsenault. Please, go back to being serious."

"I'm sorry, I'll apologize to your ribs."

"Here, just apologize to my mouth."

He caught his breath in surprise, but she stretched upward and pressed her lips to his before he fully realized what was happening. An instant of contact, that delicious moment of anticipation and invitation that happened with a first kiss, and he felt like he was eighteen again. Her mouth was so warm. She tasted faintly of honey and kacin tea, and that soft place behind her ear was warm beneath his thumb, and he just wanted to get this godsdamned pillow out of the way.

But when he tugged on it, she made a small sound of distress against his mouth. He pulled away in alarm.

Her eyes were closed. In pain this time.

"S-sorry. Arsenault."

Damn. "I'm the one who should be saying sorry. I've hurt you again."

"We'll make a rule: no apologies." But she didn't open her eyes, and she was shivering. The papers on the bed slid with her movement. He reached down to collect them, his hand trembling, too. She pressed her forehead against his cheek, and he held her against the pillow that remained an awkward barrier between them. He lifted the papers behind her head to see where she'd left off reading. But it wasn't the letter. It was one of his sketches. He must have left it in the stack of papers.

So, she'd seen the bed, too.

"It's not this bed, is it?" she mumbled against his skin. Now he noticed the chapped, dry edges of her lips, evidence of the battle she'd been fighting, just as serious as the one she'd fought on the battlefield. "You wrote runes, but I didn't recognize all of them."

"It's a bed I would like to build. For us." He didn't know why the admission made him uncomfortable. It just felt...strange. To think about a future, any kind of future. He had no idea how long this reprieve would last, and her health was so godsdamned precarious. But he couldn't stop himself from clinging to a shred of hope, though it felt impossibly brave and also foolish.

"Maybe it's ridiculous to think about right now. But I'd hoped some day we might have a home. Perhaps I could bring you to Orienne, to the vineyards. And I'd build a bed. For us."

"Two gavaros pretending to be farmers?" she said with a twist of a smile, and he remembered how she used to tease him about doing farm chores at the villa.

"There are worse things. You'd like Orienne. It's down south, so it's warm, but the ocean breezes keep it from getting too hot. The vineyards go on for leagues. Everyone moves with the seasons—tending the grapes spring and summer, and then the harvest with its new wine, monitoring the barrels in their caves over the winter... When I worked for your father, the first year, the silk plantation reminded me of Orienne. The ordinary chores, anyway. Bandits don't raid the vineyards."

"You never told me you were a Vençalan noble. Why did you need to be a gavaro if you owned vineyards?"

"Would it were true, and I would have stayed forever. Grown old over and over again while drinking wine on my veranda."

"Brooding, no doubt. People would think the place was haunted."

"Maybe so. The vineyard doesn't belong to me, though. It belongs—"

To my descendants. He stumbled over the words, caught short by the truth. Those brows rose again and he cursed himself for an idiot, though he wasn't sure if he felt more like an idiot for bringing it up in the first place or because it still felt wrong to introduce her to the tangled mess of all his pasts.

"—to a family I've become part of over the years," he finished.

"Why didn't you ever tell me about this family?"

Why hadn't he told her about Orienne?

"I hold it close, I guess. If I'd told you, I would have had to come dangerously close to telling you the truth of me. But they keep a library of my books there. I rune a direction on them so they'll wind their way back. That's why I wanted you to go after I gave you the arm. I'm forbidden from telling you about my curse, but Enri isn't."

"Jon could have."

"For better or worse, Jon keeps my secrets, too." She gave him another of those looks. "You'd do the same, wouldn't you?" he asked softly.

Her expression grew troubled. "We both kept your secrets, just different ones. I always thought he took more from you than he gave, but then I suppose the same could be said for me since I stayed in Rojornick so long and left you here."

"You just did what I asked."

"It didn't help you runed my arm with Sanctuary," she said like she was accusing him of something. "My arm had its own ideas about keeping me safe. I hated it, every day, every hour. And still, I stayed too long. I could have come sooner." She sighed. "Seems like it would have been easier for you to stay in Orienne instead of getting involved in all our hopeless battles, though. Why did you leave?"

He frowned, trying to remember. "I think there was always a person asking me. I had lots of ideas for the place. Last time I visited, they wanted to expand the winery. And I've always wanted to add to the main house. I thought if I did stay, I'd build a whole new wing. Ship in timber from Rojornick, take time to carve doors..."

She was laughing at him, turning her face into the pillow to hide it.

"You know," he said, relaxing, "there's a leak somewhere in the roof of this house and it's driving me mad. The woman who owns the house is one of Jon's contacts and it seems the least I can do, but I can't climb on the roof yet. I got halfway up the ladder and—"

Kyrra fiddled with his braid in a soothing way. "I'm not sure I share your fondness for roof repair, but boring might be nice for a while. What's the bedroom like in this new wing of the chateau we're going to live in?"

"I never stay in the chateau. They keep a cottage for me, on the grounds. In a grove of live oaks, overlooking the grapes."

"Room for a bed?"

"I'll build it out of oak. Seal locks of our hair into the frame, the way we did in Tule. We'll have a dog, like the dog I once had. A wolfhound, used to lie on my feet in front of the fire."

The memory was so vivid it stopped him. The wolfhound lying on his feet in front of the fire and the man sitting next to him... Someone else he'd lost. Now it was too late to have him back, or the dog. His chest ached suddenly, hard and hot.

Kyrra hesitated. "Are all your stories sad, Arsenault? I thought we were talking about the future, not the past."

He tried to swallow the hurt and his voice came out gruffer than he wanted. "I went to that island to hide from everyone. But I couldn't stand the loneliness. I came down to the village and there was someone there, a friend, who died—twenty years now, it's been. I've only just remembered him."

Kyrra was silent for a moment. When she spoke, a reflection of his grief shimmered in her voice. "There had to be some peace in your lives, didn't there?"

"Shoveling snow off a pigsty roof, sewing with a serf girl..." He waited for her to react and thought she might have laughed a little, quietly. He pressed her closer. "Guin taught me how to build furniture."

"And there was a dog?"

"Artos liked to hang around the shop. He was older, lame in his back leg. Kittens from the stable would play with his tail and he would give us such a look. As if we'd failed him, allowing him to be victimized so by the young and energetic." Arsenault couldn't help chuckling. "Poor long-suffering old man."

"Nibas and I rescued a litter of marten kits once," Kyrra replied in a dreamy voice. "He snuck one back to the barracks. It never stopped attacking its reflection in my arm. Gods, that thing was annoying. But I miss it—and those days, too, when Markus was alive. Nibas has Razi, though... Surely Razi survived. I made sure he got better care than I did..."

Arsenault stiffened. *Razi*. The Nezar he'd shot. The guilt there was like a fresh piece of shrapnel. Not only had he nearly killed her friend, he could have killed *her* and never realized it.

Damn Erelf to the bottom of the deepest hell. He hoped the god heard him.

"It's time to go back to Orienne. Open up that old cottage again, get some life back in it. Put in a kitchen garden out the back door."

"Do you know how to garden, Arsenault?"

"Enough to survive. We'd have time to learn to do better. This is my fantasy, Kyrra; I'm pretending to be a farmer, remember?"

She paused, a little too long. "What is it?" he asked, looking over her in concern. "I haven't disturbed your ribs again, have I?"

"If I did continue to be Kyris in the world," she said slowly, "would it bother you? I'm not sure I could ever pretend to be a farmwife, unless we grew silk and I kept the books and bargained the transport fees. The only other thing I can do is fight. I don't want to hide anymore and yet...I can't imagine life as a woman and a gavaro."

I don't want you to have to fight anymore. That's what this fantasy is about, he wanted to say. But maybe that was selfish.

"You know, there are places in the world where women carry swords the same as men. Like Dakkar."

"But not Eterea. Or Vençal. It wouldn't bother you?"

He looked down at her. Her earnest expression, the hollowness in her cheeks, all the world's expectations stripped away until it was just the two of them, stealing time to be who they were for once.

"Kyrra," he breathed. "I don't care how it looks to the world. I just want to stay with you for as long as you'll have me."

⚜

He had to get up eventually, but he dragged out the process as long as he could. He set the papers on the nightstand, pushed up her sleeve, and checked the cut on her left arm that had festered. It looked less red and puffy, and it had stopped weeping. The honey compress made it sticky, but it smelled clean and only the smallest edge still gaped.

"You'll turn the corner soon. Then we can talk about Fixing your arm."

"It doesn't hurt," she murmured.

"I don't think that's a good sign, Kyrra. You should be able to feel it."

"Maybe the metal's inside me now. Maybe that's why there are so many voices. The feeling in my arm will come back eventually, won't it?"

Taken by surprise, he looked down at her. Her eyes were closed, her fingers curled loosely around his bicep but not gripping.

Drifting again.

It disappointed him, but he was surprised she'd stayed awake this long—that she'd been able to read at all. This was a lot of progress, even though it seemed like one step forward and two steps back. It took a long time to make a journey that way, but eventually you would get there. Her breath settled to a faint high-pitched wheeze that was his real worry.

The magic wouldn't leave her alone. It was eating her up from the inside and her body couldn't handle it.

"You didn't answer," she accused him in a slurry mumble. "What does that mean, Arsenault?"

"I'm sure I can Fix it," he said again, more firmly. But he wasn't, and that was the hardest part. He could tell her stories of all the things they would do in Orienne, draw her pretty pictures of an idyllic landscape of grape vines and wineglasses and long afternoons lying in the sunlight in a bed he'd made for them, but if he couldn't Fix her arm, if he couldn't stop the magic...they might never have the chance.

He held her until he was sure she was asleep. Then, as quietly as he could, he untangled himself and got up.

He pissed in the chamberpot, poked at the fire, splashed his face with the water left in the pitcher, and ran his damp fingers through his hair to slick it back out of his way. His hangover had subsided to the point where he felt hungry, so he let himself out into the hall without bothering to dress in more than shirt and trousers. He heard more voices than he expected and stopped.

The extra voices belonged to the woman who owned the house and her two boys. They stood near the entry, wrapped in cloaks, Jon beside them.

"Every time you make this trip, you put yourself in danger," Jon said to the woman. He turned to one of the boys. "Why can't you keep your mother away, eh? She thinks we're not going to take care of her house?"

The boy laughed. He was tall and sturdy, about thirteen or fourteen, almost old enough to take over the farm himself. "You know Mama won't be running away if you have people to mend."

"Besides," the woman said. "We have the gun in the wagon, and we all know how to use it."

In her hooded brown cloak, Miranda was the sort of woman who might slip through life unnoticed, almost as if a glamour hid her. The calm in her dark eyes and the streaks of gray that swept through her wavy black hair made her seem as if she had experience you could lean on when you needed it. Most men wouldn't see the strength—only the food on the table, the clean clothes handed to them by raw-knuckled hands. They'd only realize she was keeping them going when she was gone.

He knew Jon trusted her implicitly. Jon had brought them straight to her house after the battle, when they were all covered in blood and mud and magic. Those memories were a mess. The only clear thing was Kyrra's ashen face and her torn and bloody body as he and Jon loaded her in on a stolen blanket.

He hesitated, feeling emotionally naked and physically underdressed, though Miranda had seen much worse of him over the past twelve days. She'd treated the wounds on his back while Mikelo was busy with Kyrra. As he stood in the hallway, the boys loaded up a basket of maroon yarn from beside the big spinning wheel in the corner of the room. It reminded him of his own mother, who'd died so long ago her name had been forgotten by everyone. He remembered how she sat spinning at her wheel, the clack-clack-clack a comforting counterpoint to long, dark winter days when they huddled together around lanterns from what should have been dawn to what should have been dusk and was instead constant, bitter night.

These small fragments of peace, like still pools inside a maelstrom, felt so fragile. Anything could shatter them—one of Kyrra's dreams, a word from Cassis, a tiny, overlooked cut that festered.

But he couldn't spend the day stuck in the hallway, unable to move forward or backward. He forced himself to walk into the common room.

Jon looked up immediately. The boys gave him a nod and disappeared out the door in the kind of gawky tumble brothers made at that age. "It's nice to see you, ghost," Jon said. "I thought you were going to sleep the whole day away."

Arsenault started to run a hand through his hair, but his shoulder protested the movement, reminding him muscles took their own time to heal. His hair remained hanging about his face, like a wild man's. "It's not that late, is it?"

Jon looked at the clock on the mantel—one of the new ones, with springs and gears and a hand that turned and told the hour. Arsenault forgot it was there sometimes, except in the middle of the night when he had nothing to do but watch it and wish he could take it apart to see how it worked.

"Eleven of the clock," Jon said with a hitch of his brow.

"Where are Mikelo and Silva?"

"Outside. I made them go together, for safety. Mikelo needed the time away. He gave Kyrra tea and broth earlier. They tried not to wake you."

Arsenault frowned. "Didn't know I slept that hard." That couldn't be allowed to continue; it wasn't safe.

"You needed the sleep. I wouldn't feel guilty about it," Miranda said. "I'll get you something to eat, Arsenault. The boys can handle the wagon." She moved past Jon to the kitchen without removing her cloak or taking her hood down.

"You need to leave before the weather comes in," Jon called to her.

"If you keep me talking too long, we will be caught in the weather!" She disappeared into the kitchen and the sounds of cooking soon put an end to their conversation.

Jon made a frustrated noise between his teeth. "Go on, then. Get a luncheon for his majesty. Will you sit with me, ghost?" He patted a chair at a low table covered in papers. "How is your back?"

"Better," Arsenault answered warily as he sat. Jon rolled out a large piece of parchment over the table's surface, pushing a stack of missives to the side to make room. "What is this, Jon?"

"I commissioned a survey of the area. All the maps we had were hideous, inaccurate. This was drawn mathematically. I found a navigator down in Liera working with those new map projections."

"We have another Oji la Kaif on our hands, do we?" Arsenault murmured.

Jon gave him a curious glance. "Well, we won't go overboard. I don't know how Oji got his start, but I'm not sure this man will go on to be a great scholar of the Eterean world. He is a good navigator though. I checked his numbers; they seem to work."

Arsenault let his gaze rove over the map. It was meticulously drawn, from the High Peaks of the Irondels to the Villa d'Aliente and the area around the hunting lodge, Karansis and the towns of the coast that faced Kavo and the pirate-infested waters of that coast, and then Liera, its sister city Amora, and the bay between them.

Their location in the farmhouse was lightly marked with a penciled x, just northwest of the Aliente hunting lodge in the Irondel foothills.

"It's a lot better than the maps I had," he said in grudging admiration. "Kyrra and I were mapping Aliente lands when everything fell apart, but once you get into the hills, it's harder. The mountains? Forget it. Most of the terrain is impassable anyway. Your mapmaker was lucky he made it through this area here. It's traditionally fought over by bandits, and I imagine it only got worse after the wars when the Houses discharged their armies. All those gavaros out of a job."

Jon settled his elbows on his knees and leaned forward, tapping his chin with his steepled hands. "Which is why I'm worried about Miranda traveling back and forth. Geoffre's gavaros have dispersed all over. I've heard about them here, here, and here, on the road. They're not organized into companies by all accounts, but they're doing a lot of damage. Stealing food. Accosting travelers and landowners."

Jon looked worriedly over his shoulder toward the kitchen, where the sounds of cooking continued.

"I'd like to rune the whole place," Arsenault told him. "But it's hard to work magic without calling down even more on Kyrra. It will kill her if it keeps up; her body's not strong enough to handle it." He tried to speak as if reporting a handful of facts. Jon didn't need him breaking down before lunch.

Jon shot him a troubled glance, then scowled thoughtfully at the map again. "I have *also* heard that something happened with Cassis the day before yesterday. Miranda came to pass the news along. I'm happy to have it, but I wish she'd let someone else run the risk. I know she was accustomed to using this house as a letter stop, back when her husband was fighting with the Aliente, but..."

Oh, so that was it. Arsenault's stomach knotted. "Her husband fought for me, didn't he? For some reason I didn't put that together."

"How do you think I met her? They used to run letters to me in Rojornick. From you, ghost, after you refused to send them by raven."

"If one of those ravens had been Erelf's bird, Geoffre would have learned all our secrets. You could have let me make a cup of coffee before you started in on this. Did her husband die at one of my battles? Or was he fighting for one of my other captains up here?"

Arsenault moved a paper off the stack and picked up the charcoal pencil lying next to the map. He needed something to do with his hands. "What was his name?" he asked, bracing himself with a thick, black curve.

"Iacomo, I think. And you didn't have anything to do with his death. He was caught carrying a message to the Caprine in Liera and executed by firing squad along with a dozen or so Aliente prisoners of war." Jon paused. "So you see why I thought I could trust Miranda."

Arsenault faced him. "I'm not sure I can. What if she blames Kyrra or me for her husband's death instead of the Prinze? I'm surprised she's still running information for you."

"You forget how it works, ghost. The Prinze took the boys' father, ruined their lives. And now here you are, Geoffre's dead, and there's Kyrra in their back room."

"Do they know who she is?"

"Nothing has been said aloud, but they have an inkling."

For some reason, the idea bothered Arsenault more than it reassured him. Responsibility sat heavy with him. It seemed like every person for whom he'd ever felt responsible, in every life, was trying to edge back into his mind. The men he'd lost on the battlefield. The friends he'd lost to circumstance and his own bad decisions.

Names drifted through his memory. Guin, the man he'd been telling Kyrra about, and so many more. Their memories were on the tip of his mind, but with everything crowding together, he couldn't sort through it. He wanted to do them all the honor of grieving, but it was too much all at once.

"Why are you telling me this now?" he asked.

"Because we have a lot of problems. Cassis took a group of gavaros to parlay with Devid and there was a skirmish."

"Did Cassis come out of it or is there one less Prinze to deal with?"

"No, he survived. I'm not sure what Devid is thinking right now. Adayze sent me a bird recently with news about the shipping lanes. The Prinze apparently don't have the iron grip on trade they assumed they did. The Qalfans are pressing them, and also the Arak on the northern borders of Dakkar. But if we destabilize the Prinze too much too fast, Qalfa will rush in to fill the gap."

"How does this relate to Miranda and her boys? To Kyrra?"

Jon lowered his voice. "I think we're going to have to pick a Prinze who will listen to reason sooner than we thought. Qalfa is pressing on one side of Dakkar and the Sugar Kingdom on the other. If I was forced to choose one or the other, you know it would be Qalfa, but once they come in, they never leave. We need someone to hold the vultures so we can put Adayze back on the throne where she belongs, and *then* we can negotiate our own agreements. The situation is tipping again. I don't like where it's heading. I rolled cowries five times this morning and some of the numbers were downright evil."

Jon's words flew around Arsenault's head like birds. He attempted unsuccessfully to catch them. Finally Jon seemed to notice the trouble he was having paying attention. "What are you doing, ghost?"

Arsenault looked down. The outline of a flower bloomed on the page, like his hand had known what it wanted even if his mind didn't.

I'll carve an orchid on the headboard for Kyrra.

"Jon didn't tell me you were an artist, Arsenault."

Miranda appeared behind Jon, carrying a cup and a steaming bowl with a piece of bread balanced on it. She set them in front of Arsenault and pulled a spoon from her apron pocket. The bowl was filled with the ubiquitous northern Eterean broth made from hard cheese rinds and dotted with tiny pork dumplings. It reminded him suddenly of meals he'd eaten in Pallo d'Aliente's gavaro barracks—before the war, before they were under siege and hungry—and with that memory came others, of all the men he'd lived with and fought with who'd died at Kafrin Gorge. Because he'd led them, or because he hadn't been there to lead them—like Miranda's husband. The feeling ambushed him out of fucking nowhere.

"Arsenault?" Miranda asked again, hesitantly.

He looked up at her, feeling thick and stupid, caught in the unexpected rush of grief. Her gaze softened to a calm, sympathetic brown.
Jon was also looking at him with a troubled expression, one he kept
seeing. Was it concern or pity for his curse? Well, no more, or at least,
not now.

"How's your shoulder?" she asked. "And your back?"

"Fine. Healing. I was—a lot of Fixers also draw. I learned somewhere along the way, that's all." He shoved a dumpling into his mouth
and chewed vigorously. When he tried to swallow, it stuck like the
lump of feelings that threatened to choke him. He reached for the
cup. A robust red, watered, but a good vintage. Not the stuff he'd been
drinking last night. He felt guilty about taking her best. Now that he
knew about her husband, he felt guilty for taking any of it.

"Did you hear anything I said?" Jon asked softly.

Arsenault put the cup down, empty. "Yes. The Prinze are
collapsing in on themselves as we'd hoped, but now we're caught in
the rubble and we'll be trapped when the walls fall in."

"Perhaps he needs more time before you put all that weight on his
shoulders, Jon," Miranda said. He wished Jon hadn't told him about
her husband; now that was all he could see when he looked at her.
"Can I check your wounds, Arsenault?" she asked.

He laid his spoon down and tried to still himself. Her touch was
gentle, but he still felt like a spooked horse when the magic trickled
out of her and into him. Conjure magic was deep and old, less wild
than the magic he used. The unpredictability seemed to be growing
over time, getting angrier as people used it to commit more and more
violence. Surely it hadn't been this vicious when he was a boy. But it
had been younger then, and perhaps more innocent.

As the whole world had seemed.

As Miranda probed at his wounds, the balance of magic in the
house shifted. It was subtle at first, and then the world seemed to tilt
and run downhill, like a giant wave about to crash in on them.

He caught Miranda's arm. "Stop."

"Arsenault, you need help, no matter what Jon says."

"It's not me. It's Kyrra. Using even a little magic calls to her. I can't
risk that." He pushed himself up. "I can't risk her with your politics
either, Jon. The gavaros bother me. We're too close to Cassis's camp."

"If you think either you or Kyrra are well enough to face gavaros *on
the road*, Arsenault—" Miranda began.

Jon rose and interrupted her. "*My* politics? You think the woman
lying in that bedroom isn't politics? Mikelo, out in the barn—a giant

snarl of politics. Are they not also *your* politics? I'm trying to protect them, Arsenault!"

"You were protecting Kyrra by keeping her a secret from me?"

"When there was no way to talk you out of getting yourself killed? When we were trying to keep her away from the Prinze? I tried to keep her away from you, too. You didn't remember her, and you wouldn't have recognized her—"

"Because of the curse—"

"Because of that blasted *arm*, Arsenault! You opened up a well of magic and now you need to face the consequences if you want to save her. She set all this in motion by killing Geoffre, and if you back away from it, you're throwing away everything she accomplished!"

"I'm not throwing it away, Jon," he said through gritted teeth. "But I'm not throwing *her* away either, just to play some godsdamned game of Houses. You can do what you need to for your home and your family, and I'll back you on it if I can, but I'm not a player anymore. I am off the godsdamned board."

Jon surprised him by grabbing his right hand. He yanked the bandage off to expose the fresh cut and the other two faint scars on Arsenault's palm, so unobtrusive they might have been created by anything in a lifetime of war. Jon forced his fingers back and the new cut pulled. He hissed in a breath and Miranda cried out. "Jon!"

Jon ignored her. He pressed his thumb, hard, into the second scar. "And who is this scar for, Arsenault?"

The B'ara. Because the B'ara became my people, too.

He couldn't say anything. He jerked back his hand and gave Miranda a stiff bow. "I think I'll eat later, lady, thank you."

Then, clenching his hand into a fist, he stormed through the room to the back door.

❧

HE GRABBED SOAP FROM THE KITCHEN AND WENT OUTSIDE TO SCRUB everything off—memories, feelings, Jon's politics. The water from the pump felt like ice, but the pain was welcome. He rolled his sleeves up and lathered his hands and forearms with the harsh lye soap, scrubbed it through his beard, and rinsed it off. Put his head under the stream of water as if he could wash the worry out of it. The water poured in a steady stream into the mud at his feet as long as he could stand it, making a puddle that lay on top of the half-frozen ground.

A reflection shimmered on the surface of the water. It looked like his own at first, but no, the mouth was different. The hook at the corner turned down more sardonically than his did. The features were a little less defined, a little younger, a little cleaner—no scar, no beard. The eyes were...

He shouldn't have been able to see the color so exactly. Not in a reflection like this. But he was sure those eyes were green.

Not me. Tavi.

"Dammit!" he said out loud and grabbed for the pump. Just as his fingers touched the metal, a shadow appeared behind his brother's face—a flare of dark auburn hair, the curve of a woman's cheek, the gleam of a pale shoulder, an emerald dress, a feeling of wildness—

"Sella!" Arsenault exclaimed. His brother began to smile, but at that moment, Arsenault's hand came down hard on the pump, completing its motion, and a burst of water let go over his head, startling him and splashing down to obliterate the image.

Arsenault cut off the pump and stood, shaking and shivering, dripping water over his shoulders and his back and into the mud at his feet.

So many fucking ghosts.

They were all determined to pull him backward. "I'm not going, do you hear me?" he muttered through gritted teeth as he rubbed his hair dry with a towel. "You can't suck me back in. What's done is done. I'm headed forward now. New life, new chances. Reprieve. It was a victory, dammit!"

CHAPTER 3
MIKELO

MIKELO SAT ON THE RAILING OF A HALF STALL WHILE SILVA KNELT in the straw beside a pregnant goat, feeling her belly.

"I'll bet she kids in the next few days," Silva said, as if Mikelo ought to be paying attention. "Four days at most."

Mikelo made an absent-minded affirmative noise and studied a budding snowdrop he'd plucked near the house. The barn seemed far enough away from Kyrra to chance working a little magic. The tightly closed green bud was like the doe, still days away from birthing its flower. Flowering was the stalk's whole purpose in life, and it wanted to grow. A quiet humming lived deep within it. Just a nudge with his magic, and—

Even with such slight encouragement, his magic burst from its gates and up through the stem like an eager colt. The bud swelled and turned a deep green. Cracks appeared within it, and suddenly the white bell-shaped flower burst forth, stamen heavy with yellow pollen.

He tried to pull his magic back, but he lost his grip and it barreled through the plant until the white petals loosened from their base and floated to the straw. The stem browned and shriveled now that it had nothing to do but die.

"Damn," Mikelo swore, throwing the withered stem into the straw. His hand felt like it was on fire. He shook it out as if that would heal the burn. "Damn!"

Silva leapt to his feet, staring at the dead flower and then at him.

"I didn't mean for it to die," Mikelo said apologetically. "But I can't seem to shut my magic off in time."

Silva stared at him in astonishment. "But why? What were you trying to do?"

Mikelo shifted on the rail and flexed his tingling fingers. He'd had the same problem after healing Kyrra, except worse; by the time they'd made it to Miranda's farm, he'd been shaking with exhaustion and half his body had been numb.

"I'm just wondering if Kyrra is like the snowdrop. Maybe when I tried to undo what I did to help her defeat Geoffre, I took back too much. Maybe I killed her arm like I killed the flower—because my magic could only see her arm as a hunk of metal, like it was in the beginning."

The little doe butted Silva in the thigh and he absently scratched the space between her nubby horns. "I thought you came out here to take a break. Why don't you spend some time with the animals?"

Mikelo eyed the pregnant doe skeptically. The snug barn smelled pleasantly of straw and animals. "It is good to be out of the house..." he began. "We had pigs and goats in the village where I grew up. But when I picked up work, it was usually as an errand boy."

Silva bent to grab a bucket and cocked a brow at Mikelo while he refilled the goat's trough. "You had to work, did you? I thought with Geoffre as your uncle, your life would have been posher."

"Everybody thinks that," Mikelo grumbled. "I'm a bastard, Silva. There was nothing posh about my life until Geoffre brought me back to Liera, and even then, I'm not sure you could call living the way Geoffre did *luxurious*. He didn't throw his money around like Cassis, and certainly—"

"Did you wear silk? Sleep in a bedchamber in one of those fancy beds with a...a roof?"

Mikelo found himself squirming a little. "It's called a canopy. You owned your own silk shirt, didn't you?"

Silva's eyes narrowed. "I'd hardly call my life working at the Youth *posh*, would you?"

"That's my point. Sometimes you can wear silk shirts and your life isn't posh, not by any stretch of the imagination."

Silva gave him a grudging look of acceptance and wiped his hands on the thighs of the worn trousers Miranda had lent him. "I'd rather be in here with the goats," he said as he settled the bucket in the straw and pulled a carrot out of his pocket like he was comfortable being a farmer. The little goat snapped it up with her square teeth. "My family kept goats and sheep, though we had no house like this one. We used abandoned farms sometimes, old Eterean dwellings, tents. Depended on the season."

Mikelo cast a brief, furtive glance over him. Silva would look posh no matter what he was wearing, which seemed odd for the son of shepherds. The faint scrub of brandy-colored stubble along his jawline didn't make him look any rougher than his borrowed farm clothes did. Or the straw in his brown curls, which the goat had tugged loose from their leather tie. Mikelo wore similar clothing, but the sleeves of his tunic were a little short and pulled awkwardly above the knobs of his wrists. He hadn't looked at himself in a mirror since they'd fled the battle.

"You don't seem like you belong with the goats," he said before he could stop himself.

"You don't seem like the kind of person who kills flowers, but here we are."

Mikelo sighed heavily. He wasn't sure what to say to that, but while he was thinking, the barn doors rattled open and Miranda strode in, followed by Jon.

Mikelo's stomach sank. *What's gone wrong now?* Silva flicked him a concerned, questioning glance and leaned on the rail next to him.

"I can take care of myself, Jon," Miranda said. All Mikelo could see was the back of her head—her hood, really—but her voice was firm. "And I have my boys for help. Your friend needs you, and there you are, dumping more on his shoulders, which haven't even properly healed."

"You don't know Arsenault like I do, Miranda."

Silva's brows rose slowly and Mikelo felt the same way, except more panicky. *If something is wrong with Arsenault, will I be able to take care of it? Will I be able to take care of Kyrra by myself?*

"All men have limits," Miranda replied.

Mikelo cleared his throat. Silva nudged him, but he couldn't keep listening in. "What's wrong with Arsenault?"

Jon looked up suddenly, but he must have known they were there.

"Speaking of another man who doesn't know his limits," Miranda said. "You're all the same, not allowing yourselves space to grieve or weep or feel. But a body and a mind can only hold so much. And what does being a martyr accomplish when you can't be there for the people who love you?"

"Maybe this is actually about your husband?"

"That was extremely condescending, Jon Barra. I deserve an apology."

Jon looked chagrined. He took one thumb out of his swordbelt and reached up to tug at his locs. "All I'm saying is wars don't give you much space. When Jemma died, there was no time to take. And there is still no time. The war isn't over, the front has just changed."

Jon's admission surprised him. Jon hardly ever talked about Jemma. Usually only with Arsenault, because Arsenault seemed to remember her—a whim of the god who'd cursed him.

"I thought we were done with the war, now that Geoffre's gone," Silva interjected.

"Wishful thinking. Geoffre's death leaves a wide open space for anyone strong enough to take it. Our war won't end until we regain the Ibuu's Seat. And even then, this conflict doesn't obey borders, much less confine itself to a single House."

Miranda caught Jon's sleeve. "Ignoring your body's needs will kill you in the end, Jon. Ignoring your feelings will do the same."

They looked at each other in a way that made Mikelo uncomfortable. He wondered if Miranda was doing more than running information for Jon...if, with their histories, they had ever taken a moment themselves.

Unbidden, a memory from the mirror in Cassis's stable flashed across Mikelo's mind, an image of himself doing terrible violence to a person. Violence he didn't want to recall, didn't even want to think about. Mikelo sucked in his breath and ruthlessly pushed it away.

How long could he put off his moment? Indefinitely, he hoped.

"Once a captain, always a captain," Jon replied. "The captain's job is to keep going until the war is truly over. Or he's dead. Arsenault will come around, but sometimes you need to push him a little. He digs in his heels."

Miranda's eyes flashed, breaking her usual calm. "But *you're* the captain in this situation, Jon, and you need to know when to stop driving your men like you drive yourself. You won't let Kyrra heal either?"

Mikelo couldn't help snorting. Silva shook his head as Miranda looked at them in surprise. "In another week, we'll be forcing Kyrra to stay in bed," Silva told her. "The real problem is trying to stop her from doing what she wants."

"I hope you're right," Mikelo said. "I still wonder if I made some mistake."

Stop second-guessing yourself, Mikelo.

He wasn't sure if the voice in his head sounded like himself anymore or if somehow it had changed to sound like Kyrra goading him. Sometimes he swore he could also hear Geoffre. Compared to his uncle's twisty, ruthless reasoning, Kyrra's blunt challenge felt like a shield against the dark.

"And what will it be like when she's strong enough to get up but not strong enough to keep Ires out?" Jon asked. "Arsenault needs to pull his head out of the sand. If he thinks that god will obey this agreement..."

Mikelo jumped down from the rail. "Miranda's right, Jon. Arsenault probably needs to take more moments than all of us combined."

"And we need him. The gods are part of this war and he knows how to fight them. Do you think I *like* what I'm doing? Somebody needs to keep his eye on the cause. Even if—well, godsdammit, I'm not a monster, but sometimes that's what it takes."

Sometimes that's what it takes...

"That's a slippery slope, Jon," Mikelo said, refusing to entertain the immediate assault of monstrous images he'd seen in his reflection in Cassis's mirror. "I don't know if victory is worth that cost."

He tipped his head to Miranda in an awkward imitation of Arsenault's courtly bows and walked out of the barn.

❧

THE WAY THE PATH WAS LAID OUT, MIKELO SAW ARSENAULT AND Miranda's boys standing beside Miranda's wagon before they saw him. An old-fashioned fancy carriage was still housed in the barn, as if this land holding had once been much more prosperous, but Miranda wisely traveled back and forth in a simple farm wagon. Incongruously, one of the boys held a big wheellock pistol with two hands as Arsenault adjusted his grip. The boys were dressed for the weather in coats and scarves and gloves, but Arsenault only wore a cloak thrown over his shoulders.

"There you go," Arsenault was saying. "Remember to compensate for the kick of the barrel when you aim because the gun will knock you backwards. You'll be more likely to hit close targets, but don't let them get too close before you start priming the damn thing, understand? Otherwise, you won't get an opportunity to take a shot at all."

"Yes, ser," the boy answered. He looked tense, like he was putting all his concentration into the gun. Mikelo tried to remember his name. *Fillipo*. The younger brother—*Hani*—darted Mikelo a glance as he walked up. Hani was dark to his brother's bright. Slender, quiet, a little wary. Mikelo didn't think Hani missed much. He hung back now, watching his older brother with eager but worried brown eyes.

Arsenault took the gun back as he handed the key and powder to Fillipo. The smooth metal bottles of powder hung like charms from a leather bandolier with a worn brass buckle. "Wear both key and powder around your neck so you don't have to stop in the middle of battle and fumble around in your pockets or your bag or, worse, on the ground. How many times have you fired a gun? What about your mother?"

Fillipo settled the bandolier over his chest, then hung the key around his neck. It clinked against the bottles. Fillipo was already into his growth spurt, but the bandolier was made for someone with wider shoulders and a wider chest. It drooped low on his hip, rattling when he moved.

Hani laughed. "Don't let them fall off, Fillipo. You look like a scarecrow wearing wind chimes."

Fillipo moved around so the powder jars knocked together and did, indeed, sound like wind chimes. "Maybe it'll scare the gavaros off. They'll think I'm a ghost." He stretched out his hands and wiggled his fingers. "Get off my land—"

"You couldn't scare a gavaro out of a piece of candy, Fillipo."

"You should wear them, Hani. All you'd have to do is show them your face."

"Boys. It doesn't matter what you look like as long as you can use the gun. If I had two pistols, I'd give one to each of you. But I imagine Jon doesn't have another to spare."

The boys traded guilty glances. Then Hani said hesitantly, "Jon let us fire the gun a few times, to make sure we could all do it. Mama, Fillipo, and me, too."

"Papa never had a gun when he was fighting in the wars." Fillipo picked up the key that hung around his neck and clenched it tightly.

Shit. Maybe he should just walk on. Maybe he should leave.

Arsenault rested a hand on the boy's shoulder. "It's all right," he told Fillipo softly. "You don't have to talk about your father if you don't want to. But it gets in your body when you practice a lot, so my advice is for both of you to practice the motions even if you don't shoot. Keep doing it until you're fast at it. The three of you are a team. If anything happens, you'll all have to get yourselves home safe, not just the one with the gun."

"Papa met you once," Fillipo said suddenly.

Arsenault looked caught off guard. "Jon said—he didn't fight under me, did he? You'll have to forgive me if I don't remember..."

"No," Hani said. "He rode information through the battle lines. He brought you a message. The only time he ever saw the Villa d'Aliente, he said."

"What did he say about me?"

"He said you were doing the best you could with what you had. And it wasn't your fault you didn't have enough."

Arsenault sagged like a weight had settled on his back. *Miranda was right. He does need to take a moment.*

"Aren't you supposed to be resting, Arsenault?" Mikelo said, moving quickly toward the wagon. "I thought you were with Kyrra."

Arsenault blinked like he was returning from somewhere else. The war maybe. He pushed his hair wearily out of his face. "She's asleep. I thought I'd see Miranda off."

From what Jon had said in the barn there was a lot more, but Mikelo kept Jon's secrets and turned to the boys. "Arsenault helped me the same way, you know. Put me through arquebus drills over and over until I could use it, but I don't like guns. I never had an occasion to shoot, really."

Hani frowned. "Why was he showing you how to shoot? You were with the Prinze in the war, weren't you?"

"It's a long story," Arsenault said. "I didn't meet Mikelo until after the war ended. I was operating undercover for a time. For a lot of reasons, but Mikelo here was an important one."

It still felt strange to know Arsenault and Jon had known who he was long before he'd had any clue himself. It shouldn't have taken him so long to realize all Geoffre had wanted out of him was his magic.

"I wasn't allowed near the fighting in the wars," Mikelo said. "I know it was a privilege, being isolated like that, but—well, it was a blessing, I guess, that I don't have actual blood on my hands. Now I'm just angry at how my uncle duped us all and wrecked Liera. All for revenge and power."

Fillipo kept his eyes on the gun as he cranked the wheel with the silver key hanging around his neck. The muscles in his face tensed as he worked it. Round and round, tightening the spring. An expensive gun, the kind only Jon could get reliably. Polished cherry wood stock.

"They're good words, mestere," the boy said finally. "But they won't bring my father back."

For a moment, Mikelo felt like he stopped breathing. Suddenly he remembered—the boy's father had been killed by firing squad.

He didn't know what to say. The firing squad days had been the worst, worse than the battles, the cannons, the hand-to-hand fighting in the streets of the city. Mikelo had been little more than a clerk, but he'd processed prisoners' belongings. Had their father's belongings passed through his hands? Had he handled their father's life tangentially even if he hadn't pulled a trigger to take it?

It was so small, what a life came down to. A weapon, a pipe, a pair of boots. If the belongings were good, the men came to claim them. Everything else—the little things, the irreplaceable, individual things—they threw into the canals with the trash, to be swept out into the lagoon by the tide.

He remembered picking up a watch. It had fascinated him, this pocket clock, so new and strange, and he was trying to buff away a smudge to read the engraving on the case. But then the roar of arquebuses went off in rapid succession in the yard, right on the other side of the wall.

He never had learned who that watch belonged to. He had never had the courage to find out.

"I..." he began, because the boys were still looking at him. So was Arsenault, with an appraising, concerned squint. "Yes," he said, bobbing his head. "Of course. You're right. I'm sorry."

He backed up, brushing past Arsenault as he walked toward the house. He didn't know if he was doing the right thing, but his eyes were hot and blurry, and he could barely see where he was going—

Arsenault caught him by the arm. "It's true. Mikelo can't bring your father back. But he didn't have a choice of fathers any more than you did. You should thank the gods you had a good man for a father. And now Mikelo's here with us instead of standing with the Prinze down there in the valley, so what do you think that says about him, eh? How much do you think it cost him to desert his House?"

The boys traded hangdog looks. Mikelo couldn't blame them; he'd feel the same after being upbraided by Arsenault. He smiled miserably. By all the gods, he must look like he'd suddenly developed rigor mortis. "No, they have a point, Arsenault. I wish I could do more, but all I can say is I'm sorry, and I wish I had, well, I'm not sure what I would have done if I'd known everything earlier, because I needed Kyrra to take me hostage to escape that compound. So"—he tipped his head again—"I think I'll check on her now. Safe travels."

"Mikelo."

"I'll let you know how she's doing," Mikelo replied and kept walking.

"I'll be in shortly!" Arsenault called after him. Mikelo could tell he was frustrated, but he didn't know exactly why.

He'd lived in such a bubble under Geoffre's guardianship. Geoffre had supplied his food, his clothing, regular meals, a bed—books! It had all seemed like a dream. He *had* willfully blinded himself to the misery caused by his House. He'd known too well what he would have been without them.

Hungry.

Hunger lived inside you like an animal, using your belly as its den. It never slept long enough to be forgotten. When it woke, if you had nothing to feed it, it would gnaw an ever-growing hole into the part of you that was still human, the part that believed ideas like "love" and "peace" and, for the gods' sake, regular meals existed in the world. But when you lay awake in the dark feeling as if you were feeding your own guts to an insatiable demon you had no hope of ever satisfying, those things only seemed to exist for other people.

Geoffre, damn him, had realized that. He'd fed Mikelo as soon as he'd arrived in the still smoldering ashes of Mdembu harbor.

Fried fish, clams, prawns, flatbread and olive oil, greens and plantains and yams, beans cooked slow with salt pork, and, most importantly, a trifle layered thick with cream and mangoes and dusted with sugar, washed down with hot coffee steaming in delicate Qalfan cups.

Blatant bribery. But how could he have resisted, as poor and hungry as he'd been then? The fear of being poor and hungry again had made him ignore all the evidence of his eyes for years. Thinking these things now wouldn't bring the boys' father back, but he wished he could say them. He knew it would only sound like so much whining justification coming from a Prinze, but he still wanted desperately to explain.

He scraped his boots on the rock beside the back door and pushed his way inside. The kitchen smelled like the most perfect afterworld, especially after being assaulted by his memories. Everything was quiet except for the pop of the fire and the creak of the floor. He fumbled at the toggles of his coat—his fingers colder and stiffer than he'd realized—worked it off his shoulders, and hung it on a peg on the wall. He sat on the bench beneath the row of pegs to pull off his boots and stood them neatly underneath. He'd tracked some mud in, unavoidable in this weather. He wiped it up with a towel and hung that on a peg, too. After he finished the comforting ritual, he finally gave in to his awakened or imagined hunger and grabbed a hunk of day-old bread from the board under a cloth.

A strange thump on the ceiling stopped him. Kyrra was in her room and everyone else was outside. The room above the kitchen was the one he and Silva shared. He froze, listening for more, but all was silent. Probably the cat Miranda kept for mice. It didn't seem too interested in mice, but it did like to sleep upstairs on his bed.

Mikelo stuffed the bread into his mouth and—another thump, louder this time. The bread suddenly felt like a mess of dry crumbs, sticking in his throat. He reached for the bottle on the counter to wash it down—

"Ah, gods," he gasped. Imya. He set the bottle down too hard and the pottery chinked on the stone counter, not loud enough to cover more thumping from upstairs. Mikelo wiped his mouth with his sleeve and put a hand to the hilt of his knife.

Up the stairs, quiet in stockinged feet, slipping a little on the wood risers. He stopped outside the room and edged his knife out of its sheath. His heart drummed hard as he pushed the door open a crack wider.

It's going to be the cat, and then you'll feel ridiculous...

It wasn't the cat.

It was Kyrra. Lying on the floor with the Prinze sword unwrapped before her, staring into the mirror of the blade.

CHAPTER 4

KYRRA

IT WAS STRANGE, NOT BEING IN CONTROL OF MY OWN LIFE. RELYING on other people to do the simplest things—to eat, to drink, to get out of bed to piss and shit. Great events and history could have been happening outside my window, and yet, in my life, the simple act of getting out of bed loomed largest. It reminded me too much of the time after my arm was first severed, when months could have been years or moments, blurred by pain and fever.

In that hazy period after the Circle had severed my arm, I remembered falling off the chirurgeon's cot because I'd needed to use the chamber pot. It was dark, but it could have been the middle of the day; the chirurgeon kept the shutters closed because the light hurt my eyes. The chirurgeon's boy was gone and the chirurgeon had needed his sleep; it was a luxury for me to have any sort of attendant at all.

So, in the dark, alone, I'd rolled off the edge of the cot, hit my knees, and, unthinking, put both hands out to catch myself, not remembering I only had one. The strange movement set me off balance and I'd collapsed onto my festering stump instead.

It's hard to remember pain well enough to describe it. Memories remain of what it's *like*, but any word you use to define it—*red, hot, gnawing, excruciating*—feels inadequate. Pain eats you alive, but after it stops, all you remember is its distant imprint. After my arm was severed, there were many nights I begged the chirurgeon not only to let me die but to kill me. I had nothing to live for and my whole world had shrunk to pain and guilt, both of which were too huge and heavy to bear. Whenever the waves of pain eased, I would think, *no, I don't want to die. I want to stay alive so I can visit this pain on Cassis di Prinze, I'm afraid of dying, I want to...*

I hadn't known what I'd wanted. I was sixteen years old. That night, almost ten years ago, my arm on fire, my vision wavering with fever heat, the only thing I had cared about was reaching the chamberpot.

It was one of my first lessons in what it meant to be missing an arm. Actions I had always made instinctively now needed to be planned with care. To crawl, I had to support my weight on my left arm alone, which shook with every halting movement. Then, I had to sit back on my heels, grab the edge of the bedside table to haul myself to my feet and lower myself to the pot. Getting back into bed after was the matter of a drunken stumble. The trip across the floor felt like leagues but it was in reality only a few steps. I'd lain there afterward, panting and sweating with exertion while the room whirled around me, thinking, *Thank all the gods, I did it.* It felt like a great victory, at least as important as winning a battle.

I couldn't help remembering that night when I woke, older and more experienced, in the big farmhouse bed with the soft goose down mattress. My skin felt hot and paper thin, my throat dry and painful. I was muzzy with kacin tea, and yet my ribs still burned with pain when I moved. But I needed to use the chamberpot.

My metal arm kept dragging me down as I tried to rise. A wall of pillows wedged me in place on either side and I shoved them onto the floor. Then I grabbed the edge of the mattress with my weak and aching left hand, and I slowly worked my arse over to roll onto my side and sit myself up. When I finally made it upright, I stopped to catch my breath. My wheezing was so loud I could hear it. It felt like I was being slowly suffocated with a pillow while somebody punched me in the ribs at random intervals. Every now and then, I suffered a bout of what Mikelo called *magical pneumonia* and the coughing wreaked even more havoc on my ribs.

I didn't know how much time had passed since the battle with Geoffre. The whole experience had become really fucking frustrating. I needed to get up, out of bed, needed to...

I was sure I needed to do something. If I was safe—if *we* were safe —surely I wouldn't have felt so panicky every time I woke. Especially when I woke alone.

They could be outside, fighting Geoffre's gavaros. Godsdammit, there could be a marauding army outside and Arsenault wouldn't tell me. Maybe Cassis wants Arsenault back, maybe Erelf...

Arsenault might have accepted his reprieve, but I didn't trust Erelf. I knew this war wasn't over.

I pushed myself onto my feet. My healing muscles didn't like that, nor did my fevered brain, but after a moment the ache and vertigo calmed. I looked up and—

I wasn't alone after all. A man rocked slowly in the chair. His burnished bronze hair glittered in the firelight. But when he faced me, his eyes were a strange, unnatural color: black, edged with a rim of deep glimmering ruby that only appeared in the right shadow.

"Ires," I swore. "It is you, isn't it?"

"Hello, Kyrra. It's nice to see you again."

He smiled. It seemed genuine and even warm, the way you might greet a comrade after a long absence. Not the sort of expression one expected from the mad god of war. He rose and, nervously, I moved back against the bed. It seemed as if he might want to hug me, but the iron shackles fastened to his wrists clanked when he moved. He gave them a look of disgust.

He was the most beautiful man I had ever seen, his features chiseled like a pristine Eterean statue. I'd only spoken to Ires once in person. His image, or whatever it was, had picked up some imperfections since then: a few dents in his bronze breastplate, a tarnished smudge here and there, a spatter of dried blood marring the skirt of his gleaming white chiton. I knew I wasn't seeing *him*, just a simulacrum. Or maybe it was all a dream of getting out bed?

Dreams didn't usually hurt this much.

I swallowed, trying to take hold of my dizziness and surprise. Shadows moved in the corners of the room, in the corners of my eyes. The flutter of big, glossy black wings, a glimpse of blue skin like stone, strangely elongated human forms that disappeared when I turned to look at them full on.

Vanth. Ires's guards.

"Is it nice to see me?" I asked, hoping my voice wasn't cracking and trembling as much as I thought it was.

His smile returned. "Of course it is. I'm happy you're still on this side of the underworld and not the other."

It hadn't occurred to me I might be seeing him because I was dead or dying. I knew Ekyra must have sent me back for a reason, but the idea was enough to make me shaky.

"How are you here, though? Why am I seeing you? You're still shackled."

I cursed my voice for faltering, but I could barely stand. I put my fingers down to the mattress for balance.

A turbulent expression passed over his features. "You invited me in to fight Erelf. That made more of a connection between us. You've become quite a lodestone for magic these days."

"My arm," I groaned. If not for the sling Arsenault had made, I wouldn't be able to hold it up. It hung off my shoulder like a dead weight.

"Perhaps the magic thinks it's found another champion."

"A...what? Why would magic need a champion?"

"Because it's abused. Tekus and his brood are power hungry. They don't care how they achieve their ends. They never have."

"They're gods."

"You think being a god means you have less responsibility than a human being? Eternal life, incredible abilities, magic at your beck and call...and yet, somehow that gives a god a pass? Shouldn't you acquire wisdom at some point if you live forever?"

"I thought they were just bored," I mumbled.

"You'd destroy lives, pit families against each other, burn cities, all for something to do?"

I winced. That hit a little too close to home. Liera was in ruins because I'd been a bored girl in search of passion. "Ah..."

"You were a girl with a fleeting mortal life. Let an opportunity pass by and it's gone forever. You can't claim responsibility for the destruction Erelf and his worshippers have wreaked on the world. No. What we need now is justice."

His eyes flashed, as if *justice* might be a synonym for *vengeance*. I was tired and everything hurt and I needed to use the chamberpot. I didn't want to think about justice or vengeance or whether my sins mattered anymore. I would always take responsibility for what I did, but the longer I stood, the weaker I felt.

"Right now, my battle is just getting out of bed," I told him. "Could you..." I wanted to wave, but I couldn't spare my hand. "I need the chamberpot."

"Would you like me to help you over?" The heavy iron chain binding his manacles chinked as he held out his hands to me. It made a lot of noise for a dream.

"No!" I jerked away, too quickly, then put my hand to my side as if that could cure the burning pain. I had to pause for a moment, take a deep breath.

"Maybe you could just look away?" I said when I could speak again.

I glanced at the shadows. "And send your vanth somewhere else. I don't need them watching me either."

He gave me a peeved look. "Oh, all right. Do what you need to, but don't go back to sleep. I have a lot to ask of you and not much time to spare."

I wanted to pull my hair out in frustration. But I did what I needed to with the chamberpot, and Ires paced while he waited. His image—or whatever it was—grew thin and ragged around the edges. The folds of his chiton were almost transparent as they fluttered in the draft.

I stumbled over to the rocking chair he'd left empty and leaned on it, staring stupidly at the cane seat. I wanted to use both hands to lever myself down slowly but another moment of frustration passed as I tried to figure out how to sit without hurting myself.

Ires touched my elbow. I looked at him in surprise. This close, the faint spice-sweet scent of myrrh and lilies clinging to him swallowed me up. The odor of funerals, stifling and claustrophobic. Seeing my reflection in his dark, ruby-touched eyes was like looking into a mirror made of blood.

His mouth bowed down in a worried and distracted expression as he helped me into the chair.

"If you're a dream, how can you touch me? How can I smell you?"

Ires let his gaze rove over my face. In a man, I might have said *fondly*. But I didn't know what that look meant for a god.

"Does it matter?"

An *infuriating* god.

"Of course it matters! If I'm dreaming, I'm still out of my head. Anything could be happening and I wouldn't know it!"

"Or... it means you're *in* your head. And you're the only one who can know what's happening there."

I bit my lip. I wasn't sure how to reply to that. My body hurt as I sat back. Dreams never carried real pain, so maybe I *was* awake and he was just refusing to answer the godsdamned question.

Finally, I said, in a voice I struggled to keep calm, "But I've found Arsenault. He's been granted a reprieve from his sentence. Erelf agreed to leave him alone, I don't know for how long. What more is there for me to do at this moment?"

Other than figuring out what to do about this godsdamned arm. And making sure Cassis stays out of our affairs. And that Erelf doesn't cheat.

How long would Arsenault's reprieve last? If the answer wasn't *forever,* it was the wrong answer, but I didn't know what I could do about it.

Yet.

Ires gave me a sharp look. I wondered if he could hear what I was thinking. Dealing with gods was a pain in the arse.

"We'll call Ari's reprieve a temporary victory. But true justice has not yet been done. Ekyra is maddeningly inscrutable, but it was hard to take her aid to you as anything other than a strike against Erelf. Perhaps Ekyra *is* maneuvering against her half-brother. You know the gods are still angry at Attrasca for releasing magic into the world. They'd captured it, shackled it, made it into their servant, so they could be gods in the first place. Now Fixers can imitate gods, and people like you—"

"Dream about gods? Eavesdrop unwillingly on conversations they have no right to hear? Foul things up, generally?" I was starting to get tired. I rested my elbow on the arm of the chair and propped my head on my outstretched fingers. My metal arm was a counterweight that didn't allow me to slip too far to the left.

"I wouldn't have put it quite that way. But magic isn't always polite, is it?" The leather harnesses of his breastplate creaked as he knelt before me, an action that surprised me into raising my head again. He gripped my thighs as he held my gaze. "Kyrra. This isn't over. You chose to put yourself under my vow. If you want proof of what I say, you can find it in the sword Erelf stole from me."

"When did I put myself under your vow? You chose me! No vows were exchanged!"

"You asked me to fight for you. And I did. But that means you agreed to be my soldier. To serve under the same vow I do. The new gods shackled my power so I can't use it to force you, but force is *their* way, not mine. My soldiers follow me because they choose my war."

"And what war is that? The war of revenge? Ires, I've spent the last nine years consumed with your war. It's eaten up what's left of my soul. Now I have a chance at a new beginning and I can barely get out of bed! You're trying to trick me into putting blood on a blade for you."

Anger overtook his features. He was still beautiful, but now he was also frightening. And sad, in a way, as if he was grappling with a heavy load of grief. He leaned toward me suddenly and I recoiled into the back of the chair. But there wasn't any escape.

"That's what everyone assumes I want," he said viciously. "The blood, the bodies, the death. Did your captains glory in the destruction wrought by their petty little wars? Did you, after my magic helped you win and you realized what you had done?"

As if he had summoned them, I was hit with a cascade of memories.

Vargis Pass.

I remembered coming to my senses in the snow and bitter cold, surrounded by steaming corpses carved into pieces by my blade or shattered to bits by artillery fire. Some of them enemies but too many of them friends; men who'd fought at my back. And yet I hadn't been able to save any of them, no matter how many terrible things I had done. Bloody heaps of meat were all that was left. As if the battlefield was a slaughterhouse where butchers turned us into raw cuts like sheep and cattle.

Shanks. Shoulders. Ribs.

I wanted to close my eyes, but I'd only see more images of dead men.

"No," I said slowly. "And I cursed you for it. You must have heard me."

One of Ires's perfect brows quirked, bitterly amused. "Everyone curses me, though I help them find justice and stay alive. As a general, my whole purpose was to protect. To defend. Then I was attacked and betrayed. I loved Tekus. I thought our friendship could withstand his insatiable desire for power. But it poisoned him and everything he touched—his children, the magic they used like it was a dead *thing*, a tool for all their twisted desires. Then they said *we* were the stupid ones, silly and old-fashioned, with our vows and our duties..."

His face wrenched in disgust. I watched, fascinated in spite of myself.

"Magic...isn't...a thing?" I asked.

"Does it *feel* like a thing?" Ires asked angrily. "When it's writhing inside you and *begging* you to do or feel or see something? Do you think it's a *thing* then, Kyrra?"

"It's a... What would it even be? A creature?"

Ires inhaled sharply. "It's magic. Something none of you can imagine. Tekus and his brood subjugated it, bound and crushed it, the way they buried me in the underworld so I couldn't visit the same justice on them that they'd brought down on my family. As if we weren't the ones who built the world!"

"So, it *was* you who put war into the world. That much is true?"

When he whirled to face me, I cursed my mouth. I cursed all the kacin tea I'd had to drink, and I cursed my inability to let anything lie.

He did not answer my question. Instead, he took a breath in through his nose and composed himself. Back to the perfect Eterean statue.

"It was my desire to be loved that made me blind to Tekus's ambition," he said in a clipped voice. "A general should be more objective about the company he keeps, and yet, living in constant fear of betrayal is like feeding yourself poison instead of bread. Sometimes, all you want is a proper meal."

A cold draft slunk underneath the shutters and swirled about the room, flattening the ends of his chiton against the hard, sculpted muscles of his thighs.

I wondered suddenly if he created such a perfect image because his reality was ugly and scarred. Perhaps this was what he wanted to be, or perhaps he longed for something better than being chained beneath a volcano like a demon made of ash and fire. I didn't want to relate to Ires. I wanted him to leave me alone. At the same time, I needed to know how this connected to Arsenault and if Arsenault was in danger because of it.

"You may think it was too long ago to matter, but I assure you, time doesn't matter to a god. Don't think Erelf isn't working outside the boundaries of the agreement the other gods made him honor. They only made him honor it because it's something new to break up their eternity."

"All the other gods?" I asked. "Even Ekyra? And Adalus?"

"Your patrons? Adalus's ability to constantly forgive his brother is maddening, but I really can't begin to know how they feel. I'm in prison, remember?" He held up his hands and stretched out the chain between them.

"Doesn't seem to affect your ability to travel."

"Believe me, it does. It also affects who I can talk to and how much. I've said a lot to you, Kyrra, but it's only because you have a piece of the Old World in your arm and another in Ari. The Old World isn't forgotten, nor are the old gods or the old magic. You must ask yourself: To whom should they be entrusted? To what purpose should they be put? And perhaps the deepest question: Is it right to put them to a purpose at all?"

His aura flared with light. For the first time, he looked like a god. His eyes were nothing but bloody darkness. "Follow where that sword leads you. If not for your own sake or the sake of your people, at least do it for Ari."

CHAPTER 5

KYRRA

So, I was a soldier in Ires's army, was I? Bound by a vow that had left more marks on my body than the one I'd made to Arsenault—one I would gladly make again if it meant saving him. If only I knew what I had promised the god in the first place.

I was going to have to find that fucking sword. But how was I supposed to find one sword in a sea of swords with so little to go on? What sword had Erelf stolen from Ires?

I sat in the rocking chair, thinking furiously. Then it hit me—Ires couldn't give me direct instructions, but he also wouldn't risk torture for anything vague.

He must mean the Prinze sword.

Kinstealer.

I had seen Geoffre di Prinze carrying that sword my entire life. It had come down in their family since the days of Attrasca. The Eterean emperor was supposed to have gifted it to the founder of their House. I'd always thought the Prinze named it *Kinstealer* because they liked to swagger to hide their insecurities, the way men made outrageous claims for their cocks. Ires seemed to be making claims both more and less outrageous. The Prinze sword was a beautiful weapon, but the weapon of a god? A weapon that had killed other gods, used in a war of myth and legend?

It had to be more of Ires's mad babbling.

But whose kin had it stolen?

Follow where that sword leads you, he'd said. If he'd said, *Use it to murder the rest of the fucking Prinze, then throw it down a well so nobody can use it again,* it would have made more sense. Most swords led down a path of hate and destruction; opportunities to use them for nobility and justice existed few and far between. As the symbol of the Prinze, this sword would lead first to the Householder's Chair and then to the Circle of Liera. I didn't have a right to either; why would I want to take them?

An aching haze filled my head. I wondered where Arsenault was, and Mikelo, too, since he would have the godsdamned sword if anyone would. Ires's retreat left a buzzing magic in the room, as nerve-wracking as a swarm of bees. I wondered if I should ask Arsenault before I looked for the sword myself, but then I thought no, maybe Erelf had appeared in disguise to trick me, or the magic had tried to trick me, and anyway, Ires was insane.

Except he had sounded so reasonable.

The magic fog beckoned again, as seductive and deadly as sleep to a man in danger of freezing. But if I sank into it, I wouldn't have to *look* for the sword, I could just See Arsenault or Mikelo...

No.

It was like the godsdamned chamberpot all over again. It would have been smarter to go back to bed. And I could have pissed my sheets instead of making the effort to get up; I'm sure I had when I wasn't in my right mind, and Arsenault or Mikelo had dealt with it. It wouldn't have killed me.

But I needed to see for myself what Ires was talking about. I needed to discover if I could See truth in the Prinze blade, as mad as that sounded.

Because it wasn't about me. It was about Arsenault.

I pushed myself out of the chair and shuffled toward the door.

I could swear it was the biggest room in which I'd ever stayed. It seemed to take forever to reach the door, one small, wavering step at a time. But I finally made it. I rested against the frame for a moment and then had to reach across with my left hand to drag the door open. It was an awkward movement and my torso didn't like twisting.

You never realize how the world is built for right-handed people unless you need to use your left hand for everything. I'd relearned to be right-handed after Arsenault gave me my metal arm. Now I wished I hadn't. My right arm clanked uselessly against the door as I ungracefully pulled it inward and tried to step out of the way at the same time. I clung to the handle after I got it open, panting, wheezing, and then I stepped into the hall only to be confronted by a warren of rooms and corridor.

It was the godsdamned fever, making the house seem so improbably large. It had to be.

I forced myself to listen to that small voice of reason so I wouldn't be completely overwhelmed. I'd never known how many muscles were necessary to take a single breath. It felt like Erelf had cut every single one and Mikelo had only been able to repair some of them. It should have been easy, just walk out into the hall, look for the sword with its fancy hilt and glittering sapphire eyes, so damn useless in battle... Except it hadn't been useless in Erelf's hands. Geoffre—or Erelf—had slammed that sword against me again and again. I could still hear its blade clanging off the metal of my side, could feel the hot blade slide into my flesh, lubricated by my blood...

I gulped in the biggest breath I could and squeezed my eyes shut. *Think, dammit.*

Arsenault had called this place a *farmhouse*. He'd said it was north of the lodge. I knew what those houses looked like; I might even have passed this one on my way to Rojornick. Northern Eterean farmhouses were made of stacked stone and stucco, with slate and tile roofs. Modestly sized, if they were prosperous, but not so big I couldn't find my way through, not like the villa in which I'd grown up.

I opened my eyes, hoping everything would return to normal, but the house still seemed so *large*. The hallway yawned toward my left and right with doors on either side and a dim opening—*the common room*, I thought, trying to latch onto something familiar. I decided to walk the opposite way first, so godsdamned slowly, using the wall for support. I gripped the handle of each door as hard as I could and tried to push inward, but none of them budged even when I fell into them.

"Damn," I mumbled. It made sense Jon and Mikelo would keep the sword behind a locked door.

But what if they didn't?

I wanted to give up, go back to bed, but I was already up so I might as well keep going.

The only other direction to go was into the common room, which I navigated with the help of the furniture. There was a lot, thank the gods. There were also a lot of papers, which I accidentally knocked off a table onto the floor in a cascade. No one was there to notice my transgression and I began to feel a little panicked. I told myself of course they wouldn't have left me alone completely, they'd probably just stepped outside, but my heart beat harder all the same. Being abandoned in my illness was an old fear, fueled by memories of the months I'd spent cast off, burning with fever and pain in the chirurgeon's back room. My heart refused to slow and it grew harder and harder to catch my breath.

I finally made it through the common room into the kitchen but then I had to rest. I sagged against the doorframe and closed my eyes while the world spun. The kitchen smelled savory and yeasty, like soup and bread, but it only turned my stomach. I thought again about retreating to my room, but I wasn't sure I could get there by myself. Surely Arsenault would come back soon.

Thinking about Arsenault's absence stirred the panic again. *No, I told myself sternly. Arsenault's swordbelt is slung over the chair. His sword is in its scabbard. He's not out to fight anyone, calm down, dammit.*

My heart finally began to slow. Not only because the presence of his sword told me wherever he was, he hadn't expected trouble, but also because I'd grown to think of that sword as mine. Never mind I couldn't lift it now; I felt better for simply knowing it was there.

Only one place left to look. Upstairs.

I was vaguely aware I hadn't really *looked* for the Prinze sword, I'd just stumbled through the damned house. But I thought it unlikely they'd stuff a Prinze treasure into a cabinet next to the flour and lentils, and a staircase yawned into the darkness just off the kitchen. These farmhouses often had lofts; I'd holed up in more than one abandoned farm on my way north. It was an excellent place to hide something you didn't want anyone to find, especially if you were a Fixer and could rune the whole godsdamned place. It was strange that I hadn't encountered any runes yet, but better for me. Nothing prevented me climbing up there to look.

Nothing except my own body.

The day was gloomy and there were no windows in the stairwell. The stairs seemed to climb forever into nothingness. When I stepped on the first riser and fought my leg up to put it on the second, I felt like I was climbing a mountain. The rail was on the wrong side, another aid meant only for the right-handed—or at least people who still had their right hands. There was nothing I could grab to pull myself up the staircase; I steadied myself precariously by laying my left hand on the opposite wall, and the muscles of my torso throbbed each time I raised my leg to put my foot on another riser. By the middle of the staircase, I was panting, sweating, dizzy, making a noise that maybe...no, it *was* a whimper. But I was stuck. It would be just as hard to go down as it was to keep going up.

I sank to my knees, carefully, slowly, reaching down with my fingertips and wishing I had my right hand to help, afraid of falling and trying not to anger the healing wounds in my torso. My metal arm hit the wooden stair with a ringing thump, but I felt it as a distant frisson, not pain. I squinted up at the top of the stairwell, trying to gauge if there was a door or just an open room.

"How many steps," I gasped, speaking aloud, but to all hells with it. I needed to hear my own voice to know I was still alive. "Count, count... One... Two... Four... Five..."

I groaned and rested my face on the stair above me. Five stairs seemed impossible. Grit bit into my cheek. Why was I doing this? Because I thought Ires had been real in the midst of my fever? He hadn't even given me details. And what if the sword *was* in a locked room and all this effort had been for nothing?

I wished Arsenault—someone—would help me sensibly back to bed. If I fell and no one heard me, what would happen? Did I have a plan for that?

Dear gods, quit being so dramatic. You'd just slide down on your stomach. Get moving, you're almost there.

When I finally struggled onto the landing, I lay there a moment, catching my breath and cradling my aching ribs. I thought I heard noises in the kitchen, but maybe that was only my pulse thudding in my ears. I pushed myself laboriously onto my knees and crawled in my lurching, painful way to the door. If this door was locked, I'd lie there and weep. I was sure someone would find me eventually.

But the door moved when I pushed on it with my shoulder. I rocked back on my haunches and used the edge to pull myself up. Then I stumbled inside.

Another big bed, with lots of quilts neatly folded and stacked in a pile at the foot. A washstand with a porcelain jug and basin. A cloth-covered folio lay on the bed. I thought I recognized its frayed cover from my imperfect memories of Mikelo sitting with me, reading. I collapsed onto the bed and opened it, but there was something wrong with my eyes. The pictures and writing blurred before me. Botany, I thought. Plants, pressed and drawn in ink. An herbal. Yes, that made sense.

Where the hells would he have put that sword?

There was a wardrobe against the wall. To look through it meant I would have to stand again. I groaned out loud. "Fuck you, Ires," I whispered. "And I hope wherever you are, you hear that. Fuck. You."

I shoved myself upright. Too fast. Much too fast.

A blinding pain shot through my side. I folded up with a cry. My knees smacked the wood floor, adding another layer of pain to the throbbing white glare pulsing in my midsection. I tried to catch myself, but as I had done so many years ago, I forgot I couldn't use my right hand and fell flat on my face. My chin knocked against the floor so hard it drove my teeth into my lip. Blood flooded my mouth, hot salt and copper.

"Gods, gods, gods…"

I found myself eye level with the space under the bed. A long, dark lump rested there. A sword-shaped lump.

Gritting my teeth and blinking away tears, I stretched forward and dragged the bundle into the light. It felt like metal. I fought myself into a sitting position and pulled the cloth away.

I was staring at my reflection in the pristine mirror surface of a longsword. My bruised eyes, lips rouged with blood, hair a mess of dirty ropes like fraying strands of hemp. A serpent snarled atop my wavery image. Its deep blue jeweled eyes glittered malevolently, the twisting mass of its body that formed the guard far too bright for the amount of light in the room.

"Mikelo, you beautiful fool," I whispered, startled into wheezy, painful laughter. The irony of him hiding his House's most prized treasure—the sword that had almost killed me, a *god's* sword—in the dust and cat hair under the bed…

Movement in the blade's surface caught my eye. Startled, I stopped laughing and stared at it. It no longer showed me my reflection.

Instead…

Cannon fire and ships.

The steel gray waters of a harbor hung with mist. Ghostly outlines of masts and sails limned with red light. A spray of sparks crackled into the mist followed immediately by a throttling, rattling boom and then a splintering crash, a terrible creaking noise, men shouting and fleeing to escape a listing, falling mast.

A huge silver form coalesced suddenly out of the smoke and mist, a giant thing of scales and feathers and teeth. It snapped its huge jaws closed on the stern of the ship, crunching its beams and timbers as if they were matchsticks. Bodies dangled from teeth as big as the staves of a portcullis.

I gasped and grabbed the sword. But in that moment someone cried, "Kyrra!" Boots thumped toward me, fast, and a man grabbed me by the shoulder and yanked me backward.

Mikelo, it's Mikelo—

"Let me go!" I cried, struggling. "I need to see more! Mikelo—dammit!"

"It's too much magic, Kyrra, you're hurting yourself!" He pinned me against his chest. I tried to throw an elbow into his ribs but my arm was useless. And then I started to cough.

When I had served Markus Seroditch in Rojornick, I had once been assigned guard duty for his wife. The magic she'd wielded to protect Markus had been killing her, and now I sounded just like she had in those last months before she died. The soupy paroxysms of coughing scraped and burned my lungs, going on and on until I couldn't *breathe*...

As if that wasn't enough, they also mercilessly worked the muscles of my midsection. I felt like I was being stabbed and suffocated at the same time.

Maybe Ires wanted to kill me, oh gods, I wish this would stop, why doesn't it stop...

Eventually, the coughing did stop and the white light flaring from the runes on my arm dimmed. Mikelo was bracing me against his chest. He smelled like the outdoors. His shirt was damp. I took a breath, as deep as I could without hurting myself, and let sensations from the real world fill me. Not a world created by magic, full of violence and horrible creatures, where there was no division between reality and dream and I was at its mercy.

"Did you See it, too?" I asked Mikelo. "It was like the wars, except that creature at the end."

"The dragon," Mikelo replied shakily.

Dragon. Yes. Just like the fancy twisting serpent on the hilt of the sword itself. The magic was trying to trick me. Fucking Ires, what did he think he was doing?

"You shouldn't have stopped me," I rasped. I carefully sat up.

"The magic's eating away at your body. The more it takes you, the more damage it does. It lodges in your lungs like... Do you know those pools on the other side of Mount Kosemi, the hot springs ringed with colors?"

"I don't see—"

"Supposedly they dissolve anything that falls into them. Men have tried to take samples, but the water eats straight through every container they try—wood, pottery, metal, glass."

"Those springs aren't magic, though. It's probably some element—"

"Kyrra. The magic is like the water in those springs."

I wasn't sure what I thought about my lungs being eaten by acid. It wasn't the kind of enemy I could fight, except to keep trying to get back up when I was knocked down.

"I suppose you would know what it looks like," I conceded reluctantly. "The wife of the lord I fought for in Rojornick—the Lady Serodnaya—died of magic poisoning, but I thought she'd willfully used it too much. She was trying to protect her husband from too many threats and it overwhelmed her."

I looked at my arm in its sling. The runes had stopped glowing and now it was just...dead. A chunk of metal that invited Ires and his magic to torment me.

There were old Eterean stories of strange, fantastic monsters, of course. The most authoritative were written by a Qalfan explorer named Oji la Kaif.

Oji had begun as a caravan clerk and ended up traveling the entire ancient world, experiencing everything it had to offer and meticulously recording his impressions, complete with sketches and paintings. My tutor, who'd believed in an efficiency of education, had made me copy out long passages from reproductions of la Kaif's work, hoping to improve my penmanship while teaching me ancient history. He'd always chosen the most boring parts, about trade routes and the qualities of virtuous women. I suspected la Kaif had included those only because he'd been forced to. Whenever my tutor left the room, I would sneak glimpses of his other stories, of bloodthirsty griffins and poisonous basilisks and sea serpents and shipwrecks—doomed romances and passionate affairs that always seemed to end with Oji escaping the local authorities. I'd always sympathized with his longsuffering companion, never named, who faithfully and consistently searched for Oji whenever he ended up in a filthy prison at the ends of the earth.

My tutor's copy had been reproduced by a mediocre artist, but my father had brought me to the Doge's Library in Liera once and I had seen an original manuscript, its parchment crumbling at the edges with age but the illustrations still so vibrant they looked as if they had been laid down by magic.

Dragons. Fairy stories. Legends written to impress the people back home.

Ires was trying to force me ever further into irrational acts of revenge. What would it serve to steal the Prinze sword from Mikelo, who would need it if he wanted to claim the Prinze Householder's Chair from his unworthy cousins?

"I don't know what I Saw," I groused. "It was all jumbled up. I don't know what Ires wants me to do." Another cough surprised me. I wrapped my arm around my stomach in pain. "Damn. Oh, damn, that hurts."

"Kyrra," Mikelo said in exasperation. "Stop using your magic."

I hadn't been aware I was, but the runes on my arm glowed softly, lighting up my reflection in my right hand, which was curled loosely into a fist poking out of the sling. I willed the godsdamned thing to move, but it only showed me the glimmer of the room and the feverish glow of my own face.

"Mikelo, *things are going wrong.*" I wanted to pace. It made me even more frustrated that I couldn't. "Who's fighting now that I've killed Geoffre? How many wars will be laid at my feet?"

"You're not yourself, Kyrra. You didn't cause the first war. It was Geoffre then, and if there's another war it will also be because of Geoffre, and you know you don't regret killing him. This isn't you talking."

Was it not? The blurred image reflected in my fingers began to change.

"The magic is trying to tell me something. If only I could listen better." I growled in frustration. "You know this isn't over. What is Erelf doing? He won't leave Arsenault alone, I know it. What does it have to do with this godsdamned sword?"

Something in me knew I wasn't making sense. I'd jumped over information I should have told Mikelo—or had I? He'd seen the vision in the blade, too.

"I agree with you. But we have to push the magic back or you won't be able to help Arsenault at all. Maybe Erelf's attacking you with magic because he knows you can't control it?"

That was a terrifying thought.

"I don't think..." I moved and the pain got me again. "Ow. Godsdammit, Mikelo, why does it hurt so fucking much?"

"You know how I know I'm talking to you and not the magic? When the magic has hold of you, you don't swear this much."

I glared at him. "If you think magic has better manners, you're a fool. I don't know whose responsibility it is, but I don't think Erelf has anything to gain by telling me magic has a mind of its own."

Mikelo's expression changed, like he'd never considered magic having a mind of its own either and it scared him. Or... I didn't know what the hells it was like to be a Fixer; maybe he already knew.

"But if it kills you trying?"

The images in my hand caught my attention for good this time. I wanted to open my palm so there would be a bigger canvas, but instead I was left watching the minuscule scene trapped in the knuckle of my thumb, my silver fingernails like convex crescent mirrors, showing...what?

A man sitting on a... Was that a throne? He looked familiar, but I could only see his silhouette, a deep green coat, dark hair. A woman stood beside him, half-hidden in shadow but with her hand on his shoulder. A glint of smoldering auburn... Was that her hair or firelight behind her? And the curve of a giant wing, like a vanth's...

"Who is that?" Mikelo breathed. "Where are they?"

Panicked thudding on the stairs jerked me back to reality. Mikelo and I stared at each other in surprise, and then the door wrenched open and Arsenault burst into the room, looking wild and fearful.

He dropped to his knees and shoved Mikelo aside to take me by the shoulders.

"Are you hurt?" he asked breathlessly. "I was only outside for a little while, not even an hour by that mantel clock..."

"I'm all right, Arsenault."

"Dammit, you're bleeding! And you're burning up again!"

Then he saw the sword.

"I took it away from her," Mikelo said hastily, like we were children caught misbehaving. "As soon as I found her."

His words made me angry. I opened my mouth to reply but then I found Arsenault's gaze settled on me, unguarded and terrified.

"Why did you want that sword, Kyrra?"

I wanted to lie. I wanted to say some half-truth or a non-answer he could take two ways, the way he'd answered me when we'd lived in the gavaro barracks at the villa. It had become a habit with me now, too. But the healing cut on my left hand throbbed to remind me of our vows, and as the fear in his gray eyes grew the longer I took to answer, I couldn't.

"Ires told me to look for it," I mumbled, casting my gaze down at my hand again. No reflections now, just smears of dim light from the window. "He said Erelf stole it from him."

Arsenault and Mikelo both stared at me, dumbfounded. I sighed and my wheezy lungs sounded like a bellows. "Why are you looking at me like that?"

"It's not Ires's sword," Mikelo said. "It can't be. It's the sword the Prinze Householder needs to claim his right to the Chair, that's all. An heirloom. Why would you listen to Ires?"

"Because I was curious. He told me I needed to follow where the sword led. Maybe he just wanted me to get off my arse."

"It's made of tiaannamir," Arsenault said suddenly. "The same metal as your arm."

I looked at him in confusion. I had suspected as much, but... "You think it's like calling to like?"

"No, I don't. Here, Kyrra, get up onto the bed. Let me see where the blood is coming from."

"My mouth. I bit my lip. Arsenault, *dammit*, will you stop fussing?"

"When you can get onto the bed by yourself, I'll stop fussing. There's too much magic in this room."

I lay back on the pillows Arsenault had plumped behind me. Slowly the muscles of my torso relaxed. I thought about having to go all the way downstairs again and wondered if I'd only succeeded in taking over Mikelo and Silva's room.

"*Is* it Ires's sword, Arsenault?" Mikelo asked. "*Did* Erelf steal it?"

"I don't know." Arsenault leaned closer to me, examining my lip. "Do you have a towel up here, Mikelo? Water in the basin?"

"R-right," Mikelo said guiltily. "Of course. I don't know why I didn't think of that sooner..."

"It's not his fault," I told Arsenault. "He hasn't had a chance to think about it till now. I could just use my sleeve."

"We've been trying to keep you from bleeding on that shirt, Kyrra." Mikelo handed Arsenault a towel, then moved the basin to the bed and poured water from a pitcher into it. Arsenault nodded his thanks and dipped the towel in the water, then touched it to my split lip. It stung a little and I winced.

"It is just your lip," Arsenault murmured in relief.

"I said so, didn't I?" I grumbled. "I just... I fell. I forgot I didn't have a hand."

"No feeling in the arm yet?"

"Pins and needles sometimes. I was tired when I asked you to let it be, but now I wish you'd Fix it. Even if I could only have partial use of it."

He turned his troubled, thoughtful gaze to my arm, but his eyes didn't light and I couldn't feel him using his magic. "It seems like there's metal missing. I suppose that sword could have cut it out of you. I've been trying to think of how to Fix it without recasting it. But I'm worried some recasting may be inevitable."

"Do you mean you'll have to amputate it again?" I asked in alarm.

"Arsenault," Mikelo interjected quickly. "I'm not sure her body can handle that."

Arsenault shook his head firmly. "I wouldn't risk it anyway." He continued to examine me with what I could only describe as an artisan's eye. I had seen the same expression on blacksmiths as they examined a broken sword. It was a little disconcerting to find Arsenault looking at me that way, although I had often watched him approach mechanical problems in just such a fashion.

"If I was repairing a statue that had taken this much damage," he went on, "I would be forced to melt it down and pour it in the mold again. You're not a statue, but I'm afraid the principle is similar. The metal will have to be molten so I can work it. I *might* be able to do it a little at a time, but the forearm... I'm not sure I can repair the damage there without using new metal. And mixing new tiaannamir and old might have other effects."

He rubbed his jaw thoughtfully and looked down at the floor.

I found myself a little faint at the thought of my arm being recast, but when I noticed what he was looking at, I grew even more alarmed.

"You're not thinking of putting the Prinze sword in my arm, are you?" I asked, aghast. "Ires said to follow where it led, not make it part of me."

Arsenault recoiled. "Gods! Put *that* in your arm? If I had my way, I'd melt it down and throw it in the caldera of Mount Kosemi. I was thinking about the metal. All tiaannamir has its own character. It begins in its origin, then evolves through use. I gathered the metal for your arm from antiquities markets in Liera. I was under magical proscription, but I tried to make sure it would be compatible. There's something about that Prinze serpent, though..."

"The hilt? What do you mean?"

Arsenault folded the towel carefully over the lip of the basin. He wasn't looking at me, so I knew whatever he had to say, I wasn't going to like it. I tried not to tense, but I didn't succeed.

"Tiaannamir fell from the sky in the battles the old gods fought with Tekus and his children. From their molten, destroyed swords. And...from their bodies. The old gods could take any form they wished and many of them chose to become monsters. If you think about it like that, Erelf might have stolen this sword from Ires. The metal came from his kin."

I stared at him. Eventually he looked up at me, chagrined.

"Have I finally succeeded in rendering you speechless?"

"You made my arm out of *Ires's metal?* And your sword and the Prinze sword are both made from the same thing?"

"The metal that made your arm didn't belong to Ires. He's still alive. Perhaps to one of his family members, but not—no, not Ires himself... No, I didn't... Gods." He brought his fingers to the bridge of his nose and closed his eyes. It was such a familiar gesture that even in my shock and astonishment, it made my heart twinge. He was here with me but only so recently. I wasn't used to thinking in years and I was suddenly terrified he would be taken from me again or I would be taken from him. Maybe he was right about going to Orienne. But the gods would be able to find us there, too.

He looked at me sideways, still rubbing his brow. "You see how I keep failing you, Kyrra."

His words snapped me back to the moment. "Stop feeling guilty for giving me my arm. As if you think you made *me* into some kind of monster."

He winced like I'd hit him. "That's not what I meant. Your arm probably magnifies the assaults the magic makes against you. It doesn't surprise me Ires keeps whispering at you, after you let him in to fight for me. A mad god will do or say anything to get what he wants, and what Ires wants is vengeance against Erelf."

What Arsenault said seemed reasonable... As reasonable as the things Ires had said. Trying to sort out this mess was exhausting. Maybe it would be better to let it lie.

"You're probably right," I said grudgingly. "Maybe it was just a vision. But I've spoken to Ires before. He knows about you, and—"

"They all know about me. And I'm grateful to him for helping you survive that battle. But gods don't have human hearts. I made that mistake once, treating a goddess like a woman. But she wasn't, and Ires isn't a man."

I traded a startled glance with Mikelo. "You're talking about your wife."

It seemed strange to hear Arsenault say the words so matter-of-factly. I had read both his book and his letter. I'd heard every accusation Erelf had made against him. He'd even confessed with his own tongue. But it still felt odd as a topic of conversation, as if his wife—Erelf's daughter, a goddess—was someone I could know, like a gavaro's woman in another town.

Arsenault hesitantly touched my arm. I barely felt his fingers on my forearm, when before, his human skin had felt like fire against my metal flesh. Now it was only a dim echo in a vast, aching emptiness.

He stretched my fingers out and began to rub them, although the only reason I knew was because I was watching.

He kept his gaze on our hands, too. "I experimented. Steel was too heavy. Bronze too soft. Silver was pretty, but it wasn't hard enough and it turned black. I knew tiaannamir would be the perfect metal, but I went through the other options first. And then I thought, why am I trying to do something difficult and dangerous if something simple might suffice?"

"The wooden arm, you mean. The one you threw out the window."

He nodded. "You didn't need simple. You needed difficult and dangerous."

His words squeezed something in my chest. I didn't know if I wanted to be difficult and dangerous anymore, but then again, he was the only one who'd ever accepted it, who hadn't tried to force me to be wooden and simple.

"Well," I said, embarrassed. "The metal you chose works well most of the time. My arm got me out of some difficult scrapes. Earned me a fair bit of coin, too. My company used to enter me in arm-wrestling contests so they could bet on me. I looked like such a scrawny weakling the odds against me were always astronomical."

"Wonder you weren't murdered for cheating," Arsenault murmured. At least I'd coaxed out that reluctant hook at the corner of his mouth.

"We could only do it once per town. In the camps, we went company to company, but only for a single night. Word traveled fast after that. Ergus and Nibas always backed me up, which was fortunate because not every man was happy at being duped." I fell silent for a moment. "This is ridiculous, Arsenault. Why don't you Fix my arm now? Then I'll be able to sort Ires."

He hesitated. "Now? The process won't be gentle. I haven't done it yet because you asked me not to, but I don't know if you could have borne it anyway."

"I'm not sure you can bear it now," Mikelo said. "Are you sure—"

"If it will help me recover faster, just...do it. Get it over with. I can't feel worse, can I?" The tortured look Arsenault gave me made me regret my words. "At least Mikelo's here," I amended guiltily.

"Oh, *that* doesn't put any more pressure on me." Mikelo ran a hand through his hair. "Could I at least eat the midday meal first?"

"Stay here while I see if it's even possible," Arsenault said. "Just...a moment."

He began untying the sling. I tried to ignore how close he was, the way he leaned over me to fumble at the cloth. Perhaps Ires was more perfect in all his proportions, but I loved Arsenault's scruffy black beard, newly grown to hide the bottom of his scar again. His nose that was perhaps a bit too long, too sharp, his shadowed gray eyes, and the way his hair always slid into his face. I loved the feel of him, how the muscles of his shoulders moved under his shirt as he fought with the knot, the intent way he focused on his fingers, and the scent of musk and soap that spoke more of life than death.

Mikelo cleared his throat. "Shall I leave?" he asked hesitantly.

Arsenault looked up suddenly and caught me watching him. My cheeks flamed. Arsenault grinned. "No, Mikelo. Stay. In case."

To me, he murmured, "I think your fever's talking."

"It's five years talking," I whispered. His brow hitched and then he had the knot open and pulled the sling away from my arm.

All three of us looked at it. It was just as mangled as it had been the first time I'd seen it. A twisted, dented thing that hardly looked like an arm anymore. It made me sick. A big, pommel-shaped divot caved in my forearm, all the way to my elbow. It obliterated the dent Arsenault had made when we had fought in the alley. That divot matched the pommel of the Prinze sword lying on the floor, unscratched, undented, unbroken. The serpent's blue eyes winked at me from the hilt like a monster waiting to sink its fangs into my heart...

Arsenault touched my arm and I gasped.

"It will be uncomfortable," he said. "It might hurt. I just want to see if I can even it out instead of adding more metal."

His voice trailed away in a swirl of magic that caught me up in a rough embrace. His magic always took me by surprise. I never expected it to feel so much like him. All that strength and power under such tight control. I was never truly afraid in its grip, but—

It might hurt...

Arsenault's magic burned away all the numbness. I felt every dent, every scratch and pit, every unnatural twist as if it was flesh and bone. Through the pain's red haze I heard a sound and realized I was crying out—caught a glimpse of Arsenault, the muscles of his jaw strung taut with effort—watched my metal arm heat, red to orange to white... It looked and felt as if my flesh was boiling.

"Arsenault! *Arsenault!*"

"Hold on, Kyrra—"

But I was too weak. I tumbled into the well of magic he opened around me and spread out in the blessed, pain-free darkness as if I had become the surface of the sea.

CHAPTER 6

CASSIS

"WE'VE GOT A PROBLEM, MESTERE."

Cassis glanced up blearily from his desk. Lobardin stood in the doorway, looking grim, but Cassis couldn't remember telling him to come in. His desk was covered in an ocean of correspondence. The days after the skirmish in Devid's camp had been a blur, a continuous chain of nothing but problems.

"Can't it wait? If Vokavik's not about to come over the walls, I still need to go through all this." Cassis gestured helplessly at the papers.

Instead of answering, Lobardin pushed the door shut and moved over to Cassis's desk. He leaned on the desktop, so close Cassis could smell the scent that lingered on his clothes. Cooking. Cassis looked up at him in surprise.

"It's about the food," Lobardin murmured. "I think you'd better come see for yourself, mestere."

FOOD WAS THE MOST SENSITIVE, CRUCIAL PART OF THEIR WHOLE operation. The men didn't know how low their stores had gotten. The wily, brutal Vokavik was starting out with fewer troops, but he'd retained most of Geoffre's ammunition and supplies and was using them to good advantage. Yesterday, Vokavik had torched the nearest village, put its residents to the sword, and stolen what remained of their harvest—all to prevent Cassis from taking it.

Cassis regretted his former smugness. It felt now as if he'd simply been tempting fate.

Vokavik had also been nettling them with constant bombardment. This deep inside the lodge Cassis couldn't hear it, which was another reason he'd escaped to this room. The sound of crashing cannon and arquebus fire made him want to crawl out of this skin. Perhaps he could leave his life as Cassis di Prinze and live as a new man in some other, more peaceful world. Every whistling ball gave him more bizarre thoughts about how to make his escape. If it went on much longer, he might go well and truly mad. He missed Driese. Her presence had anchored him. Without her, there was nothing to push back the darkness.

But even news of Driese and the baby was missing from the sea of correspondence. Ironically, his first wife Camile had sent him a pile of letters; she seemed determined to ruin him as much as Devid did. Demanding more coin again, as if he hadn't left her in possession of the townhome in Liera.

"You need a secretary, mestere," Lobardin muttered, retrieving a pile of papers that had slid off the corner of the desk.

Cassis snatched them back. "Are you volunteering?"

Lobardin looked affronted. "I've of course had the *training* a secretary needs, but I've been your liaison with Jon Barra for some time now. Maybe you don't want to make me privy to *all* your most sensitive secrets."

Cassis scowled at the overflowing pile of papers. "Probably nothing Jon doesn't already know, damn him. Reports of Dakkaran pirates as far north as the Onzarran archipelago and what with all the rumors about Renzo... The *Hind* is already late coming in. We needed that shipment of guns and wheat months ago."

Lobardin's mouth bowed downward. "Just put all the papers in a drawer and lock it, mestere."

That seemed reasonable. Cassis hated to leave everything out of order—surely he could force this little piece of his world to make sense—but instead he shoved it all into a pile with the corners going every which way. He felt itchy inside as he carried the papers over to a tall cabinet painted with a mural of Attrasca surveying his empire. Everything in Pallo d'Aliente's study exuded an ancient Eterean past that hovered ominously over his shoulder. Cassis wondered if Attrasca had ever felt like his world was falling apart because his papers were in disarray.

He thumbed apart the Eterean puzzle lock, which had only

protected the stable and kennel roll books and not a map to the Legacy of Attrasca as he'd hoped, stuffed the papers in the safe, then straightened his tunic. "Well?" he asked.

"The larder," Lobardin answered grimly.

The kitchens should have been bustling with pre-dawn activity, as he remembered the kitchens in the Villa di Prinze when he was a boy —fire burning cheerily in the hearth, smelling permanently of sizzling fat and bread and the sweets the cook had baked for his mother, who'd had a terrible sweet tooth. He and his mother had spent more than one secret afternoon closeted in the larder, eating sticky buns and avoiding Geoffre.

His campaign cook was a wizard, but without bread, it would be difficult to keep the men loyal. Stomachs won out over reputation eventually, every time.

The servants all seemed to be going about their routines as usual, though an older woman standing against the wall looked nervous. She ran a towel through her hands while another woman stood beside her, patting her shoulder. A Qalfan woman, Cassis didn't know what her name was, but he thought he'd seen her before, down by the creek doing his men's laundry. She seemed to come and go, but with Vokavik's bombardment, they were all stuck here, under siege.

He nodded to both women absently as Lobardin stopped to light a tallow candle and led him into the larder and its connected storage rooms. They stored all their food here, in the center of the lodge, where it would be available if they had to fall back quickly.

The larder seemed untouched—and distressingly spare. But there were still some cheeses on the shelves, jars of pickles, and a few crates of salt pork and ship's biscuits the men grumbled about but which kept them fed. The lids to the biscuits were askew. Cassis frowned at them.

"Shouldn't those be closed so the moisture stays out?"

"Aye," Lobardin answered. "They should." He pushed open a door at the back of the larder and gestured Cassis into the dark room beyond. The guttering candle cast large, ominous shadows on the far wall. Bins and crates and bags. Cassis looked around the darkness in confusion, and then—

"Here, mestere. This is your problem."

Two men lay on the floor in the gloom, both bound hand and foot and gagged tightly. One was limp, his eyes closed, a great clotted mass of dark blood sticking in his hair.

"What's this?" Cassis asked in surprise.

"They were caught poisoning the biscuits, mestere. The cook heard noises when she came in to get the fire going. The washer woman was here picking up kitchen towels and together they managed to apprehend them."

"My cook and the washerwoman?" Cassis asked incredulously. "Where were your guards?"

"On patrol. They said they didn't see anyone go in or out. Fortunately, the women reacted quickly. The cook took an iron kettle to this one's head; I'm not sure if he'll survive. The other, your washerwoman, is a fair hand with a butcher knife. Let your chirurgeon stitch him up and he'll be right as rain. Leave that wound and..." Lobardin shrugged.

"Are you saying my washerwoman left him alive on purpose so we could question him? Maybe I should be paying her a gavaro's coin."

Lobardin snorted. "Fortunately, I was picking up a bit of early breakfast. The kitchen boy didn't have to run far to find me."

"How the hells did we let them in? Or have we been betrayed by our own?"

"I haven't questioned them yet. No one saw them come in, but you and your brother still have the same colors, mestere. They wouldn't have even had to change armbands. Vokavik's a weasel, but in a lot of ways, he's like Arsenault—if he can win with a ruse, he'll do it. Unlike Arsenault, he'll send men on suicide missions."

"Arsenault would have ordered men to do the same."

"Men would have *volunteered* to do the same for Arsenault. Vokavik's leveraging the few gavaros who remain loyal to Geoffre, that's all."

The conscious man bound on the floor glared up at them murderously. Lobardin nudged him roughly in the ribs with his boot and earned a muffled expletive. "The poison is over there in a sack. Doesn't take much to spoil all our stores."

Cassis steeled himself to ask the question he didn't really want to ask. "How much did they ruin?"

"Not sure yet. I thought perhaps we might have him tell us. The poison is esoteric, but I recognize it. Don't touch it with your bare fingers; it will seep into your skin. According to legend, Attrasca used it to demolish Barca's army in the war against Tiresia. Killed all his elephants, too."

"Elephants."

"That's the story. You've heard it, surely?"

"Of course I have. Devid seems uncharacteristically interested in ancient lore these days."

"Perhaps it's time to hear their story." Lobardin dug his boot into the man's side again, and this time the man definitely sounded like he was in pain. Sweat glistened on his forehead in the candlelight.

"Undo his gag," Cassis ordered.

Lobardin knelt and fumbled at the knot with his thick leather gloves. Cassis studied the man while Lobardin jerked him around. Geoffre had included Fixers among his army, but surely if the man had magic, Lobardin would have warned him. "Whatever my brother is paying you, it can't be enough to throw away your lives like this."

"We didn't do it for coin," the man spat. "We're Prinze and we're standing for our House. The House you're trying to tear down!"

Cassis caught his breath. His godsdamned relatives. "Do I know you?"

The man's expression grew surly. "My brother and I aren't main branch. But unlike you, we're faithful. We know a House needs a strong foundation."

"Spare me the rhetoric or I'll have Lobardin gag you again. How did you get in? Surely you didn't just *walk* in."

The man went stubbornly silent.

It always came down to this, didn't it? He hated it, just wanted all the fucking violence to end. "Lobardin," he sighed.

Lobardin took a barely audible breath, like he was also steeling himself for this process. Then he drew back his boot and drove it into the man's wound. Hard.

The man howled and Cassis flinched before he could stop it. Lobardin took a quick breath.

"How did you get in?" Cassis asked the man on the floor, who was still writhing in pain.

The man squeezed his eyes shut and said nothing.

"I can keep doing this all day," Lobardin said. "Or you could tell us what we want to know and we could kill you quickly. Your choice."

"We just walked in," the man said.

Lobardin shoved his boot into the man's wound again. "Liar."

"It's true. We used the fucking armbands, and your pathetic sentinel—"

"Lobardin," Cassis sighed.

Lobardin drew back his foot like he was preparing for another kick. The man on the ground tried to squirm away—there was a scuffing sound... No, the sound came from a different direction. Cassis grabbed Lobardin's shoulder.

"Wait, stop. What was that?"

The darkness suddenly felt dangerous and thick. The scuffing became a grinding noise, and now Cassis could place it. It was coming from one of the storage rooms at the back, the one that housed their emergency water supply. The storage rooms were underneath the lodge; had a cannon hit above them?

For an instant, his fear of being trapped in rubble blinded him. His heart started pounding, he was sweating—*dammit, not now!*

Lobardin's voice finally encroached on the panicked dark. "Mestere! Look there."

Lights bobbed—torches, not candles—and the shapes of two men resolved, hardly more than shadows. The torchlight glinted off spectacles and Cassis swore in surprise. His momentary panic transformed to rage. He gripped the hilt of his sword in reflex so hard the wires cut into the palm of his hand.

"Devid's fucking Empirist! What in all the hells are you doing here? Poisoning my food!" He turned to the men on the floor. "You used a tunnel!"

The Empirist bowed his head as he came closer. "Tomas and I aren't here to poison your food, mestere." He dusted cobwebs and stone dust off his shoulders as he straightened, and the gavaro with him—*Tomas*—did the same. Tomas was Tiresian by the look of him, his mass of black braids beaded with glass glittering in the light—but wearing Dakarran gold in his ear like Jon fucking Barra.

If Jon had anything to do with this—

"In fact, we're here to help you. These two were about to block off your water supply and bring the whole lodge down on your heads."

❧

CASSIS STARED AT THE MAN IN SHOCK, HIS ANGER SUDDENLY frozen. What was his name? *Lupa.*

"You're here to *help*? How? Why?"

"I did a job for Devid di Prinze. That doesn't mean I'm loyal to him. I'm a scholar. A gavaro of knowledge, if you will."

Lobardin's brows lifted. "Pardon, ser, are you trying to say you're a spy?"

Lupa gave them an embarrassed smile and fiddled with his spectacles, settling them on the bridge of his nose more firmly. "Perhaps it isn't the best metaphor. The heart of the matter is the Eterean heritage contained in this lodge. I couldn't allow it to be destroyed in an internecine feud."

Cassis frowned and glanced at the bound man on the floor, who was staring up at them in bewilderment. "You make it sound so...petty."

"Forgive me, mestere. You and your brother simply lack the knowledge to see the larger tapestry. I'm sorry to say I did have something to do with the discovery of the tunnel. I knew it had to exist because both Eskylus and Carpachi mention multiple passageways, and if one overlays their descriptions on a map—"

"Just get to the point. They were going to block my water supply?"

"The aquifer. In the cave beneath the lodge. That's what your well accesses. The tunnel ingeniously bores into the cave system that riddles these mountains. It follows the aquifer and comes up in a staircase near the well. The ancient writers speculated that perhaps Attrasca had hidden his Legacy in the cave, but—"

"But Attrasca's Legacy is a bunch of fairy dust, Lupa, and what's important here is, *did these men poison our water supply?*"

Lupa removed his spectacles and began polishing them on his shirt. "I'm not sure. Tomas and I were too far behind to see exactly what they were doing, and of course, we were following them in the dark so they wouldn't see us. Did you notice anything, Tomas?"

Lupa's gavaro drew himself up. He was so quiet and well-trained Cassis had almost forgotten he was there. But when he shook his head, the beads in his braids chinked together. The sound seemed louder in the charged silence. "No, ser. They laid the powder—"

"Powder?" Cassis repeated in alarm.

"And a fuse. I don't know which of them has it or how long it would take to burn down if they lit it."

"Gods, man, why didn't you just say so right away!"

The gavaro's glance flickered back at Lupa, who jumped as if he'd been pricked with a needle. "Oh, yes! Of course! I've been distracted! I did think we had time, because they'd need to get back down into the tunnel and look for the treasure—"

"They were looking for treasure, too? They know about the treasure?"

"Well, Eskylus—"

"I don't want to hear about bloody Eskylus!" Cassis turned suddenly to the man on the floor. "You're going to tell us exactly what you were doing down there and where the godsdamned fuse is and if there's poison in the water. *Now* if you want to live."

"I'm willing to die for my House!"

"You've no idea what issues are involved here. You're not even of the main branch!"

"If you'll permit me, mestere?" Lupa said. "I think I know which questions to ask."

"Be my guest," Cassis said tightly and stepped aside.

Lupa knelt beside the unconscious man on the floor. The other man eyed Lupa warily. In the candlelight, his face was pale and waxy, his dark eyes shadowed by dirty dark hair.

Cassis didn't know what he expected out of Lupa. Questions, certainly. More references to bloody Eskylus probably, though they were surely running out of time. But Lupa reached into his pocket for a pair of gloves and drew them on efficiently. He set his gloved fingers to the unconscious man's neck, feeling for a pulse. "He's still alive," he announced, then sorted through the man's hair for the wound made by the cook's iron kettle. "Ah. A depression here. Tomas, will you put your fingers on it for me? Can you feel it?"

The gavaro knelt silently—hesitantly—to put his own fingers in their heavy leather gloves, like the ones Lobardin was wearing, against the man's wound.

The other prisoner's eyes flickered back and forth, watching.

"I think his skull is fractured," Lupa said. "Press down, would you, Tomas? Slowly now. Does the bone move?"

"I don't—"

"Just slowly, Tomas. But use a little pressure. We need to see how much the bones move, don't we?"

Oh gods, no, we don't.

For a bewildering instant, Cassis wasn't sure what Lupa was doing. Was he really trying to get medical information? Was he torturing the conscious man, torturing his gavaro—torturing *them*? Tomas started to press down, then stopped, a fine sheen of sweat glistening on his forehead.

"Ser Lupa, there's a soft spot, I don't think I need to push to know."

Lupa sighed. "Move out of the way, Tomas. I suppose I'll have to do this myself. I may be able to repair the wound, but I was hoping to get a little help."

Cassis traded glances with Lobardin, who looked deeply skeptical.

Tomas moved away, relief washing over his face. The other man on the ground looked relieved, too.

Maybe they'd be able to avoid torture. Maybe it was a good idea Lupa had, holding out the carrot instead of the stick. Interrogations made Cassis sick to his stomach, but it was damn hard to motivate a hero.

Then Lupa began pushing on the head wound.

He did it with agonizing slowness. The wound made a squelching, grinding sound that grew worse the more pressure Lupa put on it. Fresh crimson trickled down the man's temple and the smell of blood mingled with the dusty food smells of the larder turned Cassis's stomach. His palms began to sweat and the conscious man whimpered. The unconscious man didn't move at all, just lay there while Lupa felt around his skull, and somehow that made it so much worse.

"Well?" Cassis forced himself not to look at Lupa. It was the only way he could put the steel he needed into his voice. *Don't look, don't ever look. Don't think about the way they all eventually break, how fragile their bodies are, the way Geoffre used to—the way he—*

It had been easier to be cruel to Arsenault. Anger was fuel and if you were burning with fire, the flames would blind you, so you couldn't see what you were doing.

"I think this is probably where the handle got him."

Lupa pressed down, hard, with his thumb.

The unconscious man twitched. One leg stiffened and his bootheel began rapping time on the stone tiles—*tap taptaptaptap*—rattling and thumping. His leg jittered all down its length and his body jerked like a fish. Cassis had seen men with head wounds fall down in fits before, but this was so much worse. The other man cried out in anguish, but Lupa kept pushing and the injured man kept up his fascinating, horrible dance, never opening his eyes though he began gurgling and his neck arched as if pulled on strings—

"For the gods' sake, stop!" his compatriot shouted. "Are you monsters?"

Cassis's stomach turned. "Think he'll come back to haunt you? Will he blame you for this when he's dead?"

"You said you could repair it! You said—"

"I said I might be able to," Lupa answered in a reasonable voice. "If you tell us where the fuse is, what you were supposed to do on the way out, and who you were doing it for."

"Gods! Just—stop! Stop! I'll talk, for the gods' sake! It was a long, slow fuse and it was his job to light it! I didn't see what he was doing because I had the poison. We did the food first. We were going to do the water on the way back—"

"I think you're lying," Lupa said. "He looks like he's lying, doesn't he? If you were going to block the aquifer, you'd want to poison the well on the way up. And you wouldn't want the whole supply to be poisoned, would you, because Vokavik wants to take this lodge. You had another goal, didn't you?"

"The treasure?" Cassis asked.

"No, it—yes! The treasure, the Legacy! Devid said it was supposed to be here and that you had it because Geoffre had found it, but all we ran across was a lump of tarnished metal. That's it, I swear!"

"And where is this metal?"

"Ser," Lobardin broke in. "Who fucking cares about the metal? Where did you lay that fuse?"

"Behind us!"

Lobardin grabbed Tomas. "Help me look for the damn fuse. The end of it must be here somewhere—"

"Now the metal," Lupa said calmly.

"He put it in the pack. Just—please, let go of him and repair him like you said you could!"

Lupa did let go, but only to grab the pack that lay beside the sack of poison. He pulled out a chunk of metal just as Lobardin crowed, "Found it! Bastards just left it lying behind the wine."

"Good—" *Good job* was what Cassis had been going to say, but his voice died in his throat as Lupa rubbed the metal with his sleeve. It shone bright silver.

Just like Kyrra's arm.

Lupa leaned over the man and said, "Now tell us why Devid di Prinze and Captain Vokavik wanted the treasure. What were they going to do with this?"

"I don't know, I—"

Something very strange happened to the man then. His shirt began to glow, like something was showing through his chest, and he started choking. Lupa ripped his shirt down. Etched into the man's skin was a thick black design, a long black line with a curve wrapped around it that drove down over the man's heart. His skin gleamed in the light, but too much for candlelight to be solely responsible. The mark glowed faintly.

"A rune," Lobardin swore from across the room. "A fucking rune!"

"I'm sealed!" the man cried. "I can't tell you anything even if I wanted to! Please, please, let us go!"

Cassis began to tremble. He didn't need Lupa's knowledge to know who could have sealed a man with a rune and would also want that particular kind of metal. But a gavaro wearing Dakkaran gold... He didn't understand any of this; was Tomas's presence just a coincidence? "I think that's enough," he said. "Lobardin, give his brother a merciful end. Then make him taste our food and water. Let him have the death he meant for us."

❧

CASSIS WATCHED IMPASSIVELY THIS TIME AS LOBARDIN SLID A KNIFE into the unconscious man's side and spilled a pool of blood onto the stones. Quietly, thank the gods, without all those obscene movements. Just ordinary death throes, which he had seen dozens—hundreds—of times. Then Lobardin hauled the other man up by the collar and dragged him over to the well, where he forced a cup of water down the man's throat. Within moments the man began frothing at the mouth, contorting in paroxysms.

"It might take hours for him to die, mestere," Lobardin said.

"Fine. Leave him tied. We'll take his corpse out and burn it later."

The man looked at him out of pleading, terrified eyes, but it was far too late for that now. Cassis turned to Lupa's gavaro. "Does the name Jon Barra mean anything to you?"

"He has some importance in Liera, I believe, mestere?" Lupa said as he peeled off his bloody gloves. Behind them, the poisoned man was still choking and gasping. His boots came down hard on the stones in spasm. Cassis suppressed a shiver.

"I wasn't talking to you, ser. I was talking to your gavaro. That's Dakkaran gold in your ear, isn't it?"

The gavaro cleared his throat. "I'm sure with your background, mestere, that you know Dakkar is only called so because of the people who ruled it for so long? But there are three different peoples who make up the country—Dakkar, Arak, and Dininga. The rings mean I'm Dakkar. Perhaps like this Jon Barra. Not Arak or Dininga. Three groups, one territory. One very large territory. Mestere."

Cassis frowned at him. The gavaro was sweating, though his words were well-formed and sounded like truth. His reactions were perhaps to be expected after what he'd just witnessed and he did look young. He couldn't have many years of experience under his belt, would probably have only been a boy when Geoffre had attacked Mdembu. Still.

"You wear a Tiresian's beads," he said skeptically. Though *Tomas* was an Eterean name.

Tomas drew himself up straighter, squared his shoulders. He had the height and build of a swordsman, the bearing of a soldier, not a secretary. "I'm an orphan foster, mestere, from everywhere and nowhere. My father died and my mother couldn't care for me, so I was placed with a sea captain and his lady. I wear the gold in honor of my mother."

"Are we to interrogate my secretary now? Shall I bring out some poison sandwiches for him?" Lupa asked.

More thumping, gurgling, and wheezing from the man dying behind them. Cassis scowled at Lupa, but Lupa gazed back as if he didn't realize how cheeky he'd been. "I'm hardly to be faulted for being careful where I place my trust, Ser Lupa."

"He had very good references when I hired him. The name Jon Barra never came up."

"What do you know about the mark on the man's chest?"

"Qalfans use such marks to ensure magic is never used among them. They think magic allows the Dark One too many opportunities to do his work. Perhaps he's encountered someone who wishes to prevent the Dark One from whispering his secrets."

Cassis didn't know much about Qalfan worship of the Magnificent Sun, but there was something wrong with Lupa's explanation. Any mention of dark gods made him shiver now. "The men were Prinze, though."

"Your father was rumored to have uncovered troves of magical knowledge, wasn't he?"

It *could* have been his father's fault. But this whole situation sat badly with him, and Lobardin's expression, half-hidden in the dark, told him he was shaken, too. The sounds of the man on the ground made it damn hard to think. Why couldn't he just die? Cassis rubbed his jaw in frustration.

"Can I show you something, mestere? If you'll follow me?"

"Why not? What else can happen before breakfast?"

What little of it they might have to eat. Right now—fortunately— he didn't find himself very hungry. Lobardin edged closer, hand on his hilt, which made him feel more secure.

Predictably, Lupa lectured them as he led them down the narrow staircase into a damp passageway. Water dripped off the roughhewn ceiling and formed chilly rivulets down the back of his neck, like the touch of a ghost. They'd have to find a way to tap into another water source if they were to maintain the lodge. Cassis tightened his hands into fists and tried to focus on Lupa's constant commentary.

"Most people attribute the advances of the ancient world to the Etereans, but they only built on the foundation their ancestors laid for them. If those people had a separate name for themselves, it's lost in the mists of time. But they were the ones who built this lodge. Attrasca wasn't Eterean at all. The Eterean Empire was what he built, not the other way around."

"I think that was because he was lowborn, wasn't it?" Cassis replied absently. "He didn't want to remember his origins, so he just wrote them out of history."

The shadowy painted shapes on the wall looked like ghosts. Cassis wondered if the man they'd left in the room above had finally died. Was Lupa luring him to his own death now, hidden beneath the mountain? It didn't matter. He needed to know the particulars of his water source and if any other of Devid's men might attack through this passageway. They would have to block it off, at the least.

"Perhaps." Lupa lifted the lantern to observe the walls more closely. The light revealed a brilliantly colored but grotesque Eterean fresco of half-human, half-animal monsters tearing through a group of men in chitons. Bodies dangled, torn and bloody, from teeth and claws as the men tried to flee into a dark forest. Their horror was palpable, even in the flecked and ancient stone. Cassis shuddered.

"Damp down here, isn't it," he muttered.

"We're under a mountain in the presence of an underwater river," Lupa answered. "Rivers, perhaps. The sources I've consulted are inconclusive."

"How far are you going to lead us down this tunnel, Ser Lupa? I'd prefer not to walk into my brother's camp. We just need to fill this with rubble. Then find a way to take our water upstream from the poison."

"Well," Lupa said, "I believe you'll also want to see this, mestere."

He lifted the lantern and lit up a giant cascade of glistening rock that looked like a frozen waterfall.

Cassis gasped. Lobardin did, too. He gripped his hilt as if he might be in the presence of an enemy, which did nothing to calm Cassis's nerves.

"Amazing, isn't it?" Lupa said. "But wait!" He darted into the gloom and then a dazzling glow lit the whole chamber.

"What?" Cassis breathed in amazement.

Beside him, Lobardin looked around in dumb wonder. The ceiling of the chamber towered far above them, dripping long, glittering icicles of rock. The room itself was quite large, easily the size of his father's bedchamber in the Villa di Prinze. Scattered about the floor daggers of rock thrust upward, smooth and slick with water. A giant block of rock in the center looked like an altar. But the walls were what truly took his breath.

Immaculately preserved Eterean art covered every inch.

"It's the Gods' War, in its entirety!" Lupa exclaimed, exactly like a child who'd been gifted the most extraordinary pony for his birthday. "I knew there must be a way to light the chamber, so when we came through, I marked the quartz towers, and I was right! Is it not an ingenious way to light the room? One sets the lantern on a ledge and the crystal magnifies the light a hundredfold. Such a thing is described in the writings of Aronimus, but I never thought I'd discover a cavern myself. Not a cavern like this! Were you aware this system was down here, mestere?"

"No," Cassis said, stunned. "There have always been rumors about a hidden Aliente treasure. I asked Kyrra about it once. She just shrugged and told me she'd been all over the lodge looking, but the most interesting thing she'd found was some dirty graffiti in the wine cellar."

"Kyrra, mestere? Kyrra d'Aliente?"

"Yes," Cassis said in a clipped voice, brought back to earth by the way Lupa said Kyrra's name. "I'm sure you know that story, ser. They like to tell it in all the cafes when they're complaining about the wars."

"Tawdry melodrama plays well in the theater, I suppose."

"Tawdry melodrama? I'd hardly—"

"It's a pity she's not here now. Are you quite sure she was telling you the truth?"

"She had no reason to lie to me *then*."

"The Aliente have always played their genealogy close to their vest, have they not?"

"My father was of the opinion that Carolla's genealogy mattered more," Cassis said bitterly. "And she was a distant Caprine."

"And now there aren't any Aliente," Lupa sighed. He shoved his spectacles back onto the bridge of his nose with passion. "*This* is what is frustrating about this peninsula, mestere. Here you are, standing in the middle of one of the great monuments to the human spirit—it was perhaps in *this very room* that Attrasca ended the Gods' War by releasing magic into the mortal realm—and your petty House divisions have practically laid it all to waste. I understand your father was searching for Attrasca's Legacy, but he didn't really *unite* the peninsula, did he?"

"If you mean, did he want all the Houses to kiss each other in peace, you know very well he didn't, or you've been living underground for the past twenty years. He wanted to 'unite' the peninsula by ruling over it. Making the Prinze into emperors like Attrasca and all the other Houses vassals bowing to him. Like an Amoran."

Lobardin gave him a look at that but didn't say anything.

"It's true. A strong, central government makes for a strong country," Lupa said in a strange, thoughtful way. "But have you ever considered, Mestere di Prinze, how much might be gained from an alliance with the Aliente now that they've been turned into a mere symbol? Have you ever thought what stood to be gained if you could *legally* claim the Legacy of Attrasca?"

Cassis's mouth went dry. "I don't know what you're talking about. All the Aliente are dead and I claim the lodge—as long as I can hold it against Devid."

"But how long *can* you hold it against your brother, mestere, now that your food and water have been poisoned? And with your uncle possibly returned from the dead to claim the Chair you all struggle to hold..."

Dammit. Lupa was going to add substance to the rumors about Renzo, too. Maybe he *had* faked his death. It was so hard to tell reality from his father's invention. He knew from all the whispered stories that had circulated through the Houses after Renzo's loss that there had been no body in Renzo's coffin.

"You know," Lupa continued, "people are saying an Aliente champion killed Geoffre di Prinze."

Cassis's throat felt like it was seizing up, down here with the whole weight of the lodge on top of him. "That's preposterous," he managed, but something about the way Lupa looked at him made Cassis feel as if the man could see every secret that seethed beneath his surface.

"They're saying one of Ekyra's own. Or possibly even one of the old gods returning to seek revenge."

"That's even more preposterous."

Lupa shrugged. Lupa had a powerful frame for a man who'd been cooped up copying manuscripts his entire life. The shrug brought attention to the breadth of his shoulders.

"Preposterous though it may be, it's what people are saying. A rumor wielded by the right hands is more powerful than a sword or even a barrage of cannons, really. It could help put people on your side. Win their hearts. And their coin purses."

As Lupa paced around him, Cassis suddenly began to feel very nervous, like he was being hemmed in. He wanted—inexplicably—a sword in his hands. He noted Lobardin still had a hand on his hilt.

This is ridiculous. Lupa is one of those intellectuals who has more regard for knowledge than people, but he's not even armed. His gavaro is young and nervous, a secretary, not a soldier. Get hold of yourself.

"And how do you propose I do that? With some nostalgic epic poetry about monuments to the human spirit and a flighty campfire story about a Silver Warrior with a magic sword—"

"Your brother seemed to think Geoffre di Prinze might have been murdered by Kyrra d'Aliente herself."

Cassis mercilessly strangled his emotions. "My brother thinks a lot of things that turn out to be wrong in the end."

"It would be too bad if it turned out to be just a rumor, mestere. Too bad if you knew the truth and didn't act on it. *If* Kyrra d'Aliente *were* still alive, wouldn't it seem magnanimous of you to pardon her? To welcome her, perhaps, as your bride? I hear you're currently in need of one."

They were such innocent-*sounding* words, but they fell into the room with the echoes of a thunderclap.

"*What?*" Cassis gasped.

"You heard what I said, mestere. The Aliente are a symbol now. If you want to unite Liera behind you instead of letting your brother or uncle take it, you'll make Kyrra d'Aliente your wife."

CHAPTER 7

LOBARDIN

"Godsdammit, I need a smoke."

Lobardin stared at Cassis. It seemed an incongruous statement to make after lighting two human bodies on fire, but Cassis rarely joked. Lupa and Tomas had been given a set of chambers under guard. Lobardin had stuffed the bodies of the two dead infiltrators into burlap sacks and dragged them out of the kitchens as if they were wheat. He took them to the midden and spent gods knew how long trying to get a fire burning in the icy dawn fog. Now the bodies were roasting in the flames. They smelled like pork—a sick reminder of all the food Cassis's men wouldn't be eating because of them.

By all the gods, he needed a smoke, too.

He wanted to strip off his bloody, possibly poison-tainted gloves and hurl them as far from his own body as possible. To blot out the memory of the way the magic from that binding rune had crawled over him, worse than watching the man writhe with the effects of the poison on the floor. And Attrasca's cavern... Despite the way Cassis had scoffed, there had been some*thing* down there. A throbbing, sullen *presence*. Why had he decided that now was a good time to give up kacin?

"Sweetweed," he said. He couldn't even manage a complete sentence. That was nice. "Junei—"

At Junei's name, Cassis gave him a vicious glare. "What information has Junei been passing to Jon? He and Arsenault were trying to get me out of the way, and I know he doesn't give a shit about any agreements he makes with me. It must be Arsenault who did this, not

Devid, or maybe Arsenault's working with Devid. That mark! But Lupa, and Kyrra—*Dammit*."

Cassis slammed his hand against the wall behind them.

Lobardin let his breath out. He couldn't think yet. His thoughts were all a jumble and the gloves were too big and heavy to fumble in his tunic for his pipe and sweetweed, which he *had* begun to carry with him because Junei had said it might ease the rest of the transition.

Would she have tricked him so these men could sneak in and poison them all? She was a firebrand of a woman, so impassioned with her role in Jon's... It wasn't an army, so what was it? An organization? It didn't make sense that Jon would send men to poison them *and* to save them, so which was it?

Tonight, he would take her to bed. And then he'd ask her the questions.

"The sweetweed's in my tunic," he said to Cassis. "My pipe, too. I can't take off my gloves here."

Cassis gave him a strange look but did as he asked. He fumbled blindly for a moment, searching for the muslin packet of sweetweed and the new clay pipe Lobardin had secured beside it. Kacin was baked into his old pipe, blackened and sweet, so he couldn't use it anymore. At the moment, Lobardin missed kacin more than anything else in the world—with the exception of Ires, whom he'd *never* thought he'd miss, but he'd never realized how much he needed that blessed black space of surrender to the god. And the smell, the gods-damned *smell*. The wind was blowing the rotten smoke from their little corpsefire straight into his face.

Finally, Cassis's fingers closed on the packet and pipe lodged against his breastbone. Lobardin wished he could make the familiar gestures of packing the pipe because he needed to do something with his hands. It seemed to take forever for Cassis to tamp down the leaves and then he looked around stupidly, like he was thinking about using the corpsefire to light it.

"There should be matches, too," Lobardin said roughly.

"Oh yes, yes, of course," Cassis stuttered shakily. He found the small packet, drew it out, and lit the pipe. The leaves burned orange for a moment, then Cassis thrust the pipe into his own mouth and took a few heavy puffs until the cherry glowed red. He exhaled a cloud of fragrant smoke, which disappeared into the mist around them, and the tension in his shoulders relaxed.

The godsdamned entitled fool.

Cassis finished his smoke and finally handed the pipe off. Lobardin grabbed it brusquely and shoved it into his mouth. The feel of the clay between his lips made him feel immediately better, more relaxed. Just going through the motions of smoking... Holding the pipe, dragging the smoke into his lungs, the scratchy burn in his throat, the tightness in his chest as he held his breath—*one two three four five six*—then blew it out... It wasn't what he wanted, but the routine calmed him. He found himself needing something in his mouth all the time; he wanted to eat constantly, even when he wasn't hungry. Seeing these bastards poisoning the food had made him furious, as if they'd insulted him personally by fouling the ship's biscuits, which had been foul enough already. The only thing keeping the maggots from hatching was the cold.

Cassis looked longingly at the pipe and Lobardin took a few more puffs just to extend the moment. When he'd finished breathing the last bit of smoke from his lungs, he stretched the pipe out to Cassis. "Care to share again, mestere?"

Cassis eyed his glove warily.

"If my jaw locks up and I start frothing at the mouth, then you'll know you should worry. But we've probably moved past that moment. And if we haven't, I don't care. Maybe it'll put me out of this misery."

"What *was* Kyrra doing all those years we thought she was dead? Maybe she really is in league with this faction of Aliente-sympathizing Empirists—"

Lobardin shook his head. Thought returned bit by bit as the smoke slowly swirled the tension out of him. It didn't hit as fast and completely as kacin, but at least it helped him think. "This isn't Kyrra's style, letting someone else do her dirty work. It wouldn't be nearly as satisfying to her if she heard about your death secondhand. And for all that she holds a grudge, I think she'd pause before poisoning an entire garrison."

Grudgingly, and he didn't know why except that so many things about this situation didn't make sense, he added, "That was more Arsenault's style anyway."

Cassis took the pipe out of his hands. "Maybe he's her captain now."

"I think he was always her captain, mestere. At least, it never made sense that he'd fight for Pallo d'Aliente like he did. Not after Kyrra hanged. But I'm not sure he could orchestrate this now himself, with Kyrra like she was after that battle and after what Geoffre did to him. Andris was a different man. You took advantage of that, didn't you?"

Cassis drew another broody smoke from the pipe. With the fire-light flickering over his face in the dim early morning light, his eyes seemed darker, the hollows of his face starker. The Cassis Lobardin had known in Liera had always been cleanshaven, fashionable, silk-clad. The dark stubble lining Cassis's cheeks made his expression more complicated and hooded as he thought through...whatever he was thinking about. Probably all the people who had reason to kill him, the revenge he had taken on Arsenault, memories of Kyrra hanging maybe. For all that Lobardin had hated Pallo for kicking him off Aliente land, he was glad he hadn't been at the Villa to see Kyrra's hanging.

Or maybe Cassis was thinking about what it would have been like to make Kyrra his wife—Kyrra with two arms. That was also not what Lobardin wanted to think about; it was better for him to stay the hell away from Kyrra d'Aliente and all these webs of politics and magic she dragged behind her. He didn't want to feel sympathy for her, but he remembered, in a painful, reflexive flash, exactly what she had looked like lying in the mud after she'd killed Geoffre. Like a torn and broken doll, not the fierce and brave Kyrra he knew. And the look on Arsenault's face...

Cassis took the pipe out of his mouth. "But the sign. On the man's chest. I saw Arsenault with Mikelo once. Arsenault was making those marks on a piece of parchment, naming each like they weren't pictures or letters but...ideas. *Sanctuary. Peace.* Lying to Mikelo just like he'd lied to me. He didn't want *peace* for Mikelo. He was just working for Jon."

Lobardin shifted uncomfortably. "He's not the only man to know runes, Cassis. I'd bet a handful of your father's Dagmari Fixers use them."

"Seems strange, though, doesn't it?"

"Well..." Lobardin said slowly. "Devid hired Lupa."

"You think my brother bought into my father's crackpot magical schemes? He hates Geoffre so much he's not even going to bury him."

"Your father *did* have similar magical connections, though. Or are those rumors not true either?"

Cassis shifted uncomfortably. "I don't know all the connections my father had. As the years went on, he trusted fewer and fewer people. Maybe it was because of Arsenault, maybe because of all the betrayals he orchestrated himself, maybe it was me. I don't know. Perhaps the god made him paranoid. I thought all his talk of empire was a symptom of his madness. It began with Kyrra. I had to stop him."

"I suppose it doesn't matter in the end if it's madness or not if it drives men to action. We need to rig a new system for the water, and we still need to get rid of all those biscuits. Not much wheat to make more. It will rot—"

"I know that," Cassis snapped. Lobardin shut his mouth. Not without effort. It still stung after all these years, being reminded how far he'd fallen from his birthright. He tried not to be bitter. His role was a damn sight better now than it had ever been.

Cassis sighed, apparently remembered he was holding the pipe, and put it in his mouth again. When he took it out, he exhaled a cloud of sweet-smelling smoke that drifted around Lobardin's head. Lobardin couldn't help sniffing in the dregs. Old habits died hard, even though it didn't give him what he wanted. Then again, the kacin hadn't either.

"Do you think," Cassis ventured slowly, "there's truth in what Lupa said? About marrying Kyrra?"

Lobardin froze. Even as the youngest, throwaway Cozin son, he wasn't reckless or stupid enough to ignore the implications if he answered. "Mestere, are you asking me for counsel?"

Cassis handed him the pipe. "Yes. I suppose I am. My life seems to have been upended recently and apparently it hasn't turned completely upside down yet. I thought I could fight my father into a draw so I could marry Driese and force a truce between the Houses that way, but—well, I thought Kyrra was dead, didn't I? But she had the chance to kill me, and instead she killed my father. Do you think, for the sake of Liera..."

In his mind's eye, Lobardin could see his father leaning against the fence of the training ring, watching one of his prized Ipanzers being broken to the saddle. He must have been eight or nine in this memory, and it had been a privilege to attend the training with his father. But his father, as always, had made the afternoon a lesson in politics. *The key is to have a very soft touch on the reins. Then the colt will go wherever the rider wills him as if it's his own idea. People see the crown of the king and think power lies in the symbols, like people think power lies in the horse. But real power lies in the whispered word that goes to the king's ear.*

Lobardin had run away from the position of counselor, his family's birthright. Having learned to ride from the time he could walk, he'd always known that no matter how good a rider was, he could still be thrown and trampled.

And yet, he was tired of burning bodies and sleeping in the muck.

"I think, mestere, that I trust Lupa and his gavaro as much as I trust a pair of vipers in a box. But there might be truth in what he says. Fighting against your brother and your uncle, with this lodge as your only asset while they both have access to Liera itself... It would help if you could sidestep that conflict entirely or at least gather some allies. I'm just not sure how you would ever get Kyrra to agree to it."

"Damn," Cassis muttered. "I need to know if all these rumors about Renzo are true or if this man is an imposter showing up to throw a rod into my wheels. Jon and Arsenault *must* know something, and by the gods, I'll make them tell me. Clean up and meet me at the stables, Lobardin. We're going to see Kyrra."

CHAPTER 8

ARSENAULT

KYRRA KEPT MUTTERING IN HER FEVERED DREAMS ABOUT DRAGONS, but Arsenault felt like he was waging a war in his mind, too. A war against the deluge of memory.

It always began innocuously, like a gentle rain. For instance, here was the splinter of an image: Kyrra walking barefoot into the trees behind the Aliente gavaro barracks. Head down, short golden curls springing up and down with every step, jaw set in determination. He liked watching her walk. She always looked like she knew where she was going, even if she didn't. But he didn't know why she never wore shoes. It always drew his attention to the turn of her ankle, the curve of her calf, the shape of her thigh beneath her skirts, and then he'd start thinking things he had no business thinking. She needed someone far better than him. Someone who would remember her, who at the very least wouldn't *die*.

In this memory, she was wearing the blue guarnello he'd talked her into buying. He couldn't stand the plain undyed clothes she wore like she was bleeding her personality away, struggling to fit into them as if they could make her invisible. The blue guarnello did bring out the color of her eyes, just as he'd said it did, and seeing her in it always brought a feeling of satisfaction to his days.

Discovering what she clutched hidden in her skirts became his excuse for following her. He didn't know where she was going; maybe he hadn't talked to her that morning. He wanted, generally, to be up and out of the room before she woke so she could dress, but kitchen work started before dawn, and dawn came earlier and earlier on summer days...

So, no. Her shuffling on the dirt floor had woken him that morning. Water splashing in the basin as she washed her face. He remembered the warm, diffuse glow of the candle through the blanket screen, her silhouette as she combed her hair, slid into the guarnello, tightened the laces of her bodice one eyelet at a time by hooking her finger under the string.

He'd lain in bed, afraid a single breath might break the moment or else break him. He wanted to believe the blanket between them was as solid as a wall and he was made of steel. But there was no metal in him; he was just a man. With every breath, his resistance leaked away, and he wondered what purpose this box around his emotions served, why he wanted to keep his heart so safe. It felt like both of them were locked inside a prison built by their fears.

What a godsdamned idiot he'd been.

So much *time* they'd wasted. It was strange thinking of time as a treasure to horde instead of a weight to bear. They'd been like two crippled soldiers, unaware they were holding each other up and yet completely unable to walk on their own.

That summer day, he'd followed her to the hidden grotto with the broken statue and discovered she was hiding the blunt practice sword he'd given her in her skirts. He knew he should let her know he was there. But she'd come there to be alone and probably didn't want or need him to stumble into the moment.

He couldn't resist watching anyway. It was ridiculous to do weapons training without shoes, and yet...there she was, stepping out the sword runes in her bare feet. She moved like a dryad: skirts spinning, revealing the golden skin and taut muscles of her calves.

He had never known how beautiful swordwork could be until he watched her doing it. She didn't move perfectly, but she handled the sword like it was a part of her body. Every bit of what would make her a swordsman and what made her beautiful to him were on display. The confident and dangerous way she manipulated the blade. The way she always climbed back up, no matter how many times she tangled her feet or lost the beat of a rune, throwing herself into the task until *finally*... Gods, the way her face shone with the victory of meeting a challenge. The moment made him ache with desire and something more, something he hadn't felt in a very long time and had never expected to find again.

She stumbled and swore—*dammit*.

Dark clouds streaked past the sun, bringing an angry stormlight with them, and then, ravens, ravens everywhere.

Shit, it's a different memory now. When is this?

"Arsenault?" Kyrra asked hesitantly. *Does that even sound like her?* Had she ever been that tentative? Or had he never really known her? Maybe the image of her barefoot with the sword was something he'd invented, something he'd wished for...

Dear gods, the ravens.

He was not in the grotto now.

The trees were not the manicured flame-shaped poplars of Eterean estates. They were tall mountain conifers, thick with ravens and eagles. Kyrra wore a gavaro's jerkin and trousers and boots, one entire side of her body made of metal as if she'd transformed not from serving girl to soldier, but to a discarded, broken blade lying in the mud beneath Geoffre's mangled body. Geoffre's whip had left Arsenault's back in tatters, the horses had wrenched his shoulder out of its socket, but he barely felt the pain as he stumbled, then crawled in the icy, bloody muck to reach her. He stretched out to grip her hand, as if by holding onto her, he could tether her in place, keep her alive—

"Arsenault?"

The ravens perched on the ground now, croaking, gorging on war dead. He looked around for Kyrra, bewildered, and a whiff of scorched grass and charred meat blew past on a hot wind. Flames roared up around him. He turned to run but there was no running, the only way out blocked by a wall of fire that suddenly sprang up in front of him like a hungry, snarling beast—

Oh, gods, not Kafrin...

"Arsenault!"

Kyrra was leaning over him. Her eyes shone in a bar of moonlight that slid through a crack in the shutters and her mouth turned down worriedly at the corners. For a moment, he didn't know where he was. He thought he was back in the gavaro barracks at the Villa d'Aliente and his heart began to pound. *Did I say anything in my sleep I shouldn't have?*

"Arsenault. It's a nightmare."

He was lying on a pallet on a hard floor. She hung off the side of a bed, looking down at him.

"I'm supposed to be taking care of you," he whispered, brushing an errant curl from her face, but she was already pulling him closer and when her mouth touched his, he began to tremble. Gods, he wanted her. But he couldn't bear to hurt her anymore... And he couldn't bear for her to whittle away at the new box he'd built for himself, the box that kept all the raw, ugly things locked inside, all the memories he didn't want, so they wouldn't seep out like pus from an infected wound.

She gazed down at him, her eyes accusing, angry.

"So, you made that promise...out of guilt? Just because you were *sorry*?"

"No!"

He startled himself awake—for real this time. Caught off guard by the scent of woodsmoke and the low, sullen glow of a banked fire, his heart raced as if it would pound out of his chest. The almost healed cut on his palm twinged in pain when he slammed his hand down on something wooden—*chair arms*—his feet smacked a hard floor—*stone tiles, wearing wool stockings, no boots*—and finally, he realized he was sitting in a rocking chair in the farmhouse bedroom.

He looked wildly to the bed to make sure Kyrra was still there. His attempt at Fixing her arm had set her recovery back days; the fever had returned with a vengeance and the ravaging magic meant she was rarely lucid, which had been dangerous for everyone. Suddenly he was *sure* Kyrra was the dream and his reality was back in Liera, leading yet another double or triple life that would end by sword or bottle.

But Kyrra wasn't there. The bed was empty.

"Hells," he swore and shoved himself up. His scabbed-over back throbbed with the sudden movement and his stiff shoulder refused to cooperate. His heart nearly stopped when a figure rushed at him out of the dark, metal flashing bloody red in the firelight.

Arm, no—knife, godsdammit—

He couldn't stop his forward motion and collided with Kyrra, but at least she didn't have space to stab. He grabbed her wrist, her fingers spasmed open, and the blade dropped into the space between them, barely hitting his chest and leg before it clanked on the floor. She uttered a soft cry, curled her fingers over the scabbed black slash of their vow, and tried to kick him.

She was barefoot and too weak to do much damage, thank the gods. He tightened his grip on her arms and pulled her away from the blade on the floor. One of his whittling knives. He must have left it on the bedstand and fallen asleep in the chair like an idiot. She shuddered awake while he held her, and then her head tipped against his bad shoulder and she sank against him. Unsure whether it was even all right to breathe, he drew her closer, wincing when the movement pulled at muscles made sorer from sleeping in the chair.

Her hair and forehead were damp against the skin of his collarbone, her shirt—gods, she was soaked. Her fever must have finally broken. It had been touch and go for a few days; he hadn't even used that much magic on her arm, but he hadn't realized how tricky and angry the seething sea of magic that had collected around her truly was.

"Did I hurt you?" she asked breathlessly. "I heard cannons. I thought you were fighting or I was at Vargis Pass or maybe you were in the war—"

"I was dreaming," he said, trying his damnedest to reconcile what was going on to reality. "But everything's fine. It's fine now. You're all right. I'm all right."

Her eyes narrowed skeptically. "If everything was fine, you'd be asleep. You were dreaming about guns. There was a reason I thought of Vargis and grabbed that knife. I didn't do it out of nowhere."

"Vargis," he repeated, trying to place the name, disturbed by her casual reference to *his* dreams. Gods, maybe he shouldn't even be sleeping beside her. "Kyrra, are you seeing my dreams, too?"

"Doesn't matter. Your dreams, my dreams—it's all war." She shivered. "There was so much snow at Vargis Pass."

Her shivers grew worse. The tremors moved through her metal arm, and then she began to cough so hard she clutched at her midsection.

"Oh. Oh. Balls. That hurts. Dammit."

"Just a moment, Kyrra."

He scrabbled at the laces of his shirt as she kept coughing, her arm pressed into her midsection as if she was trying to hold in her guts. The coughing echoed in the small room, terrifying because he had no way of stopping it.

Finally, he got the laces of his shirt unknotted. He stripped it over his head and threw it on the back of the chair. Hopefully the honey from his flogmarks hadn't seeped through the linen bandage wrapped around his chest. He hurriedly began unlacing Kyrra's shirt, a strange and ironic mirror of his dream. In the latent throes of coughing, she tried to smile at him.

"Didn't know. Coughing. Made me. So attractive."

Gods. Just a joke, but he was living in a constant state of frustrated desire these days. Desire, anger, love—whatever the hell it was, he was a mess.

He tried to keep his voice wry. "I don't know if you'd be up to that.

You can have my shirt. It's dry, and then we'll sit by the fire under a blanket, get you warm again."

She'd stopped coughing at least. He could feel her gaze as it rested on him. He wasn't sure what would be worse—if he turned his gaze to hers or if he kept his attention on this knot resting between her breasts. Sweat had soaked the knot tight and he couldn't get it apart. Especially since his fingers had begun to tremble.

"In R-Rojornick we c-carried blankets in our packs," she said. "If we got lost in the snow, we were supposed to strip and get under the blankets together."

He looked up in surprise. Her mouth twitched at the corner, like she wanted to smile, but instead that left brow just climbed slowly like she was daring him to take the bait.

"You sure whoever told you that wasn't trying to get you into bed?"

She laughed a little, despite the shivering, and he dug harder at the knot.

"Who tied this godsdamned thing," he muttered.

"I d-don't even remember putting it on. Maybe it was you."

He grunted. Probably had been.

"It's t-true, though. Skin-to-skin body heat will save you if you're too c-cold."

"I used to tell girls the same thing when we went walking up near the glacier. *If we're trapped in a snowstorm, I will do the brave thing and strip for you.*"

She grabbed his forearm with her shaking hand. "Is th-that what you're doing now? The b-brave thing?"

The knot fell open, exposing the curve of her breast, the greening edge of a bruise, and the scarred edge of one of the long slices Erelf had left on her body. It was a complicated feeling to have her flirting with him—had she ever flirted with him before?—wanting her and yet wanting to weep at the same time. To rage over what had happened to her and ask her what in all the hells she had been thinking, and also to wrap her up in his arms and hold her.

Her smile faltered and she resumed trying to hug in her shivers. "If it's that bad, you could just tell me," she mumbled.

"It's—" he began, trying to say *it's not that bad*, but she would know if he lied. Silently, he unknotted the sling that supported her right arm so she could take her shirt off. The arm immediately fell, heavy, limp —if metal could be called limp—reflecting the firelight like blood. She stared at it in frustration.

He grasped the hem of the shirt and helped her work her way out of it. When she was naked, she looked down at herself and made a strange noise that was half gasp and half whimper.

Mikelo had done the best he could. The wounds that should have killed her were only puckered pink scars. Countless smaller cuts and slices, ones Mikelo had been forced to leave, remained in various stages of healing. Old bruising covered her whole torso, in that yellow and green stage which looked particularly like hell. The cut on her left arm that had festered had finally closed, the color of her skin faded from red now to a normal olive, gold in the dim light.

"Will I be left like this forever?" Anguish broke her voice. "First my arm and now—"

Arsenault tried to sound hopeful. "The scars will fade in time. Mikelo didn't want to accidentally seal in any rot. I don't know enough about Shaping flesh, I wasn't sure how it worked, and my back, I—"

"Are you trying to say my scars are your fault? G-gods, Arsenault, you really haven't changed." Then she laughed bitterly. "Wh-what's another s-scar, really. M-might get b-better j-jobs on the T-Talos now if n-nobody thinks I'm a pretty b-boy anymore."

A pretty boy. That image hit him uncomfortably hard. Reminded him how he'd tracked her through the alleys of Liera, thinking he needed to get her—him, Kyris—out of the way.

She felt so thin and fragile as he took her by the shoulders.

He heard her sharp intake of breath as he pressed his lips to a bruise along her collarbone. Her skin tasted like salt. He couldn't help lingering, wishing he could kiss all the pain away, wanting to taste her, to feel her, to have her on his tongue and hold her in his hands. Like all those times he had forgotten and now remembered as if he'd only experienced them in his dreams.

The fire popped. The sudden noise, the smell of woodsmoke, provoked an irrational fear left over from Kafrin and he clutched her against him. She made a noise in her throat. He tried to rid himself of it by running his hands down her arms to her hips, fitting her to him more firmly. Her breasts crushed against his chest and he wished he wasn't wearing the bandage, so he could feel her skin-to-skin. But the smell of smoke, the dream...

He fumbled for the shirt he'd thrown over the back of the chair. "You're cold. You should go back to bed—"

"*Arsenault.* For the god's sake, not without you." She touched his face, then slid her hand into his hair and pulled him to her with surprising strength.

It was not like the dream kiss, not just the *idea* of a kiss. It was all Kyrra. Nothing tentative or indecisive about it. She gripped his hair roughly and forced his mouth open with her tongue. His body surged with desire and recognition—*yes*, he remembered this; *yes*, this was the way things were when they took each other in the grass in the dark; *yes*, he remembered the dreams when her Sight swirled them together, before Kafrin, before the fire, *before Geoffre*.

No, no, don't let the thought of him in, not now—

He pressed angrily against her, and though she couldn't know where the anger came from, she met him. Her metal arm banged against his thigh and the magic she couldn't control swirled out of it, wrapping around him like a tether.

He pulled away, gasping, and she stared at him.

"I don't want to hurt you again, Kyrra," he said raggedly.

"I'd do it all over if I had to. But you can be careful of my ribs, can't you? Because, by all the gods, five years is a *long time*. Maybe we should play one of those games they play at courting parties."

"What, like the Game of Chastity?"

Kyrra stared at him. "You have been to some truly horrid courting parties."

"Well, I don't think you're up to the games they played at the other parties I went to."

Hesitantly, she touched his face. "You're afraid, aren't you?"

He wanted to look away, but his gaze snagged on hers and he couldn't.

When Tonia di Sere had set him to follow her, he *had* thought she was one of those pretty boys down on the Talos trying to get by on their looks. Then he'd watched her scale a wall and stand on a rooftop with the winter Lieran moon gilding her hair, and for the first time in a long time, it had made him *feel* something. And then it had only made him angry that his head could be turned by a lithe form and some golden hair in the moonlight, and he had fallen back into that cynical cruelty that seemed so rampant in Liera since the war—all of them trying to keep themselves safe by refusing to let in any beauty at all.

The fierce anger in her eyes took his breath. She'd always been able to stab unerringly to the center of him, whether or not she was using her Sight.

She leaned past him and took the shirt herself. "Help me on with this," she said, "and then get me out of this godsdamned room."

CHAPTER 9

KYRRA

I WANTED EVERYTHING TO BE EASY, BUT IT WASN'T.

When I had first returned to Liera and seen the wanted posters placing a bounty on Arsenault's head, I'd thought, in my hubris, *Maybe no one else has been able to find him, but I will. I'll turn him up and everything will be exactly the way it used to be.*

I had spent the previous year hunting men like a wolf hunts deer. Hiding in my Kavol colors, behind my mercenary mask of cynicism, greed, and brutality, searching for and killing all but two of the conspirators involved in the death of my lord, Markus Seroditch.

I had tried to put all that behind me in Liera. Leaving unfinished business bothered me, but I had been waiting so long to come home. I had built up my reunion with Arsenault in my head. With peace declared in Liera, we would be able to live where and how we wanted. I wasn't sure what that meant for me, a female gavaro with a metal arm and a talent for chaos. My vision danced ahead of me like a mirage: a farm somewhere I'd never have to wade through snow drifts again, a good wine cellar, a decent library, excellent coffee... And I'd dress as a woman when and if it pleased me, or as a man if I liked, and Arsenault would build all our furniture and spend as much time as he wanted mending the roof.

In the nearer term, I spent many nights torturing myself by imagining the night of our reunion.

Over the years we spent apart, I imagined a lot. Sometimes, I would be able to put him out of my mind, but then the wild, uncontrollable magic that plagued me would throw us together in my dreams. In my dreams, I could feel his hands on my body, taste his lips, his skin, hear his voice—but when I woke, it was always smoke and fantasy.

Now I realized just how much smoke and fantasy it had been.

The reality I had won from Geoffre and his god was far better *because* it was real, no matter how tattered and torn it was. But if Geoffre's body had been lying in front of me in that moment, I would have run it through a thousand more times just to make sure he was dead.

I couldn't stop shaking as Arsenault settled a blanket on my shoulders and helped me into the common room. The fight and fear that had woken me had peaked, leaving me an angry mess, burning with desire the way I'd recently burned with fever.

It was an ugly desire and not the kind I had imagined for us. A need to stake my rights to his body smoldered and flared at the core of me. I needed to reclaim him from the men and women who had abused him and perhaps even loved him while the god had used him as a plaything. To grind the memory of Geoffre and Cassis into the ground until it was lost in the tiny grains of dirt Arsenault trod on.

Those fucking, fucking Prinze.

I stood in front of the fire Arsenault avoided, shivering as I stared into the flames. It wasn't the same as Seeing in mirrors, but it made my vengeance burn brighter.

"Kyrra, sit down. Don't hurt yourself," Arsenault said from the entrance to the kitchen where he had gone to retrieve a bottle, some leftover bread and cheese, sweetweed, tea...something. I didn't know what he was doing.

When had my world come down to these narrow walls? I didn't know if the house was a refuge or a prison with its polished wood and its hearth outfitted with its small household gods that seemed oddly familiar, and all this fancy furniture that didn't belong here unless we were being hosted by a fallen householder. All my tangled, ugly emotions throbbed hot inside me. I wanted Arsenault; I *needed* him. I needed his touch and his presence to moor me to the present, or I would just drift.

He came up beside my shoulder with a bottle in one hand, a cup in the other. It was a plain clay bottle, probably imya or leftover loose wine, not anything like the fancy brandy we'd used to drink together.

I didn't know what to do. I just knew that he needed not to be scared and I needed to know he still wanted me, despite Geoffre, and in spite of my dead, mangled arm and all the scars and bruises on my body.

I grabbed him behind the neck and pulled him down to kiss me, hard. His hands were full, so he couldn't defend himself. I had a feeling the magic was amplifying my emotions again like the wind drove waves in Liera's lagoon, but it was too late.

He broke away, breathing raggedly. He looked torn, and I hated it. "Kyrra," he breathed.

"*Now*," I said. "Or don't you want me anymore? Maybe my injuries have made me too ugly—"

He flinched backward like I'd slapped him. "You earned those scars for me. Do you think it matters—"

"I don't know what to think! I don't *want* to think. I just want you to fuck me and gods damn my ribs, I don't care how much it hurts, I want you now!"

His eyes snapped, hot and dark, gray as the ashes of a smoldering fire. Then whatever had held him back snapped, too. He shoved me roughly up against him, still holding onto the bottle, and took my mouth with his.

Our kisses felt like we were fighting a war, a battle against the darkness that wanted to swallow us both. The bottle pressed hard into my shoulder blade as he held me against him, too tightly for me to escape even if I'd wanted to. His teeth caught on my skin and his beard rubbed rough over my mouth as I tried to kiss him everywhere all at once. The pain and fury burned together with my desire until it was all the same flame.

"How could you ever think I didn't want you?" he rasped between kisses. "How could you think you would ever be ugly to me?"

"You kept pushing me away, what was I supposed to think?"

"Exactly what I said, I didn't want to hurt you!"

He propelled me over to the couch. Or I dragged him, I wasn't sure which. The back of my calves hit the cushions and I barely noticed. Arsenault still held the bottle and cup, but his hands dropped to my hips and the pottery knocked against my bones. He kissed the bare line of my shoulder, not gently, as if he wanted to punish my disbelief with his desire. When he was done with my shoulder, he leaned forward and caught my breast with his teeth through the thin fabric of my shirt. He might as well have thrown a match onto a cache of powder. It had been so long since I had been touched as a woman. I was not prepared for the way it made me feel.

But that was what I loved about him, that we matched up so well. My ribs had been broken, my side sliced open, my arm dented, but I didn't need or want him to be gentle. Five years of loneliness, of desperation, fear, and anger. Five years stolen from us by Geoffre and his god.

No, I didn't want him to be gentle.

I wanted him back. I wanted him inside me, to drive away the awful feelings of the past and fill me with the belief that we could rescue our old love from the ashes and go on to build a new one. A gentle, slow, romantic wedding night was not for us, as a wedding had not been. Our vows had been said in desperation on the blade of a knife, and we clung to each other as if we would both be lost if we let go.

He kissed his way down my body, hitting the floor on one knee and then the other, finally setting down the bottle and cup on either side of me. Then he slid his hands over my hips and pressed his lips to one thigh and then the other, bunching my linen shirt in his fists. Every hard gesture set me on fire. I wanted to tangle both hands in his hair and pull him to me even harder, but my metal arm still dangled at my side, useless. He kissed it anyway, taking my metal fingers in his.

"Every cut," he said viciously. "Every bruise, every scar, every terrible thing done against you I have marked. It makes me want to weep, but not because it's ugly. It makes me want to break anyone who has ever hurt you, anyone who has ever touched you—"

"Do you think I feel differently about you?" I asked helplessly.

His eyes were a storm of emotion. "Sit down. Now. Let me have you."

He pushed me down firmly. Not a shove. Just firm enough to let me know he was putting me where he wanted me. I wanted to be there, too—gods, how I wanted it.

The couch was upholstered in silk and too luxurious for this house. I smoothed my hand down over the arm and my fingernail snagged on a hole, but that felt right too as I bunched the torn silk with my fingertips and dug my nails into the fabric.

Arsenault shoved the long shirt up my legs and ran his callused fingers up my thighs to push my legs apart. He fit his palms around the bones of my pelvis, drew his fingers slowly down the joints, so close to where I wanted them and yet so far away. His lips lingered warm on my flesh as he leaned forward to kiss the back of my knee and then made his slow, torturous way up the inside of my thigh. I shoved my fingers through his hair and tugged him forward to where I wanted him.

He locked his big hands around my hips, bracing me. The silk slid cool against my skin as I arched against him, but he held me down so firmly I couldn't move enough to hurt my ribs. The anticipation, the restriction of him holding me in place so I couldn't move the way my body wanted to under the maddening coaxing of his tongue was excruciating and wonderful. It had been so long, in barely any time at all the pleasure-pain of ecstasy crested within me, burning, seething, taking me over.

Describing ecstasy is as impossible as describing pain. They both walk the same edge. I bit my lip on the cry that wanted to rip free of me, and the pain of it blended into the pleasure that kept rolling on until they melded into one feeling. Arsenault continued mercilessly and I kicked something—*shit, the bottle*—but I didn't care. And after everything, after the grief and the anger and the pain, it turned out to be brandy and not imya after all. It spilled its hot, bright scent into the room.

I lay back on the couch as spent as the brandy when Arsenault finally relented. Then he lifted me in his arms and carried me to the bedroom, where he closed the door with his foot and laid me down oh so gently on the down-filled mattress. And when he was finally inside me, when I realized there was even more pleasure to take and to give, when I held him fiercely against me and felt the muscles of his back working beneath his skin... When he looked down at me, intense and dark, and he filled up so much of me with his presence, and neither of us could catch our breath, and when he said my name like it was wrenched out of him and we both cried out together...

My home had never been the city.

It had always been him.

And, now, finally, I was home in truth.

CHAPTER 10

KYRRA

SOMETHING WOKE ME WHEN THE DARK WAS STILL THICK AND black. A breath of cold air, the brush of a touch not wholly kind. I blinked awake, confused, but Arsenault was asleep. One arm rested heavily over my hip. He had tucked his hand under my body, to hold me against him. His breath fluttered in my hair, calm and slow, and his skin against my skin kept us warm under the blankets.

A draft, I reassured myself uneasily. *Nothing more.*

I tried to close my eyes, but I felt it again. More than the touch of the wind, like something physical. Icy. Scaly. I lifted my head and looked toward the door.

It was open a crack. Arsenault had gone to clean up the front room and bring back a drink, but I was sure he'd closed the door behind him when he'd returned. Maybe the draft had blown it open. The hallway was dark and our fire had burned down to glowering embers of red and orange.

A sound scuffed the silence. I lifted my head a little more.

A white hand materialized out of the darkness and closed slowly around the door.

I leapt out of bed, terror blocking any pain I might have felt. A voice in the back of my head protested that the hand probably belonged to Mikelo or Silva, but surely, they wouldn't be so ghostly? Then again, why did I think a ghost—or a god or a monster—would have to open a godsdamned door?

Arsenault's whittling knives lay on the bedstand where he'd left them, but I propelled myself to the wall where his sword—my sword

—hung. I fumbled it down, but I couldn't hold it up and the blade clanked against the pine floor. As soon as I gripped it, all the runes on the blade lit up, bright white.

"Kyrra?" Arsenault said in alarm as I stumbled through the door, dragging the blade along the floor after me.

The hall was dark and quiet.

I paused. Nothing but Arsenault's quick, heavy footsteps behind me.

Ahead of me—the swish of a garment.

I cursed the runes that blinded me and heaved the sword up.

"Kyrra. Come back to bed. You're dreaming again." Arsenault spoke in a low, careful voice.

"I'm not," I said through gritted teeth. I was breathing hard already, beginning to wheeze, and pain encroached on my vision, barely kept at bay by my thudding heart. Once a soldier, always a soldier, and I knew what I'd seen. Not a vision from the magic, but some*one*, some*thing* in the house with us.

If Ires was playing mindgames, I was going to stab my godsdamned sword straight through his simulacrum, god or not. Maybe it would lay down some rules between us.

If it was a ghost...or Erelf...

"Come out and fight," I said, teeth gritted with the effort of holding the sword. I scanned the darkness. The fire in the common room was very low; the fucking sword was the problem, too bright in the darkness to see past. "Show yourself instead of skulking around!"

"Kyrra," Arsenault tried again. "Put the sword down, there's nothing—"

"Look!"

He stopped talking. I could feel his frustration, but he looked where I gestured. His body tensed, as if maybe he did see something. I knew from experience that I had a few more moments of clarity—such as it was—before the battle magic would fizz in at the edges, muddling things up—or worse, that whatever primed my body to fight would leak away into a mess of pain and fear. "If these godsdamned runes would go out—"

Suddenly they winked into darkness. I looked up, startled. Arsenault was lowering his hand. He must not have used much magic, or the shot of fight running through me gave me better defenses against it.

"In the kitchen," he murmured.

I didn't need more encouragement. I thrust the sword forward and stumbled into a run. Its weight dragged me along with it, so my run was more like a long, barely controlled fall, clumsily kept upright by the furniture that provided a course through the room. Ahead of me, I saw the swing of fabric—a shirt or dress—headed for the outside door.

I shoved it open and fell down the steps into the icy mud. My knees splashed into the muck and I barely kept my hold on the sword. All around me the woods lit up with the shades of people who had died here. It was an old, old land and there were so many of them. I struggled to my feet and kept going into the dark yard, with Arsenault clattering down the stairs behind me and cursing.

"*Who are you?*" I yelled as I chased the figure into the woods. It was Erelf, I thought. Or Geoffre's ghost. Or maybe just marauding gavaros...

My clarity had gone. Pine twigs stabbed my feet. I slipped on icy, wet leaves, but the ghostly figure flitted through the trees just ahead of me. A woman, her white petticoats gleaming when her green gown swung free of them, auburn highlights in her hair glinting like the embers of our dying fire...

The woman in Geoffre's sword... A flash of memory renewed my spirit. What in all the hells had she been doing inside the house— inside our bedroom?

Suddenly, a giant form stepped out of the trees before me, unfurling huge wings the color of night. I collided with them. Feathers swallowed me, soft and cold against my face. The world became a night spangled with stars, like I was drifting in a black sea with no division between sky and world until it was all the same.

I gasped and let go of the sword. A large hand closed on my hair and tugged my head back so I would look up at its face.

I stood shuddering, trying to breathe and not to panic, but making a poor job of it. I was staring up at one of Ires's vanth. *Of course.* Its face was impassive, blue-gray, as if carved from stone. No emotion broke the line of its mouth as it leaned over me.

"*Stay away*," it said, its voice like crackling ice, its breath the fetid, musty air of a tomb. Its gaze caught mine, filled with the agonizing span of infinity, and I stood, frozen in its grip.

"Let her go," Arsenault said in a low, dangerous voice. *Thank the gods he can see the vanth, too!* Maybe I wasn't entirely mad.

The vanth turned its head toward him. The movement was like a boulder moving—ponderous, inexorable, like watching something heavy begin to tip. An aura of magic crackled in the air, like the instant before a lightning strike. Words spilled out of me in sudden fright. "Don't hurt him! He's trying to protect me. Just let me go and leave him alone!"

It tugged my hair again. I closed my eyes, trying not to cry out. The vanth mobilized the magic of the grave, the fear of death, to frighten their victims. I'd recently been almost dead, so the fear was fresh in me. I didn't know why it was protecting that ghost, a woman who, for all I knew, had been long dead; I just knew it couldn't have Arsenault. I didn't know what he could do to a vanth, but he was clearly preparing to do it. Magic sizzled around us like an approaching wildfire.

Then—in an instant—the vanth disappeared. I dropped forward, and then I did cry out, in pain and alarm.

The magic disappeared abruptly. Arsenault caught me so I wouldn't fall on my sword. I thought I had dropped it, but it was still in my hand. I sagged against him because it hurt to hold myself up.

"Kyrra!" he exclaimed. "You're all right? It didn't hurt you?"

"Fucking vanth," I gasped. For the first time, I realized how cold and wet it was, and that I was barefoot and wearing a nightshirt. I started to shiver and Arsenault wrapped his arms around me, though he was barechested, too, but for his bandages. "Ires sent them to watch me. Did you see the ghost? The woman?"

He paused. "I saw something. Maybe it was a woman."

I wondered if he meant he was reserving judgment until he had a chance to think about it more, and if so, why he would. Or if he was just trying to calm me down so we could go back inside.

It didn't matter. The vanth's warning practically guaranteed I needed to know more.

CHAPTER 11

ARSENAULT

"HOW MUCH MAGIC IS TOO MUCH?" MIKELO MURMURED. "HOW much magic will Kyrra feel in the other room?"

Arsenault sat in the common room by the fire in the early morning dark, the sketch of the marriage bed he wanted to make laid out on a table before him while he tried to ignore how it made his skin creep to have Mikelo and Jon examining his back. He'd been jumpy ever since he'd settled Kyrra into bed. When the house grew quiet again and what was left of the night felt darker, thicker, full of a presence he was trying to convince himself he hadn't seen.

Surely the ghost Kyrra had chased outside had been the ghost of some other woman. An apparition raised by the magic picking up on all his worries. Or Erelf trying to find a loophole in his reprieve, torturing him with the reminder of Sella just when he thought he had taken a step forward into a new and better life.

The presence of the vanth, though... The vanth had *not* been a mere phantom. It had been a genuine guardian of the underworld, walking through the forest right outside this quiet, cozy little house, grabbing his wife by the hair.

His wife.

Their vow was consummated now, which would make it more likely to count as binding in a court of law, though the courts often ignored gavaros' love oaths if it was convenient. But *wife* was a strange, terrifying, and magical word. Like sleeping with her in his arms, skin to skin, no secrets, no need to justify anything to anyone.

Free.

How much magic was too much? He'd build a sanctuary of iron that would keep even the gods out. Why—*why*—would an apparition of Sella wake Kyrra so violently? And why now? He'd always expected her to haunt him, but goddesses went...elsewhere, he supposed. Not like his brother, who followed him everywhere. It would have been like Tavi to frighten Kyrra, but Tavi didn't have a good relationship with the vanth, who barred his entry to the afterlife.

He needed to lay some runes.

"Arsenault," Mikelo said, bringing him back to the moment.

He tried to focus on the orchids he'd drawn on the imaginary bed's headboard. "It depends, I guess. I don't know if there's a definite answer. Why?"

"Because you have pulled this scab open here at the top, ghost," Jon said, touching his shoulder blade. "It was fine last we looked at it, so what have you been doing?"

He flushed. He knew his run through the forest wouldn't have pulled those wounds open. He'd been thinking sometimes, in his more hopeful moments, of what the first time with Kyrra should be like. A marriage bed, a feast—hell, at least *dinner*. But that had never been the way it went for them. It had turned out right anyway, and he'd take her again a thousand times, however she wanted him.

"I've been living," he mumbled. "Being alive. Or trying to be anyway."

"I don't know if I should Fix this," Mikelo murmured. His magic hovered tentatively just below the surface. "There are so many things I don't know. Would it do harm to close an old wound? Is it even possible? When I try to See, it all looks... confused. Angry."

"Maybe you're seeing the man and not the wound," Jon said.

Arsenault twisted around to look at him. "Next time you're cursed by a god, let me know."

"I didn't say it wasn't justified, but maybe you need to be a little more careful. Whatever it was you were doing."

He gave Arsenault a meaningful look and Arsenault rolled his eyes. "Are you my mother now?"

"Mmm," Mikelo answered. A swirl of magic, followed by the sharp smell of imya and a sudden cold swab against his back made Arsenault flinch and swear.

"Sorry, Arsenault. I'm doing my best. I've never practiced with real wounds. All I had were tutors."

"If you keep those wounds clean, they'll heal," Jon said. "You don't have to know much medicine or magic."

"Miranda's book says I should have rubbed salt in the wounds. But I didn't, and I don't have that much salt now. Miranda says it's better to treat them with honey, but what if—"

"Mikelo. If Miranda says it's better, it is. I tend to agree with her. Salt keeps wounds dry, but..."

"It hurts like a son of a bitch," Arsenault growled at the floor as Mikelo did something uncomfortable to the wound. "I'm happy for you to use honey, Mikelo."

"Miranda and Silva have been teaching me about herbs, too. At least her store is labeled; all the plants here are different and Geoffre didn't seem to care..."

Mikelo's fingers stilled on Arsenault's back for a moment before twitching into motion again, maybe a little harder than strictly necessary. Arsenault traded a glance with Jon, who didn't look happy. They'd both been witness to how Geoffre had treated Mikelo.

"You're doing fine," Arsenault told him again. "Your Sight will help even if you don't Fix the flesh, Mikelo. Just be careful not to let it run away with you. It's not just Kyrra; you need to worry about yourself, too."

"This advice seems a bit hypocritical coming from you, ghost," Jon said.

"So, it's both then," Mikelo said. "Two things to worry about if I use magic to See into this wound. I might set Kyrra off or lose myself in the magic."

"Or you might See too much into him, Mikelo, and we can't have that."

It was like Jon to make jabs. They'd known each other for a long time. "Jon."

"I forgot. You have safeguards, don't you?"

"I don't. Wouldn't it be easier if I could just tell everybody the truth?"

Jon laughed, but there was a bitter note in it. "I'm not sure it would make it easier on everyone, ghost."

Before Arsenault could reply, Mikelo poured more imya on his back. He bit off a curse. "Why don't you let me have a drink, too, Mikelo. I think I might need some to get through the rest of this process."

"It's not even dawn. Why does it matter to Kyrra if we use our magic?"

Arsenault shifted, wincing. "The easiest explanation is because magic is a great sea. You know how the seas all have different characters and yet, they're still connected? Magic is like that, too. It expresses differently in everyone who uses it, but we all draw on the same ocean."

"Why can't Kyrra control hers if it's all the same? Why does she keep drawing more in?"

"People write treatises on that subject, Mikelo. You can't expect me to explain it all while you work on my back."

Mikelo huffed in frustration. "I've read some. I couldn't make heads or tails of them. Geoffre threw a copy of *On the Nature of Magic* in a bonfire. Said it was useless to dither about the ethics of using magic when we were fighting a war. I'm fairly certain none of those books covered Kyrra's situation, though, or I would have remembered."

"I—" Arsenault began, but whispers of memory in the back of his mind stopped him. *Which treatises? What books had survived?* "I can't remember how I knew to do what I did with Kyrra. The knowledge was just there. Part of being a Fixer is cultivating a relationship with the magic. When to listen to what it's telling you, and when to...not."

"You're saying you didn't know what you were doing when you gave Kyrra that arm?" Jon said in disbelief with a deep undercurrent of skepticism.

"No, I... I knew how to make it work. Somehow. The only time I don't have my basic knowledge of how to make magic work is when Erelf takes it from me. The way he did after Kafrin when you found me. But no one knows for sure why magic acts like it does. Some magic is wild. Some magic is the province of women. Like sailing from the Sheltered Sea down around Thunder Cape. Some seas are wild and dangerous, some placid and calm."

"Thunder Cape is an actual whirlpool of magic, though," Mikelo said. "Actual magic rushing up into our world, not through any person. I didn't think we were going to make it around."

More memories stirred. He should be able to remember rounding Thunder Cape now. And yet...

"The magic that leads to Fixing was what Attrasca unleashed on the world after he tricked the gods."

"Tricked them?" Jon said sharply. "I always heard the gods *gave* Attrasca the gift of magic. His Legacy. When before it was all violent like Thunder Cape, unable to be harnessed. The province of the gods."

"It—I don't know. Tricked, gave—same thing. I think Kyrra's arm is just an open conduit, like an aqueduct. If you or I use our magic within her range, Mikelo, there's always the danger of backflow."

"You're sure it's not Ires fouling things up?" Jon asked. "You didn't see her fight in Rojornick. You haven't heard the stories of the revenge she took on Markus Seroditch's assassins. She's spent five years with Ires as a close companion. You don't know what that's done to her, ghost."

Arsenault stood. Mikelo took a quick step backward. "Jon, speaking respectfully, as your friend, you can go fuck yourself. After you find me another godsdamned shirt. I gave my last one to Kyrra when her fever broke."

Jon stared at him for a moment, then chuckled. "Respectfully... Fuck you too, ghost. You're just going to keep chasing her into the woods? Ires won't let go of her until she does what he wants. You can't escape a god just because you leave the territory. I know you're thinking of heading off to Orienne again."

"So what if I am? I told her to go to Orienne after I gave her the arm, but I didn't make her *promise* to go. She hung around Rojornick waiting for me, Jon. I *have* heard some of those stories about Markus Seroditch, and it doesn't make a damn bit of difference."

Jon sighed. "I suppose I do have a shirt for you. Come on."

Arsenault left Mikelo to clean up, glad to be done with whatever healing he had given him.

"How did you die that time in Orienne?" Jon asked as they were walking down the hall.

"Of fever. In my sleep. I got to see a few children grow up, I think." A rare blessing. There must have been more children through the years, but he couldn't remember them yet. Or maybe he'd died or left before he'd been able to know them. He didn't know which thought was more depressing.

Jon looked troubled but didn't say anything. He led Arsenault to the wardrobe in the second bedroom and produced a good wool shirt, a scarf, and a sturdy coat. Arsenault eyed him as he laid out the clothes on the bed. "How often are you coming up here?"

Jon shrugged. "Often enough. It's not important."

"It is important if Miranda means as much to you as it seems."

Jon sighed heavily and gripped the footboard of the bed. His knuckles flexed tight before he answered, like he had to physically wrestle his thoughts on the matter.

"I don't know. Jemma..."

He stopped, the way he always did when he talked about Jemma.

Arsenault began the too-slow process of getting his stiff shoulder to cooperate in pulling the shirt over his head while he waited for Jon to say more. He wasn't going to press. He'd always felt retaining Jemma's memory was a small mercy; in a strange way he was thankful for the ability to properly grieve her.

"I can't forgive myself for not being there when Jemma and my boys died in the fire," Jon said finally. He smoothed the front of the coat he was holding with long, deliberate gestures. "Their death wasn't my fault, but it was everything to do with who I was that I couldn't be there. It's been—gods, is it six years now? Every time I think about being with another woman—not just for a night or two but seriously, in a relationship—I can't stop comparing it to what Jemma and I had, and it always comes up wanting before I even start. So, if it will never measure up, why try in the first place? But maybe... I don't know. I don't want Miranda and her boys to be hurt because of me, and yet... It's not like you and Kyrra. Jemma can't come back from the land of the ancestors. Sometimes I feel her watching, though. Keeping an eye on me."

"I'm sure she is, Jon. But I'm also sure she'd want something good for you. Sometimes you just need a friend."

"A certain kind of friend, you mean?"

"Both, sometimes. Just because you need a quiet, easy love doesn't mean it won't grow if you water it. And what's wrong with quiet?"

Almost against his will, he thought about Orienne again, and Rie. How *would* Kyrra feel about Orienne? Rie had been dead a long time. He didn't know if he'd ever properly grieved her or if her vague presence, which the gods had allowed to persist in his memory all these years, meant he'd never dealt with her death at all. Their relationship had been...easy. Not passionate, just convenient. But because it had been easy, Orienne was the place he kept going back to when he needed to heal. The rolling green and yellow hills, the twisted and yet orderly forms of the grape vines trained on their strings, the espaliered fruit trees against the garden wall, the ocean, glistening blue as a sapphire in the distance. Would Kyrra understand that he wanted to share that feeling of permanence with her, as if there was something good in the world that wouldn't change?

The journey was too hard to make now, with her health the way it was and sanval season upon them, keeping west-sailing ships in harbor. But when the spring storms ended...

Jon tugged wearily on his locs. "I don't know, Arsenault. What if I bought Miranda some goats? Would that be too much? The winter was cold, and she lost a few..."

Arsenault laughed and reached for the coat. "Jon, you furnished her house. The chairs in the common room are mahogany. The couch obviously came out of some householder's collection, although the upholstery is a crime. The table is a solid piece of Dakkaran teak."

Jon snorted, but he looked embarrassed. "You and your tables."

Arsenault winced as he shrugged into the coat. "I enjoyed building tables. The man who taught me had an artist's eye and a lot of patience. Wood's not my talent, but I appreciated having to slow down and put it together."

Jon gave him an odd look. "You're talking about Guin, yes? The man you lived with on the Outer Isles? Do you remember him?"

Arsenault frowned, suddenly uneasy as he wound the scarf around his neck and began to button the coat. As he looked down, he realized he was still barefoot. He would need his socks, boots, and swordbelt to go out and those were in the other bedroom with Kyrra. His sword was propped against the wall in the common room, where he'd left it after he'd brought Kyrra in. It made him nervous no one was in that room to watch it, but maybe Mikelo was back by now.

I could melt it down to Fix Kyrra's arm, but how much blood has she fed it fighting all those wars in Rojornick and Kavo?

He hated to admit it, but maybe Jon was right about Ires.

"Ghost," Jon said, tugging him back to the moment. Damn, he was tired. "Do you remember Guin or not?"

Arsenault took a deep breath. He wasn't sure he wanted to remember Guin; just bringing up his name was painful. "Guin is dead, Jon. He's not coming back. I suppose I'd forgotten him, too, but it doesn't seem like there's any use remembering him now if I can't do anything to help him, only to...grieve."

Jon gave him a sharp glance. Stepped forward and smoothed the wrinkles of the coat across his shoulders. It was definitely Jon's coat; it fit him well, even a little loose in the chest. "I sent a letter to my sister Adayze, telling her that I finally solved the puzzle of your curse."

"I suppose you had to report that," Arsenault murmured.

Jon's eyes narrowed and his hand stilled, making Arsenault think there was more there Jon wasn't telling him, something else he'd forgotten and hadn't remembered yet. He did remember Adayze and her little boy Edo... Grown now. Gods, so many names, so many people. He just wanted to do the fucking chores.

Jon's face cleared and he patted Arsenault on the shoulder. "You think I should buy the goats?"

"Buy the godsdamned goats. If she keeps coming to check on you —if she lets you fill up the house with all your damn furniture—it probably means she thinks somewhat *more* of you, too. Now if you want to stay in her good graces, I better milk the goats. Next one jumps over the fence, I'll let it go and you can buy the woman another one, all right?"

❧

BY THE TIME HE WALKED OUT THE DOOR, DAWN WAS BREAKING. A thin orange line like embers shot through a layer of rumpled, ash-colored clouds. It seemed like the world had been locked in ice for an eternity; it could have been years since the battle, but the weather had been shit for most of it. When the wind blew, the ice-coated firs creaked ominously; broken boughs littered the ground, scenting the air like a Longest Night party in Dagmar.

Arsenault spared the trees an anxious glance and pulled his scarf up over his nose, then kept walking, tugging on a pair of wool gloves he found in his pockets as he went.

He didn't mind the weather so much. It was miserable, but in a way that made being alive so long bearable. It was easy to lose track of what living meant, to sink into the idea that sorrow and pain would never change. The natural world was always a reminder of what was *real*, the tiny little things that had nothing to do with people, their wars, politics, and conspiracies. Like the clutch of snowdrops blooming at the corner of the house's foundation, encased in ice like white jewels. If the stories were true, these last cold snaps were merely the pangs of Adalus, murdered by Erelf, rising back to life.

He could relate to that. Coming back from death was never easy.

The sun's first light lit the ice like fire before it died back into the brooding gray clouds. Arsenault stopped to look at the sky. Probably more ice on the way, or snow if they were lucky. If his shoulder and back would allow it, he'd haul away some of these branches. Dried and seasoned, they could be burned as firewood; none were big enough to be sawn and planked for building. They'd need to watch that tree leaning over the house...

Movement in the corner of his eye caught his attention. He put his hand on his sword and whirled, only to be faced not with an animal or a man, but an inhuman creature drifting out of the trees.

Huge black wings unfurled, scattering ice from the branches. Skin gleamed blue—flat, hard eyes like chips of jet tracked his every move.

Not another fucking vanth.

Anger boiled up in him, too fast to stop. Before he realized what he was doing, he was stomping toward the vanth, hand on his hilt.

"What in all the hells do you think you're doing? Is Ires sending you to torment us? Or are you in league with Erelf now?"

The vanth stood silent, as devoid of emotion as a statue.

"Is it Tavi then? Why did you tell Kyrra to stay away? Were you protecting her or threatening her?"

A connection, a memory, itched in his brain. Something about fear-conjured images, something he remembered about *apparitions* that was important. It was like having a word on the tip of your tongue that you knew but couldn't quite say.

He waited for the vanth to answer, but it only stared into him with its black eyes, as dark and suffocating as the inside of a coffin.

"Go fetch some other ghost," he told it in exasperation. "You know it's not my time. And stay away from Kyrra."

He thrust his hand into his trouser pocket and closed his fingers on an old bit of metal he'd picked up in the barn yesterday, a rusty piece of horse tack. He was a little close to the house, but probably far enough away from Kyrra that he could chance it. He couldn't rune the place against Ires, and if he used too many, it would hurt Kyrra. But maybe just *one*.

The magic came tentatively at first, a little trickle warming his fingers in the cold dawn. He'd been forced to use his magic clandestinely or not at all for so long that it was hesitant to obey him; calling it to work on Kyrra's arm had been like prying free a jammed wheel. He coaxed it past the learned fear and it rushed, relieved, into the metal in his palm, casting off the rust in red flakes that floated to the ground like snow. The old buckle shone silver, then glowed orange and yellow, and with his gloved thumb and forefinger he stretched the soft metal into a different shape, lengthening one side of the rectangle before squeezing the gap in the buckle closed with his fist.

He waited a moment, holding his breath, conditioned to feel the weight of the gods' displeasure at him for transgressing his old boundaries. The feeling of unresolved expectation made his skin crawl. He hadn't gotten used to it yet and didn't know if he should.

His anxiety infected his magic and it struggled to escape its bonds like an eager hound—to seek out the deep pockets of ore beneath them and turn the whole place into a fortress instead of a farm. The farm would be impregnable if his magic could only merge with the unpredictable stream of magic pouring through the house—

"*Dammit*," he muttered and cut the flow abruptly, sealing off the rune and damming the rest of the magic behind his gates. He hurled the metal rune to the ground and stamped it into the frozen mud as deep as it would go. Blue light crackled around it, limning a filmy host of wandering souls in its glow. Any of them could have been the ghost who'd tormented Kyrra last night; maybe he'd just seen what he'd been most afraid of. The vanth gave him one last unfathomable glance and swallowed the ghosts in its glossy night-colored feathers. The fire of dawn dwindled to the steady silver light of a cloudy morning and both vanth and ghosts disappeared.

"I'm just trying to do the chores," he said through gritted teeth. "Stay in your hells and leave us alone!"

A wind swirled through the trees like Ires's mad laughter. Arsenault glared and stomped off toward the barn and the goats.

The females that had recently kidded were separated out in their own pen, and Silva must have put the doe about to kid in her own stall last night. They all bleated at him when he walked in. The horses hung their heads over the stall doors and whinnied nervously. One of them—the big gray—kicked the side of its stall so loudly it sounded like a gunshot. The whole stall rattled with it and the goats set up an angry bleating, the pig squealed, and a couple of barn cats streaked out of the corners where they'd been curled up.

Arsenault frowned. Why were the horses so riled up? Usually, they were happy to see him, eager for their morning oats.

The animals' noises died down and in the sudden silence, he heard a shuffle of straw from the wrong direction, not heavy enough to be a horse. He'd barely touched the hilt of his sword before two men rushed him from one of the empty stalls.

Arsenault threw himself out of the way, banged his bad shoulder on the frame of a stall, and tasted pain. A heavy metal hilt slammed into the wood beside his face, splintering the edge, and Arsenault jerked against the stall door.

Two skinny young men wearing blue tunics smeared with dirt and old bloodstains stood before him, one with a short sword, the other holding a long, rust-speckled knife.

"It is him!" the man with the knife whispered. *Gods, he's little more than a boy.*

"Told you." The other smiled a stupid nervous grin, the kind men got when too much fight pumped through their bodies. "Heard it in camp last night. Jon Barra'd found the Aliente captain." He moved to stop Arsenault as he tried to slide down the line of stalls. "Still a bounty on your head, isn't it? Twenty thousand astra!"

The godsdamned scar. All those fucking posters.

"Easier if you come with us." Knife twisted his hands on his hilt. He looked sweaty and nervous. "Better if we can bring you in alive."

"We'll kill you if we can't. Two of us, and you're not armed."

"More men outside if you try to escape."

A feed bucket hung on a post slightly out of reach. Arsenault twitched the fingers on his opposite hand. The men were so fucking young and strung so tight, they did exactly what he hoped they would. Both swung in that direction, the bigger one with the sword in his fist, but Arsenault was already lunging the other way. He yanked the bucket off its hook and swung it in a wide arc—smashed it into Knife's head so hard the metal band holding the slats buckled. The man staggered backwards, cursing as he brought a gauntleted fist to his head in reflex—only one hand gripping that knife now—and before his comrade could get space to maneuver his sword, Arsenault brought the bucket down hard on top of his head.

Splinters shattered everywhere. The horses whinnied in the stalls and one of them slammed a hoof against the door. The man Arsenault had hit staggered to his knees and dropped the knife. Arsenault grabbed it just as the swordsman's blade cut down at his shoulder. He barely got the rotten, warped steel blade high enough to meet it.

In a moment of reflex, the magic he'd just forced behind his gates poured eagerly into the knife. The blade leapt for the man in a fount of hot metal that filled his mouth, splashed over his face, and froze into a death mask of dark steel. He fell to the dirt floor like a doll and Arsenault finally succeeded in slamming the magic off. Then he picked up the man's sword and skewered his frightened compatriot through the midsection.

The man dropped, gasping and writhing, to the ground. Arsenault jerked the sword out and the blood started pumping, pooling. He died quickly after that, the light gone from his eyes even before his limbs stopped jerking.

Arsenault let his breath out shakily and sagged against the barn wall, dazed. It was so fucking useless. Two men throwing away lives that hadn't even begun for twenty thousand astra they probably wouldn't have been paid now Geoffre was dead. So, what was the fucking *point?*

A muffled metal clang outside the barn made him draw up in surprise. *More men outside if you try to escape,* the man had said.

"Dammit," he muttered. He wished he had a gun, but even if he couldn't shoot, he could get a better view from the loft.

The leftover fight running through him blocked the pain of using his bad shoulder to climb the ladder. In the loft, he ran as quietly as possible over the creaky floorboards to the small door under the eaves used to toss hay. He grabbed a pitchfork and pushed the door open a crack to see outside.

Four men. Two on the ground, injured or dead, and two in dark cloaks standing over them. The cloaked men turned in the direction of the house as if they were about to start walking.

Dammit, he couldn't let them get to the house. He shoved the door open and hurled the pitchfork to the ground. It sank into the icy muck beside the shorter man's boot and quivered there. The other, taller man cursed loudly, raised his hands in surrender, and turned his face up so Arsenault could see it.

They stared at each other in surprise. Then the man in the cloak started to laugh. "Godsdammit, Arsenault," he said. "All we need is for you to hand Devid the Chair with a fucking pitchfork."

Lobardin?

He wasn't imagining things. It was really Lobardin standing down there with two dead Prinze gavaros on the ground at his feet. "What in all the hells are you talking about?"

The man he'd almost hit with the pitchfork flipped his hood down and looked up at him. "Arsenault."

No, dammit, not him.

He'd almost killed Cassis di Prinze.

CHAPTER 12

ARSENAULT

"WHAT IN ALL THE HELLS ARE YOU DOING HERE, CASSIS? I thought Jon made it clear you're not welcome! Are these your men?"

"They're independent or they're Devid's," Cassis said in a measured voice, hands still raised.

"I told you we should have used new colors, mestere," Lobardin said.

Cassis threw a sour glance at Lobardin. "We're not here to cause trouble, Arsenault. We just want to talk."

"Do you have another pitchfork or can we put our hands down?" Lobardin interjected.

Arsenault leaned against the frame of the loft opening. "No pitchforks, but my magic works and I'll use it. Throw down your weapons. Over there, by the fence." He gestured a long way from where they were standing.

Lobardin and Cassis traded nervous glances.

Good. Best if they imagined the worst of what he might do to them.

In reality, the fight had worn him out. Fluid dripped down his back from beneath the bandages, something sticky and viscous. He hoped it was just honey. More magic—destructive, protective, big magic— would overrun him and cause more problems than it solved. But to protect Kyrra and Mikelo, he could damn well make it work.

"Now!" he snapped.

Cassis slowly unbuckled his pistol belt. He tossed it as far as he could in the direction Arsenault had indicated. "Will you at least come down to hear what I have to say?"

"All your weapons. You, too, Lobardin."

Arsenault watched as they disarmed themselves, then let his gaze skim off toward the trees. He didn't think Cassis would have come without a guard, but if he had, they were keeping well back. This wouldn't have happened if he'd runed the farm. It was too risky to put off doing that anymore.

"Don't move," he said when they put their empty hands up again.

Arsenault disliked letting the two men out of his sight, but he had to get down from the loft somehow. The goats bleated as he walked past the gavaros he'd killed, the does still needing to be milked, their udders heavier than they liked. The bleating was strangely distressing amid this violence.

His bad shoulder protested with a deep, burning pain as he hauled open the barn doors and drew his sword. "Where's that last knife hidden, Lobardin? Arm? Back?"

"I don't know what you're talking about—"

Arsenault let the tip of his sword fall forward and rest against Lobardin's chest.

"Back," Lobardin said.

Carefully, Arsenault reached around Lobardin's body into the waistband of his trousers to pull the knife he had hidden there. It was so small it fit into the palm of Arsenault's hand. Cassis twitched him a worried glance but didn't move.

"I'll want that returned," Lobardin told him. "It was expensive."

Arsenault hefted it, testing its balance, then flipped out the blade. A wicked, useful little knife. He closed it and shoved it into the pocket of his coat.

"You look like hell," he said to Lobardin.

"Kyrra hit me. And I haven't had a smoke in twenty-one days."

Arsenault tilted his head. "So, she beat some sense into you?"

Lobardin's mouth twisted into a smirk. "You could see it that way. You don't look so wonderful yourself, Arsenault." The smirk faded to puzzlement. "Though more like you used to... Were you scarred again or—"

"It's not that kind of scar," Arsenault replied shortly. "But the men wanted the bounty. You didn't put them up to it?"

"I did not," Cassis said. "I couldn't have paid them anyway. But why would I give up twenty thousand astra to get something I'd already had?"

Cassis's flat expression barely covered a tumult of anger. Arsenault shifted his grip on his sword. His shoulder hurt from holding it one-handed. He hoped the other men couldn't see the blade tremble as he patted Cassis down with his other hand. Cassis stood for it, clenching his teeth, but not—to his credit—protesting.

When he was satisfied Cassis didn't have any hidden weapons, Arsenault rested the blade against his shoulder and leaned against the doorframe of the barn, letting the other men sweat for a moment as he took in the scene more closely. The dead men lay at their feet, both of them with neat wounds as if Cassis and Lobardin had taken them by surprise. He squinted back toward the house. No movement there yet. Maybe he could deal with Lobardin and Cassis and send them on their way before anyone knew they were here. Kyrra surely didn't need to get wind of Cassis's presence.

"Well," he said. "If you're here in good faith, you might as well help me deal with these bodies. And I still need to milk the goats."

⚜

THE GROUND WAS TOO FROZEN TO DIG, SO THEY COULDN'T BURY the men. Arsenault thought about putting them on a pyre to burn, but that took a lot of work and watching. He didn't want to disrespect the corpses, but there were four dead men to deal with and he didn't have the time or strength to do it properly, especially not with Cassis breathing down his neck.

"We'll take them to the ravine," he decided. "Throw them down for the birds and wolves, and I'll...I'll rune them, I guess. Can't make sure their souls make it to the underworld, but at least they'll be far enough away from the house."

"Reminds me of the Forza bandits we killed," Lobardin muttered. "After they raided the Aliente. You didn't rune any of them."

"I couldn't predict when the gods would punish me for using my magic. I had to choose my battles. Not all magic was worth the gamble."

"Their ghosts are probably still wandering the countryside, wreaking havoc. I was a bit of an innocent; knifing them in their sleep felt ruthless then. Good thing we're not close here. Are we?"

Arsenault shook his head. *I suppose we were all innocent before the war. Even me.* It shouldn't have been possible, and yet it felt that way. "Other direction. Come on. We'll use the horses. It's a fair distance. Where are your horses, by the way? And your men?"

"Down the road," Cassis replied. His gaze tracked nervously over the dead men in the barn, catching on the man with the metal filling his mouth. "Arsenault, this sits ill with me. I don't want to commit more transgressions against the dead. Devid had Geoffre's body and I don't know if he'll have him buried properly."

"Didn't realize you were such an innocent too, mestere." It wouldn't help to goad Cassis, and yet...being able to speak his mind in Cassis's presence felt like a right Arsenault needed to assert.

Cassis glared at him. "I've spent the last weeks—the last five *years* —burning corpses. I was *in charge* of the men I burned, they died *for me* because of what I ordered them to do! And you'll throw barbed comments as if you're untainted by guilt?"

Arsenault bristled. Ire rose hot in his chest. "I've also burned my share of men who died on my orders. It's a burden of command, not something to be whined about as if you're too special to have to deal with it. You can take your pious squeamishness and shove it up your arse."

"You don't think I'd be worried about my *father*—"

"About Geoffre? You came at him with an army! Did you think he was going to see you at that lodge with all those shiny cannons and finally take you seriously? Wave a white flag, get down on his knees, and beg for forgiveness?"

Cassis's jaw twitched. A sheen passed over his eyes, like he might be fighting tears. What gave *him* the right to be upset? What gave him the godsdamned right to tug on Arsenault's empathy?

"Fuck you, Arsenault. You're so godsdamned high and mighty, *fuck you*. You think I didn't know you were sleeping with Viela before she died? She was my wife, Arsenault. My second wife, but still my *wife*."

Arsenault tightened his hand on the hilt of his sword. "After everything you put me through, you'll try to justify it with Viela? The woman you married solely to bear you a child, then abandoned because you were too lost in your kacin haze—"

"You should have known my father would find her out!"

"You should have protected her from him!"

Lobardin put a hand on Arsenault's chest and gave him a sharp look. Arsenault turned angrily toward him. "So you're his bodyguard now, Lobardin?"

"You get rid of him, we're stuck with Devid," Lobardin replied in a low voice. "Jon made a mistake. Maybe Devid is weak, but he's wilier than we thought."

"Godsdammit, both of you!" Cassis shouted.

Arsenault stared at him. "I thought you got what you wanted. Can't you be content with your victory?"

Cassis took a deep breath. "That's what I came to talk to you about—you, Jon, Kyrra, Mikelo. All of you. About this so-called victory, where Devid is pushing things, and what the hell you and Jon think you're doing. Two men tried to poison our food stores a day ago, and if either of you had anything to do with that, you can damn well tell me. But it starts with my father's body, Arsenault, whether you want to hear my pious bullshit or not."

Arsenault wanted to keep being angry with him. To shove him down the path and not have to speak to him, and failing that, or maybe prior to it, to give him a taste of the debasement Cassis had forced him into over the past months. Make him kneel and beg. Except that kind of cruelty felt like it would start a rot in his own soul. It wasn't the way he wanted to restart this life.

But being accused of a plot to poison Cassis's food stores confused him. It didn't sound like Jon; Jon would only do such a thing if he could get men in and out without being caught.

"Whatever Devid does to Geoffre's body will be on his own head. If Geoffre's shade wanders the land forever, at least he'll be bound here along with all the others. It's a very old land and there are a lot of ghosts."

"So, you don't think he could come back? Because the god—"

"Is that what you came here to ask me?"

"I just... I thought you might know. That's all."

Cassis's hesitation seemed strange. Arsenault studied him for a moment, then shrugged. "Well, I don't. Geoffre made himself a vessel, but *he* wasn't a god. He was a man the same as anyone else."

"But you're different. You come back."

"Geoffre wasn't cursed like me, was he? Maybe he'll haunt Devid. Are you afraid, Cassis?"

Cassis's brows rose. "Aren't you?"

It was too direct a question with too simple an answer. Of course he was afraid. He had no desire to meet Geoffre again in any fashion, but especially not as a reanimated corpse full of rents and tears made by the sword he'd forged hundreds of years ago and given to Kyrra. He had no desire to see if Erelf preferred walking around in stolen human form.

"I'll get the horses," Arsenault said curtly. "You two find the rope. In the far stall."

"Si, Captain," Lobardin answered in a mocking tone, but he and

Cassis both went. Arsenault let out his breath and went to take the gray gelding out of its stall.

The horse whickered as Arsenault approached, stepping around the man killed by his magic. Arsenault tried not to notice the way the dim overcast light gleamed dully on the metal pouring from the man's mouth, as if his dying scream had taken physical form. The horse butted his chest and Arsenault rubbed its velvet pink and black nose, thankful for the distraction.

"No carrots today, lad. We both have work to do before breakfast."

His shoulder and back hurt as they tied the bodies two at a time to long ropes behind the horse and dragged them out, through the barnyard, down the path through the trees to where the hillside sheered away into a ravine. Even though they weren't in the Irondels proper, the landscape was rocky, steep, and treacherous in the ice, and the dragging bodies made the horse skittish. The horse slipped and slid on the trail, but with him and Cassis at the bridle and Lobardin making sure the corpses didn't slide forward too fast and tangle in the horse's hocks, they made it in two trips and cast the corpses—torn and scraped—over the side.

Arsenault turned away before they hit the bottom. He couldn't stomach watching the men bounce and flop over the rocks and roots as if they were dolls. *May birds clean their bodies and their souls return to the light of the sun from which they came.* He didn't know why this prayer to the Magnificent Sun was so ingrained in him—he doubted the Magnificent Sun would have him—but it quieted his soul to say it. He broke off a branch from one of the bare trees overhanging the ravine, sending ice clattering everywhere, and used it to trace a line of runes over the path.

Sanctuary. Ward against evil. He finished the last emphatically and the shapes he'd drawn gleamed faintly white as if they'd filled with ice.

It wasn't much, but it was something. He swayed as the magic ran out of him, put a hand to his head, and pitched the stick into the ravine with the bodies. When he turned to Cassis and Lobardin, Cassis looked as pasty as old porridge.

"Is that it then?" Cassis asked in a clipped voice. "Are you ready to talk now?"

"If you want to talk, you'll do it while we take care of the animals. I hadn't done my chores when I was interrupted."

"Godsdammit, Arsenault—"

He whirled on Cassis. Lobardin had a hand on him in an instant, but all they had were their fists and neither of them knew how tight a leash he had on his anger, that Cassis wasn't lying in the mud right now, or worse.

He stabbed a finger at Cassis's chest, shoving Cassis backward. "You're on my territory, so you'll follow *my* rules for once. Kyrra's not well enough for you to traipse in there, and then you'll have Ires *and* me to deal with, because I will take you down in a heartbeat if I think you're threatening her. So. My space, my people, my rules. Do you understand? If you don't, collect your men and go back to your camp, but don't expect safe passage from me."

"And your rules include milking the fucking goats?"

"The animals deserve more respect than you do. If your goal is to talk, you can wait. Or better yet, help."

"You *were* trying to get me killed in that battle."

Arsenault tugged on the horse's bridle and began walking back up the path. "That was the plan, mestere."

Cassis swore but jogged to catch up. Lobardin followed in a flap of black cloak that made him seem supremely tired of the conversation. Fuck Lobardin, too. Fuck him for trying to clean himself up after Kyrra bashed in his nose. It put a crook in the bone that made him look even more like a raven.

"Jon misjudged if he thought Devid would be what Liera needed," Cassis said, trying to keep pace with him. "In possession of the Chair Devid's weakness will be dangerous. And there are rumors, Arsenault. A lot of rumors. I need to talk to Jon."

"You want him to kill Devid? Put *you* on the Chair?"

"I'd like to say it to Jon. And there's something I need to talk to Kyrra about, too. Something important. It's not just the Chair that's at stake here, Arsenault. It's Liera."

Arsenault walked in silence for a moment, the only sound the clopping of the horse's hooves against the frozen pebbles littering the path and the crash of an overburdened branch as it succumbed to the weight of the ice. The mud was miserable to climb in, slippery under the horse's shoes and his boots.

"That's going to be more difficult," he said finally.

"You're making decisions for her now?" Cassis replied angrily.

Arsenault flicked him a glance, trying to gauge why he was suddenly so worried about Kyrra's right to choose. "Well, it will depend on whether she's awake and lucid, Cassis. Turns out, it takes a while to recover from doing battle with a god."

Lobardin suddenly pulled on the horse's bridle, stopping the horse and him. "Arsenault. She isn't... I mean, I saw her. On the battlefield. I brought the cart..."

The look in Lobardin's dark eyes brought him up short. The expression on his face, the faint green remains of a bruise that colored the hollows above his cheekbones, the shiny new scarring that marred the bridge of his nose. A sliver of shared memory took form between them, binding them together like ropes: Kyrra lying in the mud with her torn clothes and broken skin, blood slick in a pool all around her. Mikelo wheezing as he wrestled his magic, trying desperately to save her.

For a moment, Arsenault thought he could actually see it all reflected in the black sheen of Lobardin's eyes. But it was only his own face, contorted and surprised by grief.

He turned away abruptly, tugged the horse too hard and regretted it. The horse had no role in their drama.

"Thank you," he said gruffly. "I didn't know where the wagon came from."

"You didn't answer my question, Arsenault."

"She's...not, no. Mikelo healed most of her wounds. But she lost a lot of blood, and then there was a fever, and now it's magic doing the most damage. She's weak and she can't control her Sight." He took a deep breath and looked at Lobardin and Cassis squarely. "That means, if you try to lie, there's a good chance she'll See it and Ires might take over. I don't know what happened between either of you and Kyrra back at the lodge, but she can't keep Ires out and you need to be aware of that. Nobody brings weapons near her, not even me."

Cassis frowned. "Does that mean you'll let me talk to her?"

"I suppose that will be up to her, won't it?"

CHAPTER 13

MIKELO

MIKELO CARRIED A TOWER OF BOOKS AND NOTES DOWN THE DARK hallway, topped off with a jar of ink and a quill balanced precariously on top. The names of the plants he thought Kyrra would need to ease her breathing felt like part of the stack, too, just not anything he could hold onto. They kept slipping out of his mind no matter how many times he repeated them.

He was so godsdamned tired. It felt like someone had scrubbed sand into his eyes. His nightmares seemed to be intensifying, not abating, with time; now they were disturbing Silva. That damn mirror from Cassis's stables. As if reliving what he'd seen in his own awful reflection wasn't enough, Geoffre often stared back at him now with a smug, self-satisfied smile.

I refuse to become my uncle, even if I am forced to compete for the Chair.

You're getting ahead of yourself, Mikelo. No one's forcing you to do anything yet.

That was true. He couldn't even remember a simple list of herbs. How did he expect to remember political treaties and tariffs and taxes and...

Focused on the voices in his head, he'd passed Kyrra's door and had to backtrack a few steps. He adjusted the stack of books and papers in his arms, trying to balance the ink well on top while he reached for the door handle. It slid to the edge of the book cover, but he finally got a hand on the twisted iron handle—

The door abruptly swung inward. He stumbled; the ink slid; he lunged to catch it...

He caught a flash of mussed up golden brown curls, the edge of firelight gleaming off wide dark blue eyes, and then the ink crashed to the floor and the papers followed. All his work lay in a puddle of glistening glass shards and black ink, spreading across the floor like a pool of asphalt on Qalfan sands.

"Oh—no—gods*dammit*—"

"Mikelo!" Silva exclaimed. "Oh, gods, I'm sorry!"

Mikelo dropped to his knees and cast the books aside to gather the papers, shaking the ink off them in desperation. The ink continued to spread over the floor, sinking into all the little pits in the stone. He lunged to rescue more of his papers—*no, gods, no, how could I be so stupid?*—and then Silva was there with a towel, sopping up the ink and wiping up the glass. Mikelo realized for the first time that he was kneeling in it. Tiny bits ground into his knees.

"I'm sorry, Mikelo. I didn't mean to frighten you. I thought Arsenault was coming back for something."

"It's fine," Mikelo mumbled, still picking up papers. "We didn't wake her, did we?"

Silva twisted to look over his shoulder. "I don't think so..."

Kyrra's knees twitched and she murmured something as she shifted a little. Mikelo held his breath, but she stilled. She was wheezing again, though.

"Peppermint, horehound, ivy," Mikelo muttered. "No, that's not right. Thyme? Spearmint? Dammit." He sat back on his heels and pressed his fingers against his closed eyes.

"Mikelo. What are you talking about?"

"The herbs to ease her breathing. Except I can't remember them, and—" He opened his eyes and looked down at his ruined papers. "Oh, damn."

He was so *beyond* tired. Watching the ugly black splotches bleeding through his carefully penned notes and the valuable blank sheets of paper he probably wouldn't be able to replace... Tears rushed up to press at the back of his eyes, so hot and gritty already. Now they burned with frustration and shame.

He moved to rub them. Silva made a sound and Mikelo blinked in surprise.

"Ink. On your fingers. And your—" Silva gestured at his own face.

Mikelo flushed so hot he felt like his cheeks must be glowing. He swiped at his face with his sleeve—probably just making it worse—and looked at the mess on the floor. "At least I saved the book," he choked, in a way he hoped came out as laughter and not despair.

A light touch on his shoulder made him tense. When Mikelo looked down, Silva drew back his hand, leaving a big black ink smudge on Mikelo's shirt.

Silva's eyes widened. "Dammit, Mikelo, I didn't mean to add *more* to the mess. How long have you been awake?"

"A while? I wanted to spend some time reading, but Arsenault needed help."

"I'll bet you haven't had coffee or breakfast either."

Mikelo stared at him. *Coffee? Breakfast?*

"Did you eat supper last night, or did you just go to sleep?"

Mikelo started to rub his eyes again and remembered the ink just in time. "Can't remember," he mumbled.

"Right. Go. I'll see what I can save."

"But, Kyrra—"

"No buts, Mikelo. Sleep will be what she needs. *You* need food."

"All-all right." Mikelo stood hesitantly. Silva had been nothing but helpful, which had worn down Mikelo's distrust, but... Well, he supposed he was just tired.

"Mikelo, I said go," Silva whispered.

Mikelo jerked, realizing he was watching Silva's hands as they expertly rolled the ink-soaked towel into a bowl to hold all the glass inside. Those long, dangerous fingers. He turned quickly aside.

"All right, I'll just—I'll—"

He grabbed his book and backed out into the hall.

Dawn lent a silvered brightness to the front room and the kitchen. He managed to navigate the furniture without smearing it with ink and let himself out into the cold yard, where he washed his hands and face briefly in the painful, icy water from the pump. Then he went back inside to collapse, shivering and dripping, into a chair at the kitchen table.

His mind still felt bruised. For a moment, all he could do was stare around the kitchen. The copper pots hanging from the mantel reflected the glow of the fire, and the astringent scent of dried herbs mingled with the scent of woodsmoke and the lingering smell of alliums in a comforting way. But it was still somebody else's home, somebody else's life.

A clank startled him. He blinked blearily at Silva, who was digging a scoopful of grain from a tall jar in the pantry.

"What are you doing?"

"What does it look like I'm doing? I'm making you polenta." The tiny pieces of grain rushed into the pot with a reassuring musical clatter.

"I can just have some cheese. A cup of wine. There's no need—"

Silva poured water in the pot, then covered it with a lid and hefted it onto another hook over the fire. "You didn't eat last night, and you've been up long enough this morning, you should have something warm."

He moved efficiently on to another task, scooping a handful of dark beans into a mortar. Mikelo felt as if he were watching the workings of a kitchen in an inn. Silva began smashing the beans with a metal pestle and a rich, dark smell filled the room.

Coffee, thank the gods. The smell took Mikelo back to Baleria, crouching under the banana trees and watching the village men perfect their eyi strategy. He could almost hear the sound of beans and stones falling onto worn wooden boards. There were many mornings he'd had to content himself with the smell of coffee alone, unless one of the village women took pity on him by giving him a bean cake or a cup of millet porridge.

Silva went through the motions of coffee-making, then poured out a small, delicate, Qalfan-made cup and placed it in front of him.

"You're cooking just for me?" Mikelo asked skeptically.

Silva threw Mikelo a confused glance. "I thought I'd eat with you unless you don't want me to. Drink that coffee quick, before the grounds settle." He walked back to the pantry and stuck his head inside the closet. His voice continued, slightly muffled. "What do you like in your polenta? There's honey, of course, preserved lemons... Oh! Sugar! Jon must have brought it."

He came out holding up a little jar, face flushed in triumph and wearing a happy grin.

Mikelo smiled in return as he put the cup to his lips—*sugar*—but he couldn't hide his confusion. He drank the coffee, grateful for the strong, bitter heat of it. "You don't have time for this, surely?"

"Didn't anyone ever tell you it's rude to refuse a gift? Arsenault's doing my chores and Miranda's not here, so I suppose I can cook. You don't seem to recognize what you're doing is difficult."

Mikelo frowned. How to explain that he felt his tasks were not merely difficult but impossible?

"Well—imagine someone gives you the gift of a beautiful, wild, and very fast horse. You don't know how to ride, and yet you're forced to ride this horse in a race. The horse is so fast that if you're lucky enough to hang on, you might win. But in the next race, you might fall and be trampled, or maybe you'll do something that will hurt the horse or the other riders. You don't have any knowledge *or* skill. Just dumb, fickle luck. That's me and my magic right now."

Silva gave him a strange look. He was frying thick rashers of bacon in a skillet and even the smell seemed like an unspeakable luxury. "I doubt you're as ignorant and dangerous as you make it sound."

"But it only took Arsenault eight days to recover from—" He stopped abruptly when he realized who he was talking to.

"You healed Arsenault," Silva said tightly. "And Kyrra would have died if you hadn't been there. Maybe you can't help Kyrra because she can't be helped? Maybe she just needs time."

Mikelo blinked, a little flustered by Silva's faith in him. He tried to recover by laughing. "Are you saying I'm being arrogant?"

One of Silva's brows hooked as he scraped the bacon out onto a plate, then walked it over to Mikelo. The smooth, practiced way he placed it on the table reminded Mikelo even more strongly of being served at an inn. *Because he was a server, you idiot. A courtesan.* As Silva straightened, Mikelo felt like he was seeing him—really seeing him— for the first time. The careless brown hair that glittered with gold streaks like a wildflower honey, the clean, strong lines of his features as if someone had sculpted them, the warmth in his deep blue eyes.

Silva looked toward him, mouth twisted in an exasperated smile. "Eat your bacon. Would you like some cheese, too?"

"This is the largest breakfast I think I've ever eaten."

"I thought you'd be used to fancy food. Partridge pie every morning. Cream puffs served to you in bed."

Mikelo couldn't help snickering at the thought. "As if the servants would have bent to that."

"Surely it was more than *porridge*."

Mikelo shrugged. "Geoffre was a believer in working breakfasts, so mostly it was food we could eat while walking—buns, coffee, cold meat and cheese, sometimes a glass of wine. He often locked himself in his study all morning. He had a lot of claims on his time. Suppressing the other Houses. Controlling Liera's trade. Attending Empirist meetings."

He didn't want to remember the Empirist meetings. Geoffre's were different than the endless conversations one heard in cafés. The secretive locations and the masks worn by the attendees had always lent the proceedings a vaguely sinister air. Mikelo wished Geoffre had never brought him along.

He picked up a piece of hot bacon and put it in his mouth. It was crispy and fatty, and it tasted so good it blotted out Geoffre entirely. Mikelo sighed in contentment.

Silva chuckled as he peeled the rind from a wheel of cheese. A handful of almonds lay on the board, too. "Well, that's a compliment."

"Silva. This is too much."

"When I worked at the Youth, our meals were always topsy-turvy. Most of us in the house worked the brothels, so we ate our family meal at what should have been breakfast. I don't know if everyone's forgiven me for being such a hotheaded idiot, but I thought I could find little ways to make up for it."

Mikelo paused in the act of stuffing more bacon in his mouth. "So this breakfast is penance?"

Silva gave him a stormy frown. "I am sorry I made you ruin your notes, but if I was giving anyone penance, it wouldn't be *you*, would it? You needed to eat, I like to cook."

"Really," Mikelo said skeptically.

"Mikelo, if you find one more thing to disbelieve, I'm going to shut you up by stuffing this cheese in your mouth. I'm not trained, but if I was lucky, the cooks would let me help in the kitchen instead of serving tables or going upstairs. Made less money in the kitchens, but I was a poor courtesan anyway."

"I'm sure *that's* not true," Mikelo murmured as he reached for more bacon.

Silva's brow quirked. He left the cheese to ladle the polenta out of the kettle into two bowls. Steam painted a flush along his cheekbones and gave his lashes and the curls hanging over his forehead a wet, shiny look. He laced the polenta with sugar, almonds, raisins, and a big pat of butter, then set a bowl in front of Mikelo and sat down across the table with his own. "Doing penance, too, are you?"

"No! I mean—I wasn't. I—" Every word felt like a step that sank him deeper into mud. Mikelo looked into his bowl in helpless, awkward appeal and realized it was millet polenta, the same as he might have eaten back in Baleria.

When he looked up, Silva was watching him with an amused smile that seemed to hide bruised feelings.

Mikelo tapped his spoon definitively on the edge of his bowl. "I don't know how much you'd like to be reminded of working as a courtesan, but I think anybody would have been lucky to have you."

Silva blinked in surprise. His mouth opened like he was going to speak, then closed again, like a fish. He stood abruptly and went to pull a bottle off a shelf. "That's...that's kind of you. I-I think I would like some wine, too, if you don't mind?"

With that flush still on his cheeks, Silva seemed even more beautiful. *Dammit, maybe he's sensitive about his looks. But that wasn't exactly what I meant—*

"To be honest," Silva was saying as he poured himself a glass that looked strong for morning, "all this food worries me. Gavaros are all over the countryside after a battle, just looking for flush farms like this one. Especially now, the lean time of the year. At most they're living on favas and lentils left over from last year..."

His voice trailed away and Mikelo looked up uneasily. Silva was staring through the small window in the back.

"Is that Arsenault? There are two men with him."

Mikelo rose and walked over to stand next to Silva. "I can't tell who's with him—"

His shoulder bumped Silva's and he broke off suddenly.

For the gods' sake.

Mikelo forced himself to remain still, trying not to notice how the heat of Silva's body contrasted to the thick, cold waves of window glass. Their breath fogged it and Mikelo wiped it off with his sleeve in big motions that made their shoulders touch again.

If Kyrra were here, she'd say, *Mikelo, if you were any stiffer, you'd be cast in bronze,* and he'd feel like melting into a scarlet puddle on the floor. Then again, maybe it would be safer to turn the feeling into a joke.

It was just a *feeling* after all. He was accustomed to fighting those back. For five years he'd watched his cousin Cassis give in to every desire he entertained. The havoc those desires had wreaked was obvious in every ragged, burned-out building in Liera, every raft of corpses ferried out to the islands beyond the lagoon to be buried. The Prinze blamed it on Kyrra, but what if Cassis had simply told himself *no?*

Mikelo's own life had happened the way it did because a man couldn't keep his cock in his trousers.

He didn't know if he'd be forced to continue with the betrothal negotiations Geoffre had instigated or not, but he wasn't going to be that kind of man, a householder who thought he had the right to do whatever he wanted with whomever he wanted, breaking vows and promises—*people*—as if they were dishes to be replaced with a trip to the Day Market. Silva had probably had enough of householders who came through Karansis thinking of him as nothing more than a piece of arse to grab on the side before they went back to their wives. The same as the meal they'd eaten downstairs, bought for a handful of coins to restore their "vitality".

"Mikelo," Silva murmured, gaze moving, puzzled, over Mikelo's face. "I think you'd better get the door."

Mikelo flushed and threw open the door to find Arsenault standing on the other side, a new purple bruise marring his cheek. Behind him, a man he'd never expected to see here tipped his head in greeting.

Speak of demons—it was *Cassis*.

Everything rushed back to him—the prison, the mirror, the *things* he had seen, the *things* he had watched himself do, Cassis's guards beating him, and that guard he had turned into a monster... It poured through him like boiling water scalding him from the inside.

"No," he said, trembling. "No, Arsenault, I'm not letting him in."

CHAPTER 14

MIKELO

"Mikelo. Breathe. That's it. In—out—"

"But he can't come in here! What does he want?"

"You're reacting to the magic Kyrra's drawing into the house. Just breathe. Find your feet if you can't start with your breath."

Arsenault's eyes seemed to fill his vision. Those gray eyes, the color of mist or metal. Mikelo couldn't escape the temptation to stare straight through the black pupil into the aqueous lens behind it, the tiny, wriggling blood vessels, the wrinkled brain matter—

"My feet," he grumbled, but he closed his eyes, mostly to make Arsenault happy, and forced himself to think about his godsdamned feet.

He was still in his socks. The cold air swirled around his ankles. He rubbed a foot back and forth, feeling out the bumps in the fired clay tiles of the kitchen floor, rolling around the little pieces of grit and mud someone had tracked in. Maybe him, when he'd gone outside to wash.

"Good," Arsenault murmured. "Now fingers."

"Why fingers?" he asked, bringing his head up again. "Why not ankles, or the big bones of your legs—"

"Fingers, Mikelo." Arsenault's voice was gentle but firm. Like he was talking to a skittish horse. Mikelo had heard that voice before. *Oh, you beautiful boy, quiet, quiet.*

Half of magic seemed to be taking fucking breaths. Another, and he went to the place in his mind Arsenault had told him he should visualize when he was being purposeful with his magic. Arsenault talked about gates and water, but what Mikelo saw was the huge fortress wall in Mdembu with its giant ironwood doors still standing though most of the city had burned to ash.

The tide of magic and fear subsided. He dropped his hands and stepped backward.

"Better?" Arsenault asked. Silva must have run for Jon because Jon hovered over him, too, looking concerned.

"The boy needs rest," he said to Arsenault.

The door snicked softly shut. Cassis stood inside, shedding water onto the floor, and behind him, wearing a black cloak, his black hair gleaming and wet, was Lobardin. The last time Mikelo had seen Lobardin, Kyrra had smashed his nose with her metal fist. The memories lingered physically on Lobardin's face in the last vestiges of a bruise. Silva glared at him while holding a kitchen knife at the cutting board.

Lobardin gestured with his head at Silva. "Is your watchdog making us breakfast, Arsenault?"

Silva tightened his grip on the knife instead of putting it down. "You've no right to this food. You're lucky Arsenault didn't cut you down where you stood!"

"Bark, bark, bark," Lobardin said laconically, but the room felt charged with tension.

"Kyrra can sleep for the moment," Cassis said, clipping his words short. "I have some questions to ask you all first." He pulled off his gloves and laid them on the table. Water immediately pooled on the wood.

Arsenault dragged in his own deep breath. "Cassis. Get your gloves off the table before they ruin it."

Jon shot him a glance, grabbed a towel, and wiped up the water himself, then moved a chair out from the table with a clatter and draped his long frame into it. "Well? We're waiting. It must be important, to brave Arsenault's wrath."

Cassis looked shaken, but he took off his cloak and hung it carefully over the back of a chair, like he was prepared to stay a while. "I have several topics I'd like to discuss with the three of you. One— where is the Prinze sword? Two—did you try to poison my food stores? And three..."

He reached into an inside pocket in the cloak and pulled out a wrinkled broadsheet. He slowly unfolded it and threw it on the table.

Mikelo leaned forward to read the headline spread across it in big bold print:

RUMOURS ABOUND ON THE MERA! RENZO DI PRINZE RETURNS FROM THE DEAD TO BATTLE FOR THE CHAIR OF HOUSE DI PRINZE!

⚜

IS RENZO DI PRINZE ALIVE?

With the recent Death of Geoffre di Prinze, the Houses once again battle each other in the Circle for Supremacy. As Geoffre's Sons face off for Possession of the Prinze Chair, an intriguing and alarming piece of News has surfaced. Renzo di Prinze, Brother to Geoffre and long assumed to have been lost in Dakkaran Waters, is rumoured to have survived Shipwreck and Fever to return to Liera.

New Information has come to light regarding Arms, which Officials assert have been moved legally using an unknown Prinze Seal associated with the long-missing Renzo. Caprine Dock Channels regard this Information as reliable, though the Prinze deny all Knowledge. In addition, there have been unconfirmed Sightings of a Ghost Ship drifting toward Liera, rumored to be the Hind, *a Ship commissioned by Cassis di Prinze for the Trade Run to Dakkar. A sailor who reported these Sightings says the Ship was plundered by Dakkaran Pirates and implicates the Weapons diverted by Renzo di Prinze, although he refused to give any further Information for Fear of stirring up the Vengeance of her Dead Crew.*

Could Renzo di Prinze be building a Pirate Fleet to take the Prinze Chair? Will a third hat be tossed into the Fray? Tensions in Liera mount as neither Devid di Prinze nor Cassis di Prinze have appeared before the Circle with the Sword Kinstealer, leaving the Chair of their House officially unoccupied. Dissatisfaction within the other Houses is growing amid Empirist Rumours that Geoffre di Prinze was killed by a Silver Warrior fighting for the Aliente and the Legacy of Attrasca...

Mikelo read the story over again for what felt like the tenth time, but none of it changed. He slammed the paper back on the table. "What in all the hells is this? It's just a bunch of rumormongering—"

He stopped suddenly, caught by Jon and Arsenault's expressions. Cassis's visit must have taken them both by surprise. For a moment, Jon didn't look like a man who thought the press was rumormongering to sell more papers. He looked like a man who knew something and hadn't expected that knowledge to become public. And knowledge dawned on Arsenault's face like the morning had earlier seeped into the dark house.

Maybe Arsenault had forgotten Renzo. Maybe the recognition in Arsenault's eyes was from a memory returning, and not because Arsenault had purposely withheld the information from him that his father was alive. Arsenault as Andris had been just another gavaro, and yet, who else had noticed he'd existed as a person and not merely Geoffre di Prinze's nephew? Who else had stepped in to tell him to breathe and to focus on his feet when his Sight overwhelmed him? It had always felt like Arsenault was on his side.

"It's not true," Mikelo said suddenly. "The broadsheets need another scandal to fuel their sales. Or maybe the Caprine House-holder is trying to fuel unrest, or-or the Amorans! They'd love to see us at each other's throats."

"You'll pardon me, mestere, if I take offense that my beautiful city should ever want to visit such pain upon yours," Lobardin said mildly, in the process of making himself a cup of coffee. "These aren't the sort of rumors a Cozin would start without at least *something* behind them."

"I thought the same at first, Mikelo," Cassis added. "I almost discarded the rumors outright. Then I did some digging." He turned to Jon. "How much do you know about this, Jon? Do you think there's a chance Renzo wants the Chair and that's why he's coming back? Nobody seems to know if he faked his death, or if everyone in Liera only assumed he had died. I always thought Geoffre had him killed. But if that's not true..."

The way they were calmly talking as if it was just another thing, like saying *tomorrow is Third Day and we can have lentils for dinner...*

"He's been gone for over twenty years!" Mikelo burst out. "People don't just return from the dead!"

Lobardin coughed and looked pointedly at Arsenault. "Well. *Most* people."

Cassis also looked to Arsenault, and Mikelo felt as if he would explode out of his skin like a pottery grenade. "Ordinarily I would scoff at such a thing, but he *is* Geoffre's brother."

Arsenault's wary expression gave way to a touch of astonishment. "You think *Renzo* pledged himself to the god and now he's coming back to finish what Geoffre started? That's really what you think?"

"You *did* know my father?"

Mikelo didn't want to be this bare and raw before Cassis, but he felt as if he'd been stripped down to the bones and was too damn tired to care. Silva edged closer and Mikelo felt an irrational rush of gratitude for his presence—for *someone* who wasn't involved in all these tangled conspiracies.

Arsenault fiddled with his coffee cup. It looked ridiculously small and fragile in his hand, winking in the dim light as he rotated it with his thumb.

"Yes," he said finally. "Yes, I knew Renzo."

The whole table seemed to rearrange itself. Mikelo thought he heard Jon groan, but maybe that was just the chairs scraping against the floor.

"You knew my father and *you didn't tell me,*" Mikelo whispered.

"All I knew when I worked for Geoffre was that you were Renzo's bastard. I had forgotten about Renzo himself."

"But you must have spoken to Jon, and Jon knew where he was all this time?"

"I never said that," Jon said. "I did know him, long ago, but I don't know where he is at this moment."

"So, he abandoned his family? Abandoned—"

Me, Mikelo wanted to say, but his throat clenched shut on the word and he couldn't utter another sound.

"Mikelo, I feel sure he didn't abandon you," Arsenault said.

"You *feel* sure?" Mikelo seethed. *He* felt like a rumbling volcano. Any moment he would erupt, scattering ash and fire over everyone. "You feel—"

"Yes, I *feel,*" Arsenault snapped. "I haven't run all my memories down yet and I'm unlikely to dig them all up anytime soon. I remember Renzo now, but it's been a while since I saw him last. Twenty years at least. I don't know what he's been doing in the meantime. I'm sorry I didn't tell you, but dammit, sometimes it's best to let sleeping lions lie."

"Arsenault. My *father.*"

"I didn't say it was easy, Mikelo... Hell. I didn't say it was right either." Arsenault ran a hand through his hair helplessly.

"Couldn't you have at least told me you knew him?"

"He had no magic," Arsenault said firmly. "The god wouldn't want him."

"How am I supposed to know that?" Cassis interjected angrily. "I was only a child when Renzo left for Dakkar. I barely remember him at all. There must be some connection with these Empirists, and the last survivor of the main branch of the Aliente is living in your back room!"

"You think Kyrra is going to cooperate with a Prinze who has the same agenda as Geoffre?" Arsenault said. "Cassis, that doesn't make sense."

"Gods. I don't know what I think. The point is not that there's a conspiracy here—though I think there is, and I think you know all about it, Jon. I know you're a member of the old Ibuu's family. Geoffre helped put your enemies on the throne of Dakkar, stole your guns, and—"

"Killed my wife? My children? My family?" Jon barely moved, but his voice was as forbidding as those ironwood doors. "Geoffre di Prinze was a demon. I think we all agree on that. I don't care if he gets a proper burial and I hope the fila torment him in the next world if your gods won't. But I haven't done any scheming with Kyrra to bring back the Eterean Empire. That's ridiculous. I knew Renzo twenty years ago at my father's court. What he's been doing since..." Jon shrugged. "That's on his shoulders. Were you just coming here for confirmation?"

Cassis slammed a hand down on the table. The silverware rattled. "Dammit, Jon! You haven't confirmed anything!"

Jon crossed his arms over his chest and leaned back in his chair. "Why do you want Renzo?"

Cassis pushed himself up from the table and started pacing.

"Now that Renzo has entered the equation, we're splitting our power three ways. Devid wants to maintain his power with the same iron fist Geoffre used, except Devid's is made of lead. It's heavy, it will crush everyone, but in the end, it will be too soft to withstand much. He knows that, though, so he's shoring himself up with outside support wherever he can find it. The other Houses sense weakness and they will exploit it. *Then* there are the Empirists, whom I always assumed were crackpots, but apparently, they have more sway with the general population than I knew. And maybe the Legacy of Attrasca is a real fucking thing, and it's buried *somewhere* under my base of operations."

Mikelo tried to digest what Cassis had just said. "You *don't* know Renzo is alive, though. You're just afraid he is. Everything you said is based on fear and suspicion."

Cassis gave him a contemptuous glance. "Stop being such a gods-damned idealist. What else do you think politics is based on?"

For a moment, rage blotted out Mikelo's vision. *One day I'll know where my hands are because they'll be punching Cassis in the face.* "I'm asking if you have any evidence," he said in a voice as tight as his clenched fists.

Cassis threw him another glance, then sighed.

"My father placed spies in the trading and customs networks of Dakkar. They watch to make sure the Arak-Prinze monopoly on guns is upheld. A shipload of guns was diverted from Mdembu by someone using an authentic Prinze seal. Renzo's seal, which was assumed lost. Then there's the issue of *my* ship. What do you know about Dakkaran pirates, Jon?"

"I navigate pirates for my shipments the same as you, Cassis. And who's to say the thief didn't use a stolen or counterfeited seal? Why assume it's Renzo himself? Why are you afraid he's going to move against you?"

"What else would he be acquiring guns for? I hope I can negotiate with him, but I'd be an idiot to assume he's going to *give* me the Chair."

My father's just another fucking Prinze.

The sword—the symbol of Prinze power with its winking sapphire serpent hilt eyes—was hidden in *Mikelo's* room, in *his* possession. If he brought that sword into the Circle, it would make him the de facto Householder of House di Prinze. But he hadn't taken the sword. Jon had found it on the battlefield and given it to him days later when Kyrra seemed to be healing.

Had he always just been a bargaining chip to Jon and Arsenault? A placeholder until his father returned?

The thought hurt more than he wanted to admit. Maybe he *was* an idealist. A godsdamned *naive* idealist.

"You said you needed to talk to Kyrra, too," Arsenault said. "What does she have to do with any of this? It sounds like a Prinze matter to me."

"If Aliente sentiment rises again, it will rip the city apart with vengeance and blood feuds. We'll be so busy fighting each other, the Qalfans could take all our trade routes and we'd never notice. You know they moved in on them during the last war."

"That doesn't answer the question of what you want with Kyrra," Arsenault pointed out.

Cassis took a deep, ragged breath. "Kyrra...is slightly more complicated."

He took the rucksack he'd set on the floor and opened it onto the table. Pulled out a chunk of tarnished metal that gleamed dully in the dim light. They all stood staring at it for a moment, trying to sort out what they were looking at. The magic in the room hummed around it, as if the metal were alive.

A shadow moved behind Mikelo and something thumped. He turned around in surprise.

Kyrra staggered into view, a blanket wrapped around her shoulders, the hem of Arsenault's shirt fluttering around her calves and wool socks on her feet like boots. She stumbled into the wall with her right arm. Her metal elbow thudded hard against the stucco. Then she caught sight of the metal on the table.

"It's a dragon's arm," she said. "Just like mine."

CHAPTER 15

ARSENAULT

IT FELT EXACTLY LIKE CASSIS HAD THROWN DOWN A GAUNTLET AND
challenged them all to a duel. Suddenly, Kyrra's visions took on a
whole new dimension of urgency.

The Old World. Here. In this house.

The thing on the table was, as Kyrra had said, an *arm*, though
clearly not human, covered with exquisitely rendered silver feather-
scales, its three-fingered "hand" tipped with slim stiletto claws.

The metal sang to him mournfully. Of the fathomless black of a
long northern winter, metal corpses lying on the ground. A time
before time, when gods and people mixed. The longer Arsenault
stared into it, the more the firelight flickering in the old, tarnished
surface twisted, forming blurry images that could have been pulled
from his own mind: the hearthlight in the old house in Tule, his children's faces, Tavi...

Sella.

The memory of her hit him like a punch, realer than any other
memory he'd kept. Had the rock-solid history on which he based his
whole identity *also* been subject to Erelf's twisting and corruption?
Was that why she felt so much closer now, why he kept seeing her in
reflections, in ghosts—in this leftover piece of ancient history?

The thought made him feel as if the earth had suddenly moved
beneath him.

Then Kyrra stumbled forward and the room snapped into motion.
Chairs screaked as Jon and Lobardin leapt to their feet. Mikelo caught

her as she fell. Silva kicked an empty chair out from the table with his foot and she collapsed into it.

Arsenault shoved his way in front of her and fell to his knees, scabbard clattering against the floor. The thin shirt bunched beneath his heavy gloves as he put his hands on her legs, smearing the linen with dirt and hopefully nothing worse. "You're supposed to be sleeping," he said.

A high-pitched wheeze edged every breath she took. "Am I"—*breath*—"supposed to"—*breath*—"just lie there like some useless—"

"Like some useless woman who just fought a god?"

It was supposed to be a joke. Instead, the helplessness and anger in his own voice stopped him. Kyrra stared at him as if it startled her, too. He tilted his head against hers. "You don't have to fight every battle," he murmured in apology. Or explanation—hell if he knew.

"But this battle is mine. I need to know what I set in motion by killing Geoffre." She squeezed his shoulder and pulled away from him. "Lobardin? I thought I was dreaming, but it is you."

Lobardin moved warily closer. "Dream about me often, do you?" He put on a smile, but it was easy to tell how shocked he was. It made him seem too human.

"You wish I dreamed about you," Kyrra shot back with some semblance of herself. But then she peered at Lobardin intensely and reached out to touch the bridge of his nose. Lobardin startled backward. Her slow, fuzzy movements were strange, as if she had shifted in her mind from reality to dream again. Everyone in the room seemed to be holding their breath. The aura of the god-touched made everyone uncomfortable, but the fact that it was *Kyrra* felt like a fist squeezing his heart. He wanted so badly to find a solution to this problem, but there didn't seem to be anything he could do besides raging at the gods for leaving her like this.

She pressed her thumb to the knot. "I put a crook in it, didn't I?"

Lobardin winced and pushed her hand away. "You could have pulled up somewhat on the force."

"Ergus used to tell me to never hit a man unless you mean it and always mean it when you do."

"Wish you'd paid a little less attention," Lobardin grumbled, rubbing the bridge of his nose as if it still pained him.

"He would have handed me my arse. He wasn't much for letting me slide out of things."

"You fought with him in Rojornick," Arsenault said. If he could keep her talking, maybe he could get her back to her room without anyone getting hurt.

She nodded. "He was our Dagmari armsmaster. Nibas bunked on the other side. I don't—" She stopped and rubbed her forehead again. "Lobardin. When you're in Liera, you'll find out about Razi for me? I need to know if his arm healed."

Gods. That was a stab in the heart. She had to know there was a high likelihood her Nezari friend had died of fever. A gunshot wound was far dirtier than the clean axe blow that had taken off her arm. There would have been powder burns and little bits of cloth driven into the flesh. What if he had really killed the man? Would she be able to forgive him then?

"*When* I'm in Liera?" Lobardin asked, confused. "Kyrra, I don't know if I'll ever go back to Liera. We're entrenched, under siege by Devid's forces. We snuck out in a tunnel." He shot a glance sideways at Cassis. "That's one of the things we came here to talk to you about. The passageways."

Passageways? Beneath the lodge?

Kyrra continued to mull over the Nezari gavaro like she hadn't heard Lobardin at all. "Nibas was talking about going north again, so maybe he'll take Razi to Rojornick with him. Or maybe the Nezari took Razi back into the temple. Maybe he's making a quick recovery. Hasn't been that long. Has it?"

She shivered, pulling the blanket tighter with her left hand, and looked up at all of them with a confused expression that made Arsenault feel even more like he'd been knifed. Wild magic flared around her suddenly in a nimbus of white light. "You're all hiding something. Not just that godsdamned chunk of metal on the table. Did you dig it up from one of those pits by the wall?"

Lobardin blanched. "We were shoring up earthworks."

"Bullshit. What is Cassis looking for? Arsenault says the metal comes from the old gods and that thing has claws, so what did it come from and why are you bringing it to me? I saw a dragon—"

"A what?" Lobardin said shakily, his brows pulling down together. "You mean a statue of a dragon? Do you know where the limb came from?"

"No, that's what I was asking you, dammit." She leaned forward to look at it over Arsenault's shoulder. "You know the Etereans had dragons. What does Cassis want with this metal, Lobardin?"

She looked up and Arsenault knew immediately where her gaze landed.

Godsdamn Cassis di Prinze.

Cassis's face was an open book of disbelief. Maybe he hadn't believed the stories about Kyrra killing Geoffre, even though he knew they were true. Maybe...

The magic raged into an out-of-control inferno in an instant. Kyrra elbowed Arsenault in the face, knocking him backward before he could scramble out of the way. "Kyrra!" he gasped, grabbing for her, but she dodged him—tripped over his leg, fell into the table with a crash, and lurched across it to snatch the cheese knife.

Jon jerked Cassis out of the way of her clumsy strike. Arsenault struggled to his feet and pinned her arm against him. The knife fell to the table with a clatter.

She struggled, her eyes blank of sight but full of fury. Not *her* fury but the wrath of Ires.

Leave this alone, Ari! You'll regret walking this path!

Like hell he would. He lifted Kyrra off her feet, ignoring the burning pain in his shoulder and back, and hefted her into his arms before the battle magic could launch another assault.

The sudden movement must have jarred her. The magic gave way and she started shouting. "Arsenault! Dammit, put me down! Let me walk! What did I do?"

He carried her out of the kitchen, through the common room, and down the hall into the bedroom. He kicked the door shut behind him and laid her down on the bed. She was shivering so hard she curled up as soon as he put her down. He piled all the blankets on top of her until only the top of her head and a few strands of blond corkscrew curls indicated she was there at all. Then he collapsed heavily beside her.

The door flung open. Lobardin hurled himself into the room, slammed the door shut, and threw the bar.

"Lobardin!" Silva bellowed from the other side. His fist shook the door. "Leave her alone!"

"I don't want anything out of her!" Lobardin yelled back through the wood, then turned to Arsenault with a deep breath. "But you really need to talk to Cassis."

"You Etereans can stuff all your scheming plans up your arse. She's in no shape to deal with your fucking plots."

"Cassis needs information. Or Devid will grind us all into meat between his need to prove himself against the memory of his father and those lunatic Empirists. You might think Cassis has his head up his arse, but he cares about his city. He's against your—your god, in any case. And you, you're free—"

"To tell you to fuck yourselves."

"Have you ever not been free to do that?"

What was the answer to that question? He'd always been free and not free at the same time. "It's not about *me*. I'll be damned if I'll let the petty politics of your godsdamned Houses suck Kyrra in again. She lost an arm and almost died *twice* because of the bloody Prinze."

Lobardin's black eyes flared, then his lids lowered with a deceptively lazy look. "I thought this time she almost died because of you, Arsenault."

Arsenault's control snapped. He grabbed Lobardin by the collar and slammed him against the wall. The sound of a blanket being thrown back stopped him before he hit the other man.

Kyrra struggled to sit up. "Don't talk like I can't hear you," she said bitterly.

Shame flooded him. He cursed and let go of Lobardin, who looked dazed. "Pardon, Kyrra. It's been a difficult day."

She looked at him with some of her old heat, then turned it on Lobardin.

"It wasn't Arsenault's *fault* I fought for him. I fought for us all, so we'd be free of Geoffre and free of Erelf's meddling. Why does he want Liera..."

Her brows pinched over the bridge of her nose and the runes on her arm suddenly glowed blue through the fabric of the sling.

Dammit, not again.

"*Kyrra*. Stop. I don't care what Erelf and Devid are doing. I can't lose you!"

"Do you think I want to lose *you* again?"

"If you'd killed Cassis with a cheese knife, it would have caused you more problems than he's worth. Kyrra, *breathe*."

She took a big breath. It rattled in her chest, but not as badly as before. Lobardin saw his opportunity and took it, moving past him quickly to drag the rocking chair close to the bed.

"I'm sorry." He took her hand as if Arsenault wasn't standing right beside him. "I don't know if that head wound had anything to do with what's happening to you, and I don't honestly know what happened to me before...before you hit me. But I just—I feel like I need to apologize." He glanced nervously at Arsenault before looking back at Kyrra. "Even with Arsenault scowling over me like a northern bear. I've been off kacin since the battle. I know it doesn't sound like much—it's not, I guess—but I just... I felt like I should apologize. For, well, for a lot."

Kyrra turned all her attention to Lobardin.

"I hate being stuck in this fucking bed. And now Cassis and that limb... All these damn gods. I feel like I'm going mad."

Lobardin put a hand awkwardly on her good arm even though Arsenault *was* scowling down at him like a bear. "It's not worth it, being Ires's tool. Ires is the mad one. He makes revenge and hatred sound like something you need more than anything—more than love. How many years did I throw away to anger and kacin? I could have been living, but the god's voice was always in my ear."

Suddenly, Arsenault realized what Lobardin was saying. Ires was never going to let her go. The magic was just going to keep eating at her. It was in the metal of the old gods. The metal he had fused into her body. She kept telling him it had saved her, but...had it only put her at the mercy of another god now that it was twisted and torn?

"I don't know if that's the way of it," Kyrra murmured. "The new gods wrote all the history. Maybe if we had Ires's side of it..."

An enormous shiver wracked her and she started to cough again.

Arsenault hauled Lobardin out of the rocking chair. "Out. Now. We're done talking."

Lobardin jerked out of his grip. "You're making a mistake."

"You don't even know what I'm doing yet." He shoved Lobardin into the hallway and, with a guilty twinge, shut the door and barred it to make sure Kyrra stayed in until he got Cassis out. He didn't know why he was offering Cassis his protection, except that Kyrra would hurt herself if she attacked Cassis again and Cassis wasn't worth that.

Ires wasn't worth it either.

He pulled his sword as he walked Lobardin down the hall.

"See? It *is* a mistake. Arsenault!"

It was true. What was he was about to do might be a mistake. But how else would he be able to Fix Kyrra's arm? He'd make sure the limb was safe first. Run down all the strange memories he'd seen reflected in the metal. He'd *remember*.

Cassis backpedaled, startled, when Arsenault strode into the kitchen with the sword. The runes on it flared bright white as he stretched it toward Cassis.

"Tell me everything you know about that godsdamned piece of dragon. Then leave it on the table and get out."

CHAPTER 16

KYRRA

THE WALLS SEEMED TO CLOSE IN ON ME AFTER ARSENAULT AND Lobardin left. I wanted to follow them, but my body was taking its time catching up to my intentions.

If Aliente sentiment rises again, it will rip the city apart with vengeance and blood feuds.

Cassis had been talking about Aliente sympathizers before he'd dumped that dragon limb on the table, linking my House *again* to the kind of destruction I'd seen reflected in *his* family's sword. What did Ires think I should deduce from this mess of disparate clues? I was too bloody exhausted to even start drawing the lines.

There were no "Aliente sympathizers". People who sympathized with the Aliente cause perhaps, Lieran citizens who chafed under the yoke of the Prinze and felt cheated by the taxes they paid in tribute to Geoffre and his House. But an organized group with the power to challenge the Prinze and restore my House? There was nobody to restore *to* it.

Only once had I discovered anything resembling an organization of Aliente. But it turned out they were more interested in smuggling banned Aliente silk. Otherwise, Aliente sympathy was limited to endless conversations in cafes and useless flyers Prinze night watchmen burned to warm their hands.

If Cassis thought I knew where Attrasca had hidden his magical machines, he would also be sadly disappointed. But I needed to know how he thought the dragon limb and Aliente sympathizers were linked, and what he wanted out of me.

I needed to talk to him.

I clumsily swung my feet onto the cold floor and stood unsteadily. Dizziness washed over me, but I waited it out. Surely there had to be clothes in this room? I didn't want to talk to Cassis in my nightshirt.

My gaze fell on a chest snugged against the wall. Maybe there.

My struggle to lift the heavy lid one-handed ended in defeat. The carvings on it looked like runes but they didn't light; if there was magic on this godsdamned thing, it could at least help me get into it if it didn't want to keep me out.

The lid suddenly wrenched upward as if it had responded to my thoughts. I stood dumbfounded for a moment and then realized I was staring into a gavaro's war chest. The dim light sliding through the shutters glistened on a burgundy silk armband.

Shit. Was this Arsenault's chest? What kind of *farmhouse* was this?

More than one armband lay inside the chest, though, along with a tattered standard. Leather jerkins, greaves, a cuirass. I searched for the golden daisies Arsenault had Fixed from his daughter's flower crown and the carving of his wife I remembered from the villa but didn't find them. The cuirass was dented in the shape of a ball that had surely left a body bruise if it hadn't broken bones. Beneath the armor lay a light saddle of well-worn leather, the kind messengers used to minimize the weight the horse would have to carry. That surely couldn't be Arsenault's.

Wedged in along the side, though, was a weapon I did recognize.

Arsenault's Dagmari battle axe.

I suddenly felt dizzy again, like I had stepped off a cliff. I picked up the armband and rubbed the silk between my fingers until the light played off it in the way only silk had. Dark splotches marred its edge —blood, from the look of it. I crunched it in my fist.

"All right," I whispered to the magic or who in all the hells knew. "Perhaps you could help me find some trousers?"

I dug through the pile of folded clothing. There were tunics— Aliente, too—and in the bottom, thank the gods, a pair of dress trousers, as if my father had given his gavaros actual dress uniforms.

I wasn't about to wear an Aliente tunic to meet Cassis, and these trousers would be hell to pull on with my arm in a sling, especially since they were made for a man taller and bigger than me. Maybe they *were* Arsenault's. There was a cloak, too, a nondescript brown one. I wished for boots, but at least I was still wearing the socks Arsenault had put on my feet earlier this morning. A pair of slippers sat neatly beside the bed, which had to be Arsenault's doing as well; he must have retained a vain hope that I would be civilized enough to wear them. Practical as ever, he had ensured they were leather, not silk, and lined with warm wool.

Getting the clothes on was a battle. The magic couldn't help me or didn't want to. I supposed I'd always known magic had a mind of its own, but it was strange thinking of it as a partner in crime. I found a belt without enough holes to hold my trousers up. I couldn't tie the leather in a knot with only one hand, so I did my best to pull it tight and twisted it around my hips. I sat on the bed to roll up the cuffs, shoved my feet into the slippers, then stood and fought myself into the cloak.

By the time I finished, I was out of breath. I needed a weapon, but Arsenault was wearing his sword. Though I eyed it enviously, I didn't think I could carry his axe. It would be too much temptation for the battle magic anyway. Any weapon would, but I didn't trust Cassis and Lobardin enough to go without one.

It was strange seeing Lobardin after what had happened at the lodge. Meeting him in the kitchen seemed like it had happened at least as long ago, like I'd been moving underwater. A small voice in my head raised concern about why things should change so violently from one moment to the next, and I wondered if maybe I still wasn't thinking *so* clearly...but it didn't matter. All that mattered was that I caught Cassis before he left.

I gave up trying to find a weapon—Arsenault had been thorough in making the room safe, except for his axe—hitched my too-big trousers up over my hips, and walked to the door. Grudgingly I admitted that the slippers did make it easier. The cuts on my feet only twinged, cushioned by the soft wool. The world still felt precarious, but I was walking better. I could do this.

The fucking door was locked.

"Dammit," I growled. I should have known, though. It was just like Arsenault. Locks on the inside *and* locks on the outside.

I turned to the window.

In some ways, I had changed very little from the girl who used to drive my nurses mad. In others, I had changed so completely I was no longer the same person. But my relationship with windows remained as friendly as ever.

The shutters were closed of course, but shutters never latched from the outside. These had heavy iron bolts at the top. I had to stretch to reach them, which caused me a great deal of pain, and then, I couldn't wrestle the godsdamned bolt back through the cylinder. My vision swirled with blackness and light as I collapsed onto the sill, huffing. Maybe I wasn't thinking clearly after all. Maybe I should stay in bed, as much as I hated it—

The bolt suddenly rattled above me. I looked up at it in surprise, and then it slammed free on its own.

"You know," I muttered breathlessly to the magic, whatever it was, "I could have used your help a few times before now if I'd known you were good at locks."

Nothing answered and I felt immediately ridiculous, like I'd been talking to myself. It didn't stop me from throwing open the now-unlocked shutters. I clambered painfully and ungracefully on top of the nightstand and fell more than climbed through the window onto the half-frozen, muddy ground. The cold air cut into my exposed skin and sliced its way into my cloak too easily. I should have worn one of the tunics; it wasn't as if Cassis didn't know who I was. But it was too late now. I needed to find some cover where I could wait on him.

The farmhouse stood at the top of a hill. On a clear day, you'd probably be able to see several leagues, but in this weather, I could barely see to the edge of the farmstead. The meadow grass surrounding it had frozen into yellow tufts, spangled with ice and bowed down nearly flat. I disliked the idea of having to walk all the way down the lane to hide in the trees at the bottom. Cassis had undoubtedly hidden his men there. Instead, I made my way around to the corner of the house where a few espaliered apple trees clung to the relative warmth of the wall.

I crouched to hide among their branches and ended up sitting on my bum in the cold mud. Waiting for Cassis and thinking about the chest with all the Aliente artifacts, and Ires wanting the Prinze sword but wanting to get rid of the Prinze, too. If Ires had even been the one who'd driven me to attack Cassis.

That was a strange thought. Was the magic out of Ires's control, too? Frantic, vengeful, impulsive, and panicked in the kitchen with the remains of a dead god on the table, at least according to Arsenault, but eager and helpful in the bedchamber when I had wanted to escape?

It was strange thinking about anything being out of the control of a god, even an imprisoned one. We Lierans weren't pious by any means, but I had still been taught all our standard religious teachings —first in the form of little stories parents tell children and later, in the form of boring theological treatises my tutor made me argue as formal proofs. Whatever else my father might have done, at least he had provided me with an excellent education, more than the equivalent of many of my male peers.

All the theology I had been taught agreed: There was no power outside the gods' effect. They had conquered both time and death. Magic was their servant and they had guarded it jealously until Tekus presented it to Attrasca as a gift. Instead of hoarding it as the gods expected, Attrasca had let it loose on an unsuspecting world. Only then, my tutors explained, had magic begun to degrade. We were being punished for Attrasca's betrayal, for the way he had dared reach beyond his station, his assumption that human beings deserved a life on par with the divine. Attrasca's presumption was the reason for the constantly declining births among Attrasca's Eterean descendants.

Ires hadn't talked about magic that way, though. Was that what made him mad?

I wished I had something to eat while I waited. I was hungry, for the first time in a long while. I looked up into the branches of the winter-dead apple tree, hoping to find an old frozen apple. Leftover fruit and root vegetables had saved me on my journey from the lodge to Rojornick after Arsenault had given me my arm. A glimpse of red caught my eye on one of the lower branches. I snaked my arm in between the slick, spiky twigs to twist it off just as the door creaked open and boots clattered on the step.

"We came here in good faith," I heard Cassis say.

"You came here because you wanted to believe we were behind the attack on your garrison, which would have been an easy solution," Jon replied. "I don't know what you thought you were going to do, threaten Kyrra or twist Arsenault or somehow convince us we should all be on your side, but you got yourself into this, Cassis. Now it's up to you to sort the hard parts."

"Renzo, Jon! And the Empirists! You can't tell me you don't have your fingers in all those pies. Your people are threaded all through my camp. The games you're playing will destroy Liera. Your petty paranoia and need for power—"

There was a scuff, like bootheels dragging over stone. Cassis's voice choked off. Jon must have grabbed him. I couldn't blame Jon, but I was surprised Cassis had cracked his temper.

"When your father was alive, it served my purposes to treat you with civility," Jon said in a tight, false-calm voice. "Now that Geoffre is dead, I will make one thing clear: It no longer serves my purposes to allow you to believe you are in control of anything. We can work together, in cooperation, toward a mutually agreeable end, or I can discard you. You're only alive today because Arsenault and Kyrra considered you irrelevant. You should thank your gods you weren't important enough to care about after all. Tonia di Sere didn't pull Kyrra's name out of the air for that job; Kyrra has a whole list of men who've lost their lives to her revenge. You wouldn't even be the first."

Jon never did or said anything carelessly, so he must want Cassis to know about the men I had killed to avenge Markus for a reason. That bothered me. Cassis had no idea how complicated Jon's networks were.

"And I'm trying to tell you, Jon, for our *mutually agreeable ends* that the Chair is more important to Devid than Liera or Eterea or his House. If you think he'll let it slip through his fingers without a fight now that he's so close to having it, you're telling yourself stories. He'll invite in Qalfa, let Alozh Vokavik butcher all of us, sign up with the Empirists—*anything*."

I stiffened. *Alozh Vokavik*. What did he have to do with Devid di Prinze?

"Why not give him the Chair then?" Jon said. "Make him leave you alone and assassinate him quietly?"

"Do you really believe Devid would let me or my men live after I rebelled against Geoffre?"

Jon grunted.

"I know you have something to do with Renzo, Jon, and I will find out about it. Make sure you keep Kyrra under wraps until she's well enough to talk to me, because I-I have a proposition for her, for the good of Liera, and until I can make it, she just needs to stay out of the way."

Stay out of the way, was it? At least I knew he hadn't changed.

"You better be sure to stay out of her way, too," Jon said. "Or I don't know what Arsenault will do to you. I can't promise you anything, Cassis. Just that I haven't tried to poison you and Arsenault hasn't been working magic against you. Go away and let them be."

"Arsenault can stick his head in the sand for as long as he wants, but I don't think his god is going away."

I didn't either, as it happened, but I also couldn't say that Arsenault's desire to tell Cassis and everyone else to fuck themselves was misguided. I wanted to tell them all to fuck themselves, too. But I could see now that no one was going to leave us alone.

The door closed. Cassis swore. "We better be heading back soon, mestere," Lobardin said. "There will be more gavaros. All we need is for you to be murdered by accident in the dark."

Cassis sighed. "Of course, how ridiculous. I just hope we're not haunted by those men Arsenault threw in the ravine this morning."

Those men Arsenault threw in the ravine? Arsenault was going to have a lot to answer for when I finally got to talk to him. He must have thought I was safely locked in because he wasn't out here now, looking for me. I probably didn't have much time, though.

I took a big bite of my frozen, dried apple. It didn't exactly crunch, but it made some noise as the cold sweetness rushed painfully into my mouth. I couldn't help myself up by grabbing a branch, so I had to thrash out of the winter-dead tree by putting my knee in the mud and lurching upright. My midsection protested, but I made it to my feet.

I expected Cassis and Lobardin to draw their weapons, but they stood frozen, with empty hands.

"Kyrra!" Cassis exclaimed.

Lobardin edged warily in front of him. "Is that you, or will we be talking to Ires again?"

I took another bite of apple. "Depends on how reasonable our discussion is."

"I don't..." Lobardin's voice trailed away as he looked at my feet. "Kyrra, are you wearing slippers?"

Cassis edged nervously out from around Lobardin. It would have been comical if it wasn't so pathetic. I finished the apple and tossed the core into the mud. "I'm still recovering. Doesn't mean I'm help-less. The magic comes and goes, so it's in your best interest to talk quickly."

"About what?" Cassis asked warily.

I rolled my eyes. "You came here to talk to me, didn't you? You threw a piece of Eterean junk onto the table like it meant something. If you've got a proposition, let's hear it now. I want to know what you thought I was doing over the last few weeks. Aside from getting rid of your father for you."

He tugged his tunic down and I suffered a... If I called it a pang of memory, it would summon too much sympathy. But the gesture reminded me so much of how young we had both been. I'd seen him make the same motion while talking to my father, when he thought no one was watching. I'd found it endearing before I realized it meant he was hiding something.

I pushed my memories away. We were living in a new world now. One *I'd* created. Not him.

"A scholar—an Empirist, by all accounts—and his gavaro helped foil an attempt to poison my garrison by following men from Devid's camp through a tunnel that led under the lodge. The men my brother sent to poison me found the metal limb in the tunnel. Lupa, the scholar, thought the Legacy of Attrasca might be down there and that you'd know more about it. *I* thought Arsenault must be involved, but Arsenault denies it, and well...Lupa had a plan."

"A plan to...what? The metal can't do anything on its own, no matter what it came from. And the lodge is riddled with passageways; I used one to escape. But I've never found one that led into the mountain and came out in the valley."

"I told him I didn't think you knew about it, but Lupa refused to listen. He still claimed the information had been passed down through the Aliente line."

"Lupa..." I repeated thoughtfully. The name drew no associations for me. Had I missed something, if this Lupa knew so much more than I did about the lodge where I had spent all my summers as a child?

"He has a gavaro named Tomas. Dresses like a Tiresian but wears Dakkaran gold."

"I don't recognize anyone by that description either. And you know how my father felt about magic. He admired Attrasca's politics and character, but he felt that magic had its place in legends, not in the modern world."

Cassis shifted uncomfortably. "Perhaps that changed for him. After—"

"I said he felt it had no place in the modern world," I snapped, not wanting to think about what Cassis meant by *after*. "Not that he didn't believe in it. Why didn't you just give the scholar and his gavaro a reward and send them on their way?"

"They have some bizarre notion that the Aliente are the key to a new empire, and that as the last one, you could be a potent symbol."

I laughed. "I'm a symbol, all right, but not the kind that's a key to an empire. Cassis. Do you really think they'd want *me*? I don't have to remind you that I'm not even Aliente anymore, do I?"

"We might have taken away your titles, Kyrra, and your arm, but no one could take away your House. That was clear when I watched your father hang you. It's even clearer to me now."

So, he wasn't going to let me out of remembering my hanging. I found myself rubbing my neck where Arsenault had made me a new vertebra. "You think I killed Geoffre for my House?"

"Didn't you?"

"Are the Empirists making me out to be a hero? Is that it?"

"They don't know who killed Geoffre. As far as I know, no one does."

"I think it's best we leave it like that. Tell everyone you killed him, for all I care."

"I'm afraid it's too late to stop the stories, Kyrra," Lobardin interjected. "A lot of men saw you fighting Geoffre; they just didn't know it was you."

"They wouldn't believe it if you told them. I'm just a kinless girl without a right arm. A *dead* kinless girl without a right arm."

"But what were you doing all those years between then and now?" Cassis asked, obviously frustrated by the blanks in my history. "Where were you? How did you learn to use a sword, dress as a man? Jon said you'd assassinated people. Who were you working for? How do I know you're not lying to me? Maybe it was always your plan to return and bring back Arsenault, raise your own army—"

I laughed bitterly. "Trust me, if I could have done such a thing, I might have. Well, once. But there aren't any more Aliente. Your House killed them all. It's just me, and you can see the state of things." I swept my arm out so he had to look at me in my borrowed cape and too-big trousers, the sling that supported my right arm. My slippers were soaked through and my toes were half-frozen even in the wool socks. "I'm not raising an army. But you still have a price on your head. If you threaten Arsenault..."

"I'm not here to threaten Arsenault."

"Then what do you *want*, Cassis?"

"Lupa suggested..." Cassis stopped. It wasn't like him to seem so nervous. But even Lobardin shifted sideways with the air of a gavaro waiting for trouble. Had I done something impressive when I'd attacked Cassis in the kitchen? I doubted it; he wasn't wounded at all.

Cassis tugged on his tunic again. "Lupa suggested that I should sidestep my uncle and my brother by issuing you a pardon, restoring your titles, and...marrying you."

Which froze me more—his words or the weather?

Long ago, I had lit candles in the shrine of Adalus and spent many desperate hours praying—longing—for this moment. I had imagined him kneeling to take my hand, telling me he'd received my father's permission, asking me in his sophisticated and courtly way if I would consent to be his wife. And then—after my father chased him off our land—I had imagined him riding in to rescue me in the moonlight, disguised in black to evade our sentries, standing beneath my window and calling up to me, *Kyrra, Kyrra, will you marry me?*

I started to laugh.

I couldn't help it. It wasn't the laughter of battle madness—not quite. It hurt my ribs, but I couldn't stop. Lobardin and Cassis stared at me in alarm, and then Cassis colored, high on his cheeks.

"You can't be serious," I gasped.

Cassis stiffened. "Don't you think we both have a duty to Liera? It wouldn't have to be a love match."

"Good gods. You *are* serious. What kind of duty to Liera do you think I have? You don't think I did enough by getting rid of Geoffre?"

"Geoffre's death left a giant hole in the power structure. I thought I'd just be fighting my brother, but now my uncle Renzo is back from the dead and, Kyrra, we're under siege. I'm trying to save the city, godsdammit. Our *home*."

"And I'm sure Camile would swoon to have me as her co-wife. Replacing your other poor, unfortunate—"

"Don't talk about Viela that way," Cassis snapped. "You don't know, Kyrra. You don't have any idea."

"I know she died of poison. At least that's what all the rumors said. It would be easy to poison me, too, wouldn't it? Marry me for Liera, and then, oh no, poor Kyrra, she took sick and died."

"You don't know anything! Geoffre poisoned Viela and he did it because... Ask Arsenault, Kyrra. Ask Arsenault about Viela, see what *he* has to say, how he defends his actions."

"Are you suggesting Arsenault poisoned your wife?"

Cassis pressed his lips together tightly before he answered. "He played a role. Don't think he's so innocent. Anyway, Camile hates me. She'd welcome being put off so I could marry you and Driese."

I was glad I wasn't still eating the apple, or I would have choked. "Oh, me *and* Driese. How magnanimous of you, Cassis."

"Dammit, Kyrra. I love Driese. I planned to marry her after this battle was over. That was why I started the godsdamned war. To rid Liera of my father and his heavy-handed policies so we could unite the Houses and marry who we wanted. Do you think I wasn't scarred by— did you think—gods, Kyrra. Driese is carrying my *child*."

The wet air froze me to my bones. Suddenly I felt exactly like ice —cold, brittle, fragile. So easily broken.

"That didn't seem to matter to you, once," I said. My voice didn't even sound like mine.

He flinched like I'd hit him. And suddenly I was boiling over with fury, not icy at all. I thrust my hand with its barely healed cut in his face and he stumbled backward. Lobardin put a hand to his empty scabbard and grabbed him.

"I made a vow to Arsenault," I said through my teeth. "You can take your fucking proposal straight to the deepest pit of all the hells while Camile and Driese watch you burn. Or they can burn with you, for all I care. I'd have done them a favor if I'd shot you."

Cassis swore. My hand itched to go to a hilt, but I remembered I didn't have one. I turned my back on him, though my skin crawled to do it. Seeing my back would squeeze Cassis's honor like a fist, and right now I needed that. The pretentious bastard.

"Godsdammit, Kyrra. Liera is at stake again! Wasn't the first time enough?"

I kept walking.

❧

BY THE TIME I REACHED THE TOP OF THE HILL, I WAS EXHAUSTED. My side hurt so much I could barely stand. Arsenault was there to meet me.

"You went out the window, didn't you," he said breathlessly. "Gods fucking dammit, Kyrra!"

"I needed out," I said, beginning to shiver.

Grimly, he helped me in. As soon as we walked in the door, chairs clattered and men appeared around me.

"I was sure everything was locked!" Silva said.

I should have told them what I'd done and why. They all had to suspect it. But—later. My grasp on the world had begun to disintegrate. Everything was fuzzy and hot around the edges even though I was shivering, and there seemed to be a lot of activity going on around me, movement, voices...

Soaking wet, dammit. Get a blanket, some tea, we'll put her in front of the fire. Come on, Kyrra, let's get those wet slippers off and the cloak...Where did you get these clothes?

"Th-there's a chest," I said. "It's very strange. I don't know why it's there. I was looking for some trousers. I would like to be dressed, that's all, and have breakfast, or luncheon—or supper? What time is it?"

Arsenault had wrapped me in a blanket like a Tiresian corpse. Gradually I began to feel like I might one day stop shivering. "Midday," he answered. "Silva will bring you some porridge."

"Polenta," Silva corrected him. "Millet. Would you like sugar in it, Kyrra? Almonds?"

Almonds made me remember Devid's poisoned buns and killing the women in the bathhouse. It made me think of what *would* happen to Liera—and to Mikelo—if Devid, Cassis, and Renzo di Prinze fought a three-way war for the Chair of their House. Which Prinze would the other Houses back? What would Jon do to fan the flames? What stake would the gods take in the proceedings? Cassis's last words echoed in my head. *Wasn't the first time enough?*

My stomach turned over. Silva was still waiting on me to answer, watching me worriedly with those eyes the color of twilight. I had thought killing Geoffre was a new beginning, but the colors of sunset and sunrise were too similar. The sky was just as dark at dawn.

"A little honey," I answered weakly, struggling to re-enter the real world of blanket, couch, and hearth. "And raisins," I added quickly. I had always eaten rye polenta with raisins when I was a girl. From Imisi grapes, the ones not good enough for wine. Polenta with raisins suddenly seemed like a message from an old world that was lost, like an ancient Eterean artifact.

Arsenault rubbed my feet, his mouth bowed into a worried frown. His beard didn't hide the new bruise on his cheekbone. "Why did you dump men in the ravine this morning?" I asked.

He looked up at me, startled. "How did you—"

"Geoffre's gavaros, weren't they? Looking for food?"

"For me," he corrected, still looking bewildered. "For the bounty on my head."

Silence fell but for the crackle of the fire. The flicker of flames glimmered on the worn blue upholstery of the sofa. But I'd made the hole in the fabric of the arm bigger by bunching it in my fists, and now it revealed...

The gleam of burgundy.

I caught Jon watching me from the doorway to the kitchen. He was leaning on the doorframe, arms crossed over his chest, studying me carefully.

He knew where I had learned about the men. He knew what I'd been doing outside. He knew about the chest in the room and the burgundy silk on this sofa, and he had to know about Renzo di Prinze, just like Cassis thought he did. And like the axe in that chest and the Aliente standard, it was more of Arsenault's past. But did Arsenault know?

I remembered my vision before Ekyra sent me back. I remembered watching Attrasca walk the halls of my ancestral villa and Ekyra's words. *Eventually he inflicted this dream, this shattered pearl, upon the whole world, and all men and all gods were called to its defense or its damnation.*

His idea had never really gone out of the world, had it? It had only slept. Now it was awakening again, and here was Arsenault... How long had he lived? Who was he really?

Did *he* even know who he was?

Cassis was wrong. I did care about my city. And he was right, too. Even though the Prinze had cut off my arm, stripped my titles, thrown me down in the dirt, and hanged me, I would always be Aliente.

Damn Ires. To find the answers, I was going to have to do exactly what he'd said.

I needed to follow the magic.

CHAPTER 17

ARSENAULT

OLD HABITS DIED HARD, BUT THE IMYA MADE IT EASIER TO SIT HERE staring at the dragon limb he'd taken from Cassis. Watching his own reflection flicker in its claws. Wondering if he had, as Lobardin seemed to think, made a mistake.

"Why did you keep that fucking dragon claw, ghost?" Jon said. "All that Eterean metal causes is grief. You remember—"

He didn't remember. He looked at Jon in mute appeal, but Jon closed his mouth, took the imya bottle, shook his head.

"I don't need your pity, Jon," he said angrily, grabbing the bottle back. "What I need is answers. Real ones."

"My real answer is to get rid of it. Bury it as deep as you can and find some other way to Fix Kyrra's arm. Step out of this web your gods have woven around you, I beg you, Arsenault. I don't want to see you digging yourself ever deeper into pain. You said it yourself: Sometimes it's best to let sleeping lions lie."

"And if I asked you to tell me?"

Jon pulled the fingers of Arsenault's right hand back to expose his palm and the two faint old scars that lay below the new one he'd made with Kyrra. Jon touched the middle one. "This vow still holds, yes? Your vow to the B'ara?"

"You know it does."

"Then my answer is that I can't answer. I wish I could, but... Forgive me, Arsenault. My mouth is also bound closed." He left Arsenault alone at the table with all his questions, an open bottle of imya, and the ache of a promise he only remembered in intent, not circumstance.

But Jon was probably right. The limb shouldn't stay in the house with Kyrra.

He staggered outside drunkenly, the dragon limb awkward under his arm and the imya bottle clutched in his other hand. Just holding the limb awakened in him memories of the Old World, how it had felt to wander through a landscape alive with magic, to watch a sea dragon crest the waves of the harbor, the flash of its sapphire eyes as breathtaking as a storm. How powerful it had felt to love a goddess, to feel her hair spilling over his hands and watch her slip gracefully and quickly through the trees, always just ahead of him...

Why did this limb call up so many memories of Sella?

He should get rid of it. Nothing good had ever come of their relationship. But that wasn't entirely true, was it? Their children. Meeting Kyrra. And Kyrra needed metal for her arm. It was damn convenient to have the thing he most needed drop into his lap—onto his table—exactly when he most needed it, but he pushed that thought aside. He'd been drinking; it was easy.

Magic laid a path for him through the woods. He wondered if anyone else alive today would be able to see the sprites lighting his path. Their colors swirled like the skyfire of his long-ago home as they danced in the frosty treetops.

Gods, he missed it. The ice, the sea, and the dragons. The satisfaction of Shaping a lump of ore into an object which only came into existence because he touched it and yet was exactly what the ore had always been destined to become.

He wouldn't have knowingly forged anything into Kyrra that would trap her in the webs woven by the gods or her treacherous Houses. The first time he'd seen her, battling that bucket at the well, he'd known freedom lived inside her. It made up her bones and her flesh. That anyone could think of her as his creation infuriated him. He'd hide the damn limb, and when she recovered enough, he'd know if it was safe to use in her arm.

The sprites twittered in the trees, their lights curved, and the path veered to the right. A fallen stone wall loomed in the shadow, the building next to it mostly intact. He ducked beneath the crumbling lintel and found himself in an abandoned forge.

The history of the place reached out for him. The life the smith had given it by shoeing horses and making plows and rakes and kettles —tools of peace. The smith's rusty implements hung on the wall, and through another door was a room with a workbench, a rack of chisels, a lathe—a carpenter's workshop.

Miranda's farm had once been part of a whole village. Maybe that was why it was full of so many objects that seemed strange for a single farmstead. The noble's carriage that sat dusty in the barn. The furniture.

He ducked to peer through the door into the night woods. The whole place lit up in ghostlight, the way it had looked long ago. Now it was only a village of ghosts. Eternally tending animals, milling wheat, baking bread, plowing fields...

Building tables, like he had once.

He turned away from the roving dead who reminded him too much of himself and went back into the small, abandoned forge. Dropped the metal limb to the ground with a clang and took another burning drink of imya while he studied it. The forge would be a fitting grave for it if Jon turned out to be right. But the limb was tiaannamir and even the thought of burying it twisted him up. It would be like burying a creature still half-alive.

Surely putting away the drink, which had been killing him before Kyrra had found him, would be more useful than burying the gods-damned limb, which he could use to Fix Kyrra's arm. Except the limb was from a dragon and Jon had said, "You remember..."

Jon's reaction made him think maybe he shouldn't want to. But he needed to.

For himself. For Kyrra.

He sat on the cold ground, and, in the company of ghosts, he took his book from his pocket and began to write.

PART II

A giant maelstrom of malevolent magic spins in the sea off Thunder Cape, birthing storms and high winds that dash even the sturdiest ships to pieces. It is rumored that inside this maelstrom lives a giant serpent of insatiable hunger, whose rage can never be quenched. I questioned the captain of our ship as to how he braved it thrice without losing ship or sailor, and he explained that the chances of a successful voyage could be increased by carrying even the tiniest bit of magic. Carrying a Fixer on board was considered good luck, even by the Qalfan sailors, who otherwise abhorred magic. In the worst cases, the captain told me, they threw the Fixers overboard to satisfy the serpent's hunger.

—Oji la Kaif
   Sea Voyages to Distant Lands

CHAPTER 18

ARSENAULT

KYRRA,

Shall I begin my story like the Qalfans do: "Once was, once wasn't..." Or like a Dagmari poet raising his mead horn in the hall: "Sing, o Songmaker, the deeds of a great man, a captain, a leader of souls and commander of magics—"

That's rubbish.

Instead, I shall have to begin the way my people did, simply, with the facts:

"There was a man named Ari, son of Gunnar, outlawed and cursed for killing his wife and his brother. He was captured by a pirate, chained to a bench on a galley, and brought as a slave to the far ends of the earth."

The fatespinners love irony, and Erelf loves it, too. I'm not the man you think I am, Kyrra. Let me warn you now.

I can already see you rolling your eyes. But *I'm not the man you think I am* doesn't stop with a name or clothes or a story about a man in search of Truth and the goddess who betrayed him.

I heard you tell my story once in the hall after supper. I drank too much and you followed me down to the grotto and asked me what I was thinking. I said, *I'm thinking about the way the stars looked*, and you told me about climbing onto the roof with a spyglass because your tutor had said some stars had rings. *That must be a bit of poetry*, I scoffed, but you said, *No, and seeing the rings was worth being confined to my room for a week.* Your eyes shone in the moonlight and your mouth turned up at the corner in that hopeful way you had sometimes when we were alone together.

Perhaps this memory isn't true, but I'll accept needing to invent it. That innocence is what I hope the edge of your gavaro self hasn't cut away. I look into your eyes and they're full of questions because you don't know who we are together. Husband and wife, but also somehow strangers. I don't know what you had to do to become your own version of *not the man you think I am*, and you know I have other scars on my palm. Vows I made long before we met.

I've always remembered just enough to realize the man I saw in the Ice at my Scrying—the killer, the drunk, the selfish, self-absorbed, too-proud man—wasn't a dream-conjured nightmare but my reflection.

I know you've read about the Dagmari raiders, those vicious northern wolves who plundered Dagmar, Vençal, and the Outer Isles for silver coin and golden-haired men and women to sell to Eterea as slaves.

I remember when I told you Jon had once owned me. The galleys stole our rights, however we came to the oars—as criminals or kidnapped labor. Jon had no reason to believe I was anything other than a common murderer when I was first dragged off that ship. The Qalfan Empire filled its eternal need for unskilled rowers by condemning criminals to galley service, but if a pirate was clever, he could make an enormous amount of coin selling men to the galleys using forged papers that listed the many horrible "crimes" for which they had been "sentenced." In many cases, the pirates would falsely brand their captives with the symbols Qalfan prisons burned into their most violent criminals, ensuring the men would be chained to the galley bench until they died, whether they deserved it or not.

But I remember the horrified look on your face. You had been made a serf by your own father. You could not choose to leave, to marry, to carry a weapon, or to sell the labor of your own hands and reap the rewards for yourself, except for the little sewing jobs the gavaros gave you. Your father had made you a slave in everything but name, but you weren't ready to accept the idea. Would you continue to tell me how the Householder is responsible for the lives of everyone who resides in his House, his immediate family, his serfs, his servants...even the kinless girl who draws water for the gavaros? Would you justify your father's right to decide who in his House should live and who should die even though you were a casualty of that right?

In my homeland, we had no slaves, no lords or kings or householders. Everyone who owned property had a say in our governing. When I became an outlaw, I gave up all my rights and slaughtered the ideals of my homeland on hunger's altar. The local Dagmari jarl liked to hire outlaws to do his killing and stealing. In exchange, we slept with a roof over our heads instead of freezing in the snow, and the bread and mead in our bellies kept our minds away from thorny moral questions.

You saw the best man I could be and loved me because of it. The nobler path would have been to die of starvation again and again instead of staying alive by raiding. At the very least I should have left Dagmar sooner. But my first step on the road to Liera came as a twist on those lives that faded into mist so long ago, when I was still trying to live close to my home. I left Dagmar finally—ended up in Vençal and found different wars in which to sell my sword—but the gods didn't forget the choices I'd made. They couldn't; their memories are eternal.

Eventually, I tired of being a wolf. I couldn't bear for anyone's life to touch mine when I knew I would die and go on to another life without remembering them at all. So, I built a cabin high up in the mountains of the Outer Isles and hid in the wilderness, alone, for years.

The people of the island began telling stories about me as if I were a nature spirit guarding the peaks. Finally, I couldn't take the loneliness anymore. I reckoned I could kill myself and I'd wake up young again, but Erelf would never take away the pain. So, I packed up what coin and food I had—which wasn't much—and decided to go down the mountain, seek out the local blacksmith for work.

It sounds like a reasonable plan, but it wasn't. Spring storms were unpredictable and brutal. A stream spilled from a cleft in the rocks near my cabin and grew into a river as it tumbled to the sea. It was already swollen with snow melt before I left, and soon after I set out, the wind began shrieking through the rocky hollows, whipping the river into a frenzy, lashing me with pellets of ice as I picked my way carefully down the steep, slippery path.

I was almost down when I slipped on a rock and plunged into the water.

Drowning is a death I would prefer to avoid. It's a wrestling match with panic; you're trapped inside yourself, trying to fight your way out with no possibility of escape, your body constantly driving you to breathe the very thing that will kill you. I could have let myself go, but what would have happened to my body? Would it wash out to sea? Would I awake to find my new situation worse than the first?

Somehow, I wedged my sword into the rocks and clung to it for what felt like hours. When I finally climbed out, my bones felt as if they were made of ice, cracking with every movement. By the time I stumbled into Avelbris, the thought of dying began to seem like relief. Surely, if I died, I would also warm up.

I found a small barn on the edge of the village, dug into a corner of an unused stall beneath a pile of straw and horse blankets. I don't know how long I dozed in and out of sleep, but I was still there that night when Guin put his horse up and discovered me.

Erelf stole Guin from me, too. It's strange how I've forgotten some of the most important players in my story, and now that they're coming back, I think, *how could I ever have forgotten?* Sometimes it feels as if my mind is a wilderness. I break out of the trees only to find myself stranded on the edge of a vast crevice I can't cross because a bridge is out.

Guin is a bridge. If Guin hadn't found me in that stable... If he hadn't brought me into the house... If he'd been yet another hardened, jaded soldier instead of a carpenter...would I have ended up in Mdembu? Met Jon and Renzo? Followed Jon north to Liera?

Met you?

But Guin wasn't a soldier. He didn't belong to the violent life I'd fled when I built my lonely cabin. Guin lent his cloak to the pale ghost of a man huddled in a corner of his barn, then took him into the kitchen for a bowl of soup.

His voice was soft, the kind horses and dogs like. I was half-animal at the time, so maybe that was why I liked it, too. "Take a bite," he said. "Slowly, just a sip."

You can't imagine how good that soup tasted. Silky and hot, swirling with egg yolk. Alongside, he gave me a cup of tea with plenty of honey. The biggest feast in the royal palace of Ris could never compare.

"Let's get your boots off. Warm your feet."

Guin knelt and worked off my wet boots, and I put the bowl down, surprised. He said nothing else as he wrapped my feet in wool and placed them on a fire brick that had been heating on the hearth. After a while, the food and the warmth and the kindness began to turn me into something human, and I noticed details about the house: the snugly stacked and mortared stone walls, the tightly plaited thatch roof above us. The shaggy giant of a wolfhound stretched out in the corner eyed me warily.

"His name is Artos. Mostly he holds down the floor. That's right, boy, don't give me that look. There's no shame in claiming your place now your hunting days are behind you."

Guin ruffled the dog's ears. His fingers were long, like the rest of him—lean and spare. All these details are branded into my mind; it feels so strange that I had lost them. I used to watch Guin go about his work sometimes, the way all his focus was on what he was doing. A chair went together for him in a way it rarely did for me. I slammed pegs and arms and legs together by brute force, but Guin taught me to slow down, to find the beauty in the wood and coax it free.

It was a talent that went beyond his Sight, a natural eye for the possibilities in a knot or a plank or a person. Flecks of gray had begun to show in my beard, but he was the one who taught me the world wasn't all blood and dirt, that there was still compassion in it, and hope.

The dog closed his eyes in contentment as Guin scratched him. "Wolf took a chunk out of his hind leg. It healed lame, but he gets around the shop well enough, scares away the rats, keeps me company."

"No woman?" I asked. My voice was so unused it felt as if flakes of rust fell to the floor when I spoke.

"Just me and Artos. Small village. Never found a girl I felt like sharing the wedding gilt with. Never felt like leaving either. So..." Guin spread his hands and shrugged. "Here we are. And good for you, too, eh? There's space by the fire."

When I stumbled into Guin's stable, I didn't realize he would offer me more than a bowl of soup and the brief pleasure of a dog who wanted a scratch behind his ears. I wasn't like Artos; I was a stray cur afraid of being kicked.

"Thank you," I mumbled. I gave the soup a longing look, but the thought of staying in Guin's house was more terrifying than being swept down the river. How long had it been since I'd seen a human face? There had been the little sprites who'd played around the stream, dryads in the forest...

No, those don't count.

"Thank you," I said again. "But you've done enough. I can't pay you..." I started unwrapping my feet, not knowing where I would go or what I would do when I got there.

Guin stopped me with a hand on my shoulder. The human touch made me feel like a spooked horse. I had a feeling my previous life was best forgotten, and yet there must have been something good in it for Erelf to torture me by stealing it.

"You're running away from a lot, aren't you?" Guin murmured. "You don't need to pay me coin. I'll make you up a pallet. You can sleep on the floor and wear my extra shirt and trousers. Perhaps you'll feel more like talking in the morning, eh?"

Artos's tail thumped on the hearth rug as if he agreed with his master.

My shoulders slumped. I didn't know if I was giving up or giving in, but I didn't have anywhere else to go.

So, I stayed.

⚘

IT'S HARD FOR ME TO JUDGE TIME. A YEAR CAN FEEL LIKE AN instant or an eternity. Some lives feel as if they're over in a blink, and others... Well, those go faster if I'm drunk for the duration.

I didn't mean to stay with Guin as long as I did. But I came down with a fever the night he found me in the stable. He nursed me through it and withstood my moods as I recovered. After I recovered, I felt as if I must repay him. So, I worked with him in his workshop, making tables and chairs and spoons and other implements of peace. After that, I couldn't leave because I didn't want to.

You asked me once why I kept track of mending roofs and shoveling snow. It isn't just that I know I'll forget those days. I forget small and large events alike, minuscule details and enormously important ones.

I write down the ordinary days because the little moments, the ones no one pays attention to, are what make a life. It's the slow buildup of days when there are no wars to fight, no fevers to cool, no famines to suffer, no deaths to grieve. The days that come down to the simple act of planing a board—shaving off the thin curls of wood onto the floor so the whole shop smells like pine, feeling your muscles work with every scrape of the lathe.

Learning to work wood Talentless was a relief and a joy. I was always grateful to Guin for giving me that gift—the gift of routine, of steady rising and sleeping times, and meals made on a schedule, cooked on a proper hearth. The quiet way he used to sit with his feet up in the evenings. We'd smoke a pipe or drink some ale and he'd

whittle little figures or pick out a plaintive island tune on a flute—
though he wasn't very good. And faithful Artos, sleeping on top of my
stockinged feet, keeping them warm.

I'd lived long enough to get a pain in my knee, but even that
stopped aching so much.

The day the pirates arrived was no different. The ship anchored
offshore in a hard mist, making it difficult to see anything but the
Empire colors they flew. One of the new Qalfan merchantmen, people
said, and they were eager to get a look.

I remember standing in front of Guin's workshop, wondering why
the lines of the ship made me uneasy. I'd been staining a table. My
fingers were colored a deep walnut brown, and I rubbed them with a
towel to no avail. The small boat the merchants had dispatched to
shore bobbed on the choppy waves.

Guin came up behind me to watch. "Looks like we'll be having a
party tonight. Best close up shop early." He didn't sound displeased.

Perhaps I've imbued this memory with the foreboding I think I
should have felt, but you're Lieran, you know how merchants and
pirates play a one-up war with each other. To fight pirates, merchants
charter the big, sea-going galleys. Cutters don't always work against
them because the galleys hire archers and crossbowmen—or they did
in the days before arquebus and cannon. What hasn't changed is how
it's handy for a pirate to disguise itself as a merchant galley. Nothing
about the ship advertised its true nature, but maybe all the raiding I'd
done long before had lodged itself in my bones. My body remembered
what my mind didn't.

"Something wrong, Arsenault?" Guin asked.

I was trying to lead a peaceful life, so I shoved my worries aside as
paranoid scraps of a former existence. "Just worried about that stain
drying properly. You're right; we should close up and get down to the
beach."

Many of the Dagmari raiders I'd worked for had settled in the
Outer Isles, taking Isles women to wife, raising golden-haired children
in the very place where they had once been feared. And when Tule
cast out its outlaws—like me—there were two places to go: Dagmar
and the Isles. A lot of magic swirls around the place. Most of the men
who remained in the village that day were Fixers who worked as artisans. Guin was a Fixer; he worked in wood like I work in metal.

As the crew of the Qalfan ship dragged their boat on shore and
straggled up the rocky beach, magic misted in the air like rain. At
first, I thought the crew was using it, but I quickly decided that wasn't

the case; perhaps, like me, the others on the beach were struck by how much rougher this crew looked than typical Qalfan merchants and were using their Sight. But if that were true, shouldn't someone have protested bringing them into the village?

The captain wore his urqa and allaq carelessly, not like a believer veiling in respect for others and the Magnificent Sun. When the headman of the village asked about his wares, the captain's black gaze slid over the old man's face in oily disdain. But when the captain opened the casket at his feet, the gold and silver, ivory and amber within shone forth as if the crew had brought the sun. And then, rarest of all, an ingot of tiaannamir, gleaming silver even on a cloudy day.

Such riches blinded everyone. But surely someone among us had to have Seen that it would end in fire?

If they did, they threw themselves into the flames along with everyone else.

❧

I HAVE A LONG LIST OF DEATHS I DREAD, BUT FIRE, WATER, AND rope cluster near the top of the list.

You could call my life as an oarsman an extended death, beginning in fire, spooling out in exhaustion and starvation, and ending in water and blood. The villagers threw the ship's crew a grand party. I sat against the wall, watching the women's bright skirts spin as they danced, listening to the pipes trill and the drums beat their rhythm. Guin sat next to me and stamped time with his feet while we shared a horn of mead.

The hall was warm, with the fire flickering in the pit in the center of the hall and the feeling that there was no reason life couldn't go on like this, if not forever, then at least for a long time.

"Annika looks especially fine tonight," I teased Guin.

"Oh, she does," he agreed. "And I'll be leaving her alone, won't I, because Matteu has already spoken for her."

"What about Wren?"

"No, she's like a sister to me."

"Branna?"

He screwed up his face. "Branna? I used to pull her pigtails when she was just a wee girl."

"All right, well what about Evin?"

He stopped to let me know I'd surprised him. Evin was the stonemason. Beneath his woolen shirt and dusty leather apron, he could have been an Eterean statue: *The Beautiful Youth*. He had big brown eyes and long black lashes, and the women swooned for him.

Guin took a drink and shook his head. "You're worse than my mother, may the gods grant her peace, always trying to see me set with someone. If you want to give up your space in the house that badly, Arsenault, maybe I'll take old Hew in as a lodger. The poor soul could use the company, and you..." He brandished the horn at me.

I snatched it out of his hands. "Me, what, Guin?"

"Oh, don't give me that look. You're doing it on purpose, to make me uncomfortable."

"So, Evin?"

His cheeks fired a bright red. "By the gods, old man, sometimes I think you've barely hit puberty. Why don't you dance with one of the women? Old Lady Hithestan is about your type."

I chuckled. Truth was, I might have been interested in dancing with a few of the women—maybe not Old Lady Hithestan, who was a sprightly ninety-two—but most of the women I admired were married and it was a very small village. I did enjoy teasing Guin, though. He was easy company, and unease had been twitching at me all day, like a chill in the air whispering, *summer will be ending soon.*

Across the fire, I caught the captain looking our way a few times. He used his long, handsome smile to charm the ladies, bending to kiss their hands with manners from the continent, but his eyes always slid away as if he were keeping track of the men in the room.

Counting warriors?

I didn't want summer to end, but I couldn't quite ignore my instincts; they'd been bled into me too often. I rose and took the horn from Guin. It was empty anyway. He had been looking sadly into it for a while, as if more mead might magically appear. "Time to go," I said.

"What, already?"

"Artos will be whining to be let out."

Artos got through to him. He lurched up from the bench in a haphazard muddle of limbs that said a great deal about how long we'd been drinking. Island mead is strong, sweet stuff. I'd been pacing myself, but I can't say I'd done a perfect job; my memories, newly returned, have kept their blur. Guin flashed me a grateful but rueful grin as I caught his elbow and righted him. "All right, spoilsport. Lead on. Perhaps we'll find the door faster with you in front."

"Perhaps we will. What kind of line is that you're walking?"

"What's the fun in walking a line? Here, Arsenault, let me have your shoulder and I'll be able to stay on the floor better. It keeps tipping."

I snorted, but I let him take my shoulder as we made our way through the crowd. I spoke politely to all who stopped me and to the members of the crew who kept their eyes on us, but finally I shoved Guin through the door into the cold, damp night.

An onshore wind whipped bitter off the sea. Guin hunkered against me. "Gods. What a fucking night."

I grunted something in response as I pulled him slowly down the slick cobblestones. The temperature had dropped, turning the mist into a patchy, thin coating of ice, which made the footing treacherous. The wind thrashed the beachgrass about in a wild dance. I thought I heard sounds above it—the ringing of a man's hobnailed boots on stone, the knock of a body against a wall, a muffled curse. I stopped to listen.

Guin stared at me blearily. "It's bloody cold, Arsenault. I want to go home."

"I know," I murmured, peering into the darkness. "Just thought I heard something."

Guin dug his fingers into my shoulder and tugged on me. "Come *on*, Arsenault. You were the one who wanted to leave in the first place." He forged onward against the wind, and I had no choice but to skid down the icy slope after him.

Guin fetched up against the door with a thud and laughed, with me right behind him. He fumbled at the latch and we both tumbled inside, tripping over Artos. Artos shot out the door past us with a yelp. I lit the candles by the sullen glow of the banked fire while Guin swayed in the middle of the room. The calm yellow light of the candles and Artos's whining at the door—he was quick about his business in the cold—bestowed a sense of normalcy on the night.

Guin collapsed on a bench and began tugging off his boots while I let Artos back in. Artos descended on him at once, licking Guin's face, wagging his long, shaggy tail enthusiastically. It was hard to be worried with such a dog around, and watching a drunk Guin try to shove him away without success tugged a smile out of me.

"Artos," I said under my breath. As if the dog ever thought I disapproved of him. I grabbed him by the collar, trying unsuccessfully to drag him away, until Guin said, "No, my boots, just take off my boots." I obliged him and he fell back on the bench and stretched out, closing his eyes and wriggling his toes in their blue wool socks with the yellow zig-zags.

It's funny how I can remember little details like this—the color of Guin's socks, the thread pulling off from around the toes on the right where it would need to be darned again. I remember thinking, *Maybe I'll take it to the smith's daughter, see if she'll do it for me.* Does memory work like this for everyone? It's been so long I've forgotten what it's like to remember.

"Arsenault," Guin interrupted, face turned eagerly toward me, eyes open now. "I was thinking. If we traded the spoons for cloth and we traded the cloth to the smith for a new saw and we traded the saw to one of the whalemen for some bone and we tooled the bone and then we—"

"Guin. None of those trades are trading up. You're drunk. What is it you really want?"

He stared at me for a moment. Was it the firelight that made his gaze warm or—

I backed up, almost tripping over the dog. I remember how furious you were when I talked about *entanglements*, and you were right, I was a selfish bastard trying to protect my own heart. But only because it had been broken too many times to heal properly. And that night, when I thought Guin might want something more from me than friendship, I remained too much of a wary stray to do anything more than run away.

"You're all right then," I said. I knew I was using my gruff veteran's voice from the way Guin drew back, hurt, despite the alcohol. "Sleep it off and—"

Something thudded against the door. Artos barked, two short, sharp sounds, and suddenly both the dog and I were our old hunting selves.

"Somebody else slid down the hill?" Guin mumbled, pushing himself up on an elbow.

I didn't answer. Instead, I knelt and thrust my hand under my cot for my sword. I hadn't had occasion to use it in a long while, but there was something odd about the night that made me want the feel of steel at my side.

Guin shoved himself fully upright, eyes round as saucers as I unwrapped the sword from its linen shroud and buckled my sword belt around my waist again. Thank the gods for the extra notches; I'd been a much leaner man when I'd worn it last. "Are we still talking about trading?"

"I'm not trading my sword. I'll be back in a moment."

"Surely it was just somebody sliding down the hill!"

"Probably," I agreed.

As soon as I touched the door handle, a muffled scream split the night. I froze and the moment cost me. Something scuffed against the door. I shoved my shoulder into it, but a weight on the other side held it closed. Cursing, I slammed my body into the door, but it didn't budge. By now, Artos was up on his feet, barking madly at the ceiling. The thatch of the roof rustled, someone cursed, and then—

Fingers of thick, black smoke slid through the gaps in the plaits.

"Guin!" I shouted. "The door!"

He didn't hesitate. Magic washed out of him in a wave, squeezing the door in its grip until it cracked in two with a sound like a thunderclap. The top half of the door crashed inward. I shoved Guin out of the way but the ragged edge of it swiped my arm; Artos was barking so loudly now I couldn't hear anything else—just *barking, barking, barking*. I choked on the smoke billowing down from the roof. Somehow, I managed to get my hand on my hilt, to climb over the broken top half of the door that still blocked our way out. I shoved open the listing bottom half of the door that hung drunkenly on its hinges.

A row of faces greeted me as I staggered, coughing, out of the house. Men from the ship, men we'd been drinking with, grinning that stupid raiding grin, as if violence was as intoxicating as kacin.

"Fucking dog!" one of the men hissed. I didn't know if he was talking to me or Artos. Artos leapt with a growl and I jerked my sword free and hurled myself at them, too.

The world fractured into details, with no sense or meaning. I don't know what it's like to be taken by battle madness, but memories of fighting are always like dreams to me, disconnected from fear, which ambushes me later as formless panic in the dark. I remember Guin crying out, Artos snarling and growling as he tore open a man's thigh; he was a damn good dog. Guin was grunting, wrestling with a pair of men trying to lash his hands with a rope. His captors ripped his shirt open and made a rough, swooping gesture over his skin.

I stopped, paralyzed momentarily by the fear that they were cutting him. Instead, light flashed, blinding white. Guin cried out in anguish and I realized—they were binding his magic.

I drove the pommel of my sword into a man's gut and leapt over the bodies lying on the cobblestones. But my boots were the smooth-soled boots of a craftsman, not a soldier. I slipped, cracked my knee, and a cudgel whistled down at me out of nowhere.

One stumble, a single moment, and the whole world jerks off its path onto another. I watch everything in my memories as if it exists in an unreal, timeless space where I ought to be able to change things. That stumble was what put me on the boat that led me, eventually, here, and for that, I can't fault it.

But surely more than one path could have led me to you—one which involved less pain for all of us?

CHAPTER 19

ARSENAULT

TWENTY YEARS AGO

THE UNDERDECK, WHERE THE GALLEY SLAVES STRAINED, SHACKLED to their oars, stank.

It smelled of waste and sweat and wounds gone wrong, but he had gone numb to it unless one of the pirates hauled him up top into the air. Every now and then, one of the pirates would need something: entertainment or an extra hand with a sword. Sometimes the captain wanted someone to torture to keep the others in line. Somehow, he knew the beatings, the exhaustion, the foul food and fouler water hadn't destroyed the responsibility Arsenault felt for the other men, especially Guin, so he made Arsenault watch to keep *him* in line.

Guin had changed in the past months—they all had. Down to skin and bones and muscle, their clothes in tatters, skin marred with flog stripes and peeling sunburn—black binding runes burned into their chests, all of them, including him. Such a damn waste to bind a man like Guin whose Talent was wood. What could he have done to hold the ship together on a long ocean voyage? Or to break it apart if it came to that?

Arsenault wouldn't let it come to that. Chained together on the same bench, Guin had spoken in the dark about how he dreamed he died, and would that be so bad? Arsenault knew only too well that kind of longing, but all the men on this ship had only one life to live and they'd put it in his hands; one hundred forty-seven lives on his ledger, and he was determined not to lose them if he could help it. He tried to lend his strength to keep Guin alive the way Guin had once kept him alive, but Guin wasn't made for this world. He was wasting away, retreating ever further into his own mind until he had almost stopped speaking at all.

Thunder Cape had seemed the logical place to stage a mutiny—the only time when chaos would be on their side instead of the pirates'. The hold was full of looted Eterean metal and the ocean had suddenly become a magical multiplier; the pirates didn't know the danger they'd created by binding the Fixers but leaving tons of magical artifacts free.

Thunder Cape was supposed to be impossible to round, but the Qalfan doctor the pirates used to bind the galleymen Fixers kept pointing out that Oji la Kaif had made the voyage more than once, repeating Oji's stories so many times everyone *almost* believed him.

The doctor wore his urqa pulled tight up over his nose all the time like a godsdamned Nezar, and like a Nezar, he could be in turn charitable and vicious, mercifully tending the men's wounds but binding their magic at the captain's orders, making sure none could escape their shackles. Sometimes Arsenault thought the doctor's eye was especially on him, just like the captain's—that even though the doctor was Qalfan and probably bound himself, he could still See that Arsenault's Talent was for metal. There was something about the doctor's eyes, so dark they were almost black, except for the golden rim around the outside of the iris, which inexplicably made Arsenault think of flower dust.

But that was probably because the doctor's favorite story was the one about Oji la Kaif and the magic river, in which Oji outwitted a group of thieves by throwing handfuls of daisies into the water until they turned to gold. But when the thieves dove in to pick up the flowers, the illusion dissolved and the thieves all drowned.

"If only we had some of those magic flowers now," Guin sighed, and in the painful, dark nights locked away from the stars in the hot, smelly underdeck, Arsenault missed Pippa and her golden daisies so much he wept. And silently he wondered why he didn't do exactly as Guin said and give up—slip away into death and let them throw his body overboard to wash up somewhere in a new life.

He fought against that wish as he had life after life because he knew it wouldn't matter. What *would* matter were the lives of the men on this boat. He only knew a handful of names, but they were all so close, stripped until they were nothing but straining, stringy muscle, naked chests and raw hearts still beating in the face of despair and brutality.

Nothing in words or illustration gave the scale of the Maelstrom at Thunder Cape.

The furious swirl of water dragged the ship toward its center for days. Trapped in eerie, storm-whipped darkness, the mast glowed white magic like hoarfrost. Sheets of water pounded down onto the deck of the *Gannet* every time it plunged into another deep trough, flooding the dark underdeck until men cried out that they were drowning. But the overseers kept beating more and more effort out of the oarsmen as if they were horses. Arsenault felt like his heart might burst with one more drag on the oars, but miraculously, he kept making them. Without the galleymen, the ship would be sucked into the maw of the whirlpool, ripped apart and dragged under.

But finally, the moment came, as he'd promised the men it would.

The ship's boy was supposed to open the door to the hold while the crew was distracted with the Maelstrom. The ocean, wild with magic the bound Fixers couldn't use themselves, would aid them by pouring in on the tiaannamir the pirates had stowed in the hold. Then the boy would give Arsenault a signal and the rowers would attack the overseers.

Balanced on the crest of a wave, anything might have happened. The fatespinners had not yet decided on a design. But then the spinners passed a thread through the warp of the loom and all their lives plummeted toward the crash. You could plan a mutiny down to brass tacks, but in the end, it was a game of chaos, and Fortune judged the winner.

What did Ekyra think when it was all over? When the decks were slick with blood and the surviving rowers were back in their shackles, their situation unchanged except for the empty benches and Guin's empty eyes, reflecting the nightmare of watching their brethren thrown overboard to feed the giant serpent at the center of the whirlpool. The scraps of Eterean metal that rattled together to form a metal monster as if they had been attracted by lodestones. In addition to a hand fashioned from daggers, it had been armed with his own sword, which it wielded indiscriminately against both slave and pirate, who died with indistinguishable screams.

This was the chaos Arsenault had hoped to create, but it was not at all what he wanted. And who would have predicted that in the end, it would be one of his own who betrayed him, who looked him straight in the eye, and said, *I'm sorry, Arsenault,* then drove a dagger through his flesh.

❦

"ARSENAULT."

Whispers in the heavy, hot dark. A cool, wet rag across his lips.

"Arsenault, we've docked."

The ship's boy. Zim. They threw him down the hold to bring the rowers food and water and haul out the waste buckets when they thought about it. He huddled beside Guin. Both looked at him like... Arsenault had seen that look before.

"If you want to get out of here, you can't let them know you're sick."

He tried to rouse himself. A throbbing, hot pain filled his gut, like he'd swallowed a firestone. The stab wound hadn't been enough to kill him quickly but was plenty good enough to fester.

"Three more dead this morning," Guin said. "The Ibuu's men will be coming to the docks to unload the ship. *Arsenault.* You have to get up or they'll throw you overboard."

He was still chained to his bench, but he couldn't remember when he'd stopped rowing. Couldn't remember who else they'd put beside Guin—four rowers to a bench, him, Guin, who else—

"The serpent," he croaked.

"No serpent. We've docked. Arsenault."

"Where?"

"Dakkar. Mdembu."

"Mdembu," he repeated.

"The royal city. The Ibuu won't like the condition you're in. Put yourself and all the men at his mercy." The boy spoke in a quick voice, like he was afraid of being caught.

"How?"

"Throw yourself at his retainers' feet and beg."

All right. He could do that. He could beg.

"You," he began as the boy helped him sit, but the world became a fetid, black blur and erased whatever he'd been going to say. Then it was just the boy peering at him in the dim light of a candle. The boy's black hair hung down spiky in his thin, dusky face, and his dark eyes pulled tight at the corners with concern and fear. The boy's expression planted its fear in him, too. He looked around wildly to make sure Guin was still there.

Guin was only behind the boy, thank the gods. With his scraggly beard and his skin paper thin over his cheekbones, Guin seemed like a different person. And that look... Yes, Arsenault had seen that look many times before. His wound wasn't going to heal, was it?

The boy bent in close again.

"You'll remember me, won't you? My father, too? All of us?"

⚜

THE BOY'S FATHER—THE DOCTOR—WAS DEAD. THE MAGIC-animated metal had swept him into the side of the cabin. Arsenault remembered the sickening crunch of the man's skull as it slammed against the wood.

"Write," he gasped as the boy and Guin shoved him upright against the curved bones of the hull. The boy was slim and ragged, thirteen or fourteen years old, much shorter and many stone lighter than he was. "Write your story. Both of you. So I don't forget."

"You told him that already," Guin said as the boy slid a crumpled piece of parchment into the waistband of Arsenault's tattered pants. Guin's voice was confused, hurt, almost angry, but also... Arsenault couldn't parse it. It took too much effort.

"Someone will find it," Arsenault mumbled. "Someone will know."

"Surely you won't forget me, Arsenault? If we're separated? I don't know what's happening. Will they sell us to another ship or—"

"If I die," Arsenault interrupted him, hoping it would make sense. His voice crackled like burning paper.

"Don't talk like that!" Guin hissed. "You can't die now! We've made it all this way!"

Arsenault wanted to explain. Instead, he said, "You're right. An old stubborn man like me," and Guin relaxed a little, but the fear didn't leave his eyes. Maybe it was just the fear of being left alone, but it was better than the nothingness that had deadened Guin's eyes for so long.

"Ask for protection," the boy said in a low voice, close to his ear. "The Ibuu is merciful, but some of his nobles aren't."

The boy's hands left his shoulders. In the next moment, the bench rattled and other hands untied his ropes and hoisted him up by his armpits. His feet felt like plumb weights. The men had to drag him up the ladder and onto the deck after Guin.

The day was hot and humid, only slightly less oppressive than in the underdeck. Sunlight speared his eyes. The sky became a blue lake, flooding the world.

His head dipped as if he were a puppet with its strings cut. He sank into the man beside him.

The man shook him. "Oh, no. We don't want none of that. If the inspectors quarantine your people to the ship, what will the Captain do, eh?"

Arsenault squinted at him. It was the Vençalan mate, and on his other side, the big Tiresian sailor with his braids spilling out of his headcloth down his back. The mate's breath, so close to Arsenault's face, smelled sour, of wine and garlic, and his grizzled gray-brown beard seemed to fade into his skin. The gold in his ears flashed painfully bright in the Dakkaran sun.

With difficulty, Arsenault turned his head. The whole earth seemed to turn with him. "Captain's fault if it happens."

The Vençalan chuckled, but not in a nice way. "Thought we beat that attitude out of you."

"Put me down on the docks with the others. I'll make sure we stay off your ship."

"Course you will. Come on. Captain has a buyer's agent wants to make sure you're healthy."

How in the name of all the gods would anyone think he was healthy? But he concentrated on putting one foot in front of the other and made it down the gangway to the dock.

❧

SOLID GROUND WAS A REVELATION. IT DIDN'T MOVE LIKE THE SHIP and he nearly fell.

"Been a long voyage," the mate laughed to someone. "They'll have to find their land legs again."

"I can see that," a deep, lilting voice answered.

They were speaking Qalfan, but the man's accent was different. Arsenault raised his head. The man was young, very tall with broad shoulders and ebony skin, dressed in a red silk tunic that shimmered painfully in the sun. A flashy crimson ribbon gathered his long locs into a knot at the nape of his neck, but the curved knife at his side didn't look decorative.

Beside him stood a woman wearing the same red and gold silks, carrying a similar knife. *A uniform?* A hat obscured her face, but when she looked down at him, he caught a glimpse of dark eyes wide with horror, while the man briefly wore an expression of distaste.

Men armed with pikes stood behind them.

And all around—people.

Haggling vendors, the thrum of conversation and laughter... Skin of a hundred different shades. Clothing in a riot of color, fabric, and style—tunics and trousers and bright-colored skirts, head wraps, toggle-fastened robes, Tiresian glass beads, and Qalfan veils.

Parrots chattering amid rustling palm fronds.

His knees wobbled and he knew he was going down.

He hit the dock hard and threw himself prostrate, arms spread like a bird's wings. His cheek brushed the man's leather boot.

Both the man and the woman jerked backwards, but Arsenault grabbed their ankles.

"Asylum," he rasped in Qalfan. "We ask for asylum from the king, all of us here. For the boy on the ship, too. We were wrongfully stolen. Abused. The *Gannet*'s a pirate."

He pressed his face into the dock, at the end of his strength.

The pirates laughed. "He don't know what he's talking about," the Vençalan said. "He don't know nothing, him. He's a galleyman, for sale. Making things up to escape his sentence. A murderer or a thief, like the rest of them."

"Asylum," Arsenault gasped again. The man and woman both stepped backward and his weak grasp on their ankles slipped free. He had once been too proud to beg, but no longer. It wouldn't make up for the lives lost on the ship, but Guin was still alive, so—Guin. "Mercy. Please."

"I don't think—" the man began, but the woman cut him off.

"Are they all in the same shape?" she asked the mate.

"They're standing here," the mate said. "You can see them well enough. They're all walking."

"So many of us died," Arsenault said—aloud, he hoped. "Worked to death. Starved. Beaten—"

The mate kicked him. Pain blacked him out for an instant. "...troublemaker. Tried to start a riot, this one. Best leave him alone."

"No, you have to listen—"

The woman's boot creased and her knee settled on the dock in front of him.

"Adayze," her companion said. "Don't touch him. Look at the shape he's in!"

The language had shifted from Qalfan to Dakkaran. The words were a jumble of sounds until some buried knowledge made sense of them.

"I don't think it's catching," the woman—Adayze—said. "Smells like a wound gone bad."

Her fingers slid beneath his chin and tipped it upward. He didn't have the strength to resist if he'd wanted to, but the ever-present pain of moving escaped his lips in a combined whimper and moan. She leaned closer to study him.

"Found my curiosity, did you?"

The captain. One of the pirates must have run for him.

Arsenault tried to pull away, unable to stifle a growl, but the woman caught his chin and held him firmly.

"He's a Northman. Tulan," the captain went on. "That group in the middle, they're all from the Outer Isles. They put up quite a fight, but of course we bound their magic. Thought they would be helpful going around the Cape, but it's difficult to beat the evil out of them. I'm transferring their contracts, so it's not my problem anymore."

The captain shrugged, an elegant lift of his shoulders. The blue silk of his coat pulled and shimmered with the gesture. He had a whole wardrobe of clothes that made him look like a fucking noble. The oil he used on his hair and beard cloaked him with the smell of cedar and lemon, but he'd methodically put entire crews to the sword for a few scraps of metal.

A light entered the woman's eyes as they tracked over Arsenault's face. The binding on his chest writhed with unfamiliar magic and crushed against his sternum. She turned his head to study his profile, and he forced himself to remain still though he struggled to breathe.

"The treaties," he said in rusty Dakkaran to the surprise of both the woman and the man. His throat felt like someone had filed it. "Island belonged to Vençal. No raiding Vençal."

"Outlaws, all of them," the captain said in Qalfan. "That's the only reason for those outposts. Tule used to set its outlaws adrift."

"What made you think we would want starving, sick Tulan outlaws you've had to beat the magic out of?" her companion asked. In the wake of the woman's gaze, an aura of light surrounded him, too, wavering like a heat mirage.

The captain dusted an imaginary piece of lint from his shirt. "Because one of your trading agents paid me a finding fee in advance. He said something about 'rehabilitation experiments.' It sounds dangerous to me, but you Dakkarans all seem to be moral philosophers. I've come through on my side of the bargain, in any case."

"Do you have the agreement with you?" the woman asked, standing.

"Of course." The captain produced a set of papers from inside his coat. He handed them not to the woman but to the man, and she frowned. Deeply.

The man scowled as he read them, then shoved them at the woman.

"Your papers are in order," she said reluctantly when she finished reading. "You can take your galleymen to the exchange. But even criminals have a right to be treated like human beings. Don't think you can get away with this again without being fined or denied docking privileges."

The captain sketched a bow that stopped just short of mocking. "Of course, madame. We live to serve."

Arsenault tried one last time. With his final shred of strength, he flung himself again on their boots.

"No," he gasped. "Grant us mercy. We've done nothing wrong—"

The captain pressed his heel into the base of Arsenault's spine. It forced him against the dock and put so much pressure on his bad wound that it gave way. Fluid gushed over his stomach. He cried out and pain erased him for a moment, as if he didn't exist outside of it. When awareness trickled in, he realized he was trying to scream, but screaming had become too hard; sound was just wheezing out of him like a broken instrument, pathetic.

"No," the woman said suddenly. "I've changed my mind. I'm fining you right now. That galleyman. Give him to me."

"But the agent will dock my pay—"

"You've worked these men to skin and bones down in that filth. This man, right here. I'm claiming him in the name of the Ibuu."

"Adayze!" the man beside her exclaimed. "If the agent wants to broker his contract to a noble who wants to rehabilitate him, why do you need him?"

Adayze flashed her partner a glare. "I want him, and I want him now."

Dammit. They were going to grant him asylum and send everyone else off gods knew where. "No! Mercy for *them*, not me; don't separate me!"

"Take him then," the captain spat, removing his foot from Arsenault's back. Arsenault curled around the pain in his stomach. Warm liquid soaked his shirt, oozing over his hipbone. "And good luck dealing with him. You've probably done everyone a favor."

"No—Guin!" he tried to shout. Arsenault stretched for their boots again, but they lifted him off the dock. The pirates stared smugly at him. Guin stood in shock, then struggled to pull out of line.

"Damn y—" Guin's voice cut off abruptly as an overseer stuffed a rag in his mouth.

Arsenault watched in horror as Guin fought and choked. The overseer jammed the rag in further until Guin turned red—

"Didn't you hear him?" Arsenault shouted helplessly. "Look at him! He can't breathe!" He struggled, too, but maybe he was only yelling in his head, maybe this whole life was a nightmare he could wake from tomorrow, if there was a tomorrow...

They put him in a wooden cart, but Guin's growl echoed in his mind as the horses snorted and stamped. He tried to throw himself over the side, but then the cart clattered on cobblestones, and he fell back onto the hard slats of the wagon. Pain burned away his ability to do anything but lie still.

And that night, he died.

CHAPTER 20

ARSENAULT

THE IBUU'S PALACE, DAKKAR, TWENTY
YEARS AGO

IT WASN'T THE FIRST TIME HE'D DIED. NOT EVEN THE TENTH. BUT it still took him by surprise.

The cart bumped and rattled away from the docks, through the city streets, up the sandy bluffs toward a looming stone wall whose towers looked like beehive skeps. The fever painted everything in heightened, painful colors and crazy, blurred washes. Round metal tubes poked out of holes in the wall. They looked like giant spyglasses, but the only spyglass he'd ever seen was the small one the captain of the *Gannet* had used.

The Dakkaran man and the woman rode in front of the cart, but sometimes their voices drifted back to him.

"What are you going to do with him, Adayze? He won't live long."

"We'll have him treated."

"Why?"

"He's a man, that's why. Jonawak!"

When they were inside the gates towering in the sky, the cart stopped. Adayze and...Jonawak—he assumed that was a name, too—leaned over the cart to study him before the men with pikes lifted him out.

"Look at all that blood and pus. It's a bad wound; he's going to die."

"Then let him die here with dignity. Or should we let him die like a sick cow, on a journey to the fila know where? No one will be rehabilitating them; that agent was a liar, and you know it."

"But the other men are with the agent," Jonawak said. "Perhaps it would have been more merciful to let him go with them."

"I would have given asylum to all of them. But I need to find out who that agent is working for. Here, Jon, take his legs. Watch that wound."

They settled him on a mattress. Water splashed his lips. The sound of ripping fabric told him they were cutting off his shirt.

Arsenault caught the woman's arm.

"Lie down now," she said. "We'll take care of you."

"Give my body to the sea when I die," he said.

He hoped they wouldn't bury him.

His greatest fear was always that he would wake up in a coffin. A shallow grave was better; he could try to dig himself out. But the coffin had been an endless cycle of waking, panicking, screaming, and dying slowly of thirst, until he'd begged the other gods of the Tribunal to make Erelf stop. Even they had thought that punishment too terrible for his crime. Otherwise, Erelf would probably have let it go on forever. He had certainly seemed to derive a great deal of enjoyment from it.

Arsenault wasn't looking forward to seeing Erelf again. But as the day went on and coherent thought flickered in and out, his hope in healers failed and he realized he wasn't going to make it. Whatever the captain had done to the wound was speeding him on his way. He hoped Guin was rehabilitated, whatever that meant, and that Guin would remember him, maybe come back...

No one ever came back.

It was hard not to sink into the feeling of failure that washed over him. The black sense of futility and shame always conquered him in the end. *This* was his eternal prison.

Life slipped away in the quiet time of night. One soft exhaled breath and he came unmoored from the body lying thin and ravaged in the healer's hut, surrounded by mosquito netting and attended by the healer and the woman, Adayze. He admired her determination, but he was still angry at her for separating him from Guin. How would anyone be able to track Guin down if he forgot?

Then he was standing before the Tribunal of Gods.

The gods were arranged in a half-circle as they always were. Tekus, their father and king, sat on his throne sculpted from the bones of drowned men and the opalescent carapaces of long-extinct fish. He cupped the rounded balls of hip joints with his big hands and leaned forward, his slick black hair falling in kelp-like strands over his bare, brown chest. Erelf stood before him, separate from the other gods, black hat in his hands in respect for his king. His scar—the mirror of Arsenault's own—jagged down his temple like a lightning strike framing the thundercloud blue of his eyes.

Arsenault sank wearily to one knee.

"You had a longer run this time, Ari Gunnarsson," Tekus said.

Arsenault lifted his head. Futile tears had left sticky tracks on his cheeks. He'd long ago given up asking to be sent back to the life he'd left but abandoning this life hurt. "I did, sire. But I'd like to stop running."

He knew asking to be released from his sentence was also useless, but he did it anyway. By now, it was part of the ritual.

"Surely he's been tormented enough?" Cythia's melodious voice interjecting on his behalf wasn't unwelcome, but the goddess of love never did anything without wanting something in return.

"He's mine to torment," Erelf snapped. "And no amount of torment will ever wipe away his sin."

"That's true," Arsenault murmured. "But once again, I ask the gods for mercy."

He'd learned early that flinging himself at the gods' feet as he'd flung himself onto the boots of the Dakkaran officials achieved nothing. Words drew similar results, and yet he kept saying them. The Dakkaran officials had at least been kind. The gods could only ever be gods.

"Did he give my daughter mercy?" Erelf asked. "Or did he spurn and murder her, casting her body down on the beach?"

"I never spurned her." Arsenault wished he'd had the presence of mind and the courage to have walked away from Sella far earlier, to save her fate being tangled with his, but he'd never spurned her. Nor had he worshipped her. Mostly, he'd simply loved her. "Are you going to send me back again?"

"It remains my son's decision, but I think we are," Tekus replied. "Do we still support the verdict?"

It was possible for the gods in assembly to overrule one of their own, which they had done when he was caught in the coffin. But it didn't happen often. Arsenault tried to gauge their mood.

Mostly, they looked bored. His visits must be growing tedious. A movement in the back snagged his gaze—Ekyra, shifting on her seat. She smoothed her doeskin tunic and allowed one of her eagles to clamber from her leather-armored shoulder to her gauntleted hand.

She fed it a strip of meat, then looked directly at him, taking his measure.

It was too hard to guess what Fortune would do. Though she was one of the most powerful gods, she rarely spoke. The fatespinners were always listening. She raised a blond brow, but who in all the hells knew what that meant.

Tekus settled back on his throne. "Since I hear no dissent, I shall take that as affirmation. Ari Gunnarsson, you shall return to the world to live more lives until my son Erelf's vengeance is satisfied."

"And my vengeance shall never be satisfied," Erelf said with his cold knife-slash of a smile. "But I'll allow you to keep more memories this time, Ari. I'll allow you to remember your failure."

At least they didn't bury him.

He woke from a nightmare of being shackled to a ship hull, starved, beaten, responsible for a hundred people he couldn't possibly save, into a new nightmare of linen binding wrapped tight around his entire body—even his face.

It was almost worse than the godsdamned coffin.

In a panic he thrashed and shouted. Did they plan to put him in the ground like this? Seal him into a stone tomb?

Dear gods—embalm him?

His hands were bound too tightly to tear the strips away from his face. He sucked linen into his nose and mouth with every breath, and when he struggled, he slammed into something hard beside him.

"By the gods! The fila send us demons!"

"I'm not dead!" Arsenault tried to shout around the linen in his mouth.

The man—whoever he was—went quiet. In a moment, the boards of the cart thumped with footsteps. Fingers scrabbled, trembling, at the bandages and in a moment tore the linen away from Arsenault's face.

Arsenault took a deep, dragging breath and stared into the terrified face of a middle-aged man with walnut-brown skin.

That's right; I'm in Dakkar.

He remembered that at least. It was something, an anchor to hold onto.

"I wasn't dead." Arsenault tried to sound calm though his voice was ragged. "Someone made a mistake."

"How? Lord Jonawak brought me your body. He said the Lady Adayze had been treating you for charity and had ordered your body handled with dignity. How is it they both made a mistake?"

Fever. I died of fever this time.

"I don't know. Unwrap me and bring me back to them."

Maybe Lady Adayze and Lord Jonawak could tell him why he was here. Where Guin and the boy and the other men on the galley had gone.

Erelf thought knowing his failure would torment him, but that was only partly true. It also gave him back a purpose.

⁂

"I DON'T WANT TO MAKE A FUSS," HE SAID AS THE CART CLATTERED uphill away from the ocean that broke in white breakers against the thin strip of beach. "That might not be what Lady Adayze wants."

If the man had slid him into the water while he was wearing the graveclothes, he would have drowned again and again. He'd have to specify *no wrappings* next time.

They fluttered in the wind, puddling loosely around his hips. The pungent, sweet-smelling funeral oils left his skin sticky and supple. Anyone they met would have thought him a ghost, but thankfully the road was empty except for the insects singing loudly in the trees.

It was always a thrill and a relief to be alive and new again, to hear, feel, smell, see. In some lives waking made him feel like weeping, but it was also like getting out of bed when you were ill; he'd be better once he got going.

The carter eyed him but said nothing until they were almost to the gates of the fortress. Then he stopped the cart and made Arsenault lie down so he could cover him with the graveclothes he'd already unwound. Arsenault waited until after he heard the carter speak to the guards at the gate, then pushed the bandages away from his eyes and propped himself up to look over the side as they drove into the quiet courtyard.

A palace, built of white marble and decorated with glittering tile mosaics, reigned resplendent in the center of the courtyard. A fountain played at the bottom of a sweeping front staircase, and the orange glow of torchlight revealed spires of tall, round minarets soaring far above him into the night.

If waking after dying was like getting out of bed after being ill, it was also like waking the day after a big battle. *Take stock of your resources. Survey the terrain. Determine your position and formulate a strategy.* Having a task to focus on allowed him to shove all the emotions surrounding death and judgment somewhere... He didn't know where they went. They weren't at the forefront of his mind anymore, which was a relief. Time to get on with the business of living.

The carter drove them hastily past the palace entrance, onward to a handful of low mud-brick buildings some distance away. He stopped the cart in a palm grove behind the buildings.

"Wait here," he said. "Do not move. I have sprinkled the cart with herbs against ghosts."

"Fine," Arsenault said and climbed out of the cart as soon as the carter left.

The palm grove formed the entrance to another garden; Arsenault couldn't tell what purpose the building served in the dark, but it was empty now. Arsenault wondered how long he'd been dead this time. The moon was sinking into the far horizon, but how many nights had passed?

"If you are a ghost, I have defenses against you."

Arsenault whirled, surprised, to face a barefoot, brown-skinned woman in a headscarf and a silk dressing robe, armed with a drawn scimitar.

Slowly he raised his hands. His mind felt like a wagon with a bent wheel. It was always like this after he died; Erelf delighted in leaving him some memories but not others, especially ones he needed. The woman looked familiar; he was sure he knew her, but her name wouldn't come.

He took a guess.

"Lady Adayze. I am not a ghost."

The blade in her hands trembled slightly. "Jon and I saw you die. We felt your chest; we tested your breath with a mirror. You were dead. We laid you out for two days and rubbed you down with myrrh and wrapped you in the burial cloths. There was no life left in you."

Magic fuzzed brightly around her. "Use your Sight," he ventured. "You could tell if I was a ghost."

"Are you a corpse then? Reanimated by magic?"

"Is that possible?"

"I wouldn't know." She steadied the sword and stepped toward him. "If you're not a corpse or a ghost, how is it you're walking around? I know of no magic that can cure death."

"It's a curse. Laid on me by the gods."

"Why? What did you do?"

"I committed a crime. Against one of their own."

"So, the captain was right. You're a criminal and deserved to be on that galley."

He struggled to remember if any of the men had committed the crimes for which they'd been enslaved or if it had all been forged. But the memories he'd retained felt like fever dreams, sketches of men and fragments of names and stories that didn't match up.

"No one is like me, as far as I know. At least I can't remember meeting anyone."

"Did the captain also know about this curse?"

A murky image floated into Arsenault's mind, of a blue silk coat and black eyes, but it was gone before he could catch it, leaving only a low, banked feeling of rage.

The captain is my enemy.

"I doubt it," he said.

Adayze looked less frightened, but more skeptical. She took another step toward him. "What about your wound?"

He looked down at his torso. The graveclothes didn't hide much, but he couldn't remember if he'd had a wound or where it had been. He pressed his fingers to his side and frowned. Adayze surprised him by laying her hand in a different position, searching his ribs, while the sword remained in her other hand. Her fingers ran over the bones that stood out too much under skin that was too thin, her touch light and hesitant at first, then more aggressive. He didn't know if he should pull away or submit, so he remained, frozen.

"It's not there," she murmured. "It was an ugly wound. A gash leaking pus. But now... It's as if you were never cut, and the binding rune on your chest is gone, too."

She left her hand on his side and looked up at him.

The distance between them was not that great. She was wearing her nightdress, and he could see down it to the curve of her breasts.

She drew her hand back quickly and gripped the sword with both hands again.

"So, you're not a ghost, and you're not a corpse, and now you can do magic. I don't know how you've come to be standing here, but you should know I am a married woman and the heir to the Ibuu. Also, I can use this sword."

He flushed and twisted the graveclothes tight against his hip, so they wouldn't fall off when he bowed. *Heir to the Ibuu.* Gods, he hadn't meant to offend her. He dipped his head low. "Forgive me. It will take me some time to be myself again. Being brought back to life requires some adjustments. I meant no harm."

"If you're not yourself, who are you then? You never told us your name."

Arsenault straightened and she took another step backward, but it gave him an extra moment to decide what to tell her. He never went by Ari anymore. Ari had died as soon as the magic-forged blade sank into Sella's ribs.

Adayze regarded him curiously, and he realized he was taking too long to answer. What name had he used in the village?

"Arsenault." Relief flooded him. "Arsenault is my name." *Of course.*

Saying it recovered a memory of a woman with tawny, sun-kissed skin pulling him from the bottom of a small boat. One of the first times he'd been sent back, he thought. It hadn't been a stinking underdeck, but he'd surely been adrift, and when he'd woken, he'd needed a purpose, something to beat back the guilt.

What was that other woman's name? Rie. That sounded right.

Women were always pulling him out of boats, saving him from drowning, setting him back on his feet after he died. He never knew if Erelf used them to drive his guilt ever deeper into him, or if one of the other gods was having mercy on him. Or maybe it was all random, some quirk of the universe. There were men, too, but they tended to sink into the past, so many lives he'd been responsible for and failed to save. Like Guin's. He struggled to remember what Guin was like as a *person*, but all he found was emotion—the remnants of friendship, brotherhood, grief. A hazy image of a man chained to a bench, back bowed and strings of salt-stiff brown hair obscuring his face. And, inexplicably, a dog.

The sound of Adayze's scimitar sliding back into its sheath brought him back to the present, where he was standing nearly naked and smelling of funeral oils in a garden thousands of miles from his home. Adayze stood with one hand on the hilt of her sword, studying him closely.

"Arsenault is a Vençalan name, isn't it? You were asking about a boy and another man. I think his name was *Guin*. When we took your clothes, we found a note."

Something tickled his mind, just beyond the edge of what he could grasp. "A note?" he echoed dumbly.

Adayze's stance lost more of its wariness. "I saved it. Why do you think the captain wanted men from the Isles specifically? Did you know the captain wanted to bring you to Mdembu when he took you?"

Arsenault struggled to recall details, but all Erelf had left him was a jumbled mess. Fear, fighting, a long ocean voyage, day after day spent hauling on the oars. Slowly, he shook his head. "All I remember is that the raid came at night. They were flying Qalfan flags—Empire flags. I will gladly answer all your questions, Lady Adayze, but could I have some clothes and something to eat first? I've been dead for two days."

Adayze jumped as if just realizing where they were and what he looked like. "I suppose that would be best. It will look strange if someone catches us out here like this. Even if you are made of sticks."

"I suppose no one would believe I'd just come back from the dead."

"It would be one of the more creative excuses for a man and a woman meeting at night. Go into the garden and hide. I'll leave clothes and food in the magus hut. After I decide what we're going to say about you, I'll send Jon."

"You won't come yourself?"

"It will raise too many questions about where I was two days ago and why. My father isn't a fan of magic, my husband is at sea, and you've admitted to being an outlaw."

Arsenault rubbed his beard, which was slick and soft with oil, as he tried to absorb Adayze's explanation. "What are you going to do with me then?"

"You'll be Jon's responsibility. There's too much I don't understand to let you go free just yet."

CHAPTER 21

ARSENAULT

TRUE TO HER WORD, ADAYZE RETURNED, DRESSED FOR THE DAY THIS time, wearing a long tunic of light blue silk, blousy white linen trousers, and rope sandals, a style of clothing much better suited to this hot and humid climate than the heavy skirts and petticoats he was used to seeing women wear. Arsenault watched from behind a thicket of thorny bushes as she left a compact bundle in a small mud-brick building, then dropped the key into the tangled flowers beside the door. She walked down the path to where her guards waited. Arsenault gave them a head start, then scooped up the key and let himself into the building.

The "magus hut" turned out to be a well-appointed workshop. Cabinets with hundreds of tiny gilt-labeled drawers lined the walls, whittling knives hung in racks, and projects in various stages of finish lay on tabletops. Some of his tension unwound at the sight of the sturdy worktables, their legs expertly carved with markings he couldn't read but that pulsed lightly with magic like runes.

The long, polished metal mirror in the corner bothered him, though. Arsenault moved hesitantly in front of the reflective metal, trying to ignore the flashes of images in the corner of his eye as he unwrapped the bundle Adayze had left on a low stool. Two bladders fell out—one of water, the other a sweet-smelling, cloudy drink—as well as some golden fried cakes, a pot of fermented brown paste, and a bar of soap.

His stomach rumbled painfully, reminding him he was truly alive again. He ate everything as fast as he could. The cakes were made of mashed beans, crunchy and soft with a hint of spice, and though the paste was sour to his palate, he was so hungry he licked the last tiny bits from his fingers. He drank the sweet cloudy drink and tried his best to scrub away the smell of funerary oil with the water and soap. Then he dried himself with the graveclothes and pulled on the clothes Adayze had wrapped around the bundle.

An undyed linen shirt and trousers, both the color of dead grass. A hemp belt. A pair of rope sandals like Adayze's. Everything fit well, which was a surprise. After he dressed, he walked hesitantly to the mirror.

Seeing himself after he died was always a revelation. Sometimes, if all his memories had been rubbed clean like polish from a blade, his magical knowledge stolen, he reverted to *Ari*—no scar or silver streak, no breaks in his bones or crowsfeet or worry lines. Other times he kept bits and pieces from his past life. Sometimes death left its mark, too.

This time the scar and the gray-white streak in his black hair remained. He expected to see gray in his beard and lines at the corners of his eyes, but only hollows gouged by hunger and work marred his younger face. Adayze had said he'd had a binding mark, but that was gone, too. The gods had again locked him into a prison of free will. They knew the greater torture was for him to choose to submit to his sentence. They also knew that, in his freedom, he could never adhere perfectly to their impossible rules and that his inevitable mistakes would also guarantee he would never meet the terms of release which they had also set.

Still. There were worse things than waking up twenty years younger.

The snick of an opening door stopped him before he could check the mirror for watchers on the other side. "My sister says you are not a ghost or a corpse," a big male voice said in Qalfan. "Are you a necromancer instead?"

Arsenault turned. The tall man leaning against the doorframe wore the same uniform as Adayze's guards, but gold glinted in his ear, stirring memories of ships that made Arsenault uneasy.

Jon. That sounded like a nickname. *Jonawak?*

"If I was a necromancer, I would have chosen a more well-fed body," Arsenault replied.

"It must have been a terrible crime. To be sentenced by your gods."

"I've no quarrel with you. But I'd rather be on my way all the same."

"To go where? To do what?"

Good question. He hedged. "To make my way back home."

Jonawak laughed. "Oh, no. Whatever you did in your past life, you were a leader to those men. All we need is for the Ibuu to bear the blame for your misguided sense of honor when you try to free them."

Arsenault's fingers twitched, seeking out a sword hilt that wasn't there. "I had an obligation."

Jonawak gave him a canny glance at odds with his youth. Arsenault had to remind himself that he barely looked older now himself. "You were their chief? Lord? King? I don't know what you Tulans call yourselves."

"Tulans don't have kings. Or lords. But someone had to take over, so I did."

"A man who's nothing won't take charge of that many people."

Arsenault shrugged and turned away only to find himself facing the mirror again. He hated mirrors. Anyone could be watching, and there was no telling what horrible, reversed image of *honor* and *obligation* the magic might decide to show him in his own reflection.

"A man doesn't have to be a lord to be a leader," he said. "I'm a carpenter. If you've no use for me, why don't you let me go?"

"Because Adayze told me to keep you."

"I thought she said you were her brother. Can she order you around?"

"Her younger brother. She assumes the throne from my father. I take my orders from her."

"So, are you...her right hand? Her Champion, the way they do in Dagmar?"

"Here in Dakkar, every Ibuu has a Dagger to do the dirty work behind the diplomacy and lawmaking. But everyone knows the Ibuu has many children and many wives and concubines, spread out all over the country. Adayze's Dagger is probably one of my siblings."

Arsenault rubbed the side of his head. He wished he knew what questions to ask, but with so little memory, he needed to know everything. There didn't seem to be a place to begin.

"The Ibuu has a Dagger, though... Who is he?"

"*She*. My aunt is the Ibuu's Dagger. She and the Ibuu have declared her position, so it isn't a secret anymore." A smile hooked up Jon's mouth. "Surprised?"

Arsenault tried to draw up any knowledge he still possessed about

Dakkar, but it was like winding a bucket down into a dry well. "A little," he admitted.

"Adayze likes to harness me into her schemes because we have the same mother. We grew up close. She didn't want to be recognized down on the docks, so she made me bring her dressed as a court official. And now here I am, saddled with *you*. I've just been appointed command of the Palace Guard, so maybe—I know you can row a boat, but can you fight?"

"Aren't you a bit young for command?"

Jonawak stiffened. "My father commissioned me for the position. If you think I haven't had to earn it, you'll learn your lesson soon enough."

So, he *was* young for command and he knew it, and Arsenault had stuck him in his pride. "All right. My lord. Am I supposed to kneel now?"

"You're very bold for a stick man."

"I've no intention of hurting the Lady Adayze. Why would I when all she wanted for me was a death with dignity? But I think she wants to use me for something and I'd like to know what that is. Why was she down on the docks in disguise in the first place?"

"You're a corpse and a slave. How is it you're asking me questions now?" Jonawak sat heavily in one of the chairs. "Have you drunk all that palm wine already?"

"Being dead for two days makes you thirsty."

Jonawak eyed him askance. "Adayze said you didn't know why you were taken."

"None of us expected to be brought all the way to Mdembu, as far as I know. Almost every Qalfan port is closer."

"The boy who wrote the letter..."

"Do you have it? What did the boy write?"

"Mmmm. Check your pockets."

Frowning, Arsenault did. A wrinkled piece of parchment was folded inside.

My name is Zim la Hallad, son of Miha, a doctor from the city of Joffra. Pirates kidnapped us from a trade ship in Vençalan waters bound for Onzarro. My father was on his way to take a post with the Qalfan legation there. The captain knew we were Qalfan citizens and broke the law by taking us as galleymen.

Please, if someone else is reading this letter because Arsenault is too sick... He took a deep wound in a mutiny against the pirates. Everything he has done has been to keep these men alive and to set them free. The men trust him. He says he was only a carpenter, but if you saw him use a sword, you would wonder.

If Arsenault is still alive, keep him well. Pass this note on to the Qalfan delegation in Mdembu, so they will know the captain of the Gannet *has been enslaving Qalfan citizens.*

Arsenault refolded the letter carefully. "The boy took care of me." Uneasily, he added, "He doesn't say anything about Guin."

"Guin is the man you were with?"

"We were captured from the same village. I thought I asked the boy..." He shook his head. "Never mind. I suppose I was just fevered."

"The boy probably figured you were his best bet, if what he says about you and swords is true. Is it?"

It was useless denying it, even if all he retained was the memory of failure and betrayal. Surely *Guin* hadn't betrayed him? It was dangerous to make any assumptions about his previous lives; Erelf delighted in twisting the most basic information.

"I think you've come to your own conclusion already."

"Well. A man cursed by the gods to immortality for a violent crime..."

"I'm not immortal. I've just been consigned to the whim of a god. When his whim runs out, I'll die. It could happen tomorrow or two thousand years from now. Who knows."

"Why don't you sit down? Go ahead; I give you permission."

Maybe Jonawak was being pompous on purpose or maybe not. Arsenault cast him a curious glance and folded himself into the chair. As soon as his backside hit the pillows, exhaustion washed over him like a wave. Being dead for two days was not like sleeping. What he had told Adayze was true; his body had to make a lot of adjustments.

Jon put his boots up on the table and his hands behind his head as he leaned back in the chair. "This captain of the *Gannet*. I've been asking around about him. He seems to be well known on the docks for smuggling rum—but it sounds as if the rum might be a front for something more valuable. I hear he also runs antiquities and exotic artifacts. Customs officials in Mdembu are supposed to stop and certify those shipments, to ensure dangerous magic isn't changing hands unknown to the Ibuu—and that no one is selling our secrets. But it's a lucrative trade and hard to eradicate entirely."

"Don't you enforce the laws?"

"Unfortunately, black market rum and antiquities go mainly to the nobility. They keep it quiet by paying off the dockside officials. We've been trying to root out the corruption, but the whole world comes through Mdembu. It's like trying to stop a plague. How much do you know about us?"

"Not much."

"Well then. We're a country made of... Qalfan is inadequate. If I translated literally, I would have to call them *bindings*. Promises. Some of those promises were made long, long ago and have spun out to include hundreds, even thousands, of people. They're like spider webs, growing ever bigger, catching more people in their threads."

Arsenault tilted his head back on the top of the chair and closed his eyes. "You're right," he murmured. "Translations must be inadequate."

"Heh. I'll try to explain, though I'm not sure why I should. Adayze is just putting you off on me."

"I doubt that. She sounded like she had an agenda."

Fabric rustled and boot heels thumped on wood as the lord shifted in his seat. Arsenault kept his eyes closed. "Once upon a time," Jonawak began, "when the fila walked the land and men had just been made, the world was a dangerous place. There were no cities, no walls, no fences, only bush. Leopards lay in wait in the trees and big snakes took men in the underbrush, and when men went down to the rivers and lakes to bathe, they were eaten by crocodiles. In the ocean, there were sharks—bigger than you've ever seen."

"I don't know," Arsenault said skeptically. "I've seen some big sharks."

"You were chained to an oar underdeck."

"It wasn't my first ocean voyage."

"Your Qalfan is very good. Did you sail with them?"

Had he? Ghost-like images of caravans and mountains moved behind his closed eyelids like mirages, but not ships. "No," he replied slowly.

"Well," Jon went on. "These sharks could eat a big man and come back for more. And they did. Men did not live to be old. Their children and women were eaten, too. Finally, the people went to the fila. 'Why would you put us on this earth only to serve as food for lions?' they complained. 'If you don't want us, put us back into the earth peacefully, but save us from becoming food.'

"The fila got together to talk about it and finally they thought, 'Who will give us kacin and beer if all the men die? Lions do not offer us any of these things.' They came back to the men and said, 'We think there are enough of you that maybe if you banded together, you could defeat the lions and the leopards and the crocodiles.'"

"Not the sharks?"

"It's hard to build cities on the water."

"But, boats."

"Here, let me tell the story, would you? I'm coming to a point. After the fila gave men this advice, the men wandered back into the bush and tried to do what the fila told them. But it was too hard to stay together, and sometimes the men you asked for help would forget and then the lion would take you anyway. Finally, a man named Nambutu had enough.

"'We are going to stop wandering the forest,' he told his family. 'We will clear these trees and build houses and a wall, so the lions can't get in. And we will dig a well, so we can find water without being taken by crocodiles.'

"When the rest of the men saw how safe Nambutu and his family were, everyone wanted to come into the village. But Nambutu said no. 'Not without making me a promise. If you live in my village, you will promise yourself and your family to me and my family, that if we should ever need aid, if we are ever attacked by lions, you will help us. Anyone who refuses shall remain outside in the bush at the mercy of beasts. And if you fail in this promise, then we shall throw you outside, and we will not save you from being devoured.'

"'We promise, we promise!' all the men outside the wall cried. But Nambutu didn't have that much room. 'I can only allow a certain number of you inside and the rest will have to make villages of your own.' There was grumbling, but what could Nambutu do? He let in the first families and then shut the gate, and he told the men who remained outside how he had built his village. The skilled among them built their own villages and took in pledges. Soon the forest was beaten back and dotted with villages, and that is how my country got its start. I am descended from Nambutu's people, but there are other bindings, too—the Arak and the Dininga, and smaller bindings which do not wield the same power as the larger three."

"And have all the bindings lived in peace as they've grown larger? Are their main concerns still beasts?"

"Beasts of a different sort. The Dininga wolf sleeps peacefully for now, but the Dakkar lion and the Arak leopard have not always been allies. Promises are like nets; you pull on one string and the whole thing closes. My father has collected everyone under his aegis for now. The Arak have given him pledges in exchange for defending their eastern border, but the Arak have their own net of pledges. We have been hearing...rumors."

"You think the captain was selling the galleymen for someone to use against you?"

"When you died, my sister treated you like a free man, not a criminal. Now she gives you clothing, a place to sleep, food, and drink. These are promises she made to you. Tell me why anyone would need a shipload of magic-bound galleymen."

Arsenault lifted his head and opened his eyes. Jonawak was tapping his steepled hands against his mouth and staring thoughtfully at the opposite wall with its rows of drawers and cabinetry. He was still stretched out in his chair, boots crossed at the ankle. Awfully casual for a man sitting next to a corpse.

"You think the buyer's agent was lying about selling their contracts for rehabilitation? It sounds like a humanitarian cause."

"You don't need to know the particulars, but that agent was found floating in a drainage ditch yesterday afternoon. Seems like a strange way to reward a man for doing good. Adayze has other concerns, too, which influenced her decision to take you from the captain."

"I thought she did it from the goodness of her heart."

"We'll be clear here, ghost: My sister does have a good heart. Sometimes it is too good. But she's been raised as the Heir, and her first and highest duty is to her people. Can you, with your sense of honor among thieves, understand that?"

Sad to say he understood it more than if she'd picked him sheerly out of altruism. He hated politics. "All right," he said. "Maybe whoever bought them will use them as bribes."

Jonawak turned to look at him. His brows crept slowly upward in surprise. "Bribes?"

"Maybe he doesn't really want the men. The ship was carrying something else, too, something I can't—I don't—remember, but it was important. Metal. Antiquities. Maybe the men are just a front for the cargo and they'll go with the metal to sweeten the deal."

Or they really will be sold to fill the benches of Qalfan galleys, and how will I find Guin then?

"Then we're back at the beginning. *Why?* Why go to the effort of asking a pirate to go to all the ends of the earth for magic? We have magic here."

It was a frustrating question because he didn't remember enough to even attempt to answer the question. "How should I know? I'm a carpenter."

Jonawak gave a short bark of laughter, then pushed himself up from the chair. "Go ahead and sleep, carpenter. I'll be back for you later."

"To do what?" When Jonawak gave him a disapproving glance, he added, "My lord."

"I'm sure I'll find something appropriate. Why don't you take a knee now?"

Arsenault slid out of his chair and went down on one knee, inclining his head in silence. This seemed to satisfy Jonawak, who nodded and left, locking the door from the outside. When he was sure Jonawak was gone, Arsenault threw the chair cushions onto the floor and grabbed a whittling knife from the rack. He lay down with his hand curled tightly around the wooden hilt and pushed the knife underneath the pillows.

For a moment, his mind wandered. He thought about promises and bribes and someone watching him from the other side of the mirror. But he slid off into sleep before he could figure out who it was.

CHAPTER 22

ARSENAULT

ARSENAULT SPENT TWO DAYS IN THE MAGUS HUT, WAITING, BEFORE Jon woke him from a muddled vision that was half memory—dragging his brother Tavi away from Sella, Sella hurling herself between them, and the glint of the knife just before it sank into Sella's breast. But because it was a dream, when Sella looked up at him, she was no longer only herself but a long line of women falling to the floor beside the bed. Blood washed over the pine boards like floodwaters—an inch, two inches, three—creeping up his ankles toward his knees, as if the bedroom were the hold of a ship and he would drown not in water but in blood.

And then *snick!*—like the trapdoor to the hold was being locked shut.

He came awake fast. The room careened around him; the furniture, the dirt, the heat. Moonlight pooled in white puddles on the floor. His hand shot underneath the pillows and closed on the whittling knife. As the sound of soft footsteps came closer, he tried to lay still, waiting.

Boots stopped beside his head.

"Ghost," a male voice he knew said. "Wake up. It's time to hunt."

They'd eaten, he'd dressed, and now he was walking with Jonawak through the dark palm grove outside the magus hut. He felt the absence of a blade at his side as keenly as if he'd forgotten to put on trousers. It wasn't the first time he'd lost his sword, but he hoped the rune he'd put on it would bring it back to Vençal. It hadn't let him down yet, but he didn't know if the magic would last forever.

Jonawak led him down a winding trail to a gatehouse in the far wall. Arsenault stopped for a moment, struck by the view illuminated by moonlight under a sky dusted with a million unfamiliar constellations. A rolling silvered plain spilled out before them, each stem of long-bladed grass, every island of flat-topped trees and rocks frozen as if coated in frost.

"I think I've forgotten what open places are like," he murmured.

"You speak Dakkaran, though. Surely you've been to our country before?"

"More likely I learned it from someone else who spoke it. I've... traveled quite a bit, but I think that was my first time around the Cape."

"You think?"

"It's been a long time."

They made their way downslope from the wall to meet a group of people who held several panting dogs on leashes. Arsenault held out his hand to be sniffed, but then an animal howled and the dogs stiffened and growled. He slowly lowered his hand and stepped back as more somethings howled, like the unbalanced laughter of a warrior possessed by battle magic. The sound made his skin crawl.

"What is that?" he asked.

"Hyena," Jonawak whispered. "They follow the lions, hoping to steal their kills. A few days ago, before you threw yourself at our feet, the Ibuu's chief herdsman lodged a formal plea for help. The lions have become bold or desperate enough to walk right into the villages. They're protected by bramble fences, but those won't stop a lion."

"I've no experience hunting lions. You don't want me to get the rest of you killed, do you?"

"I'm not asking you to be an expert lion hunter. I've a special job for you."

The lord began walking. Arsenault thought briefly about slipping into the dark night, rounding the back side of the fortress to find a different way down the bluff to Mdembu. But with dogs and lions about, not to mention *hyenas*, he probably wouldn't make it far.

When they joined the small party standing at the top of the cleft in the hills, Arsenault counted four men and a woman. She was dressed the same as the men, in tight-wrapped dark folds and a hood, a pack on her back and some sort of long scabbard slung over her shoulder. It surprised him when he realized it was Adayze.

"You brought our ghost," she said to her brother.

"I thought his talent of not-dying might come in handy."

Uneasily, Arsenault looked down at his clothes. He stood out from the others not only with his light skin but also because he still wore the beige clothing Adayze had given him two days ago. The moon, only a few days past full, made them glow.

Adayze's hood obscured her face entirely. "We have no way of knowing where the lion is," she said, as if she were picking up a prior conversation. "Or if the murderer even *is* a lion. The latest victim was a young man walking at night to see his lover. They heard him scream, but when they came out, he was gone. The lions may be dragging their victims into the wash near the village, but so far no one has found either body or bones. We may find nothing; the grazing lands are very large. I don't want to be gone too long."

"The nurses will take good care of Edo," Jonawak said. "You baby that boy, Adayze."

"He is a baby, Jon. And I'm his mother. What else am I supposed to do?"

Jonawak made a noise, as if it were an old argument between them, then pointed into the distance.

"Do you see that place down there, where the rocks jut up into a hill? We'll stop there and survey the land. If we haven't encountered lions yet, we'll let the dogs sniff them out. A maneater will be active at night."

"My lord—my lady," Arsenault said, bowing stiffly to Adayze, "I still don't understand what you mean to do with me."

Adayze sighed heavily. "My brother wants you to walk ahead of us. Alone."

Arsenault looked out across the still plain. The hyenas sent up more laughing in the night. It was hard not to take their laughter personally.

"You want me to be bait," he said.

"You could choose not to do it," Jonawak said. "We would go down to Mdembu tomorrow, find a Qalfan galley in need of a rower so you could serve out your sentence. Or…"

"Prove to us you're telling the truth by helping us here," Adayze said. "And we will help you find your man Guin and discover what happened to the rest of the men the pirates took. Perform a feat of courage for your people and we will trade pledges."

Damn everything, he hadn't been alive three days yet. He'd never been devoured by a lion and wasn't keen to experience it.

He scrubbed a hand through his hair in frustration. "Your choice is no choice at all. You've got shackles on me the same as I had on that ship." Useless to protest, though. They must have gambled that a man who'd thrown himself on their boots for mercy would say yes to this ridiculous test, and fuck him, but they were right. "Tell me what to do and I'll do it. But don't send me out there unarmed."

"You can have a stick," Jonawak answered. "The same as the herdsmen carry."

For all the good that would do. He looked around for anything else he could request, and when his gaze fell on the dogs, an idea bloomed. The gods might not like it, but he was allowed self-defense. "Do the dogs' leashes have metal fastenings?"

"You can't think you'll leash a lion."

"Consider it a dead man's last request."

"If the lion charges you," Adayze told him, "freeze. If it's twitching its tail, it isn't hunting you, but if it goes still, you're in trouble. We have guns. As soon as we see the lion approach you, we'll take the shot."

For the first time, Arsenault studied Adayze and the men with the dogs closely. Maybe the strange, blocky hilts that protruded up past their shoulders weren't hilts but *guns*.

"What are guns?" he asked.

Jonawak laughed and slipped the strap off his own shoulder. He held the gun out toward Arsenault but not close enough to touch. Arsenault leaned forward to get a better look, but Jonawak pulled it away from him before he could get a good look.

"We put a lead ball down the barrel and set firecracker powder aflame inside it. When the powder explodes, it forces the ball out of the tube at a very high speed. The impact can kill a lion from a safe distance. But first we must draw the lion out."

"We could have used a cow," Adayze said.

"You're the Heir," her brother said. "You could refuse my plan."

Adayze glanced back at Arsenault, her gaze a flickering gleam in the dark. "Unfortunately, I see the use of it."

A cattle path led in a meandering fashion around islands of trees and rocks toward a deep wash just north of the village. Unfamiliar night sounds surrounded him as he walked ahead of the rest of the party—not just the wind in the grass, but also an enormous chorus of insects and the annoyed chittering of birds disturbed from sleep by his presence. He couldn't identify any of the calls. Orienting himself in a world without memory always gave him emotional vertigo, but not even being able to identify the natural world he was walking through—the stars, the animals, the geography—made him physically dizzy. Facing a lion seemed a fitting part of a larger experience that might as well be a dream.

Arsenault swung the stick he'd fashioned from a tree branch with the dog leash and its metal buckle at the end, making a lot of noise. After a while, he began humming a melody he remembered, though he'd long forgotten the words.

A line of trees loomed up ahead of him, marking the edge of the wash. He stopped for a moment. He could take the branching path through the grass, skirting the wash, or he could follow in the hoof-marks of hundreds of cattle down over the lip of the wash into the bottom.

"Dammit," he muttered. He'd much rather go around, but if he was going to draw out a lion, this would be the way to do it.

He tightened his grip on the stick and tried not to think about what else might be down there at night.

Snakes. Leopards. Crocodiles.

Poisonous spiders.

You're supposed to try not *thinking about that, idiot.*

He wasn't prepared for the way the path dropped as it went over the lip of the wash. His heel skidded on gravel and he barely caught himself by shoving his stick against the ground. The clay hadn't seen rain in a long time. It was hard and slippery beneath the pebbles scattered over its surface.

He started again more cautiously, using his stick, until he came to the bottom and crossed to the shallow trickle of a stream that wound through it.

A soft coating of grass grew here like hair, low against the ground. He kicked through it and a cloud of insects rose around him. They buzzed around his sweaty skin, biting all patches of visible flesh. Cursing, he beat them off, shaking them out of his hair, and backpedaled to the bare ground at the edge of the grass, against the side of the wash.

When he looked up, eyes stared down at him out of the night.

Feline eyes.

The lion lay on the rocks jutting out of the side of the wash. Arsenault had seen lions before—probably traveling the Spice Road—but he was sure he'd never seen one this big. It had to be ten-span long, over one and a half times his own height. Moonlight dripped silver into its dark mane and turned its coat white-gold, as if it were a giant statue forged of precious metals. Then it moved. Muscles rippled in the hulking shoulders as it stretched. It shook out its mane and yawned, showing all its teeth.

Was it twitching its tail or not?

Did it really matter?

Arsenault glanced over his shoulder, but there was nowhere to go. A few trees grew from the sides of the gully, hanging tenuously by roots that looked like fingers, all of them higher than he could reach except by climbing. He'd lost the cattle path trying to beat out the cloud of bugs and Adayze and Jonawak had given him too much distance and wouldn't be able to see him down here, in the dark.

The lion tensed on its front paws, its rear end bunching beneath it.

Its tail was not twitching.

Arsenault reached for the metal leash clip on his staff. Just as his fingers closed on it, the lion's muzzle curled up in a snarl and it launched itself off the shelf.

Trained reflexes saved him. Otherwise, he would have turned and run, and the beast would have been on his back in an instant. He shoved back the protective gates on his magic and it surged upward in quick, joyous relief, flooding the metal he clutched in his hand. Panic forged it into a blade that shot down half the length of the staff. He thrust it above his head even before it was fully formed.

His makeshift magic-made spear tore through the loose skin above the lion's leg. It roared in pain, trying to twist away, and blood spattered Arsenault's face. The lion's big front paw still hit his shoulder, and its claws raked his chest.

The magic coursing through him saved him from the pain, but the impact knocked him flat on his back. The lion hit the ground next to him with a tremendous thump. Arsenault scrambled to his feet, blade still in his hands, and whirled to face the lion. It had also climbed to its feet and was limping sideways, snarling—a low growl that vibrated the very ground.

"Well, dammit," Arsenault shouted, "are you going to eat me or not? If not, you'd best be gone!"

The lion staggered backward on its wounded leg. Arsenault stood his ground, aware suddenly that something warm and wet was soaking his shirt.

Blood. Dammit. His, not the lion's.

He adjusted his grip on the staff and stepped toward the lion.

The lion growled and shook its mane. Would it spring or run? If it sprung and he did it right, he could ram the blade straight down its mouth...

But there was something strange about this lion—a soft white-gold glow surrounding it, an angry sadness in its eyes, an almost human softness...

The residual magic dripping from Arsenault's blade suddenly flared outward, a blindingly bright white spark. Arsenault threw his arm up to shade his eyes. When he lowered it, there was no lion.

Only a man with heavy black braids wearing a lion-skin mantle, running as fast as he could toward the far end of the wash.

FOR A MOMENT, ARSENAULT STOOD STUNNED. THEN HE GAVE CHASE.

They were both running on fear and fight. When the man reached the end of the wash, he seemed to run straight up the side in long leaps. Arsenault stumbled in surprise. *Stairs carved into the hard clay.* He threw himself at them, breath knifing in and out of his chest, making him light-headed. By the time he struggled to the top of the gully, the man was already out into the long grass, not slowing down. Damn it all, shouldn't he be limping at least a little? It didn't seem fair. Arsenault tried to run harder.

Shouts came from behind him, in the trees. Adayze and Jonawak. Baying dogs.

Arsenault hurled his blade down in the grass and turned around to face them, arms outspread, hands empty.

"The lion isn't what you think it is!" he shouted.

"Get out of the way, ghost!" Jonawak yelled, bringing his gun up to his shoulder.

"Jon—no!" Adayze called.

There was a loud *crack*! It sounded like a rocket from Saien. White smoke and sparks rolled up in a cloud around Jonawak, and an impact ripped across the top of Arsenault's shoulder, burning deeper into the claw wounds.

It knocked him backward and surprised him so much he tripped on his own feet and went down. The magic swirled away and heat and pain squeezed him like a fist.

"Gods*dammit*," he cursed through clenched teeth. Ahead of him, the lionskin shimmered back into powerful limbs. The lion galloped, silver-gold in grass the same color, amid more loud cracks and the smell of sulfur and smoke, until it disappeared.

Arsenault let his head drop and gripped his shoulder. Some fucking test. He wondered if he'd passed or failed.

Footsteps pounded towards him. When he opened his eyes, Adayze knelt beside him. Jonawak loomed over her.

"You shot *him*," she said viciously as she stripped Arsenault's ripped sleeve away from his arm. "Not the lion."

"Why did you stand in my way?" Jonawak asked. "You were chasing a lion, that was courage enough! Why did you try to save it?"

"It wasn't a lion," Arsenault gasped. "It was a man. What in the gods' own hells went through my shoulder? It feels like someone hammered a spike into it."

"A lead ball," Adayze said. "Thank your gods our gunsmiths are still working on the accuracy of our guns. If Jon had hit where he was aiming, it would have gone straight through your chest."

"It was a man doing evil, killing cattle and other men, and I was doing my duty shooting at it! There was no reason for you to stand in the way!" Lord Jonawak was practically shouting as he defended his actions.

"Perhaps the man wasn't doing evil by his own will," Arsenault interjected, his voice raspy with pain. "Maybe he's been cursed. Wouldn't you have wanted to question him?"

Adayze had been poking at his shoulder. He gritted his teeth in anticipation of more but realized after a moment that both she and Jonawak had grown quiet. Brother and sister were looking at each other, not at him.

"You knew it wouldn't be a real lion," he said slowly, feeling like a dupe.

"We knew nothing but what I told you. We thought it *might* be a lion, but we weren't sure. And because we weren't sure, my father thought it best to send Jon and me. To keep it quiet."

"And why me then? Were you really giving me a test to strike a bargain, or were you only throwing me to a magical beast because you could? Just because the gods resurrect me doesn't mean I enjoy dying."

"We thought it was a reasonable way to take two birds with one stone. We needed to find out about you. We knew you had come back to life once and these nightmare stories are growing more prevalent. There have even been apparitions inside the palace despite our magical protections. That was why, when a captain showed up with a cargo of bound Fixer galleymen... Well, I wondered if the two weren't related. Did you recognize the lion man? Is that why you tried to save him?"

"Do you see these claw marks? If we were allies, why would he attack me? Why would he run?"

"Who knows what goes through the mind of a man when he is a lion," Jonawak said.

Well, that was probably the gods' truth. Arsenault struggled to sit up. "Gods' balls," he said through gritted teeth, then realized he was cursing in front of Lady Adayze. She didn't seem the sort of woman to be offended, but he tried to calm himself anyway. "If I had known the damage *guns* could do, I wouldn't have stepped in front of it. But I've never seen a gun before, so how could I know?"

Adayze sat back on her haunches, watching. She didn't say anything for a long time. Then she said, "I think you're telling the truth. And I don't make pledges I don't mean. The word of the Heir is as binding as the Ibuu's. That means your word is binding, too. You're bound to help us find out what is happening with the men and cargo your captain brought in, as we're bound to help you find the men."

Arsenault frowned. That wasn't quite the way he remembered making the deal...

Jonawak barked a mirthless laugh and dropped to a squat next to him. "Between you and me, ghost, you must be more careful when you talk to my sister. I'm not sure you know what you've gotten yourself into, but I'll make sure you keep your word."

CHAPTER 23

CASSIS

LIERA, PRESENT

GODSDAMNED PIRATES.

The ship drifting in Liera's harbor carried no cargo but corpses. All that remained in the hold was a pile of bodies surrounded by a sticky lake of congealed blood. And the seal of his own uncle, Renzo di Prinze, like a godsdamned calling card.

"I've seen enough," Cassis said through the rag he held over his nose and mouth. "You don't have to prove to me all the cargo's gone." The harbor official nodded, his eyes a brief gleam between his hat and his mask, and made a little tick on the list he carried. Disgusted, Cassis climbed the ladder to the deck.

Why had they needed him to look around the hold? It was obviously empty except for the tangled heap of dead, gnawed-on flesh which didn't even seem human anymore. The officers had all been shot or stabbed and tossed into the hold like pieces of meat. Every crate of guns, every scrap of food, every bar of gold that should have come in return for the silk, salt, and spice he'd provided at a heavy cost to himself—gone. Just the bodies left, like a message written in blood.

Lupa stood on the deck, waiting for him, his body rocking with the gentle motion of the ship as if he were an experienced sailor. "Well, mestere? Where will you go, now that you have proof your uncle has returned from the dead?"

Cassis squinted at the vast expanse of the Sheltered Sea that stretched toward the horizon in the hazy distance. Before Geoffre had died, the sea had seemed safe, like an extension of Prinze territory.

Now it felt like a cruel frontier, an unfamiliar wilderness where monsters, murderers, and thieves lurked, just like Liera itself. He was taking a huge risk by being here. But he had not planned for these contingencies.

If Arsenault hadn't kept the damn dragon limb, he might have sold it. Now he was forced to find his coin in more dangerous, legitimate ways.

"I suppose there's nothing else but to continue to the next item on my list. Thank you for accompanying me, Ser Lupa."

Cassis hadn't trusted Lupa at the lodge and he didn't trust him free either. He wanted the man within arm's reach. But perhaps the feeling was mutual—Lupa had insisted that Tomas, his gavaro secretary, stay with Lobardin at the lodge to "help." Cassis had tried to ensure that Lupa knew Tomas would be less a spy than a hostage, but Lupa had ignored him breezily and continued packing his battered leather satchel full of papers. Cassis would have preferred to bring Lobardin, but Lobardin was the only man he trusted to oversee operations at the lodge. If these last-ditch efforts didn't pan out, it almost didn't matter; he'd be well and truly bankrupt, forced to let go of his army anyway.

Cassis turned toward the official who'd followed him out of the hold. "Burn the ship with the bodies on board and send it back out to sea. I don't want to watch it; just make sure it's done."

The official nodded and went to speak to the captain who'd towed the ship into port.

What a waste it was to burn a ship, but Cassis didn't need more ghosts dogging his nightmares. He kept seeing his father's corpse as it had been laid out in Devid's tent and waking in a sweat, night after night, when the corpse sat up and said, *Cassis, don't be a fool.*

News of Geoffre's death had traveled faster than he'd thought, and Liera had responded by falling apart. He and Lupa clomped into a seething kettle of confusion.

The docks, usually busy with longshoreman and stevedores, walked a thin line between disorder and riot. A captain stood nearby, loudly refusing to pay the silk tax demanded by a Garonze official. Not much farther away, a Prinze detachment wrestled with a gavaro wearing Caprine green, who kicked open a shiny, leaf-wrapped bundle at his feet. White kacin powder exploded all over the dock, drawing kinless addicts like vultures to a kill. People elbowed each other out of the way; the Prinze soldiers belted the Caprine gavaro in the face and wrenched the kinless away from the kacin, but more people swooped in—a woman, rubbing her hands in the white power and licking it off her fingers—

"Gods. That's a thousand astra worth of kacin they're sweeping through the cracks." He had a sudden urge to drop onto the docks with the kinless woman, to scoop up the white powder and stuff it in his pockets for later... A lick off just one finger would calm him...

Get hold of yourself, for the gods' sake.

"Devid's men are losing the monopoly," Lupa said. "He'll be getting desperate soon if you can just hold the city."

Hold the city... Cassis didn't even have a grip on it, and he was in real danger of losing the hunting lodge and any territory he'd gained after defeating Geoffre.

After Kyrra defeated Geoffre, the traitor voice of truth in his mind responded.

All Lupa had talked about since leaving the lodge was his wild scheme to marry Cassis to Kyrra. Cassis wanted her out of his head—the way she'd shoved Arsenault's name at him, how frail and thin she'd looked. And yet she was still stronger than most men he knew, like she was burning herself up with her own passionate flame.

"What errand are we running next, mestere?" Lupa asked.

He dreaded the next item on his list almost as much as he'd dreaded dealing with his plundered ship. "You and your Empirists can rendezvous with me for supper in the Night Market. I need to see my wife about selling our townhouse."

❊

"GET OUT! OUT! OUT!"

Camile threw something made of porcelain or crystal at him after every word, destroying pieces of art like exclamation points. The objects crashed against the wall, the furniture, the floor, littering the fine Tiresian carpets with their dagger-like shards.

An irreplaceable vase from Saien exploded beside his head. Cassis ducked, heart pounding, then stretched out his hands and strode toward her.

"Camile, calm down. I'm sure we can talk this over..."

She swept the last remaining object off the harpsichord, a crystal decanter half full of wine. "We. Can. Not!" she hissed, hurling it to the floor. He lunged for it, but it splintered on the tile in a scarlet flood, soaking the white skirt of her chemise as if she'd been stabbed. The servants had tried to tell him she was indisposed, but when she'd heard his voice, she'd run down the stairs in her undress, a manic gleam in her green eyes that made her look like a mad dryad.

She drew in a deep breath. Her whole body rose with it, and then she let it out slowly. Fuzzy black strands pulled wildly out of her thick braid. She'd been beautiful once, just like Liera, but her beauty was now as ravaged as everything else in the city.

"There is nothing left to talk about," she said in a clipped voice. She lifted her skirt and stepped carefully around the puddle of wine and glass in her bare feet. "I will not be cast off as a common whore, and I won't be *poisoned* like Viela. I'm going back to my family. We'll have the marriage annulled. I'll give you till the end of Fifth month to repay my dowry."

Frustrated, Cassis followed her. There was no way he could repay her dowry. He tried to pick his way through the wreckage of the room but chips of porcelain and crystal ground beneath his boot heels.

Gods, the carpets.

"No one will annul this marriage, Camile. Are you planning to lay the issue before Cythia? Or Pana, perhaps? Hope one of them has sympathy?"

Camile stopped walking and faced him again, green eyes snapping. "I'm your first wife, Cassis! I have recourse to the queen of the gods! And I'm sure Ahra will be favorable to me, since the gods know she's been on the wrong side of Tekus's affairs often enough."

Cassis couldn't help wincing. Not for the first time he wished he'd risen above allowing the truth to wound him. He stepped around the broken bowl of a vase until he stood close to her. "Nothing will hold up in a court of law, you know that. We married in good faith and consummated the marriage many times, and I shouldn't have to remind you I'm not the only one who's broken my vows."

Her eyes went wide. "You practically threw your gavaros at me!"

"That's a lie, Camile. I saw how you used to look at Arsenault."

"Arsenault had far too much honor to lay it down like that. You didn't *want* to father an heir—"

"Well, it's a good thing then, isn't it, considering you were never able to bear me one?"

The old hurt bloomed and died in her eyes like the last gush of blood from a mortal wound. After all these years, the daggers they wielded against each other retained their edge. The familiar feud only brought home how much his life had changed, how different it had been to fight with Kyrra. If Kyrra had thrown that Saien vase, it would have connected with his head. She wouldn't have destroyed hundreds, thousands of astra in a useless exhibition of anger.

Kyrra's presence in his life always seemed to turn it upside down—or whatever was worse than upside down. But this argument with Camile had been coming for a long time. Perhaps it had been inevitable from the moment their fathers had sealed their betrothal.

"You couldn't sire a child on Viela either," Camile said. "It wouldn't do for Viela's indiscretions to get out, would it? Not while the precious Prinze had their reputation to protect. Your father might have had her poisoned, but he did it with your consent, didn't he?"

Camile didn't know how sick Viela's death made him. She was just an innocent girl who'd been far out of her depth trying to play the Houses' games. His father hadn't killed Viela because Cassis couldn't sire a child. After all, Driese had discovered she was pregnant about that time, and everybody knew about Kyrra's child... He was the father of two children, neither of which he could acknowledge, only one of whom might still be alive.

No, if Viela had been barren, he could have just cast her off. But she hadn't been, and it hadn't been his—and the child of a common gavaro and a wild Forza daughter couldn't be allowed to pollute the Prinze line. He still didn't know how his father had discovered Viela's pregnancy; Cassis had been prepared to claim the child as his, to save both her and the baby, even if Arsenault had been one of the gavaros Viela invited into her bed, damn both of them. *That* would have been ironic, him raising Arsenault's child. The worst part was, he was relieved his father *hadn't* found out about Arsenault; the magical testing Geoffre would have put both mother and baby through might have been worse than death by poison.

"You know it never mattered to my father whether I consented to any of his schemes or not," he said angrily.

Camille rolled her eyes. "Oh, yes. Viela was your new plaything. I was the old, boring, barren woman. You would have poisoned *me* instead."

"It wasn't *like* that, I tell you."

"You think I didn't watch you treat her just like you treated me? As soon as you were bored with her, you were down to the smoking dens, parading with that *Caprine* girl. Kyrra d'Aliente didn't teach you anything."

His hands began to tremble. "Leave Driese out of this."

"Leave her *out* of this? You abandoned me for a *Caprine*—*left* me here with your father while you kept *her* safe and planned a war. And it's all because of Kyrra, isn't it? I was your second-choice wife. You never wanted me. It was always Kyrra, and you couldn't have her because she cheated you—"

Fury flooded him. He grabbed her by the shoulders. She tried to twist away, but he drove his fingers into her flesh, into tendon and bone, as if by doing so he could relieve this old anger that still felt like it would burn him alive. She gasped in pain.

What the hells am I doing?

"Enough," he spat, letting her go. "Driese is nothing like Kyrra. I can't pay back your dowry because I need the coin to provide for our defense. Everything you just destroyed would have bought rations for an entire squadron for a month. I'll give you five thousand astra and another cut from the sale of the house and you can do whatever you want with it."

"Five thousand! But that's barely enough—you're selling the house? Cassis, where will I go?"

"One of your father's country houses, I imagine, if you live frugally. It's all I can give you right now. Ask Ahra's acolytes to hear the annulment case, but I guarantee they won't. Then I'll sign the papers casting you off and you can live however you care for the rest of your life, Camile di Sere. I'm sorry for the mess my father put you in, but I don't want to ever see you again, and I imagine you feel the same about me."

She stared at him, her face pasty and wan, her lips a tight, bloodless line. Then she laughed, but it was a tired, hopeless sound.

"I'm right, aren't I? You never wanted me. Now that your father's dead, you don't have to put up with me anymore. If Kyrra d'Aliente were alive right now, you'd have her installed in my place within the month."

Gods. If only she knew. If only Kyrra would listen...

He turned and began picking his way through the ruined conservatory like he was walking through a minefield. "Pack whatever you want. But I want you gone in the morning."

THE NEXT ERRAND ON HIS LIST WAS THE SERE COUNTING HOUSE. Dealing with the ship and then Camile in immediate succession had left Cassis feeling bruised and drained, but the ordered bustle of the financial district soothed him. Even at this hour, criers manned their stands outside the counting house, trading information. Scribes recorded the best of it in the large, leatherbound books the Houses used to set commodity prices and forecast trading enterprises. Inside, clerks changed numbers on slates, counted coins, finished up contracts.

Everything operated with the precision of clock gears. Arithmetic was one of the rare facets of reality his father couldn't manipulate. Two and two always equaled four, regardless of what his father wished it was. Sometimes, in an effort at escape, if only in his mind, Cassis tried to imagine life as a clerk. To have his day's work laid out for him every morning, predictable and precise. And then to return home when it was finished, perhaps even to a wife he'd chosen himself, without tipping the whole of the Eterean peninsula into the ocean. Maybe this imaginary wife would even have been happy to see him.

He might as well wonder what it was like to be born on the moon.

He strode up to a vacant desk, his hob-nailed boots ringing on the marble tile. A lot of gavaros were hanging around inside the counting house and the way they watched him made him nervous. Coming alone might have been an act of hubris, but Camile wouldn't leave unless he provided her the funds to do so.

"Mestere Prinze?" the clerk at the desk said hesitantly. "May I help you?"

Frowning, Cassis worked off his gold signet ring and threw it onto the desk. The heavy thunk echoed in the building's soaring ceiling. "How much coin can I withdraw at once? I've experienced a setback with a trading expedition and time is of the essence. There should be thirty thousand astra in the account and I need at least fifteen of it."

"Mestere—"

"I'm in a hurry."

Gulping, the clerk laid his hands on the table instead of pulling out his ledger. "I'm sorry, but Mestere Geoffre di Prinze put a freeze on those funds before he died. Which the new Householder has maintained."

He'd left the money with the Sere in order not to alert his father to his revolutionary intentions, but he'd thought he'd hidden it well enough that he'd eventually be able to gain access to it...

Oh, Devid, you bastard.

His hands shook. "Those funds belong to *me*. *I* raised them with my own ships, trading in salt."

"I'm sorry, mestere, but until we have word from the Prinze Householder—"

"Devid isn't the official Householder! He hasn't been installed in the Circle; he's not in possession of the sword—"

"The prior Householder's wishes take precedence until the new Householder can be properly installed."

Cassis's temper snapped. "The hell they do," he growled and unthinkingly put a hand on his sword.

The moment he touched steel, the room came alive with gavaros. The clerk's chair clattered as the clerk stood up, scabbards thumped and hissed as men loosened their blades, and hands grabbed at his tunic. He tried to twist away, thrusting his palms up to show he meant no harm, but a gavaro grabbed his arm and wrenched it behind his back. Another man seized his other arm, and suddenly, he was bent over in the middle of the marble-tiled, gold-trimmed Sere counting house like a common criminal.

"But I've only come to claim what's mine!" he gasped.

"Mestere Cassis di Prinze, you're under arrest by the order of the Head of your House."

CHAPTER 24

ARSENAULT

FARMHOUSE, PRESENT

CORPSE SHIP IGNITES MOB

Late yesterday Evening, Lookouts from the Armory spied a Ship floating toward the Lagoon with a splintered Main Mast, quickly identified as Cassis di Prinze's Ship, the Hind. *Upon boarding, Officials smelled such a Stench that they immediately took Steps to protect themselves from vengeful Spirits. The Crew had all been killed and left in a Pile to rot in the empty Hold. Assumed at first to be the work of Dakkaran Pirates, a Prinze Seal was found near the Captain's mutilated Body, which identified the Murderer as none other than Renzo di Prinze himself.*

The growing Empirist faction in the city has used the Corpse Ship as evidence that a stronger, more unified Eterea is necessary not only to protect Shipping and consolidate control of the Dakkaran Weapons Trade, making it harder for our Neighbors to acquire both Guns and Powder, but for the survival of Liera itself. Protests against Prinze control of Prices turned violent yesterday when two Officials were stoned in the Day Market. The leaders of the Mob were hanged as Cassis di Prinze's Ship was set alight in the Lagoon to lay its Ghosts to rest. It sank quickly and now lies at the bottom of the Sea, guarding the Gate to Paupers' Island...

ARSENAULT SLAMMED THE BROADSHEET DOWN ON THE COMMON room table. "Dammit, Jon! What are you doing? This is you, not Renzo, isn't it?" The raven that had brought it squawked and danced away from him, talons skittering across the wooden surface. Kyrra, sitting in a chair next to the table, eyed the bird as fearfully as it regarded him.

Jon barely looked up from the letters he was reading, a pair of spectacles with half lenses perched on the end of his nose. "Cassis di Prinze was not supposed to be alive. We could have dealt with Devid on his own, but Devid fighting Cassis is a different matter. We can't let Cassis have a shipment of guns, but my designs for them are different than you think."

Kyrra put down the broadsheet she was trying awkwardly to keep open next to a steaming cup of tea. Before the raven had come, she'd spent the longest time yet working her left arm in sword forms. Her lucid times were lengthening as her body grew stronger, but he was still nervous having one of Jon's ravens next to her, and he could see she was, too. A lot of news was coming out of Liera these days. Jon had decided to spend more time controlling his underground empire from here while he kept an eye on Cassis at the lodge. Or waited for Miranda to come back—his true reason for staying, Arsenault suspected.

Either was fine with Arsenault. He wanted Jon where he could see him. Kyrra might be growing stronger, but he wasn't sure that meant she was getting *well*. He felt like he was constantly rebuffed in his search for the information that would help her by his own mind, a hunk of dead metal, the wily twisting of a force nobody *really* understood, and Jon's godsdamned political scheming.

"And you'd still rather have Devid than Cassis?" Kyrra asked.

"I'd rather have neither Devid or Cassis," Jon replied. "I don't trust either of them to be good for Dakkar, or even tolerable. Mikelo should be in that seat, but he needs time."

Arsenault leaned back in his chair and rubbed his eyes. "Let's hope to the gods Mikelo doesn't find that godsdamned clipping. He's not ready for Renzo the Bloodthirsty Pirate either."

One benefit to the way Mikelo was avoiding him lately—he wasn't here for this. Arsenault didn't know where he was; he blundered through every magical protection Arsenault had laid on the place as if he didn't even notice them. It was maddening.

Kyrra gave him a look. "Don't you think Mikelo deserves to know the truth about Renzo, even if it's ugly? The worst thing about being a householder is how many people want to keep you in the dark. You start to feel like all your relationships are simply 'strategies.' *Are* you faking this, Jon? *Is* Renzo a bloodthirsty pirate?"

Jon regarded her for a moment. Then he put the letter down, like he'd decided doling out some information would be acceptable, the bastard. "My sister has a large network of privateers. They've been preying on Prinze shipping for the past five years. Sometimes we use the cargo, sometimes we store it. Most of the time we sell it and bank the coin."

"With the Sere?"

"In Vençal. Safer to move it that way. The Sere say they're neutral, but you know now that Tonia was following Geoffre's wishes when she hired you to kill Cassis."

Kyrra tapped the table in front of her cup like she was thinking. Arsenault had watched her make the same motions with her right hand when she'd been Kyris, all those little habits he'd never seen because she'd had no right hand when he'd known her. She stopped tapping, turned the cup around, slid her fingers backward through the handle, and took a drink. Even her smallest actions took more thought and time since she was back to using only her left hand.

"But it is true that Driese di Caprine, Tonia's sister, was with Cassis," Kyrra said. "Cassis told me he'd sent her away because she was already far gone with child. Tonia must have wanted Driese back in the fold any way she could."

"I think you ascribe higher motives to Tonia," Arsenault replied wearily. His life as Andris had seemed to be divided between Cassis humiliating him and Jon asking him to cozy up to powerful women, who used him for their own purposes—Tonia as a tool, Triente as a status symbol. Tonia, at least, had been strictly focused on business. "I worked for her for weeks, following you. Her father-in-law, the Sere Householder, is getting old, his son—her brother-in-law—is a fool and likes to squander their fortune. But Tonia..."

"Geoffre killed Tonia's husband so he could possess the sole claim to the monopoly on guns and kacin. She threw me to Geoffre because I was a necessary sacrifice to get her sister back. If she could also use me as a bargaining chip to get rid of the Prinze, so much the better."

"I don't think the other Houses have thought through what will happen if a Sere who knows how to leverage their position controls the Chair," Jon said. "We've contacted the Sere, of course—I have accounts with them—but we'd be fools to rely on them. I've stashed coin for Adayze in every country and Eterean city. Geoffre knew he hadn't gotten rid of all the royal B'ara when he hit Mdembu. He tried to chase the funds. That's why we used so many dummy accounts. Fortunately, now we have a network. I can trace the coin that comes in from that gun shipment on the black market."

"Why do you need to trace the coin?" Arsenault asked. "You don't want Cassis to have it, but you'll let the highest bidder take it—on the theory that anyone who buys black market guns is anti-Prinze?"

"It's not a bad assumption, but—no. Guns have been moving on the market lately. That's why the Prinze were cracking down—why they sent a whole contingent of guards, including Andris, for a simple dikkarro sale to a common gavaro like you, Kyris. The problem is we don't know where they're going."

"Cassis had to get his guns somewhere, didn't he?" Kyrra asked, not even stopping when Jon used her male name. It was an uncomfortable reminder that she and Jon had a whole history he wasn't privy to. "Didn't Arsenault know what you were doing with the coin?"

"*Andris* didn't know what we were doing with the coin," Jon pointed out and Kyrra frowned.

She ran her thumb up the handle of the teacup and took a broody drink, like she was digesting everything Jon had implied by using the name *Andris*. Andris hadn't been privy to important secrets because Andris had been drinking himself to death, and Jon knew it. Did Kyrra? Or was she figuring that out now?

"Cassis ordered most of his guns through legal channels, then diverted them," Arsenault offered. "He kept Geoffre in the dark a long time, looking like he was just doing what he was supposed to do."

Kyrra put her cup down. "You still haven't answered my question, Jon. *Is* Renzo a bloodthirsty pirate? Did he hit Cassis's ship to run a ruse for you, or is he really setting up to fight Devid and Cassis for the Chair?"

"All I can tell you is that we're in possession of some of Cassis's guns. We're curious to see where they go and where the coin to buy them comes from. We need to know if there is another player in this game. Cassis's Empirists, perhaps?"

Gods, the Empirists. "They were all on Geoffre's side," Arsenault said roughly. "The money will probably lead back to the Sere, who won't tell you anything because it violates all their contracts."

"Well." Jon picked up his letter again. "We shall see."

Kyrra sighed and picked up her broadsheet, too. "I feel like we need one of those Hamari gameboards to keep track of all these moves. The one they call the Game of Kings. Except perhaps we should rename it the Game of Queens."

"I think too many people involved see all this politicking as a game." Arsenault shoved himself off the couch. He had to pace this anger out or he was going to explode. He didn't have anywhere to go, so maybe he'd just collect his tools and fix that damn leak that kept *dripping dripping dripping* in the background. It was driving him mad, but he couldn't find any water in the house. "That was the whole problem with the wars: None of the Householders in charge were on the ground dying beside their men. It's not just toy soldiers."

Jon angrily tore the spectacles from his face. "You think I don't know that, ghost? How many wars have I fought on the ground? Some of them were beside you! Ask Kyris where I was for the last one!"

Arsenault stopped, brought up short by this second, instinctive use of Kyrra's male name, the unknown past shoving its way into the present again, just like Renzo killing an entire ship's crew and leaving them for Cassis to find like a—like a—

Gods, the memories of pirates. He swiped his hand across his eyes, wishing he could wipe them away. When he put his hand down, all he could see was another memory overlaid on Kyrra's firelit face as she looked, troubled, between them, the broadsheet crinkled and forgotten. Watching her swagger into The Lady and the Vine as Kyris, her glittering Rojornicki black and silver making her face seem like winter. *His* face. Kyris was a different person, a person he hardly knew.

Kyrra took a deep breath and the present settled precariously into place again. "It's hard to explain what it's like to be a householder. Perhaps I did feel like life was a game when I was young, and that was why I got into trouble. But all our generations have seen war. In my father's childhood, Liera and Amora were fighting over control of the bay. Peace never lasts more than a few years. It begins to seem like something you only read about in ancient books. It doesn't cost anyone anything to keep doing more violence. It feels safe, in an odd way. Familiar. Laying down weapons, forgetting old feuds, making a true peace... That costs much more."

HOW HAD HE BEEN PART OF THESE SCHEMING CIRCLES FOR SO LONG? He knew the answer before he asked it, but it didn't make him less angry. The three scars on his right palm flashed at him mutely as he pulled on a pair of fingerless gloves Miranda must have knitted for her husband—another man he hadn't been able to save. His scars and promises were all tangled together now, impossible to honor one without violating another. He was making inroads into recovering his memories and figuring out that dragon limb, but not fast enough if these damn Lierans were poised to tear apart their city and the surrounding countryside. *Again*.

Did it ever end?

He tried not to think about it as he walked to the shed to haul out the ladder and then a bucket, which he began to fill with rocks—thin, rectangular chunks of shale that had weathered out of the hillside behind the farm. They were cold and slick in the mist, and his fingertips soon grew raw and numb. At least patching the leak in the roof gave him something to do. He was spending too much time in his head lately, running the mystery of that limb through his mind over and over.

For Kyrra. That's all.

Because Jon was wrong and they might come to a moment where she needed the metal, any metal, but also because he was right and the damn limb might be too dangerous for her. It still only spoke to him in tantalizing, frightening whispers. He'd need access to an excellent library and a lot of time in order to run down its origins without using Sight, if that was even possible. Though the Etereans *had* been compulsive record keepers, and there was always Oji la Kaif.

Miranda owned a modest library, which was a little odd for a mountain farmer, but he wasn't one to question a gift horse. A reproduction of la Kaif's most popular *Travels* with mediocre illustrations resided on her shelves, along with a collection of the major Vençalan poets of the last several decades, a thick tome containing the stories of the gods, and *On Agriculture* by Haurans, which assumed the kind of warm, lowland fields Miranda and her family didn't have and must have been acquired only for curiosity's sake.

None of those were much help. He'd given into the temptation to look himself up in the book of the gods, but it was something to realize his whole story with Sella merited a single sentence: *The goddess hid herself in Tule as the wife of a Smith who had pledged to discover True Beauty, not knowing he already possessed it, and in a fit of jealousy killed her and was cast out, to wander the world forever.*

To wander the world forever. He had a thing or two to say to the author about thinking he'd ever "possessed" Sella, but hopefully his reprieve also meant his wandering might one day come to an end. He didn't want to look ahead to what would happen when he died again, but if he couldn't figure out what the magic was doing with Kyrra, what he'd done to her in giving her that arm...

Though it was enough just to have a second chance to *be* with her again, she deserved more. He knew she could live life perfectly well with only one arm, but he wasn't going to give up until they had come to her *best* life. And fuck all those scheming Houses.

He hauled the bucket—heavy now—to the side of the house by their bedroom window and set the ladder against the rock wall as firmly as he could. As he began to climb, footsteps scuffed behind him. Kyrra, hunched up in a quilt, looking miserable and frustrated in the drizzle.

"Why are you out here?" he asked, exasperated.

"You're not planning to climb on that roof in the rain, are you?"

Arsenault eyed the pitch of the roof. Even the ladder was slick now. The water in the air couldn't properly be called *mist* or *fog*, even by him. It sluiced down the back of his neck and soaked his shirt inside his cloak, which felt increasingly heavy and wet on his shoulders. At least the rain was dousing his anger. But now he was committed to fixing the damn roof.

"I can't find the leak if it's not raining," he said. "But I can't figure out where it is. It seems like I can hear water dripping everywhere in the house, but it's never dripping on my head. Maybe there's more than one leak."

"Well, hurry up then. It's cold and wet and I'm not going back in without you. Somebody needs to make sure you don't slip and break your neck." She looked like she wanted to fold her arms over her chest, but of course she couldn't, not while holding the quilt on her shoulders, so she just gave him a stubborn blue glare.

He was in it now and they were both wet, so he could at least look at the bloody roof. He climbed up a few more rungs and decided to risk a little magic, just to get this over with quickly. A tendril eased out of him, seeking flecks and veins of ore in the huge slabs of shale that formed the roof. There were little bits of pyrite, a lot of mica, a tiny, surprising deposit of copper over the eaves by their bedroom, but—

"If it's not dripping on your head, maybe you're just imagining it," she said.

"Is there an attic somewhere?"

"J-just the loft—"

"Kyrra, go back inside before you catch your death."

"So will you. Is...is that smoke or mist in the distance?"

He squeezed off the thin trickle of magic that continued to spread over the shale like a spider web. The slabs wanted to be a whole and tight roof. They had been a roof for many hundreds of years, back into Eterean times, but there was indeed a leak. Something didn't match up... The roof seemed too big for the house, and yet it wasn't. He wiped water from his eyes to see better.

"I think it's smoke..." she said uncertainly.

Smoke. The word brought him back to the moment. White smoke rolled out of both chimneys, lifting in puffs through the rain-soaked air like smudges of paint on canvas. No smoke anywhere else; the runes he'd set on a wide perimeter seemed to be keeping Geoffre's gavaros away well enough for now, but he hadn't let down his guard.

Kyrra shivered, clutching the blanket around her shoulders to keep it from sliding off. Damn—*magic*. The smoke was a vision. A troubling vision if it was on the horizon or down in the valley with the lodge.

He climbed down the ladder and pulled the soggy blanket forward, so it rested more securely on her shoulders. "Go in. I'll follow you soon."

"You'll stay out here in the rain until you've filled every tiny gap, and then you'll come down with fever and ague. Are you really attempting a new life so close on the heels of the last one?"

"All right," he sighed. "You win. There's a big space between the windows on that wall..."

His voice trailed away as he stared at the wall. It was surely bigger on the outside than it was on the inside, which would account for the larger expanse of roof...but that would mean there was a hidden room and the leak was inside it.

"Kyrra," he said excitedly, grabbing her right elbow in his haste. "Come on, let's go in."

"Now you're in a hurry?"

"I think I figured out the mystery of the leak."

❧

He tromped back into the house, shedding water and mud all over the floor. He hung up his dripping cloak on a peg and Kyrra's sopping quilt beside it, then grabbed her by the hand and pulled her through the common room, passing a surprised Jon on the way.

"What are you doing, ghost?"

"Fixing a leak."

Kyrra was shuddering by the time they reached the bedroom. Arsenault deposited her in the rocking chair, yanked a dry blanket off the bed, and tucked it around her. "Now. Try to keep track of where your hand is, your fingers, your feet. Your...nose maybe, I don't know."

"My nose?" she asked in confusion.

"I'm just looking for something you'll remember. I'll have to use magic. If I'm right, there's a room behind this wall somewhere—"

"Like a safe room?"

"I don't know why I didn't think of it before. Eterean houses were often built with heart rooms. They stored objects associated with the *heart* of the family, like—"

"Votas? We had a room like that in the villa. Behind my father's study. He kept our House seals in it, the deed to the land, the genealogy scroll that proved our House descended from Attrasca…" She rose, trailing the blanket behind her, and joined him as he pressed his fingers into the grout, searching for cracks, runes, depressions— anything. She smelled of rain and damp leaves, and when she looked up at him, he realized he had been watching her instead of the wall.

"Have I said something odd?" she asked, brows pinched in confusion. "I accidentally trapped myself in that room once, you know. It was hours before the servants found me. Felt like every ghost in the house was huddled right behind me in the pitch dark."

"That sounds awful. How old were you?"

"Eight, nine. You know, if you keep looking at me like that, I'm going to wonder if you really did want to come in here to fix a leak."

The cold of the rain disappeared in the warmth of her eyes and the small smile playing at the corner of her mouth. He gave her his own crooked smile and went back to pressing on the wall. "It ought to be here somewhere, I think, but I may have to feel it out by matching it up with what I felt on the roof."

"I didn't know magic was useful for home repairs."

"Well. If you know what you're doing."

He pushed his thumb on a crack in the mortar, but nothing budged. "Dammit—"

She moved closer to the wardrobe that stood down the wall, near his war chest, which he hadn't known Jon had stashed here. Her expression grew vaguely thoughtful. She let the blanket drop and then—

It kept happening lately, that the magic didn't seem to move through her or him or Mikelo, but just appeared, as if it twisted up out of the earth and sought the easiest course, like a stream of water. He and Mikelo weren't easy, but Kyrra was, and so—

Dozens of glowing magic marks suddenly appeared on the wall. He hadn't used any magic and she hadn't moved, but there they were, hundreds of years of Fixers scribbling over each other to keep the room hidden. He'd been so preoccupied, so exhausted and injured for the past few weeks—so focused on Kyrra—that he hadn't realized how much magic was in the godsdamned *room* with them. The locks had piled up over so many years with the same intentions from so many people that they'd become practically invisible. It was like the magic was tired of waiting on him to figure it out and had decided to take matters into its own hands.

"Arsenault," Kyrra breathed. "What is it? They're not runes, are they?"

"No," he said, bringing himself back to the moment. "They're not all runes." Trying to read the marks was like trying to read a manuscript written on a piece of scraped vellum, where the old writing was still faintly visible beneath the new words.

And the new words...

Damn. He recognized some of them.

"Jon!" he bellowed. He left a bewildered Kyrra in the room and threw himself through the door into the hall, almost running into Jon, who was standing outside the door, startled. "*You* hid this room! Those are Dakkaran locks, with runes beneath them! What were you hiding? What kind of house are we in?"

Jon put his hands on Arsenault's shoulders. "Calm down, ghost. I'll open them for you if you like, but it didn't seem like the time—"

"You've been hiding an awful lot from me lately, Jon."

"You weren't ready for it. Trust me when I say I was just trying to keep you safe."

Arsenault flung out his arm angrily. "What's in that room then?"

Jon set his lips in a tight line. Then he pushed past Arsenault into the room. He looked down at Kyrra, who was uncharacteristically quiet, staring up at him with wide eyes—maybe still in the grip of the magic, which buzzed franticly around the room, as if it was tugging at their coats to get their attention.

Jon put both hands on the wall. The marks slithered and spun like snakes unwinding their bodies.

"Hah!" Kyrra crowed in victory. "I knew you had more magic than you said you did, Jon. All those battles, always in just the right place at the right time."

Jon flicked a sour glance at her, then grunted as the door slid back, revealing a room the size of Miranda's pantry. The drip-drip-drip was louder now and it smelled musty, like...

Kyrra coughed, a great, soupy, rattling, cough. "Wet books," she gasped.

"Damn," Jon cursed. "Damn! This is where the leak is?"

Arsenault shouldered his way into the room. The dim shapes of chests and crates greeted him, stacked against the far wall, but also shelves of scrolls and books. He moved closer for a better look, trailed his finger over a spine that was splashed with the water trickling through a gap in the beams. A leatherbound book, stitched with gut, just the right size to fit in the inside pocket of a cloak.

Comprehension struck him like a fist. He stared at the shelf, dumbfounded.

"My books," he breathed. "From the Villa."

Kyrra looked at him, astonished.

"When you asked me to keep an eye on Kyrra in Rojornick, you said no one could know she was alive. You gave me all your books to hide," Jon explained wearily. "I knew if I gave them back and you learned everything about who you had been, eventually Cassis and Geoffre would weasel everything out of you. I hid the books in a safe room in Liera at first, but after we got involved with Cassis, I didn't trust Geoffre not to search the house. And I was right. It was broken into at least three times with nothing of value stolen."

"So, Miranda knows..."

"We used this house as a stop on the smuggling ring out of Rojornick. During the war, this room stored powder and arms—what I could get to you anyway. Miranda doesn't know your books are yours; as you can see, I brought them in with many other manuscripts."

"How old are these, Jon?" Kyrra asked as she pulled a thick leather and gilt volume off the shelf. The cover was styled with intricate golden Qalfan designs, closed like an envelope with a leaf that folded over. She put it down on a trunk and opened it carefully.

A faded crimson dragon greeted them, twisted horns rising from its head like those of an ibex, feathers painted in exquisite detail—but the paint had burned a hole in the paper over the years, as if the dragon had charred it with its fiery breath.

"It's Oji la Kaif's *Journey to the Dragon Isles*," Kyrra said in surprise. "My tutor didn't even think this book existed. He said it was apocryphal."

"Your tutor's education was lacking. Oji wrote many more books than are credited to him, but an astute collector can search them out."

"It's about Medeas," Arsenault said suddenly. "The island. Medeas was full of dragons."

"You're saying that as if you remember," Kyrra said.

"I...suppose I do." Images of dragons—too painful to even think about, what the world had lost. What *he* had lost. He began pulling his own books off the shelf. One, two, three...six books in total. Three for his years at the villa with Kyrra. Three for the war.

Seeing his lost memories made physical kicked him in the gut the way it always did. He took his six books out of the small, musty room —six years of his life—placed them carefully on the bed, then opened the one on top randomly, to the middle.

Kyrra let out an involuntary gasp. "It's my arm! You used to write and draw at night in the candlelight. You were drawing sketches of my arm?"

He glanced down at her, amused. "You didn't think I'd cast something I attached to your body on a whim, did you? Just toss it off freehand?"

"I suppose I never thought too much about how you made it. I don't know how magic works, but the date on that, Arsenault. I didn't know you worked on it for so *long*."

"First I had to track down all the tiaannamir. I knew I could find worked metal because there's a lot of old Eterean stuff floating around the curiosities and antiquities markets. Finding an unworked ingot in the Day Market that day we ran from Cassis, though—that was a stroke of luck. I returned to question the vendor about his source, but he made me go through a lot of middlemen."

All the sketches of Kyrra from another time tugged at his heart— burrowed into it was maybe a better description, a sweet, sore ache. He tried to talk through it. "I thought I'd made your arm entirely from unworked metal, but this confirms it. See? A list. Eighteen ingots. A fortunate number. Two nines, six threes."

"*Eighteen* ingots?" Jon exclaimed.

"You paid a whole astra for one small ingot," Kyrra said. "How much did the whole arm cost?"

"The price didn't matter. I had a lot of back pay coming to me."

Jon frowned. "You mean coin my sister owed you?"

"Yes, I suppose. Now that I have my notes and my memories, I'll be able to make more progress." He turned to smile at Kyrra, but she was still studying his book, stunned.

"Progress," she murmured. Her gaze skated over a sketch of her arm that filled a full page, orientation palm out and open, dimensions all question-marked, notes about the casting process at the top.

"Progress in Fixing your arm," he elaborated. "Without hurting you. Surely, I wrote down the origin of all the ingots, what I Saw in them... I think I was able to get most of them from the same source..."

"You Saw something in the metal you used for my arm? Before you worked it?"

"It was unworked tiaannamir, which meant it came straight from the old gods. I told you that the metal absorbs character from the uses to which it's put. Far safer to use unworked tiaannamir than something already given a Shape."

Like that damn dragon limb he'd hidden in the abandoned forge. It wasn't like he had a choice, though, and anyway, he wouldn't use it if it turned out to be evil. It didn't *feel* like evil, but... He just wished everything was clearer. He needed more time.

"I thought the Shape already existed inside the metal. And you just pulled it out."

"That's...almost true. I had to get around the proscription on my magic, so I saved it for the very end and cast your arm like I was making a sculpture, using a lost wax mold. Then I pulled out the metal in you and the magic in the arm and made them one." He stopped to check her reaction; she was frowning slightly. "Very few things have only one Shape," he went on. "Like a person who can be many things at once—good, evil, angry, joyful, sorrowful, dutiful, irreverent. If I take an ingot of tiaannamir and Look inside it, it might embody courage, duty, love, vengeance, and hatred. The old gods were all those things. Pure magic."

Monsters. Heroes.

Dragons.

The slight frown grew deeper. "So, if that's true...what did you See inside the metal you used to make my arm? Am I trying to change it to be more like me or is it trying to change me to become more like it?"

"That's the question, isn't it," he replied softly.

"Does the mold still exist?"

"No, the technique destroys the mold in the process of casting. I could have made another mold to copy the arm after I cast it, but... that would have assumed that if you damaged your arm, I would have to cut it off and start over. You're not a statue; we've been through this before."

"And there would have been a mold for me to hide," Jon said grimly. "Which there wasn't, and I thank you for that, ghost. Keeping an eye on the arm attached to her body was enough."

Kyrra looked up at Jon sourly. "You make it sound as if you were my bodyguard. We didn't even fight for the same lord."

"Nor on the same side after a while. But by that point, we had a common intention that overrode promises I had made to someone in a different life."

Jon was looking pointedly at him. Arsenault tried not to think about why—tried not to let memories of Geoffre and Kafrin flood back in. A droplet of water splashed onto the open paper, which he hastily wiped away with his cuff. He looked up into the darkness of the ceiling, searching for bright gaps in the beams and roof. "I'll have to repair that quick, there's so much water—"

Kyrra suddenly frowned. "Where are Mikelo and Silva? Why aren't they here with us?"

Arsenault stopped and looked at Jon, who seemed to be thinking the same thing he was. "He's probably just out again. I'm trying to give him time. But why notice now, Kyrra? Is there something—"

"About water," she murmured, staring up at the shiny silver beads lacing the ceiling beam. One began to detach itself from the rest, clinging for a last, long instant. "There's something about water..."

Then the drop of water fell and Kyrra collapsed into his arms with it.

CHAPTER 25

MIKELO

FARMHOUSE, PRESENT

WHY THE HELLS COULDN'T RENZO HAVE STAYED DEAD?

The woods behind the house were damp with mist as Mikelo trudged blindly up the slippery, rocky slope. The few runes Arsenault had dared lay around the perimeter buzzed at him as he passed through; they were tightly controlled, and Mikelo wondered what it would feel like if Arsenault ever truly let his magic go. He found he wanted it a little, perversely—to break the man's iron grip on himself, to make Arsenault shout back at him.

The path climbed hundreds of feet in a short span. Snow still lay in thin scars over the fallen fir needles and gold and brown beech leaves. By the time he reached the top, his breath puffed out in white clouds that disappeared quickly into the icy fog. A strange peace reigned here, a hush that seemed to exist only in this spot. The fog muffled the steady drip of melting ice, the otherworldly call of a bird, the gurgle of the stream that rushed down the slope.

He'd discovered the little clearing early in their stay when he'd just needed to be in a place without blood and pain for a few moments, to remember there was still a world outside the walls of the house. The clearing was a good place to look for the low-growing, silver-green plant Miranda's book said made a good wound salve. It grew around the foundation of a small cabin in the trees that was falling to rot. He pushed some leaves aside with his boot and studied the wet leaf litter for signs of the plant. It was better than rolling thoughts about Renzo around and around, like a wheel.

His father's absence had always felt like a giant hole in his life. It was as if someone had begun building a house but had left one wall permanently unfinished. No matter what he tried, nothing helped; there were no magical runes, no sorcerous protections that would make the structure sound.

A twig cracked and someone cursed. Mikelo gripped the hilt of his sword and whirled around, heart hammering, expecting to see gavaros —*why didn't I tell anyone where I was going? I'm an idiot...*

A golden-brown head appeared over the crest of the hill, dark with damp, and a hand gripped a wet tree branch. Mikelo let out his breath; it was just Silva. He was wearing a heavy wool cloak, but he looked almost as miserable as Mikelo felt—curls bedraggled and wet, face flushed with the cold.

"It's hard to keep up with you when you're running away," Silva said, breathing hard as he walked into the clearing.

"I'm not running away."

"Well, that's good." Silva came to stand beside him in the middle of the clearing, shoved his hands into his pockets, and looked around. "I was getting a little tired of being stuck in there with Arsenault and Kyrra acting like lovebirds."

Mikelo blinked at him stupidly for a moment before he realized the corner of Silva's mouth was twitching upward and that he was joking.

"You're an ass," Mikelo told him.

"You're an easy mark. Were you looking for something?"

"I needed time to think. Can't I be alone for a while?"

He immediately wished he could call the words back. He sounded like a whinging child.

Silva breathed out heavily. His breath rolled over his head in a cloud, but it didn't hide the way his face dragged downward. "I'm just trying to be your friend, Mikelo."

Friend. A strange warmth fluttered inside him, followed quickly by a guilty flush. "Pardon, Silva. I...I've never had many friends. No one wanted much to do with the son of the local whore."

Silva scowled at the ground. "I suppose that would be a reason. I'll just leave now, shall I?"

Mikelo, you idiot. Silva used to be the local whore.

"No!" Mikelo shouted as Silva turned to go. He had wanted to be alone, but only for a moment; he didn't want to drive Silva away from him, too. "Stay. It's-it's all right."

"You're ashamed of your mother, that's easy to tell. Maybe it also makes you ashamed to keep company with me."

Mikelo shoved his fingers into his hair in frustration, accidentally pulling some strands out of the tail that wasn't doing much to keep them back in the first place. He surprised himself with a helpless laugh. What a mess he must look.

"Yes. I am ashamed of my mother. I'm ashamed of being ashamed. She had a hard life. But sometimes… She just forgot about me. Not like she was preoccupied; she forgot I needed to eat. When she'd had too much kacin."

Silva's expression transformed from wariness to horror. "So, you didn't have a father, and you barely had a mother." He stepped toward Mikelo, his hand out to touch him. Mikelo panicked. It had taken bravery just to say the words and now Silva wanted to *touch* him? He'd come here to get a grip on his emotions, not to wrestle with all these brand-new ones.

He jerked away in reflex and caught his toe on something hidden in the leaves. Before he knew it, he was falling. He shoved his hands out to catch himself and when he picked himself up, blood smeared his fingertip.

Silva stood over him, studying him in exasperation. "Mikelo. Are you hurt?"

"No, I'm—"

Silva slid his hand under Mikelo's armpit and hauled him upright. At least this touch was firm and necessary. He looked down at the ground to see what he'd tripped on.

"Dear gods."

"What is it now?" Silva asked angrily. "You don't want me to help you up?"

"No… Silva, I think I know why this clearing feels the way it does. Look."

Silva, his arm still locked around Mikelo's, glanced down. "A gravestone!" Then he stared in alarm at Mikelo's hand. A thin trickle of blood snaked down Mikelo's finger. He could barely feel it, but Silva suddenly squeezed his hand tightly, hiding the blood.

"Don't bleed on the bones, for the gods' sake! The magic in your blood—you don't know how they died!"

"That's just a superstition." Mikelo pulled out of Silva's grasp, relieved to have an excuse. The gravestone he'd tripped on was small, just a rough gray rectangle sunk into the ground. Near it another gray corner peeked out of the leaf cover. Mikelo kicked the leaves away, revealing another gravestone. He kept kicking and discovered another right next to it. And a fourth, at the edge of the clearing.

Mikelo absentmindedly sucked the blood away from his finger. In Dakkar, they told stories of ghost-criminals who devoured the living to regain their lost kin ties. His Eterean mother had told him other stories about ghosts—men bent on revenge, who were denied the underworld or refused it, choosing instead to wander ceaselessly.

He bent to read the gravestones. "*Anna, Gino's daughter.* Gods. Just a little girl. Died of fever during the last war with Amora. Two more children, and damn, here's the mother. It looks like they all received the correct treatment, though. We haven't disturbed any graves."

"What do you call this?" Leaves rustled as Silva kicked at the ground. Something dull yellow and hard appeared in the black humus.

"A man's leg bone," Mikelo said in surprise.

The bones were scattered, as if animals had gotten to the body. The skull rested some distance away, tucked unnoticed into the hollow of a beech tree, the jaw unhinged and covered in dirt.

"So, they all sickened with the plague passed on by the fighting," Mikelo said slowly, putting the story together in his mind. "One by one he buried his family. Then, there was no one left to bury him."

"If he died up here with them, maybe we're safe. They could guide him to the underworld. Otherwise..." Silva raised his head and squinted down the path. "Don't you think this is a bad omen?"

Maybe it was a bad omen, but Mikelo couldn't find it in him to be afraid of a man who had died in such sorrowful circumstances. For such a man, all he felt was pity.

He began gathering rocks to build a cairn, but Silva wouldn't let him touch the bones. Silva put them in a pile next to the woman's grave. He and Silva were both sweating with exertion even in the wet cold before the cairn was partially formed.

"Kyrra would understand," Silva mumbled. "She grew up in the north. She knows about murder markers and omens."

"You sound like one of those old Eterean soothsayers. All we need is a deer liver."

Silva flung his hand out angrily. "Why don't you find out for sure then? Use your magic to see what happened. Just don't bleed on any bones. My uncle once stumbled across a whole line of murder markers east of the Villa d'Aliente. Before he could drive the sheep away, a pack of huge black wolves surrounded them. One grabbed a lamb and tore open its throat on top of a murder marker. The blood poured into the ground and a dead man rose out of it. A Forza, with a big knife slice across his neck. He turned to my uncle and said—"

"This will be a good way to scare your nephew when you tell the story around the bonfire?"

"Shut up, Mikelo, and let me finish. He said, *We were all killed here by trickery. Help avenge us by seeking out our killer!"*

"And you don't think your uncle told that story so no one would make him pay for the sheep?"

"The sheep's throat was torn out. It was definitely killed by a wolf."

Mikelo scratched the stubble on his cheek. "That was sheep blood, though, and Ires had something to prove, whatever it was. It doesn't mean anything will happen if I bleed on these graves."

"It doesn't mean it won't. After the past few weeks, why is it so hard to believe a god—maybe Fortune herself—is warning you to be cautious?"

Mikelo let his gaze sweep over the little graveyard that had suddenly sprung up in the very place he went to think. At the man who had buried his entire family one by one, then died alone.

What was it like to be Renzo, the man who had abandoned his family, leaving them to the ravages of history—kacin, poverty, illness, murder? What was it like to be Arsenault, the man who buried everyone?

He sighed. "Would it make you feel better if I did try to See? I can't promise you anything. But we ought to be far enough from Kyrra that I shouldn't cause her any problems."

Silva's jaw twitched. "If it will convince you to be more careful, please do."

"All right." Mikelo let his breath out. "Let's move over here by the stream so I can sit down." He arranged himself cross-legged on a flat rock. It was wet, but the cold seeping into the fabric of his trousers gave him a hook to concentrate on. He let his awareness spread from the dampness into the pockets of moss and lichen growing in the grooves of the big limestone boulder, the skeletal fingers of beech branches rattling above him. The beeches were nearly ready to bud. Sap flowed sluggishly up from the roots...

I don't need to know what's happening with the plants, he thought in exasperation, but then realized—if he wanted to know about the people who'd died here, he needed to feel his way into them just as he had with the trees. Except they were bones and decaying flesh buried in the soil, beetles and worms crawling over, tunneling through—

He opened his eyes with a gasp, hoping to see Silva, there to rescue him as usual.

Instead, a man stood before him. But it wasn't the man who had died.

It was Geoffre.

CHAPTER 26

MIKELO

GEOFFRE'S MOUTH CURVED UPWARD IN THAT COLD SMILE MIKELO remembered only too well. But now a starburst scar marred his forehead from the gunshot wound that had killed him. His silver hair fell over it, in a way it wouldn't have in life. Mikelo had never seen him with a single hair out of place.

"Hello, Mikelo."

Mikelo tried to force himself to breathe normally. *It's just a vision. It's not really happening.*

Dammit, Mikelo, you fucking goatherder, you don't have to sit through this!

Kyrra's voice again—or was the magic trying to sound like Kyrra on purpose?

"How is that harlot?" Geoffre asked.

"She's not a harlot," Mikelo answered and cursed himself for the way his voice quavered. "You're just a vengeful, jealous, dead man, upset you failed your god."

"So, you've some fire in your belly after all."

"Leave me alone."

"We're blood, Mikelo, linked by family and magic. You're a Prinze, and you'll do whatever needs to be done."

"I will. I'll rid this House of your vile ways and everything you've touched."

Geoffre shook his head mournfully. "Go ahead and hate me, but I won't have my sons burning our House down. I raised you better than to take part in petty posturing. You're more *powerful* than that, Mikelo."

"I just heal people."

"You Fix flesh, Mikelo. That's different than healing."

"It's wrong to use it—"

"For your House? To stop Devid giving Liera up, and Renzo and Cassis battling over guns, and Cassis mooning over every Caprine tart who walks by?"

Mikelo gritted his teeth. "Some things shouldn't be done."

"Even if doing them could stop a war?"

"My talents aren't enough to stop a war. I'm *one* person, and not even that important. I can Fix holes in people; how does that translate to diplomacy?"

"It doesn't translate to diplomacy. It translates to intimidation. It translates to ascendance. If you knelt before the right gods, think what they could do with your gifts. What kinds of creatures you could create. You could be the next Attrasca."

"Me, Attrasca?" Mikelo laughed.

"Why not? Think how much advantage a ruler could gain using Sight alone."

"Arsenault says if you use magic too often, it will wash you away in the end. It's eating Kyrra up."

"That's because Kyrra is nothing, just a conduit. The gods use her because she happens to be in the right place at the right time. As soon as they're through with her, they'll throw her away. She's a pawn, just as she's always been. But think about all the things *you* could do. Wouldn't your health be a worthy sacrifice to achieve such noble ends?"

Healing diseases. Helping the kinless. Ending all these godsdamned wars.

Wasting away would be a noble sacrifice if it was the price to pay for peace. But could he do it? Was he strong enough?

He squeezed his eyes shut against the temptation. If his uncle was saying it, it must be a trick. And yet, it sounded so good, so…heroic.

A hand settled on his shoulder and startled Mikelo's eyes open. Geoffre leaned in close. The sulfur scent of gunpowder and the musty smell of the grave accompanied him. Mikelo tried to pull away, but there didn't seem to be anywhere to go.

"Just because you Saw it in the mirror doesn't mean it's evil," Geoffre said in that reasonable voice he'd used to draw Mikelo in before. "What if you hadn't turned that guard into a creature in the prison? Would you and Kyrra have been able to escape?"

"If I hadn't Shaped the guard, *you'd* still be alive."

Geoffre's mouth curved upward. "And obviously, since you thought

I was evil, anything you did to eliminate me must therefore have been good..."

His uncle's eyes, glittering in the dreamlight, were the same as they'd always been—shrewd, calculating, but not insane. Through everything that had happened over the past five years, he had always been able to convince Mikelo that the House di Prinze was the most important thing, not himself or Mikelo or any of their relations. *The role of the Householder is to strengthen the structure, building ever upward, making sure the fortress holds strong for future generations.*

"You're twisting things," Mikelo whispered. "Making evil seem good, trying to manipulate me to your point of view."

"I never had to convince you of the importance of duty. You always knew it in your heart."

Geoffre touched Mikelo's cheek. The tips of his fingers were cold and smooth, and his touch made Mikelo's skin crawl.

Mikelo lurched forward, grabbing at Geoffre's arm, trying to shove him away. Instead he pitched into the air with a ragged cry. He'd been arguing with a phantom, and now he was back in the real world.

He scrabbled for purchase on a body that didn't exist and fell, face-forward, into the rushing, snowmelt-fed stream. It all happened in an instant—his hand slipped on the slick rocks and the current smashed him against the opposite bank. He kicked out and his foot slid into a hole between two rocks and stuck there, tight.

The water wasn't that deep but panic had cost him; his cloak snagged in the roots sticking out of the bank underwater, but worse, so did his scarf. He jerked his head, even more panicked now, but every movement tightened the knot around his throat. He yanked his foot, hoping to be able to twist, but the more he struggled, the more tightly he was bound.

He thought somebody was trying to grab him by the shoulders— Silva, of course!—but Silva didn't know what was catching him and he couldn't *do* anything. His lungs burned and then his breath ran out, and his body betrayed him by reflexively gasping in water instead.

After everything that's happened, I'm going to drown in this stream?

He barely felt the hands that heaved at the rocks trapping his foot. Then a blade cut through his scarf and the hands hauled him out and threw him onto the bank like a fish.

He fell on his shoulder, coughing up the water he'd breathed in. Somebody pounded him on the back with hard, painful blows and water kept spewing out of his mouth—gods, would it never *end?*

"Silva," he gasped when he finally stopped coughing. "Thank you." He rolled onto his back and wiped the water from his eyes.

For the second time that afternoon, he was surprised to see someone he didn't expect. Silva *was* there, kneeling beside him. But standing in front of him, hands on his knees, panting and dripping, was Arsenault. When he looked up at Mikelo, his eyes were silver as steel.

"*Stay inside the runes*," Arsenault said between his teeth. "Or are you trying to get yourself killed?"

৩৩৩

THE TRIP BACK DOWN TO THE FARMHOUSE WAS EXCRUCIATING. HE was so cold, he felt like he would never warm up, and all because... Why? Had his magic run away with him? Had he just not realized?

"I'm going to teach you more magic defenses," Arsenault panted as he and Silva supported Mikelo down the path. It hadn't seemed nearly as hard to walk up as to walk down the slippery slope. His ankle hurt, too. "I could only do so much when you lived with your uncle."

"It's my fault," Silva said in anguish. "I pressed him to use his magic, to see how the family died."

"I'm r-right here!" Mikelo said. "I c-can w-walk f-fine, I've caused enough p-problems."

"Hush, Mikelo," Arsenault said. "The cold is affecting your thinking. We'll get you dry and warm as soon as we get to the house."

"I'm s-sorry, both of you. Arsenault, I-I've been an ass, I was j-just s-so angry—"

"I bet you're a morose drunk, too," Arsenault grunted, skidding on a patch of gravel and catching himself.

"M-Miranda's book says t-tea."

"What? Mikelo, try to make sense."

"F-for cold. T-tea, not brandy. B-blankets. Firestones. Or hot w-water bottles."

"Well, I'm not getting in bed with you," Arsenault said wryly. "You're not my type."

"You only like women who can k-kill you," he shot back and Silva snortled with laughter.

"We had a man fall in the spring once, in winter, at the Youth," Silva said. "The girls thought he must have fallen in on purpose because he didn't have money to pay for another night, but since he was freezing, he got a free bed and a bottle of brandy. And free company, too, because Bethe was that kind of girl."

"What kind of g-girl?"

"Soft-hearted. My sister Meli had a hell of a time with her, trying to get her to understand she was being taken advantage of. But she liked her job, I guess, and she got bed and board, which was all she really needed."

Arsenault made an *mmph*. Mikelo didn't know what it meant, aside from the fact that Arsenault-as-Andris had also known bathhouse girls, and that led to him remembering the women Kyrra had killed—*Geoffre's spies*—and another fit of shivering he couldn't stop. He felt like his thoughts were caught in an icy sludge, slowing so much they were going to stop.

Would it be so bad, though? Maybe he could get some sleep for once, not plagued by images from Cassis's mirror or by Geoffre. It was like being trapped in the swirling silver-blackness of the stream...

"Mikelo," Arsenault said sharply. He blinked and realized they'd stopped. Silva shook him, not gently.

"I h-hope one of you is m-my type," Mikelo tried to joke. "I'm s-so c-cold." Both Arsenault and Silva looked too concerned. He didn't like that look on Arsenault. He didn't know if he was genuinely sorry about being angry at Arsenault or if he was just afraid of drifting away with Arsenault thinking he wanted Arsenault to leave, when he was just...angry. But if Arsenault left, who else would he have?

"I r-regret b-being angry at you, Arsenault," he said, trying again. "I just want to know why my father left us. I-I w-want to know why a man would do s-such a thing. That's what I can't forgive."

"You had a right to be angry. I should have put myself in your shoes. We're almost there. Stay awake and I'll tell you what I remember when we get there. But don't drift away."

"Y-yes..."

"And you'll tell me about your vision, too, yes? What Geoffre said to you?"

"J-just like always, twisting his words. It was...nothing, just *worries*."

"I'll be the judge of that," Arsenault muttered. They were limping across the courtyard now. Kyrra threw open the door and stood in the entry holding, of all things, a wooden spoon.

"Kyrra," Arsenault called. "What are you doing?"

"You took your sword. I didn't feel comfortable without something in my hand."

"Get the boy in now," Jon said—from somewhere—and then Arsenault and Silva were hauling him into the kitchen. The warm air felt like a hug and at the same time he felt like he would never be warm again.

"Here, here," Jon said. "Get those wet clothes off him, use Kyrra's blanket."

"In front of Kyrra?"

"We've had this discussion before, Mikelo!" Kyrra exclaimed.

"You-you told me to stop. Goatherder. I knew it was you. Or-or the magic s-sounds l-like you."

All the while Arsenault, Silva, and Jon were stripping off his wet things—cloak, boots, socks, trousers, tunic, shirt, everything—then wound him in a blanket. When he looked up from the whirlwind, Kyrra was staring at him in shock, and then Silva gently pushed him down onto the couch and his feet were up and Arsenault was wrestling new, dry socks onto them. His feet had gone completely numb, but now they felt like they were on fire, and the foot that had been trapped in the rocks throbbed.

"I Saw you," Kyrra said in astonishment, and then gruffly, "Goatherder. Talking to Geoffre!"

The room seemed to still. It took him a moment to realize it was because they were all watching him. He took a deep breath—or tried to. He was still shivering, worse now, and it still felt like there was water in his lungs that he couldn't cough out. Silva shoved a mug into his hand. Brandy, not tea.

"I'll get you a hot water bottle," Silva said.

"B-but—"

"Just drink the brandy, Mikelo."

Obediently, he did. It tasted like honey on fire—deliciously, wonderfully warm. He took another drink, and another, and Silva returned with a bladder filled with hot water from the kettle always on in the kitchen—so they could have made tea, dammit, though right now he didn't care. Silva slid the warm leather bottle inside the blanket, against Mikelo's chest, with a tight look of concentration. Mikelo didn't know which sensation was more comforting: the heat of the water bottle, the blanket, the fire, the brandy—or simply to be cared for. Maybe, *maybe*, one day he would be warm again.

Until Kyrra said, "Geoffre, Mikelo."

He took another drink of brandy, noting the generous amount left in the mug, as if Silva or Arsenault had treated it as tea. "I didn't know

I could hear you in the magic," he finally said. "I thought I was making up your voice. But if you Saw me, then I wasn't?"

She settled into the wing chair beside the couch and adjusted her metal arm by cupping her elbow with her left hand, wincing as she did. Now they were two invalids. "I didn't know that you did. But I Saw you with Geoffre and Arsenault said you were outside the runes. The magic just..." She ran a violent hand through her loose curls, mussing them even more. "Arsenault found a secret room full of books. But it's leaking and there was water and I was hit with a terrible feeling about you, and I guess I fainted. Arsenault left to find you, and I had to do *something* to distract myself so I made Jon get me the *Mythos* off Miranda's top shelf, and suddenly it was just *Geoffre*, and I can't kill him anymore than I already have."

Mikelo blinked. "A secret room? Oji la Kaif? Is it because I'm so cold I can't follow you or are you all right?"

"It's the bloody kacin. Makes me run at the mouth like—what's the equivalent of a drippy nose?"

Mikelo hunched deeper into the blanket. "I don't know what happened. Perhaps his spirit isn't at rest. When I tried to See what had happened to the family who'd died in that spot, suddenly I Saw Geoffre. It was just like always—him twisting up his words, my thoughts. But maybe it wasn't him; maybe it was just me."

"Cassis said Devid had Geoffre's body," Arsenault said. He was sitting on the hearth, barefoot, next to all the clothes that had been laid on the bricks to dry. His expression was complicated, but he didn't seem to like what he was thinking.

"You're worried it really was Geoffre's ghost?" Mikelo asked in surprise.

"I *told* you that place was no good," Silva interjected.

Arsenault flicked Silva a glance, but Silva didn't seem to notice, just held onto his surly look while he warmed his hands by the fire. Mikelo felt even more ashamed of himself, as if it took much, sitting in the common room naked and wrapped in a blanket.

"I don't know if it had to do with the place," Arsenault said carefully. "But I don't know what Devid did with Geoffre's body. Cassis was certainly worried."

"I wish Geoffre would haunt *him*."

"I don't know that I do, Mikelo," Jon said. "Cassis is in possession of an army. I wish Geoffre was put to rest in the ground and trapped in the underworld forever. Let your Ires sort him out." Jon looked troubled and rubbed the back of his neck. "But it makes sense Geoffre would haunt you. He wanted you to be his heir. And you have the sword."

"Only because it fell on the battlefield. If I showed myself in the Circle—if you thought that would work, you'd have me down there right now, wouldn't you?" Jon didn't answer, so Mikelo knew it was true. "I'm so far down the line of succession. Was Geoffre planning to kill off everybody ahead of me first?"

"I wouldn't put it past him," Kyrra said.

Mikelo took another drink of brandy and eyed her skeptically. "Seems chancy, doesn't it? I think he just wanted to manipulate my magic. He said—"

Mikelo bit down on the words. Thank the gods there was a lot of brandy in the mug.

"What did he say, Mikelo?" Jon asked.

"Why don't you ask Kyrra if she Saw it," he replied tightly.

Kyrra rolled her eyes. "You boneheaded arse. I didn't hear your entire conversation. Why did you talk to him anyway?"

"Why did you talk to Ires?" he snapped back. "I wanted to make it clear how much I hate him. For betraying us. For making me think I actually had a *family*."

His angry gaze caught in the glass on the mantel clock. It threw his reflection back at him—a scruffy, lonely figure wrapped in a blurry crimson blanket, his naked, bony shoulder peeking out over the hem. All around him loomed the shapes of objects that should be furniture but were instead...

Creatures.

Geoffre had said he could create *creatures.*

They huddled beside him, there in the mirror of the clock, as if time was just ticking down to his inevitable fate. Grotesque *things* that weren't animals or humans but instead *monsters*, like the paintings unearthed in Eterean tombs. Twisted animal-people with horns and fangs—people-animals, snake-birds, dragon-wolves, bones and flesh sculpted like clay—

And, oh, the cat! The poor cat had become a mewling, spitting, hairless *thing*—

He cried out and hid his eyes. Then fur brushed his hand, his face, and a deep purr vibrated against his neck.

He started shaking. *It's just the cat, the sweet cat, it wants a rub, that's all.* Why in all the hells would he hurt the cat? He hugged her as tight as he could against his chest, burying his face in her soft fur as long as she would let him.

No one spoke. Something rustled and Mikelo lifted his head to see Arsenault throwing a piece of fabric over the clock. "Give us a moment," he said to everyone else.

Kyrra pushed herself up out of the chair with a wince and Jon caught her elbow. "Mikelo..." she began, but Jon tugged on her and she closed her mouth. Thank the gods; Kyrra never knew when to shut up. He could hear himself being testy in his mind, but he was too frightened to stop.

"Geoffre thinks I can use my magic to control people...and make *things*," he told Arsenault. "But I won't."

Arsenault was shivering, too, as he stripped out of his soggy shirt and trousers. He grabbed a blanket and the bottle of brandy, drank it straight, without bothering to pour himself a cup. "Kyrra told me about the stables," he said as he sat in the chair Kyrra had vacated. "You did what you had to."

Mikelo took a deep breath. Finally without shaking and shivering. "I know. I don't regret it. But why won't it go away? Why is the mirror so much worse than the actual...*thing* I Fixed? I didn't even know I *could* Fix flesh that way until I Saw myself doing it in the mirror. And then it seemed as if the next moment Kyrra was asking me if I could. But it was like you said. She didn't force me to do it; it had to be done."

Arsenault took another drink of brandy and stared at the bottle in his hands. The refractions from the glass functioned too much like a mirror. Mikelo looked abruptly back to Arsenault's face, but Arsenault appeared to be looking somewhere far within.

"I was about the same age as you when I did my Scrying," he said. "Life was peaceful. I was married, with one boy and another on the way. I'd done my schooling and my apprenticeship as a smith, and I was out on my own, providing for my family. I could have left it there and probably should have. I had enough control over my Sight to work metal reasonably well. Tavi had more Talent than I did. He was on track to be a powerful Fixer. But there was always something more I needed to understand. To make a better sword, a more beautiful blade. So, I asked Calden to take me to the Ice."

"You *asked* to have that done to you?"

"It's different when it's voluntary. We had rituals around it to prepare. I grew up knowing that to be a Fixer, I would have to face the Ice. To see Truth in things outside myself, I first had to See inside myself."

"So those monsters... They actually *are* the truth of me?" Mikelo whispered. "Geoffre said..."

"The Ice reflects both good and bad. Reality and potential. There's nothing about fate in the reflections, it's just a mess of what might be. When you See into flesh, it's like that, too, right?"

"It isn't exactly flesh I See, though, it's more...life. A person, a flower, a cat. Life is a riot. There's just so much of it."

Arsenault looked startled. "Life," he breathed. "Gods."

Mikelo laughed shakily. "Your reaction doesn't instill confidence, Arsenault."

"I didn't know exactly where your Talent lay, that's all. The point I'm trying to make is, when I did my Scrying, I *thought* I faced my dark places. I used the idea of honor I had built for myself as a shield to hide behind, but it wasn't made of anything real, anything strong. It was easy to think I had turned away the darkness in a time of peace. But the images from the Ice haunted me in my dreams, and I poured myself into work to get away from them. If I'd simply owned up to the darkness in the first place, maybe..."

Arsenault sighed heavily and took another drink. "It's a continual battle, that's all. Your talent is extraordinarily strong and vanishingly rare, but the true test of power is to be able to hold all this conflicting potential inside you without breaking. To accept the struggle."

"Maybe there's a reason it's a rare Talent," Mikelo murmured darkly.

"There's a unique darkness in everyone, Mikelo. You've just lived closer to it than most."

"If you're talking about life with Geoffre—how could I have been more naïve? I believed Geoffre when he said we were fighting for our House. Without him I would have been kinless on the street, so it didn't take much to fool myself. It would have been better if I had been kinless. Why didn't I just leave?"

"You can't fault yourself for surviving, Mikelo. When Geoffre found you, you were little more than a child. You're looking at your past from the hindsight of escape. Now that you do have a choice... Well, choice shouldn't be terrifying, but it is. In my experience."

Arsenault clutched the blanket around his shoulders and stood, setting the brandy down on the table next to him.

"If you find yourself trapped in another vision, use the Sanctuary rune. Put all the light into it you can—all your loving and being loved. That's where safety lies. It's one of the most powerful pieces of magic you can conjure."

Being loved.

A broadsheet sitting next to the bottle caught Mikelo's eye, his father's name in bold, black print the way it had always seemed to be written across the blank page of his life.

"Arsenault... I'm not even sure what it *means* to love or be loved. All I have are ideals."

"Then use your desire to be loved, Mikelo. Your hope for a better world. And throw it in the face of the darkness."

CHAPTER 27

ARSENAULT

THE IBUU'S PALACE, TWENTY YEARS AGO

Arsenault felt like Guin was slipping away from him.

He knew he was lucky, as a galleyman, to have made it into Lord Jonawak's Palace Guard. The crimes galleymen had committed bound them indefinitely, so they would never earn the pay the indentured soldiers were paid after their seven-year service ended. Jonawak still kept the forged papers detailing his supposed "crimes," but he hadn't revealed them to the Ibuu. It seemed a dangerous game for the young lord to play with his father, but Jonawak appeared to like games. Every day since Arsenault had begun recovering from his gunshot and lion wounds, Lord Jonawak took him aside to play a game of indij, which also served as a way for them to discuss the little that had turned up in the search for Guin and the other galleymen.

Having a position in the Palace Guard was only to his advantage, but some nights he lay on his pallet surrounded by sixty other sleeping men and he felt so alone, so *stuck*, he bit his pillow to keep from weeping tears of sheer exhaustion. As more time passed, he fought to recall even the most basic details of Guin the man, to separate him from the crushing feeling of failure Erelf had transferred from his past life.

Sometimes he wondered what would happen if he walked out into the night and just kept walking. But somehow, he always stayed where he was. He rose every morning, played his daily card game with Jonawak, and did his duty like all the other men with whom he now lived, following any crumb of information about Guin whenever he could.

At least Lord Jonawak remained true to the deal, in his mysterious fashion. He tended to stride in unexpectedly with something for Arsenault to do, or to talk about magic or Guin or life on the galley, and Arsenault would struggle to complete the task or remember as best he could what the lord wanted to know.

Like the day the lord walked in with his deck of indij cards and announced that the customs office had suffered a serious fire set by a basilisk.

"A *basilisk,* my lord?"

"I didn't believe it either. But look, a witness sketched it."

Lord Jonawak pushed a piece of paper—real papyrus paper, not hemp or linen—across the table. Arsenault winced as he sat to get a better look. The gunshot had festered; for a time, he'd feared he might die, and if he did, would his memory of Guin survive a second death? Only brief images and his stubborn dedication remained; if either disappeared, he'd have no reason to keep going but to follow orders and wait for the sword thrust that would inevitably kill him again, as in countless lives before.

The sketch did, indeed, depict a basilisk—beak open wide, tongue a stream of flame that exploded into an inferno in the hastily drawn arched doorway of a building. A little out of proportion, but...

Arsenault pushed the paper back to Jonawak. "The artist must have had balls of steel. Just sitting there drawing it."

Jonawak finished dealing the hand and replied absently, studying his cards, "You'd think there would have been injuries, but only three people were hurt and the surrounding buildings didn't catch fire. The basilisk disappeared almost as soon as it appeared."

Jon had dealt him a crap hand. "It's a magic creature, I suppose. Perhaps its fire—"

"Hmmm. Maybe that's it. It selectively burned all the files kept by the agent who brokered the *Gannet*'s contracts because it's magic."

Arsenault jerked his head up in surprise. Jon laid down his hand and smiled blandly. He'd won, of course, the bastard.

"I think you cheat."

"Like the basilisk?"

Arsenault snorted. "Basilisk, my arse. Somebody's working illusion to cover their crimes, just like they're trying to cover up the path of my galleymen."

"Well, the fire was real enough. The office has been bumbling around for a while now in delivering the contracts and Adayze got tired of it. So, out of nowhere, a basilisk. Just another evil apparition like the others that have been plaguing Mdembu for months, so sorry about the bad luck, what is the Ibuu doing about this, Lady Adayze? At least now we know there was something in those contracts worth hiding. I think it's safe to deduce somebody in Dakkar bought their contracts but didn't want my father to know they were doing it."

"Someone capable of making basilisks?"

Lord Jonawak frowned thoughtfully. "You said most of the galleymen were Fixers."

"We were all bound, though...I think."

"And the apparitions began before your galleymen ever docked. But it is strange how they seem to be linked now, isn't it? Only...I don't know of any Fixer in our registers who could shape an imaginary basilisk that breathed actual fire. That's something out of the legends of the Nightmare Man."

"The Nightmare Man?" Arsenault asked in disbelief.

"It's an old story. Mostly told by children to frighten each other these days. The Nightmare Man lived during the time of the fila, when the world was thinner. He stole people's dreams and Fixed them into reality. It only makes a good story if he mostly Fixes nightmares."

"Seems like a horrifying Talent," Arsenault agreed. "You register all your Fixers?"

"We are a people of meticulous recordkeeping. At least, of some things. Our more traditional knowledge is kept inside the heads of our Historians. Some would point out that if we continued to store knowledge in our own memories, a fire wouldn't have destroyed the information we needed."

"Some?"

"All right, me, I am the some. But it's very strange, ghost, these monsters that disappear before we can find out anything about them. Hah, here, you beat me this hand so I can't have been cheating. Tell me why you played those cards together. They shouldn't have won. And then you can tell me all about the mountains of fire on Tule."

The indij games didn't end when the nurses proclaimed Arsenault well enough to move into the barracks. The game there was eyi and every time Jon joined in, his men would groan. At first Arsenault thought it was because they would be forced to lose, but Lord Jonawak played all his games fair and still won time after time.

They were just setting up a game after a long, hot day of drill when Jonawak walked into the barracks and gave him his first real lesson in court politics. The young lord was dressed not in his everyday uniform, but resplendent in a burgundy silk tunic embroidered in gold lions, a belt fashioned of mother of pearl links wrapped around his waist. His locs—usually tied back casually with a plain leather strip—were bound by a scarf of gold cloth.

All the men in the barracks leapt to their feet in surprise. Jonawak barely acknowledged them. "Arsenault," he said, pointing. "Come with me."

Everybody knew Arsenault was only in the Palace Guard because Lord Jonawak had put him there; he hadn't earned rank yet and he didn't carry a sword. But Jonawak unpredictably pulled him out of the barracks, sometimes for baffling reasons, like walking in the gardens. Playing with his nephew Edo, Lady Adyaze's son. Or playing indij. Eventually Arsenault wondered if there wasn't more behind the lord's erratic and entitled behavior than met the eye. If he wasn't making sure that Arsenault dangled before anyone who might know about the galleymen like bait. In which case, he could damn well be bait.

"My lord," Arsenault said, looking at his sweat-stained, untucked shirt, his dirty trousers and dusty bare feet in the plain rope sandals issued to every man in the barracks. He'd smashed his big toe with the end of a halberd pole during drill and the nail was already turning blue and black. He'd lose it soon enough. "I thought I was off duty. Do I have time to dress?"

"No, don't worry about that, you'll do just as you are. Come on, quick."

He grabbed Arsenault by the arm and pulled him away from the other men. Arsenault hoped this treatment didn't seem special in their eyes; he already had to fight harder to gain their respect and Jonawak's actions didn't make it easier.

Jonawak spoke quickly as Arsenault followed him out of the barracks. "We have a situation. You are going to spar with my Aunt Neyane."

Arsenault stopped dead. "The King's Dagger? A woman?"

Jon stopped with him, looking both vexed and worried. "Yes, a woman. Why does that make a difference? She's been fighting men like you since she was a child. You don't think you're going to win the spar just because you're a man?"

"No, I—it's just—in most of the countries where I've fought, women aren't warriors. It's not that I think women are weak, but men aren't supposed to—"

"It's different here, ghost, and this is political. I'm trying to protect my sister. I hope you can fight, but if you can't, I suppose it will show something if Neyane decides to wash the ring with your blood."

"Forgive me, Lord Jonawak, but I haven't been out of the infirmary that long. I'd rather not have to go back in so soon." He hesitated. "This isn't a fight to the death, is it?"

"I hope not, because then people will talk. And they've already been talking enough. Some of the nobles will seize any excuse to undermine the Ibuu's authority—the Arak, but also the families of the Dakkar who have something to gain by weakening the B'ara. If Isa was here, perhaps it would be different. He's a diplomat, related to half the audience. But we must do without him."

"Who is Isa?"

"Adayze's husband. He's still...on his journey. Hopefully he will return soon, to put an end to this posturing."

"And what am I supposed to do?"

"Just let my aunt see you, ghost. Let her see that you are a man and not another apparition like the ones that have been plaguing us, or a criminal bringing danger into our court. Both stories are going around. That godsdamned carter started spreading his story about you coming back to life as soon as we brought you back with a gunshot wound. Thank the fila he didn't also see that you began old and rose again young or he'd have more proof."

"You shooting me was an accident."

"Don't worry; Neyane has upbraided me for not thinking more about the consequences. Nothing is ever an accident to her. I paid the carter a handsome retirement and sent him back to his village to live out his old age with his daughter and her family, but the damage was done—the story had already spread."

"I see. You and your aunt want me to bleed publicly."

"It wouldn't hurt. But it also wouldn't hurt to see you prove your-self and swear fealty to the Ibuu. Neyane wants you to bleed, but Adayze needs you in place in court to gather information. I'm gambling here, Arsenault, but a public spar with my aunt seemed the best way to shoot two birds with one arrow."

"You want me to lose and win at the same time?"

"Hah. Neyane will knock that attitude out of you, ghost. You're going to be watched, is my point. Adayze wanted to keep your pres-ence quiet, but there will be no quiet unless we face these issues."

They had reached the parade grounds.

A crowd had gathered around the dirt arena—people from a multi-tude of nations and cultures, all dressed in clothing that would cost a soldier a year's salary or more to afford. He still picked out Adayze easily. She was wearing a necklace of braided gold and a burgundy dress the same color as her brother's tunic. She sat easy in her finery on a carved wooden stool, bouncing her baby son on her knees beneath the shade of a parasol.

"What is the occasion?" Arsenault asked, dumbfounded.

"Seventh-day luncheon," Jon replied. "Once every moon, the Ibuu hosts games, competitions, petitions—lately it's mostly been a bunch of twits competing for Adayze's attention."

"She is very beautiful," Arsenault mumbled as he buckled on a sword belt, then pulled on a pair of leather gauntlets Jonawak handed him.

"Very powerful, you mean. Very rich. Beauty doesn't hurt, but those men would beat each other to their bones even if she had the face of a spined toad. They're not the ones you should watch out for, though. Adayze doesn't care about shows of strength."

"What does she care about then?"

"Ah, ghost," Jonawak shook his head. "Just go out there and give everyone a good time, eh?"

He handed Arsenault two curved Dakkaran swords, like the ones he wore.

Frustrated and nervous, Arsenault spent a moment getting the feel of them, their balance and heft. The smith who had forged these blades had done an excellent job, but it had been a long while—he was sure it had—since he'd fought with a curved blade.

"These aren't practice swords," he said.

"No, it's all real. Practice swords would not show bravery in this competition, but the fight will be stopped at first blood."

That probably meant a lot of fighting at the bind, punching instead of stabbing, and he wasn't sure he could punch a woman. "All right," he said skeptically. Jon motioned him into the ring.

Neyane was already standing there, wearing her fighting leathers with her hair woven in many braids and entwined with ribbons of crimson and gold. The symbol of her office—a long, jewel-encrusted dagger—jutted up at her hip and she gripped a long, curved sword in each hand. If she meant to look daunting, she did. Everything about her spoke of power, strength, and agility.

His greatest advantage as a swordsman was always that his body had worked the forms for so many years they'd been burned into his very muscle fibers. And thankfully, those muscles were now approximately twenty-eight again. On the other hand, he had a stiff shoulder and he'd already been worked hard most of the day. The sun beat down on the dirt of the ring and he was thirsty and flushed in the heat.

"Well?" Neyane said. "Are you ready? I think the Onzarrans have odds you are a northern demon who'll turn to smoke and disappear as soon as I cut into you."

Arsenault glanced at the crowd. The Onzarrans were easy to pick out with their big hats and their Eterean House colors, though Arsenault had no idea what any of them meant. "Why would they say that?" he asked. "The Etereans hire Dagmari gavaros. They know I'm not a demon."

Neyane chuckled. "Because they make more money that way. And because they are allied with the B'ito and it will help that family to spread preposterous rumors about the B'ara. It's our job to make those stories work for us; the Onzarrans know it will gain them coin one way or another."

"You're not worried I'll turn to smoke, though."

"My niece is going to be a good Ibuu, but she needs to learn to allow her Dagger to work for her instead of masquerading herself as a customs official down on the docks. Blades up and bow."

Arsenault lifted his swords and bowed as instructed. Neyane stepped back with hers raised in a guard stance and rested lightly on the balls of her feet. "Do you know how to fight, Tulan?"

Arsenault assumed his own guard stance. His muscles settled in from old memories and long years, actions his body remembered even if he'd forgotten the details of all the many battles. "I do, lady."

"Then fight."

He didn't expect her to be as fast as she was. She attacked with both blades, one high, one low, and he barely got his up to block. He stumbled backward, his feet finding the fighting runes on their own as he tried to fit the unfamiliar blades into familiar patterns. *If only I had my own sword*, he thought, and Neyane almost landed a punch in his face with a hilt.

Godsdammit, focus.

Neyane was such a good swordsman Arsenault expected to sense her using magic, but hers was a purely physical talent. He took one hit after another, and the impacts rang through his arms and set his teeth on edge. He took a few punches to the face and groggily shook off the pain, but as long as he kept meeting her blades, he wouldn't use his knuckles and she couldn't cut him.

"I'm impressed, Tulan," Neyane said breathlessly as they broke apart and circled for what felt like the millionth time. The chattering of the crowd buzzed in his ears. A baby cried—*Edo*.

"I sold my sword," he panted. "I had to be good."

"None of that fancy Vençalan dueling?"

"Only if you want."

Neyane laughed and swept one blade at his hand. He jerked away and she came down with a hard, high cut at his shoulder. He twisted, threw a punch at her face without thinking. His knuckles connected hard with her cheekbone. Saliva flew from her mouth and she grunted in pain, staggering to the side, and for a moment—a long, agonizing moment that was probably only an instant—he panicked.

Their eyes met and he thought crazily, *She knows*. It didn't matter that he was in a totally different situation and Neyane had already left bruises on his face, the terror bubbled up from where it was stored inside him. He had never meant to do violence against a woman and especially his own wife—

Neyane's jaw clenched. She swept her sword into his arm. He tried to jump backward, but not fast enough. The blade ripped through his shirt and left a long thin burning line across the skin of his chest. Blood feathered crimson in the torn, fluttering fabric of his shirt. Biting his tongue against the pain, he dropped his blades, raised his hands, and hit the dirt on one knee. Blood and sweat dripped into the dust, and he watched them mingle in little black wells—isolated from the rest of the world by the sound of his own breathing and the drumming of his heart.

Both Neyane's blades hovered over his neck, their hot steel eager for a kill. He didn't know if he was shaking with exhaustion or memory. The first months of a new life were always so fucking hard.

Finally, the tip of one blade touched him lightly on the shoulder.

"Get up, Tulan. Everyone can see now how you bleed and that you have not turned to smoke."

Arsenault struggled painfully to his feet. "My lady."

She leaned close before the other guards came to lead him away. "I hear you've been asking a lot of questions about your fellow galley-men. My advice to you is—don't. If you continue to lead my niece and my nephew astray, I will be forced to take care of it."

CHAPTER 28

ARSENAULT

HIS BATTLE WITH NEYANE SEEMED BOTH RECENT AND ANCIENT AS he stood guard in the Ibuu's court, with her standing beside the Ibuu in her court clothes. Arsenault was sure she was keeping a clandestine eye on him as they waited on the Ibuu in this large and varied court, which moved according to the Ibuu's whim. This afternoon, the Ibuu was hearing business contracts on the veranda.

Arsenault wore the same long red silk tunic as did all who bore service to the Ibuu, the same loose trousers, the same wrapped leather boots. He carried one curved sword at his side and felt better for it.

But the Ibuu's appointments had been staring at him all day.

His braid had been cut to keep the bugs out of it while he recovered from the lion and gunshot wounds, his beard shaved, too. He kept trying to convince the Guard's barber to let his beard grow, but the man kept trimming it down to a small circle around his upper lip and chin in the Dakkaran fashion, leaving his cheeks clean-shaven and his scar bared in its full-length gory wonder.

He hadn't seen the length of it in many years himself and it had startled him, too, when the nurses had brought him a mirror. It was the exact shape of the knife that had killed Sella, and nearly as long. He tightened his hands, resisting the urge to rub it, and shifted minutely. Jon caught the movement and shot him a look.

Guards were supposed to be the human equivalent of the stone statues that formed the veranda's columns. The fila—twelve gods with various animal attributes. The statues would have made him nervous, except he had no history with the gods of Dakkar and the afternoon had dragged on so long already. They'd just seen the next to last supplicant, a livestock trader with sycophant aspirations whom the Ibuu had put firmly in his place.

"That's a man who just pulled his ass from a jackal trap," the guard next to Arsenault said out of the corner of his mouth. Haq was a young guard, a Tiresian-Qalfan whose mother was a nurse. The smattering of freckles on his nose and cheeks made him look younger than he was. He wore his thicket of dark hair in a single braid instead of adopting Tiresian braids and beads—just as Arsenault would have worn his if Haq's mother hadn't cut it all off. It had grown back a bit now, just long enough to make his neck itch, but he still felt like everything about his appearance made him stand out. He didn't dare acknowledge Haq's remark even though it was true. The humor was a welcome break in the droning afternoon.

Haq moved his head imperceptibly to the right so he could look out the door, then lifted his small finger.

One more appointment.

"Promethi dom Arak, accompanied by his retainer Renzo di Prinze," the crier called from the doorway and stepped aside to let the two men in.

Di Prinze.

Everyone looked up at the unexpected foreign name of the retainer, but something half-remembered struck a chord deep inside Arsenault. The pirates, Eterean metal... *Prinze* was a name he had heard the pirates speak, he was sure of it. But why? Damn Erelf, it was all a blurry glimmer, like reflections on the sea.

Arsenault hastily pasted his neutral, unseeing expression back on and angled his head downward as a Dakkaran man dressed in blue silk robes walked calmly into the room, followed by a dark-haired Eterean man.

Few Etereans from farther north than Onzarro made it this far south, and those who did rarely ended up in the Ibuu's court. Prinze was not an Onzarran name and the man's pale olive skin was not the deep tan of natives from that southern trading city. The other guards and nobles in the room openly stared at the new visitors, and the Ibuu's ancient Historian tucked his hands into the voluminous, gold-trimmed sleeves of his robes, the deep furrows of his face crinkling as he clearly made an addition to his ongoing mental narrative of the Ibuu's reign.

"Promethi," the Ibuu said in a cheerful voice that bore an undercurrent of wariness. "To what do I owe the honor of this visit? How is your brother?"

The Dakkaran noble bowed his head and shoulders, but not his whole body. He had a proud nose and a hunter's aura. His silk robes looked expensive, light blue patterned with darker blue swirls, with a headcloth cut from the same fabric.

"Lord Dirik's health is somewhat erratic, my lord Ibuu, after his accident. But he continues to persevere."

The wariness remained in the Ibuu's voice when he replied. "I'm glad to hear it. But on what business does he send you? Haven't I already set my seal to the ventures we spoke about on your last visit?"

"I come on my own business, Lord Ibuu, not my brother's. May I introduce my associate, the Lieran silk trader Mestere Renzo di Prinze?"

Renzo swept a deep bow to the Ibuu in the flowery Lieran style. His silks were a bright sky-blue slashed with silver and stitched in gilt thread—probably his House colors. A silver clasp winked in his dark hair as he bent his head, but a few long, curly strands had slipped free and plastered themselves to his temples with sweat.

"Liera, is it?" The Ibuu frowned and stroked his short beard. "That's quite a distance. Most of our Eterean traders are from Onzarro or Carrazone."

"I bought passage on a Qalfan trader out of Joffra to investigate more outlets for Lieran silk, my lord," Renzo answered. "I belong to a merchant House and we'd like to expand our network."

"We've traded pledges with the Onzarrans already," the Ibuu replied.

"Onzarro's Houses differ from ours."

"The Camerani doesn't rule you?"

Renzo's mouth twitched. His Qalfan was very good; he'd caught that little glitch in the language, too, conflating the House name with a ruler. It was easy enough to do; power in the Eterean cities seemed to change hands like dishes on a menu. "No, my lord. The Camerani are the ruling House of Onzarro. Liera is ruled by a Circle. A group of representatives from the noble families."

"So, you do not have the power to make treaties. Or pledges."

"All the Houses make their own treaties and pledges, my lord. My brother, the Prinze Householder, gave me full authority to negotiate with my lord dom Arak and you, my lord Ibuu. Any agreements I make are binding to my House."

The Ibuu turned to Promethi. "And have you been negotiating with this lord Renzo, Promethi?"

Promethi shrugged. "We've been in talks. Silk for kacin."

"Is kacin what you desire, Lord Renzo?"

"Kacin is in high demand in Liera, sire. But we would also ask the Dakkar for pledges in return for silk. We hear you have developed a weapon called a *gun*, sire."

The Ibuu stared at Renzo. Then he laughed. "You want guns, do you? Promethi, is this why you brought this man to see me?"

Promethi crossed his arms over his chest and bowed from the waist. "My lord Ibuu, you are very brave and very wise, and you have eyes watching your bindings. We wish you to know that the knots remain tight. We offer this Eterean and the gun he traded as proof of our good faith."

At Promethi's words, one of the Ibuu's guards approached, carrying an arquebus. He laid it at the Ibuu's feet and the afternoon light gleamed, dangerously beautiful, on its teak stock and its barrel of polished steel.

Not steel. *Tiaannamir.*

Arsenault could hear its song from here, and with it, the certainty —not a true memory but just knowledge—that tiaannamir had been what the *Gannet* had been carrying. Of course. *Antiquities.* The gun had been Fixed, which didn't surprise him after seeing the B'ara magus hut, but the metal, the name Prinze...

Was tiaannamir banned here in Dakkar? Gods, he wished he could remember...anything.

Renzo looked around nervously. "I can offer you duty-free thrown silk at far lower rates than you are accustomed to—"

"We are not talking about silk now," the Ibuu said. "Where did you come by this weapon?"

"I—a trader. My lord dom Arak said—"

"I don't know what he's talking about, my lord Ibuu. I fear he may have been treating with a pirate."

"A pirate! I assure you, if he was a pirate, I didn't know. I thought trading for a gun was a legitimate enterprise—"

"It is, with the Ibuu's seal. Otherwise, it is against the law. And this weapon has been made using magic, has it not, out of that strange metal your ancestors distributed to the world?"

"I don't know—that's Eterean metal? I had no idea! My lord, you must believe me, if I have committed an offense, it was not intention-al." Lierans had a reputation for political cunning, but Renzo di Prinze looked as if he had suddenly realized how far from his city he was. He bowed again, so deeply he nearly lost his balance.

"Jonawak," the Ibuu said. "Send your men for powder and shot. We'll see this weapon in action before we decide what is to be done about it."

"I assure you, my lord, I'll give you any information I can—"

"Quiet," the Ibuu snapped. Renzo paled and shut his mouth. "We will wait. Then Jonawak, my son, you will give us a demonstration."

"Of course, Father," Jonawak said, but he looked troubled as he signaled to Haq. Haq spun quickly for the door—probably just happy that *something* was happening on this long, hot afternoon. When he returned with powder and shot, Jonawak took them and walked to the table where the gun lay, gleaming wickedly in the late afternoon sun. His aunt Neyane watched everything impassively, but Arsenault would have paid to know what was going on in her head. He didn't dare use his Sight.

He hadn't listened to her warning, of course, and when he'd told the lord what his aunt had said, Jonawak had merely stroked his beard with the same troubled look he wore now. Arsenault had decided to keep his own watch on Neyane. Easier said than done, since he had a job and he had to assume that like any good spymaster, she had eyes everywhere.

But what did she know about that metal?

Jonawak examined the gun for a moment. The ones they used to train on were plain, serviceable arquebuses, but Jonawak had demonstrated a new gun the smiths had been working on, a *pistol*, which would allow a man to fire without having to light a fuse first. He could prime it, cock it, and hold it in one hand until the time came to pull the trigger and fire.

This gun was a work of art but there was no wheel. Jonawak ran his fingers over the stock and barrel, and the designs that chased it lit with magic when he touched them.

Runes. Dammit.

Jonawak laid a finger on one—*courage*. Another—*sharp sight*. Jonawak went methodically through all the steps of loading and priming the gun, then lit the fuse and lifted the gun to his shoulder. He sighted along the barrel at the target that had been set up on the outside porch. When he stroked the trigger, the last rune appeared. It must have been cleverly worked into the shape of the trigger itself.

Fear.

Jonawak pulled it. The spark ignited in a loud crack of orange flame and white smoke, and fear leapt into the room.

It was impossible to tell if the ball had hit the target at first because the smoke boiled up into a monstrous shape of teeth and claws, a shadow of the old gods—a *manticore*. The crowd uttered a collective chaotic gasp, then people responded to the raw emotion released by the rune. Chairs crashed to the floor as courtiers shoved each other out of the way. The ball smacked into one of the pillars of the porch and chips of stone shattered in a puff of dust that seemed to hang in the still, humid air longer than it should have. The injured statue stared through it—the fila Lion, patron of the Dakkar.

Jonawak lowered the gun slowly, looking stunned.

The Ibuu shoved himself to his feet. "Enough!" he roared. A magic-laden wind rushed through the veranda, shredding the remnants of the apparition.

"Take that Eterean away," he ordered, "and lock him in his chambers until I find out more about where this gun came from."

⁂

IF RENZO HAD ANY SENSE, HE WOULD HAVE THROWN HIMSELF prostrate on the ground. But he remained frozen, looking around wildly.

Jon gestured to Arsenault, Haq, and their other bunkmate, a tall, thin man named Banye, who had come to Mdembu from one of the villages beset by lions. "You three. Take him upstairs and remain there with him."

Renzo grabbed Arsenault's tunic and began rambling in what Arsenault assumed was Lieran. "I swear I didn't know I was doing anything wrong! I had no idea the gun would work like that!"

Arsenault's Eterean dialects were as rusty as his Dakkaran had been, but he picked up the gist of Renzo's words.

Arsenault removed Renzo's fingers from his tunic, and he and Haq each took one of Renzo's arms. "Calm down, mestere," he answered in Vençalan, which he assumed Renzo understood. "You're not going to a dungeon; you're going to a room."

"Do you think I don't understand what the Ibuu meant?" Renzo hissed.

More hair had pulled free from his clasp and his face had gone pale except for the red flush lining his cheekbones. His dark blue eyes were stormy and wild. Something about him reminded Arsenault of an old

Eterean statue he had seen once with similar features, the tossed hair, the aquiline nose and large eyes, the way the statue stretched out its hand, as if pleading with a god for a touch or a pardon...

So many lives ago. Before silk came to the peninsula, before kacin, before Houses. When the gods whose skeletons formed Renzo's gun had only recently walked the earth. Arsenault tried to make sense of the deja vu before it was gone. But it sank into the depths of his mind as quickly as it had surfaced.

He tightened his grip on Renzo's arm. "Come on. Be quiet and pay attention, and you might get out of here."

Arsenault and Haq walked Renzo down the marble halls and up the wide front staircase inlaid with glittering carnelian. Banye trailed them, while Lord Jonawak went to speak to his father. Jonawak seemed shaken up, and why not; everyone had seen the apparition this time. *Find out whatever you can about him and these pirates who sold him the gun*, Jon had murmured before he'd left. *I don't care how*.

This was the guest wing of the palace, where visitors lodged. The rooms on the top floor were more secure—farther away from the family's chambers, too high to easily escape. The B'ara left little to chance.

"That Promethi's a snake," Haq said as they walked, talking past Renzo's head. Renzo's Dakkaran had seemed poor, but Arsenault wondered if he understood more than he could speak. "He'd deal in guns if he could get around the peace agreements and stay in the Ibuu's good graces. He doesn't want to do anything that might endanger his chances with the Lady Adayze. But it's not because he wants peace."

"So, he wants to be a second husband? What do these men think will happen when her first husband comes back from sea?"

Arsenault still hadn't quite figured out how marriages worked among the Dakkaran noble families. The Ibuu had many wives and concubines, a nursery full of children, but they all bore their personal rank according to their mother's status. The nursery was an active, happy place, a bittersweet joy to visit.

"They think he's not coming home, is what," Haq said as they arrived at the corner room. "He's been lost at sea almost two years now. He came home long enough to get the Lady Adayze pregnant, then he's back out on another diplomatic mission and gone. She just doesn't want to admit he's dead. Nobody does. Except the suitors like Promethi."

Everything suddenly made sense. All those men who had watched him fight Neyane—they weren't competing for second place. They were competing for first. Adayze's pained and mournful expression when she'd passed through the groups of men made more sense now, too. Arsenault felt for her, a woman unsure whether to keep waiting on her husband or to mourn him. The common lot of women who lived in partnership with the sea.

"None of those men are worth the Lady Adayze. Is Promethi not either?"

"Hang around long enough, Arsenault," Banye said as he slid the key into the lock, "and you'll realize much of your job will be fending off suitors. Haq is right. I don't trust that Promethi. You can't tell me the Arak meant the terms of that peace. They're just biding their time until they can challenge the Ibuu again."

Arsenault squeezed Renzo's arm to get him moving, and Renzo looked up at him, startled. "Will you get me out? I can't understand much of what they're saying."

"The Ibuu's a fair man. There's no reason to be afraid if you're telling the truth."

Renzo gave a short laugh. "This is politics. There's nothing fair about it."

Banye stepped aside for Haq and Arsenault, then closed the door behind them. The entry didn't look much like a prison, that was sure. Intricate blue and white tile designs covered the walls and the curved ceiling. Haq gave Renzo a push and they walked into the bedchamber. Renzo stumbled on one of the big sitting pillows scattered over the floor, the only place to sit but for the glistening burgundy silk bed and a lounging couch upholstered in the same color. Curtains of fine muslin mosquito netting hung from a frame built over the bed and a citronella candle was already burning to keep the bugs away. The mere presence of flame seemed to make the heat in this third-story room more stifling. Banye threw open the shuttered windows to the rumpled gray sky of rainy season. A weak breeze rippled the netting that stretched over the windows but did little to help.

Renzo tested his freedom by walking to the open window and pushing the netting aside to lean out. Palm fronds shivered against each other near the window, but the trees were too far away to aid a climber. Below, flowers Arsenault had yet to name grew in tangled, thorny vines. The view was spectacular, though. In the gray afternoon light, the sea in the distance had turned a deep emerald green, and it rushed onto the white beach in foamy breakers. The city of Mdembu was hidden from sight around the turn of the cliff.

Renzo braced himself on the window ledge. "It's still a prison, isn't it?"

Arsenault didn't see any point in arguing. "For now."

Renzo's blue gaze roved warily over Arsenault's face, his body, his weapons, as if he were figuring his odds at escape or survival. Arsenault remembered, vaguely, stories he'd heard about the Eterean city-states and the politics they practiced there—diplomacy accompanied by deceit, poison, torture.

Renzo finally seemed to come to a conclusion. "Perhaps you'll be able to translate my story so it makes more sense." He cast himself down on a set of pillows and tilted his head back against the wall, looking as if he were playing a tragic hero in a play.

Haq and Banye both cast him a curious glance. "Good luck with that one, Arsenault. Lord Jonawak says we're on the door."

Arsenault gave them a sardonic nod as they walked out.

"So," Renzo asked as soon as the door clicked shut. "How did they get their hooks in you?"

"I was brought here on a Qalfan ship."

"*Brought* here? Do you mean you're a galleyman? Good gods, I didn't know the B'ara used criminals as bodyguards!"

"I said I was *brought* here, mestere, not that I was a criminal. I've earned my place."

Renzo eyed him shrewdly head to foot again. Arsenault wished he knew what was going on behind that gaze. He found himself unconsciously pulling his shoulders back.

"Some of the galleymen I've seen..." Renzo murmured. "You don't think the B'ara will sentence me to indenture, do you? I'd just like to get back home to my wife and children. Although if I return with nothing to show, I doubt my brother will be more merciful than the Ibuu." Renzo frowned to himself, then looked up abruptly. "What's your name, or can't you tell me?"

"Arsenault, mestere."

Again, that calculating expression. "You don't look Vençalan."

"Outer Islands."

"And it truly doesn't bother you that your life still belongs to another man?"

"I was a sellsword. It's not so different."

Renzo arched an eyebrow. "On the one hand, Arsenault, that's a very gavaro thing to say. On the other, I doubt any gavaro would say it. You don't care that you don't have a contract that would allow you to change sides? To hire on a caravan and be free again?"

"I've thought about it, but I doubt it'll happen tonight. If you're trying to tempt me."

Renzo's face fell. "That obvious, was it?"

Arsenault chuckled. "I can't blame you for trying, mestere."

"Well, it seemed like the best alternative. You'd knock me on my arse in half a minute if I tried to grab your sword, and I'd break my legs if I jumped out the window."

A knock at the door interrupted him. He raised his head nervously. "Is that the Ibuu sending for me already?"

"I doubt it," Arsenault replied as he went to open the door. "It's probably dinner."

Although Renzo *was* technically a prisoner, Lord Jonawak had ordered a huge feast. The rich smells of beef and cumin made Arsenault's mouth water painfully. It had been a long time since he'd eaten. Renzo perked up at the food and the wine jugs, but as the serving girls arranged the food on a low table, his expression grew wary. "If this meal is to be my last, I would appreciate it if you shared it with me, Arsenault."

"No sentence has been passed, mestere."

"If a gavaro rejects this feast, I'll *know* it must be poisoned," Renzo replied.

Arsenault fought back a sigh. He was *almost* positive the food wasn't poisoned. A dead Renzo couldn't give the Ibuu the information he wanted, but what about Neyane? If she wanted to keep the connection between the galleymen and the metal quiet, as the Ibuu's Dagger, she would certainly have access to poison...

A glance at Renzo, though, and Arsenault realized he wouldn't get his information any other way. He inclined his head, trying not to do it wearily. "If that is what the mestere wishes."

"Yes," Renzo said in relief. "It is definitely what the mestere wishes. And perhaps you can also help me understand exactly what Promethi hoped to accomplish by throwing me to the lions."

Arsenault pushed a bowl of a thick, orange soup toward Renzo. "Groundnut stew. Good eaten with rice or with these fried millet balls or the bread. The bread is very sour and soft; you can bend it into a scoop, like so."

Renzo's brows V'ed together as he watched Arsenault scoop the stew into his own bowl with the bread. Arsenault reached for a platter of skewered meat.

"Beef," he said, holding up a skewer like a sword. "Spicy."

"Mmmm," Renzo said, but he still made no move to eat anything.

"These are fish balls. And coconut rice and plantain. Smoked fish over here. And this paste, you eat it with your fingers. Very sour. The Dakkarans are great fermenters."

Renzo still looked nervous, so Arsenault scooped out several fingers of bean paste and demonstrated how to eat it neatly out of his own hand. The sour notes Dakkarans preferred in their bread and pickles had quickly grown on him and they went well with the heat of the spices coating the meat. He suspected the plain fish stew he'd subsisted on in the Outer Isles would taste hopelessly bland to him now.

When it became clear that Arsenault was going to survive his meal, Renzo's shoulders relaxed and he reached first for the jug of red. Wine of all kinds was served in bowls and Renzo poured himself a generous portion, then grimaced as he took his first sip.

"Oh. It's that stuff made from berries, isn't it? So sweet. It's not bad, but not what I'm expecting from the first sip, you know?" Renzo lowered the bowl and looked at him. "You're Vençalan; you ought to know wine."

"It's been a long time since I've had any."

"The Qalfans I sailed with had a nice stock of Vençalan whites. Rather extraordinary, actually. If only my brother had sent me for wine."

Renzo's long, thin fingers played over the small dishes, rearranging them before he took a beef skewer, some coconut rice, plantain, and fish.

"Here, I'm talking to you as if we're equals. You've probably never tasted a fine white wine. A fisherman, were you, before you sold your sword or rowed the galleys?"

"Carpenter."

"On the Isles? Haven't they been completely denuded?"

"I came from Avelbris on Hefne Island. There are still forests there. Your ancestors didn't take all the wood."

"Mmmm." Renzo took another uncomfortable sip of wine. Then he grimaced and looked up. "Would you like some?"

"I'm on duty," Arsenault said. "I'm not really supposed to..." In counterpoint to his words, he reached for the pitcher of palm wine and poured himself a very small amount in the bottom of a bowl. Renzo was right. A Vençalan gavaro would never refuse an offer of food and wine from the lord's table.

"Of course." Renzo poured him a little more. "I did request your company, though. And we're locked in here until the gods know when."

Oh, so it's to be a drinking contest.

Getting him drunk was a lot subtler than a lunge for his sword, Arsenault had to admit.

He settled back on his heels and took the barest sip from the bowl. Renzo watched him thoughtfully, then picked up the beef skewer. It smelled like it was coated in spice and groundnuts, a combination Arsenault appreciated, but Renzo flushed as soon as he bit into it.

"Dear gods," he gasped. He took a big gulp of his wine, then stared at it regretfully.

Arsenault chuckled. "You should be more careful. My lord."

"Apparently," Renzo said. He took a smaller bite this time. "So, Qalfan pirates took you, did you say? Must have been a long voyage from the Outer Islands. Were others taken with you?"

"A few men from my village," Arsenault replied carefully. "The Lady Adayze pulled me off the ship as a fine for the conditions. All the other galleymen either died or were sold as rehabilitation experiments."

"Rehabilitation," Renzo repeated slowly. "Experiments."

Was it his imagination or did Renzo pale?

"I'd be dead without Lady Adayze's attention," Arsenault went on. "I consider that she's rehabilitated me, but I would still like to know where the other men went. Does Lord Promethi also believe in rehabilitating criminals?"

"Lord Promethi and his brother use a lot of indentured labor, but I would have no idea where they acquired the contracts. Arak lands butt up against the mountains. The work of keeping back the wilderness and tending kacin bushes is neverending."

Renzo looked out the window like he was brooding over a memory, then his eyes flicked back at Arsenault. "The rain in Arak lands does break the heat. If it would only rain *here*, perhaps we would also have some relief."

He suddenly leaned back from the table and stripped his silk tunic off over his head. The linen shirt he wore underneath clung to his chest with sweat. Renzo wasn't a bulky man, but he had the lean physique of a man accustomed to activity.

Arsenault watched for a moment in confusion as Renzo shook out his tousled hair with his hand. Then it occurred to him what the single, flickering glance had meant. Etereans had a long tradition of using male courtesans. Renzo wasn't bad-looking, as much as Arsenault was a judge of such things; he preferred women in general, but he'd lived far too many lives and some of them almost exclusively around men to have confined himself only to women. It made him wonder for a moment about Guin. Had he lost more memories there? But even the thought of resuming a friendship was painful. So much of it would have to be rebuilt from nothing.

Arsenault schooled his face and poured Renzo more wine. Trying to figure out the Eterean was beginning to fascinate him a little. He certainly seemed determined to escape this apartment.

Renzo tossed his tunic on the couch. "I suppose if I'd come down on a caravan, I might have adjusted better. But my brother wanted me to sail. He thought the other Houses were being short-sighted. *The future lies in Dakkar*, he said. *Whoever controls that trade controls the fate of the peninsula*."

"Seems like he'd want the charts then, not your notes."

Renzo stuck his finger in the little pot of sour brown paste and licked it off before he answered. "Gathering intelligence, are you? Want to know if I was trying to steal the charts?"

"I'm on duty, mestere," Arsenault replied calmly, picking up the jug to pour Renzo more wine. "I can't help you unless you tell me what happened."

Renzo took a clean bowl and the jug when Arsenault finished and poured out another bowl of wine. He pushed it over to Arsenault.

"Why don't we abandon the fictions, Arsenault. I know I'm the goat about to be slaughtered, even though I'm telling the truth about that gun. Promethi needed a sacrifice to keep himself in the Ibuu's good graces, and I was handy. But I've been the goat since my brother called me into his office to send me on this journey. So, do me a favor. Allow me to believe—just briefly—that I am sharing a meal with a fellow traveler and not with my executioner."

"Lord Renzo, I don't—"

Renzo put his hand up. "Perhaps you were once a carpenter, Arsenault, and perhaps that scar came from a slip of the chisel, but you don't get a position in the royal guard by building tables. I'm requesting this as a courtesy to a condemned man. Take off your tunic and eat your meal. And call me Renzo, will you?"

"QALFAN VESSELS ARE A SIGHT TO BEHOLD—SLEEK, FAST, STRONG AS iron. But those rocks would rip holes in anything. After the storm, it was a wonder the ship didn't sink like a stone. We had all hands on deck, everyone who'd ever reefed a sail, and round-the-clock bailers in the hold. We had to put in at the nearest harbor, not even in Dakkaran territory yet. It was a wild place. Nobody around for miles, just...jungle."

Renzo made a loose gesture with his bowl of wine. The sweet, dizzy smell of kacin rose from the pipe he held in his other hand.

"We cut some trees for wood to patch the places where the hull was breached. I helped as much as I could, but I'm not a shipbuilder. I asked if I might take a few members of the crew to explore the area, to look for fresh water. The captain gave me a few men and we walked off into the jungle.

"Do you know how easy it is to lose yourself in a jungle? As soon as you step into it, it closes around you. Everywhere you look—hot, green. Full of bugs. And snakes. One dropped from a branch..." Renzo shuddered and took a long pull on his pipe.

Arsenault leaned back on his pillow with his own pipe, packed not with kacin but with a mild mix of sweetweed. The smoke from Renzo's pipe was bad enough. He didn't know if Renzo knew Arsenault had tricked him when he went to the door to request the pipes from Haq, but maybe he did. Renzo was difficult to pin down. On the one hand, he'd bumbled straight into Promethi's hands. On the other hand, he was keeping up the wine contest. As soon as Arsenault's attention wandered, he found his bowl full again and Renzo requesting him to try the spiciest thing on the table. *Please tell me what that's like, Arsenault. I think I have burned my mouth. I can't seem to taste anything anymore.*

Arsenault *had* drunk more wine than he'd intended, and Renzo's request for him to take off his tunic had been blatant, but then again not. And why wouldn't he lie down on the pillows if Jon wanted information out of Renzo? It was, after all, information Arsenault also wanted for himself.

His tunic lay folded over the back of the couch, leaving him in his plain, linen shirt as Renzo had requested, but he still wore his sword.

"I've not been to the interior," Arsenault said. "I have no experience with snakes."

"You should thank the gods for that. They say there's a snake in Arak lands that can kill you with its eyes."

"How? Does it cry venom?"

"Dear gods. That sounds awful. Dying from snake tears?"

"There are worse ways to die." *And I could mention a few…*

"The venom turns you inside out."

"Literally inside out?" Arsenault frowned, trying to imagine. Even with magic… "I don't think that's possible."

"Figuratively, maybe—how the hell should I know? I'm just telling you what I heard. Do you have to know how everything works?"

"It helps."

Renzo shot him a strange look. "The important thing is we got lost. We spent the night in the jungle, and in the morning, we stumbled on a village.

"You've never seen a more ragtag establishment in your life. Tents and hammocks, monkeys, chickens, pigs, all milling about together. We had no idea where we were; we hoped Dakkar, but instead, it was a slice of no man's land between the Wastes and civilization. This *village* we'd stumbled on was only a way station on the Serapo, a place where the caravan captains trade on their journey to Mdembu. Full to the gills with pirates and their women.

"They were so very helpful, too. Brought out surprisingly good brandy, asked all about our misfortunes—just like you're doing now, Arsenault, except at the end of the night, they offered…entertainment." Renzo glanced at him.

Arsenault pretended not to notice. "I thought you were married."

"For whatever it's worth. I return to port long enough to kiss my children and remember how lucky I am to be married to the woman my mother chose for me, then my brother ruins everything again. Before, it was always some damn fool trip to Tiresia or Qalfa. It's his way of making sure I don't challenge him as Householder."

"Would you?"

"Me? What would I want with the Householder chair?"

"Aren't you Lierans always competing for something? I don't know very much about your politics."

"That much is clear. You eat like a man who's never had to worry about being poisoned by your relatives."

Renzo was watching him in a measuring way, his eyes far sharper than they ought to be, considering there was *kacin* in his pipe. Before Arsenault could catch him out, he faced the window, where a gray afternoon had turned to a hot night muffled by clouds. Candlelight glimmered in pools on the table and moths hurled themselves at the screens, drawn uselessly to it.

Renzo tapped the ashes from his pipe, sighing heavily. "You can probably guess what happened next. The pirates helpfully led us back to our ship, only to attack us once we got there. They killed the captain, his mate, and most of the crew and hauled off everything valuable, as well as those of us they thought might be worth something."

Renzo's mouth stretched tight in a strange expression that wasn't a smile, though it looked like one. "My fault. All of it."

"I wasn't there, mestere, but I don't know if you can assume responsibility for the crew's deaths. If you were stranded, you needed help."

Renzo looked bleakly amused. "Are you giving me an out? Suggesting it's not really trust if you don't have a choice?"

"I don't think it is. It's merely the thing you do when you can't do anything else. What's done is done, mestere; best let it go."

Easy to say, harder to do. Arsenault drank his wine again, hoping the bowl hid the twitch he got under his scar every time he thought about what was done and the thousands of things he could or should have done instead, all of them under his power and ignored in the moment.

"Call me Renzo. Go ahead."

"Best let it go...Renzo?"

"Such conviction." Renzo let his head sink back into the pillow. "I've no power over you here, Arsenault. We're both free men taken into custody far from home. Perhaps we shall discuss philosophy. Is it really trust if a man has had all his choices taken away?" Renzo seemed to consider this. His features drew downward. "Would that I had the Sight my brother has."

The way he said *Sight* made Arsenault bring his head up immediately. He looked for the tell-tale aura of magic washing around the other man but saw nothing.

"You think your brother would have acted differently in the same situation?"

"My brother is good at ferreting out the weaknesses of other people and exploiting them. Doubtless, he would have made some sort of deal with the pirates. But I'm not sure the crews' lives would have figured positively into the equation."

Aside from a resigned and somewhat mournful cast to the man's features, there was nothing to indicate how Renzo felt about the fact that his brother was cruel. Or did he mean his brother was merely practical? "Did the pirates send your brother a ransom note?"

Renzo shook his head. "It would have taken months. Geoffre would never pay a ransom for me anyway. He'd consider my death a windfall. No, I think they were hoping a caravan captain would purchase me as a hostage or an indenture. The tongue they spoke was all mashed-up—Qalfan, Dakkaran, Onzarran. I couldn't understand it very well. But they made us work. They weren't terrible masters if we did what we were told.

"Then a caravan came floating down the river, the pirates brought us out, and business was conducted. The new captain was Onzarran and after I traded him most of my silks, he decided he was sympathetic to my plight. As well he should have been, because all my silks were Aliente. Don't tell my brother I said so, because he hates the Aliente, but their silk is the highest quality you'll ever find. It fetches an enormous profit, but the merchant Houses all know it and take a higher percentage of carrying fees out of them. If Pallo had his own ships, he could get around it, but he doesn't, which is so much the better for us. I even had some burgundy, like that bedspread. The moths that spin burgundy silk are the size of hummingbirds. Only the Aliente grow them. But the captain took all my silk in exchange for my freedom. Thank the gods the bastard left me my House tunic. Without it, I might as well be a fisherman."

"Sometimes it's easier to be a fisherman."

"Or a carpenter? Didn't seem to help you much, did it? But I continue to do my duty to my House for some ungodly reason." Renzo shifted closer—close enough Arsenault could smell the wine and kacin on his breath. He couldn't help catching Renzo's gaze now. His eyes were a little darker than they ought to be, the pupils dilated until they swallowed most of that brilliant blue, almost certainly because of kacin and candlelight. "You know, you don't look Vençalan," Renzo said in a low voice. "And you don't sound Vençalan. Not even from the Outer Islands."

Renzo's clumsy and half-hearted attempts at seduction were more amusing than appalling. It might be kinder to put a stop to them now, but two could play this game and he didn't for a moment believe Renzo would let things go further than having a chance at—

Go ahead and think it. He wants to grab your sword. Arsenault stifled a groan at his own bad humor.

"Are you trying to tell me something, Renzo?"

Renzo leaned away to put down his empty wine bowl.

"When we reached the Arak stronghold, the captain took me straight to lord Dirik and his brother Promethi. As I understand it, the two oldest siblings have special relationships in these cultures, don't they? Lord Dirik was indisposed, so his brother kept me there—

in quasi-freedom—for an entire season, inviting me to dinner, allowing me access to his library, walking with me in the kacin plantations..."

Arsenault cleared his throat. "You think it's possible the galleymen from my ship might be working the kacin farms?"

Renzo shot him a curious glance. "One might be surprised. One might also be surprised at what else indentures are used for in the Arak holdings. It's not just to make kacin."

"For...entertainment purposes?"

"Assuredly for entertainment purposes." Renzo moved even closer. "But there's a difference between an indenture and a galley slave, isn't there?" Hesitantly, he touched Arsenault's arm. When Arsenault didn't pull away, his fingers settled, then moved up Arsenault's bicep in a touch that couldn't be interpreted as anything but a caress.

"Renzo," Arsenault said softly. Renzo's gaze snagged hopefully on Arsenault's. Arsenault leaned forward, his face inches away from Renzo's.

"*I'm not the entertainment.*"

Renzo flushed dark red and pulled back. An embarrassed, crooked smile lifted the corners of his mouth.

"Damn. I am married, you know. I should apologize for my inexperience at this sort of"—he waved his hand—"thing."

"So, you weren't used for entertainment purposes?"

"Ah. No." Renzo rolled onto his side and pushed himself up next to Arsenault. His face went suddenly serious and Arsenault got the feeling they were done playing, that whatever Renzo said next would be unquestionably true.

"I think I've seen your galleymen. They aren't the ordinary sort of indentures and they certainly aren't being *rehabilitated,* whatever that's supposed to mean."

Arsenault shoved himself up, but Renzo stopped him. "I'm willing to trade what I know. But in return, you are going to get me out of here. Otherwise, I can't help you find who you're looking for."

CHAPTER 29

ARSENAULT

Dammit.

Renzo had played him like a fiddle. All he could do was strike a bargain with the Eterean, promising to free him from the Ibuu's custody in exchange for information about Guin. A host of hazy and desperate plans shuffled through his head as he reported to Lord Jonawak, but not one seemed workable in the real world.

It was almost dawn when he finally left the lord's study to seek his own bed, but the thought of staggering into the middle of the shift change smelling like kacin smoke didn't appeal to him much.

He stopped at the pump behind the barracks, stripped out of his tunic and shirt, and sluiced water over his hair and shoulders, probably longer than necessary. Even tepid water was a relief in this heat.

A noise caught his attention as he straightened.

There was a lot of noise in the palace compound at night. The chirp and whir of millions of insects, the trill of nightbirds, and distantly, hyenas and their crazy laughter. This was different. He dried himself with his shirt and listened.

The scattering of pebbles.

The sound raised the hair on the back of his neck. It could have been another guardsman coming into the barracks. It could have been one of the many cats and dogs that hung around the outbuildings.

It could have been a lot of things, but it didn't *feel* like any of them. He set his shirt on the wooden rack that held the buckets and pulled his knife.

He edged down the path that led away from the barracks toward the small village of artisans and field hands. Between them there was a large garden and then the stables and kennels. Further downwind stood the pigsties and a few small enclosures of goats.

The shuffling sounded like it was headed toward the garden.

A pair of mango trees, laden with heavy fruit, framed the entrance. Arsenault didn't like walking under them. They made the already dark night even darker. He wouldn't be able to tell if anyone was waiting in the branches until it was too late.

Or there could be snakes...

He ducked under the trees as fast as he could. When he looked up, a tall shape moved on the path before him.

He froze. The shape, oddly formed, turned—

A woman. Holding a child.

"Adayze?" he said.

The woman jerked and the child she held tucked up against her shoulder made a noise and pushed against her.

"Shh, Edo. It's all right. It's only our carpenter playing with us, yes?" She let her breath out in exasperation. "*Arsenault.*"

He sheathed the knife quickly, but the feeling of danger didn't disappear. "Were you walking by the barracks?" he asked in a low voice.

"We have been walking almost everywhere. His nurse was at her wit's end. I should have brought my wrap, but I thought he would go right to sleep, he's been up so long." She grunted and shifted the toddler, rolling her shoulders as she did so. "Edo, little one, how can you be so heavy?"

"I'll take a turn, if he'll come to me," Arsenault said.

Adayze turned her head, so he knew she was eyeing him, probably noticing he wasn't wearing a shirt. He had too much alcohol and secondhand kacin in his system to let her look go by without it affecting him.

"You know people will talk if we keep meeting like this. You, only half-clothed."

He forced a chuckle, but her words only reminded him how long it had been since he'd had any kind of meaningful connection with a woman—a simple touch, a kind word. He'd kept to himself in the months he'd been at the palace, unwilling to form more webs of relationship than had already been woven for him. He didn't recall a woman on the island. He'd gone there to be alone. Instead, he'd ended up responsible for a ship full of men.

He tried to keep his voice amused and mild. "What—you, me, and Edo? Sounds like a perfect recipe for a midnight tryst."

Adayze laughed, thank the gods. "Edo. You like the carpenter, don't you? He wants to carry you for a while. Give your mama a break."

When Edo realized he was being handed off, he wriggled and looked at Arsenault with large round eyes.

Arsenault held out his hands, relieved to turn his focus to the child. "Come on, Edo. Ari will walk with you for a while. We'll go see the fountains."

Fountains turned out to be a key word. Silently, Edo lunged forward. Arsenault caught him, settling him securely into the crook of his arm. Bittersweet memories of holding his own children ambushed him suddenly—Erelf never wiped those away, both a blessing and curse.

Damn kacin. Made him maudlin.

He hugged Edo briefly, a pitiful gesture that cheered him regardless, then bounced the baby on his arm so Edo could see over his shoulder.

"Arsenault. I want him to sleep."

"He doesn't look that tired to me."

"*I'm* tired. I spent many hours with the Ibuu and his court, trying to maintain a civil conversation with Promethi. I am exhausted."

"Perhaps he'll fall asleep as we walk."

"He loves the fountains. See? He's not even putting his head down. Maybe I shouldn't have given him to you. You can't be more awake than I am." Adayze paused and sniffed. "And what is that smell?"

"Lord Jonawak had me prying information from Renzo di Prinze."

"And did you?"

"Some." Edo squirmed against him, a warm, wriggling ball of toddler, and Arsenault adjusted his hold. "I don't mind taking him to the fountains."

"It will be light by the time he goes to sleep."

Arsenault looked down at Edo. "Do your ears hurt, little one?" he murmured. "Or perhaps your teeth?"

In response, Edo wiggled his hand free and pointed over Arsenault's shoulder. "Unh," he said. "Unh, unh."

Arsenault smiled. "I apologize, young sir, for taking too much time. I shall quicken my pace."

"You spoil him," Adayze said in an amused voice. "My mother says he won't talk unless we make him use words."

"He'll use words when he's ready."

"My mother says both Jon and I were talking by this age. She's convinced my husband has brought bad luck down on our whole family."

"That's ridiculous. Neither of my boys talked at all until they were almost two. After that we couldn't get them to be quiet."

Slowly, Adayze turned her head toward him. "Your...boys? Do you have children, Arsenault?"

"Had," he choked—*damn* the kacin, it always made him talk too much. "I *had* children. They've been...gone. A long time."

"Oh. In one of your other lives."

"Yes."

"Only the two boys?"

How could he answer that? Maybe he'd fathered other children, but if so, Erelf had wiped away the knowledge like rubbing wet paint from a canvas. He was left looking at a blank surface instead of the rich and colorful landscape of which he might have been a part.

He exhaled heavily. "And a daughter. Two boys and a girl."

Edo laid his head on Arsenault's shoulder. Arsenault gave him a squeeze.

"My mother is convinced everything is my husband's fault. She watches Edo like a hawk, waiting for anything odd. The not sleeping. The not talking."

A smile tugged at Arsenault's mouth. "Chasing cats? Pulling up the flowers in the garden? Eating dirt?"

Arsenault could almost hear Adayze roll her eyes. "Our nurses raised us. My mother has no idea what we did daily, and she doesn't understand why I am taking such an active role. *You are supposed to be the Heir, Dayze!* she tells me. *It is beneath you to change that dirty nappy!*" Adayze shook her head. "How can she understand? Her family married her to my father for expediency, then she ran back to her relatives half the year. I never questioned that she cared for us, that wasn't an issue, but her whole life was based on doing her political duty. She had to keep those ties between her family and her husband tight, and they were constantly threatening to pull apart. She left us because she didn't have a choice—but what if she had created a new choice? Could she have done it? Did she try? I don't know."

Adayze sighed as if the sound was pulled out of her by an old, familiar weight. It pressed on his heart, too.

"Eating dirt is normal toddler behavior, Adayze—lady. I thought one of mine lived on it. He had to live on something. He certainly didn't eat much of anything else."

"It wasn't because he was cursed? Turning into a monster?"

"All two-year-old boys are monsters. But usually they grow out of it."

She paused for a heartbeat. "You called me by my name."

Arsenault felt like he'd broken cover on a sortie, exposed himself by accident. His heart drummed until he scolded himself. *You are being dramatic.* "Forgive me, lady. I didn't mean to cause offense. It's late. Early. I'm tired." He paused, then added, hoping she'd take it as explanation, "Renzo di Prinze was smoking kacin."

"I have so few people who call me by my name," she continued wistfully, as if he hadn't said anything at all. And there was that loneliness again, calling to his own.

Edo's limbs were softening, his thumb in his mouth, his head heavier on Arsenault's shoulder. In a few moments they would be out from under the dark umbrellas of the cycads and into the clearing where the fountains played. The sound of splashing water threaded itself faintly into the sounds of the night.

Finally, Arsenault trusted himself to speak. "I shall call you whatever you wish, of course."

A flick of movement in the darkness made him think she was rubbing her temple. "Arsenault. That isn't what I meant—"

The long, palm-like leaves of the cycads behind him shivered, too loudly to be the wind.

Adayze paused. "You said you heard something at the barracks?"

"I did. Probably it was a cat, but—"

The leaves rustled again. Arsenault stopped walking and stood very still. Beside him, Adayze did the same.

The soft slip of something moving in the ferns.

Adayze caught his eye. Silently and slowly, he transferred a now sleeping Edo back to her. Edo stirred and began sucking his thumb again. Adayze tucked the baby under her chin as Arsenault worked his sword out of its scabbard.

By unspoken agreement, Adayze backed away with Edo and began walking down the path toward the fountains, slowly at first, then faster. Arsenault pulled his knife with his other hand and waded into the ferns and cycads, weapons ready.

Something big shot through the undergrowth in Adayze's direction. *What in all the hells...*

Adayze broke into a run and Arsenault lunged at the *thing*.

Silver flashed, the sinuous overlapping of moving plates or scales, a thick body about as big around as a cycad's trunk. Without stopping to identify it, he drove his sword downward as hard as he could.

The blade shrieked through the plates like metal piercing metal. Weird green liquid poured from the wound and spattered the ferns with a burning hiss. Arsenault cursed when the creature buckled and he lost his grip on the sword and fell over the steaming, writhing body. The creature's blood seared his bare chest like acid. He gritted his teeth, trying to scramble back over the tail, but too late—it slithered over his calves.

An enormous, hooded snake rose in front of him.

How had a monster that big hidden in the ferns? Its tongue flicked past gleaming silver fangs and its scales glittered like metal, but surely that was a trick of the light.

He let his magic move through him and the snake lit up in his Sight like a torch.

"Gods*dammit*."

Arsenault barely got his knife up to block its strike. The blade clanged off its fangs and cut into the side of its mouth. Enraged and in pain, the snake jerked its head away, leaking more hot green fluid. Its whole body squeezed itself around Arsenault's waist.

"*Shit*," he wheezed. Frantically, he brought the knife down, but the point slid off the scales and Arsenault had to wait again to thrust into a gap between the moving plates.

The snake's tail thrashed, but instead of letting him go, its powerful muscles only constricted tighter. Arsenault struggled as it tried to pick him up off his feet and roll him over. The pressure on his ribs was excruciating. He dropped the useless knife and grabbed for his magic.

Surely this counts as self-defense! He didn't know any other way to fight the damn thing. He struggled to See deeper into the snake's body—what it was made of, how it worked, what it *was*. Not metal, exactly, but like metal, built somehow of living gears and cogs—

"What..." he began in surprise. That was enough pause for the snake to kick him out of its space. The magic snapped back into him and the snake's pink maw hurtled downward out of the night.

Desperately, he did the only thing he could think of. He welded its mouth closed.

His magic hit it like an explosion of gunpowder. It flung its head back with a hissing cry, its lips flaring cherry red, but not before its blocky jaw swept past Arsenault, charring the hair on that side of his head. He shouted in pain as the snake unwound its coils and shot off down the path, wrapped in the thick, noxious odor of sulfur.

Arsenault fell forward onto his hands and knees, gulping air. It took him a moment to realize he wasn't actually burned. His hair wasn't really on fire. But now the snake was free to chase Adayze and Edo.

❧❧

SWEARING, ARSENAULT SWEPT HIS SWORD OFF THE GROUND AND ran down the path. The snake moved faster than anything he'd ever seen, almost as if it disappeared and reappeared again in the place it wanted to be. But broken branches and leaves from its passing littered the path and made the footing treacherous in the dark.

Adayze and Edo had made it past the fountains. The path from there led into the palm grove by the magus hut, which must be where Adayze was headed.

Silver scales glinted ahead of him. Edo was crying. Arsenault put on a burst of speed and nearly tumbled down the slope leading into the palm grove.

Adayze backed against the door to the hut, holding Edo tight against her hip with one hand while she sorted through a keyring with the other. The snake towered above her. Its head swayed, hood out, like it was preparing to strike.

She was singing a lullaby under her breath in a shaky voice.

"Hush, now, baby, day is done..."

Keys rattled. She found one and slowly reached toward the lock, but the snake darted forward. With a soft cry, she stopped, closing her eyes briefly as she stood absolutely still. Edo clutched her and whimpered in terror.

The snake drew back as if it were trying to get in a better position to strike. But why didn't it strike now? Was it chasing one of them, but not the other? And if so, did it want to kill Adayze or Edo?

"Hush...hush now, baby... Cows are...cows are...sleeping..."

Arsenault moved slowly around the back of the snake.

"Hush now, baby, night comes creeping..."

"Adayze," he said softly.

She lifted her chin, just a tiny movement, but the snake caught it.

"No, don't turn your head."

"I can't find the key."

"You don't have it?"

"No. The keys keep slipping. I keep picking up the wrong one. Like a—"

Edo's face pulled like he would start crying again.

"Hush, hush," Adayze sang in a low, choked, tuneless voice, "dreams will keep...keep you..."

Then she finished what she had been saying to him, "Like a dream."

Not just a dream. A nightmare.

Arsenault continued to move softly around the snake's coiled tail with his sword out, wishing he had an axe. Or his *own* sword, dammit, the one the captain had stolen.

"Adayze. What do you see?"

"What do you mean, what do I see? It's the cobra demon the fila cast into the sea. Oh, shh, shh...Edo, don't move..."

"Silver?"

"Black! Why—"

Damn. They were seeing two different creatures. Him, an Eterean machine—her, a monster out of Dakkaran legends. It was just like Jonawak's Nightmare Man story.

He kept his eyes on the snake as he approached its field of peripheral vision. "You'll have to See the keys through the magic. It's confusing us with some kind of illusion. Can you do that?"

"Yes." He heard the brief ting of metal. "Got it. I think. It's...hard to hold the magic this long, Arsenault. With Edo."

"I know. When I count three, put the key in the lock and run inside as fast as you can."

"All right."

"One... Two... *Three*."

He smacked the side of the snake with the flat of his sword. It swung its head around and Adayze jammed the key into the lock.

Then it spat a fine spray of burning green liquid at him.

It pattered down like rain, searing his skin before he threw himself out of the way. The pain was excruciating, like a handful of simultaneous hornet stings. The snake lunged back toward the hut, flinging more droplets of venom from its mouth. Adayze shoved on the door, which had stuck with the humidity. A drop of venom caught in her hair and she cried out as smoke curled up from her head. More sulfur scent filled the air.

Arsenault bellowed and hurled himself at the snake.

He drove his sword deep into the snake's body. It writhed, but Arsenault curled his fingers around its scales and used the sword as a

step to boost himself on top of it. If he could Shape the cogs inside...
The snake's violent movements knocked him loose. He scrabbled for a
grip, slid down its back—*dammit*—got a brief handle, and then the
snake snapped its tail and he fell, banging his chin on its tough scales.

The impact drove his teeth together, ringing his head like a bell.
Clenching his jaw, he dug his fingernails into the scales and dragged
himself upward again. Adayze slammed the door open with her hip.
The snake's hood collapsed and it shot after Adayze as she ran
through the door. Fucking hells, this thing was fast. He didn't know if
he could—

Edo wailed in terror.

With renewed determination, Arsenault clung to the snake's head.
It slammed him into the doorway lintel so hard his vision went black
and he lost his grip on his magic.

When his vision returned, he was somehow still holding on, but
for how long? They needed to take the monster down *now*. Adayze
faced the snake, holding two pitifully small whittling knives. Edo
sobbed in the corner, tucked into a ball.

"Stay there, baby," Adayze said. "Edo. Stay. There."

The snake tried to roll. "Pull its head back, Arsenault!" she
shouted.

Yes, that could work. They had one chance. He slid his hands into
the scales in the snake's hood and yanked its head upward. Adayze
charged forward with the whittling knives and he drove his magic into
those odd whirring cogs like a sword. Her blades sank deep into the
snake's tender throat while Arsenault Fixed the cogs, melting them
back into piles of slag.

The snake rolled and thrashed in its death throes. Arsenault barely
jumped off before the snake crashed to the floor, smashing and scattering chairs and tables. Adayze ran to Edo. She scooped him up and
held him tight to her breast, pressing herself and him into the farthest
corner of the room.

The snake's thrashing became shudders, then shivers. Finally, it lay
still.

Arsenault limped painfully over to it.

"Is it dead?" Adayze asked in a shaky voice, shielding Edo with her
back. Edo made some of his noises and Adayze bent her head over the
baby's.

Arsenault took a deep breath and kicked the snake. It didn't move.
"Yes."

"We should get my brother. Tell the Ibuu."

Arsenault made a noise in assent.

"What do you think it is?"

"I don't know."

"Where do you think it came from?"

"I don't know that either."

The room lightened suddenly as the sun rose over the horizon. At first it was just a trickle of gray, but quickly the gray tinged pink and then bright, bloody red. The light spilled over the silver beast lying on the floor, and in an instant its colors and lines grew fuzzy. Then...

The snake dissolved into a mist, which swirled away into the air, leaving nothing but a room full of wrecked furniture, a splintered doorway, and a few blackened metal cogs.

CHAPTER 30

ARSENAULT

ARSENAULT STRODE THROUGH THE ROYAL QUARTERS NEXT TO Adayze and Edo, barely noticing the way chambermaids and manservants alike scattered before them.

"I think you're scaring them, Arsenault," Adayze murmured.

"Too bad."

He scowled down at a male servant who appeared in their way and just as soon scurried out of it. He could imagine what he looked like. Half his hair burned close to his skull, his scar standing out livid, and red welts everywhere the venom had touched his skin. He *had* rinsed the snake's fluids away at the pump and retrieved his shirt and tunic. The servants who worked in the barracks had gone running as soon as they'd seen him striding up, shirtless, next to a trembling Adayze carrying an exhausted, sleeping Edo.

"They are only trying to do their jobs," Adayze said.

"*Someone* tried to kill you. It's too much of a coincidence that Renzo showed up with a gun runed and made from tiaannamir at the same time *this* monster attacks you. I'll drag Renzo out of his room as soon as I get you and Edo situated, lady. He knows something. I mean to find out what."

"You need a healer first. And..." She stopped talking long enough that Arsenault turned to look at her. "I will be unable to sleep unless you are guarding my door."

"But, lady—"

"Call me *Adayze*. A man and a woman who fight a giant snake demon together ought to be on a first-name basis."

"I was merely—"

"You weren't *merely* doing anything, Arsenault. This is the second time you've risked your life for my family."

"I'd probably come back," he mumbled. "If I died."

"You feel pain, though, don't you?"

At the moment he was feeling a lot of pain. It felt like a hammer banging the inside of his skull, and every time his shirt rubbed against a venom burn, he wanted to scream. Every muscle in his body ached and he had been awake since yesterday morning before sunrise.

"I was only doing what any other man would have done."

"Any other man would have climbed up the back of a giant snake and... What *did* you do, Arsenault?"

He slid his hand into his pocket to finger the cog he'd stashed there. "It wasn't a real creature," he said thoughtfully. "And yet again, it was. It seemed to be made from something...metal-ish. I've a Talent for metal."

"So, you *are* a Smith. I wondered when we found the blade you made to fight the lion."

"Don't think of transferring me to your blacksmiths. I won't be able to magick any weapons. There are proscriptions on my Talent. It's part of my curse."

He wasn't sure he should be saying that much. Not after what he'd just done. The gods' attention weighed on him like a pack on his back.

"We've more respect for our Smiths anyway. Why do you think my father was so interested in that gun Renzo di Prinze showed him? It had to be made by one of *our* Smiths."

Despite his resolution not to be drawn into this conversation, he turned toward her.

"That's why our guns are superior," she continued. "And also, why we're guarding the knowledge."

"Well, why don't you carry one of your fantastic guns around with you? Probably would have killed that godsdamned snake faster."

She glared at him. "Our Smiths forged the knives for the magus hut, too. That's why I went *there* instead of running for the palace. It's where we keep all the materials to make our fetishes—the objects that store the power granted us by the fila and our ancestors. If I'd only had one to throw at that snake..." She trailed away thoughtfully. "But it was all like a dream, wasn't it? A nightmare."

Arsenault rubbed his scar. "Either it was intended for you more than me and what I saw were the underworkings, or I was also seeing an illusion. It was like an Éterean machine, but I haven't seen one of those in—"

He finally noticed the way she was staring at him. Éterean *machines*. How long had they been out of the world?

They rounded a corner in the hall and came up against her brother and a wall of guardsmen, nursery women, and chambermaids standing in front of Adayze's bedchamber. She tightened her hold on Edo.

Jonawak had been about to say something, but instead he stared at them in shock.

"By the fila, ghost! What happened to you?"

Arsenault ran his hand through his charred hair. Little burnt flakes of ash sprinkled his fingers, releasing the foul smell of sulfur into the corridor. "Go get Renzo, my lord. Ask him about Promethi and if he won't answer, tell him I'll be in later to throttle the information out of him." Arsenault turned to Adayze. "Are these guardsmen sufficient to protect you, lady? I'd put two by the door, two by the window, a couple at the foot of your bed."

"Arsenault, I told you. I don't care how many guardsmen there are, I want you by the door. Inside the room. In case that thing comes back."

"Adayze!" Jon exclaimed. "Arsenault can't stay in your room!"

"He can and he will, Jon."

"He looks like he needs two days of sleep. Adayze, give Edo to the nurses—"

"No! Edo stays by me. I'll nurse him and he'll sleep right here. Don't contradict my orders, Jonawak, *I* am the Heir. Do your duty and question Renzo di Prinze as Arsenault suggested."

Jon glared at her. "What am I questioning him about?"

"Ask him what Promethi dom Arak is doing with the galleymen from my ship. Ask him what he knows about the ship's cargo. It was carrying metal, I'm sure it was—and this is just too much of a coinci-dence. It *must* be linked somehow," Arsenault said. "Tell him our bargain is canceled if I have to deal with more nightmare creatures."

Jon frowned deeply. "*Your* bargain?"

Arsenault eyed him level. There was a clatter of boots and weapons as all the guardsmen reacted to the anger he didn't bother to hide. Jon might take it out of his hide, but to hell with it. He was tired of being a galleyman, a convict, an indenture. Tired of being ordered about by both gods and men.

"*My* people, *my* bargain," he said. "Tell Renzo if more of *my* people are threatened, I'll see him to the hanging tree myself. If you have any consideration for your sister and your nephew, you'll see to their comfort now and worry about everything else later. My lord."

"You know what your problem is, ghost? You have no respect for authority."

"Authority comes and goes. Integrity and compassion last."

"You'll take a knee to the Heir and to me right now," Jon said. "Since it seems as if you might need help remembering your place."

Arsenault glared at Jon. His knees felt like a rusty gate as he forced himself down onto the hard tiles of the hallway. With effort, he bent his head and supported himself with the fingers of his right hand.

"My lady," he said.

"Jonawak dom B'ara," Adayze said, her voice almost as full of venom as the snake. "It is my desire as the Heir that this man be rewarded for his service with a position as my *personal* guard. It is also my desire, as Heir, that this man shall be a personal guard to my son, as I trust him with our lives. He will stay by my door tonight, and my son *will* stay with me, and now—Jonawak—you can take a knee right beside him."

A muscle in Jon's jaw twitched. But he went down on his knee next to Arsenault and bowed his head, crossing his arms over his chest, holding his fists against the balls of his shoulders. When he went down, all the other guards and nursery women dropped, too, pressing their foreheads to the floor.

Adayze took a deep breath. "Now get up, both of you. I'm exhausted and Edo needs to eat."

❦

ADAYZE'S CHAMBERS WERE LARGE, BUT SURPRISINGLY SIMPLE FOR the heir to a kingdom. A big bed, a lot of floor pillows, and some rugs and chairs, all done in patterns you could find down in the market. A basket of toys in the corner, the front legs of a sewn hippo doll hanging over the side. Renzo's chambers were more impressive.

Arsenault and the other guards made a circuit of the chamber first. In the dressing room, Arsenault waited for them to leave, then turned Adayze's long mirror to the wall. After a moment's consideration, he also carried it into her closet, where he hid it among the tunics and dresses. He flipped over a hand-held mirror on the vanity and pushed it into the corner amid the collection of small pots that held hair oils, lotions, and Adayze's other cosmetics. He didn't trust any portals for Sight, especially not tonight...this morning.

When he stepped into the bedchamber, the guards had arranged themselves and Adayze had settled down on the bed with Edo. She sighed as she leaned into the pillows propped against the headboard and pulled down the neck of her tunic before shifting Edo to her breast.

Arsenault looked away to find a small, middle-aged woman standing before him, wearing a white robe. Here in Dakkar, there seemed to be a large population of people of mixed ethnicity, children of the Mdembu-to-Qalfa trade networks that had been operating probably since Nambutu had built the first city. The woman didn't braid her thick black hair Tiresian style, nor did she wear the urqa and allaq the way Qalfans did, but with her golden-amber skin she could have been either or both... Or perhaps one of her parents had been Hamari or even from Saien. You could see that a little, too, in the shape of her black eyes.

She bowed her head slightly. "My name is Chayma. Lady Adayze's personal healer. You may not remember me."

He bowed in reflex, even as he struggled to recall her. There was something familiar about her, maybe her voice, or the way she twitched the flowing sleeve away from her wrist. "Vaguely," he said.

"I treated you the day you came to us. I didn't think you'd survive that wound." She eyed him shrewdly. "But you seem to have made an excellent recovery; you look years younger."

Arsenault straightened. The healer tilted her head back to keep eye contact—the top of her head came only to his collarbone—one dark brow raised as if daring him to put the question off.

"It amazes me, too, lady, how much vitality a festering wound can steal. The gods must have taken an interest in me; that's the only way I can explain it."

Adayze made a noise and covered it by coughing.

"Well, miracles happen," Chayma said in a mild tone. "Please sit so I can treat you now."

"In front of the door," he answered, happy to be off the subject of his recent death. Chamber women moved around him, setting up pillows where he indicated. The sight of the pillows pulled all the fear and fight out of him. His legs began shaking so badly he collapsed the rest of the way to the floor.

"Take off your shirt," the healer said calmly.

He'd put the shirt back on for propriety, but the fabric rubbing against the venom burns hurt like all the hells. Getting the shirt off again was a relief. The healer leaned forward to examine him, as if she needed spectacles, then dug in her robe for a small white pot of oint-ment that smelled of sandalwood and camphor. He pulled backward before she could apply it to his wounds.

"I can do it myself."

The healer smiled slightly. "I treated you when you looked worse than this—what's your name?"

"Arsenault."

"Arsenault. Lie back. I'll do a more thorough job and it will help me gauge how deeply the venom has worked its way into you. You're lucky; if it had hit your eyes, you'd be blind."

"You know this venom?" he asked in surprise.

"It's more common in the interior, but not unknown here. Now, lie still and close your eyes. It will feel better."

Stiffly, he lay back on the pillows and closed his eyes. She touched one of the wounds with her ointment-laden fingertips and he flinched. It was so damn hard to lie still. And not just because it hurt. She began working the ointment into his chest and a pleasant warmth spread through his muscles in counterpoint to the cool ointment, but the aftereffects of the battle were hitting him and he had to fight to keep his eyes closed—always sure he saw a flicker of silver at the edges of his vision.

Soon, his exhaustion got the better of him. The pressure of Chay-ma's fingers and the soft, warm lapping of her magic were lulling him to sleep. Hands moved behind him, helping him sit so Chayma could bind his chest with soft cotton bandages. By the time she was finished, he was drifting.

Chayma pushed him gently back into the pillows. "Rest now, so the ointment can draw the poison out. It may draw up...other things, too."

He struggled to open his eyes, knowing how many *other things* lurked inside him, worse than the poison.

"*Rest*, Arsenault," the healer said more firmly. He brushed his fingers against the door, reminding himself that anyone trying to come into the room would trip over him first. Her magic washed through him again and he sank into a warm darkness. He didn't know for how long, but Adayze's voice brought him back to the surface.

"The wounds will heal, won't they?"

"Yes. You need your sleep too, lady."

"Give me a moment, Chayma?"

"Of course, my lady."

Fabric rustled. Arsenault tried to push himself up, but his limbs and his eyelids were so heavy. "Adayze."

"Shh. Don't move. I just want to know...what you said to Jon about *my people*...are Edo and I your people now, too?"

He remained silent, unable to answer. He *had* gone to that island to be alone. And this was why.

Look what happened the moment he couldn't stand the loneliness anymore. All these tangled relationships, these hurts and pains. Everything they needed from him or that he wanted to give them but couldn't. He wasn't strong enough or good enough to save them all. Not Guin, not the ship boy, not the other men on the ship, not Adayze or Edo either. He'd break and betray them, lead them farther into danger...

Die and forget all about them.

He forced his eyes open. Adayze leaned over him, more scent than vision in the dimmed room. Cloves and citrus. Smooth skin. Her fingers remained on his shoulder, still touching him lightly.

She was married, and he was just a man who'd been lonely far too long.

"I'm not anyone to rely on, Adayze," he said hoarsely. "I just do my best."

Her eyes narrowed. Then she took her hand away, which was both relief and disappointment. "Edo went to sleep on the bed. I am going to sleep with him. I want you to remain here until he wakes. Do you understand?"

"Yes, my lady."

"Good night, Arsenault."

"Good night, lady." When she paused in the center of the room, he cleared his throat and corrected himself. "Adayze."

She started walking again.

☙◊❧

THE OINTMENT PULLED MUCH MORE TO THE SURFACE THAN JUST THE venom in his skin. Or perhaps it *was* the venom that made these nightmares stalk him through the dark.

He walked perpetually through gardens, unable to find a way out and pursued by *something* in the undergrowth he could never see. Something large and dangerous—but beautiful, too, seductive and deadly as the remnants of the magic still swirling through him. He wanted to stay away because he knew how it would end. Too weak to close the gates on his magic, or his jealousy and anger, he knew he would end up hurting everyone and everything he loved. Finally, he dreamed that he discovered the narrow trail leading to his old cabin.

Walking it was hard, impossible in the winter when storms whipped through the cliffs and snow often blocked the trail entirely. Arsenault clambered over rockfalls and scree past the spring that burbled, sweet and cold, year-round until he finally reached the green cleft where he'd built his home.

Inside, a woman stood before his hearth.

Her back was to him. Her long hair shone like beaten gold and caught in the furs she wore on her shoulders when she bent to turn the spit. Thin drops of fat dripped from the two rabbits skewered on it and sizzled in the flames, filling the small room with the rich smell of roasted meat.

A floorboard creaked under his weight. The woman turned her head so he could see her profile. Cold, chiseled features. Northern pale.

"Ekyra," he breathed.

She faced him, her mouth hooking up at the corner. Maybe it was a smile, but her frosty eyes were too cold to tell.

"Hello, Ari. It's been a long while since we've spoken, hasn't it?"

"A long, long while. Do your brothers and sisters know you're talking to me?"

"Would I be here if they did?" She peeled off a gauntlet. Her birds were nowhere to be seen, but that meant nothing.

"What do you want from me, lady?"

She threw the glove on the table. He'd built the table himself, before he'd met Guin, so it was less elegant than it might have been. But all he'd had was time, and he'd spent it cutting and milling the planks, sanding them smooth, oiling and finishing them until they felt like silk. The table, like all the tables after, the chairs, the stools, the spoons and chests, had been about building. Not destroying. Seeing her gauntlet cast carelessly down on it—a reminder of all the wars he had fought—soiled it, as if she'd laid down a bloody sword in a sacred space.

"I came to warn you," she said. "You've used a lot of magic since my father sent you back down."

"I'd hardly call twice a lot. Once to defend myself against a lion and the last, we were attacked by a giant snake. It was self-defense."

"That's debatable, Ari. Both cases began as the defense of others."

"What else was I supposed to do?"

"Just go lightly. Don't allow yourself to be discovered if you're still working for redemption."

"Erelf will never grant me redemption, and you know it."

"Erelf is not the only one who can grant it."

Talking to gods was always an exercise in craftiness. Arsenault regarded her in silence a moment, trying to pick up any clues from her body language—a dangerous game and futile, in any case. "Are you telling me the other gods will go against him?"

"I'm telling you there's something in the air. Power shifting. You need to tread carefully. There are jealousies at work here, old hurts and grudges and long-plotted betrayals as my siblings try to put themselves in my father's favor...or position themselves against him."

Arsenault frowned. "Who's trying to depose Tekus?"

She laid a finger over his lips. "I can't tell you that, can I? It would give away both sides."

He caught her hand. "And what side are you on, Ekyra?"

She smiled. "Ari. What I have seen of you pleases me, but you know I can't tell you that either. Time that seems a mere stitch to me —or to you—spins out like a long thread to mortals. This is a long thread. Perhaps it begins here, but..." She ran her hand over his chest. "Who knows when or where it will end up."

"*You* know," Arsenault said. Her thumb traced his collarbone and he reached up and stilled it. "You're Fortune."

She shrugged and pulled her hand away. "I don't predict or control the future, any more than you control the outcome of a game of cards. I merely steer things the way I wish them to run."

"You play the future like a game of dice you've weighted."

A brief, twisty smile appeared on her lips. "Perhaps. Here is my throw today, Ari. You have my support, but I must keep it secret until the proper time. It won't do to show my hand too early. Keep your magic close. I won't help you in the Tribunal if you're sent up early."

"But how will I know if I'm doing what you want? Will you control my actions?"

"All men have free will, Ari. You know that."

"But some choices aren't choices at all."

"If I like the look of your decisions, I'll support them. You're a good man, Ari Gunnarsson. Keep being a good man."

She put her hands on his shoulders and pushed up on her toes to brush his lips with hers.

KYRRA

IN THE MAGIC

SOMEHOW I'VE FOLLOWED THE MAGIC INTO A REVERSED WORLD—INSIDE a mirror with Arsenault looking in from the other side. All those times I turned a mirror to a wall, was someone trapped there as I am? I feel as if I've become nothing more than the silver backing of the glass.

The Arsenault who first met Jon looks the same as he looks now—a little younger than he seemed when I met him, though I was younger then, too, and the crook in his nose made him seem like he'd been battered around a bit, like a cloak that had seen some wear. But now that I see how much of his scar he usually covers with his beard, I realize... All those years ago, I never understood how deep his hurts dug in.

Arsenault leans close enough for me to catch the variations in his familiar metal gray eyes, the fleeting emotions he tries to suppress. I reach out to him without thinking, but my knuckles only bang against the glass.

"Dammit," I swear, raising my hand to my mouth like a dog licking a wound. Arsenault looks puzzled, then raises his hand, too. The barrier between us ripples like water.

I catch my breath, stand as still as I can to freeze this moment. He cocks his head as if he hears me thinking—him in his burgundy tunic, Aliente silk from a more prosperous time, and me in my over-sized, borrowed men's clothes, my bare feet, the ragged sling that supports the metal arm Arsenault crafted for me out of love. The burgundy reminds me of the barracks at the Villa, the way the Aliente colors he wore shone in the sunlight—the bougainvillea that framed him, his hair hot and sleek as a horse's hide.

What would happen if I pulled him through the glass and skipped all our history?

But—Jon's sister Adayze walks into the room.

Her son stretches out his arms and Arsenault lights up. He swings the toddler in the air and Edo squeals in delight. Adayze smiles at them both.

I can't help feeling a twinge of jealousy, though it's twenty years past and I know him well enough to realize that perpetual patient frown is his armor. It protects the heart that sends him into battle again and again though he knows it's a losing fight. The heart that reaches out to a lonely mother who everyone sees but no one sees and the child she is fighting to raise as a real human being, not merely as a title in a history book.

No. What I'm feeling isn't jealousy. Not of Adayze, at least. It's a feeling without a name, a longing for a similar life for us—the child reaching out and me there with Arsenault instead, experiencing the actual touch of a child's hand, not just the brush of ghost fingers in a future I've always thought wasn't for me.

The only salt I taste now comes from my own tears.

I fight them back, like always. Remind myself that in the present there is no glass between me and Arsenault. The godscursed magic has taken my desire to help as permission to do anything it wants. "Why don't you just tell me what you want me to know?" I fume. But it's my own fault; this is what I agreed to, though I can't control it and it can't speak.

Whatever happens in this past world, I know he will hurt. I always wondered why Arsenault wrote about his ordinary moments, but now—dear gods, what I would give for an ordinary life.

As if my desire whispers through the glass, Arsenault glances at the mirror with a strange expression. He hands Edo to his mother, then, when Adayze and Edo have left the room, he strides over to the mirror again and purposefully grips the top.

"No, Arsenault, wait—"

The world flips upside down.

❦

IN AN UPSIDE-DOWN WORLD, THERE'S NO SUCH THING AS LOVE THAT lasts—only lies and treachery and pain. In an upside-down world, promises don't matter.

That was the world to which I was born. The game of Houses. The Houses like to claim it isn't a game, *just life*, as if life itself was the prison that kept us shackled inside.

My desire to reach for the world I sensed outside the cage started a war. My missing arm no longer feels like a loss so much as the symbol of my escape. I'd lay it on the chopping block a thousand times if that was the price I had to pay to define my own life. Maybe this life isn't perfect, maybe it's hard, but by all the gods, it's *mine*.

When Arsenault flips the mirror, he turns my world upside down again.

I'm standing in the portico of Tekus's temple in Liera. Wearing a dress.

But *such* a dress.

Voluminous burgundy silk skirts trail behind me like a pool of blood. Golden serpents with glittering eyes of jet twine down my sleeves. Hundreds of tiny seed pearls spill down the bodice, clicking when I move. How many thousands of worms died to transform me into this living display of wealth and power? The stiff stays hug my torso and make it impossible to bend from the waist; the high-heeled satin slippers pinch my feet. Every shoemaker my mother ever brought me to tried to pretend my feet were smaller, more feminine.

I feel again the same urge I had as a girl, to kick them off and run away barefoot in rebellion. What is the harm in making a pair of shoes that *fit*, for the gods' sake?

But if this is a vision, why can I feel so much? The breeze tugging at my curls in their prison of pins. The air, laced with the faint tang of salt from the sea and the lingering imprint of incense and smoke drifting out of the temple. The noise of a shifting crowd behind the giant oak doors, carved with a scene from the Gods' War—Tekus stabbing a giant wolf with his trident while it writhes on the ground.

A ceremony.

Oh, gods—a wedding?

In the days of the Empire, aristocratic weddings were always held at the temple. Only after the Houses carved out their own territories were weddings held in the groom's household—like my father's wedding to Claudia d'Imisi, which I ruined when I killed Ilena the combergirl.

I feel suddenly like being sick. My mother might have commissioned a fabulous dress to display our wares, but it would never have wasted this much profit in the train. Only one House is rich enough to afford this finery and arrogant enough to stitch its standard all over me like my body is its banner.

I told Cassis he could burn in the deepest pit of all the hells. How could he think...

I try frantically to remember if I've ever seen my own future. *No, no, only the lives of others.* But this isn't a past—not even a different version of my past—because *I still have my metal arm.*

I hike my skirts as well as I can, but when I run up the massive marble staircase in these slippery heels, I trip on the hem and barely catch myself on the doorframe with my right hand.

It feels good to use my hand again, but if this is my future, how did Arsenault fix it? What did he use?

I fling the door open. Gods, I was right. The temple is packed—householders dressed in their finest silk; up in the gallery, free men in their cotton and linen; huddled in the shadows on the fringes, the kinless in their worn and tattered cloaks.

And Cassis.

This can't be my future. I refuse to believe it.

Cassis sits in a gilt chair before the altar, brooding and handsome in his finery—a circlet clasped around his loose, mahogany hair as if he thinks he's a godsdamned prince, the Prinze sword at his side. The sapphire serpent eyes on its hilt wink in the light that streams between the columns.

A dragon looms behind him.

It looks like one of those images that haunted me from the cave wall of my cell while I waited for my father to hang me. Its body gleams like metal, and it's covered in silver, gold, and bronze feathers like a bird, but instead of a beak it pants with a long wolf-like snout full of wicked, curved teeth. It clicks its taloned feet against the tile floor, settles its giant wings against its back, curls its scaly tail around itself like a cat. When it rolls its black, inscrutable eye at me, it's like looking into the gaze of a vanth. Except for the glimmer of ruby in the iris, which I can see even from here.

I hesitantly step onto the carpet that has been rolled down the center aisle—burgundy, too. What *is* this? Is it like Cassis said, a symbol? Are people really willing to accept me as Aliente again, a peace offering to the city?

A little voice in my head says, *Peace offerings are slaughtered and burned.*

For that matter, why in all the hells is Cassis just *sitting* there, propping his chin on his fist, like he's the only person in the world? Does he know there's a dragon behind him? Why does the dragon stay?

A heavy chain clanks against the floor, attached to a manacle snapped around the dragon's ankle. The chain anchors to a thick ring set into the stone wall. Surely such an enormous, powerful creature could simply pull the chain out of the wall—

"Kyrra." Cassis rises from his chair and holds out his fucking hand.

I grab my skirts and kick off the damned shoes. "All right!" I shout. My voice echoes off the bones of the building. I'm not sure who I'm talking to—the gods, magic, what. "Why this? Why now? Are you trying to frighten me? Well, I'm not frightened! This ridiculous vision could never happen! Let me go back!"

"Are you sure, little bird?"

I jerk, startled. Sitting on the bench to my left, Erelf looks up at me from beneath the brim of his black hat—his scar, his gray-streaked hair like a blasphemy of everything good about Arsenault. He smiles at my surprise—cold, twisted, just like Geoffre.

I will not let him see me tremble. I will not show him my fear. But a memory of his sword slamming against my metal body lances through me—the hot-cold feel of the blade as it pierced my side, the sensation of falling, into the blood and muck—

My hands immediately seek hilts, but cold, slick silk brings me back to the moment. I lift my chin, not meaning to, but by all the gods—by this god—I'm going to fight this vision.

"We had a deal. You're supposed to leave me alone."

"I believe the terms were that I would leave Ari alone for the time being. No one said I wasn't allowed to talk to you."

I shut my mouth tight and try to sort my words, thoughts, feelings. I need to be careful. "There are terms laid on you by the other gods, aren't there? What about Ekyra?"

"The goddess of fortune is a cruel and fickle mistress. Haven't you realized that by now?"

The god of knowledge and magic grows his words like the gnarled and twisted roots of a hollow tree. I settle my feet in guard. It feels better to stand like I have a sword, even if I don't. "Arsenault flipped the mirror and made everything upside down. That's what happened."

Erelf's brow climbs. "Do you think so? Do you think a mere scar on his palm will make any difference? You're not the only scar there, are you?"

That feels like a smack in the face. "No. But Arsenault and I both have our pasts. *My* other scar's sitting up there by the altar."

"Your past is so much shorter than his. How many women has he promised himself to, then abandoned? Do you know? Could you count?"

"Because you take all his memories," I say through gritted teeth.

"But how can you compete with a goddess?"

Bastard. I can't reply to that quickly enough, it hits a little too close to home. "He's here now. With me."

Erelf laughs. "Look at what your singlemindedness will reap, little bird."

He sweeps his arm out expansively toward the doors still open behind me. The same voice that encouraged caution before tells me, *Don't look back!* But as ever, my curiosity gets the best of me.

The city—my city—is burning.

This is worse than the vision I saw in the sword blade. More than a ship demasted in the harbor, a splintered hull in the wake of cannon shot. The temple of Tekus is built on the highest point in the city, an artificial island created by the Etereans in the center of the Temple District near the charred ruins of the old imperial palace. From here you can see most of the city, or at least a sea of rooftops riven at intervals by the canals, and then off to the east, the lagoon, which should be sparkling white and green in the afternoon sun.

The sun is shining today but there is nothing sparkling about the lagoon.

Ships list and smolder like the carcasses of sea beasts left to rot. Instinctively, I search for the Mera di Capria, the lifeblood of Liera, but giant chunks of stone block its mouth. Thick black smoke envelops the docks, but plumes of smoke lift here—there— throughout the city. Gods, that must be the Day Market. Was it full of people when it was destroyed?

I look at Erelf in horror. "Is this what the Prinze do, fighting over the Chair? Cassis, Devid, and Renzo?"

"You've left someone out."

"Gods, there are more?"

"Mikelo di Prinze. Yourself."

"It's a future I'll have no part of! The Prinze started this conflict, not me or Mikelo."

"Suit yourself. Or perhaps ask your patroness what Fortune has in store for you and your city, if you do your duty or if you shirk it."

"The mirror is upside down!"

"He's only turned it to reflect you. And what do you see in the mirror, Kyrra? Are you prepared to face your dark spaces? Your own deepest fears?"

"You're talking about Scrying. My magic is wild. All it does is torment me."

That's not entirely true since I've agreed to let the magic show me what it wants, but does Erelf know?

"So, being a victim spares you the responsibility of being self-aware? Is it that pure in there?"

"That's not what I said!"

"I see. So maybe you are just running away from it."

Talking to gods is infuriating, this one more than all the others. I clench my hands into fists and my metal hand pops and tingles.

"I'm trapped here with you for the time being," I say. "Obviously I'm not running away. And I'm only too familiar with my fears and dark spaces; I've been living them for years."

"Answer a question for me, Kyrra. If you let Ires wreak his madness through you, are you the victim or the perpetrator? Ires is a convenient excuse to keep from having to acknowledge your own rage and bloodlust, isn't he? But is it Ires or is it *you*?"

"You think I'd *choose* battle madness?"

"I don't know, little bird. Would you? Do you?"

"Enough." I close my eyes, trying to get some of that rage—all mine now—under control. "I still don't know what this has to do with Arsenault or what happens to the city."

"Turn around, little bird. If you're so experienced in facing your fears, why don't you face them now?"

I'll apologize to Mikelo later for being so godsdamned self-right-eous about Geoffre. I want to curse Erelf, but my voice refuses to obey. Damn my curiosity, but I have to know.

I expect to see more destruction. Instead, I'm staring at a pair of thrones.

Another old Eterean ritual: King and Queen of the Temple. For a moment, I feel like I've been punched in the gut; the king looks like Arsenault.

He *looks* like Arsenault, but he isn't. I catch my breath, relieved, and in the next instant—

Damn me for a fool.

Arsenault might not be king, but he's here, standing behind the queen, whose auburn hair blazes like the ruddy gold of the dragon's wings. She reaches one slim, possessive hand up toward him, as if she has no doubts about his allegiance.

"Arsenault!" I shout.

Arsenault looks right at me. For a heartbeat we stare at each other.

Then he encloses her hand in his and brings it to his lips.

Oh gods, he's made his choice long ago.

Suddenly Cassis fills my vision. The faint scent of jasmine from that long ago summer wraps around me in a heady haze. Nine years later and he's still the same moody, handsome man with the little cruel twist at the corner of his mouth, ambition and anger burning his dark eyes like coals, and his sudden entrance steals the last of my breath, leaving me dizzy and reeling.

"This is for Liera, Kyrra," he whispers. "I knew you wouldn't abandon your House."

His lips, when they brush mine, are both strange and familiar. And as in the old fairy tales, the kiss grants me knowledge.

I know why the dragon is bound to the wall. The dragon burned the city, and now the dragon must be sacrificed. *I* am the dragon, and Cassis isn't leaning over me at all...

It's Arsenault, and he's holding a knife.

"No, oh gods, no!"

I startle myself by shouting. But I'm not in the temple or Arsenault's mirror. I'm flat on my back looking up at ceiling beams, shifting firelit shadows—

Firelight. My heart drums in panic.

"Kyrra!"

I turn wildly in the direction of my name. Arsenault leans over me, different than he looked in my upside-down dream—scar, silver streak, scruffy beard, the fading bruise on his face, earnest gray eyes, all illumined by the low red light of the hearth.

"Breathe," he says. "It was only a dream. I'm here, I've got you."

"I was in the temple," I say too quickly, still in the grip of fear. "It was a wedding. Cassis was there, but so were you. *So were you.*"

"Who was being married?" he asks carefully. He sounds confused.

My mind is like a pond in the pouring rain—overlapping ripples, splashes, waves—too hard to sort. "The city was burning," I gasp. "And there was a dragon. I told him no, the bastard, but he won't take no for an answer."

I look at Arsenault—*please understand me*—but I must have left something important out.

"You told Cassis no?" Arsenault repeats slowly.

"Arsenault." I tangle my good hand in his hair to hold him here. He looks back at me, bewildered. My voice sounds urgent in my own ears, the way it so often does when I say or think his name. It took so long to admit I loved him, and yet why has this love always felt like an emergency? Maybe because he always feels like he's slipping out of my hands.

"Erelf was showing me the world turned upside down, not what's really going to happen," I say, trying to convince myself.

Arsenault's expression grows shadowed when I mention Erelf. In some corner of my mind, I realize I'm still not making sense. It's like the magic remains in control of my tongue and its thoughts—if it has thoughts—flit here and there, never in a straight line.

Arsenault pushes the hair back from my face with a gentle, comforting touch. "Kyrra. Slow down. I'm trying to understand, but I don't want to jump to conclusions. Describe the little details to me. What did you See?"

I don't want to go through the little details. I want to forget everything. "How did you handle it when you were forced to look in the mirror at your Scrying??"

His brows pinch with confusion. "Is that what's happening? Scrying over and over?"

I try to slow my panicked breathing. "I don't know. The city was burning. I married Cassis to save it, except I *know* that won't work. Only, the cut you made on your hand didn't matter, your promise... You had already given me up."

I dare not mention his wife's name, or Erelf's again, but from the storminess in his eyes, he's made the connection. He doesn't mention it either. He sinks down on his elbow, still stroking my hair. I feel like a spooked horse and a gentle touch is what I need to calm.

"The mirror offers temptation. To assume that the reflections it shows you are real—the real world, the real you. But a reflection is just an image, it's—"

"Upside down?" I whisper. I run my fingers over his face, as if I'm still trying to prove to myself that he's real, that *this* is real, because— well, I could feel sensations in my vision, couldn't I?

"Kyrra. I will *never* give you up again."

His voice is rough. His promise burns in his eyes, which are lit with that silver glow that used to flash by too quickly to tell. My arm is glowing, too. The magic wraps around us—*his* magic, his vow. Relief surges within me—thank the gods, this *is* the right world—and I tighten my fingers in his hair, pull him down to put my mouth on his mouth, to chase away the smell of blood and jasmine with the warm, sweet feeling of his lips against mine.

But maybe this is a dream, too. Maybe I'm lost inside the magic, in a vision of what I want to be true. Or maybe *this* is one of my dark places, this wild need that's always lived inside me, clawing to be released—

"Don't leave me, Kyrra," Arsenault whispers raggedly in my ear. "Kyrra—*please*."

The pleading in his voice reels me back. I blink and—

⚘

THE WORLD SUDDENLY SNAPPED BACK INTO PLACE; REAL, PHYSICAL, the ache in my muscles, the grip of Arsenault's hand. We were in Miranda's farmhouse. The goosedown mattress sank as he put more weight on his bad shoulder to lean over me and make sure *I* was here.

"Did you know Sella was a goddess when you met her?" I blurted out.

His eyes widened and he tensed. But he must have seen something in my face that let him know I was back, as if *oh yes, that's just the sort of insensitive question Kyrra would ask*.

"Gods, no," he said finally. "We were little more than children. She...arrived one day. Spindly, half-drowned. Like she'd climbed out of the waves. No parents. No history. Mostly hair. Calden—my teacher— adopted her. Brought her into our lessons."

"Just you and—"

"No, the group of us children on the island, like a...schola? I know all you householders have private tutors, but there used to be a word for it. There were about ten of us, and she walked in one day, all that auburn hair like tangled seaweed. Sat right in front of me. So, I did what boys do."

"Somehow I knew you must have been horrid."

He lay back on the pillow as if he were relieved and chuckled dryly. "I couldn't see past her hair. There was so *much* of it. I wrapped it around the back of the chair. I figured I'd untie it when the lesson was over and no one would be the wiser. But I forgot. When it came time to rise and she realized she was tied to the chair, she turned around and gave me an icy glare I've never seen the like of since. Then she took a knife out of her pocket and cut it off herself. Left a hank of hair hanging there like a fox tail so it was clear to everyone what I'd done, including Calden. I hadn't intended it to be a prank, but when she cut her own hair, nobody else thought it was a prank either."

"She didn't play by the rules," I murmured.

"No," he sighed, staring up at the ceiling. The firelight threw shadows over his face. "She never did. The war was on from that moment. Sometimes I think that's all our love was, really. Every now and then she relented and made me think I'd won...but it was always only so she could claim another victory."

I thought about the woman sitting on the throne in my vision. The way her hair had shone like molten bronze. The way she'd held herself, like she belonged there.

"She was a goddess; she didn't have to play by the rules," I said. And then, because my treacherous tongue always freed my thoughts in the end, I asked, "If she was a goddess, how do you know she's dead?"

Arsenault shoved himself up so violently it hurt my ribs. I sucked in an involuntary breath, but he didn't notice.

"Of course I'm sure she's dead! Dammit, Kyrra, what kind of question is that?"

"A legitimate one!" I snapped. I used my heels to push myself up on my good elbow to partially face him. "*You* don't die, and the gods used their magic to give you your sentence. Why would they let one of their own perish? Unless they've been fooling us all along, making us *think* they're immortal just to play their games for them?"

Arsenault stared down at me wildly. His chest moved like a frightened animal. "No," he said. "No, it's just—"

He pushed himself up straighter and took a deep, ragged breath through his nose. He looked as if he wanted to make one of his old-fashioned bows even though we were in bed, half-naked. "Pardon, Kyrra. I wasn't expecting it, was all."

His voice had returned to the clipped, iron control I remembered from long ago. It made me want to scream at him, even though I also did want him to calm down and treat the question I'd asked the way I'd intended it—as a *question*, not an accusation or a shovel digging up old bones.

I took my own deep breath to calm down. It was hard to support myself on my elbow, so I lay back on the pillows and tried to use my heel to shove myself further upright. I didn't want to lie down for this conversation. Flashes of pain in my side accompanied every movement, and I clenched my teeth to avoid cursing at all my uncooperative muscles. Why in all the hells did everything have to be so godsdamned *difficult*?

"It was just, when you framed life like a game for her," I said, hoping I sounded reasonable though I had to flop like a fish to sit up and now I was out of breath. "You said you didn't know she was a goddess when she came to your island. That she was pretending to be a half-drowned orphan child. Did you know she was a goddess before you—" I stuttered to a stop before I uttered the words on my tongue, *before you killed her.* "Before she died? Or was she still pretending?"

Arsenault ran a hand through his hair violently, then did it again. It left his normally straight, smooth hair a rumpled mess hanging in his face. He took a breath, like he was preparing to forge into battle, not conversation.

"She revealed herself to me before we were married. It was a secret; she didn't want her father to find her. I let it slip to Tavi, though. He was more scholarly than I was, and I thought he could help me figure out exactly *why* she was hiding because she never told me. It was so long ago, though, Kyrra—before the gods had gone out of the world. You call it the Old World like it was some kind of paradise, but it was just...home. Tavi must have suspected she wasn't who she claimed to be even before I told him. He was always drawn to her like a moth to a flame. I just didn't want to see it."

Hearing him talk about the Old World like it was a country I could visit made me wonder exactly how many years had passed since he'd found his brother in bed with his wife. Time didn't seem to have healed those wounds; if anything, it seemed to have dug them deeper. I wondered how much time it would take to truly heal the wounds I had been dealt, the wounds I had caused. Would there ever be enough time?

I swallowed the despair that accompanied that thought and forced myself to continue my inquiry. "How did she hide being a goddess, though? She must have been beautiful."

I knew that I had opened a dark, dangerous place inside me, and yet, I was the sort of person who often ended up in dark and dangerous places and then cursed myself afterward.

"I don't know how anyone couldn't see she was a goddess," he said in anguish. He looked like he was lost in the past. "But she counted on me to protect her. And not only did I fail to protect her, *I* became her downfall."

"Seems like a heavy role for a mortal. Being the protector for a goddess."

Arsenault flicked a curious, confused sideways glance at me. "I appreciate you trying to exonerate me, but—"

"I'm not trying to exonerate you. I'm just trying to put all the pieces together."

He recoiled from me. My damn mouth. As a sort of penance, I hastened to pry the dark place open a little more. "Perhaps...I am afraid. I can never measure up to a goddess. I can't even measure up to

Jon's sister, Adayze. And Guin, your friend—what a kind soul *he* was. What happened to him, Arsenault? How did you come to be stuck with me?"

Arsenault tilted his head like he was having trouble following my train of thought. He hooked a strand of hair behind his ear as if he needed the time to decide how to answer. Finally, in a stunned voice, he said, "*Stuck* with you?"

I looked at my battered arm in its sling. I was wearing one of Miranda's old flannel chemises and more than one new pink scar edged above its scalloped neckline. I sighed. "I should think you're scraping the barrel for the dregs now."

I became aware he was staring at me—in amazement, I thought— and I thrust my chin up defiantly. I didn't know what I had to be defiant about or why my eyes felt hot, but—dammit.

"What has Mikelo been giving you?"

"Nothing! Just that tea that tastes like dirt. Don't try to distract me."

"I'm trying to figure out how you've lost your sanity."

"*My* sanity? Arsenault, I'm just being realistic. I have no idea how many lives you've lived, but I know you've had many women before me—or were there men, too, that you loved? Like Guin? And if a goddess decided she wanted you for a protector, I don't see how I—"

"You're not yourself, Kyrra."

"If I'm not myself, then—dammit—tell me, *who am I?*"

It exploded out of me—the grief, the uncertainty, the anger, the lingering terror that I wouldn't be enough for him and he'd leave me again or make me leave him. Where would I go this time?

He's already made his choice.

What if she's still alive?

I waited for him to say something, anything. His image blurred through the tears in my eyes; godsdammit, he was right, I *was* losing my sanity. Five years of battlefield experience and I was reduced to tears by *this?*

"Kyrra," he said softly. He'd lowered his head, and now he slid his fingers under my chin and tilted my head back so I had to look him in the eye. "I know exactly who you are, no matter how much you change."

"Then tell me, dammit, because I don't have any idea."

"You're the one I love."

He bent to kiss me.

The touch of his lips made me feel like I was a candle—soft, formless, burning up. He tangled his fingers in my hair and I thought—hoped—the kiss might go on forever. Instead of straightening up when he pulled away, he shifted so his body lay against mine and he pressed his forehead to my hair and wrapped his arms around me, collecting me to his bare chest. His beard and breath brushed my cheek.

"I hope we'll be able to figure out who we are, together. That we'll both have the chance to be new, together. We'll escape Cassis's damn army, go... Somewhere, I don't know. Sanval season will be over soon and we can sail for Orienne. I'll build that bed for us..."

I was lying on my left arm so I couldn't reach up to touch him like I wanted. "Is that how you feel about your lives? That it's a chance to be new again?"

"I haven't felt that way in a very long time. You won that for me."

Maybe he was right. This was our chance not to retreat into old fears and old patterns. But did a new beginning bring with it the responsibility to choose rightly over the wrong you'd once done? Given the opportunity to prevent a war instead of igniting one, what kind of person was I if all I considered were my own desires?

Arsenault rubbed an unshed tear from the corner of my eye with his thumb and let his gaze rove over my face as if he could See me even without using his magic. But I wondered if he could, really. I wondered how well we did know each other now, with so many years wedged between us. Were we really trying to make a new life, or were we simply clinging to the old one? My brain wouldn't let go of the mystery, *how had he killed a goddess*. At the same time, I was afraid to work out the answer. Regardless of what Arsenault said, Erelf's words still reverberated in my mind. *How can you compete with a goddess?*

If Sella hadn't *actually* died, wouldn't that negate his sentence? If she had used the knife as an excuse to hide?

But if I solved that mystery, I would lose him.

Just as I would lose him if I chose duty over love for the sake of Liera.

CHAPTER 32
KYRRA
FARMHOUSE, PRESENT

"Most of my father's library burned with Mdembu," Jon explained as we carried the manuscripts into the common room. After Arsenault and I worked out my dream in bed, we had breakfast and coffee, and he had seemed excited to get the day going. He helped me dress—I hated that I needed it, but socks continued to defeat me—and then he put on all his now dry clothes and walked outside to mend the roof over the heart room. Silva joined him after finishing the animal chores.

That left Jon and Mikelo and me to assess the damage, which did nothing to soothe my lingering jumpiness. I tried hard not to dwell on Erelf's words, because I knew I was letting him win by thinking about the vision over and over, but the image of the king and queen of the wedding, Arsenault with the knife, all of them arrayed like a triptych at the altar, kept intruding into my thoughts. I felt like I'd hardly slept, but the last thing I wanted was to sit with all these fears. So, against the protests of the men who now considered themselves my mother hens, I helped haul out all the books and scrolls.

"I recovered as much as I could," Jon continued, "the same way I added to the Ibuu's library and to my own over the years—by keeping a finger on the antiquities markets. Libraries have become fashionable again, thank the fila. Old manuscripts are expensive and new ones are cheap. I was able to reacquire the Dakkaran manuscripts for a modest amount—they're all modern."

About half the works were by Dakkaran authors—treatises on art, moral philosophy, metaphysics, and more scientific matters, like metallurgy, alchemy, the production and acquisition of textiles. Jon didn't voice it, but grief and anger ran like a current beneath his words. Some of the Eterean manuscripts looked like ones I had seen in my father's library. But those manuscripts would have been burned along with everything else.

I dumped my load on the table and sat to catch my breath. Mikelo eyed me worriedly as he walked in carrying his own stack of books. He seemed none the worse for wear for his near-drowning in the mountain stream, but he was staying close this morning. Silva said he hadn't slept well.

"Are you sure you're up to this?" Mikelo asked me. I supposed I was wheezing. I was always wheezing, at least a little bit.

I opened my mouth to answer, but Arsenault's hammer set up a loud tattoo that pounded inside my head. "Yes," I answered, more peevishly than I'd intended. "Let's just see what we're dealing with here. Everything smells wet."

In fact, the papyrus immediately in front of me was disintegrating at the edges. It must have been damp for weeks, even months. I tried to roll it out carefully, but soon realized that was impossible with just my one working hand. I sat back and Jon took it from me.

It was amazing how painstaking and delicate the man could be, though his hands were so large. I remembered watching him take apart the trigger mechanism of a wheellock. Sitting in a tent, our breath condensing and freezing on the canvas, dripping back down as rain in the warmth created by our bodies. But Jon had focused patiently on the metal parts, laying them out with surgical precision while he had listened to me report.

Now he put on his spectacles and from his other pocket pulled a metal stylus like the one Arsenault used to draw in his books. Carefully, he unrolled the thin layers of papyrus into a long scroll that covered the entire length of the table. Fuzzy spots of mold dotted the manuscript in between weird burrows that branched like the drunken designs of a mad artist. Evidence of bookworms.

Jon swore. "I thought I'd treated these properly before I stored them, but the damp must have been too much. Mikelo, in the back room you'll find a chest where I store my ink. Get it for me, please. I'll have to scrape the mold, then treat the whole thing with cedar oil."

Mikelo nodded, then quickly set off down the hall.

I frowned at the unfamiliar script. "What is this, Jon?"

"Before any of our modern cities were built, back in the days of

Nambutu, the fila lived among us in a green land, possibly located in what is now the Wastes. The people who lived alongside the fila used this script. This papyrus is thousands of years old—much older than your Attrasca. Older than Arsenault, too, I sincerely hope, though I don't think he knows how long he's been dying. Sometimes he says things and I wonder."

"Now you know how I felt trying to make him add up. He still doesn't, but maybe that will get better."

"Maybe," Jon said absently. He pointed with his stylus at a section of manuscript. "It tells the story of the fila. How they created the world and came to live in it. The words all sound strange, even to me. It has nothing to do with Dakkaran."

"Is this the script of your gods then?"

"It's not sacred, if that's what you mean. It's writing, created by human beings. Our scholars managed to puzzle it out when they discovered a version written alongside a translation into Hamari. See, here, this is the section where the fila bring their magic into the world. I'm a bit rusty, but I think it tells how Spider showed women to weave, Lion showed men to hunt, and Wolf brought metal—silver from the moon. In return, we give the fila their due—keep them happy—so they will continue in this relationship of reciprocation."

I frowned at his mention of Wolf and metal. I had lost Arsenault's wolf somewhere along the way, which troubled me. I didn't like thinking of it crushed into the mud of Cassis's battlefield. But this new connection to the Old World troubled me, too, particularly after what Arsenault had said about it being *home*. The sound of his hammer tapping in pieces of shale above us and the muffled sound of his voice as he called out to Silva were comforting. Sounds of the present, not the past.

"When you say giving the fila their due, do you mean sacrifices?" I asked.

Jon shrugged. "If that's what they want. We used to slaughter a steer, have a great feast for them. Lots of beer. That's what the fila like. Good food, good companionship, for us to remember them. They've gone out of our world, but they still maintain the Land of the Ancestors as part of our continuing relationship. And they come back into our world when they need to."

"It sounds like the story of the old gods in the *Mythos*," Mikelo mused as he walked back in carrying a compact cedarwood chest. "They created the world because they were Shapers—Fixers—and their magic wanted to make things."

"As if the magic predated them," I murmured as I watched Jon pull out a small pot and a brush from his chest, where ink pots, gum blocks, and a stylus were laid out in a cushion of faded burgundy velvet—made from silk our worms had spun long ago, by the look of it. It was worn thin in a few spots.

Jon cast me a strange look, then went back to his work. The astringent, fresh smell of cedar filled the room when he pulled the cork out of the little pot. "Magic is a primordial force," he commented mysteriously. "All the old legends from many lands have that in common. The bounty of creation."

He sat and began rubbing at the moldy spots of the papyrus with a handkerchief soaked in imya, then carefully brushed on the cedar oil.

The bounty of creation. Magic felt more like the bounty of destruction to me, especially when I was caught in the grip of battle madness. And at other times, simply the bounty of chaos. Then again, I wasn't a Fixer, I was just...what? A repository? An exchange to keep some of the gods happy, to keep my city safe?

I didn't like that thought very much.

"Do they talk about dragons in this manuscript, Jon?" I asked.

He didn't look up. "There is a dragon in it, yes."

I waited for him to say more, but he didn't.

"And?" I asked impatiently.

"It sits at the bottom of the great river running through the fila's paradise, waiting to eat everything good the fila make. In the end, it tries to devour the world. But the fila and their human compatriots manage to defeat it first. In the end, it is only able to eat paradise, leaving behind a wasteland where nothing can live."

❧

It took us all day to spread the manuscripts out in the common room, there were so many of them. We ate a pantry meal of wine and cheese for supper, with toasted bread left over from the day before. All the candles were being kept well away from the precious and highly flammable stacks of linen, hemp, parchment, and papyrus.

Arsenault sat on the couch in his socks, pipe and wine at hand, frowning thoughtfully at one of his books. If every flat surface in the house weren't covered in stacked and opened manuscripts and folios, we would look like a bunch of gavaros waiting out the weather for campaign season to start.

"The vendor claimed the ingots were all from Tule," Arsenault said. "I'm not sure it could ever be proven, but I'm assuming wherever the man got them, they didn't all come from the same deposit. His supplier was an antiquities scholar and dealer by the name of Bruzzia. I tried to run him down, but he'd left Liera at that point, saying he was going to sail to Tule. Quite an accomplishment since Tule's been closed for years."

"I thought Tule was a legend," Mikelo said from his seat on the floor, where he was idly stroking the cat and reading through a large folio—not the herbal this time, but one of Oji la Kaif's books. "How did this man find out it wasn't?"

"The better question is how he thought he would get into port. Tule's been protected by magic for—I'm not sure how long. They were tired of being plundered for antiquities, as I heard it."

Drying out the manuscripts was one thing, but it was another to become the subject of study once we'd begun the inventory of what we had and Arsenault had sat down with his books. I felt like a specimen in a Qalfan medical college.

I probably wasn't being fair. I was testy, exhausted, and aching after a long day, trying my best not to use more kacin. I hated kacin, but I also missed it, and that was a sign I needed to stop. I'd known enough injured men who'd ended up slaves to the drug long after their wounds had healed. At least my uneasy alliance with the magic meant I could now fidget with a table knife without everyone diving to take it from me.

"Does it matter if all the ingots for my arm came from the same place?" I asked.

Arsenault had just stuck his pipe into his mouth. "Yes," he said around it, then took a long drag before saying anything more.

The balance of the knife was a little tricky and twirling it gave me something to focus on. But it also set my mind free to think. In the lacuna of Arsenault's explanation, it returned quickly to *a dead waste where nothing can live.* What if my dream of the dragon was true, what if I was the one who would cause Liera's destruction if Arsenault couldn't discover how to Fix my arm without killing me—or if I didn't acquiesce to Cassis's proposal of a marriage alliance.

Also, twirling the knife made me think of Razi, who'd taught me how to do it and who'd also suffered at the hands of my chaotic tendencies.

With every flip of the blade I caught a glimpse of him or Nibas huddled in a cart—perhaps traveling north, the way Nibas had been threatening for months. Razi losing his arm to our House machinations—to *my* machinations—had undoubtedly been the last straw for Nibas. But if the reflections in the blade were true, at least that meant Razi was alive and they were both out of Liera, which was for the best. Neither was likely to sign up to fight in a Prinze war, even if the coin was good, and it was strange and disconcerting to remember that Arsenault had shot Razi *as* a Prinze gavaro. Sometimes it seemed like this situation didn't have *sides* exactly. It was like an Eterean puzzle box; I thought I got one door open only for another to snap shut on my fingers.

"Kyrra." Arsenault touched my leg and I looked up. "Do you want to hear the long answer or not?"

"And put the knife down, for the sake of your ancestors," Jon said. "Before you slice that book apart by accident."

"Sorry," I mumbled, still distracted by images of Razi. He'd looked cold and miserable, wrapped in a cloak and veiled tightly. I wondered if he was waking at night the way I had after I'd lost my arm, convinced it was still there and on fire. I wished I could apologize, but perhaps he'd find an apology from me as useless as a glove for his missing left hand.

I sheathed the knife reluctantly. Arsenault darted it a wary glance before settling against the couch again.

I tried to settle, too. "What happens if the ingots come from different places? Is it better or worse?"

"Depends. If we knew the ingots all originated in the same geographical area—say, the island of Tule—it would give me, or anybody who could do the scholarship, a reasonable idea what gods we were dealing with. In the Old World, every land had its own guardians. Tule was no exception. But if the ingots could be traced to the same *deposit,* their origin and character would be narrowed down much further, perhaps even to a single god. Which would be... Well, it's been a long time. I'm not sure even the metal would remember. Some is older than the Gods' War. It's just what happened when the old gods died."

"Seems odd, thinking about a god dying," Mikelo murmured absently, flipping a large, crackly page of parchment filled with black handwriting. Beside me, Arsenault stiffened, but Mikelo wasn't paying attention. "I know they must have been able to die, because Adalus did... But then again, he didn't really, because he rose again with spring. *His sacrifice watered the ground*, the tutor my uncle hired used to say. But then Geoffre fired him and got me a new tutor with religious teachings more to his liking."

"All your old gods must have been able to die if they were killed in the numbers the epics give for the Gods' War," Jon put in, shaking his dice in his hand.

He looked distracted, like he expected to see something dangerous lurking outside the window. The *clink clink clink* of the dice made me even more nervous. I knew he was rolling to cast the future, the way he did before important decisions or battles. He'd spent all damn day anxiously working on his books. I'm sure he had other things to do, but he and Mikelo very carefully didn't talk about Renzo di Prinze, and I was starting to wonder *why* Jon was spending so much time with us here in the mountains, so far away from Liera.

I'd caught him looking at some portraits earlier. Images of his wife and children, small, exquisite paintings done in oil. His wife had been a pretty, fresh-faced woman who looked...happy. His boys so young, dressed in finery you could tell they couldn't wait to strip off. They peeked out from under his fist as he looked out the window yet again.

I grabbed my knife. There was too much past in the room suddenly and it made me claustrophobic, like I needed more air. "*My* tutor used to say it was a great mystery, which was what he always said when I asked too many questions. What happens when you mix the ore—say, from Tule and Dagmar?"

"In theory, it spreads out the influence of any one essence. In practice, it's a little more chaotic."

Jon threw his dice and drew in a sharp breath. "Dammit," he swore softly. "That seems like an understatement, ghost."

Arsenault frowned at him and stretched to pick up another book, a small, battered leather folio with black smudges on the cover. When he opened it, the binding cracked and we all winced.

"This is a guide written by the Ibuu's Chief Smith on the production and Fixing of metal for guns. He gives percentages of raw ore for forging steel—no magic involved there—but for a gun for the Ibuu's armory, he recommends adding tiaannamir however you can find it. *A little goes a long way in Fixing*, he says. *Perhaps best to alloy samples from various locations with iron from the mines in the interior. The combination yields a particular fierceness to the resulting metal and focuses the quality with which the Smith wishes to imbue the weapon, to the exclusion of other qualities that may compete for ascendence.*"

"That sounds like it was written back in my grandfather's day," Jon said. "The first guns had a problem with the barrels cracking with the heat, then blowing apart. Our Smiths spent a lot of time perfecting the casting technique."

The feeling of being a specimen under study intensified. "Are you suggesting that I've become analogous to a weapon?" I tried to sound like I was amused. In truth, I was tired. Tired of hurting, tired of being a mystery for all these men to solve—for *me* to solve, now that my world had changed yet again, leaving me suspended in between.

"How did you cast that arm, Arsenault?" Jon asked, trying to sound placid. But he was shaking his dice in his hands and we both knew something was going on.

Arsenault scowled. He'd put his pipe between his lips when he'd finished reading, but now he yanked it out angrily. "Has no one ever tried to read your arm, Kyrra? Do you think I would have made you into a weapon on purpose? Or even by accident?"

"I'm just trying to decide which quality you wanted to imbue into ascendance for me."

"I think you'll find Sanctuary is the rune written deepest. Also, Love and Courage." He sighed in exasperation and rubbed his brow with his forearm, still holding the pipe. The smell of sweetweed drifted over me. "It doesn't matter. The point is, when an object—a blade or a machine or a prosthetic—is cast or forged from pure tiaan-namir, the number of qualities that can be accessed increases if the source of the metal is mixed. It's the difference between a single singer and a room full of voices."

"The Ibuu's Smith was writing about how to make a chorale then," Silva said. He sat on the floor next to Mikelo, his hands tangled in maroon yarn, making a cat's cradle the actual cat regarded with bored green eyes. "Harmony and melody, singing together."

"Yes!" Arsenault exclaimed, and Silva jumped, startled. Mikelo and Jon both looked up sharply at his uncharacteristic burst of enthusiasm. "That's exactly the way it is. Every metal has its own song. Some songs are more complex than others. But when you layer them all together..."

"So, you heard the metal in my arm...singing?" I asked timidly.

I liked to throw it back in his face that I wasn't a monster, but the truth was I *had* done a lot of violence in the last five years. Killed so many people, both directly and indirectly, and Razi could still die because of me, too. He and Nibas were probably the closest friends I'd ever had, after Arsenault, of course—but Arsenault's friendship was bound up in love and passion, like the most complex of melodies. As we spent more time together, I was coming to realize the extent of the chasm we were trying to bridge, and it just seemed to grow wider and deeper the more I looked at it.

I hadn't told him what Cassis had asked me, either, beyond whatever I had said to him about my dream. I told myself it was because the proposal was ridiculous—which was true—but really, I was just afraid. Saying it aloud to him would grant it legitimacy. It would put it into the realm of action.

Arsenault caught my gaze. When he looked at me like that, it always made me catch my breath. He wasn't using magic, but I always felt like he could See me—which was exhilarating and frightening at the same time. Cutting someone down with a sword was far easier than consenting to be loved.

"Of course the metal in your arm sings," he said. "I chose every piece of it so the songs would blend together and see you safe and well."

"From that first day in the market?" I asked skeptically, remembering when he had bought the first ingot and told me to buy a dress that matched my eyes—long before we ever came together.

"You never knew how much I needed you."

The heat rose on my neck and I reached for my own glass of wine, feeling flustered.

We will continue this discussion later, I thought at him. *In bed.*

As far as I knew, telepathy-in-magic was off the table unless it was Mikelo having horrible visions, but Arsenault seemed to catch my meaning anyway. His gaze darkened and I think if we hadn't been sitting in the common room, he would have leaned over and grabbed me. Or I would have grabbed him.

Jon cleared his throat. "If you two newlyweds could spare a moment, have you found any mention as to why the chaos of your songs has intensified? Most tiaannamir has that tendency, doesn't it? It's not entirely predictable."

"You know, Jon, I'm never sure whether you're trying to look out for me or get rid of me," I said.

Arsenault put his hand on my leg. "No. It's true. It's because tiaannamir isn't exactly a metal, like iron or copper. It was once alive and made of pure magic."

And Arsenault had resurrected it only for it to be bashed and battered, fed on the blood, gore, and fear of battle. Then the god had left it mangled and dead...

Or like Adalus...was my arm really dead? Had the magic run to me because it thought it had found a host or because it had found a protector?

If the metal was made from the gods...

Why did some gods die...
And some live forever?

❦

"Arsenault, I've been trying to remember... Did Cassis have the dragon limb with him when he left?"

We lay in bed later, having happily continued our discussion. The blessed mattress was so soft, I swore I would never move again. Mostly I tried to get through the days without thinking too far ahead, but sometimes it hit me in a sobering way—the world was precarious and I was not used to being weak. Not that long ago, I had walked from Iffria to Karansis under my own power, not to mention fighting a battle with a god. I knew I was getting better, but I wasn't getting better fast enough.

"Arsenault," I said again, nudging him with my shoulder.

"Mmm?" he answered muzzily, a half-asleep, rumbly vibration. It was warm under the blankets, skin to skin, and he had collected me against him, curled up so his nose was in my hair.

"The dragon piece Cassis brought. Where did it go? I didn't see him take it."

"Dragon..."

He'd always slept heavy from time to time, as if his body gave out in rare, safe moments to account for the constant vigilance he was usually forced to maintain. I resisted the urge to elbow him, then remembered I couldn't because he was sleeping with my right arm wedged against his chest. The metal didn't seem to bother him. I wondered if he could always hear it singing, and if it was even possible, in all these manuscripts, to find out why the song had grown so discordant—even before I'd fought Erelf. Was it my fault for feeding it blood and revenge? Or was it some deeper root within? Was that what the magic—what Ires—was trying to tell me?

"Oji la Kaif says dragons were endemic to the peninsula, as if they were animals like lions. That limb isn't the same, is it? With tiaan-namir we're not talking so much about *creatures*, we're talking about the old gods, about Ires's family."

"The world used to be shiftier," Arsenault murmured, like he wasn't concentrating on his language. I waited for more, but he didn't elaborate, so I had to parse what he meant by *shiftier*.

"Do you mean changeable?"

He drew me closer and snuggled down into my hair. "Magic shifts forms."

"So, the old gods could go back and forth between whatever forms they chose? Or did they have particular forms? Or did everything go back and forth?"

"Kyrra," he sighed.

"I'm just trying to work it out. If Cassis didn't take the dragon limb, where is it?"

He paused a beat too long. He wasn't asleep now. His muscles tensed, like he was thinking about lifting his head. Then he relaxed again.

"Jon said to get rid of it. So, I did."

A tiny, cold sliver of doubt edged its way between us. I sat with it for a while before it hit me:

He was lying. But why?

CHAPTER 33

ARSENAULT

IBUU'S PALACE COMPOUND, TWENTY YEARS AGO

ARSENAULT AWOKE WHEN THE DOOR HIT HIM IN THE BACK.

He kicked off the sheet and scrambled to his feet before the dream of Ekyra had entirely left him. A woman's startled exclamation brought him completely to himself, and he realized he was standing in Adayze's room wearing only his trousers and some tight linen bandaging around his chest. A Dakkaran woman he didn't know, dressed in an exquisite burgundy silk robe, glared at him.

Aliente silk, Arsenault remembered absurdly. *Moths like hummingbirds*.

"What are you doing in my daughter's room?" the woman exclaimed. "Adayze, who is this?"

Adayze awoke with a groan. "Ma?" she said in a dazed voice. Edo began to wail.

"Adayze, are you having an affair with a guard?"

"Edo, hush. Arsenault, let my mother in."

Arsenault bowed. "As you say, lady."

Still trying to shake off the effects of sleep, he dragged the pillows and sheets away from the door. Adayze's mother stepped inside with a haughty glance. The Lady Omalade was tall, like Adayze. It was only up close that one could see the silver beside the burgundy yarn threading her black braids. Otherwise, she didn't look old enough to be Adayze's mother.

"You're that Tulan my daughter took from the pirate ship, aren't you? I thought you were my son's responsibility."

Arsenault dipped his head. "I'm part of Lady Adayze's guard, my lady. You heard about the attack last night?"

"I was coming to check on my daughter. I did not think I would have to trip over a soldier lying on the floor like a sack of rice. I shall mention it to Jon."

"Ma," Adayze said. "I ordered him to stay. If he hadn't been with me when Edo and I were attacked, we wouldn't have survived."

Omalade looked Arsenault up and down. "Even though he was injured and should have been on duty with Jon? Adayze. You must start thinking more politically. If you've moved on after Isa, you should focus on choosing from your suitors instead of running after your brother's guard."

"Ma! There are six other guards as well as Edo in this room; do you think I am depraved enough—"

Arsenault was having a hard time controlling his expression. As flushed as he felt, he was sure everyone could see the color on his cheeks. Probably all down his neck, too.

"No, no," Omalade said, flicking another gaze up and down him. This time the haughtiness was replaced by an appreciation that made Arsenault turn even redder. "I can see his appeal. It's a good thing you're moving on, Adayze. It's time."

"I am not moving on!" Adayze shouted. She swung her legs off the bed and stood up. Behind her Edo burst into tears.

Please dismiss me, Adazye, Omalade, anyone...

Adayze swept her son into her arms. "Oh, sweetie. I'm sorry, I didn't mean to scare you."

Edo tunneled into her shoulder, gulping big sobs.

"Why don't you let the nursery women take him?" Omalade said. "You need your rest. You're spoiling him. How will he grow up to be a man with you spoiling him like this?"

"He has many years before he's a man. If I let him sleep with me one night—"

"It hasn't just been one night, Adayze. Villagers sleep with their children. Not royalty. You are the *Heir*. I thought as you grew up you would begin to act like it, but now you are a woman and *still* you don't think about how your actions will look."

The other guards were staring at the floor or the wall. Arsenault wanted, more than anything, to put on his shirt and tunic—though the heat in this room was already stifling—but he didn't dare draw Omalade's attention by moving.

"This only looks like something in your mind," Adayze said, hugging Edo.

Omalade's face grew serious. "It looks as if you love your son too much, Adayze. That will matter to whoever made this attempt on your life. It will give a person ideas."

Adayze leaned toward her mother, holding Edo tight against her chest. "Which is all the more reason to keep him close to me, isn't it?"

EVENTUALLY, ARSENAULT WAS ABLE TO WASH HIS FACE, COMB HIS hair, use the chamber pot, and dress in Adayze's dressing room. The nursery women came for Edo and Adayze sent them away again to bring her wrap and some food. True to her word, she kept Edo close, wrapping him on her back with a long length of blue fabric. After she settled Edo, she armed herself with two curved knives, one on each hip. Edo's feet kicked the hilts, but he couldn't reach them.

"Your mother had a point," Arsenault said as they walked down the hall to the Ibuu's private receiving chamber. The air inside the quiet palace was thick and hot, like a garment you couldn't strip. Sweat trickled down Arsenault's breastbone, making the skin beneath the linen wrapping itch. Three layers of fabric on an afternoon like this was an abomination.

"About what," Adayze answered in a flat voice.

"About Edo. He'll be Heir after you. The reason you have suitors is because they want to bring themselves and their families close to the Ibuu's seat, perhaps some day to sit upon it. If one of those suitors wanted his progeny on the throne, he would have to get rid of Edo." Arsenault scratched the stubble on his cheek, which was beginning to itch with sweat. "Have I got it right?"

"What am I supposed to do then? Not love my child?"

Arsenault closed his mouth. Was there an answer to that question?

"Love can be tender, or it can be fierce," Adayze continued. "My mother doesn't understand that I *have* considered how it looks. I don't want to raise my children based on an image. How will he learn to be a leader, to love his people, without first learning how to love in his family? I was lucky to have had good nurses and that, for the most part, my father's other wives didn't see me as a threat to their children. There were moments, real moments, when my mother became a person, not a royal figure, and those are moments I treasure. I know the politics. I could have gotten them from my tutors. What I needed was my family." She threw him an imploring glance. "You understand. You had children."

Grim, Brant, Pippa.

He suddenly remembered them viscerally, as if they might be in the next room. He could see and, by all the gods, even hear them, talking and laughing together. Feel their ghostly weight on his back the way Adayze was carrying Edo, as if their arms were locked round his neck. He could even smell the scent of fresh air that seemed to live in their hair.

What hurt the worst was knowing his children now only lived in his imagination. Sella's sons and daughter had all been mortal, and he had forfeited his right to see them grow up. *What they had needed was a father.* The sound of his boots echoed in the marble hall like the inexorable march of time.

"I had children," he said, when he could speak again. "But I didn't have to choose to drive them away by not loving them and thus keep them alive or to love them and expose them to the assassin's knife."

Adayze gave a decisive nod. "I have decided love matters more than fear."

Arsenault stopped, hit by the force of her words. But she kept walking with a long, determined stride and soon disappeared around a corner, forcing Arsenault to hurry to catch up.

❧

LORD JON WAS WAITING FOR THEM OUTSIDE THE IBUU'S CHAMBERS. Adayze disappeared inside with him, leaving Arsenault without a backward glance.

"What happened last night?" Banye asked. "We've only heard bits and pieces of the story."

"Lord Jon dragged that Eterean out of his quarters and took him down to the Ovens this morning," Haq added.

A couple of hours in the Ovens would probably bake the information out of Renzo, especially since Renzo had no real reason to hold out if it meant dying. "Did he tell Lord Jon who did it then?"

"No. Just started blabbing something about machines. Lord Jon left him down there."

Arsenault fingered the blackened cog he'd shoved into his pocket before leaving Adayze's rooms. This was the closest he'd been to Guin since Adayze had taken him; what if the heat was too much for the Eterean and Renzo died before giving up his information?

"He'll talk more sense tomorrow," Banye said, "once he spends a night in that hut with the rats and snakes. I would invent information rather than stay in the Ovens."

"Scared of the rats, Banye?" Haq teased.

"There's worse than rats down there. Ghosts."

"You been listening to your granny again."

"My granny knows. She's a conjure woman. Anyone who dies in the Ovens dies in disgrace and shame, cut off from their family. No one to pray them to peace. No one to remember them. So they wander around, cursed and angry, just trying to get hold of a live person."

"Why would they want a live person?" Arsenault asked.

Haq wrinkled his nose. "To eat, of course. To gnaw the flesh off his bones and dig out the marrow with his fingers and lick it off, just like sugar frosting."

He stuck a finger in his mouth and sucked on it, then grinned at Banye who was scowling at him.

"You make light, Haq, but would you spend a night down there?"

"Eh, ghosts don't go for foreign food, do they?"

"I bet you taste just like chicken."

"Hah. You wish you knew."

Banye laughed, too loudly in the way he had, then darted a glance at the Ibuu's door and squared his shoulders against the wall. On the other side of the door, Haq mildly did the same.

Banye leaned toward Arsenault. "Don't listen to this asshole. The ghosts only eat you because they're trying to put on your body. They need you and your live soul inside them to rebirth a body of flesh. Then they go walking around like a new person, and nobody ever knows what happened. The prisoners are going down there to die anyway."

Arsenault looked at the door, which didn't seem to be in danger of opening soon. Voices rose and fell behind it. He couldn't break Renzo out of the Ovens without more time, but maybe there was something he *could* do, though it would be risky.

"I'm not sure I believe you, Banye..." he began, then swayed and blinked. "Damn poison."

Haq and Banye traded alarmed glances. "If the healer's medicine is wearing off, it can eat into you," Haq said quickly.

Arsenault swayed into the wall.

Haq pulled him back upright. "We can't leave our posts. Do you think you can get to the healer on your own? Lady Adayze's healer has rooms just down the hall. You better hurry, though."

Arsenault gave them a smile he hoped looked shaky. "Thank you. I'll be back...soon, I hope."

He started off down the hall, listing to the side and trailing his hand down the wall.

Behind him, he heard Banye say, "He could be a corpse by sunset."

"Quiet, Banye; he'll hear you."

When Arsenault turned the corner, he smoothed his tunic and went to rescue Renzo from the ghosts.

⁂

THE OVENS FORMED THEIR OWN SMALL COMPOUND OUTSIDE THE walls of the palace. Built on bare cliff rock without any shade, the small, octagonal mudbrick huts quickly reached dangerous temperatures in the Dakkaran sun. If criminals weren't tried and executed right away, they often died waiting. Adayze said it was an old practice she hoped to change.

The sky had begun to cloud up like it did every day about this time during rainy season. He'd have to hurry if he didn't want to get soaked.

After peering in through several small, barred windows, he finally found the Eterean in a hut close to the edge of the cliff. Renzo lay, shirtless, upon a narrow bench made of the same mudbrick as the walls. Jon had roughed him up a little. His ribs, bruised and slicked with sweat, moved in and out slowly, like he was sleeping.

The ghosts Banye had mentioned hid in the cliffside below them, like nightbirds nesting during the day. Their malevolence ran up through the ground the way the sea flooded the caves at the bottom of the cliff.

Arsenault shivered despite the heat and pulled his knife. The magic he was planning wouldn't be as large as killing a giant snake demon, but it would still send ripples out into the ocean of magic, ripples that could be seen and traced if anyone was watching. The trick was keeping it so small and quiet no one cared.

He took a deep breath and centered himself. *Just this one hut*, he thought to the magic, which scented his intent like a dog. *Just here, this one place, only for tonight. Quickly, run into these runes I'm drawing for you.*

What was magic really like? Water, the way Calden used to explain it? Molten metal? A lion that turned into a man? A giant snake demon?

It was all those things.

Arsenault drew the protective runes on the outside of the hut with his knife. The magic flowed willingly through him into the metal blade and from there into the runes he scratched into the mudbrick, lighting them briefly blue before they faded to chalky white.

He was drawing the last line when Renzo's voice came hoarse and urgent from inside the hut. "Who's there?"

The magic faded away. Arsenault pressed himself to the door and spoke quietly through the barred window. "I can't get you out right now, Renzo. I'm sorry. Just don't go near the door after dark, even if you hear knocking."

"Arsenault?" Straw rustled on the floor. Footsteps scuffled nearer. "Is Lord Jonawak coming to kill me? I told him what I knew."

Arsenault glanced in through the bars. Renzo stood with his palms and his forehead resting against the door. His eyes were closed. Moving—speaking—seemed to take a lot of effort.

"Everything?"

"Everything *he* wanted to know. He didn't need to know the information I'm keeping for you."

The Eterean's words made him suddenly, irrationally angry. He should erase the runes and let the godsdamned ghosts eat the man. "Do you know who sent the snake to attack the Heir? Were you behind it?"

"How in all the hells could I have anything to do with that? I was with you all night. It must have been Promethi, and you know it. Why else would he betray me to the Ibuu if it wasn't to use me as a scapegoat?"

"You can't have it both ways, Renzo. Promethi knew you were locked up and that you'd have an alibi. Why would he try to hang it on you? It doesn't make sense."

"You're twisting your logic. If it doesn't make sense for Promethi to use me as a scapegoat, then you can't blame me either." The door creaked as Renzo pressed harder against it and his voice became more urgent. "Listen to me, Arsenault. The way Lord Jonawak talked, Lady Adayze was attacked by a monster, an animated machine. No one had to be present and it was made of Eterean metal, so what would make more sense than to blame the Eterean? But why would I be so blindingly stupid as to connect the dots for everyone like that? And what would I gain from such an attack? It wouldn't release me from my prison, would it? Ask yourself: Who stands to gain the most from such an attack?"

"Promethi wants to marry the Lady Adayze. Why would he want to kill her?"

"Consider this: Perhaps he wants to marry the *lady*, but does he want to be stepfather to her son, too?"

Dammit. That did make sense. But something still nagged at him. "It sounds good, Lieran, but Promethi would also know that if you didn't have a good motive, he'd be an idiot to blame it on you."

"Oh, I have a wonderful motive, that's why he locked me up. My brother wants the Ibuu's guns. He wants the magical knowledge that goes into making them *and* he wants the trade securely in Prinze control. I was prepared to negotiate for diplomatic and trading relations under the theory you catch more flies with honey than vinegar. But Promethi has already been filling the Ibuu's head with lies about me; he said I was trying to kill his Heir for a threat and a distraction, trying to break the dynasty. Making me out to be both cruel and stupid."

"Are you?" Arsenault asked in a clipped voice. "Or was it again only a matter of trust for which you can't be faulted?" He moved away from the hut. "I'll be back when I can."

"Arsenault," Renzo called, and then more urgently, "Arsenault! Don't leave me here! Dammit, I thought we had a deal! Don't you want to know how you can help your man? Arsenault!"

CHAPTER 34

ARSENAULT

"There are things we need to talk about, you and I," Jonawak said as they walked away from the healer's chambers, where Arsenault had gone as quickly as he could after finishing with Renzo, just in time to avoid a deluge. The air was cooler now, making Arsenault's new bandages marginally bearable. "Things I will have to tell you in private."

The lord led him up one of the back staircases that spiraled upward into a small minaret and a small, round room ringed with windows. Curved bookcases lined the walls. The craftsmanship was damned impressive. Arsenault ran a hand over the smooth lacquered surface of the wood before looking at the books. Some he recognized as classics hundreds—even thousands—of years old. From the look of the tattered fabric and battered leather covers, not all of them were copies.

"Take a seat," Jonawak said. "This won't take long."

He gestured to a wicker chair next to a table, then dragged a chest away from the bookcases on the far side of the room and flipped its latches open.

Arsenault lowered himself slowly into the chair and ran a thumb along the nicked edge of the table. In contrast to the bookshelves, its top was scarred and battered, as if someone had taken a knife to it on purpose. A shame, since it was mahogany.

"From the outside, this minaret looks like a guard tower," Arsenault said.

"It is a guard tower. It's my guard tower. I used to come here when

I was a boy. I liked to watch the ships on the sea, imagine I could sail them to distant lands where I could be anyone I wanted to. And I liked to steal books from my father's library and run away to read in peace."

Arsenault glanced up at him. Lord Jonawak was staring out the windows with a wistful expression, his hand on the spyglass set up in the corner, as if he still might happily become an anonymous sailor, given the chance. His other hand, wrapped in a bandage, rested casually on the hilt of his sword. Arsenault wondered if any of the bruises on Renzo's body matched the bruises on Jon's knuckles. Interrogation laid a burden on the soul, and so did the authority to imprison a man in a place called "the Ovens."

"Who did you want to be?" Arsenault asked. Jonawak blinked at him, as if he'd been startled out of a daydream. "My lord," Arsenault added. "When you were a boy watching the ships?"

The lord smiled as if he were embarrassed and waved his hand vaguely. "Oh. You know. An explorer. Steering my ship by the stars. Always somewhere new just past the horizon. I had a head full of dreams when I was a boy."

"You were a better boy than I was, my lord, if these were the books you were reading. *Lial l'Aq on the Wars of the Qalfan Empire. Navigation and the Heavenly Spheres. The Mathematics of Harmony and Dissonance.* Heavy stuff."

Jonawak laughed. "I had to work my way up to those. But the boy's books are here, too."

"Do you still come up here to read, my lord?"

"When I can. The time seems to grow ever shorter, the responsibilities... Well. Here." He strode over to one of the bookcases and pulled out a worn blue folio, which he laid on the table in front of Arsenault. "This was one of my favorites."

"*A Journey Through Eterea.*" Arsenault traced the gold-stamped letters, then lifted the cover. The binding crackled. "*Being an Account of the Strange Flora, Fauna, and Customs of a Northern Empire.*"

"I did find Eterea a curious place. Exotic and barbaric. I made my father engage a tutor who knew ancient Eter, just so I could read *The Dance of the Heavens.*"

"*The Story of the Old Gods in their Strange Forms,*" Arsenault murmured absently as he turned the old pages of the book in front of him.

"You know it?" Jonawak asked eagerly. "The merchant who sold it to me said it was a rare copy, but perhaps in the north—"

"No. The merchant was telling the truth. I—who was it written by?"

"The Emperor Attrasca commissioned it. There are many rumors about its author."

"Some poet, I'd imagine," Arsenault said dismissively.

Another memory itched at him—a dragon emerging, dripping, from a cold northern sea, a seal hanging limp in its teeth. The old gods, the Old World—now, just fading ink. He had not experienced the kind of wanderlust Jonawak was talking about in a very long time.

"Some poet," Jonawak snorted in derision. "Here you make me believe you've had an education, carpenter, but you're just as practical as ever, aren't you?"

Now it was Arsenault's turn to shrug. He focused on the book before him.

The text was hand-lettered and illustrated, pre-dating presses. Colorful and fanciful creatures bordered every page and sometimes earned entire pages of their own. Arsenault recognized otters and lynxes, Irondel rams with spiral horns, mountain cats, chestnut trees, apples, plums...even the cloudberries of the very far north.

A large, labeled sketch of the life cycle of the giant Aliente silk-moth spread across two whole pages, beginning with the blind white worm and proceeding to the deep burgundy chrysalis. If the perspective was correct, the worms were huge, the moths as big as a man's hand.

Arsenault slowly turned the page to a series of drawings of a lion with the head of a man and eagle wings folded along its sides. The wings and claws of the creature shimmered with silver and gold gilt paint as if they were made of metal. He squinted at the flourishes of Qalfan writing accompanying them and traced the curve of a wing lightly with his finger, trying to sort the idiosyncrasies of the artist's brush. Almost, he could see the charcoal lines beneath the paint, where the artist had corrected himself. It seemed familiar somehow, the way old things did sometimes.

The Etereans build fanciful creations out of metal, stone, and pottery. These creations adorn their fountains, their villas, their public buildings, even their tombs. Some of these elaborate sculptures move and speak as if they, too, were animated with the breath of life. Indeed, I have witnessed just such an event, in which a large and handsome sphinx lifted itself from a fountain to prowl about a crowded plaza. This seemed to me an unwise display of power, since the sphinx possessed claws and teeth the size of a man's index finger. At any moment, it might have succumbed to its lion nature and torn the onlookers limb from limb...

"Ah," Lord Jon said, leaning over his shoulder, "the sphinx. Always one of my favorites. Do you see the drawing in the corner?"

In the right-hand corner, a much smaller sphinx crouched, its wings folded, tail out straight, lovingly done in gilt paint. In front of it the artist had painted a man.

"Flip the corners of the book. With your thumb."

Hesitantly, unwilling to destroy the old pages, he did as the lord had said.

Remarkably, there were sketches of the sphinx in many of the corners. And when Arsenault flipped quickly through them, they seemed to move. The sphinx crouched, stretched, lifted its wings, and pounced.

It caught the man in its paws and teeth and tore into his belly, spilling faded dark red paint into the very corner of the last page, where it puddled in a hard glob the same color as the Aliente silk.

Jonawak was smirking. "You see why I enjoyed this book as a boy, yes?"

Arsenault closed it. "An inventive artist."

"An original Oji la Kaif," Jonawak said proudly.

"I was under the impression that only a few of Oji la Kaif's originals were still extant. Weren't most of them destroyed in the sack of Rodis?"

His memory was a funny thing. Dates and dry historical facts never disappeared. But when Lord Jon mentioned Oji la Kaif, another itch began in his brain, one he couldn't scratch. Those damn Eterean machines. Adayze had seen something totally different in the snake than he had, and yet it must have been metal to use his magic on it. And the cogs it had left when it disappeared...

"We still have a few manuscripts here," Jonawak said, drawing him back to the present. "They were overlooked in the library. My Qalfan tutors reckoned Oji too fanciful, the way he used to embellish all his geography with fantastic tales. My father thought I ought to spend more time on the ins and outs of Qalfan politics and the strategy of Ur Kanz, the great Hamari general. You know who I'm talking about? I'm glad he did ensure I studied those things, but—to a boy—Qalfa and Hamar were known places."

"You wanted adventure."

"I wanted freedom. There's a difference."

For a moment, the words hung in the silence. Then Jonawak

seemed to realize what he'd said. He turned hastily to the chest against the wall, threw it open, and pulled out a voluminous length of fabric.

"Here," he said gruffly, dropping the cloth onto the table in front of Arsenault. "This is an abaganda. Traditional robes, but mostly worn by merchants. Watch me put on mine, then you do the same. Make sure to pull it up around your head."

"My lord," Arsenault said in surprise. "Why?"

"I didn't bring you up here just to show you my books, did I? I have work to do, down in the city, and I think I can use you. But we need you to blend in."

Arsenault looked mutely down at the fabric, wondering how he was going to *blend in* even wearing what appeared to be a blanket. But he picked it up anyway and tried to follow Jon's instructions.

It turned out not to be as hard to wear as he thought, a cross between a cloak and a Qalfan's body robes. It draped loosely across both shoulders, crossed over the chest, and hung down to the knees. Maybe Jonawak was right; if he fit anywhere, it would be in the vibrant trading community that visited Mdembu from all over the world.

"Swordbelt underneath," Jonawak said, adjusting his. On his other hip, Jon also wore a pistol.

"Who are we hiding from?" Arsenault asked.

"Everyone," the lord replied with a grin.

❧

Dusk darkened to night as they reached their destination, an inn in Mdembu's market district, near the docks. Arsenault hadn't been on a horse in a long time and by the time they rode down the rickety boardwalk, his thighs ached.

All Arsenault remembered of the city was a haze of sky and boots and dock. Now that he was looking at it upright and lucid, it seemed much like every other city he'd visited, though clumps of palms grew among the buildings and crocodiles slithered down canals draining standing water. Impressive white-stucco villas clung to the bluffs, but the buildings grew considerably less impressive the lower one rode.

Once in the city proper, Jonawak led them through narrow alleys where the houses seemed to only stand because they were all jammed together. The scent of frying bean cakes hung heavy in the air, but it didn't entirely cover the stench of rotting fish and garbage clogging the canals behind the houses. As it grew dark, women called to children and leaned out windows lit softly yellow with candlelight. They passed a drunk old man shambling home who paused to take a piss right in the street. *Hey, hey, grandfather,* a couple of younger men called out, coming to move him out of the way. *Why don't you go home? Don't you have a wife to take care of you? We'll help you get there.*

"This side of town doesn't have to be like this," Jon said in a low voice as they rode side by side. "These people should have decent water, food. So many drown themselves in rum and kacin because they have given up hope. We're trying to change things, but responsibility for the city is divided by family."

"Like...landlords?" Arsenault asked, surprised.

"Something like that. The Ibuu makes laws, and the other bindings spend all their time trying to get around them for profit and convenience. Do you see the water in those gutters? Mosquito fevers will be bad this year, but do you think the B'daro will clean up this part of the city on their own? Too much work and coin. They'd rather blame it on bad luck from the fila than fix the gutters."

"You're a hard man to pin down, my lord," Arsenault said. "I thought you were just a younger son with a military commission."

"I am a younger son with a military commission. But I am also the Ibuu's son and—" He bit down on whatever he was going to say, then shook his head. "You Tulans with all your ideas about nobility. Believing a title makes a man frivolous."

"It doesn't always guarantee he won't be. If you'll forgive me, my lord, most military commissions I've known aren't terribly concerned with gutters unless the gutters affect their campaign."

"Doesn't everything affect a campaign? Ur Kanz says so. Hunger, disease, unrest... It's my duty to ensure the safety of my city, my country, and my family. Do you think anyone is served by allowing the B'daro to drink and dine on the backs of the people *they* are supposed to be responsible for?"

"You'll pardon me if I find it ironic you've brought me to a tavern."

Jonawak threw him a sour glance as he dismounted. "I didn't say it was wrong to drink or dine, just that a noble shouldn't distill his rum from the blood of his subjects. Besides, we have work to do."

The tavern backed to the beach and was connected to the inn by a raised wooden walkway. Both tavern and inn were built on stilts, with the stables located beneath the building on the sand. They left the horses in the care of the grooms, then clattered up the gray weathered steps into the tavern proper.

It was and wasn't what Arsenault expected.

There was a bar, and a lot of people were drinking at it. But the whole back of the room opened onto a porch roofed with thatch and set with tables. An ocean breeze blew into the crowded room, keeping it from becoming an oven.

Jonawak shouldered his way through the press and Arsenault followed.

"Hey, Niki," he said, leaning on the bar top. "Is the table outside available?"

The Dakkaran woman working the bar gave Jonawak a look up and down with an expression that could have frosted a beer mug. "About time you made it in." Her gaze drifted over to Arsenault and the other eyebrow lifted. "Who's your new friend?"

"Galleyman indenture. Debt slave. He's working it off, guarding my shipments."

Arsenault fought his desire to look at Jonawak, but he was beginning to wonder exactly what kind of *work* the lord did. Was he hiding in plain sight?

"Is he guarding your new shipments or you?" the barkeep asked. Her gaze lingered on Arsenault's scar, then on his shoulders and arms, not in an appreciative way. More like she was trying to guess how much trouble he and Lord Jon would bring to her bar.

"Hey, something like that. Give me two beers and send over some food. We're starving."

She pulled out two dark pottery bowls and filled them with a ladle from a barrel. The liquid was light yellow, frothy, and smelled sweet, not like the dark northern ales Arsenault was used to. Arsenault picked up his and followed Jonawak out onto the porch where the lord sat at a table in the corner, his back to the side of the building so he could face the room. Arsenault sat beside him.

"You come here often."

"I'm also in the business of imports," Jonawak said vaguely, letting his gaze rove the crowd. "This is a good tavern. Fairly respectable. But not too respectable. If you know what I mean."

"The surprises continue, my lord. I'm not sure I can keep believing you're only one of the Ibuu's children of no particular importance."

"Believe what you want. What do I care about the opinions of a carpenter? My position at court requires me to develop many skills."

Jon's cool tone was almost as good as a yes. It was easier to think of him as *Jon* here, where they were both in disguise. Arsenault lifted his bowl of beer to his lips and watched the crowd. The men in the room were probably merchants—not too rich, not too poor. Judging by the different styles of clothing, there were the usual Dakkarans, Tiresians, Qalfans, and Onzarrans, but also a few Hamari with their henna tattoos. Some light-skinned northerners and a few men from Saien, who wore their long black hair in thick braids down their backs.

"What kind of work are we doing?" Arsenault asked, setting down his bowl. "You wouldn't have brought me here if you were just trying to negotiate some imports. Not that I don't appreciate the meal."

"You might as well enjoy it while you can. The food is good here. And fast."

Jon put down his ale bowl and sat up straighter, smiling at someone in the crowd. Arsenault followed his line of sight to see a barmaid with a tray of food propped on her shoulder wending her way over to them. Unlike many of the women he'd met in the Ibuu's stronghold, she was on the shorter side of medium height, not tall or impressive, but instead soft, curvy, and round—not a girl who would necessarily stand out. It was when she saw Jon that she transformed. Her smile made dark roses of her cheeks and lit her deep brown eyes with warmth.

"I'm pleased to see you made it tonight, Jon." Her eyes twinkled as she set the tray down before them, then handed Jon a plate of coconut-scented rice. "Thought you might have lost track of time, you're so busy." She settled a plate of blackened fish in front of him.

Jon inhaled the scent of the food and smiled a little wider. "I am never too busy for a first moon dinner at the Pepperpot. You know that, Jemma."

"Oh, it's the food you're here for, is it?"

Another plate in front of Jon. Arsenault wondered if he was going to be able to eat too.

"The food here is beyond compare," Jon replied.

"The coconut rice?"

"I was thinking more of a nice roast bird. With a tender breast."

She put her hand on the table and leaned toward Jon. "You know what I'm looking forward to? After work, I've been a promised a big, juicy haunch of—"

Arsenault coughed into his fist.

The tavern girl and Jon both looked up at him in surprise. Arsenault bit down on a smile. "I don't mean to interrupt, but would it be possible for me to take my own food off the tray?"

"Oh!" The serving girl looked embarrassed and hastily picked up another plate of rice. Jon watched her with a lopsided grin.

Arsenault took the plate with both hands, tipping his head politely but unable to keep the corner of his mouth from hooking up in amusement. "Thank you. But I don't mind getting my own."

"Jon likes being the center of attention," she said with a rueful smile. "He didn't tell me he'd hired a bodyguard." She handed Arsenault a plate of fish and then a dish of fried bananas dusted with salt and cinnamon. The smell made his stomach growl.

"Just a precaution. Looks good when you're negotiating."

She gave Jon a sour, skeptical look, but her eyes were worried. Jon pushed his rice around with a piece of spongey, fermented flatbread, either too busy to notice or ignoring her. She slid the empty tray off the table. "You'll find your usual crowd in the first-floor corner room."

Jon nodded. "And I'll find you at the end of the night, yes? Like always?"

"You take me for granted," she answered with a small smile, leaning toward him.

"Never." He pulled her into a kiss.

Arsenault concentrated on loading his own bread with fish, trying not to watch. Gods, it had been a long time since he had kissed anyone like that...or been kissed like that by someone.

In a moment, a female voice behind him said, "Jemma. Save that for later."

The barkeep frowned at Jon as he slowly let his hands slide away from Jemma's sides.

"Sorry, Niki." Jemma bit her lip. She didn't look sorry, though, and when Jon squeezed her hand before she walked away, she let it trail away much too slowly.

Niki sighed. "The other girls will be angry for picking up her slack while she talks to you."

"I'll pay you for the lost time."

"When are you going to make her an offer?"

"I'll be set soon."

Niki pressed her lips tight, then shook her head and pushed her way back through the men standing around the other tables to the bar.

"Neither of them knows who you are, do they?" Arsenault asked.

"You're very impertinent."

"I'm right, though, aren't I?"

"You could at least use my correct term of address."

"I'm right, aren't I, my lord?"

Jon gave him a sardonic glance. "Yes. But I do intend to make her an offer as soon as I can figure out how. Does that surprise you, ghost?"

"Very little surprises me anymore, my lord. But usually when a prince disguises himself to pick up tavern girls..." He shrugged. "Forgive me for being skeptical."

"I suppose you might. But Jemma's different. I'm different. Anyway, carpenters don't have these problems."

Arsenault picked up his beer. "No. But I married above my station."

"You? Were you taken away from your wife?"

"It was a long time ago. In another life."

"You must have made it work out somehow, to have actually gone through with it."

The tentative but eager way Jon asked for advice hit him with unexpected pain. Usually, it was just a dull ache, but watching Jon with Jemma suddenly made him feel the weight of all the years and loneliness. Like being trapped in a fallen house—a house he had brought down himself.

"It didn't work as well as you want to believe," he said angrily and reached across his bowl of ale for a cruet of hot pepper vinegar. He shook it viciously over his remaining fish, then stuffed the fish into another piece of bread and crammed it into his mouth.

Jon pulled back minutely, eyes narrowing for an instant. "It was a different time and place, though."

Arsenault chewed his food and tried to get himself back under control. He was tired. His chest, under the binding, itched, and what he wanted more than anything was to lie on his own cot, alone, and go to sleep. Or to get some actual godsdamned information about Guin from Renzo di Prinze. Instead, he was down here eating with an inscrutable, infuriating, pompous prince.

He took a long drink of beer to wash away the enormous amount of spice he'd cruelly inflicted upon himself and brought his gaze up to Jon's face again. "Why did you bring me here, Lord Jon? Not just to feed me dinner and make me watch you flirt with Jemma, surely. If you wanted to use *me* specifically, it must be about the pirates, the metal, or the galleymen."

"First, I want to know how much Adayze has told you about her husband," Jon said calmly as he reached for more food.

Arsenault paused, taken by surprise. "He's at sea. Possibly lost.

She doesn't believe it. Apparently, she has a lot of suitors. Your mother thinks she should move on." He focused hard on his plate again, driving his spoon into a piece of fried banana. "She is not moving on."

If Jon noticed anything out of the ordinary about his reaction, he didn't show it.

"Adayze doesn't believe Isa is dead. She believes something has been done to him."

Arsenault stopped before he got the spoon to his mouth. "Done *to* him? She doesn't believe his absence is an accident? Did she See it?"

"I don't know how much Adayze has Seen, but it's not hard to believe. Look. Isa is from the Sugar Islands. His family runs a sugar farm. They also make rum. His father is Dininga, but his mother is Arak. Promethi's aunt."

"So...that would make Edo second cousin to Promethi?"

"Neither Promethi nor his brother are married, and they have no bastards either." Jon lowered his voice. "At this moment, Edo is the heir not only to the Ibuu's throne after Adayze, but also to the Sugar Kingdom on the islands *and* the Arak's kacin estates. If he takes the throne, he will control guns for the B'ara, along with kacin, sugar, and rum exports, which provide our wealthiest families most of their coin. All of it will come under control of the Dakkar. We will have, for the first time in our history, a true king."

Arsenault settled his spoon on the edge of his plate and sat in silence for a moment. "Edo."

"Edo," Jon agreed. "My nephew, who eats dirt from the flower beds."

Dammit, Renzo had been right.

"So, the snake *was* attacking Edo, and Promethi did have a motive. To clear the way to marry Adayze and put his own child on the Ibuu's throne? Doesn't she have a say in this?"

Jon sighed. "There are laws. Whenever an Heir opens marriage negotiations, all the pledges made by the Heir's ancestors must be considered. My grandmother began paving the street that led to Edo, but perhaps she didn't foresee creating some holes. Some of her pledges seem to indicate that we are now bound to choose spouses from the Arak, while other lawyers interpret the pledges to indicate that *first* choice goes to the Arak and if Adayze takes a second husband, she can choose whomever she wants. She did the best she could for her first marriage and chose Isa. But if he's dead, maybe she'll have to choose Arak again and maybe not."

"So, if her second marriage isn't a love match, neither was her first."

The words were out of his mouth before he could stop them.

"They had a good relationship. Isa was a good man." Then Jon corrected himself. "Is. Is a good man."

It wasn't what Arsenault wanted to hear, but then again, it didn't matter, did it? In the first place, he was still a galleyman occupying the netherworld between criminal, slave, and indenture. And secondly, the last thing in the world he needed was another relationship for Erelf to twist into him like a knife. Something else bothered him, though.

"If there's a realistic chance the lawyers could decide in favor of the Arak, why so many other suitors? Just out of hope?"

Jon shifted uncomfortably. "Not exactly. There is still prestige to be gained from lower ranked marriages, especially since Adayze's next child will be her second—Edo's Dagger. The child's birth will have to be obscured somehow, but it's trickier for a female Ibuu than for a male. Some sequester themselves until two children are born, ruling from behind a wall of privacy. Some have hidden their pregnancies. Then, when the child is born, they foster it elsewhere, making it seem as if the third child is really the second. Twins are an answer to prayer. In that case, no one knows for sure if the Ibuu isn't really the Dagger. Some have asked conjure women to help conceive them."

Arsenault rubbed his thumb over the handle of his spoon. "But...if a child is kept in the second position, wouldn't it be obvious that there's another child out there?"

"Sure, but no one knows who that child is. The child is never publicly acknowledged."

"Sounds like a horrible existence for a child."

Jon shoveled up a spoonful of rice. He seemed to be concentrating on it very hard. "It's not so awful. When the child is old enough, they're told their true birth. They're brought up to be the Dagger, usually as close to the Heir as possible. They know they haven't been abandoned. Their raising is just...unconventional."

A brief flicker of weariness—almost sadness—passed over Jon's face. If Arsenault hadn't been watching him closely, he might have missed it. Suddenly, Arsenault remembered what Jon had said that day in the magus hut, after he'd died.

Here in Dakkar, every Ibuu has a Dagger to do the dirty work behind the diplomacy and lawmaking. But everyone knows the Ibuu has many children and many wives and concubines, spread out all over the country. Adayze's Dagger is probably one of my siblings.

"You're the Dagger, aren't you? Adayze's Dagger."

Jon's expression flattened. It told Arsenault nothing, and it told him everything. "I do Adayze's business. That's all."

Arsenault let out a long breath. It was good to have his suspicions confirmed. Good to know Adayze had made him Jon's responsibility because she had thought him capable of aiding Jon in her "dirty work."

Really, he just wanted to know where he stood.

"So, what are you going to use me for tonight?" he asked, trying not to sound angry—which was ridiculous, considering nothing had changed, except now he understood why the boy had escaped to the guard tower to read books and dream about freedom.

"You'll recall Isa comes from a family that grows sugar and makes rum? Your pirate captain is a well-known rum runner, though I think it's a front. My father laid high taxes on foreign spirits, especially rum, several years ago because cheap rum from the Sugar Kingdom was flooding the market. Their costs are much lower than ours, but only because they starve their workers, clothe them poorly, keep them in line by beatings...and depend on pirates to replenish their ranks.

"When my father laid the taxes, it started a trade war. The Sugar Kingdom passed even more exorbitant taxes on their imports of kacin so we would drop the taxes on their rum. The Arak—particularly Dirik and Promethi—produce a majority of the kacin exports."

"So, they have reason to ensure the taxes on rum don't work? Or they maintain their own kacin smuggling ring in the Sugar Kingdom?"

"Yes to both. Which gives us the first link from the Arak to your captain. But." Jon leaned forward and tapped the table with his finger. "There is something else. Isa was trying to expose the smuggling rings and corruption before he disappeared."

Arsenault frowned. "You think he was captured by pirates? To shut him up?"

"It was always a possibility. But Renzo di Prinze gave me an interesting bit of news. Your captain has dry-docked his ship and taken a commission with a flat-boat caravan owned by a company of Onzarrans. Moving goods from the north into Arak lands. Mostly metal. Machinery."

The cog in Arsenault's pocket felt suddenly heavy against his thigh. "Did he sell off all the galleymen? Does he still have the boy who wrote the note about me?"

"I don't know." Jon scooted his chair back abruptly. "The real reason we're here—there's a standing indij game in the first-floor room every first moon week."

"What's so important about a game of indij?"
"We're playing for information."

CHAPTER 35

ARSENAULT

THE PEPPERPOT INN, TWENTY
YEARS AGO

"WHAT'S TO ENSURE THE PLAYERS TELL THE TRUTH?" ARSENAULT asked as they walked down the boardwalk to the inn.

"Nothing," Jon answered. "If you can bluff your way to win with a pack of lies, then you've won twice over. You'll take home the purse and you won't have given anything up for it."

"Why doesn't everyone lie then?"

"Because if you're caught out lying, you must submit to a penalty. The Tiresian learns a lot of secrets in his trade. Maybe one that destroys your life…or maybe he'll sell you into indenture or throw you outside to the crocodiles. He has his whims."

"Isn't this is a risky way to get information?"

Jon laughed. "I rolled the cowries this afternoon, ghost. I only play in a fortunate moon." Then he added, just before they stepped into the luxurious first-floor room: "Also, we're going to cheat."

Arsenault stopped for an instant, caught by surprise. Jon could only mean one thing: He wanted Arsenault to use his Sight to truthtell. Damn the man; there wasn't time to let him know how disastrous that could be. Arsenault hurried to catch up as Jon sat down at a table that was already almost full. A couple of Dakkarans, a Qalfan wearing urqa and allaq, an Onzarran, all men—and a woman.

It was hard not to focus on her, not only because she was a woman in a room full of men or because she was strikingly beautiful. Vençalan, he thought, dressed pirate-style in an azure split skirt and leather stays, hair the color of dark honey swept up in a blue scarf that set off her tawny skin and dark eyes.

No. It was something more than that. Like there was no question in her mind that she belonged here, and that she and her bodyguard could take the men in a fight if it came down to it.

Her bodyguard was also a woman, lean, hard, and tall, with russet skin and dark hair pulled tight and knotted at the back of her head. Her knuckles were a mess of nicks and healed-over cuts, her shirt rolled up to her elbows like a man's, the supple leather jerkin she wore well broken-in.

Like Neyane all over again.

Arsenault tore his gaze away before the women could catch him staring and sized up the other bodyguards in the room.

They were all men, scarred, too, but in more disturbing ways. One was missing an ear. The Onzarran's bodyguard had the corners of his mouth sliced so he seemed to be perpetually grinning; that meant he'd had his tongue cut out so he couldn't tell his master's secrets. He was built like a lionhound, probably the kind of fighter who threw his size and strength around fearlessly.

The man who ran the game didn't match the fearsome reputation Jon had given him. He was a slight man whose shoulders jutted up awkwardly in his silk robe. The entire curve of his right ear was pierced with gold rings, much like Jon's, but he also wore more rings in his left ear and a gold stud through his nose.

"Gentlemen—lady. Please write down the secrets you'll be putting up for the first round."

The scritch and rustle of paper and stylus were the only sounds as the players took their provided supplies and began the game. Arsenault leaned to the left, allowing him a better look at the whippish Onzarran. The man hunched over his cards and his writing, trying to hide both with his body and his ridiculously large, round hat. His stringy black hair and pasty olive skin made him look unwell. Every now and then he took off his hat and mopped his forehead, giving Arsenault a better view of his cards.

Mediocre indij player...unless he's playing to lose as a bluff...

No truthtelling necessary to know his behavior was strange, though. He was someone to keep an eye on.

The secrets for the first few hands were sordid tidbits of gossip anybody could pick up, worth little when they were read aloud at the close of a hand.

The B'daro regulator has a mistress.

Keffre the Lender went bankrupt, is looking for a bailout.

Fifteen cases of rum came in on the Dolphin yesterday.

It wasn't worth it to cheat at this point, and thank the gods, Jon knew that, too. The trick, as the action got going, was to pick out who had written what slip of paper, but the most basic strategy was to disguise your handwriting for each round. At the end of every hand, the Tiresian collected all the slips of paper and doled them out to the winner. The bets were burned to finish the round. To accuse someone of lying, you had to choose the correct player while the winner was still reading off the information.

What happens if you accuse somebody of lying and they're not? How do they prove the truth, and what happens to you if you're wrong? Arsenault had wanted to know.

Jon had shrugged. *The Tiresian just seems to know. There's a penalty for guessing wrong, too.*

The information needed to be pretty damn important to risk using magic in this environment. Hopefully the kacin smoke fogging the room would be enough to hide it from the gods. Sometimes it helped; he didn't know why, exactly, except that it muddled his thoughts. But there was a fine line between muddled magic and letting kacin dreams take over.

Jon was playing a loose game. The information he threw into the kitty smacked of bait.

Lady Adayze dom B'ara has a Tulan guard she's been showing interest in.

Arsenault tried not to react. Weren't there better ways to introduce Tulans to the company without connecting him to Adayze?

Jon folded the paper into tiny thirds and placed it carefully in the center of the table. Then he lost the round.

The Vençalan woman, the pirate, won.

She raked the small pieces of paper toward her with a slim hand bedecked with rings, then grinned as she leaned back in her chair and put her feet up on the table. She crossed her beaded high-heeled boots neatly at the ankle.

"Oh, boys. Listen to this. Urake dom B'ero hired Captain Fourfingers out of the Sugar Islands; I wonder why he did that? And Long Sally is sending out a call for armed men; that must mean she's bringing in another shipment of rum soon, don't you think? And look here, the Onzarran legate was caught drunk with his pants down at the Paradise Inn, enjoying the tender ministrations of a number of other men, and...hmmm..." One of her beautifully arched brows arched yet higher. "Lady Adayze dom B'ara has a Tulan guard for a lover? And here I thought Lady Adayze was such a straight—"

"It's a lie!" the Onzarran cried out suddenly.

Arsenault couldn't help jerking, the man's outburst was so loud and unexpected, but he wasn't the only one; every bodyguard in the room touched steel.

"Are you accusing *me* of lying about the Lady Adayze?" the Vençalan woman asked quietly.

"No," the Onzarran said, leaning forward on his elbow to point at her. "Not about the Lady Adayze. About the Onzarran delegate. That was not in your kitty. You planted it there yourself and it isn't true. You want him off his post."

"Me? Why would I care about the Onzarran legate? Why would I care about any Onzarrans at all, D'atalan?"

"You think just because you mangle my name on purpose, *Etraney*, that I'm going to believe you? You have every reason to want the Onzarran legate off his post. Didn't he just cooperate with the Dakkarans to throw most of a shipment of your rum into the sea?"

"He's only cooperating because they've got him by the balls. Or rather, he's cooperating because the Dakkarans know all the people who've had his balls, in public no less, and that story isn't anything he wants getting back to his superiors."

"It's a lie, though! You want somebody on that post you can trick into your bed, who'll keep your *activities* out from under Dakkaran eyes."

The woman dropped her feet from the table, sat up straight, and held up her index finger.

"*One*: I don't have to trick men into my bed."

Another finger joined the first.

"*Two*: I wouldn't invite your Onzarran legate into my bed if he called me goddess and offered to immolate himself afterward. He's a disgusting man, treats his wife like a dog, and has no taste in choosing flower arrangements."

She sniffed. Then she raised a third finger.

"And *three*: If they had any inkling what that filthy bastard was truly like, your countrymen would bow before me for making up lies to depose him."

She leaned back in her chair and laid her hand over her heart. "Which—alas—I am not. Fortunately, he digs his own grave."

The Tiresian's quiet voice inserted itself into the conversation before the Onzarran could respond. "Can anyone corroborate this piece of evidence? Are there witnesses?"

"I should say there were a number of witnesses," the woman said. "It happened in a tavern."

"I meant in this room, lady."

"None of you can prove it because she's lying!" the Onzarran shouted, his voice shrill with anger.

One of the other Dakkarans in the room shifted in his chair. He was a big man, not taller than Jon but more heavily muscled. A row of gold rings winked in his ear just like Jon's and the Tiresian's. Damn. A pattern. What other secrets was Jon hiding?

"I don't think she's lying," the Dakkaran said. "My men told me there was a disturbance at the Paradise Inn a few nights ago. The City Guard came, dragged everybody out into the street."

"The legate still in his knickers?" the woman asked calmly.

"I would suppose so, lady," the Dakkaran man answered her politely.

The Onzarran lurched upward in his chair, leaning on the table with both hands. Arsenault put his hand on his sword.

"You know those Dakkarans have it in for us, they're always trying to cheat on the trade!"

The three Dakkarans at the table traded glances with each other.

The Tiresian dusted a piece of imaginary lint from his trousers, looking bored. "Who paid your entry fee to this game?"

"We take recreation pay from the Spice Company, mestere," the Onzarran answered shakily. "You knew I worked for them when you let me in. You can't accuse me of being a *spy*. Everyone in this room is either a spy or a smuggler or—dear gods, *he* runs the protection racket in the Pleasure District, doesn't he?"

The muscled Dakkaran gave the sort of shrug a Vençalan would be proud of.

"But the Spice Company." The Tiresian wrinkled his nose. "I don't like their approach." He glanced up at Tongueless, the bodyguard. "I'm going to write you a note to take to your superiors. Let them know next time they send me a player, he should know how to *play*."

He pulled a clean sheet of paper from the stack and dipped his quill in ink. "That story was true," he said without looking up. "Feed him his hat."

"*What*? Mestere!" The Onzarran laughed nervously. "Surely, you can't mean—"

"I mean exactly what I say. Guards, one of you hold the Mestere di Camerani in his chair. The other can cut up the hat and feed it to him. You might need some wine to make it go down. It *is* a ridiculous hat."

One of the men from the entry moved behind the Onzarran, brushing Tongueless out of the way. He grabbed the Onzarran by the shoulders and shoved him down into his seat. The Onzarran seemed too stunned to struggle at first, but when the other man swiped the hat from his head and pulled out his knife to slice it into pieces, the Onzarran kicked like a calf roped for branding.

"Oh, tie him down, too," the Tiresian said.

So, while the guard who had been slicing up the hat held a sword on the Onzarran, the other guard bound him to the chair. The Onzarran's own guard didn't seem to know what to do since his master had lost according to clearly stated rules. Arsenault didn't know what to do either, but Jon didn't move and the rules were clear—the Tiresian made the penalties. But what in all the hells was *this* penalty? Arsenault had expected something more like losing a finger or—gods, he didn't know.

"Play at your own risk, isn't that what I tell everyone?" the Tiresian said, looking up finally with a bland smile.

One guard gripped the Onzarran's head and pulled it backwards, securing it tight under his arm. Then he used his other hand to pry the man's jaws open by squeezing the joint.

His companion began stuffing pieces of felt into the Onzarran's mouth.

CHAPTER 36

ARSENAULT

The big guard kept jamming more pieces down the Onzarran's throat with a reed. The Onzarran choked and gasped, trying to swallow the felt and cough it back up at the same time. The guard poured a glass of wine into the Onzarran's mouth to wash it down, and the wine ran red over his face like he was vomiting blood. Then he began vomiting for real, only he couldn't get more than a few pieces of cloth up and he began to choke on the vomit, too. In what must have been only a few moments but felt like years, the man turned purple and then blue. His eyes rolled up into his head and he went limp, his throat fluttering once or twice like the wings of a bird before it went entirely still.

When the guard holding the Onzarran realized the man was dead, he let him go. The man's head rolled forward and wine continued to leak down his chin and over his green silk shirt.

Arsenault gripped his sword hilt hard to stop his hand from shaking.

Play at your own risk.

The other players and bodyguards stared at the body of the Onzarran in fascination and horror; some of them looked frightened, others merely considering. The Vençalan woman was one of these.

It wasn't that her face lacked feeling. Her whiskey brown eyes reflected emotion. But it was only a reflection, like a shadow moving in a mirror.

She sensed him studying her and lifted her eyes to his. One of her sculpted brows arched slowly and her lips settled together in thought. He turned away as quickly as he could.

"Dispose of the body in the usual manner," the Tiresian told his guards. "Get a girl in here to clean up this mess." Turning to the rest of the table, he said with a tight smile, "Please accept my apologies. I did not expect it to be this...messy. You're welcome to visit the tables in the back for drinks, food, and kacin. We'll resume our game in...a half turn of the clock?"

He stood up, bowed quickly, and left. The guards dragged the Onzarran's wine-and-vomit-stained body out behind him.

Jon was the first to stand. "I think *I* may need a drink after that. Arsenault." He gestured to the door with his chin and took a long step over the mess on the floor.

Arsenault edged around the puddle of wine and vomit and followed Jon out into the big room. As he left, he could feel the pirate's gaze on his back. He came up beside Jon in the crowded common room. "Who is she?" he asked in a low-pitched voice.

"Etranée Bizet. Runs rum and silk and occasionally other things. Luxury goods. She hits vessels all up and down the south coast as well as caravans up the Serapo River, depending on the time of year. It's storm season now, so she's in port."

"Etranée..." Arsenault repeated. "That can't be her real name."

"Why not?" Jon asked with false innocence.

"Spider Weaver, Jon? I know you speak Vençalan."

Jon shrugged and stopped in front of the refreshment tables. Young women and men dressed in tidy uniforms stood behind the tables, pouring glasses of wine and rum, offering plates of food and flames to light kacin pipes. Jon took a fried ball made from some kind of grain mixture and decorated with elaborate curls of candied lemon peel.

"She is a spider," he said. "She has webs all around the city—informants letting her know what her clients want, where the authorities will be, who can be bribed..."

"Did she set that Onzarran up on purpose?"

Jon pushed the ball into his mouth and chewed thoughtfully, then reached for a glass of wine. "In that game, one must always assume the worst of people."

"Jon," a velvety female voice said from behind them. "Is your bodyguard Vençalan?"

They both turned. The pirate stood behind them, flanked by her tall female bodyguard. It was strange to see the two of them together and to realize that Etranée—*Etraney,* the Onzarran had called her, butchering her name with that accent—was not tall, impressive, or dangerous-looking. Dress her in a gown of Aliente silk and she would fit into any Vençalan debutante fête, right down to the sweet smile she put on for them.

"Have you both forgotten how to speak?"

Jon shot him a nervous look and Arsenault bowed—deeply, in the Vençalan fashion.

"*Vou t'me couvert,*" he answered. "*Ma chiré.*"

He caught her hand and pressed it briefly to his lips. She let her fingers remain there just a little too long. Her skin smelled and tasted lightly of roses.

She pulled her hand back and laid her fingertips against the hollow of her throat. "My," she said, continuing in Vençalan. "What beautiful manners. You don't look like a Vençalan, though. What was it? Arsenault?"

"Arsenault, yes. But—no. I've fought often in Vençal, but I'm Dagmari. Came south seeking warmer climates. The Vençalese liked me, so it was a winning hand." He forced himself to smile. "They didn't like my Dagmari name, so they gave me something that sounded better to them."

"Oh, now you've made me curious. Say that Dagmari name, please, and let me judge how it suits you."

"Kenute," he said, pulling up a name he knew would sound ridiculous to Vençalan ears. "Kenute Rengveldersson."

She, Jon, and the bodyguard all stared at him.

He made an "eh, what" shrug. "My father's name was Rengvelder. Unfortunately, one isn't awarded a choice of names at birth. Or fathers."

Etranée pursed her lips together slightly and the corners of her eyes crinkled as if she were suppressing a laugh. "You know, if we were playing a game, I might call you out for lying."

"Well, whatever it was before, it's Arsenault now." He made a small bow from the shoulders. "Madame."

"Hmmm." Her eyes narrowed. Arsenault wondered exactly what she saw in him, this woman with the neat brows and the perfect bow of a mouth. She was a pirate; did she prey on ships or villages? She turned slowly toward Jon. "Did you hire him or is he an indenture?"

"I bought his sentence," Jon replied mildly. "He's a galleyman. Came in on a Qalfan ship."

Her brows lifted in genuine surprise. "If you were taken on the galleys, how did you escape? Men on the galleys usually die before they serve their sentence."

A memory shoved itself into Arsenault's mind, a brief knifelike image of night and fire, the desperate barking of a dog. He had to clear his throat. "The captain traded us in the market in Mdembu. He was getting rid of us because—"

Damn Erelf. This was not the time or place to be ambushed with memory.

"Men from that ship went everywhere," Jon said, jumping in to rescue him. Arsenault struggled not to look at him in gratitude. "I saw a bargain and I took it. The rest of them...ill-used, but their contracts were sold to be rehabilitated. Captain needed new rowers, most likely. This one, he said, had done some fighting."

"For the pirates?" Etranée asked in a cool voice.

"They used me," Arsenault replied grimly. "Wouldn't I have been an idiot not to have proved my use if it meant better treatment for the other men?"

She eyed him skeptically for a moment. Then her gaze changed, as if she were thinking about what else he could be used for. Seeing that kind of unapologetic interest in a woman stoked the heat in him, especially since—godsdammit, how long had it been, really?

He'd lived enough lives that a woman like her made him wary. He'd rather pursue the kind of relationship he imagined he might have had with the Lady Adayze had he been born to another station—or if she were free to pursue the only kind of relationship he could offer, which was a piss-poor substitute for a husband's love. But there wasn't any chance of that and it would only be a torment to keep thinking about it. He didn't have relationships, or at least he tried not to, but he couldn't avoid *people* and that in itself was a kind of curse, this perpetual dance he had to make at the edges of real connection.

Etranée brought out that sly, close-mouthed smile again. "Perhaps we've had too much talk and not enough action, eh? I think we might be late back to the game, Jon."

Jon popped another fritter into his mouth and smiled. The look in his eyes wasn't encouraging. He looked as if he were weighing kacin, trying to decide how much coin he'd get for a block.

"She likes you," Jon said in a low voice as they walked back.

"I think she wants to chew me up slowly and spit me back out."

"Same thing. You ready to play?"

"Are we going to play to the end?"

"I have no desire to die, ghost. As long as you can keep me alive, then yes, we'll play to the end."

❧

THE REST OF THE NIGHT GROUND ON, AS GRUELING AS ANY BATTLE Arsenault had ever fought. The nervous waiting was the same—when you knew someone was out there, but you didn't know where. Then finally, just when you'd passed the point where you couldn't sustain that kind of attention anymore—

Suddenly you were wading through shit and blood with no idea how you got there.

The Qalfan folded after the sixth round, bowed, and left the room. Jon had clearly wanted him to stay because he had just put a piece of information in the kitty meant for him.

Captain of the Gannet has a crew member he pulled off a Qalfan Empire ship in Vençalan waters.

Now it was down to Long Sally's man, Etranée, and the Dakkaran customs official, whose little facial tells led Arsenault to believe the man had probably been lying all night, playing for information he could use to blackmail his clients. Arsenault knew Jon had it in for the official, because he was supposed to be working for the Ibuu and instead, he was using the Ibuu's laws for his own personal gain.

Jon tapped his index finger beside his cards in the customs official's direction. Once. Twice. Three times.

All right. I can take a hint.

If he used his Sight quick, maybe the gods wouldn't notice either.

A flick of his attention and the barriers he placed on his magic dropped. The room roiled with secrets, pasts, and futures, unspoken and begging to be read. People weren't simple line sketches. They blazed with complicated color, layered in shades pushing and pulling at each other, like a dainty pink rose that bore decadent velvet wine at the center...or rippling darkness highlighted in shining white. Sight was so *easy*, and that made it much too tempting.

The customs official was a bootlicker and about as transparent as a man could be. He had been lying all night, praying desperately to get by without being caught, but the incident of the Onzarran and the hat had disturbed him deeply.

Arsenault sniffed and tilted his head up at the ceiling. Jon darted an imperceptible glance at him.

"You pulled that jester out of your sleeve," he said.

"I didn't!" the customs man exclaimed. "I won that hand fair!"

"I've been watching you pull cards out of your sleeves all night. I say you've been feeding us lies, too."

"I hear much in my line of work. Why shouldn't I bring it here to win more coin to feed my family? My mother is sick, my cousins without work. You, Jon, with your allowance from your family, you have no idea how heavy the responsibility of a working man is."

"You are a conniving little shit," Etranée interrupted. "You forced my mate to pay double the price of your usual bribe three days ago. Did he do the same to Long Sally?"

The muscled Dakkaran man inclined his head. "He's been gradually increasing Long Sally's fees for the past month. She asked me to keep an eye on him."

"Keep an eye on me? It is not *I* who decides on the fee structure. I am only a small part, like a cog in one of those new machines."

Arsenault almost swung his head up, but stopped just in time and rolled his shoulders instead, like he was adjusting his stance. Jon probably didn't need more information to prove the man was lying, but he couldn't risk the Tiresian forcing the man's tunic down his throat before he learned what the man had seen. He turned his Sight fully on the official, not holding back even a little bit.

Sight was the partner of Fixing—to create, to Shape, you first had to be able to open yourself to the way magic peeled back reality and revealed the inner truth of a thing or a person. Sometimes Truth was a word or an emotion, but other times, it came in a flood of images, as if the magic was eager to *show* you all the scenes and stories that made up another's life—everything illuminated in the glare of a harsh, white sun.

Thank the gods he'd only asked a simple question. The man's memories hit him like a wall, smell and sound, the chatter and rhythm of the docks, the very place where Arsenault had lost Guin.

Oh no, no, no. Not my memories! He couldn't trust those, and thinking of himself and what he wanted would surely alert Erelf—

Cogs! Machines!

The man *had* seen them. Coming through customs in pieces, not only gears but shells, sections of metal cast to look like men, animals, monsters...bundled in wooden cases, loaded onto riverboats.

Suddenly Arsenault felt as if all the eyes in the universe had turned upon him.

Fucking hells. *The gods had noticed.*

He slammed his gates closed. The magic scalded him as it raced through his body, into his heart, his lungs, down his arms, into his hands and fingertips, his legs and feet. The venom burns on his chest roared with pain. The magic twisted and writhed, trying to find an outlet. Little droplets of metal squeezed out of his fingers, leaving glistening streaks of silver on his palms.

The players were still arguing while the Tiresian looked on in mild interest. Etranée rubbed at her fingers, then gazed directly up at him.

He could almost hear the fatespinners snapping their threads and starting a new pattern on the loom, the silence and then the clack of the shuttle and the whir of the treadle as they began again.

"I don't care what happens to you," Etranée said abruptly. "Jon can throw you to the crocodiles for all I care, and maybe he should. But Jon, now I'm going to call you out."

Jon straightened in his chair, managing to look bewildered. "I didn't even win that hand!"

"You used magic to know he was lying."

Fuck. *Fuck.*

"I used no magic."

"Your bodyguard did."

"How do you know that?"

She wriggled the ring off her right ring finger and threw it into the middle of the table. It clinked and wobbled on the wood. The stone in the large oval setting looked like an opal, but most of it had turned black, leaving only brief spaces of shimmering blue and pink.

"The stone was Shaped to turn in the presence of magic," she said. "If it was you, Jon, you hid it well." She glanced up at Arsenault. "Your bodyguard, less well."

Dammit, he'd grown lax in his desire to chase the truth. He'd held her hand, for the gods' sake. How had he not noticed the sightstone?

Because you were thinking about your cock, that's why.

Damn him for a fool, a great fool.

"That is a clear violation of the rules," the Tiresian said in disappointment. "I thought you knew how to play, Jon."

Jon slumped in his seat. "What are you going to do to me?"

Under the table Jon's fingers twitched against his thigh. Arsenault knew he was still wearing the pistol beneath his abaganda. If he could distract the table, maybe Jon could pull the pistol...

"If I might propose a solution," Etranée said, surprising all of them.

"You wish to suggest a penalty?" the Tiresian asked, amused.

Etranée smiled that smile again. She looked like a big cat going in for the kill. "I'm sure if Jon signs over his bodyguard to me, then we'll be able to call it even."

CHAPTER 37

ARSENAULT

ETRANÉE'S SHIP, MDEMBU HARBOR, TWENTY YEARS AGO

"WHY IN ALL THE HELLS DID YOU USE MORE MAGIC?" JON HISSED, grabbing his elbow as they walked out. Etranée was folding the piece of paper that transferred ownership of his non-existent "debt" and sliding it into her stays, which gave him too many of the wrong kind of thoughts. Jon tugged on him again.

"Ghost, you were only supposed to cheat *once*. Now what am I going to do? Were you just trying to escape? You made a binding with Adayze!"

"I couldn't let the opportunity to See what he knew about the metal go past," Arsenault whispered back. "It's been moving on the docks, being shipped to Arak lands—cogs, like we found from the snake, but also full sculptures and pieces of them, like your basilisk. No lions, though."

Jon frowned, considering, then stepped away as Etranée slipped between them and took possession by sliding her arm around Arsenault's. Jon raised one finger unobtrusively. *See what you can find out.*

"Well," Jon said, smiling tightly. "Maybe I'll see you around some time, ghost?"

Etranée laughed and bumped her hip into his. "If I allow him out in public, maybe."

So, what he had told Renzo wasn't true at all. He *was* going to be the entertainment.

Damn the many years he'd spent alone and all the kacin smoke he'd inhaled tonight. It had certainly affected his judgment. Fear, anxiety, and anticipation was a dangerous combination, like the cocktails taverns mixed to tempt gavaros who'd come into unexpected coin after a battle. Jon's words—*You made a binding with Adayze!*—echoed in his head, but he had to think of his promise to Guin first, didn't he?

Etranée's ship rested at anchor offshore. It wasn't a galley, thank the gods, but a sleek cutter used to hit fast and retreat faster. A rowboat waited at the docks, manned by a large, fair-skinned man cloaked in a nondescript abaganda like his own, though Arsenault wasn't sure a man with that many scars could be called "fair." Etranée's bodyguard didn't sheathe her sword until after they clambered out of the rowboat.

"I can handle it from here, Koji. Stay outside my cabin door," Etranée said after they were on the deck of her ship, which rolled gently with the waves in the harbor. The sea breeze kept the night surprisingly cool here on the water, though on shore it had been hot and humid. After being shut up in a room full of kacin smoke with the lingering scent of wine and vomit, standing on deck beneath the wide black sky on the boundless black sea felt blessedly open. He hadn't realized how afraid he'd been that Etranée's ship would be a galley. The relief that he wouldn't be chained to an oar again left him weak.

"Captain—"

"I think Arsenault will find what I have to say reasonable."

Koji scowled at him as Etranée ushered him into her cabin. She had to know what he was up to.

"Koji will be right outside, but I'm handy enough with a knife myself. I haven't gotten where I am being soft."

"I don't doubt that's true, lady."

It was a relief to be out from under Koji's baleful gaze, but then Etranée lit the lantern and a soft yellow light flooded the room. She walked over to one wall, swung a thick iron latch out of the way, pulled a handle, and a double bed covered in a silk bedspread the color of deep twilight folded out and down with a creak. A jumble of pillows tumbled out of the wallspace onto it.

The battle his conflicted emotions were having intensified.

Etranée pulled a table out of the opposite wall and jammed it down flat on the floor with both hands. Then she flipped open the seat of a bench and rummaged around inside. When she straightened, she held a bottle secured under her arm and two glasses. She knocked the bench seat closed with her elbow.

"Brandy. Care to share?"

"What do you want from me, Etranée?"

Etranée settled the glasses on the table and poured them half full of golden liquor. "I meant what I said. I don't have to trick men into my bed. I'm certainly not going to force you." The gold hoop earrings swayed against her amber skin as she glanced at him over her shoulder. "That seems a little ridiculous anyway, doesn't it? Thinking *I* could force *you*?"

It did seem ridiculous, standing in this small cabin, where the top of his head brushed the ceiling and he felt like a giant. He dwarfed her as she leaned back against the table, slender and delicate, crossing her ankles and swirling brandy in a cup made of glass so thin it seemed even her fingers might break it.

But he wasn't going to underestimate her. Not after that game.

He tucked his thumbs into the hemp belt securing his abaganda. "I believe you have a writ of sale saying I belong to you. At least until I've paid off my sentence."

She rolled her eyes. "And what does that mean, Arsenault? That I can have you beaten into doing what I want? I don't own slaves and I don't treat indentures like that either. In fact, everyone on this ship is free. Does that surprise you?"

"After you demanded a writ of sale for me tonight in a card game? Yes, it does, lady."

Etranée looked amused. "Do you call every woman you meet 'lady'?"

"Most of them. Shouldn't I?"

"Where *do* you come from, Arsenault?"

"Dagmar. I told you."

"I've known sailors from Dagmar. They're wicked with a sword and excellent in the rigging. But you're different. And you *were* using magic, *a lot* of magic. Neither I nor my stone may recover. Surely, you didn't need that much to incriminate the custom's official; he was going to hang himself."

Arsenault hesitated, wondering how much to tell her. "Are you going to hold that other glass of brandy hostage?"

She gave him an amused smile, picked up the glass, and walked it over to him like she was making an offering in a temple. Except she was warm and close, and he was not a stone statue.

He didn't fool himself for a moment that she wanted him just for what they could do together. But using her for information left a bad taste in his mouth. He tossed back half the brandy, hoping it would burn away his thoughts, or at least the last ragged vestiges of his ethics. He reached into his pocket and threw the cog onto the bed.

She took another sip of brandy before she picked it up. "What is this?"

"Have you seen the new clocks?"

"No. I've heard about them, though."

"They're powered by lots of wheels like this meshed together like puzzle pieces. The Etereans built complicated machinery using gears and magic."

Her brows pulled downward. She threw the cog back onto the bed. "And this has something to do with the customs official? And Jon?"

He wished he knew more about Jon's disguise. The ground was treacherous here; it would be easy to step into a hole.

"You weren't playing that game for fun. What information were you seeking?"

She gave him a shrewd look and drank the rest of her brandy. Then she put the glass down and untied her head scarf. A wavy fall of golden-brown hair tumbled down and she used both hands to shake it out.

He'd been alone much, much too long.

She gave him a crooked smile. "No. I wasn't playing that game for fun. I wanted Jon. I got you instead. I consider it a step in the right direction."

"You wanted Jon...for this?" Arsenault glanced meaningfully over his shoulder at the bed.

Etranée's lips twisted into a wistful smile. "I've thought about it. I imagine many women have. But I hear he has a girl he likes. I don't think my advances would be met with the sort of approval I like to encounter in a man."

"So, you're going to try to seduce the information out of me instead?"

She stepped up closer to him. He took a step backward, but his calf hit the edge of the bed, and she leaned forward into him. He glanced downward, unable to help it, and was rewarded with the sight of her breasts curving up over the edge of her bodice; two soft, dusky crescents dusted with a light sprinkling of freckles.

Her smile grew bolder. She lifted her hand to his hair, let her fingers smooth a strand away from his forehead. "It looks to me like you're enjoying the seduction."

She leaned into him. Out of reflex, he caught her by the hips. She shifted, rubbing against him. "Mmm. Feels like it, too."

Well. He couldn't deny that. "What makes you think I'll give you any information, though?" he said, cursing the rough edge of his voice.

"Is that a dare?"

He'd been alone much, *much* too long. If he was being honest with himself, he would have rather spent the night with Adayze—but being honest hurt. Not only because Adayze was beautiful and kind and he knew he couldn't have her, but also because it hurt to have the possibility of a family dangled so tantalizingly close but in reality to be still so fucking far away.

Etranée tilted her head as she watched him. For a moment, she looked uncertain. Then she must have seen his desire to bury all those feelings that were doing him no good. Her eyes darkened, hot and wanting.

He gripped her hips and pulled her to him, roughly, before the pain in his heart could make another appearance. Etranée was warm, willing, and *here*, and everything else was a godsdamned idea and not anything that could ever be real for him.

"I suppose you can take it however you want," he said.

She laughed—a reckless sound. "However I want, is it?"

She dragged him down into a kiss.

His lips met hers angrily, but her mouth was hot and eager. She slid her hands over his shoulders and chest, feeling him out, then shoved him backward.

His calves were already pressed against the bed. There was nowhere to go but down, onto the mattress. He fell, carrying her with him, and they both sank into its soft, feather-filled depths.

"Take off that wrap," she said breathlessly. "It's like you're wearing a blanket."

He sat up with her still against him and tried to fight the abaganda off over his head, but there was too much fabric. She had to help him —leaning in, kissing him, sliding her hands against his side, brushing his cock. He threw the damn thing aside, but he was still wearing his shirt underneath it; she tugged the laces open and he ripped that off, too.

Her breath caught and her eyes went wide, and he realized his chest was still bound in linen. "You've been injured."

"It should be healed by now," he said raggedly. He leaned forward to place his lips on the inviting curve of breast before him, ran his hands over her arms, not caring about venom burns or whatever information she wanted; if she asked him, he wouldn't be able to recall it anyway. She arched her back and lifted her breast into his mouth, letting him tug on it with his tongue. He wanted her so badly he started shaking.

He pulled his arm around her to unlace her stays.

"No," she whispered, leaning backward. "Take off your binding first."

He closed his eyes briefly and caught his breath. She took the edge of the linen binding and began unwrapping it until it fell away. Every time she had to reach around his back, her breasts pressed against his chest, the leather stays rough on his skin. What was the woman trying to do to him?

"These are...burns?" she asked in confusion, tracing the fading red welts with a fingertip.

He hissed in his breath and caught her hand. "Venom."

"And these?" she whispered, running a fingertip over the claw-marks and then the bullet wound. "And this?"

"Lion. Gunshot."

She passed her hands around his back. Ran her fingers up and down, feeling out the indentations of his spine, the bands of muscle leading from it. When she reached the waistband of his trousers, her body softened against him. She brought her hands to his face again and brushed his beard with her fingertips, the stubble on his cheeks, the line of his scar where it disappeared into his hair.

"You," she said against his lips. "You're one of the lucky ones."

CHAPTER 38

ARSENAULT

WHEN HE WOKE IN THE MORNING, SHE HAD ROPED HIM TO THE BED.

A big black bird with a white ring around its neck sat in the open porthole, watching him. "Sleepyhead!" it suddenly croaked. "Raaak! Sleepyhead! Lie-a-bed!"

Arsenault jerked against the ropes with a cry. The knots dug into his skin, and he lay back, heart hammering.

"Good morning," a cheerful female voice called from the door. "I see you weren't expecting Samson. Oh, that's right. You Northerners have a thing about ravens, don't you? They belong to one of your gods. What's his name? Er—"

"Don't say it!" Arsenault bellowed. He yanked again at the ropes in reflex.

She looked startled. He tried again to calm himself, but that damn bird.

"All right," Etranée said shakily, pulling door firmly shut behind her. All her pirate gear was back in place this morning, but his visceral reaction to her pet had obviously surprised her. "Samson's just a friend of mine. Here, Samson, want some breakfast?"

She held up a scrap of meat and the raven swooped in the window to settle on her forearm. It took the meat from her fingers with its shiny black beak and then pecked at one of her golden hoops as if to say thank you before flying back to the porthole, squawking.

"He knows an easy mark when he sees one. I keep him well-fed."

Arsenault grunted. "Are you planning to keep me well-fed too?"

"I didn't want you going anywhere until we'd had a chance to talk. And you were sleeping so sweetly."

In truth, he hadn't meant to fall asleep at all. And certainly, he hadn't meant to sleep hard enough to allow her to bind him hand and foot to her bed without waking up. This was damn embarrassing.

"Give me my clothes, feed me breakfast, and we'll talk."

"How about we talk now? I want to know why a Hidden Blade has picked up a Northern magician as a bodyguard and is asking around about a cabin boy named Zim la Hallad."

Hidden Blade. Was she talking about Jon? He got the sense this was different than being Adayze's Dagger. But how?

"A cabin boy? Named Zim?" he asked.

"Cabin boy to Yasi la Fariq, who captains the *Gannet*. Zim's father is an eminent Qalfan scholar. He was en route to Onzarro when he disappeared. I must admit having Zim show up with Fariq is suspicious enough, but then for Jon to ask around about him... Arsenault. You know something, don't you?"

"The captain's name. Say it again."

"Yasi la Fariq?"

The crew had only ever called him Captain.

Captain says you're to come on deck, Arsenault. Captain says he's going to withhold food and water from the other rowers if you don't step up, Arsenault. Captain says you'd better not try anything, or your friend will feel it...

Jon had never named him either, probably on purpose.

"Arsenault."

He turned his head on the pillow. Etranée leaned above him with a concerned expression, gripping the hilt of her knife. A sliver of steel glinted above the sheath.

"What do you know about Fariq?"

"I know he's a son of a bitch. What do you know about Zim?"

"Arsenault, you're tied naked to my bed. I'm the one who's supposed to be asking the questions."

"Look, I'd be much more willing to talk if I was dressed. And fed. I worked up an appetite last night."

Watching the flush climb her neck was gratifying. Her gaze flicked away from his for an instant and swept downward. Dammit, there was no way to hide how he responded to that. But then, it was a bit late to convince her he wouldn't care. Memories of the night before played in his mind, ideas of what she might do if she left him roped here... Getting involved with her had been a terrible idea.

"I'd hate for you to waste away, but I don't trust Jon. He let you go too easily."

"He probably didn't want to have to eat his abaganda."

"That Onzarran was a spy for the Spice Company. The Spice Company will do anything to preserve its monopoly in Eterea, regardless of how it affects Dakkarans—or anyone else. They're in league with the sugar growers."

"The ones who make the cheap rum you run under the Ibuu's nose?"

She sniffed. "You know, you ought to do a little studying before you sit down with scholars. I'm a privateer. I don't have anything to do with the Sugar Kingdom or the rum they produce." She folded her arms across her chest and eyed him impassively. "Congratulations. You have successfully distracted me from my original question and without using your obvious attributes. But let's get back to that, Arsenault. Why does Jon want to know about Zim? And why, in the deepest, darkest pit of all the hells, did you risk discovery to find out about *machinery*?"

"Etranée. *Let me up*. I give you my word I will sit at your table and eat your food and speak to you like a civilized man as long as I'm wearing *clothes*. I will make no attempt to escape or hurt you or any of your crew."

She stood staring at him for a long time. Or what felt like a long time, considering he was naked and spread out on her bed, with a raven preening on the windowsill.

"All right," she relented. "But you're going to tell me how you acquired those venom scars, too, and how you know Yasi la Fariq." She slid her knife out of its sheath and leaned over him to cut the cords on his wrists, then stopped. "And one more thing. If I have your contract, you'll damn well wear better clothes."

⚜

AFTER ETRANÉE CUT HIS ROPES, SHE RETRIEVED A SET OF CLOTHING from the bench and threw it at him. Then she sat on the end of the bed, fed her damn raven, and watched him put them on.

In the daylight, her gaze pinned him more than it had in the lantern shadows. It wasn't the first time he'd dressed awkwardly in a woman's room, but this morning he felt particularly self-conscious. He should have slept on the floor and burned, and damn what Jon or anyone else wanted out of him.

He didn't have to go back to Jon, did he, if he somehow escaped the ship? Now that he knew there was an Arak connection, he could make his way to Arak territory to follow Guin's trail. There was a lot of dense bush between here and there, but he knew enough about Dakkar now he could probably make it on his own...

Or he could hire on a flat-boat caravan headed north.

Cut all his ties. Break his promises. Let Adayze and Guin take care of themselves.

He hated himself for even considering it, but dear gods, how much easier would it be to drift away like an actual ghost, to die somewhere in the bush and forget all these godsdamned promises he'd made to himself and to other people. Wanting that kind of release made him feel like a coward, but it was so tempting he stood paralyzed for a moment, clutching the shirt, too frozen even to breathe.

"Are you going to stand there naked all day?" Etranée wore her sardonic half-smile like a mask.

He pulled the tunic over his head and smoothed the dove-gray silk over his chest, straightened the notched neck, and shook out the loose cuffs with their embroidered scrollwork. It looked more like the shirt of a nobleman than of a bonded bodyguard. The trousers were silk, too, and so were the stockings.

One of these lives he was going to work a respectable job for his own coin and wear clothes of his own choosing. Stout wool carpenter clothes, and he'd live where it snowed, and his clothes wouldn't stick to him all the time.

What in all the hells was he thinking? It was like he was standing in his own guard tower, staring wistfully toward the freedom of the sea. But freedom for him was a dream, regardless of whether a writ of sale was involved or not. It was like he hadn't learned anything in all his years of living.

There was only one way to deal with these feelings.

Take a deep breath. Do the next thing.

He washed his face. Ran a comb through his hair. Buckled the swordbelt over his hips and wondered if or when Etranée would give him his sword back.

Etranée watched him the entire time. When he was done, she banged on the door.

Koji pulled it open. Her gaze went first to Arsenault, and damn, if he'd been paper, she would have burned him to the ground. "Captain?"

"Ask Cook for breakfast. For two. I'll eat in quarters with Arsenault."

Koji scowled but saluted Etranée. "Aye, Captain. You sure you don't want me in the room?"

Etranée touched Koji's arm lightly—strange behavior between a captain and a bodyguard. "Koji. I'll be fine. Seely's in the corridor?"

The large man who'd rowed them to the ship last night stepped into view. In the light without his abaganda hiding his face, all his scars and his battered nose were visible. But he was dressed neatly with a jaunty green silk ribbon threaded through his long, black braid. Etranée didn't run a slovenly ship. "I'll be happy to kick his arse for him shall he try a thing, Captain." He had an odd accent; one Arsenault couldn't place.

"I promise not to try any things." Arsenault moved behind Etranée so Seely and Koji could both see him. "I keep my word. Besides, I believe she won me fair and square."

He hooked his thumbs in his belt, trying to keep his hands from seeking steel that wasn't there.

Koji and Seely both eyed him, clearly not believing him. Was the entire crew this protective of their captain?

"So, I won you fair and square, did I?" Etranée said when they were gone, raising a brow.

"Well, you won me, Jon let me go, and I came."

Etranée's lips curved upward. "That's true. More than once."

Gods, the woman. His skin burned like a teenager's. "Are you complaining, Etranée?"

"No. But why does Jon think he needs his own personal truthteller?"

Arsenault sat in one of the chairs at the table and pulled his foot up onto his knee. "Because he's a, what did you call it? A Hidden Blade?"

"You don't know about the Blades?" Etranée's eyes crinkled slightly at the corners in disbelieving amusement.

"Why should he be telling me who he is and what he's doing?" Arsenault fiddled with the edge of the table. Whoever had built it hadn't sanded it smooth enough. Or it had been down in a raid. Splinters prickled his fingers. He dug his thumbnail into the wood. A soft wood, not the choice he'd have made.

"What are you doing to my table?" she asked suddenly.

"It needs refinishing. Or you need a better table. I'd have used teak, personally."

"You're criticizing my ship now?"

"Not your ship. Just this table. I like to build things."

"Well, Arsenault." Etranée sat across from him and leaned forward on her elbow, propping up her chin on her hand. Arsenault tried not to notice the way her breasts rested on the table or how her bodice showed them off, but it was too late for that. Memories of her lying naked beneath him surfaced all too quickly.

This whole ruse was a bad, bad idea.

She noticed him looking, of course. Her smile became a grin, about as safe as a crocodile's. "I'd like to know more about you, other than that you build tables and can offer a girl a good time. How about we start with the Hidden Blades and your contract-holder? Oh, wait—your *old* contract-holder. I'm the one giving you orders, bed, and board now, aren't I?"

She glanced over at the bed and then back at him with that damn eyebrow arched.

Great gods. Did she practice in front of a mirror?

He dropped his foot off his knee and leaned forward, settling both elbows on the table. "How *about* we start with Jon and the Blades? Why don't you tell me why it's so important to know why Jon's asking about Zim la Hallad?"

"Any time the Blades tangle with a Sugar Kingdom pirate, it's something I need to know about. If it's going to be over a *cabin boy*... well, don't you think that would set off some red flags? Do the Blades want his father?"

"How should I know?"

"Don't play with me, chiré. I don't buy this disguise of ignorance."

That was the problem with playing this game; nobody ever knew when you were telling the simple truth. "His father's dead."

She drew backward, looking genuinely startled. "You're sure of this?"

Arsenault struggled to remember. *The doctor...* A brief recollection of terror and darkness, a deck slick with blood and water—

He sank his nails into the tabletop. "Reasonably sure."

"But if Fariq picked Miha up, he'd be delivering him for money. Why would he kill Miha and keep his son?"

There was a knock at the door. Then Koji shoved it open with her hip, carrying a large tray in both hands. She set the tray on the table and bowed to Etranée.

"Cook says enjoy and your whore better know how good he's got it instead of eating in the galley like the rest of us."

"What, was she going to feed him fish heads? I didn't ask for anything special."

"She's happy to see you back, Captain." Koji darted another dark glance at Arsenault before she stepped out the door again.

"Your crew is not happy with me," Arsenault said.

Etranée smiled ruefully as she poured two cups of coffee. "Koji is unhappy with anyone I take into my cabin. But none of us trust the Blades."

He expected a traditional Dakkaran breakfast, but it seemed a mix of dishes. Delicate pastry horns, sweet-smelling porridge, coconut chutney, pickled lime, mango slices, and coffee with generous amounts of thick, fresh cream. The porcelain service was delicate, painted with drooping green palms.

"My cook is Hamari," Etranée explained. "And we're in port. So, we're spoiled. A small luxury, the cream. A tiny reminder of home." She cast her gaze downward at her coffee, and when she shifted in her seat, her eyes tightened for the briefest instant—a wince.

It might have been at the memory, but it looked more like physical pain.

Arsenault frowned. He filled the rest of his cup with cream, Vençalan style, and used one of the small silver spoons to stir it in. Etranée settled against her seat, holding her coffee in both hands, moving very slowly.

Damn. She really was in pain. Had she also been in pain last night? Had he just not noticed? Had he *caused* the pain?

"Porridge?" he asked, hand poised above the serving spoon.

She looked up at him, surprised, then wary. "Yes. With chutney. Please."

He kept an eye on her while he served. He didn't for a minute believe she wanted him as an indenture or she'd be more comfortable allowing him to serve her. People born to power took it for granted. She must have earned hers somewhere along the way.

He took some porridge and chutney, too, with a handful of sliced almonds for the top. The chutney had a little spice, but the porridge was smooth and sweet, made from cracked millet with honey. He thought about pocketing the coffee spoon just to keep some metal close to him, but the steward probably counted to make sure none were stolen.

"You know, Arsenault, another man would have been upset when my cook called you a whore. But you have bigger goals, don't you? You're trying to take down Fariq."

"Taking down Fariq would make me happy." He considered for a moment, but what did he have to lose by telling her his story? So he explained the basic facts of the raid, and Guin, and what had happened when they docked in Mdembu. "Fariq's whole ship was full of magic, and if the metal and the galleymen went to the same place, I need to know where, so I can get Guin back. Zim helped me after his father died, so I promised I wouldn't forget him. And that's my story, laid out plain. You can believe it or not."

Etranée rubbed the handle of her coffee cup as she absorbed what he'd told her. Finally, she seemed to come to a conclusion. "You'll have noticed the rings in Jon's ear. Did you count them?"

"Jon has five. Long Sally's man wears four. The Tiresian wears six in his right, two in his left."

"The Blades control most of the crime in Mdembu. The rings correspond to levels in the organization and the successful completion of various challenges. The Blades keep these very secret. So secret I've never been able to find solid evidence as to what they are. I suspect they involve assassination, but that's an easy guess. The customs official and the Onzarran representative had stepped afoul of them lately, which was why the Tiresian let them in the game. He was trying to get rid of them, and of course, Long Sally and her man and Jon helped."

Jon and his damn secrets. This web kept getting stickier and stickier. "So, what's your role in all of this? Do you need your own permissions from the Blades?"

"I work *with* them, not *for* them. I'm a pirate hunter, Arsenault, commissioned by the Ibuu's Dagger, Neyane dom B'ara. And right now, I'm hunting Yasi la Fariq."

CHAPTER 39

ARSENAULT

WHAT IN ALL THE HELLS WAS JON DOING?

Or, since Jon was Adayze's Dagger, what in all the hells was *she* doing? Were they at odds with Neyane?

He wasn't sure he wanted to be at odds with Neyane.

It wasn't that he didn't believe Jon—or Adayze—incapable of duplicity. She was the Heir after all. She'd have been raised to rule. But had Jon's indignant speech about corruption been a ruse? Were Adayze's protests against the ill treatment of galleymen faked? He wasn't sure he believed either of them would sanction criminal activity to get the kickback, but that was damn sure what it looked like. Maybe they *wanted* it to look that way, but...why?

Arsenault rose from the table and walked to the porthole—two big steps. Leaning his shoulder against the hull, he gazed out at the green sea sloshing beneath the porthole, toward the shore cloaked in a distant haze.

It...didn't look like Mdembu.

He frowned and turned around.

"So, what does Zim la Hallad's father have to do with you hunting Yasi la Fariq?"

"Miha la Hallad is a well-known artificer. He designs and builds machines. Some of his most famous were used by the Qalfans in their conquest of the Nefeth. But that warfare was so appalling Miha retired into seclusion with his family and refused to build anything else for the Empire. Because he'd rendered his service so effectively, the emperor let him go."

The doctor built machines...

It was hard to think about the man objectively. Arsenault was sure Erelf was hiding something from him...but what? Had the doctor treated his wound, and if not, why not?

No, no, that wasn't right. The doctor was dead. He couldn't have treated the wound.

"The letter the boy wrote said he and his father were on their way to Onzarro as diplomats."

"Could be true, I guess. Miha la Hallad is a polymath, well-versed in many different subjects. Maybe he was trying to make up for the destruction wreaked by his machines. That would make sense, as a narrative."

Arsenault couldn't help smiling a little. "Are you writing him a story?"

"We all have our narratives, don't we? The stories we tell about ourselves? Miha la Hallad was an eccentric genius, whose genius was used to slaughter thousands of people. Have you heard what happened in the Nefeth?"

"Not all the details. The stories sounded like any other war stories. The Empire wanted to expand, the Nefeth refused to yield. So, the Empire sent in its armies and the Nefeth was forced to surrender to greater numbers, superior weapons and tactics."

"Villages slaughtered. Farms burned. Whole cities taken in slavery."

Arsenault rubbed his brow wearily. "War."

She gave him a look he couldn't read. "Miha couldn't bear it. He had the capability to be anything he wanted. If he became a doctor, it makes sense that he would want to purge himself of the death he felt he'd caused."

Arsenault knew about the desire for exoneration—if only *he* had the ability to become anything he wanted. Then maybe he, too, could have become a healer instead of falling into his usual professions, which used his talents only too well: swordsman, soldier, killer, spy.

"Are you telling a story about him still or do you know?" he asked.

"People usually make sense if one views a person as his own sealed-up world. Like a garden in a glass bowl."

"Now you sound like a philosopher."

"My brother and I cut our teeth on metaphysics. My father was always given to long arguments with himself and whomever was in the room with him. Some things remain forever, I suppose." She glanced up at him. "You look surprised."

He tilted his head, regarding her. "No. It makes a certain kind of sense. Inside your glass bowl."

She huffed out a little laugh. "You're a strange one, Arsenault. I think it would take a long time to clean the glass of your bowl enough to see inside."

He shifted uncomfortably. He hoped he wouldn't stay long enough for her to get a peek. "So, Miha la Hallad built machines, and you think Fariq captured him on purpose for ransom. The customs official had seen big crates of cogs and other metal for machinery moving to Arak lands. Do you know why the Arak want machines?"

Etranée looked troubled. "If they were also angling for Miha, it looks an awful lot like they want to start a war."

"There's bad faith between them and the Ibuu?"

"Not just the Ibuu; all of the Dakkar. The last Arak insurrection happened when the current Ibuu was a boy. Dirik dom Arak's grandfather attacked the B'ara country house while the royal family was in residence for fever season. The Ibuu's guards managed to put it down, but with difficulty. The Ibuu died later of his wounds, and the current Ibuu took the throne at the age of ten. His mother was regent for a while, and by all accounts forged a peace by her strength of will alone. She was determined that the only way to end the violence between the two bindings was to make them family. The Ibuu's first wife—the Lady Adayze's mother—came from a distant Arak clan, but as the memory of the insurrection faded, marriage contracts were concluded much closer to the Arak seat of power."

It made sense now why Promethi had framed Renzo to get into the Ibuu's good graces. And why Adayze and Jon would be interested in Arak connections to a boatload of ragged Fixers enslaved as galleymen. He felt a little more used, but suddenly lighter for it making sense. Then he looked over his shoulder at the porthole and back to Etranée.

"Where are we going, Etranée? How far away from Mdembu are we?"

She set her coffee cup down on the table and rose—not quite as stiffly—to join him at the porthole. "I would say...about twenty leagues up the coast? We pulled up anchor as soon as I came on board. It was a calm night, but winds have picked up this morning. Is that a problem for you, Arsenault? I'm about to give you the choice to join us if you'd like."

After everything that had happened in the past few days, that finally snapped his temper. "You're giving me a *choice*? You've got a bill of sale with my name on it, you tie me to your bed—dammit, did you drug me so I'd sleep that hard?"

She laughed. "Of course not. You were just suffering the consequences of thinking with your cock."

She reached between his legs and gave him a squeeze. He nearly shot through the ceiling. The head he should have been thinking with slammed into the beams.

"*Fucking* balls and ashes," he swore, rubbing the crown of his head.

"My goodness, are you all right?" Etranée sounded as if half of her was concerned while the other half wanted to laugh. She lifted her hand to touch the sore spot and he jerked away from her.

"Don't touch me," he said hoarsely. "You're right. I was thinking with my cock. I believe I'll keep it in my pants from now on."

"I must say that sounds a little disappointing."

Damn the woman. To the deepest of the deepest pits of all the hells.

He took a big, ragged breath and straightened. Slowly. Watching the curve of the ceiling to make sure he knew where it was.

"Where are we going?" he asked.

"There's a hide-out in a little notch north of Mdembu. It's too chancy in storm season to make long voyages across open water, but if we hug the coast, we can make small daily jumps and hit quick, in and out. If your head has recovered, I believe it's time for us to go up top."

❦

UP TOP, THE SUN HAD BROKEN THROUGH THE CLOUDS AND THE weather was cooler—even bearable. He inhaled the scent of salt and water, hoping the fresh air would sharpen his wits.

They made their way to the bow of the ship, where Etranée leaned against the railing, the ends of her hair blowing out from underneath her scarf just like the figurehead beneath her. Arsenault leaned over to get a better look at it.

Godsdammit. *Ekyra.*

The goddess's polished wooden hair blew wildly around her head. Coins dropped from one hand, but in the other, she held a bloody knife. The artist had given her an expression as flat and inscrutable as the one Arsenault had seen the real goddess wear. Beneath the bust and highlighted in gilt paint was carved the ship's name: *Good Fortune.*

Arsenault slammed his fist down on the railing. Etranée looked at him in surprise.

"Something wrong?" she asked.

"No. Captain." He flexed his fingers and kept his hand open only by force of will. "I was just registering the irony of the name of your ship. What are we doing?"

Etranée held a piece of paper down on the railing, so it didn't blow away. "This is a list of our articles, Arsenault. Sign it and I'll tear up your sentence. Refuse to sign and we'll leave you in the wilderness with water and a knife. If you make it out and give us away, you'll be marked for death. It's your choice. Marooning's just a precaution if you choose the second route; you understand."

"Of course," Arsenault said with a black smile. "How could you do otherwise."

He reached for the quill she was holding, but she snatched it back, smiling sweetly.

"Read. First."

He grabbed the piece of paper.

1. All crew members have a vote in ship affairs and an equal share in the spoils.

2. Crew members take no slaves, and any crew member who comes to the ship a slave or indenture shall have his writ destroyed.

3. No alcohol or other substances of pleasure to be used when on duty.

4. Anyone who disobeys orders or shirks during a battle shall be marooned in the wilderness with one skin of water and one knife only.

5. Any crew member who spreads secrets heard on ship shall be declared traitor to their fellows and hunted down to be killed by any means possible, including blade, poison, rope, hand, rack, or torture.

Arsenault's brows rose at the last. "You're not playacting, are you?"

"You think I want you running to Fariq to tell him what I've said? We're deadly serious, Arsenault."

"You know I won't run to Fariq."

She crossed her arms over her chest, still gripping the quill tight. "When we took a vote, it was seven against, eight for. One more no vote and I would have put you out as soon as you woke up."

Arsenault looked toward shore. A white strip of beach glistened in a thin ribbon against the unrelenting forest that backed to a line of jagged, tree-covered bluffs. The green sheared away in big swathes to reveal smooth, brown sandstone cliffs. Not a hospitable place to be put on shore.

"You'd take the chance of me going back to Jon?"

"I'm going to tear up your writ regardless. Why would you want to go back to Jon? Besides, I've heard Fariq's mate and some of his crew members are holed up in that town, getting shit-drunk and whoring their way through most of its people. We'll raid them tonight. Put your signature at the bottom of this paper and you can join us."

What had Jon told him before they went hunting lions? *We're a country of promises. They're like spider webs, growing ever bigger, catching more people in their threads.*

His own promises had also spread like a spider web, but he seemed to be the one caught in their sticky threads. Guin. The boy, Zim. The other galleymen. Adayze. Edo. He even felt some responsibility to Jon, damn him. All of them had bound him somehow, and now he stood here, paralyzed by choice. Courtesy of the spider who regarded him with unreadable golden-brown eyes.

"All right," he said. "Give me the quill. I'll sign."

CHAPTER 40

ARSENAULT

ALABAD, TWENTY YEARS AGO

THE *GOOD FORTUNE* DROPPED ANCHOR AS THE SUN WAS SETTING, hiding around a curve of coast that sheltered the pirate hideout of Alabad. As dusk settled on the water, a black sliver of a boat set out from shore. It reached the ship at full dark, and a rumpled shape climbed out of it and up a rope ladder onto the *Fortune*.

The flash of a lantern revealed a small woman from Saien. Her crewmates grabbed her up and pounded her on the back in congratulations, presumably for staying alive. Her black hair was pulled back severely into a bun that hid in the folds of her abaganda, but her eyes —black in the darkness—crinkled at the corners with a smile as she greeted her crewmates. *Yeo*, Etranée called her.

While they fed her, Yeo gave Etranée the information she'd ferreted out of the hideout.

"The mate and a couple other men have rooms at the Sailor, which they've been terrorizing. Flashing lots of coin, hiring whores every night. The whores don't like them. But they've been bragging that their coin flows in an endless stream, so the girls are putting up with a lot."

Arsenault leaned into the circle sitting on the deck. Predictably, Koji glowered at him. Seely, the quartermaster, cracked his knuckles loudly. The Qalfan navigator gripped the helm but turned his head for an instant, the tail of his urqa fluttering in the wind.

Arsenault shifted uncomfortably under the weight of their attention. "I think he's running magic—metal, people. Bits and pieces of Eterean machines he looted as we went. The galleymen were mostly

Fixers. Whoever bought them must have paid handsomely. Or else Fariq has a whole side business running Fixers and it's giving him a steady stream of income instead of one big flush."

"There were rumors in town he'd just run in a load of Ceyles," Yeo said. "The little weasel-man was bragging about it. They said they set up a fake distress signal on the ship's deck and tricked a group into sending out a rescue ship. Then they captured the rescue ship and everyone on it."

"What's special about the Ceyles?" Arsenault asked.

Koji answered reluctantly. Her gaze continued to smolder but felt a little less likely to burn a hole in him. "The Ceyles are wizards. They live down south on a barely navigable archipelago of islands. People are frightened of their reefs and their magic. No one has been there for hundreds of years."

"Many people think they only exist in fairy tales," the navigator added. "The last person to land upon their shores and return to tell a tale was Oji la Kaif."

Oji la Kaif again. Arsenault rubbed his jaw. His name seemed to be turning up everywhere. He didn't know why it should bother him so much. "I suppose they'd fetch a pretty price."

"They would," Yeo replied. "If you were looking for magic, I guess. But what would you need so many Fixers for? And why go to all the trouble of searching out the Ceyles? I thought it sounded like Fariq had been blown off course in a storm and was taking advantage of it. Everybody knows he's involved in the galley trade, and he has no qualms about selling people to the nearest Kingdom isle."

"Maybe he's looking for old magic," Seely tossed in. "You know, treasure from the old gods. My mam said maps from the old times marked places where people had seen the gods fall from heaven. Surely the old magic still exists somewhere."

Damn. Fariq had kidnapped a boatload of Fixers while on a mission to find old magic, the skeletons of gods, in particular. The two *were* linked. But why? Just to make more Eterean machines or for something completely new, like that snake?

The navigator rolled his eyes. "Seely, your mam is the store of so many tales you could pin them on a fish and make a nest of eels."

"Well, what about these Ceyles then, Sandro?" Seely's accent gave the word a broad burr—*SAILies.* "I thought they were just fairy tales."

"Maybe they are," Sandro—an odd name for a Qalfan man— retorted. "Wouldn't it raise the price Fariq could demand if he said they were Ceyles, but instead they were just...people?"

"The Outer Islands of Vençal are full of northerners," Etranée interjected, eyeing Arsenault strangely. Her crew went silent as they looked to her.

"That's true," Arsenault said uncomfortably.

"I assumed the people in your village were Vençalan. But were they northerners? You're not Dagmari. You're Tulan, from a place off the maps—just like the Ceyles! You're that godsdamned Tulan guard Jon was talking about in the card game!"

He'd wondered when Etranée would put two and two together. "Tule isn't a fairy tale. Many people know about it."

"Arsenault!"

"There is nothing between me and the Lady Adayze," he said quickly. "That was a lie."

Etranée laughed. "I knew I should have called Jon out, the shit. But why in all the hells would Fariq travel so far for Fixers, unless he is hunting fairy tales—*or* it's the godsdamned metal that's the most important part of this puzzle?"

Seely frowned in what Arsenault assumed was supposed to be a thoughtful way, although it only made him seem more intimidating. "If you came down all the way from the Outer Islands of Vençal..."

"That's a hell of a lot of distance to cover," Sandro, the navigator, said. "How many of you survived?"

Hazy memories of screams, thunder, the sinuous writhing of scales under the water—a sudden image of a man's ragged leg, torn from his body. Had he known that man's name? All the men were only shadows now, even Guin—except for that perfect memory of a shorn limb. Bile flooded his throat.

"Some," he choked out. "Some were fed to the serpent. We tried to take the ship, but...without success."

Etranée's crew nodded somberly. Was their disapproval of him cracking? They seemed to know a lot about galleys and Sugar Kingdom slavers.

Etranée turned back to her scout. "Where is Fariq now? Did you find out?"

Yeo sighed. "I did not. The men were mostly too drunk to care."

"He's got a commission on a flatboat," Arsenault interjected.

Etranée smiled at him tightly, as if all these revelations were wearing her patience thin. "And how do you know that?"

"I met somebody with connections."

Somebody who's going to be in trouble if I don't get him out of the Ovens.

Would Renzo even be alive when Arsenault returned, or would the Ibuu have executed him by then?

If he made it back at all.

Etranée gave him a sardonic look. "We'll need to take the mate to find out where Fariq is and exactly what he's doing. Then we raze the place, make it look like it's just another *Good Fortune* raid. I've wanted to hit Alabad for a long time now. Too many slavers use it as a haven. If Fariq's running Fixers and his crew is showing off their coin, you can bet half those captains will be out by morning, looking for their own magicians to traffic."

⁂

THE *GOOD FORTUNE* WAS ARMED WITH TWO CANNONS—A BENEFIT OF having been commissioned by Neyane dom B'ara. Arsenault hadn't yet seen a big gun in action, but they played a key role in Etranée's strategy. He himself would be going onshore to be used as bait, but Seely gave him a tour of the cannons as he armed himself from the ship's store of weapons.

The cannons looked like chunky bronze amphorae set on their sides. "It's like playing a game of dice," Seely said, "whether it will blow front or back after you heat the shot and roll it in. See this seal here? If it's not closed the explosion blows out the back."

"Will it be worth it?" Arsenault asked. "To destroy the whole place instead of just taking the mate by stealth and being done with it?"

"Sure," Seely replied, "and if it was just about taking the mate, that would be it. But this is personal. Everybody knows Captain Etranée don't suffer slavers. Besides, if we can get a few more of the bastards along the way, then more's the better, eh?"

"Do they have cannons, too?"

"Nah. Cannon hasn't made it onto the smuggling circuit yet. Too big. Guns now... That's another matter. Have to assume some of those pirates are armed with pistols. Small guns that fit in your hand. Seen those, have you?"

Arsenault nodded curtly. Seely leaned on the cannon and folded his arms over his chest.

"The B'ara are pretty tight with their supply and they string up violators quick. But they've a leak somewhere, because captains are turning up with pistols and more are running crates of arquebus to the Sugar Kingdom for their wars. Every farm for itself in the Sugar Kingdom, and the owner, he's king. Thinks he's king," Seely amended darkly. "Or maybe a god." He kicked himself away from the cannon. "Anyway, you've seen enough here, have you?"

Enough to know Renzo probably hadn't been lying about buying that arquebus from a pirate. Still not enough to make all the connections firm. His gut tensed in the anticipation of getting the information out of Fariq's mate. He joined Sandro and Yeo on deck and in a few moments, they'd been outfitted with a small shore boat and were gliding soundlessly across the black water to Alabad and its ramshackle tavern.

"Behold, the Drunken Sailor," Sandro said as he shoved the doors open. "A study in accurate advertising."

He'd thought he would stand out wearing Etranée's clothes, but nothing stood out in this loud, garish mix. "End of the bar!" Yeo shouted. He had to lean over to hear her in the din. She barely came to his collarbone and threaded easily through the crowd he had to shove his way through. When they made it to the end of the bar, she flicked a hand at the barmaid. In a moment, the maid set a jug of rum in front of them and a big plate of crispy fried squid rings to share.

"Onzarran cook," Sandro said, grinning as he snagged one. "Enjoy them while you can." He pulled his urqa down to eat, the way most Qalfans from the diaspora did. Arsenault was surprised to find that Sandro's eyes were dark blue, his skin the same pale olive as Renzo's.

"You're...Onzarran?" Arsenault asked, but that didn't seem right.

Sandro gave him a flat stare and Yeo laughed. "Don't get him started. It's a point of pride with him that he was born and raised in Dakkar. His mother's Lieran."

Arsenault leaned forward in interest. "Do you know the House di Prinze then?"

"My mother's a freeholder, from a family of traders who dealt in silk. All I know is that the Prinze used to carry Aliente silk, but they don't anymore—there's some kind of feud going up there, after the current Householder took over from his father. I don't know if the Prinze are brilliant or stupid, refusing to carry for the Aliente. If they make it so they're the only carrier left, I guess it's brilliant, but otherwise, why don't the Aliente just use someone else?" Sandro shrugged. "My mother adopted the urqa and allaq after she met my father. Mostly she talked about wine and how she wished we had better Longest Night celebrations. She said they lit Saien rockets over the lagoon in Liera."

"I wouldn't know," Arsenault said. "I've never been there."

"Then why were you asking? Were the pirates carrying silk, too?"

"No. I ran across the name and was curious. I heard the House-holder might have some magic."

"Attrasca founded the whole damn Empire from Liera, so makes sense. Every now and then you hear a story that makes you ask what in the hells. I heard Geoffre di Prinze thought he could use magic in warfare—not just making guns or swords, but directly against *people*—and he's paying to learn how to do it. But people will say anything to get you to buy them another drink. You sure you don't want any of these squid rings? They're very good. Sin not to accept the good things the Magnificent Sun puts in our way, you know."

Arsenault frowned, trying to parse the information Sandro had just given him. "I've got a nervous stomach."

"Just so you're not nervous when it comes down to working the plan." Yeo spun a squid ring lazily around her finger. "Fariq's men like to make an entrance. When they come..."

"I'm to make a commotion, walk outside, make sure they follow me. We'll take them there. Signal Etranée so she can start shooting."

Sandro looked around the room. "Quite a crowd in here tonight, though." Conversation had risen around them and he had to lean close to be heard without shouting. "You might have to do something big."

Arsenault smiled tightly. "I think I can figure something out."

The double doors slammed open and Fariq's Vençalan mate swaggered in with a girl under his arm.

He was wearing a huge grin and gold in his ear, but not like Jon's, just a big hoop. The Tiresian and a little man who looked like a weasel followed him in. Arsenault had no distinct memories, but his body remembered—the thirst and hunger, the exhausting monotony of hauling on the oar, hour after hour, and the mate Boucher's voice... *If your oarmate can't pull his weight, Arsenault, he's out in the sea...* Boucher hadn't liked Guin.

Arsenault set the bottle on the table and cracked his knuckles. Yeo and Sandro followed his gaze.

"Shit," Sandro said. "So much for dinner."

Arsenault gripped the hilt of his belt knife, rose, and walked over to where Fariq's men had gotten themselves a good table by throwing men out of their chairs. They were hassling the barmaid now. The Vençalan had one girl on his knee, but he grabbed the barmaid, too.

"You have to have a price, *chiré*," he said. "Every woman has a price, no? Maybe yours is high?"

"She'd give *me* a lower price," the Tiresian said. "Hand her over here, Boucher. You've already got one."

The barmaid struggled. "Let go of me or I'll gut you."

"She fights like a damn swordfish," Weasel said, laughing.

That was all Arsenault could take. Yeo and Sandro wanted him to make a commotion; he'd damn well make one. He unsheathed his knife and stepped up behind Weasel. With one fluid motion, he pulled the man backward and jammed his knife into the man's back. Weasel froze, like he was surprised. Then Arsenault yanked the knife out and the man jerked forward, choking, spraying blood from his mouth. The barmaid shrieked and threw up her hands as blood spattered her face. Weasel fell forward onto the table. His head hit with a rattling thump.

No thoughts; just quick killing.

The Vençalan shoved his girl out of the way. The Tiresian had begun to lurch upright, but Arsenault jammed the knife into his gut before he could make it. The Tiresian staggered sideways and collapsed onto the floor, clutching at his side. Blood fountained through his fingers.

"You," the Vençalan said, fumbling his sword from his sheath on the other side of the table.

"Me," Arsenault agreed.

He hurled the table sideways. Weasel's body tumbled to the floor. One of the girls started crying as she stumbled out of the way.

Arsenault pulled his sword. The Vençalan lunged at him with a drunken stab that Arsenault easily turned aside. Anger made swordsmen sloppy; long practice bound his and focused it into a distant cold rage that made his movements precise and deadly. Boucher kept making wild slashes that were easy to parry. Arsenault easily avoided Boucher's next strike and thrust his knife against the man's ribs, not hard enough to stab through, just enough to hurt. Then he swung the hilt of his sword into Boucher's face.

The bone snapped, loud enough to hear. Boucher howled and sagged into the point of Arsenault's knife. Arsenault shoved him into the wall and laid the blade edge of his sword to the man's throat.

The bar had fallen silent. The barmaid hugged the shaking whore to her shoulder. Nobody seemed to want to come to the mate's aid. *Good.*

"Drop your sword," Arsenault growled.

"Magician *bastard*," Boucher spat at him, breathing hard. With every breath, his windpipe scraped against Arsenault's blade. "I knew Fariq should have thrown you overboard."

"Well, he didn't, and now he's got a problem, doesn't he? Drop your sword and move."

The Vençalan's left hand twitched at his side. Arsenault swept the knife up and jammed it deep into Boucher's forearm. Boucher screamed, but Arsenault leaned on him, driving the knife the rest of the way through Boucher's arm, pinning it to the wall behind him.

"*Drop your sword*," he said again.

Wheezing in pain, Boucher complied.

Arsenault had to rock the knife to get it out of the wall and the man's arm. Blood poured over them both as the blade pulled free. Boucher's knees buckled; Arsenault adjusted his sword so he could hold it and drag a whimpering Boucher out at the same time.

"Sorry for the mess," he told the girls. "But someone will probably be along to clean it up."

He knocked the doors open with Boucher's body and dragged him down the boardwalk that led to the docks.

Yeo and Sandro soon caught up.

"What in the name of the gods and their demons are you doing?" Yeo shouted.

Sandro scowled. "This wasn't the plan."

"I changed the plan," Arsenault answered. "Boucher and I have a history. You better signal Etranée now."

"You working for the Spider now, magician?" Boucher rasped. "That's a turnabout, ain't it. How'd you get away from them Dakkaran officials who took you from Fariq?"

"Shut up," Arsenault told him. "Yeo. The signal."

Yeo pressed her lips tight and drew a pistol from inside her abaganda. She yanked back the dog with a click, raised the pistol into the air, and pulled the trigger.

It fired with a sharp crack and a cloud of smoke.

From the harbor, closer than Arsenault had expected, a lantern flashed.

And then, with no further warning, there was a deafening boom. A red flash from the side of the ship lit up the darkness. In the next instant, one of the ships in the harbor blew open in a splintering crash. Pieces of wood erupted everywhere, splashing into the waters of the bay. When the smoke cleared, a jagged hole gaped in the ship's hull at the water line. The ship began to creak and list as water poured into it. Men scrambled over its tilting deck, shouting, screaming. Then streaks of orange and red suddenly sang over the water like

Saien streamers. *Fire arrows*. They hit another ship and flames boiled up into the darkness like a Longest Night bonfire.

Arsenault stopped dead. *This* was Etranée's warning?

He forced himself to lurch into motion again, yanking Boucher with him as the doors to the tavern behind them slammed open and people poured out. Crews fumbling for weapons, yelling orders, pushing, shoving.

Etranée's voice called over the water, much louder than it ought to. "Alabad!"

She stood on the quarterdeck with one foot up on the gunwale, a speaking horn to her lips. "That's your last warning! Harbor slavers and burn!"

Another belch of fire and smoke from the *Good Fortune* lit up the night, followed by another splintering crash as the ball slammed broadside into a ship its crew had just unmoored and started to turn.

"Time for us to go," Yeo said.

"So, you got it in for everyone now, too, do you?" Boucher said to him. "Going to burn us all?"

"You and Fariq. Etranée will take care of the rest."

As if to emphasize his words, both cannons let loose, one right after the other, turning another ship in the harbor to kindling.

"Surrender and maybe I'll leave some of you alive!" Etranée shouted.

For an instant, Arsenault regretted what he was about to do. Then he saw what he wanted bobbing against the dock. They'd docked their own boat at the end of the pier, but he didn't want it. He wanted the skiff in the middle.

He shoved the Vençalan off the pier into the bottom of the boat. The man hit with a cry and the boat bobbed crazily as Arsenault jumped in after him. Before Yeo and Sandro could follow, Arsenault sliced through the rope that held the boat to its mooring and set the skiff adrift in the choppy, debris-laden water.

❧

"You forgot something, didn't you?" the Vençalan said.

Arsenault was too busy trying to get the hell out of the harbor to answer him. He unfurled the sail and made fast the lines, then leaned on the tiller. It was a quick little boat, but the wind was not in his favor. The destruction Etranée was wreaking in the harbor raised waves that spilled over the bow, swamping them.

"I'm not working for Etranée," he said. "I'm working for me."

His best hope was to hug the coast, stay close to the mangroves that jutted out around Alabad and hide in one of the hundreds of tiny inlets the trees created in sea and swamp. It would have been safer to stay on land, but he'd have never gotten Boucher away from Yeo and Sandro that way.

"Where's Fariq, Boucher?"

"We go our separate ways a while, we two."

"Then where are you supposed to meet up with him?"

Boucher shrugged as he was dragging himself upright. "What else you going to do to me, magician?"

"If you give me good information, I might let you live."

"No, I doubt it. You're going to kill me anyways."

"I might not hurt you more before I kill you. That better?"

Boucher laughed.

Not good.

His struggle with the tiller and the wind probably gave Boucher some courage. The waves were washing the boat straight back at the *Good Fortune*. If he couldn't turn it, they would smash right into her hull.

More ships were setting sail in the harbor, choking it in their attempt to escape before Etranée blew them to pieces. The skiff was so close to the *Good Fortune* now that when Arsenault looked up, he could see Etranée standing on the quarterdeck with an arquebus set against her shoulder, taking aim at someone on another ship. Smoke and sulfur filled the night, accompanied by the crack of gunshot, the boom of cannons, and the crackle of the flames now devouring all the buildings on shore. Etranée had launched fire arrows into the tavern itself.

In an instant, Boucher leapt for him.

Boucher hit him hard in the stomach and his hand stripped away from the tiller. Arsenault fell backward and the boat rocked precariously, slopping dangerously to port. A wave shoved them from starboard and the skiff capsized.

It didn't make sense how time could slow down and speed up in the very same moment, but that's what it seemed. The mast sheared against the hull of the *Good Fortune* and snapped in two. Freed of its mast, the boat turned turtle and the world became a flash of images— the *Good Fortune*'s figurehead of Ekyra lit up with light from burning ships, Boucher's desperate and angry face as he slid toward him, the bottom of the hull closing over him like a lid on a chest.

The angry harbor water lifted him up and slammed him into the cap of the overturned boat while the ropes writhed around him like snakes.

For a moment, he was completely disoriented—floating, in pain, surrounded by black water. Then his lungs began to burn and instinct kicked in. He felt along the hull for the edge and pulled himself backward, out from under it. As soon as he was in free water, the orange glow of flames lit the surface and he kicked himself upward, toward the light.

When he broke the surface, gasping, the *Good Fortune* loomed before him. The little skiff he'd stolen bobbed upside down, helpless as a dead fish. Boucher struggled to get a grip on the hull with his good hand, but he was all tangled up in the lines.

Arsenault pulled his sword and laid it on top of the capsized skiff to keep it from dragging him down, then shoved off toward Boucher.

"Arsenault!" Boucher gasped, going under, then bobbing up, like a cork.

Arsenault grabbed him under the arm and hauled him up. Boucher lay there breathing hard a moment, his face pressed against the boat's hull.

"You know I never used a whip on you, Arsenault. I was never the one gave you any beatings. Fariq's the one told me to keep you down—"

"Shut up, Boucher. All I want to know is where did Guin go?"

"Who the hells—"

Arsenault let go of him.

Boucher sank beneath the waves again, scrabbling on the slippery hull without any purchase. Arsenault watched him pulling frantically at the ropes beneath the water for a count of twenty. Then he dragged him back up again.

Boucher sucked in air. "*Zaicré!* All right! I didn't count where everybody went, but I think that Arak noble took him with the others. That's the gods' truth! Noble hired Fariq again to transport. He's in Mirage, on the Serapo, where the caravans come in. Picking up more cargo. He just had to switch ships, get everybody certified..."

Renzo's pirate camp. Dammit.

The *Good Fortune* was growing ever closer. "Why would Promethi want Fixers?" Arsenault asked quickly.

"Promethi wasn't the name I heard. It was his brother, the recluse —Dirik! Fariq said it was for experiments, but how the hell should I know what those are? Arsenault! We have to get out of here!"

Arsenault looked up at the *Good Fortune*. Ekyra loomed over them with the bloody knife raised in her right hand, and Etranée stood above the figurehead. Her face transformed in horror as she realized what was about to happen.

"Arsenault!" Boucher shouted. "I told you what you wanted to know! Save me, please!"

There was no way he could get Boucher out of those ropes in time, even if he'd wanted to. Boucher must have seen it in his face.

"No," he said. "No, gods damn you, you bastard, no—"

Arsenault let him go.

He was still yelling as he went under, but the boat smashed into the *Good Fortune* just as Arsenault dove away in the opposite direction.

The sound of splintering wood was far louder than the sound of a drowning man.

FIVE DAYS LATER, ARSENAULT PULLED A STOLEN ROWBOAT UP ON THE beach in Mdembu and staggered over the sand to the tavern where he'd last seen Jon. He'd heard Etranée shouting his name, but in the chaos, it had been easy to hide.

Now the sun blazed down, burning hot and blinding bright on the white sand. Every step felt like he was dragging himself through hot tar. His clothes were in tatters and stiff with dried salt. Everyone he passed stared at him, but he ignored them. When he made it to the tavern, he collapsed at the mostly empty bar.

The barmaid from before—Niki—was at work again. She looked up when he threw himself down in the seat, obviously prepared to speak to a normal patron, but when she saw him, her eyes widened.

"Give me some water and a bottle of rum. A big bottle, the whole thing. I don't need a cup. And whatever you have to eat. I'm starving."

"You're...Jon's bodyguard."

"I don't have any coin. You can put it on Jon's tab, and he damn well better pay it."

"But where—"

"Has Jon been around?"

She nodded in the direction of the bigger room. "He's over there. With Jemma."

"Of course." Arsenault forced a smile. "Can I get that water? And the rum?"

"Oh! Yes, sorry, I'll—"

He pushed himself up again and lurched in Jon's direction.

Jon was too absorbed in Jemma to have noticed him come in, and he was slow to turn around.

"What do you want?"

"Right now? Mostly I'd like to punch you in the nuts."

Jon jerked his head up in surprise, then shoved his chair backwards and stood with a grin. Jemma gasped in surprise. Before Arsenault could respond, Jon grabbed him around the shoulders and pounded him on the back. Arsenault tried to stop the exclamation of pain caused by the pounding on his sunburned shoulders, but only succeeded in forcing the sound out through his nose instead of his mouth.

Jon stood back from him quickly. "What happened to you?"

Arsenault dragged in a deep breath as the pain subsided. "An arrogant son of a bitch asked me to cheat in a card game and lost me to a crazy pirate hunter who just took apart an entire town, that's what."

Jon's eyebrow inched upward.

"I was five days in a rowboat. It wasn't much fun."

"Jemma. Do you think you could get Arsenault something to eat?"

"And rum," Arsenault added. "Niki's supposed to be getting me a bottle; don't let her forget."

Jemma gave him a smile at once uncertain and genuine. She rose from the table and gave him a little curtsy before she went.

"She's a pretty girl, Jon," Arsenault said. "I'm going to sit down now. Every muscle in my body feels like it's about to come unraveled."

He fell more than sat into one of the chairs at Jon's table.

"Five days in a rowboat, eh?"

"After I swam a harbor and walked through a mangrove swamp. I found the rowboat tied up at somebody's private hideaway. North of Mdembu. South of Alabad."

Jon's eyebrows both shot upward. "So, you escaped before Etranée hit it? Word spread she took it apart with cannon. My father will have something to say about that."

"I doubt it. Etranée works for your aunt. She's a pirate hunter. She took Alabad apart because Fariq's first mate was holed up there and she's looking for a man they're supposed to have. Miha la Hallad, famous artificer, have you heard of him? I hadn't. I told her all about Fariq's smuggling history, though. You have a lot of explaining to do, Jon. You can talk while I eat. Then I'm going to drink that entire godsdamned bottle of rum."

Jon's expression went a little cagey. He looked down at his

abaganda and flicked a speck of something, probably imaginary, from his chest. "What do I have to explain? And why should I explain anything to you? You didn't have to cheat the second time, and now you're a runaway indenture or a debt slave. Not my responsibility anymore."

Niki and Jemma arrived at that moment with a pitcher of water, a bottle of good Dakkaran dark rum, and a large tray of food. Arsenault's stomach tightened painfully.

"Are you sure you're all right?" Niki asked as she put the pitcher and a cup down in front of him.

He smiled up at her. "I will be. Jon is paying for a room in the inn for me until tomorrow morning. With a bath. Aren't you, Jon?"

"Your own room? Can't you—"

"A bed and a bath. Because he's generous."

"But shouldn't you—"

"She tore up the writ," he said and closed his eyes briefly as he drank the water. It was lukewarm, but who in all the hells would care?

"She what?"

Niki and Jemma traded uncomfortable glances. "Come on, Jemma," Niki said, taking the other woman's arm. "There's more work for us to do in the back."

Jemma frowned over her shoulder at Jon as she went.

Arsenault set the empty cup on the table. "Tore it up. So technically, Jon, I'm a free man. We can negotiate a contract and you can pay me coin for my services. Tomorrow. After I eat and sleep off all the rum I'm going to drink."

He smiled at Jon. Jon looked back at him like he didn't quite know what to think.

"But Arsenault...if Etranée freed you and she was looking for Fariq...did you find out where your man and the boy are? Why did you come back?"

"Because I promised your sister I would keep them safe. Her and Edo."

"My sister..." Jon said slowly.

"And your nephew. The one who eats dirt. Now let me have that bottle, Jon, and tomorrow when I wake up again, we can make some plans."

CHAPTER 41

CASSIS

PRINZE PRISON COMPOUND, LIERA, PRESENT

"OF COURSE I'LL LET YOU HAVE THE FUNDS, BROTHER. TAKE A KNEE and promise me fealty as your Householder, and you'll have your funds by this afternoon."

"Are you mad, Devid? This is Liera. You're not a blasted king!"

Devid had let him sweat in prison for days then dragged him up to the anteroom where Cassis had used to report to his father. Now his brother sat in the heavy mahogany chair and Cassis's hands were chained behind his back.

Devid tilted his head, considering. He sat casually with one foot propped up on the opposite knee. "King Devid the First. I like the sound of that. You know it's what our father wanted. A new empire, formed from the Prinze dynasty."

"So, you plan to drag me off to the executioner, steal my coin, marry my wife perhaps? Then anoint yourself emperor?"

"Don't make me laugh, Cassis. You'd drop Camile off on my doorstep tied in a bow if you could. But what good would it do? I need a wife who can give me a son."

Cassis flinched on Camile's behalf. Perhaps he should have flinched more on behalf of Devid's wife, who had borne him only girls. *See what happens when a man banks all he has on a daughter!* Geoffre used to rail about Pallo d'Aliente, usually when he was drunk and in a rage.

Still. "I suppose you won't be forming much of a dynasty then."

Devid dropped his foot. The heel of his shoe made a harsh thwack against the tile floor, like a clap to get Cassis's attention. "If you don't swear fealty and accept my position as your Householder, I'll have no choice but to send you to the hanging tree."

"That's lovely, Devid. You could at least behead me."

"I'm being generous giving you any chance at all. You're a traitor to your House. Raising an army against the legal Householder *and* consorting with the enemy."

For an instant, Cassis froze, unsure whether Devid meant Kyrra or Driese. "The Caprine aren't our enemy anymore," he ventured. "The wars are over. We're at peace."

Devid stood. "Does it matter? The Caprine have always been our enemy. Come with me, Cassis."

He walked to the door of the study Geoffre had called his war room and pushed it open. The room was decorated in scenes from the Empire—Attrasca receiving his box of magic from the gods. The scenes remained, along with the furniture: the long table, his father's gold-gilt chair at its head. But now a contingent of foreigners faced him.

Devid waved his hand at a scruffy, sun-tanned man with bleached golden hair and creases at the corners of his eyes. "Allow me to introduce you. This is Piere Vauquelin, who commands my new navy."

Of course Vençal supports Devid; they want to break our monopoly on the sea trade.

"Trevan di Cozin, who is offering some interesting trading terms with Amora."

Cassis jerked at the Amoran man's name before he could stop himself. Trevan, one of Lobardin's six older brothers, gazed back at him in cool question, a dark, aristocratic eyebrow quirked in a strange echo of Lobardin. Lobardin's father must have stamped all his sons in the same mold. Trevan seemed less ironically cynical, probably because he retained access to the Cozin fortune, the ear of the Amoran king, and the famed ranks of deadly Amoran assassins.

"Bazidar Renko, the Grand Prince of Rojornick." A trim severe-looking man with an immaculately groomed black beard and access to guns, courtesy of fucking Jon Barra. "And finally..." Devid moved to the last man at the table, dressed in an allaq with an urqa hiding all but his bright, liquid brown eyes. "Allow me to present His Highness, the crown prince Farraj la Monazar, who has agreed to provide me with Nezari soldiers should I need them to keep the peace."

The prince tipped his head in Cassis's direction and Cassis stared at Devid, aghast. "You're bringing Qalfan troops into Liera? All you need is the Onzarran legate and your council of Liera's enemies will be complete!"

Devid's smile grew pasted on and hate flared in his narrowed eyes. "Take my brother back to his cell," he told the gavaros who'd accompanied them. "I'll talk to him after the grown-ups have finished discussing diplomacy."

❧

WHEN CASSIS HAD STOOD INSIDE DEVID'S TENT BENEATH THE falling sleet and soot, he'd never imagined how short a time it would take to end up with boring, hamfisted Devid sitting across the table from three of the most powerful men in the world and him losing control of a single old Eterean fortress, brick by crumbled brick in mud and blood, his only "allies" an exiled, kacin-addicted gavaro and an obsessive scholar. He'd spent all his time on his army when he should have been seeking outside assistance like Devid.

"Fuck," Cassis muttered after the gavaros locked him back inside his small cell. Then louder, *"Fuck!"*

He kicked the straw, staved his toe on the single stone bench, kicked it again, trying to turn his anger, astonishment, and increasing desperation into something tangible like pain instead of the amorphous ball of helplessness growing in his gut.

Devid's going to kill me, and then he's going to kill Liera.

Cassis took a deep, shaky breath. "If I just take a fucking knee to him, I can fool him into thinking—I can—oh, damn, damn. *Dammit.*"

He collapsed onto the bench and put his head in his hands. There was no time to dither. He could swear fealty to Devid and set about betraying him or refuse to swear fealty and...what? Die a noble death?

A door skreeked in the corridor, followed by a thump, then a muffled cry and boot heels. Cassis brought his head up. *Surely Devid's not coming for me already.* A key rattled in the door of his cell.

Heart thumping, Cassis stood, preparing to debase himself to Devid. If that was the only way to stay alive and keep Devid from giving the city away to its rivals, so be it. He'd have to funnel his money elsewhere. Maybe Lobardin could take it and spread his men out so it wouldn't look like he was retaining his army...

The door swung open, but his guards were nowhere to be seen. Instead, a huddle of figures wrapped in black cloaks like ravens stood in the opening, and there in the center of the group was...

Ser Lupa?

"Good afternoon, mestere," Lupa said, smiling and clutching his satchel. "I decided to bring the Council of Empirists to you."

⁂

THE EMPIRISTS HAD FORMED A FUCKING COUNCIL?

Three figures filed into the tiny cell behind Lupa. Their cloaks covered them head to foot, and they all wore masks, as if prison-breaking was a Longest Night party. One was feathered like a swan, another whiskered like a cat's, the third a disturbing creation—a vanth? The swan was quite a bit shorter than the other two... Maybe a woman, but Cassis didn't want to place bets.

Geoffre had masked himself, too. His father's interest in the Empirists had been proof to Cassis that Geoffre's mind had begun to falter, leading him into ever more dangerous obsessions, probably due to all the magic he'd soaked up from other men. He began to believe he was a god, and he only wanted the empire back because he was sure he would be its emperor. But Cassis hadn't been privy to the masking sessions. Geoffre had often called both Mikelo and Arsenault-as-Andris to assist him instead. The connections made Cassis even more uneasy.

"If you're not here to plead my case with Devid or get me out of this cell, I don't see how I can help you," Cassis said.

"That is exactly why we're here," the figure in the swan mask replied in a low voice. "First, to parlay. And then, hopefully, to move on to more fruitful discussions of mutual beneficence." The voice certainly sounded like it might belong to a woman, but what kind of woman would just *walk* into the Prinze prison like this?

Kyrra would, his treacherous mind supplied.

"Mutual beneficence." He rolled the old-fashioned words around his mouth. "That would seem to suggest there's something I can do for you, when as you can see..."

The chains clanked as he spread his arms.

"Pardon, mestere," Lupa interrupted. "But I've already shared our proposal with you. We need your answer now."

"You're talking about a literal proposal, though! You're talking about *me* marrying Kyrra, for some crackpot scheme—"

"We have guns," the swan said. "And we're willing to trade."

Cassis eyed them skeptically. Treading a middle line might be the best course of action. "A few arquebuses aren't going to make a differ-ence. I need powder. Lead to make shot. Maneuverable artillery. *Then* arquebuses and trained arquebusiers. Give me all the guns in the world but no powder to prime them, and—"

He shrugged.

The swan cocked her head. Cassis expected the cat or vanth to answer, since he'd made a point of military strategy, but she spoke again.

"I thought we would start with guns, but your main problem, as we understand it, is rations." Her voice was cool, clipped—familiar, but Cassis couldn't place it. "You're in an unwinnable situation, Mestere di Prinze, and it doesn't matter if we have one gun or a thousand, what you can't deny is our *support*. Show him, Felix."

The cat—*Felix*—reached inside his cloak and drew out a large purse that chinked with coins. He clicked it open and drew out a whole handful of astra.

"All right," Cassis snapped. "You've made your point. I need funds or I wouldn't be here now. But your proposal for me to marry Kyrra d'Aliente is insane. Firstly, because she's dead. I don't know how you expect me to marry a dead woman."

The swan spoke again. "We have intelligence that says differently. We want you to operate as our political arm. We'll put you in the Householder's Chair, but you must agree to an alliance with the Aliente first. This will do two things immediately: It will calm the Aliente sympathizers who've been stirring up trouble, and it will give you complete access to whatever magic the Aliente were able to retain."

Cassis's stomach flipped. "I don't know what intelligence you think you have, but I can hardly ally with a House that doesn't exist. Kyrra's not the only Aliente who's dead—they *all* are. And you're on with that Legacy of Attrasca bullshit again, aren't you? Well, we kept looking after Lupa pulled out that godsdamned limb and there isn't anything else!"

"If I may." Lupa worked his way in and pulled a small, leather-bound book out of his satchel. It looked impossibly old. It was tied shut with a frayed golden cord, which Lupa carefully untied with his long, ink-stained fingers. He had a few unscholarly nicks on his knuckles that looked fresh, and Cassis wondered uneasily just how *had* all these people walked into a cell in a Prinze prison?

Lupa smoothed away a smudge of dust with the cuff of his sleeve, then slowly opened the book.

Cassis frowned in confusion. "Why are the pages blank?"

"A moment," Lupa answered. "There's an old magic on this parchment and it takes time to fade." Even as he spoke, marks began to appear on the page—sketches of limbs, teeth, tails.

The captions read, in ancient Eter: *Manticore, sphinx, basilisk, dragon.*

"Is that an Oji la Kaif original?" Cassis asked in awe. *If it is, maybe I can steal it and sell it to fund my army.*

"The author of this particular book is unknown. But it was done in the same era and the same territory."

"Is it a religious book? It looks like a detail of the Gods' War, but—"

"These are sketches of the monsters that existed before the war the gods fought, yes. But..." Lupa flipped a page. "It's unclear whether the author is saying the fortress was a burial ground for the monsters that fell to earth in the war or that the Etereans buried the machines they made in the likenesses of the monsters there. In any case, there ought to be a great deal of interesting magic buried on the grounds of that lodge. But if you haven't been able to find it—"

"Has it all been plundered?"

"I sincerely hope not, mestere, but certainly some of the cache may have ended up elsewhere, sold for coin even."

"Where? How would you ever track it down? And why does it matter to me, in particular? Just because I happen to possess the land now? That lodge has been Aliente since the very beginnings of their House. You must know the story. They were sons of Attrasca himself."

"Actually, they were down the line of Attrasca's daughter. The important thing is that the metal does apply to you. I believe the Prinze sword is formed of it and that is why your House chose the serpent standard. They had stolen a piece of the Great Sea Dragon."

"That's—" Cassis spluttered. "That's preposterous. Besides, the Great Sea Dragon was a companion to Ires, and my father used that sword with the Nameless God, the god of magic, to—"

Abruptly, he shut his mouth tight.

"To do what, mestere? To fight the Silver Warrior? Whether you like it or not, magic is making its way into your world. If I tell you a story about the Old World, you'll think it's a myth. But the Old World still exists in little cubbies and crevices no one notices. Because no one *looks.* You all live your lives trapped inside a dark cave, and when I attempt to show you the sun, you screech and run back to the darkness in fear. If you choose to stay in your cave, you'll die there without witnessing the dawning of the light. Maybe as early as this afternoon."

Lupa gestured with his chin to the slit window at the top of the wall.

Cassis glared, but Lupa stared calmly back, sitting with his arms folded over his leather satchel. Finally, Cassis forced a sound of frustration out between his teeth, gave into temptation, and climbed up onto the bench to look out the tiny ventilation window.

His cell had a good view of the courtyard and the scaffold they were fitting with a rope. The platform had wheels; Geoffre had often towed his scaffolds into the streets to hang Aliente and Caprine prisoners. Now Devid was going to hang him the same way.

Lupa raised his ruddy black brows over the silver frames of his spectacles. "Well?"

Cassis dropped to the floor. "Devid has to give me another chance to swear to him."

"He does not," Lupa said. "And I daresay he isn't going to."

"How do I know you don't want to kill me, too?"

"Well..." Lupa reached into an inner pocket of his coat and drew out a snub-nosed wheellock pistol. He thumbed it back with a click and pointed it at Cassis's chest. "Because I could have killed you whenever I wanted to. But I haven't yet."

Cassis stared at the gun. The world began to spin. He felt like he was going to hyperventilate. He'd commissioned two Fixed wheellocks, to be made with teak stocks and his monogram laid into them in gold...

"That gun is from my shipment! You're the bloody pirate who stole my guns!" he blurted out incredulously.

Lupa wagged his head. The dog on the gun was still engaged; Cassis could jump for it, but any pressure on the trigger and the man would blow a hole in his chest. "We're not pirates, mestere. But we were able to *purchase* your guns for a good price."

"Renzo sold you *my* guns? Why would he do that?"

"I assume if there were guns he couldn't use, he turned them into gold on the black market. Quite astute."

"Then why don't you offer him your godsdamned proposal?"

"Am I to assume the thought of marrying Kyrra d'Aliente is so distasteful you're willing to die instead, mestere?" the swan inquired politely.

Fucking gods. How had they come to the assumption that marrying Kyrra would be *distasteful*?

An old memory hit him with physical force. The smell of the musty prison straw mellowed into the smell of the Aliente stables, the cold draft of the cell the kiss of a breeze over his hot, bare skin as Kyrra's mouth hungrily sought his and he loosed her hair, glistening gold in the afternoon light, laying her down in the fragrant hay of the loft...

Gods.

He hadn't thought about that in a long, long time.

He wiped away the sweat that sprang up on his forehead. Lupa and the three cloaked figures watched him, waiting. Cassis darted a glance up at the small window, which only showed him sky—Prinze blue, like the flag flying over the compound. It wasn't like he had a choice. He needed to stay alive, he needed to stop Devid, he needed to save Driese and her baby. Kyrra would have to understand.

"All right," he said. "Tell me what you want me to do."

Lupa raised the gun toward the ceiling to dig in his satchel for papers. He put his head down to pull them out—

One more chance.

Cassis shot his hand toward the gun. But Lupa brought the gun right back down, pressing it hard into Cassis's collarbone.

"It might be somewhat ironic for you to sit on the Householder's Chair without an arm, mestere."

"Fucking hells," Cassis breathed.

"Mestere di Prinze," the swan said. "Do you have a death wish? You're uniquely situated to become a symbol for the city to rally around. *If* you extend mercy to the woman who committed a crime against your House in the interests of uniting the Houses. *If* you show how highly you esteem your duty over ambition. Your rebellion against Geoffre di Prinze created a pile of credit in the minds of many —credit you've left lying around, unused. Many people in this city— even his supporters—hated your father. His goals might have been laudable, but he allowed revenge and naked ambition to overtake him. *You* have a chance to seize nobility. The question is *will you?*"

She took a parchment from Lupa's left hand and laid it on the bench.

"*And Attrasca knelt and said, if the gods deem me worthy, then so shall I be,*" Lupa murmured softly. "Pen and ink are in the outside pocket of my satchel."

Cassis stared down at the parchment. The crisp black ink seemed to waver.

I, Cassis di Prinze, hereby issue a pardon to Kyrra d'Aliente for the crimes committed against my House. Her title shall be reinstated and as of the day of signature, she is joined in matrimony to the House di Prinze, as witnessed by—

Was this really *seizing nobility*? To marry a woman against her will? Or was it merely *seizing*?

What would Driese say?

Or maybe Driese had found another way to support her bastard child. *His* bastard child. Maybe she had decided he wasn't worth waiting on, or maybe she'd only decided that he, a Prinze, had been lying to her, a Caprine.

Or maybe...

No, no. He *refused* to think about that. Driese had *not* done what Kyrra had. She must have had the opportunity, but she'd chosen to continue with the pregnancy. Why hadn't he received word about her then? What had happened to her, to his child?

This wasn't *nobility* at all. It was all about survival. And survival was something at which he excelled.

He reached into Lupa's satchel and took the pen.

PART III

The spot where Attrasca stood to release magic upon the world is unknown. Before Attrasca, naturally occurring magic existed only in small pockets. I have seen many of these places now, but curiosity can be both blessing and curse. Perhaps the most terrifying is on the island of Tule, where a giant wall of reflective ice made entirely of magic forms a hidden chasm. The Tulans say all Fixers must be able to face their darker selves in this mirror, but when Attrasca cracked the lock on magic and loosed it on the world, the Magnificent Sun protected his people by teaching them how to bind themselves against it. For what man, faced with a map of all the roads the Dark One might make into his soul, would be able to deny them all?

—Oji la Kaif
The Strange Artifice of Eterean Magic

CHAPTER 42

ARSENAULT

Kyrra,

All I can See in this dragon limb is my own reflection and the ocean. The memories bring back all the sounds now absent from my life. Silver waves crashing on black shores, the hiss and spit of breakers as they roll up on the sand, and in winter, the sound of the wind swirling snow across the ice and the distant smash of the waves in the rock holes, too powerful and deep to freeze.

The sound of that northern sea formed a part of my soul. I used to find myself inventing it out of insect whirr and wind. For a moment, I'd be transported back to Tule, and I'd have to force myself to think, *I am a long, long way from there.* The thought always made me ache a little, like the pang of an old broken bone on a damp day. Seems ridiculous, doesn't it, considering how many lives I've lived and how long since I've even been as far north as Dagmar?

Why does this blasted limb make me think so much about Tule? I should get rid of it, like Jon told me to. And yet...

When I made your arm, I tried to be prudent. I didn't want the gods to notice, so I only used my Sight to verify that the ingots were unworked deposits like the vendors said. In my notes, I recorded what I Saw: flashes of night sky, stars and battle, shields, teeth, claws, courage—memories as faded and tattered as ancient cloth. Your own memories—the metal of your soul—were far stronger and more cohesive.

But this dragon metal...

I can collect my memories better if I write them down, so let me tell you a little about dragons and about gods. You might know more than I do, considering the amount of time you've spent buried in Jon's Oji la Kaif manuscripts. It reminds me of the days you used to read aloud to me as I worked. I always liked watching you read—the thoughtful bow of your mouth and the way you chew on your lip, then tunnel into the blankets as if that will help you dig deeper into the text. I want to sit there watching you forever, etching every line and curve of you into my mind so I can never forget you again. Sometimes I can't believe that you're actually *you*. I thought you were dead, but you've come back. Not just to life, but to *me*.

And yes, I know how ironic that is, coming from me.

Back to dragons.

My memories are murkier than Oji's accounts, but boundaries in the Old World were murky, too. Gods, men, magical beasts, real beasts—there weren't dividing lines; it was just *the world*. The main difference between gods and men was that gods lived with magic; it made them up, a part of their being. How they got that way, I don't know. It's just the way the world was. Before Attrasca released magic to all of humanity, humans had to be granted magic, earn it, or be chosen by magic itself. Some people—like you—were lodestones. I'm not sure if anyone has ever figured out why; social status has never mattered a whit. A street urchin is still as like to wake up with visions as the richest prince in Dagmar.

The old gods were guardians and gatekeepers of magic—protectors of the land, of time, of people. The distinction between "old" and "new" only came about because of the war the gods waged among themselves. Before the war, we only had "gods"—beings who walked among us wearing whatever form they wanted. Some of them liked appearing as humans; others, you would call monsters. It was hard to tell with a dragon, whether it was its own creature or if it was a god wearing a dragon form. Gods liked the attention they got from being majestic.

If you think this is confusing, don't you have a fairy story about a hunter shooting a hind in the woods? After the arrow pierces the hind's skin, he discovers that an evil wizard had ensorcelled his lover in the deer's form. I don't know any Fixer who could turn a woman into a deer, so I think it's just an old story dressed up to look new, from a world in which a goddess could transform into a deer and a man could shoot her and she could—

Anyway, the Gods' War seemed like it took place in a faraway country. But then, tiannamir began to streak from the sky like falling stars and our guardians began disappearing, one by one. In the end, only the "new" gods were left. We tried to carry on as usual, as if the world hadn't changed fundamentally. For a while—until Attrasca—the new gods wielded ultimate control over the world and the people in it, which wasn't so different than the way it had been before, although it was also completely different. The old gods had been neither our supreme rulers nor our equals, but to some extent, *partners*. Then Attrasca altered the balance yet again and the Etereans he led discovered they could reanimate tiannamir. Predictably, I suppose, they mostly made monsters.

So why would *this* one remind me so strongly of Tule?

And not just Tule, but *my* memories of it—the sights and sounds lodged so deeply in my bones and my heart? I would gladly give those memories to you if they were *mine*. I would cut them out of my body and Fix them into metal slivers to fill the wounds in your arm.

But these are not my memories. They are something else playing on my memories, and that makes me wonder where this dragon came from—if perhaps it spent time in the hold of that ship Guin and I rowed, shackled, all the way to Dakkar. Because the other option, that this limb has some connection to me and to Tule... How could that be?

The most troubling question of all, though... The scholar Cassis called Lupa...

How did *he* know?

CHAPTER 43

LOBARDIN

ALIENTE HUNTING LODGE, PRESENT

LOBARDIN RECLINED IN PALLO D'ALIENTE'S CHAIR AND DRANK Pallo d'Alliente's aged port as he looked up at the painted ceiling in Pallo d'Aliente's study, and it was not only a hollow victory, it was fucking *terrifying*. Godsdamn Cassis for leaving him in charge. Who in all the hells left a man prone to battle madness in control of an army? He belonged on the line with a sword and a gun, following orders and just trying to keep the men in his squad alive until nightfall.

The sound of cannonfire pounding the outer wall sounded like a man taking a gut punch. Their pitiful attempts at repair would withstand Vokavik's incessant barrage a few days at best. Then Vokavik and his troops would be free to pour into the yard and bombard the lodge itself. The lodge occupied a strategic position at the Eterean entrance to the Spice Road, but Cassis wasn't paying them enough for a romantic last stand. Cassis wasn't paying them *anything* right now.

Lobardin took another drink of port, let its warmth uncurl in his empty belly, and contemplated the mural on the ceiling of Attrasca opening the box of magic. *What would Arsenault do if he were in this situation?*

He hated thinking it, but he hated more that it was the right question to ask. He immediately knew what Arsenault would do. He just didn't know if Cassis would approve.

He set down his empty glass on Pallo d'Aliente's heavy wooden desk. The men standing before him, who had just finished reporting on the sorry state of the wall, looked up expectantly.

"Bring me that scholar's secretary we locked up," he ordered. "I need to talk to him."

❧

LOBARDIN DIDN'T KNOW IF LUPA CARED WHAT HAPPENED TO HIS secretary—he suspected not—but he hadn't wanted Tomas wandering around unguarded. Tomas seemed the opposite of his employer, quiet and stolid. But the memory of Tomas's terrified expression when Lupa had asked him to torment an unconscious and dying man was burned into Lobardin's mind.

Tomas stood square-shouldered in front of Lobardin's desk now, strong and still as a piece of statuary, though Lobardin had invited him to sit and share the port. Too smart to give into the human touch.

"So, these tunnels," Lobardin asked. "Do you know where they come out?"

"Some of them." Tomas continued to stare at the wall.

"Could you lead an army through?"

That took the young secretary by surprise. His pale gaze flickered down to Lobardin and his brows lifted. "Are you asking me a hypothetical question?"

"Sadly no. Did you spend much time with Vokavik in Devid's camp?"

"I wasn't privy to his strategizing, if that's what you mean."

"I think his strategy is obvious. What did you think of him, as a man?"

Tomas kept staring straight ahead but considered. "Intelligent. Fastidious. Always dressed perfectly. He didn't have much to do with me, mestere."

"Call me Captain." That was hardly better; Lobardin had never realized more how much he'd rather *not* be in a position of responsibility. "Vokavik doesn't only defeat armies; he obliterates them. And frankly, that's what he's going to do to us. Unless..."

Lobardin paused.

Tomas waited a moment. Then he looked down at Lobardin directly. Finally. Lobardin needed Tomas to deal with him as a person, not ignore him as his jailor. "Unless?"

Lobardin leaned forward on his elbows. "Unless we can escape through those tunnels. I'm assuming that's why Attrasca built them in the first place. I'm also assuming Lupa led Cassis through one and didn't leave his body for some future scholar searching for the Legacy of Attrasca. What I'm *hoping* is that you either know those tunnels or have a map to share. Or else we'll all cross into the underworld together in a few days."

"You don't think Devid di Prinze would release you if you surrendered? Isn't that what gavaros do in your wars?"

"If this was a contest between cities, maybe. It's all a gentlemanly sport until a man gets into a war with his own family. Devid wants to mark his ledger with our blood. Unless we can sneak through the tunnels, then blow the whole fucking place behind us. I'm not sure how much powder it would take, but that's what Arsenault would do."

Tomas twitched, looking the slightest bit distressed, then resumed staring at the wall. *Interesting.* Lobardin leaned back in his chair and pulled his foot up onto his knee, trying his best to look casual. In control. The way his father would. "If you have a problem with something I just said, please enlighten me."

Tomas acted as if he was battling with himself to stay silent. Thankfully, he lost. "You mentioned a name. Arsenault. Is he..."

Hmmm. "He was the Aliente captain in the wars. Not that he wouldn't laugh to hear me using him for advice—or Kyrra would at least. She'd find that *richly* ironic, let me tell you." *Yes, let's dump a few names and see how you react, Tomas.* "But that's neither here nor there. His strategies kept the Aliente alive years longer than they should have, and though I wasn't there for much of that, the man could run a damn convincing ruse when he wanted to. I know this is what he would do, and—look, *do* you know Jon Barra? There's a good chance we'll die anyway, so I need you to be honest with me if you're working for Jon."

Tomas looked like he might be having trouble following. It was just like conning the dock officials back in Amora, this trying to get hostages to give up secrets. He'd been good at it before he'd started smoking kacin. Maybe he could still do this.

"You have my word I'm not working for Jon Barra. I'm neutral in these wars. Your allegiances mean nothing to me."

"Really? Wearing Dakkaran gold in your ear and working for a man working for the Prinze?"

"I told you before, I'm a man with no country. I wear the gold in honor of my mother. The Prinze killed the royal family. They did not kill everyone. The Arak are in control of the country now."

"I think that's the most remarkably callous thing I've ever heard anyone say. You can't expect me to believe you really feel that way."

Tomas clenched his jaw briefly, which was as good an indication as any that he'd been lying. "I think it matters to everyone whether the man who takes control of one of your Houses is just or evil. Doesn't it?"

Lobardin frowned vaguely. "And which Prinze do you think would be just and which would be evil?"

"I'll reserve judgement on that question for now."

Lobardin chuckled. Now they were back on more familiar ground. "I'm just curious why you wanted to know about Arsenault. Did you know about his connection to Jon Barra?"

"I've heard the name before, that's all. I thought he was dead."

Lobardin regarded Tomas a moment, but there was very little information to be prised from his expression. "Of course he's dead," Lobardin lied. "He died at Kafrin Gorge after Alozh Vokavik captured him for Geoffre di Prinze. I'm sorry I left you with any other impression. Believe me, I don't like using the bastard as a role model."

"You knew him, though?"

"He was a lying, duplicitous ass who would nevertheless have saved all those men from burning at Kafrin if he'd still been captain. And I know exactly what he'd do in this situation. Better to destroy the lodge and live to fight another day than to let Vokavik have it."

"A strategist, then."

"Yes, a strategist." As interested as Tomas was in Arsenault, Lobardin was having a hard time believing Tomas didn't know Jon Barra. If Jon had a plant inside the Empirists, should they then take the Empirists more seriously? More questions for him to bring to Junei, though she'd probably brush them off and they'd end up in bed as usual. It wouldn't be the worst thing before probably dying.

"Look, Tomas. Where do those tunnels come out? Is it possible to move an entire army through them? Guns, even cannon?"

Tomas frowned—and then his stiff demeanor cracked a little and he looked down at Lobardin. "I don't know about cannons. I suppose you could make a ramp down into the tunnels, but how will you even get them inside the lodge? Don't you use horses to pull the big guns? Some of the tunnel walls are pretty narrow. The floors are rough and uneven. It would take too much time, if it was even possible. Worse, the carriages might block the tunnel and then no one can get out. How many men are these guns worth?"

Arsenault would probably use magic on the fucking cannons. Lobardin sighed. "All right, it was a long shot. We'll just take the guns we can carry. Where does the tunnel come out?"

"There are two exits I know of. Do you have a map?"

Lobardin grabbed the wrinkled, worried scroll lying at the side of the desk and spread it out, weighing down the corners with whatever came to hand—the empty glass, the bottle of port, an inkpot. Tomas bent over it, brow furrowed in concentration. His beaded braids slid over his shoulder and he pushed them away impatiently like they annoyed him. He seemed unused to them, which was strange; Tiresians began beading their braids in their early teen years. It was a part of their coming of age, if Lobardin remembered correctly.

"Here and here. I think." Tomas pointed to two divergent points in the forest to the north, not too far from Kyrra's farmhouse but on the road to Padera, the city wealthy Lieran householders retreated to in fever season. "The passages twist around underground, but I do have a map." He reached inside his tunic and pulled out a creased, ancient-looking parchment, then laid it atop the map of the region. "Ser Lupa gave it to me before he left. Wanted me to search for more metal."

"He's very interested in that metal. Why?"

"He studies a lot of things for the sake of knowledge."

"Does he make any money with that knowledge? Sell artifacts to wealthy householders, perhaps?"

"That's part of my job—keeping his books. He had quite a thriving business for a while, but it's fallen off lately."

"So that's why he's here. Hoping to score a treasure he can profit from? Do you have a price, too, Tomas?"

"Captain?"

"Everyone has a price. Some men are bought with coin. Others sell their reliability for different currency. I don't want to find out Devid or Jon or Lupa paid for your loyalty when we're all trapped underground."

Tomas went stiff again. "I'm afraid the only way to prove my honesty is to see it demonstrated. Captain. But Devid di Prinze didn't buy my loyalty, and the loyalty I bear to Ser Lupa is what any worker owes to the man who pays him a wage—no more and no less."

"All I'm hearing is your price is something other than coin."

Amusement cracked Tomas's statuesque features. "You made a good case for it being my life. You don't think that's important enough to motivate me?"

Lobardin pushed himself up. "Sometimes men who aren't bought with coin also regard their lives as little price to pay for their causes." He paced around Tomas. "Like the two men who poisoned our food. Before I lead an entire army underground based on a map you pulled out of your tunic, I need to know if you are an Empirist and what that fucking *means*. Because if I can't trust you, maybe I'll just kill you and take that map."

Tomas took a step backward at the same time Lobardin unsheathed his sword. There was a minor scuffle, but Lobardin had the tip of his blade pointed at Tomas's throat in an instant.

Tomas eyed Lobardin's sword like a spooked horse. "Do you think I can kill your entire army single-handedly?" he asked incredulously. "I'm a secretary!"

"You don't *seem* like a secretary, Tomas. So, I'm wondering why Lupa left you here."

"You have my word I won't hurt your people. I don't have anything else to give you but my word. Send me down without weapons. I'll put them on the road to Padera. We'll do it at night to hide the numbers. I'll take the women first. Like that woman I see around with you, the Tiresian woman, and the woman who does my laundry—the one who knifed the poisoner? I don't know how much powder you have left, but you saw what those infiltrators were trying to do. The lodge sits on a cave system. If you set off an explosion underneath it, it won't take much to make it collapse."

"But won't Lupa be upset if his source of Eterean metal is gone? The Legacy of Attrasca? Or is there something we need to save before we blow this place to rubble?"

"That's what this is all about? It's not about saving the army at all? You just wanted me to expose the treasure!"

"To be honest, it *is* about saving the army, but if we could find some treasure doing it, wouldn't that be convenient for us? Do you know where it is?"

Tomas stared back at him with a tight, furious expression. Finally, he said, "Lupa planted the dragon limb."

"Ahh..." Lobardin smiled and lifted the blade just a little. "Now we're getting somewhere. Where did he get it?"

Tomas looked torn. Here it was—the test of trust. How much loyalty did Tomas feel to Lupa? How well did he like his own life? Or was there another, more important price that perhaps no one had asked him to pay yet? Was he willing to come clean in a situation that clearly and obviously demanded some fucking cooperation?

Another cannonball hit the wall, closer; the explosion sounded less muffled.

"Lupa is with Cassis di Prinze right now," Lobardin said. "And we're here. I hope Cassis comes back, but if he doesn't—"

"He'll come back," Tomas said quickly, like he'd made his decision. "Lupa needs Cassis. The Empirists need him. Lupa really does believe the Legacy is here, but he needed to lure you in and he thought you'd do something with the limb. He said it was like casting a gauntlet and we'd see where it ended up."

That was disturbing. "Who did Lupa think we were going to show it to?"

"He didn't—he didn't say—" Tomas sounded breathless. He pushed his hand up and Lobardin tensed. But Tomas rubbed his chest like he was in pain. "Look. I'd tell you if I knew. I really would. But I don't know that much and—"

He pushed his shirt open. There, glistening against the dusky skin of Tomas's chest, was a black inked slash mark, just like the one on the man Lobardin had forced to drink his own poison.

Lobardin almost dropped the sword. The feeling of shackled, stoppered magic writhing inside the other man was too close to what he had felt when Geoffre—no, he wasn't going to think about that. He tightened his trembling hand on the hilt. "You're bound?" he whispered in disbelief.

Tomas nodded. When he pulled his shirt back together, the feeling of frustrated and imprisoned magic subsided like the dull ache of a rotten tooth. "Soon after I was employed. Lupa said it was just a precaution; he knew I had Sight, and he didn't want me exposing any of his secrets to his buyers. Or anyone else."

Lobardin sheathed his sword. Now he knew why Tomas seemed so controlled all the time. He had to be or risk the magic in him rising. "Did you *consent* to being bound?" he asked in horror.

"What do you think," Tomas replied bitterly. "Of course not. He drugged me; I woke up bound. He found the limb in a cache that came from Tule, but I don't know anything else about it. Now do you trust me to lead you out of here?"

Lobardin considered. "More or less. I don't know what your binding will make you do or not do, but at least I know it's there. Is it wild magic or are you a Fixer?"

Tomas let his breath out. "My Talent's in metal," he said curtly. "That's why he bound me."

CHAPTER 44

KYRRA

FARMHOUSE, PRESENT

MY LIFE NEVER SEEMED TO CHANGE QUIETLY; IT ALWAYS SHIFTED with a bang. But the explosion took us all by surprise.

I was sitting on the couch with the hole in the upholstery, counting backward in my head to the last time I'd bled. I had long given up trying to focus on digging out details about the magic in Jon's old treatises; this new worry had been building for days and by now it seemed far more important than anything else. My courses had always been irregular and surely my injuries would also affect them, but was the conjure magic I'd asked Isia to perform all those years ago still active inside me?

I didn't know what I wanted and what I feared. Perhaps they were both the same thing. If the conjure magic failed, it would mean Arsenault and I could have a family, and if the conjure magic held, surely that would make me useless to Cassis—but even thinking about being useless to Cassis made me want to hide in my blanket, the way I had climbed into my wardrobe and hidden there in the dark, those weeks after my father had caught Cassis with me in the stables and my blood did not come. The wardrobe had felt like the only safe place in the villa, maybe even in the world, but its safety had been an illusion.

In the kitchen, Silva said, "Here, Mikelo, just try it; I promise it's not too bitter. You have such a sweet tooth—"

And Jon said, "Miranda should have been back by now. I'm telling you, the dice have come up with terrible numbers, no matter how many times I roll them."

And Arsenault said, "You told her to stay away and now you're worried she listened to you? Jon—"

And then there was a tremendous boom.

The sound rattled the dishes, cast sheaves of old papers off the table in the common room and onto the floor in a great, disordered pile. War memories filled the room, so palpable I could feel them. Jon, Arsenault, and Mikelo immediately ran to the windows to search the woods and sky. I caught Silva's wide-eyed gaze across the room and could tell we were thinking the same thing.

Mount Kosemi.

The mountain hadn't exploded in my lifetime, but I'd heard stories about choking ash, rocks hurled into the air for miles, mud slides that buried towns.

I jumped to my feet as fast as I could. Manuscript pages spilled everywhere. I grabbed the cloak someone had thrown over the back of a chair. Silva grabbed Mikelo. "Outside!" he yelled.

As we tumbled outside the shaking of the ground never began. Mount Kosemi stood quiet behind its ever-present gray haze at the edge of our western horizon.

There was smoke, though. Coming from our south.

Arsenault swore. I'd studied Jon's map enough to know what stood in that direction—the only thing that could explode like that.

"They blew the lodge," I breathed. "Cassis lost the whole thing."

Jon had disappeared back inside the house, but he returned now with the spyglass, moving onto the lip of one of the terrace walls for a better view. I heard him cursing from here. The day was cold and clear, and the smoke stood out in the blue sky like an ugly smear on a brilliant piece of glass.

"How?" Mikelo asked, dumbfounded. "Did that happen with cannon?"

"They blew the building with powder," Arsenault said grimly. "Probably from underneath. Either Devid's sappers got it or they did it themselves. Lobardin said Devid had somebody who knew the passages."

"It was that loud, this far away?" Silva asked incredulously.

"Tons of stone," Arsenault murmured, shading his eyes and squinting to see against the sun. "The gunpowder wouldn't be the loudest sound. It's the building collapsing to the ground all at once. The tunnels underneath it going."

Mikelo breathed an oath. "So now Devid's got Cassis out of the way—"

"I wouldn't assume that. Unless he blew the building by accident. Attackers usually don't want to explode the territory they're fighting to keep. That's a last-ditch, defensive move."

"Cassis wouldn't have the balls," I said.

Arsenault shrugged. "Maybe Devid was that vengeful then. Cassis still might have retreated first."

Jon walked the terrace with barely controlled energy, trying to get a better look, climbing further up the slope. But I was glad I couldn't see from here. The smoke was bad enough.

The lodge had seemed like it was as old as the mountains and would last as long as they would. Now it was nothing but dust. This hot ball of terrible emotion was too complicated to put into words. *Grief* seemed inadequate, like trying to paint a crow's wing using only flat black paint.

The Prinze had taken my whole family, years of happiness or at least togetherness I could have spent with Arsenault, and now they had even destroyed my memories. It all made me so angry I could barely see. How dare Cassis even steal the *places* where Arsenault and I had been together.

My arm had always been a weapon I could use when everything else failed. But now I felt again like the one-armed girl in the dirt the Prinze had made me. I thought I'd put off those old hurts and desires, the anger, and especially the fear, but they lurked under my skin and returned to prowl in the dark as soon as it became clear Kyrra d'Aliente could be resurrected whenever a Prinze needed to lay stake to territory.

Why should I care if the bloody place burns? Why should I care that the Prinze have destroyed yet another piece of my old life? It was all sad anyway.

I turned my back to it abruptly. Arsenault began to frown, like he was worried, but how was I supposed to explain what I was thinking?

If Cassis had lost the lodge...if he was still alive...would that mean he'd need me even more? Did it mean we were well and truly headed to another destructive war that would kill more people I loved? I didn't want to contemplate what it would be like to save Liera by marrying Cassis. I didn't want to give in to a truth I'd never wanted to acknowledge—that my body and Liera were the same battlefield. In the end, it didn't matter if I won or lost, the point wasn't *me* at all, it was *Kyrra d'Aliente.*

And I knew this. I *knew* it, deep in the severed bones that still sometimes ached. My stomach, my ribs, my entire mid-section, pulsed with pain. Just like the cramps from the potion my mother had given me to save my baby from the Prinze by killing him. The blood in my bed—gods, the blood. Did this pain never go away? Was I doomed to be ambushed by grief whenever I least expected or needed it? I tried to put both hands over my stomach, as if I could turn back the past and protect my child, protect my *self*, and I only realized what I was doing when my metal hand refused to obey me.

"Kyrra," Arsenault said gently. "Are you all right?"

I had made it to the door, but I needed to step up into the house. Somehow, I was frozen—I didn't know if I wanted to go in or out, but just like all those years ago, there seemed to be no safe place.

"There's some pain again," I admitted, so he wouldn't ask more questions. I needed these men to assume the pain was just more of the same, because I didn't want to try to explain that I was still afraid of Cassis di Prinze, and for some reason I especially didn't want to explain it to Arsenault. I didn't know why, except that maybe submitting my pain to Arsenault's quiet concern would give it a legitimacy I had fought for years to deny.

"I'll help—" Mikelo began, moving around toward me, but godsdammit, that was the last thing I wanted—for him to See through me.

"No!" I exclaimed, too urgently. Mikelo traded a surprised glance with Silva. Arsenault moved past them and took my elbow.

"Come on, Kyrra," he said softly, those gray eyes so earnest, so fucking sympathetic. "I'll help you in to lie down." Why couldn't he see I didn't want his sympathy right now? I didn't need sympathy. I didn't need to lie down.

I needed to move. I needed to get away from Cassis and his fucking scholar, and if Cassis was dead... *What had happened to the dragon limb? Why had he found it beneath the lodge that had belonged to my House since the time of Attrasca?*

And more importantly, what had Arsenault done with it?

All I could hear right now were echoes of accusing voices.

Erelf—*How can you compete with a goddess?*

Cassis—*Godsdammit, Kyrra, Liera is at stake again! Wasn't the first time enough?*

The magic rose in a cacophony of voices all around me, a clangor playing out of tune, out of time. Arsenault was trying to tell me something, but I couldn't hear him. I tried to stop the noise, to find the melody that was *me* in it. But I realized too late what I had done. I had made an alliance with a force I couldn't control in the mistaken belief it would act in good faith. That if I helped it, it would help me.

But it was like making an alliance with a wild animal that would snap and bite as soon as it felt threatened.

In reality, I had never stopped being that householder girl whose naivete and recklessness had landed her one-armed in the dirt. I'd thought I'd escaped, but my past was always right on my heels, ready to devour me.

The magic opened a landscape of charred, black death all around me.

I didn't want Cassis to be right.

I broke and ran.

CHAPTER 45

ARSENAULT

"Kyrra, stop!"

He should have known seeing the burning lodge would trigger the magic, but she'd been doing so much better. She shoved him backward off the step and then bolted *inside* the house.

He flailed out to catch himself on the rough stone wall, heard the clatter of chairs, grabbed the door frame and threw himself inside, just in time to see the twitch of her cloak heading out the back door and *slam!*

"Dammit!" He felt like he was repeating history.

Kyris di Nada had been the most paranoid, wiliest, or damn luckiest target Arsenault had ever tailed. When Kyris disappeared down a closed alley, Arsenault had learned to always look to the roofs. He'd watch Kyris's lithe form jump to the curb and duck into a building, but by the time Arsenault did the same, the building would be empty and Kyris lost in a maze of rubble. Kyrra had always been fast; he remembered her running the trails on the Villa grounds, barefoot, sometimes for the sheer joy of it.

Chasing Kyrra through a mountain forest was perhaps even more difficult because the magic threw stumbling blocks into his way—roots to trip on, pebbles to slip on, tree branches that snapped back in his face. Was some supernatural force actually *trying* to kill her? Magic could be so fucking subtle. He tripped on another root, hit his shin on a boulder, dragged himself over it, cursing, only to find a drop on the other side that ended in slippery leaves. He barely caught himself.

When he looked up, he couldn't find her.

Mikelo skidded down the path behind him, gulping air. "How is she so godsdamned fast?"

"I lost her. I lost her! Damn!"

"I think she went that way." Mikelo pointed. "Silva and Jon are wrapping around the other side of the house..."

Arsenault looked in the direction of Mikelo's finger. There did seem to be a figure, a woman...

A flash of auburn like ruddy bronze—no, that was sunlight—*a great wind moving through the trees, rustling needles and branches*—no, were those—*a pair of giant white wings unfurling...*

Arsenault felt like every muscle, every particle of his blood, every tiny piece of his body went cold and frozen. Why would a memory of Sella erupt so viscerally now? Was it simply the chase reminding him so strongly of pursuing Sella up the mountain back in Tule? The moment when he realized she was more than just a scruffy girl with a headful of hair like fire?

Kyrra's words, remembered, stopped him in his tracks: *If she's a goddess, how do you know she's dead?*

Then the flash of light cleared and the shock let go of him. But his moment of hesitation had cost him. Maybe everything.

Kyrra was gone.

☙❧

"How do we find her?" Mikelo asked in frustration as Silva and Jon jogged up to join them.

"There will be more men in this forest soon, if there aren't already," Jon said grimly. "I'd usually say Kyrra can handle herself, but what if she stumbles into a camp of Prinze gavaros and makes a situation?"

A situation. That was one way of putting it.

"She could handle herself if she was armed," Arsenault said. "But she's not even wearing proper shoes." He ran a hand through his hair. "I'm more worried she'll fall. What if she runs out over the ravine?"

"Surely she can't run that far," Jon said. "She'll come back to herself soon. We'll fan out, search the area, and then—Silva, I'm sending you to scout further."

"Me?" Silva exclaimed. "Why?"

"Because I'm worried about Miranda and the boys. I forbade her from telling me where they were so no one could use them for leverage if anyone did truthtelling on me. But I think that was a mistake. All the information I've been getting, and yet, I didn't know this was a possibility. Yes, dammit, it was a mistake. Arsenault and I are too recognizable, but you're familiar with the terrain, aren't you?"

Silva looked skeptical. "Yes..."

"Go, now. We'll find Kyrra. Be back at the farmhouse before dark. Make sure you have your knife. Hurry!"

Startled by Jon's urgency, Silva turned and ran. Arsenault took a deep breath, tried to call up his Sight, but was immediately lost again in a dream of Sella's ghost slipping through the woods.

He flinched away, breathing raggedly. "Mikelo."

Mikelo stepped up beside him, right away. "Where do you want me to go?"

"You told me you Saw life. Can you distinguish forms?"

"Like between a tree and an animal? Of course."

"Finer than that. Can you track a person? Not just See them, but track where they've been, where they're going?"

Mikelo frowned. "You want me to track Kyrra through the forest using magic?"

"If I try to See her, I won't necessarily be able to tell how she got where she is."

Jon laid an encouraging hand on Arsenault's shoulder. "In the meantime, I'll look for her track."

Arsenault nodded curtly to him in thanks.

"Not much of a vote of confidence," Mikelo mumbled nervously.

"It's contingency planning, Mikelo. I'm afraid she's hurt herself, so could you just give me an indication which way to go?"

Mikelo exhaled slowly and nodded as he looked for a place to sit. He folded himself down on a flat rock and closed his eyes. "I'm looking for Kyrra," he said, like he was talking to his magic. Then he muttered, "Fucking goatherder, my arse."

As always when Mikelo worked, he unknowingly drew so much raw power Arsenault was afraid he was going to burn himself. It made sense now that Arsenault knew what Mikelo worked in. Creative energy was the most powerful of all forces; Arsenault was an Artisan, he tapped into that force to make art. But when he Fixed an object, that's what it stayed. *Life* wasn't limited to a class of objects like metal or wood. Life was always changing. He'd thought it unFixable.

"Dammit, Arsenault, there's a lot to See in this forest," Mikelo said in frustration.

"People?" Arsenault responded in alarm.

"Not...exactly."

"What the hell does that mean? Ignore the chipmunks, the fucking trees, Mikelo."

"I can tell the difference between a tree and a person, thank you." Mikelo's voice was strained. "I just can't..." The muscles in Mikelo's face twitched. He looked almost like he was in pain. "It's all...burned. Arsenault, there's something wrong. I can't See, everything's dead. It's like being blind."

"Is Kyrra all right? Where is she?"

He wanted to shake Mikelo until his teeth rattled. Why had he thought this would be better than trying to See for himself?

Because you didn't want to chance having to face Sella again.

He flinched away from the thought. Mikelo's eyes suddenly flew open—wide, blue-green, but so much like Kyrra's Arsenault wondered if Mikelo's magic had made them into a mirror of hers. His urgent expression framed by all those wild blond curls only made the similarity more unnerving.

"Something's chasing her." Mikelo flung out his arm. "I think she's moving that way."

"Some*thing*? A wolf? A bear? Not a man?"

"I don't know what it is. A presence. An extremely powerful presence."

An extremely powerful presence.

When it had finally hit him that Sella was dead, he'd wanted to throw himself at her feet—to worship her, if that was what she wanted, though she hadn't when they'd been married. Anything that might repair the awful thing he had done. He'd expected a goddess to take her retribution, but instead...she was just gone.

Where did dead gods go? Had he not only killed her body, but her soul? Would her body have turned to tiaannamir the way the old gods' had? He'd hoped, in a strange, upside-down way, that Sella *would* haunt him. But she never had.

"Does this presence mean Kyrra harm?" he asked, in a voice barely more than a strained whisper.

Mikelo looked shaky and pale. "I don't know." He pushed himself up off the rock and wavered a little. "I don't know how to explain it. It existed for a moment, and then it was like the magic itself swallowed it up. If what I Saw is true, it's no wonder Kyrra bolted. Bodies, trees, land, all burned. The ground was oozing with some black substance like tar, except it felt...not just dead, but like the opposite of life. If death isn't the opposite of life, what is?"

"The Qalfans consider death a transition to another state of being.

The Dark One brings not death but evil. Obliteration. Oblivion. A fate worse than death."

Mikelo frowned deeply. "I tried my best to curse her into awareness like she does me, but I guess my cursing isn't very believable. She was in this area somewhere." Mikelo waved his hand in a generally northeastern direction.

"All right, come on. We'll spread out a little but keep in sight."

Mikelo hesitated. "You don't think the Dark One is chasing her, do you?"

"Do you believe in the Magnificent Sun, Mikelo?"

Mikelo considered a moment. "I suppose I don't *not* believe in the Magnificent Sun."

Arsenault let his breath out. "Then a few prayers wouldn't be amiss."

❧

THE TERRAIN WAS ROUGH IN THIS DIRECTION, BUT HE SOON SAW signs of someone's frightened passage and called Mikelo to him. A snapped branch, trampled leaves, and finally a footprint. Soft-soled shoes, not a boot. It led directly to a bald steep that sheared away a good fifteen feet to the ground below. A skinny path, probably traveled by deer, continued upslope into a craggy rock chimney that loomed a few hundred feet above them. Snow and ice glittered brightly up there; no one would be able to run that path. Climbing it would be hell on a recovering midsection and soupy lungs.

But the only other way out...

"Did she jump?" Mikelo asked, wide-eyed.

Surely she wouldn't. It wasn't a high enough drop to kill for certain, but it was certainly high enough to cripple. Maybe the magic *was* trying to kill her.

Arsenault looked over the edge with a sick feeling in his stomach. When he didn't see her broken body tangled among the bare, spiky branches of the underbrush, relief made him want to thank *someone,* even if he couldn't thank the gods anymore. The ground below the overhang was covered in beech leaves and pine needles, and then it continued to drop in a less precipitous way to the ruined walls ringing the old village.

Mikelo craned his neck back and squinted against the sun. "I don't see her anywhere. This was the way she was running, but I don't think she went up. It's only rock up there."

Arsenault turned toward the trail. "Is there a cave—"

It was hard to describe what happened next. It was like the world buckled beneath him, rolling like an earthquake—except it wasn't the earth. Magic so powerful metal rained from his fingertips in a scalding stream rushed through him. Mikelo cried out as all the moss and the small green plants pushing through the leaf litter suddenly charred black around him.

"I didn't do anything, I swear!" Mikelo exclaimed, staring at the dead ground in horror. "Did something trip your runes?"

"Not my runes," Arsenault rasped. "But—"

And then—a giant *crack* like another explosion and a rush of air like a million birds leaving the treetops all at once.

Arsenault threw himself prone and tackled Mikelo down with him. They both hit the rock hard before Arsenault realized it hadn't been cannon shot.

"What was that?" Mikelo gasped. "More magic?"

"Maybe. Maybe the earth—I don't know. Everything's solid here, isn't it? Maybe down in the village?"

Mikelo looked at him in confusion. "What village?"

Arsenault waved his hand in the direction of downslope. "Down there. This whole place used to be a... I forgot what they call them. Like a villa, except a collection of freeholders? Land holdings, shops, forge."

"You didn't tell us about this place," Mikelo said accusingly.

"I didn't want to let Jon know I knew about it. And I didn't want Kyrra to end up there. I'm rethinking that decision now. You don't have to rub it in."

Mikelo eyed him warily, the recent bruises to his trust over Renzo reflected in his gaze. "If it wasn't runes, what was it? It felt like one of those giant waves my mother used to tell me about, the ones that swallow islands. You don't think the lodge..."

Arsenault studied the ruins. What he wouldn't give to remember what exactly was supposed to be hidden beneath the Aliente lodge. The Legacy of Attrasca had always seemed evident to him—this mess of gods and humans trying to wrest power, one from the other. Not that the Old World had been a peaceful paradise.

"It's possible the lodge collapsed and released something buried beneath it," he murmured, feeling increasingly troubled this might, in fact, be true. "I didn't lay runes out as far as here. I wanted the village outside the sanctuary I laid on the house, and I like to keep my runes subtle. Far better to encourage intruders to confusion than to announce your presence with an overwhelming display of magic. My runes encourage enemies to kill each other, not—stop looking at me like that, Mikelo. Our main purpose here was to *hide*. How do you think we've been left alone so long? After Cassis came, I set up a perimeter as close to the house as I dared. My runes have been doing their job in the background; none of you needed to know that."

"Right," Mikelo muttered, turning to look down at the ruins again. "So, if this wasn't your runes, what was it?"

"I don't know. Come on. We need to get down there. It will take too much time to go around."

And that damn dragon limb was down there, too. He hoped like hell Kyrra hadn't triggered something in it. If it had hurt her, he would never forgive himself.

"*We're* not going to jump, are we?" Mikelo asked nervously.

"There must be a way down," he muttered, looking furiously for some clue, any clue, to where Kyrra had gone. What the hell was going on down there? There was so much *shrieking*. And a fog filtering through the trees... *There*. A torn piece of cloth caught on a knob of stone, fluttering in the breeze. *From Kyrra's sling*.

Arsenault swung himself down, using the ledge for a handhold. He stuck his foot on the knob where the fabric had caught, made it halfway down the rock face, hung for a moment, then gave in and dropped. The ground wasn't level. The impact jarred up into his teeth and his heel slid in the slick layer of mud that lay atop the frozen ground. A muffled thud of impact behind him let him know Mikelo had made the drop, too.

He thought he saw movement in the trees below, but maybe that was just a trick of the light in the rapidly dimming day. The strange fog had obscured much of the old village. The sounds, too. It sounded as if someone were yelling, but—

"Arsenault," Mikelo whispered. "I don't like this. I know this is ridiculous, but doesn't it feel like...Geoffre's magic?"

Arsenault searched the trees for a glimpse of blond hair, the flash of metal—anything. The magic formed an undercurrent of panic he was trying hard to resist. He wasn't sure what Mikelo was suggesting, but he could tell the magic had infected Mikelo with its fear. His face had turned a pasty color and he looked young. Vulnerable. It was only too akin to the way Arsenault had seen him after his training sessions with Geoffre.

"I'm sure Geoffre would have used it if he could, but I don't know if he ever manipulated anything that was, itself, evil. He took what was good—"

"And made it evil. Yes, that's exactly what it feels like. Life is good, or at least it feels *full*. But if you poison a good thing and make it evil —like if you take a good person and manipulate him so you can fill him with your poison—he's not really *full* because all the good has been stolen and he's just...empty."

That was a disturbing thought. Much too close to his own experience with Geoffre and not something he wanted to think about in terms of *fog* and *presence* and especially Kyrra running through the forest, trying to escape from it, even if Mikelo had just been using a metaphor to explain the danger they were in.

"We have to go down," he said. "Kyrra's there somewhere."

Mikelo nodded, looking troubled.

They ran down the wet, wooded slope to a stone wall that jutted up out of the leaves, about waist high. Arsenault crouched behind it and eased a knife out of his boot. The godsdamned fog lay thicker down here in the cleft in the hills. It felt like someone was yelling, but it was all just an agitated, fearful babble of magic. "Can you See anything?" he whispered as Mikelo tumbled down next to him.

Mikelo frowned in concentration. "There's something in there, but I can't See through it—"

Fear suddenly welled up around them in a wave. Mikelo made a small sound and squeezed his eyes shut. Arsenault gripped his forearm. "Stay here. Concentrate on what you can see, not what you feel, and be prepared." Mikelo gave a brief, uncertain nod. Arsenault vaulted the wall and tried to practice his own advice as he jogged toward the nearest building, into the fog.

He didn't know what he expected to see. Gavaros hauling out the dragon limb. Kyrra with the dragon limb. Something.

Instead, when the fog parted, he was looking into a hellscape of steaming fissures that rent the earth like a piece of paper. And suddenly, SOUND assaulted him, the cries of dying things, a dying world—

Mikelo was right. All of this was too familiar, but not because of Geoffre.

It felt like the Old World dying.

"Kyrra!" he yelled. "Dammit! Where are you?"

CHAPTER 46

KYRRA

I don't know how long I ran before I realized the fear wasn't all mine.

As I struggled to a stop, I cursed myself for an idiot. Manipulation only worked on tools—dumb, senseless objects that didn't know they were being manipulated. And that was exactly what I was.

I never broke and ran in battle. I thought it was my own will, but maybe I was only courageous because the magic held me steady when it wanted blood and then drove me to run when it was afraid. I had fought back against being a pawn for politics, but had I always been a pawn for magic?

"*Fuck* this." My breath knifed in and out of me, like a rusty saw blade eating into my lungs. I squeezed my eyes shut against the images surrounding me, but voices from my arm continued to clang through me like discordant bells. I was beginning to question everything I had ever felt. Sadness. Joy. Anger. Fear. Happiness. Love.

How much of me was really mine?

Madness lay in that direction. I couldn't afford to sort it now. I had conquered my fear before and I could conquer it again. I was not this person.

I opened my eyes.

I'd assumed when I started running that I was seeing the results of another war in Liera. But this was nowhere I recognized. I stood on a flat, undifferentiated, and poisoned plain, as if even the geography had been crushed. Remains of streams and structures left ghostly outlines in the ash. Some still smoldered an angry red, the only color anywhere. The rest oozed with a sticky black substance. Long, tarry fingers of the stuff gathered around me and I felt the urge again to run —far and fast. Instead, I jumped onto a small ridge of rock that jutted up from the ground like a dead monster's spine. Maybe it was, but I wasn't going to think about it. The black substance didn't flow upward, so if I kept to this slight elevation, it wouldn't touch me.

I thought.

I'd spent the past few days buried in manuscripts. While Arsenault had been combing through his books searching for clues to repair my arm, I had been restlessly reading through Oji la Kaif and countless transcribed fragments of poetry, both ancient and modern—unable to settle into anything long enough to finish it. But in one of those piles, I had discovered a copy of *The Dance of the Heavens*.

An original manuscript would have bought Arsenault's vineyard in Orienne. This manuscript had been penned carefully in the script I'd been taught as a child—the script invented by Lieran scholars specifically to copy ancient Eterean manuscripts into a clearer, easier to read hand. This told me the copy was modern and the scholar who'd copied it probably Lieran. He'd written a flowery foreword and signed it—*Bruzzia*—then stamped it with an arrogant conceit—the wolf's head symbol of the old Imperium, used by Attrasca's followers after the Empire splintered.

Arsenault had said the dealer who'd collected the ingots he'd bought to make my arm was named Bruzzia, and I didn't think this was a coincidence. Bruzzia was an antiquities dealer and an Empirist. As I looked around this desolate place, a piece of text arose in my mind. I felt as if I had been living more in books than in the world lately, so I whispered it aloud, to make sure I still had the whole thing in my mind:

"This black and blasted world, eaten by fire and darkness
Fouled by dragons
This fallen place, this death of innocence
This destruction wrought by gods upon their own
and woe to men
to meadow grasses
to songbirds
to the kine in the field
and trees that once stood
upon hills sweet with rain and sun
But no more. In this wrecked world
even stars have fallen.

And magic, once bright and golden, streams along the ground
Black and hot
Like blood from the weeping Earth."

My voice sounded strange and lonely in this empty, burned-out world. It was a commonly memorized passage, though something seemed different, as if I had misremembered a word. Markus had spoken it under his breath as we'd surveyed the carnage of Vargis Pass, and the same feeling had moved in me when I'd read the words on the page. I couldn't help seeing again the mutilated, shattered bodies, the scars of the land, snow melted by fire, blood pooled atop the frozen ground like rain that had fallen in a storm.

I'd tried to turn the page as fast as I could, as if anything would ever dispel that memory, but then a note written in the margins with a different hand had stopped me.

Ask Arsenault if he can place this—M.

I'd found the note not long before the lodge blew. I had passed it to Arsenault and he'd frowned and said *I have no idea, we'll ask Jon who did it.* But Jon hadn't been inside and I was forced to watch the troubled emotions move in Arsenault's eyes as memories crowded into his mind, too many or blurry to distinguish. *It's about the Gods' War*, he'd finally said helplessly, something I could have told him. *If the writer thought I was there, they must have known who I was.*

The thing that bothered me most of all—more than knowing Arsenault had bought the metal for my arm from an Empirist, or that Jon had found and put this manuscript in a secret collection along with Arsenault's books, *or* that Arsenault had been alive in the Gods' War—was the suggestion that *someone else in the present world knew who Arsenault was.* Maybe more than one someone. Who was M and who had he written that annotation for? Himself? Jon?

Bruzzia?

As I balanced on the spine of an ancient creature buried in sand and ash, trying to escape grasping fingers of steaming, tarry ooze, the poetry felt more like straightforward description than metaphor. *Magic, once bright and golden, streams along the ground, black and hot.* That seemed like an understatement. The realization made me dizzy.

This was a field of battle from the Gods' War. Raw magic was oozing out of the ground.

I crouched to look at it. Arsenault had always talked about magic like it was a substance that could flow, but I hadn't known it was simple truth. Then again, I'd never understood why he identified magic with a definite article—*the* magic—until the last few weeks. But

if magic was a substance that could flow out of the ground like this—
or if it had once been—why could some people manipulate it from
wherever and whenever they were, but others had no access? Nobody
drank magic or *touched* it. Well, nobody except me, and that was
because I didn't have a choice. It was grafted onto my stump.

Why did magic no longer bubble out of the ground like water?
What had the gods done to it?

More and more of the foul stuff seeped from the earth, climbing
higher and higher up the rock spine. I tried to walk more quickly; I
wasn't enough of an acrobat to run on this thin edge in my current
state. Smoke drifted past me, so thick I could barely see my feet.
Through it, I heard voices. Weeping.

There was nowhere to hide, nowhere to go in the rising tide of
magic but this narrow island. The black substance was even starting to
eat through the rock—which shouldn't have surprised me, given what
Mikelo said it was doing to my lungs. I could only hope the smoke
obscured me.

"I should have been here," a woman's voice said—raw, like she'd
been the one weeping. "Why did you send me away?"

"And what could you have done if you'd stayed?" a man's voice
answered angrily. A familiar voice... I listened more closely. "You
couldn't have saved anyone, including yourself! It's my fault, all of it.
I'll bear all this blood forever."

I gave a start. Now I recognized the voice. It wasn't a *man*. It was
Ires. And the woman? Why had I assumed either of them would be
human? This was the Gods' War, of course she would be a goddess. I
wished I could see better, but all the smoke revealed was a pair of
large white wings and a slim, hunched back that seemed too frail to
belong to a divinity. Some of the old goddesses were portrayed with
wings like Ires's vanth—Pana, for instance—but I didn't know their
names because they were all dead, stricken from human memory by
Tekus and his family.

I edged as close as I dared. This smoke wouldn't hide me forever
and what then?

"You shouldn't be here," Ires told the goddess sitting on the
broken wall before him. "They'll be wondering why I'm not dead, too,
and when they find out they can't kill me—"

"Then why don't you hide among men until you get your
vengeance?"

"Justice demands I pay the price, or what's been done to the magic
will only grow worse with time."

"How will letting them imprison you help?" she protested angrily. "You know my father has been plotting to subjugate magic for a long time. He wants *his* father to forgive him the murder of his favorite son, but you and I both know that's impossible."

"How could I be so stupid?" Ires said in a voice that was somehow anguished and vicious at the same time. "I should have seen how deep into the darkness Tekus had sunk. I should have known. I should never have trusted him!"

"You were the only one who defended us," the goddess replied bitterly. "My grandfather's manipulations poisoned all his family ties. There will be another war worse than this one, after the poison has done its work. And if you let them capture you, you won't be there!"

"Neither will you, if you keep stubbornly pretending to *be* human instead of just hiding among them."

The goddess thrust herself up off the wall and stood, rigid with fury, but I still couldn't see her face. Thank—whoever I could thank— they hadn't noticed me yet.

"I'm not like my father, Uncle. I can't convince myself humans are creatures who don't matter. I peer into the faces of my children and know I'll have to watch them grow old and die. And what am I doing to my husband?" Her voice broke with anguish. "I want to love my family the way they love me, but what will my father do when he discovers he has grandchildren? And in the meantime, there I am hiding like a coward, trying to maintain that the war is only a distant battle in the heavens and Tule is a refuge where the Old World can never die—when we both know that's a lie. I can't do it. I want to drive Ari away from me, but I love him too much and it just makes us both miserable."

I froze. *Ari*.

The goddess Ires was talking to was Arsenault's wife. And Ires was her *uncle*.

I felt—I didn't know how I felt. I wanted to run away. I wanted to shout at them. My palms broke out in a cold sweat. If Ires was Sella's *uncle*, would he really want to help Arsenault or was he just trying to convince me—

"Convince you of what?"

Startled at the voice that was suddenly right next to me, I lost my balance. I stepped off the ridge, got my foot stuck in the spines a hand span from the bubbling black acid of poisoned magic. Ires stared down at me, his perfect, beautiful face smeared with blood and ash and twisted with fury. "Look around! The magic brought you here for a reason!"

"I—" I ventured, but he wasn't finished with his tirade.

"The new gods wanted to be all powerful, everlasting beings receiving constant adulation and fear from their subjects. That's why they play games with you. Otherwise, you'd be so busy living your lives, you wouldn't pay attention to them at all and what then would be the purpose of eternity? But this is their legacy!"

"You're eternal, too, though," I stuttered, trying to make some defense, though I didn't know what I was trying to defend. "Does that mean you're the same?"

His eyes grew wide. The fury in them was breathtaking and terrifying. My fucking mouth, why could I never just shut up? This was the god of *war*. What was I doing, deliberately provoking him?

"I had to become them so I could fight them," he ground out through his teeth. "To stand in their way even if it took all eternity. Tekus's desire for never-ending power poisoned everything!"

"So, you *are* eternal? But you weren't always?"

He looked like he was struggling to be patient with a simple child. "There was no other way, Kyrra. They put magic under their control. But as long as I'm alive, if the magic is part of me and I'm part of it, it can't be entirely under their yoke. There will always be vengeance, from this moment on."

"Is that why everything is black and foul? You infected magic with your hatred to fight the gods who stole it from you?"

He stepped up close to me—so close I should have been able to feel his breath, but there was none, and somehow that was the most disturbing thing. It reminded me that I was talking to someone outside life and death—someone *not human*.

"You're not *listening* to me. *Tekus* destroyed everything. He turned on us, he fouled the magic with death. If I'd not become like them, there would be no one left to fight! He would have killed all of us. I *had* to do it."

"You're a god! You didn't have to do anything! And I've been doing your dirty work for you, haven't I? Maybe you even want vengeance on Arsenault!"

"If I wanted vengeance on Ari, why would I be fighting Erelf? I don't rule Sella the way her father wants to. You'd rather have let Erelf's pawn live out of some sweet naive desire for peace? *You* let my magic in!"

How had we gotten onto the subject of Geoffre? "Oh no. Don't you twist my meaning. Fighting Geoffre was the best thing I've ever done, but I didn't do it by being your pawn, did I?"

I had to think. I couldn't keep letting him or the magic or any other god keep driving me to do stupid, hateful things just because they fit into some master plan for revenge and control. I needed to find Sella. To learn what had really happened between her and Arsenault. Why the magic would push and pull me around like this, only to end up *here*.

I tried to shove past Ires, but he caught my shirt in his gauntleted fist. Beneath me the spine of rock began to tremble as if it really was a creature awakening. Being at the whim of supernatural forces was starting to wear me out. I rammed my metal arm in its sling into his stomach, but Ires yanked me close to him and pinned me with a ruby-rimmed gaze while I tried to keep my footing on the rumbling spines.

How in all the hells did I keep getting myself into these situations?

The sound of huge, beating wings drove off some of the smoke. I looked frantically toward Arsenault's goddess wife as she walked toward me, her expression stormy, unforgiving, green eyes as fathomless as the sea. Her auburn hair caught in the wind and danced around her face like flames.

"Who are you?" she asked.

What the hell was I supposed to say? *I'm married to the man who killed you.*

"She belongs to me," Ires growled and shoved me off my island, into the foul black sand.

⁂

I WAS FALLING. THROUGH BLACKNESS INTO THE COLD LIGHT OF A real day, where I was hanging from a rock. Where I *had* been hanging from a rock, because now I was not and it was exactly like coming back to myself after battle madness—there I was in mid-air, with no idea how I'd gotten there or where I was.

I tried to get my feet under me, but my ankle folded when I hit the slope. I threw my arm up to protect my head as I pitched forward, tucked my chin to my chest, and prayed to anyone who would hear as I tumbled down the steep hillside, arse over elbows. I fetched up against a huge, gnarled beech tree, easily as big around as a small hut. The slope had eroded out from around it, leaving a twisted mass of roots like arms encircling a hollow, which I dropped into on my side. It hurt so much I couldn't breathe for a few long moments.

Breathe, breathe, damn you.

I don't know how long before the pain subsided enough for me to tell where it was coming from. My ribs. I'd expected that. As I struggled upright, I realized my ankle ached, too, but it held as I dragged myself up by the tree trunk. I probably should have sat longer, but so much fight and fear still coursed through me I needed to assure myself I wasn't dead, that I was back in the real world where things were alive—trees, lichen, birds, squirrels, the tiny green shoots breaking through the black soil. Despite everything, spring was finally coming to this altitude.

But a mountain spring was cold and wet and icy. My clothes were soaked and slicked with mud, leaves and pine needles stuck to me all over—my shirt, my ripped sling, my hair. Twigs and rocks had ripped bloody scratches up my forearm and when I touched my cheek, it was tender and scraped raw. I thought about untying my arm to use it as a mirror, but that would do more harm than good, so I just brushed as much detritus from my person as I could. My shoulder ached as I did it. The body bruises would probably keep me in bed tomorrow.

When I looked up, figures were moving through the woods. Real ones.

Not big or tall enough to be Arsenault, or even Mikelo or Silva, and definitely not Jon...

I snatched a broken stick and thrust it out in front of me like a sword as they approached. But when they clambered onto the path, I realized they were just boys, as startled to see me as I was to see them.

"Oh," the older boy, wide-eyed, stuttered. "It's...it's *you.*"

I eyed him and the other boy. They could be brothers, I decided. The older, bigger boy had brown hair, light eyes, the younger, dark hair, dark eyes, darker skin, but their features were stamped from the same mold. They were both rumpled and out of breath, like they'd been running. The younger one clutched a basket that looked as if it was full of eggs—a strange thing to be carrying through a forest.

"It is me," I answered warily, wondering exactly who these boys thought I was. I was wearing men's clothes and a cloak, but of course I hadn't bothered with a binder. If the boys had seen me in Cassis's camps, maybe they recognized me as "the Silver Warrior" or whatever Cassis had said people were calling me. If so, they were probably surprised to see me looking even more disheveled than they did—not to mention the stick. The more I studied them, the more familiar they looked, but I couldn't place them.

"Who are you?" I asked.

The boys traded surprised glances. "You...you don't know, messera?" the younger boy carrying the eggs asked.

Messera. The polite term for a married householder woman gave me a jolt. I narrowed my eyes. "Refresh my memory."

The older boy straightened like he was reporting to his captain. "I'm Fillipo and this is my brother Hani. You were staying at our house. Our mother—"

Suddenly, it made sense. *That* was why my memories of them were so blurry. What in all the hells was their mother's name?

Miranda.

I had blurry memories of her, too. She had reminded me of Vadz's chirurgeon wife Aleya, whose house I had lodged in until—gods, that memory also felt like an ambush. Arsenault had killed him. As time went on, it seemed not as if more was put to rest between the two of us, but as if I kept rediscovering issues to divide us. I swallowed the rush of grief. I didn't even know what it was for, it was for so many things.

I knew I had confused Miranda and Aleya in my delirium. I remembered kind, firm hands and concerned dark eyes. I remembered we had spoken of things unrelated to injuries or politics—the qualities of a good bean and barley soup, the best yarns for finger-knitting. Her conversation had kept me in the world and eased my pain, and I was grateful to her for it.

I lowered the stick. "Don't call me messera. That's my mother, and I'm not allowed householder titles. I suppose you know who I am, but just call me Kyris." *No, wait—* "Or...or Kyrra." It was strange giving out my real name to someone who hadn't known me before the wars.

Fillipo looked nervously at his brother. "Of course, mess—Kyr— Oh. Yes. Yes." He stared at his shoes and his cheeks, paler olive than his brother's, flushed brick red. I wasn't used to this kind of behavior. He didn't act like he was in the company of a notorious harlot. More like the way townspeople reacted to Rojornicki nobles. Strange.

I dug the end of the stick into the mud and leaned on it to take some weight off my bruised body. "I'd appreciate if you'd lead me back. I've gotten turned around somehow and I took a fall." Not to mention—where *was* Arsenault?

"That's where we were headed," Fillipo said. "We received a letter from Mama to give to Jon. We decided it would be safest to bring it ourselves, so we put it in the egg basket. We were searched once, on the road, but they didn't find anything."

He sounded proud of this accomplishment, but also frightened. I wondered who was searching people on the road, but I held my question as his brother lifted the basket, covered with a red-checked cloth.

"They took most of the eggs," Hani said. "They left us a few because we gave them our bread and cheese and the jug of ale Fillipo was carrying."

"Kind of them," I murmured, pulling back the corner of the cloth. "But also, smart to bring a better bribe as a distraction. Whose gavaros were they?"

"They weren't wearing armbands, mes—They could have been anyone's."

I nodded. "Where is this letter?"

"We ripped it up, so it would blend in with the straw," Hani said.

I peered into the basket as he dug his hand through the straw. Long strips of parchment lay crumpled beneath it. Hani pulled one out and held it up like a ribbon.

"We numbered them. As small as I could write, so Jon could put them together again."

I could barely make out a tiny black "2" in the corner. "I think your eyes are better than mine—Hani, was it? This is ingenious, but why did your mother have to send you with a letter in the first place? Is she running information for Jon?"

Fillipo looked torn. "It's because—"

"Fillipo, she said not to say!"

"I already messed up by saying Mama sent us a letter. I can't mess up more." He took a deep breath. "Our father was a messenger in the war. People used to come and go through our house all the time. Now that we're older, Mama's been leaving us in charge sometimes because she says, as a family, we need to continue the work. Not just because of us, but because the Prinze can't be allowed to oppress everyone. She says it's our responsibility to fight the Dark One wherever he shows himself, but not all of us use swords."

While he talked, I was pushing straw out of the way, trying to match the strips on the bottom of the basket as quickly as I could. Mixed in with the dry gold and brown stalks were little flecks of burgundy sealing wax.

I rubbed my fingers together and stared at the streaks it made on my skin.

Burgundy wax. Burgundy silk hidden on the furniture. Aliente tunics.

The Prinze can't be allowed to oppress everyone.

It's our responsibility to fight the Dark One, but not all of us use swords.

"Where did the gavaros go after they took your ale?" I asked.

"Toward the road." Fillipo pointed in the opposite direction.

I matched up a few lines of the letter, but they didn't make sense. "Is this letter in code? Do you know what it says?"

The boys looked at each other guiltily. "Some," Hani said. "Not all of it."

I looked up in amusement. "She meant you to leave it sealed, didn't she?"

"Yes, but we couldn't, and we were also hiding—" Hani bit his lip.

"Hiding what?" I asked.

Silently, Fillipo opened his cloak and hooked a finger into some rough stitches holding a rip closed. They pulled out so easily they were obviously meant to be temporary. He stuffed his hand inside what I could now tell was a pocket, pulled out a couple of balls of maroon yarn, and then—

A glistening cherry stock wheellock pistol. Runes flashed white on the barrel when Fillipo brought it near my arm.

"Oh gods, you boys," I breathed. "Do you know how bloody dangerous this is? If you'd been caught with a letter for Jon *and* one of his guns..."

"But it was too important! When we saw what it was about..."

What the hell was it about? I pressed the wrinkles down and went back to work on the code. Jon had used a few different ones in Rojornick, but this was different. I frowned as I formed the words silently with my mouth. They sounded like a combination of Eterean and—

Efgar, thorn...

...and bloody *runes*. Runes *I* had once transcribed, sitting on a hillside while Arsenault worked on a map of the villa.

I swore without thinking and the boys startled. "I think I know who wrote this code," I said by way of apology.

"It's the old Aliente code from the war," Hani said proudly, and I had to wonder, why *did* he sound so proud? How did he know the old Aliente code and why were people still using it? "Nobody ever cracked it. Some said it was half magic."

"Yes, well, the Prinze didn't have to crack it in the end, did they?" I replied bitterly. "Why don't you tell me what you read instead of waiting for me to figure it out?"

"She says the lodge is under heavy fire from the forces of Devid di Prinze, so it likely won't stand. Cassis di Prinze is gone, though. He went to Liera with the scholar she doesn't like—Lupa—maybe to confront his uncle Renzo. But the scholar left his Dakkaran secretary with Cassis's forces, which are now being captained by his gavaro, Lobardin. They're going to try to get out—"

"Wait." I put out my hand to stop him. It was a lot to take in all at once, but one thing snagged me. "Your mother—was she at the lodge when she wrote this letter?"

"She didn't tell us where she was going," Fillipo said solemnly. "Just that she would come back—and then she didn't. But when we got the letter, we learned she'd been stuck there... That's why *we* came with it to Jon."

"Lobardin was the one who blew it then," I whispered. "Great gods." I put my hand on Fillipo's sleeve. I could only hope his mother had made it out ahead of time. "Take me back to the house and we'll tell Jon, figure out what to do next. Those gavaros who stopped you, they might have worked for Cassis, deserted ahead of—"

"Ahead of what?" Hani asked, frowning. "Ahead of the wall coming down?"

I wasn't much for lying to children—especially when the children were almost not children anymore and could pull off a smuggling feat like this one. But I couldn't bring myself to say anything out here in the woods. I'd feel much better when we ran into Arsenault.

"Come on—"

Before I could finish, the world rocked beneath me.

"Messera?" Fillipo caught my arm. I stared at him in shock. Hadn't he felt the thrum that had come up through the earth, the wave of—

Magic. Welling up out of the ground like it had in my vision of the Gods' War.

The ground around us cracked. Mist rose from the fissures—not steam, but a filmy veil of magic, cold and icy, like pure terror transmuted into little droplets glittering in the rapidly disappearing sunshine. When the magic fog slid by the tree branches, they blackened as if they'd been burned, then broke and crashed to the ground, splashing into the thick, black muck.

What in all the hells had been under that lodge?

It seemed impossible, but it had already been an impossible day.

"Don't let it touch you," I snapped at the boys. "Is there anywhere we can shelter from it?"

I didn't much fancy finding a cave when the earth was wrenching itself apart, and how the hell was it possible to hide from *air*? But surely there was some way to climb out of this mist.

Hani bolted down the slope. "This is the fastest way to the house. It leads through the old village!"

"We can hide in the village," Fillipo added breathlessly as he pulled me along.

I leapt clumsily over another rip that had torn open in the ground, as if the rock had become as flimsy as fabric. I prayed my body wouldn't give out. Old, ruined buildings would have to do.

The sludgy black substance oozed along beside us like a stream as we ran downhill. Hani accidentally slipped and put his foot in it. I yanked him backward as quickly as I could, but not before the sole of his boot began steaming.

"Kick it off!" I ordered. Frantically, he did, slinging a wad of goop into the air. It landed on a boulder and sizzled through its carpet of moss and down into the rock, releasing a musty smell, like the air in a cave. It had eaten a hole into the leather of Hani's boot, too, but thank the gods—or whoever we could thank—it hadn't gotten as far as his foot.

The forest around us was alive with agonized shrieking and chirping as the corrupted magic poured into burrows and nests. We'd be stranded if we didn't find a way out quick.

Fillipo scrambled up on a broken wall. "Up here! We used to climb on the ruins and play hide and seek when we were little. Come on!"

If only I were still the girl who used to play my own games of hide and seek in the ruins of the lodge, and not a woman whose body was protesting strongly at my mistreatment of it. Fillipo dragged me up onto the wall and ooze splattered my trousers. I tried to scrape it off onto the rocks, but it ate a hole into the fabric anyway. I had no doubt it would do the same thing to our flesh.

"M-messera. Look."

Fillipo pointed. The gavaros who'd taken the boys' lunch lay in a mangled puddle on the ground, the liquid around them an odd reddish-black-brown, the color of magic sludge, liquified flesh, and blood—so much blood. The bones were still steaming, as if the bodies had been cooked. Untouched beside them, the jug of ale, a block of cheese.

Hani made a noise. Fillipo looked as if all the blood had drained from his face. Godsdammit, they were only *boys*. I wanted to put my hand over their eyes so they couldn't see, but all I could do was put my hand on Hani's shoulder.

"We can't help them now. We have to keep going." I scanned the forest. "There!" I pointed at a hopefully intact building huddled at the edge of the crumbling buildings. "Inside, quick as you can."

I pushed Fillipo into motion. He stumbled on the wall, then

caught Hani by the elbow, and they both ran—light-footed—down the uneven, unsteady rubble toward the abandoned building. I paused a moment to look again for Arsenault. Was there movement on the hillside? Or, what if a fissure had swallowed him up? What if this fouled magic—

Distracted, I didn't notice the ground sinking at the edge of the wall ahead of me until it suddenly crumbled into a huge, gaping hole. With its footing partially destroyed, the wall trembled, then began to buckle and sink.

It's going to fall, too...

And me with it.

I jumped. It was like jumping roofs in Liera, except my dead right arm put me off balance. I hit the edge of the stable portion of the wall with the arch of my foot. The sharp edge of stone cut into me through the leather slippers, while behind me, a whole segment of wall collapsed into the hole—disappearing straight into the underworld for all I knew. For a moment, teetering on the edge, I peered into the abyss. I wondered—in a weird flash of cool fascination—what would happen if I fell to the underworld, too. Would I find Ires there, shackled and waiting on me? Then I wrenched myself forward and fell to my knees atop the stone.

Pain flashed, bright and fresh. Gods, I was going to feel all of this in the morning. I scrambled up and followed Fillipo and Hani into the building.

I don't know what I was expecting. Roots thrusting through the stone walls, cracks in the roof slabs, dead leaves—a whole family murdered by marauders at their evening meal wouldn't have surprised me. But a neat space with a rack of blacksmith's tools hanging on the wall, a crude workbench of freshly hewn logs scenting the air with pine and sawdust, a handmade book lying open—pages blank, of course—metal stylus lying atop it...

That, I was never expecting.

Dammit, Arsenault.

The gleaming metal carcass of Cassis's dragon sat on top of the workbench.

CHAPTER 47

KYRRA

It was dim and cold inside the forge. The earth rumbled while outside animals and birds continued to shriek. It made me nervous to stay inside a building that might fall on our heads at any moment, but for now it was safer than wandering through the mist.

"We need to light a fire," I told the boys. "Get it warm and bright in here. I don't know what runes Arsenault has put on this place, but we're not trying to defend ourselves against people; we're fighting magic itself. I imagine that changes things."

The boys jerked into motion. They were both shaking, breathing hard. I needed to get them moving, get them warm. Arsenault had cleaned up the place, but he obviously hadn't wanted to draw attention to the building because there was no wood to kindle a fire in the forge. I searched the shelves rapidly for flint and steel, matches—anything to chase away that deadly mist—but with my one clumsy hand, all I succeeded in doing was scattering sketches and bits of drawing charcoal to the floor. Finally, I knocked a box off a high shelf and a bunch of tallow candles spilled out of it. Fillipo shoved flint and steel from his own pocket at me as I smashed a candle into a holder.

"You do it," I told him. "It will be faster."

His eyes went wide, flickered to my sling, then back to his flint. He bobbed his head. "Of-of course." His hands trembled, but he got a spark and lit the candle. Monstrous shadows sprang up on the wall and light danced off the dragon limb.

"What is that?" Hani asked, pointing at it.

"It's a piece of a god," I said. "Or a magical machine. Keep an eye on it. We still need a fire. Fillipo, help me get these shelves off the wall so we can burn them?"

"Burn the shelves, messera?" he asked, astonished.

I decided to allow him a messera, considering the situation. "We can't go outside for wood. We need a fire to protect us and to let Arsenault know where we are."

The bastard.

"All-all right. Hani, get the things off—"

I handed Hani the jug, picked up the book and shoved it in my cloak, then cleared everything else off the shelf with my forearm. Little trinkets of metal and tools, both rusty and polished, cascaded onto the floor. Hani and Fillipo both jumped.

"We don't have time. Rip those shelves down. Quick!"

I'd help Arsenault clean up as soon as he explained what in the hells he'd been doing. The mist had begun to filter through the cracks in the stones. The temperature in the cabin dropped. The air felt heavy and whispery.

Voices again.

It made me think. What if magic was a creature, but not a creature with only one soul, the way humans and animals were, but a being with many souls, many voices, all connected inside the same...Thing? Most importantly, if such a being existed, what would happen if its souls had been divided against themselves? Could you predict what such a Thing might do if it was in danger and in pain?

Fear turned men into creatures that were hardly human, who did things they would never do in more rational times and not always what helped them survive. Some soldiers froze, becoming helpless targets in the face of killing strokes; strong, otherwise brave men hid or ran or pled with their attackers; others grew so frightened and angry they attacked anything that moved, whether it threatened them or not.

Then there were soldiers like me, who fought possessed.

I didn't want to admit it, but there was some truth in what Erelf and Ires had said, that I invited the madness in myself. It wasn't *entirely* true because it just happened when the battle feelings dumped in on me. But it was much easier to let Ires do the killing instead of having to look my victims in the face as I took their lives.

The black sludge, the heaviness of the air, the cold terror in the mist... If you took all the emotions from a battlefield or a disaster—or distilled them from a sixteen-year-old laying her arm down on the chopping block—and gave all that anger, helplessness, and fear *substance*... That's what the mist felt like.

How did you fight a Thing so terrified it unthinkingly destroyed everything it touched?

I didn't know if we ought to fight it or if we should try to weather it until it ran itself out. I didn't know if we *could* fight it. The only thing I could do was light this godsdamned fire.

"Fillipo, get the hammer, break these up." I held a board vertically, gripping the top, setting the bottom firmly on the dirt floor. "Hit it in the middle."

"But what if I hurt you?"

More mist filtered into the room, swirling down the chimney and spreading through the opening like breath fogging on a cold day.

"Don't worry about me. Just hit it!"

He swung the hammer as hard as he could. The board splintered with a loud crack and I pushed on the top until it snapped in half.

"Throw it in the forge, Hani, from as far away as you can."

We tossed in all the broken boards. The mist recoiled as the boards sliced through it, but then it began to thicken, to gain arms, legs, teeth—form.

I grabbed the jug and pulled the cork with my teeth, spat it onto the floor. The blessed scent of imya burned my nose and made my eyes water. I didn't like that Arsenault was drinking out here, alone, but the imya was a gift. I hurled it toward the boards, splashing the clear liquid over as many as I could, then I handed the jug to Hani and grabbed the candle.

"Stay against the other wall," I told the boys. I took a deep breath and lunged forward.

The mist was so fucking cold. Its icy fingers pierced flesh and metal, only marginally repelled by the pathetic candle flame, carrying with it overwhelming memories—

The way my wet, exposed fingers had frozen to my sword hilt at Vargis Pass. When Nibas had pried my sword from my hand, flesh had ripped away with it—

The snap of the hanging rope—

The bite of the axe—

It's all an illusion!

I hurled the candle at the imya-soaked boards. Flames immediately leapt toward the open chimney and the mist shrieked and released its grip on me. I jerked back as fast as I could, breathing hard. My metal arm groaned as if with a sudden change in temperature. Now if the fire would just stay burning...

"Mes-messera," one of the boys said.

"Kyris," I said reflexively as I looked up, rubbing the still unfeeling metal of my bicep. The boys weren't looking at me, though; they were looking at the dragon limb. Most of the mist had burned off. But not all of it. The last ragged vestiges were swirling around the dragon claw.

It creaked. The ankle joint stretched rustily. The claws spread.

My arm twinged. The feeling was so unexpected, I clutched at it.

"What is happening to it?" Hani whispered.

"I don't know," I said. Where the *hell* was Arsenault? Surely, I hadn't run far enough that I had completely lost him? "The fire is still our best defense." I didn't know that, but I wanted to sound confident for their sake. "You two move close to it—slowly, I don't know if that thing will sense you or not."

"What are you going to do?" Fillipo asked shakily.

I picked up the hammer Fillipo had dropped as carefully as I could. The ghostly outline of a dragon was forming now, running up from the metal foot to form the sketch of a body, as if the magic were drawing it in the air. I wasn't sure what a hammer would do to a ghost dragon, or if it would even put a dent in the tiaannamir—hammers never did anything to my arm—but it was the only weapon I had. Except for fire, but how hot did a forge have to be to melt tiaannamir? How did Arsenault cast it, except by using his magic?

Dammit, we were fucked.

"Just get behind me," I said, staring into the crystallizing eyes of the dragon as I sat on the hearth with my hammer in my lap. "I'm sure I'll think of something."

CHAPTER 48

ARSENAULT

IBUU'S PALACE COMPOUND, TWENTY YEARS AGO

"So, what is she like?"

Jon sat his horse lazily, his abaganda pulled up loosely over his head to block the sun that burned now and again through the clouds. It was hot and humid, but darker clouds billowed out to sea behind them, harbingers of yet another storm. They were about halfway out of Mdembu, riding uphill to the Ibuu's fortress, and Arsenault's head pounded like someone was swinging a hammer into it.

Maybe it hadn't been the best idea to drink all that rum. He'd hoped it would help him forget the look on Boucher's face as he'd disappeared beneath the waves, but it only blurred yesterday's details. He'd locked Jon out and slid down too far in the bath and come up gasping, sure he was beneath the overturned skiff. After that, he'd climbed out of the tub and into bed and slept there naked until morning when Jon woke him and his headache by banging on the door.

Now he felt like a piece of flotsam heaved at the shore. His thigh muscles ached from riding. His arms were still stiff and sore from fighting the surf with a pair of oars. His sunburn screamed whenever his clothes rubbed against his shoulders.

"What is who like," he mumbled.

"Etranée. What is she like?"

"As a person?"

"In bed, ghost. You slept with her, didn't you?"

Arsenault sighed and took his hand from the reins to rub his eyes, which felt like they were being knifed. "Ferocious. As a person and in bed. Are you satisfied?"

"You leave a lot to the imagination."

"What are you, fifteen? If you want details, you can visit her yourself. Why didn't you tell me she worked for your aunt?"

Jon shrugged. "I didn't know. Neyane doesn't have to tell me what she's doing. I tell her what I'm doing because she has the authority, but only if she asks. It's best to keep some projects quiet."

"Like your membership in the Blades?"

"Has Neyane told her who I am?"

"No. I don't know how you hide how important you are, Jon."

"We've dispensed with the *lord* then?"

"I think you owe me that."

"For condemning you to the bed of a beautiful pirate captain? Forgive me, ghost. Next time I will go myself."

"No, you wouldn't. You like Jemma too much."

"Fine. Being a member of the Blades allows me to walk through doors that would be closed to me otherwise. The Blades think the Ibuu gave me a ceremonial commission because I'm a frivolous younger son with a lot of contacts but few real responsibilities. They think they can twist me."

"Seems like you're wearing too much gold in your ear for anyone to think you're *really* frivolous. Are you taking a cut of the proceeds?"

"If I said yes, what would you do?"

Arsenault hunched into his abaganda. Jon had brought him new clothes this morning—clothes he wouldn't be noticed in. Not silk. Arsenault wanted to put his head in his hands, but he had to hold the reins.

"I've been trying to work this out," he said. "It comes down to Adayze. I don't believe she would knowingly accept coin that came from breaking laws she was sworn to uphold."

"You don't believe the Heir to the Ibuu's Chair is capable of manipulating intelligence networks for political purposes? You're putting her on a pedestal, ghost."

"I thought the dirty work was your job. Or else what's the purpose of raising the secondborn like a weapon?"

Jon's eyes grew shadowed. In the silence, the horses' hooves crunched dirt and clipped pebbles. A sluggish breeze stirred the leaves of the trees that grew on either side of the road and a deep rumbling noise that could have been thunder or drums thrummed in the distance.

"No," he said, finally. "I don't take the cut. My share of the money goes to charity homes. For the sick, widows, and orphans."

"The ones Chayma helps run for Adayze?"

Jon shrugged. "You can believe it or not. I take the money because they'd ask questions if I refused it. But what I do with it is my own business. I give it to the healers."

Arsenault watched him a moment longer, but Jon's face gave away nothing either way. He *wanted* to believe Jon, but did it really matter? It was too late to turn back now.

❧

BY THE TIME THEY ARRIVED AT THE PALACE, THE DRUMS WERE SO loud it sounded as if they were pounding inside Arsenault's head. The huge drums were housed inside the guard towers and the sound went out in a thudding, repetitive *boom-boom-boom*—pause—*boomboom*—pause—*boom*, and then Arsenault lost the rest of the rhythm in lumbering pain. Jon said it was to declare a holiday, a celebration of the destruction of Alabad. He had no time to recover from the ride and no choice but to wash the road dust from his hair and face at the pump, then change immediately into his guard's tunic. He didn't notice Adayze walking with her retainers until he was almost on top of them.

"Arsenault!" she exclaimed, drawing back in surprise.

"Lady," Arsenault said, looking up, just as surprised.

She was dressed for court: a red silk skirt and matching blouse, golden bracelets stacked on her arms and ankles, leather sandals on her feet and gold rings encircling two of her toes. Despite her finery, she wore Edo in a wrap at her side. When Edo noticed him, he stopped playing with the ropes of beads wound around his mother's neck and held out his hands.

"He has started this thing about beards," Adayze said in apology, then her tone grew accusatory. "He hasn't seen you in a while."

For a moment Arsenault felt like he was standing in between worlds, unsure which he belonged to. He realized he was hesitating, realized Adayze and Edo wouldn't know why, and obliged Edo by leaning forward so the toddler could pat his face. His head throbbed with pressure, but the air filled with Adayze's perfume—cloves, oranges, sandalwood, the same scent that had lingered in her room among her oils and lotions. He caught his breath as if by doing so he could retain a part of her, as if that would clear away all he'd done over the past eight days.

Then small fingers scrubbed the short hair on his cheeks. Chubby palms patted his mouth, feeling the hair on his upper lip. Little fingers reached up to touch his scar.

Adayze caught Edo's hand. "No, sweetie. That's not polite. Arsenault, I'm sorry."

He wasn't ready to be with people yet. He tried to smile at Edo and hoped it didn't reveal the turmoil inside him. "Edo's fine, my lady. I don't mind."

"Where did you go? I went into the audience room to talk to my mother and father, and when I came out, they said you had gone to the healer. But when I went to check on you, Chayma said you went with Jon, and now it's been eight days."

"I thought Jon sent a messenger."

"The message didn't say anything, just to make sure Renzo di Prinze had water. What were you doing?"

Killing three men. Bedding a woman who wouldn't let me see her naked. Who's now sworn to kill me.

"Working for Jon," he said instead.

Adayze's eyes tightened skeptically. She looked over her shoulder at the guards who stood behind her. They were both female, armed with big knives. "You may leave us now," she told them. "Arsenault can keep us safe."

Oh, gods.

But this is what he'd returned for, wasn't it?

The retainers looked skeptical, but then they bowed their heads and walked away, leaving him alone with Adayze and Edo.

"Are you all right?" Adayze asked when her women had gone.

"I...I've just had some long nights and the ride from Mdembu was..."

"Arsenault?"

He squeezed Edo's hand and smiled at him, then took a big step backward, away from the boy's beautiful, kind mother, who was Heir to the Ibuu's seat and, more importantly, still married. He would not—could not—violate that boundary unless Adayze made it perfectly clear she had decided it was time to put it aside. And if he wished the situation was different, he would just force himself to be happy to be her guard.

He gave her a small bow. "Forgive me, lady. I'm tired and the storms make my head ache. Were you going to dinner?"

Adayze's expression grew careful and shuttered. "Is there something I should know first? You're calling Jon by his first name. Yet you still call me lady."

He'd offended her. But how could she know why he did so?

She began walking, so he did, too. They were on the path that led to the gardens where the snake had attacked them, but Adayze took the other branch, around the gardens to the front of the palace. It hadn't rained yet, but dusk was falling on the thick layer of clouds and the day grew dark early. Torches were already lit on the palace steps. Their light flickered through the gaps of the shivering leaves of trees and bushes.

"Adayze," he said, a peace offering. "Were you safe? While I was gone?"

She walked in silence for a moment. Then she said, "I thought you'd run. That Jon had followed you. If you were in Alabad...you *could* have run. You could have hired on a ship, just kept going."

"I won't say I didn't think about it. But I made a free choice to return."

"Jon didn't coerce you? No authorities pulled you back?"

"How could they? I have no writ anymore. I'm a free man."

Adayze stared at him.

Edo chose that moment to put his hands out toward Arsenault again. "Dat," he said urgently. "Dat, dat, dat."

Arsenault turned to Edo in surprise. "What—did he start to talk while I was away? What's he saying?"

She smiled at him, but it wasn't an easy smile. "Things change fast with children this age, isn't that what you told me?"

"Dat," Edo said again, leaning toward Arsenault. Arsenault had no choice but to lift him out. He settled the baby on his arm. Edo patted Arsenault's cheeks and said in satisfaction, "Dat, Ari, dat."

"I think," Adayze said thoughtfully, "he's trying to say *datya*. Arsenault. I think he's calling you uncle."

CHAPTER 49

ARSENAULT

STILL FLUSTERED FROM EDO'S INNOCENT WORDS, ARSENAULT handed him back to Adayze and followed them into the Great Hall. Arsenault had never been inside when all the chandeliers were lit. Giant candelabras decorated with prisms hung from the ceiling, splitting rainbows upon the floor and in the gem-encrusted mosaics adorning the walls. Huge orchid centerpieces graced each table, some of them supporting golden cages housing real birds. The sound of polite chatter and string music, combined with the sudden shrieking of the birds, was disorienting, and the crazy lights knifed his eyes as he followed Adayze through the crowd of courtiers.

A man stepped out from behind a knot of chatting nobles and caught her hand, bowed and lifted it to his lips before she could pull away.

Arsenault put his hand on his sword and moved to her side in an instant.

"Lord Promethi," Adayze said with a forced smile.

Promethi smiled and rubbed her fingers with his thumb before he straightened and let her hand drop. He was wearing an abaganda made of aubergine silk and his locs were wrapped in a silk head cloth of the same color. A diamond stud glittered in his nose. Everything about the man was impeccable, not a wrinkle, not a movement out of place. And yet—Arsenault thought about the Arak insurrection and what Boucher had told him about the man's brother, Dirik, wanting Fixers for *experiments*.

"Peace and happiness be upon your house, Lady Adayze," Promethi said as he straightened.

"And yours," Adayze answered in a guarded voice. "I hope your stay has been pleasant."

"It does me good to come down from the mountains now and then," Promethi answered with the kind of smile that left one feeling something wasn't quite right.

"We're sorry your brother couldn't make the trip. Is he still unwell?"

Boucher hadn't mentioned that Promethi's brother was ill. What sort of experiments might a sick man use Fixers for? Dim shapes of long-ago memories stirred in his mind. Hadn't Fixing once run not only to arts like metal and wood but to more esoteric things, ideas like Desire, forms like...flesh? All he saw behind his eyes were horrors, remembered or invented, but only too easily applied in his imagination to Guin or Adayze or—he had to physically stop himself flinching away from the thought—Edo.

Promethi might as well have considered Arsenault a statue for all the attention he paid him. "Dirik is still recovering from his accident, yes. Not ready to venture out beyond family, I'm afraid."

"I apologize, my lord, for not making more inquiries. I thought he was happily on the mend."

"His injuries still cause him difficulties and always will, but—if you don't mind me sharing in confidence, lady—he's always been rather eccentric. And the trauma... Well, you must understand. He wanted so badly to come himself, to offer support from our binding in this difficult time with your husband's voyage so long delayed and its outcome so uncertain, but in the end, he was defeated by his health. He sent me to convey his concern."

Adayze smiled pleasantly, though she had to be seething inside. "Thank you, Lord Promethi. But until we have evidence that Isa's voyage has been lost, it behooves us to remember all the obstacles he might need to overcome. I'm sure neither the Ibuu nor I have judged your brother's absence as lack of support."

Promethi paused for a blink, as if he'd expected her to be more affected by his words. Then he gave her a secret, knowing smile. "Between you and me," Promethi said in a low voice, "I understand how difficult my brother can be. He has little patience for polite society. But underneath it all beats a heart of gold."

I bet it does, Arsenault thought. *Cold and inhuman.*

Edo babbled something and reached out for the scarf that bound Promethi's locs. Promethi didn't even look at the baby as he side-stepped Edo's hands. The look in his eyes never changed. It wasn't as if they were emotion*less*, but he looked like he was playing a game of indij. Something about the way Promethi interacted was wrong, but Arsenault couldn't put his finger on it.

Finally, Promethi turned to Arsenault. "But who's this? I heard you had a Tulan guard."

"We pulled him off a boat. The condition of the galleymen was atrocious. He said all the galleymen on that ship had been captured illegally, so I kept him for a fine on the captain and to hear what he had to say. However, we haven't been able to prove anything, because we can't find any of the other galleymen."

The opportunity was too important to let pass. "I heard that perhaps your brother bought them," Arsenault said quickly. "My lord."

Adayze's eyes widened; damn, he should have told her first, but there hadn't been time.

Promethi's shoulders lifted in a brief shrug. "Sadly, I've been traveling, so I can't confirm or deny the information. I assure you, if my brother bought their contracts, they're being treated well. He is very interested in the idea of... transformation."

"What sort of transformation are we speaking of here, Promethi?" Adayze asked.

"Just as Fixers can take a lump of metal and Shape something beautiful and useful from it, my brother wonders if the practice of chaining criminals to galleys for punishment treats men as if they're ugly lumps of ore. What if one could, through hard work and patient tending, chip away the rock and purify the ore until it also became beautiful and useful?"

Beautiful and useful to whom? Arsenault wanted to ask. As if a man was only a tool beaten out of metal. If he put Renzo's and Boucher's information together, Promethi was, if not lying through his teeth, at least talking wide circles around the truth. But so far Promethi hadn't stepped out of line himself.

"Your man looks healthy enough now," Promethi prodded. "I assume you had a similar goal?"

"He faced down a lion for a pledge," Adayze replied. "And he demonstrated his fealty recently by protecting me and my son from the apparitions that have been plaguing us. Have you encountered any, Promethi?"

"I've heard of the apparitions, of course, but I haven't had the bad luck to face one yet—outside the Ibuu's court, that is. The Lieran merchant I apprehended—*he* came in the company of many magical artifacts, so perhaps he might know something. But congratulations to you on your brave guard. *Raustr mat vel yastog vinna o kal sedaft.*"

Arsenault blinked.

The brave man shall fight well though his blade be dull. A proverb his father had often repeated when he'd complained about his swordmaster. Promethi's accent and syntax weren't perfect, but they were perfectly serviceable.

"Where did you learn Tulan, my lord?" he asked when he recovered from his surprise.

Promethi shrugged. "My brother's hobby is science, I like languages. Your language is fascinating. You have no words for *noble* or *lord,* but twenty-five variations on the word *honor.* Also, you all seem to be quite interested in ice. Everything I've seen is merely sluggish water. But after studying your language, I do not think this is what you Tulans mean by *ice.*"

Arsenault frowned, knocked completely off guard by Promethi's knowledge of his homeland. "When the temperature drops to a certain point, water becomes solid. It's important to know what kind of ice you're dealing with. If it's too thin, you'll fall through. Cold water kills."

Adayze looked at him in amazement. "Water can become solid enough to walk on? What does it look like?"

"Depends. Clear, if the wind is still and the ice is thin. Blue, if it's sea ice."

"Fascinating," Promethi said. "But I must say I find all the old Qalfan accounts of Tule fascinating. An entire island formed by magic. Surely the Qalfan explorers were lying."

No, but then the new gods stole the magic, pulled it right out of the land, and the Empire did the rest.

Arsenault wasn't sure why talking about his old homeland made him uncomfortable. Many people thought Tule existed only in ancient epics. But thinking of the land he'd left behind—the volcanos, the heaths, the black sand beaches, the mountains and glaciers—gave him an ache he thought he'd put away a long time ago. And he still didn't know exactly how they'd come to this subject. Hadn't they been talking about Promethi's brother? How had Promethi maneuvered this?

"Perhaps they've exaggerated a bit," Arsenault said. "I haven't read all the accounts."

"You've read Oji la Kaif though?"

Damn. Oji la Kaif again?

Promethi went on though Arsenault didn't answer. "La Kaif has a tendency to make the fantastic sound mundane and thus utterly believable. On Tule, he said he was led high up onto a mountain covered with ice. The ice formed a wall that towered higher than this palace, so clear it functioned like a mirror. According to Oji, *things* lived behind it —twisted combinations of man and animal, with horns and wings and teeth. Demons. Only visible during certain magical rituals."

Arsenault gave the most Vençalan shrug he could manage, considering the alarm Promethi's words provoked in him. "People like stories. It's a good way to pass a long winter night."

He vividly remembered the day his own teacher had made him face the Ice, the beginning of his lifelong battle against the dark. If Promethi was bringing up the old traditions, the old practices... *Would* he know how to conjure a snake demon made of tiaannamir?

"La Kaif also said there was a man imprisoned in the ice. Sitting on a chair made from the bones of men. The man wore a hat—black, like the Onzarrans'. A pair of ravens sat on his shoulders. And he had a scar—"

No, this was far enough. No amount of information was worth bringing Erelf into the conversation. And Erelf *sitting on his father's throne*—that was even more disturbing. "If you want to talk about *him*, Lord Promethi, I suggest you take some precautions first."

"Precautions?" Promethi looked genuinely surprised. Adayze looked surprised, too. Edo tugged at her necklace and she pulled it away from him absently.

"Are you saying Oji la Kaif's stories are real, Arsenault?"

"People who don't know talk about what they don't understand, and sometimes they get into trouble. They open doors for the sake of curiosity that ought to remain shut."

He held Promethi's gaze. Promethi's eyes were light brown, almost the color of Etranée's. Like Etranée's, they betrayed little of his thoughts beyond what he wanted to show.

"Well," Promethi said, looking down at Edo, his lips crinkling into that smile again that wasn't quite right, "I do try not to be provincial. Haven't you ever heard it said, *Knowledge is sweeter than palm wine and more enduring?*"

"But can't it make you just as drunk? If you overdo it?" Arsenault replied, then bowed and said, "My lord."

Promethi regarded him thoughtfully.

Adayze touched his sleeve. "Arsenault. I believe it's time for me to take my place. Lord Promethi, this has been a most interesting exchange. I look forward to speaking to you again."

"I hope I will have the chance, lady."

She tilted her head to Promethi as he bowed and Arsenault put himself between them as she walked to the table.

"That was rather transparent," she muttered when they were far enough away that Promethi couldn't hear.

"The man definitely knows about magic. There's something strange about him, like he's hiding something."

"I wasn't talking about him."

Arsenault looked up in surprise. Adayze's expression was hard.

She thought he'd been posturing.

Had he been posturing?

Maybe a little, he concluded guiltily. "There are some realms no one should speak of," he said.

"Why not? Who is the man behind the ice? The one with the scar—"

"Adayze. *Do not speak of him*. He controls that part of magic that gives people Sight. Don't invite his attention!"

Adayze stopped at the edge of the dais, with one foot already on it, and stared at him. "Who is he?"

Arsenault clenched his teeth so hard he felt like he was grinding them down. "A god. And that's all I'm saying, do you understand?"

"Twenty-five words for honor and not one for lord. I think I am understanding you more now, Arsenault."

He straightened, still breathing in angrily through his nose. The muscle in his jaw twitched.

"Dat, Ari!" Edo stretched past his mother's shoulder to wave at Arsenault. "Ari, Ari, Ari!"

What had he been thinking, teaching Edo to call him that name?

❧

PREDICTABLY, EDO IMMEDIATELY DOVE FOR EVERYTHING ON THE table as soon as Adayze pulled him out of her wrap—the small golden forks, the tiny silver spoons, the wine bowl, the porcelain dishes from Saien, the tablecloth, which he bunched in his fist and pulled toward him. Adayze grabbed it just in time and worried it out of his fingers. He howled in anger.

"*Adayze*," her mother whispered loudly. "You should have left him with the nurses!"

Arsenault leaned over Adayze's shoulder. "I'll take him, lady. We'll have a walk around the room."

Adayze gazed at him with mute gratitude. He swung Edo up out of her arms, then stepped back into the line of guards.

Jon wriggled a finger into Edo's belly and made the little boy giggle and squeal.

"Jonawak!" his mother said. "Save it for the nursery!" She immediately transgressed against her own directive by squeezing Edo's toes. Edo grinned and said, "Eee-ee-eee!" which was the first syllable of *eya*, or grandma, so had Edo learned to say everyone's name while he was gone? Adayze's mother smiled sweetly at the baby, then turned to Jon with an authoritative glare.

Jon sighed. "Sorry, Edo. We can't play today."

"Too bad, Edo," Haq said, leaning over to see the baby, too. "All these grown-ups are no fun. Here, you want some puff?"

He produced a small, round, fried ball of dough like magic from inside his sleeve.

"Haq," Jon said. "You're stealing food?"

"I might get faint standing here all night."

Edo grinned as he took a big bite out of the puff. It left a crumbly white mustache on his upper lip.

"You don't know where that's been, Edo," Jon said.

"My shirt's clean. I washed it yesterday."

"Well now it's covered in puff crumb. What other food do you have up there?"

"Just a piece of bread. How long do you think this dinner will last? I don't know if I'll be able to make it."

Arsenault chuckled. "Suck it up, man. You've no right to be less miserable than the rest of us."

Haq snorted. "At least we'll get the leftovers."

Edo finished eating and began bouncing up and down on his arm.

"I think that's my signal to keep moving," Arsenault said.

"Have fun on nursemaid duty," Haq told him.

Arsenault casually made a rude gesture at him, hidden by Edo's bottom, as he walked away. He stuck close to the wall away from the activity at the tables and watched as a group of musicians set up in the center of the room, followed by a line of dancers. The drums felt like they were thudding inside his skull, but Edo was entranced. He sagged against the wall and let Edo watch.

Promethi came to lean beside him. "Adayze has you doing her childcare, does she?"

"I volunteered. I don't mind carrying Edo."

"Well, he is the future, isn't he?"

Arsenault gave Promethi a sharp glance, but Promethi just smiled blandly and turned back to watch the dancers.

"You seem very protective of Lady Adayze."

"It's my job."

"Perhaps a little too protective?"

"If you're suggesting—"

"I'm not suggesting anything. I'm merely noting that a former galleyman might feel an inordinate amount of affection and gratitude for his rescuer. He might, in fact, confuse such feelings for something else. My brother, on the other hand..."

"So, your brother is competing for the Lady Adayze's hand, is that it? That is why you're here?"

Promethi's expression was placid. "The relationships of your betters are none of your business, galleyman. But I wish to point out that although my brother is a benevolent ruler entirely worthy of such affections, *he* does not use them to manipulate his subjects."

What the hell did that mean? "You think Lady Adayze's manipulating me into caring for her son?"

"The other possibility—what does the boy call you? *Ari*? That's your Tulan name, isn't it?—is that you are manipulating her. Perhaps you grew close to your oarmate. Perhaps you have been spending all your time desperately trying to find him. And now you have a clue. I heard a great deal of metal came in on that ship along with the galleymen."

"Because it went to you as well, my lord," Arsenault answered carefully.

"No, actually. Because it went to the Prinze. Renzo's older brother Geoffre—the Householder—wanted it. Presumably as part of his Dakkaran trade. Now if you'll excuse me, I believe it's time for me to prepare for my part of the festivities."

Promethi smiled tightly before he moved off, leaving Arsenault feeling like he'd just been released by a predator playing with his prey.

"Ari, Ari, Ari," Edo chattered happily until Arsenault kicked himself away from the wall and began walking again. Hearing his name in Promethi's mouth had felt like ice on his back.

"I'm going to teach you to say something else, little one," Arsenault murmured. "Maybe just 'ghost' like your uncle."

The drums thudded to a crescendo and then rumbled to a stop. Thank the gods. Maybe his head would stop throbbing. Arsenault squinted through the lights at the dais.

"My lord Ibuu," said a newly familiar voice. "Please allow the Arak to make a small gift to commemorate this occasion. Something we, too, have captured from the pirates. We make you this gift to show that we are united in our pursuit of a strong and just Dakkar, transparent in all our findings. The Eterean carried this in his cargo. It has only just now been transported here and we are eager to show it to our king."

The Ibuu and Neyane both shifted in their places, looking nervous. Arsenault glanced at Adayze and Jon to see how they reacted, but then Promethi clapped his hands and a group of servants walked in bearing a palanquin on their shoulders. A glistening gold silk blanket draped it, hiding something bulky inside. When they set it down on the floor and stepped away, Promethi set his hand down upon it.

"I think you will find it very interesting, my lord Ibuu, as I do. And perhaps a little concerning."

He swept the cover off and everyone in the room leaned forward to catch a glimpse of what was under it.

A sphinx. Glistening silver and crafted from pure tiaannamir.

Even from here Arsenault could tell the sculptor had been a master metalsmith and a talented Fixer. Strands of silver and copper tangled in the sphinx's mane as if it were blowing in the wind, the light shifting on each perfect hair. The sphinx rested so delicately on its haunches it seemed as if it might leap at any moment.

Then it stood up.

Everyone in the room gasped. Chairs clattered. Neyane stepped forward with her hand on her dagger.

Promethi put up his hands.

"I haven't had a chance to study it yet, my lord Ibuu, beyond how to wind its gears to make it move. I've never seen an ancient Eterean artifact this pristine. My conjecture is that perhaps the Lieran merchant was trading these artifacts to rogue Fixers in exchange for magicked guns. The guns were Fixed with runes. Ancient Old Magic."

Promethi stopped and looked directly at Arsenault, and Arsenault heard what he didn't say. Old Magic. *Tulan runes.*

This was not going to go well.

"Bring the Lieran out," Neyane snapped. "We'll question him here, in the presence of this machine."

Two guards entered from the shadowed hallway off the main room, dragging Renzo between them. He was a far sight from the silk-clad courtier who had walked, confident and unwitting, into the Ibuu's court. His hair hung in tangled black ropes past his face and he wore the same undyed linen shirt and trousers Adayze had given Arsenault when he'd been fresh off the *Gannet*.

"Lieran!" the Ibuu called in a commanding voice. "Tell us what this machine is for and why you brought it here."

"Why *I* brought it here?" Renzo looked around wildly, then fell on his knees and bowed his head. "My lord Ibuu," he continued in his crisp, clean Qalfan, "you must believe me when I say I have never set eyes on this machine in my life."

"And how are we to believe this? When you came to us with an illegally Fixed gun bearing runes of northern magic?"

"Lord Promethi tricked me into trading for that gun!"

"And is this all for the trade which your fellow Etereans now possess?" the Ibuu asked. "You threaten to steal our knowledge with your old and corrupted Eterean magic—"

"My lord, no! Subject me to truthtelling, please, I beg you, and you'll See that I'm not lying!"

If Renzo *was* lying, it was a bold move. There were ways to get around Sight—glamours one could cast, ways to control your thoughts to obscure the truth. They were difficult and hardly failsafe, but the margin for error was wide enough to call into question the practice of truthtelling so it wasn't immediately used on all criminals. Truthtelling took its toll on the teller. You could get a head full of another person's life, or even experience it alongside them, without being able to answer the original questions in the first place. Still, it was a damn risky gamble for a man to take if he knew he was lying.

Adayze stood. "I'll do the truthtelling."

Edo made a noise and grabbed at Arsenault's beard. Arsenault bounced him a little. "That's right," he murmured in as gentle a voice as he could muster. "I'm sure your mama will discover the truth."

"No."

Neyane. Arsenault jerked at her voice, as if she'd somehow heard and answered him. His movement unbalanced Edo and the toddler clutched at him with wide eyes.

"I'm going to take care of you," Arsenault told him in a firm, low voice, looking him in the eyes to reassure him. The whole situation was starting to make him uneasy, especially after what Jon had told him about Edo's inheritance and why Renzo thought the snake demon had attacked Adayze. The little boy looked around nervously.

"Ari?" he said. "Dat?"

Arsenault edged slowly backward, toward the big double doors at the end of the hall—too damn far away. "Shh, Edo. It's going to be all right."

"No," Neyane said again. "That is not the job of the Heir. That is a Dagger's task. With your leave, my lord Ibuu..."

"Yes," the Ibuu replied. "Let us have the truth."

It felt like a show. What was Neyane up to? Why didn't she want Adayze to See what Renzo knew?

Before Neyane reached Renzo, the sphinx suddenly took a step. Neyane hesitated and Renzo froze. Slowly it raised its shimmering silver wings and then forced them down in one powerful beat. Renzo stumbled backward, but the sphinx butted his hand with its head like a dog that wanted to be petted.

"G-good boy?" Renzo stuttered.

"What is it doing, Lord Arak?" Neyane said.

"I think perhaps it's seeking out its master."

"No!" Renzo protested.

At that moment, a shimmer moved through the room, a feeling of power.

Claws popped out of the sphinx's paws.

Renzo shoved at it hard with both hands. It tottered backward for a moment, then levered itself up with its front paws and launched itself straight at Neyane. One wing bashed Renzo in the side, knocking him over; he cowered on the floor as Neyane drew her dagger. But the sphinx streaked past her into the crowd.

"EDO!" Adayze shouted over the panicked noise in the room.

Arsenault tucked Edo into his chest and ran.

Edo wailed, high and frightened. Arsenault didn't have the breath to tell the boy it was going to be all right. The wind of the sphinx's wings buffeted him as he careened off tables, chairs, screaming, running people, shoving through them to get to the door.

Claws swiped at his sun-burned shoulder and he barely managed to wrench away, biting off his cry of pain with gritted teeth, slamming a noble in a long silk robe out of the way with his elbow. The sphinx grabbed the man instead. With one powerful jerk of its talons, it tore the man's head half off his shoulders.

Arsenault jumped over a body on the floor and threw himself out the doors.

"Ari, Ari, Ari," Edo wailed. "Ma, ma, MA!"

"We'll see your mama soon," Arsenault panted, kicking the door stop out of first one door and then the other. The doors swung back into the sphinx as it tried to shoot through the gap and sent it tumbling back into the crowd. Screams and high, inhuman shrieking followed him down the stairs and across the courtyard as he ran for the entrance to the royal wing. He didn't know how many people he'd sacrificed to keep Edo safe, including Adayze and Jon, but either of them would have done the same to save Edo and he knew it.

The guards standing outside the royal wing had drawn their swords and looked torn between keeping their discipline and running to help.

"Go," Arsenault gasped with a jerk of his head. "The family needs you."

They left immediately in a clatter of weaponry. Arsenault dashed up the stairs into the building, taking two at a time despite his burning lungs. The sound of splintering wood and the high-pitched shriek of the sphinx pierced the courtyard as it tried to escape the Great Hall. Once inside the tower, he balanced Edo on his arm and slammed the bolt through the lock, then ran up the staircase and down the hallway to Chayma's quarters.

He pounded on her door with his fist. Edo's cries were coming in big, gulping sobs, but it was quiet enough now that he began to calm. Chayma threw the door open.

"What... Arsenault?"

He barely registered her bewildered face. "Keep Edo safe," he said, handing the baby over. Edo squirmed but went into Chayma's arms as she held them up.

"What's happening?"

"Magic. In the Ibuu's hall. Bolt all your doors and windows. Can you create a Sanctuary?"

She transferred Edo to her hip, all business now. "Lay safety spells, you mean? Of course I can."

"Good. Do that on the inside. Weave them around both of you. I'll write them on your door."

"What kind of magic are we talking about, Arsenault? Is a Fixer mounting an attack?"

"Promethi brought a machine. I need to go, Chayma. Keep Edo safe."

Arsenault pushed her inside and yanked the door shut. As soon as the bolt thrust home on the other side, he grabbed his knife and began carving runes on the door as fast as he could. His magic rushed through him into the door, strong and silver. The big Sanctuary rune he wrote in the center gleamed with newly laid metal.

He didn't bother to raise his gates again. The gods wouldn't like it but fuck them. He ran down the hall toward the back staircase.

CHAPTER 50

ARSENAULT

THE COURTYARD HAD BECOME A TABLEAU OF CARNAGE. THE SPHINX had left a trail of ripped and torn human bodies, some dead, others alive and screaming in pain. Limbs, shorn from their bodies, lay in the dirt, flesh shredded and gouged.

The sphinx dipped its head into the stomach of a dead guard, tore out a piece of flesh, then choked the meat down its gullet, birdlike. A circle of defensive magic contained the beast for the moment. The guests who'd run into the courtyard to escape the hall were gone, taking shelter wherever they could. Arsenault hoped Jon had helped Adayze get somewhere safe. He hoped they were both *alive*, period.

Promethi's voice rode the wind urgently. "My king, I knew nothing! It's the Lieran's fault! You saw how it went to him! I didn't know it would run amok like this or I would never have brought it into the Hall! This is evidence, my lord, that we have all been attacked!"

The sphinx raised its head and sniffed the wind, then whirled toward Promethi's voice.

Arsenault looked in the same direction and groaned.

The Ibuu wasn't the only one standing with Promethi, though that would have been bad enough. Adayze stood beside him, holding a spear that had been a wall decoration in the dining hall. Jon was there, too, a cutlass in each hand.

"Where is my son?" Adayze asked in a dangerous voice.

With so much magic writhing around inside him, it was easy for Arsenault to make out the shield around the sphinx; Jon's magic was part of it, as well as Adayze's and Promethi's. "Didn't your Tulan guard have him?" Promethi asked in a strained voice, as if helping maintain the shield took a lot of effort. "Oh, my lady, you don't think he has something to do with this, do you? The runes on the gun, the sphinx —it's the magic of Tule. You said he came in on a ship—"

"You're suggesting *Arsenault* collaborated with the Lieran to steal my child?"

"Why does he always seem to be there when you're attacked?"

That Promethi's a snake, Haq had said, and now Arsenault could see it. But he couldn't worry about Promethi now. While they were concentrating on each other, the sphinx took a quiet, padding step in their direction.

Arsenault pulled a knife from his boot. Holding on to the magic this long without letting it flow out of him felt like trying to wrestle a crocodile. It surged forward into the blade in a scalding rush.

The sphinx hurled itself, snarling, at the magic wall before it, which should have thrown it back—except its talons ripped through the shimmering white curtain at a weak point, right in front of Adayze.

Arsenault hurled his knife at it. The blade threw sparks when it hit the sphinx's flank and sank deep into the automaton's metal flesh. The sphinx snapped its jaws shut just shy of Adayze's face, then roared in pain and fell, rolling on the ground, its great wings sweeping the dirt just as they had made eagle wings in the snow as children. Snarling, it clawed itself upright.

His magic raged out of his control, recognizing the danger before he did. It pounded down on the sphinx with the force of crashing surf, just like the waves that had swamped their ship as it rounded Thunder Cape. The sphinx fell to its knees beneath the onslaught, pink tongue lolling.

The waves kept driving him under, until finally, he dragged himself out of the maelstrom and slammed the floodgates closed.

For a moment, the night whirled around him. He didn't know where he was or who he was. And then he realized he was standing in front of the sphinx with his cutlass outstretched and the sphinx was cowering at his feet like a dog, its wings folded up and trembling.

"You see what these Tulans are capable of?" Promethi said, his voice shaking. "The creature crouches at his feet!"

"Because he brought it down!" Jon said.

"He brought it to *heel*," Promethi said. He shoved his hand into his pocket and pulled out a twisted mass of feathers. "A gift from my ancestors," he said to Adayze. She grabbed it with barely banked anger in her eyes, thrust the spear through it so that it hung at the bottom of the spear point.

The sphinx whined and Arsenault squinted at it.

Why is it still on the ground? If I didn't kill it, why won't it attack?

Promethi stepped up carefully behind the sphinx. "Could anyone else here have brought it to life? He's a Smith. He had your grandson, Lord Ibuu, but where is your grandson now?"

That's not how it was, he wanted to say. But his throat was still locked with the burning magic.

The sphinx curled up, hissing and spitting, much weaker than before. Adayze knocked it on its side with the spear. Then she drove the point with its fetish straight through the sphinx's underbelly.

Gears crunched and screeched. The sphinx yowled and then shuddered as the glisten of life left it and it became again a piece of mute machinery.

She kicked it for emphasis. The impact made a great clang, but the sphinx didn't move.

"Well?" Promethi said. "Now that the thing is dead, why don't you tell us where you put the baby, Arsenault? Or are you holding him hostage so you can get all your fellow galleymen magicians back in ransom? You were all pirates on that ship, weren't you? You weaseled your way into the royal palace just to get close to the family!"

Arsenault opened his mouth to say something angry. But no words came out. His throat wouldn't work. It wasn't just the magic.

Oh no, please.

"What were the crimes listed on his papers, Lord Jonawak? You have them, don't you? The crimes he tried to convince you weren't his?"

"They said he'd committed murder," Jon said angrily, "and when I asked, they said he'd killed his wife. But he said he didn't have a wife on that island, and that's the kind of sensational crime pirates create to—"

All the blood drained from Arsenault's face. He felt so dizzy he thought he would collapse right here, on top of the dead sphinx.

How did the pirates know my true crime?

"Arsenault?" Adayze said with dawning fear.

"Oh, ghost," Jon whispered beside him. "Oh no."

"Where have you taken my grandchild?" the Ibuu demanded.

Arsenault tried to speak again. All that came out were coarse, choking sounds, a wounded protest. He tried to sign the direction, but his hands wouldn't obey him either and while he was still trying,

Neyane backhanded him across the face with the hilt of her knife. Blood erupted from his nose and he fell to his knees in the dirt, gripped by blinding pain.

"Take him to the Ovens," she said, her voice full of spite. "We'll question him there."

But he knew he wouldn't be able to speak there either.

The gods had stolen his voice.

❦

ARSENAULT TREMBLED WITH EXHAUSTION AS JON AND HAQ WALKED him down the dark, stone-strewn path toward the Ovens. His face throbbed from Neyane's blow. On the inside, he was still sore from wrangling that much magic.

"Ghost," Jon whispered. "I don't know what happened to your wife, but you didn't really take my nephew hostage, did you?"

Arsenault gave a quick shake of his head.

"Then why don't you speak?"

Cursing Erelf, he watched his feet. All the response he got for that was Erelf's laughter.

"Ghost, I don't understand. What Promethi said *could* be true and yet—"

"I can't believe you're a traitor," Haq said. His fingers felt like iron bands digging into Arsenault's bicep. "It's bad enough you're a *magician,* but if you tricked us about where your loyalty lay, you're damn good at it."

"Is it to free your friend?" Jon asked. "You would take Edo hostage—"

Arsenault finally forced out a wounded noise and both Haq and Jon stopped walking and stared at him. He couldn't see Jon's expression in the darkness and Haq's was only marginally more evident.

"The magic...made you unable to speak?" Jon said.

It was as good an explanation as any. He nodded.

"Haq. Get me paper and a quill. Water and a rag, too."

Haq let his breath out between his teeth, but he dropped his hand from Arsenault's arm and turned back on the path, taking it at a fast jog. Arsenault sagged in gratitude.

"I've no choice but to leave you in the Ovens," Jon said. "Adayze will go insane if she can't find Edo soon, and Neyane has given orders I can't contradict. Lately I have heard some things about Neyane, but —Arsenault—you *looked* like you were guilty."

Would Neyane use this as an excuse to get rid of him? He couldn't deny the crime listed on his papers because it was true. And yet it was also not true, because the pirates would have written down anything to keep him on the galley or sell his service for coin. If only he was allowed to explain himself.

Arsenault turned toward Jon, hoping Jon saw the pleading on his face.

"Right," Jon sighed. "Come on."

Jon put him in a hut on the edge of the cliff, where all he could hear was the pounding surf on the rocks below. Blood and snot continued to drip down his throat and the heat and humidity pent-up in the little mudbrick building made him feel like he would suffocate. Jon snapped the manacle shut around his ankle and his leg immediately lit up with excruciating pain—of course the shackles were worked to prevent him using his Talent. It set up an involuntary panic inside him as the magic realized it was just as trapped as he was.

It seemed an age before Haq returned with a bag of supplies—everything Jon had requested, plus a candle.

Jon lit it, then wet the rag with water from the skin and handed it to Arsenault to wipe his face. His nose was tender, but the tepid water was a relief.

When he put the rag down, Jon had laid out paper, quill, and ink on the bench. He spent an anxious moment realizing he didn't know how to write in Dakkaran and, in pain and exhausted, he was having trouble recalling how to write in Qalfan. Then he remembered Jon knew Eter and Vençalan too. Except, what would Neyane think if he wrote in *ancient Eter?* Shakily, he dipped the quill into the ink and rested the tip on the paper. He'd barely made a stroke when his hand seized up.

His curse came out muffled and wordless through clenched teeth as he dropped the quill. Ink splattered the paper.

"Ghost?" Jon said in a worried tone.

He tried again. Unbearable pain lanced through his hand, but in shaky letters he managed to spell, *CHAYMA*.

Jon rocked back on his heels with a relieved sigh.

He decided to try for one more thing and began writing, *PRO*

But the gods were done playing with him. Blackness crept in from the edges of his vision. He fought it, but it rolled him over and he sank like a stone.

CHAPTER 51

ARSENAULT

"ARSENAULT!"

He gasped and sat up. Thin black shapes surrounded him like paper dolls cut out of the night. Their limbs fluttered in the sluggish breeze and their needle-like teeth gleamed in the moonlight.

Adayze stood in the doorway, framed by silver light.

"Don't move," she said. "The ghosts have sniffed you out."

"I see that," he rasped. He fought down the urge to press himself against the wall.

"Now you can talk?"

"The damage is done, I guess."

"I wish for once you would speak straight, Arsenault." She slowly slid her hand into a bag she wore over her shoulder. Arsenault shifted and the wraiths shivered closer, looming out of the darkness with their mouths gaping.

"Stay still," Adayze hissed.

He did his best. It wouldn't be a good way to die, eaten by ghosts.

Adayze took her hand out of the bag. She clutched something in her fist as she shuffled forward in the straw. One of the ghosts stretched out a long, spindly arm toward her, swiping at her with its claws. Arsenault kicked it away from her, but it whirled, screeching, and sliced through the leg of his trousers into the skin of his calf. Searing cold bit deep into his bones, like the nails of a coffin. The copper scent of his own blood suddenly overwhelmed him.

"Dammit, Arsenault, I told you to be still!" Adayze threw whatever she was holding into the middle of the group of ghosts.

What in all the hells is that? he thought, right before it exploded with light.

The ghosts raised filmy hands to the blank spaces where their eyes should have been, wailed and writhed. By all the gods, that was the most horrible sound he had ever heard. One grabbed at his arm and he jerked backward, cursing.

"This is the land of my ancestors!" Adayze said in a loud, commanding voice. "You are without family and you will not defile mine!"

He's not yoursss

The voices of the ghosts cut through his bones like a bitter wind.

"He's not yours either! No family came to claim you and now it is only fair for you to wander. Your time to live righteously has passed and you wasted it. Go back to the black realms and bother us no more!"

But it's so lonely

So cold

We seek warmth

A family to see us to the beyond

"I've been cut off from my family," Arsenault said in a hoarse voice. "I have no family anymore."

But there's something else in you, something we could keep going, something warm, some tasty meat...

A ghost gnashed its teeth at his ankle. He jerked it back, not quite in time; the thing's incisors sliced cleanly through the leather of his boot and sank into his foot. He hissed in pain and shoved himself down the wall, but there wasn't anywhere to go. This was going to be a hell of a way to die. Literally eaten. How in all the hells would he come back after that?

Adayze cursed. "*I* claim him, demons. Get out of my way."

She shoved through the black mass surrounding him and slashed his hand with her long, curved knife.

He cried out. It was pain upon pain, but he hadn't expected *this* blow and it startled him. He curled his hand up in reflex. Blood welled from the wound and dripped onto the straw.

The ghosts howled, showing their fangs.

Adayze whipped the blade through them and then drew it, fast, across her own palm.

"He's B'ara now, demons. Go back where you came from or face the wrath of my ancestors."

The ghosts began to keen, pulling at non-existent hair, the non-existent flesh of their faces, the clothes they remembered from being human. Their claw-like fingers shredded the blackness that created them. The breeze shivering in the open doorway blew them away like so many old leaves.

Arsenault sat against the wall for a moment, breathing hard and watching the blood drip off his thumb and onto his thigh.

"So..." he said shakily. "Does this mean you forgive me?"

⬥

ADAYZE WRAPPED HIS HAND WITH A STRIP OF SILK SHE'D RIPPED from the skirt of her dress. An identical bandage was tied around her own hand. Then she handed him a skin of water.

He drank gratefully. "I knew the sphinx was after Edo. I took him to Chayma first." He stopped, but his throat didn't feel any different. He took another drink of tepid water and went on. "Then I came back for the sphinx. I didn't wake it."

"If it wasn't you, who was it? Renzo di Prinze?"

"I don't think so. I think Renzo was telling the truth. I don't have hard evidence, but I think it must have been Promethi."

Adayze pushed herself up off her knee and sat on the bench on the opposite wall, adjusting her skirt. Her gold winked in the moonlight. "I can't See into him to tell if he's lying or not. The fetish he gave me to kill the beast was magic made by someone else. A conjure woman probably. Arak. One of his relatives."

"Did you use your Sight on me? Has Neyane done the truthtelling for Renzo?"

Adayze frowned in a troubled way. "You are all fog. I came as soon as I could, while everyone was still combing the grounds for Edo. I was going to have it out of you or die trying. Why wouldn't you speak?"

He couldn't tell her about the gods without getting in more trouble and he noticed she didn't say anything about Renzo. Maybe Renzo had already been executed. "The magic," he settled on.

"Your wife..."

"Anything I say will sound ridiculous. But now you know why I'm cursed. I don't know how the pirates knew, it happened so long ago... It was not the crime that put me on that ship. Promethi was just trying to get rid of me."

She watched him for a moment. He was afraid to look at her to find out how she felt about what he'd just said. He took another drink instead.

"Neyane didn't want to give you the benefit of the doubt," she said. "She told me I had created a problem when I pulled you off that boat and now I was harvesting the fruit of my actions. She told me I should leave the pirates to my Dagger."

"I'm not supposed to use my magic. That's also part of the curse. The gods have left me alone for a while, but it always comes back to roost at the worst time. Where is Edo now? Is he safe?"

"He's still with Chayma in her quarters." Adayze put a trembling hand to her forehead. "This never would have happened if I'd left him in the nursery."

"Adayze." He pushed himself up and clanked over to sit next to her on the bench.

She looked up at him in surprise. He tried to ignore the way his thigh lay along hers as he sat down.

"You don't know if that would have made a difference."

"People *died* because I brought my child to that banquet." Her voice was quiet, but her eyes shone.

Please all the gods, Adayze, don't start crying.

"Promethi would have found another way. And unless you had thought to put a contingent of guard in the nursery, there would have been no one to protect Edo there."

"But, Arsenault, what do I do? I can't keep him safe with me, I can't keep him safe away from me, Isa is gone and probably dead, and my people are dying because of my decisions. What do I *do*?"

She choked on the final words, put her face in her hands, and began to cry.

Oh, damn.

Arsenault sat watching her for a moment, paralyzed with the desire to hold her, the fear of letting her into his arms, and the fear that she would reject him if he did. Finally, he couldn't take it anymore. "Adayze," he said and reached out for her.

She sank against him and turned her face into his chest, gripping his shirt where the sphinx had torn through it on his shoulder. He pressed his cheek against her hair as he let her cry, holding her tight.

"You probably think I'm weak," she said, her voice muffled by his shirt.

"You killed that sphinx and faced down a circle of carnivorous ghosts. Of course I don't think you're weak."

"Papa always said I was too soft. That it was good I'd have Jon to do the hard things. That's what Neyane is accusing me of. Being soft."

Arsenault shifted uncomfortably. "I don't know about Neyane." Something didn't add up there, but he wasn't sure he could sort it either. "Jon is only responsible for himself and carrying out your wishes. No one will blame him for anything because all he seems to be is a soldier in your guard. Adayze. Edo is your son. A ruler's not an automaton. Not like that sphinx, just a collection of metal and gears."

Adayze sat up, swiping at the tears. "Sometimes I get so angry at Isa. How could he have done this to me? Gotten me with child and then gone back out to sea. He's probably at the bottom of the ocean right now, the way everybody says, and I should choose some of those suitors—more than one. I don't know if I can keep on believing in him..."

Arsenault brushed away the sticky tracks of tears on her cheek with his thumb. She tilted her head back to look up at him.

"You're not alone," he said. "You have Jon, your family—"

"That is *not* the same."

His gaze caught on hers and his breath lodged in his throat.

If she moves...

But she didn't move. His hand rested against her cheek and she was still looking up at him. In the dark, there was nothing but the heat of her in his arms and the yearning gleam the thin trickle of moonlight picked out in her eyes—the need for understanding, a connection, the touch of a man who would treat her not as the Heir, but as a woman. The line of her lips softened. And then she moved her hand slowly over his chest, and he dipped his head and kissed her.

It was barely a brush of the lips—soft, hesitant, warm. But then she made a small sound and tightened her hands into fists on his shirt and there was no going back. He slid his hand over her hip to pull her even closer, until she was crushed against him. One kiss turned into more until he couldn't even think. He tasted the salt of her tears, the citrus tang of her lotion as he lingered on the soft skin of her neck. He leaned her back on the bench and she shoved her hands inside his shirt, lighting a fire everywhere she touched. He kissed her shoulder, her collarbone...

She scooted backward with a gasp, out from under him.

"Oh," she said, covering her mouth as she scrambled up off the bench. "Oh."

"Adayze," he said, trying to follow her, his voice rough with desire.

But the chain around his ankle brought him up short with a loud clank.

"Arsenault," she said. "I'm *sorry*."

Then she whirled and ran out the door.

◈

HE STOOD IN THE SMALL, DARK HUT, BREATHING RAGGEDLY, TRYING to regain control of his traitorous body. His hands shook. It hurt physically, but the ache in his heart was worse.

With a cry that felt like it was dragged out of him, he kicked the bench. He kicked it again and again, until the pain cut through the fog of his self-contempt.

Until Adayze accepted that her husband was dead, he was still alive...*and she was still married to him*.

"Fucking balls and ashes," he muttered and sat down against the wall, breathing hard, sweat dripping from his forehead. *What a fucking hypocrite*.

He drew his knees up, draped his arms over them, and rested his head on the circle they made. Life after life and he kept being drawn into all the same dramas, even as he failed himself and everyone around him in ever new and changing ways.

Hello, brother.

The voice that whispered in the darkness was too familiar, but it might also have been a sigh of the wind, ushered in by his guilt. Arsenault raised his head.

No Dakkaran ghosts trying to eat him this time. Just his murdered brother, Tavi, squatting in the straw, grinning. *Nice to see you again, Ari*.

"You've been watching me, have you?"

Tavi laughed. Being a ghost hadn't changed him, just given his mouth a crueler twist and made his eyes look dead. When they were children, people had said they looked like twins, but he hoped he'd never looked like this Tavi, the bloody rip in his white shirt flapping open in the breeze, his green eyes the color of a cold sea, the kind that could swamp a boat and send a man straight to the bottom.

So, they put you out here with the ghosts, did they?

"The gods wouldn't let me defend myself."

You violated your sentence. And for a married woman.

"I was protecting her child. I haven't done anything inappropriate."

Gods, Ari, you always were so stiff. You haven't fucked her yet, but you want to. Enough that you came back when you really should have just kept running.

"There was a time you weren't this much of a son of a bitch. Leave me alone, Tavi."

You'd rather I left you to the other ghosts? They have a taste for meat.

"Are you keeping the ghosts away, or are you tormenting me? What step and fetch are you doing for Erelf this time?"

Tavi's face darkened. *I'm not his dog.*

"You always were. You still are. Even in death."

You can insult me as much as you like, brother, but who got the spoils?

"Sella wasn't a prize to be won," Arsenault growled, pulling at the manacle like a chained beast. It clanked against the floor of the hut, and the magical bindings burned the skin of his ankle like a brand. He gritted his teeth and tried to stop moving.

Tavi's mouth twisted up into that mirror image of his own smile, except, like a mirror, it was reversed, cynical and cruel. *You're right. The choice was hers. And she chose me.*

Unable to help himself, he took a swipe at his brother, hoping to drive him away. Tavi shifted casually, standing well out of reach as the magical protections seared Arsenault's leg again.

Tavi clicked his tongue in disapproval. *And you say I'm the dog. Ari. I came to warn you.*

Arsenault fought to catch his breath. "You-you expect me to believe that?"

No, of course not. Thought you'd mellow over the course of hundreds of years, but you're still as pigheaded as a block of granite.

Arsenault tipped his head against the wall and closed his eyes. Maybe Tavi would take a hint. "Mixing your metaphors?"

Go ahead, make fun of me. What's changed? Forgiving me would go a long way toward earning your redemption, you know.

"Tavi. You hate me. I know you do, even after all this time. Why would you warn me of anything? We both know there's nothing I can do to redeem myself."

Even Tavi grew quiet at that. It was only truth. They were both trapped by Erelf's hatred.

The gods are growing restless, Tavi said finally. *You've had some quiet spells and so have they.*

Arsenault opened his eyes and regarded Tavi uneasily. "It's not been quiet for me for a good year now. The gods aren't affected by my lives, except to be angry at me for making them work when I die."

They've found ways to use us, though, haven't they? Here I am playing the messenger, and there you are...

"Playing the what? The dupe?"

Tavi chuckled. *You make a good dupe. But the magic grows restless, too.*

"What do you mean? Like a storm brewing? Didn't Calden say—"

Speaking of metaphors, I don't know that Calden quite got it. He thought of everything as water because that's what he had a Talent for. But after you've entered the realm of magic like I have, Ari, you begin to realize how wrong he was.

"But it does feel like water, Tavi. Or...molten metal. It flows..."

You're just regurgitating the same old boring knowledge everybody does. Can't you feel it tugging at you when you use it? Would it be so hard to consider that it might have a soul?

"Does it?"

You'll have to figure that out for yourself. All I'm saying is that it's on the move and the gods don't like it. It makes them nervous. If it slips out of their control... What do you think would happen if the magic escaped its bonds and claimed a mind of its own? How do you think that might affect, say, Tekus? Or other gods that have perhaps been assumed to be more...peripheral?

This echoed what Ekyra had told him about the gods making plots and shifting alliances too neatly. "Are you saying that Erelf—"

You didn't hear anything from me, brother. It's all idle speculation, isn't it?

"But why would you tell me anything?"

It's not much of a game unless your opponent knows he's playing. What's the fun in taking a pawn?

CHAPTER 52

MIKELO

ABANDONED VILLAGE, PRESENT

"THAT ALIENTE HARLOT IS STILL CAUSING TROUBLE, ISN'T SHE?"

Mikelo huddled by the wall, wishing Arsenault had brought him along. Magic nosed around him, poking at the fear that rose so close to the surface lately, like a boil always ready to burst. It didn't surprise him to see Geoffre amid this magical disaster, but if he was so bloody Talented, why couldn't he stop being haunted by his uncle?

Concentrate on what you see, not what you feel.

By that logic, his fear was an illusion but Geoffre was real.

Geoffre looked smug as he surveyed the area. "So the poets were playing a joke on us. I always thought the Legacy of Attrasca was a physical treasure. Who would have thought it was actually a pocket of raw, trapped magic? Was Attrasca trying to protect it or just hoarding it, do you think?"

"Maybe Attrasca was trying to protect us from a magical apocalypse," Mikelo muttered.

"He speaks! And has an interesting opinion. Thank you for finally acknowledging my existence, Mikelo. After all I've given you, it seems like the least you could do. I could have left you to waste away in Dakkar."

Mikelo gritted his teeth. "Go. Away."

"You could find out what's really going on, instead of sitting here by this wall being useless."

Mikelo took a breath. *Fucking goatherder*, he told himself, trying to stand in for Kyrra. *Why do you let him get under your skin like this?* But he had a point. Mikelo squinted into the fog. Arsenault was nowhere to be found. That bothered him.

"Manipulate your Sight, Mikelo. *See* what's really happening."

That sounds like a really bad idea. But he did feel useless, sitting here doing nothing, as if Arsenault needed to keep him out of the way. He was tired of being an afterthought. An object competent men felt they needed to protect. Or worse, to use. Like some strange magical artifact.

A small voice in the back of his mind protested that maybe *this* was the sort of thinking Arsenault had warned him about, but it was too late; he was already in motion, crawling to the edge of a pit, looking down. The glossy liquid shivering inside threw his reflection back at him.

He Saw himself older. A little gray mixed into his blond hair, crowsfeet stamped at the corners of eyes he didn't recognize. They were blue-green like his, but with an edge to them, as if he'd grown cynical or even...cruel. He reminded himself uneasily of Geoffre. Geoffre's eyes had never been a free and open blue like the sky or warm like silk; something cold had always lurked in their depths. Mikelo had wanted to believe in his uncle's kindness, so he'd just stopped looking at his eyes.

Strangely, this older Mikelo who looked like Geoffre was wearing burgundy. Like...

Attrasca.

The burgundy cloak pooled behind him as he walked stately halls, followed by servants carrying trays of food. He supposed they were servants; he didn't know what to call them. Automatons and magical creatures, beings out of old stories. Dryads with long green hair and woody fingers, a metal satyr with shining silver hooves and an immaculately crafted beard, a nymph in a diaphanous gown who offered him a perfectly cut crystal goblet of deep red wine.

Were they servants or were they his creatures, brought to life by his magic?

Shaken, Mikelo watched as his older self stopped at a set of double doors intricately carved with a scene of feasting gods in a forest. A goddess hovered above a hammer-wielding smith who looked suspiciously like Arsenault, her wings outstretched as if to protect him...

Older Mikelo covered the smith with his hand and shoved the door open. He strode into his chambers, where a man in a Prinze blue uniform waited for him. The man's golden-brown hair was tied back in a soldier's queue with a blue velvet ribbon. When he turned, Mikelo gave a start.

Silva?

Silva looked at him for a moment, almost as if he were seeing through the reflective surface to the younger Mikelo outside the pit.

Mikelo, Silva said earnestly, *you need to wake up. This is not who you are.*

But everyone loves me, his older self said. *I keep the peace. We have all the food we can eat. I've worked so hard for this. Don't I deserve thanks?*

Silva motioned to the open window. *Come here, Mikelo. Come and see what it is you've done.*

Mikelo moved next to him, still clutching the half-drunk glass of wine that looked like a goblet of blood. Older Silva had grown out of his youthful beauty into something more mature, not beauty exactly but *complexity,* the way a fine wine grew deeper with age. He was still lean, but his shoulders had broadened, his features coarsened with experience but only in a way that made him look as if he ought to be painted in a portrait, especially with the feather of gray at his temples. His eyes were the same intense, dark blue, troubled as he looked out the window.

Below them, soldiers loaded a ragged group of kinless onto a canal boat, while a line of silver automata dogs patrolled the watching crowd, keeping it in line as if the people were sheep. *Is this what people will thank you for?* Silva asked.

I'm giving them work! I would have been grateful for a job that paid in bed and board when I was a boy. I know what it's like not to eat. And the machines mean soldiers don't have to do this job. What does anyone have to complain about?

You're sending them off to underworld mines to dig up poisoned magic and the corpses of old gods, to die when they're infected. Does it matter that they have food if they're not free to refuse to die for you? You've grown entitled and gluttonous. You're not the man I knew when we were young.

The older Mikelo angrily drank the rest of his wine, then threw the glass aside. It shattered in a pile of crimson-tinged shards on the marble floor. *What would you know? You'll always be a shepherd—no, a whore. You'll always be a whore, just like my mother. You don't understand how complicated it is to rule!*

Silva looked at him mournfully. *You're right. That's why I'm leaving.* He unwrapped the blue armband from his bicep and laid it on the windowsill. *Good-bye, Mikelo.*

You don't leave until I say you leave! I'm the Emperor! No one is allowed to leave unless I give them permission!

He grabbed Silva's shoulder, tried to spin him around, but Silva struggled, and there was an open window—Mikelo tried to catch him, but there was so much *air.*

You can't leave me

You can't leave me

Mikelo jerked back with a cry, his heart tripping with panic. He was leaning too far over the pit, his arm outstretched as if he could reach through the viscous black tar into his dream to pull the older image of Silva back into the window. To tell him he would never do those things, to erase the image of Silva's body hitting the stones of the piling down below...

"Gods." He thrust himself back from the edge and wiped cold sweat from his brow with his sleeve.

The mirror was showing him yet another facet of the darkness that lurked inside. *Why* did he keep listening to Geoffre? Was it just to prove Geoffre wrong? Or did the cord of their shared history still bind them together, not with love but betrayal? He wanted to cut it, but it kept reeling him back.

He took a deep breath, stretched his foot to feel where it was, and looked around for Arsenault. The fog had rolled in thick on the other side of the wall. Time seemed distorted, even muffled...

He was thinking strange thoughts. This was exactly what Arsenault had warned him about. He should follow Arsenault anyway. He turned back to the wall and was brought up short by the sight of a cloaked figure standing in the woods, watching.

Not Kyrra.

Shit.

He stood and the figure whirled and ran into the trees. Cursing, he ran after them.

He wished he were armed, and he wished he dared use his magic. He ran as hard as he could, crashing up the path, jumping over pits and fissures, breath burning in his lungs. His only advantage was that he sort of knew where he was going. The cloaked figure sloshed through a black puddle and cried out in fear.

"Take your boot off!" he shouted, remembering too late that he probably wasn't supposed to be helping, but the cry had sounded...

Like a woman. The realization hit at the same time he tackled her onto the ground and saw her frightened face. Tiresian beads stung his cheek as her braids swung out of the hood and hit him. Her boot steamed as the acid—or whatever it was—ate its way through the leather. He let her go and wrestled her boot off, then pitched it down the slope.

"My boot!" she exclaimed.

"You're better off without it. Who are you? It's not safe here."

Her eyes narrowed. "You're Mikelo di Prinze, aren't you?"

"How do you know that?"

"I've seen you around before. I need to talk to Jon Barra."

It made sense that she worked for Jon, but he was still wary. "I can take you to him, but it's not a good time. Especially if you won't tell me your name."

"My name is Junei. I have a lot of information for Jon and a message from Lobardin."

"Lobardin! How do you—"

She shrugged and stood, wrinkling her nose as she wiggled her toes in their wool socks against the wet ground. "You know this is worse than having a boot with a hole in it."

"Maybe I overreacted. But the magic is desperate and evil. You want to get away from it. I'm...I'm helping—" Dammit, should he say who he was helping or not?

Junei's next words affirmed his decision to stutter on names. "Is Andris with Jon? Lobardin meant his message for both of them. He wants to meet, if the idiot managed to get out of the lodge in time." She looked a little angry, as if Lobardin *not* being able to escape the lodge would be a personal insult. "Lobardin wants to introduce Jon to somebody. I suppose Jon is supporting you in the fight for the Chair?"

"I, uh, I think you have me at a disadvantage, Junei. When we get back to the farmhouse, we can talk, but right now you should stay here because I need to help Andris. He's down there."

"In all that fog? What is he doing?"

A branch crashed not far away, and voices suddenly carried over the rise. "My boys, Jon! Where are they? They're not where I left them! I sent a letter to you and—"

Miranda? Jon, Silva, and Miranda topped the rise, and Junei sighed. "I see she found him before I could tell him."

"We'll find your boys, Miranda," Jon said. His face was drawn tight, as worried as Mikelo had ever seen him. "Where is Andris, Mikelo? Did you find..."

Even Jon was using fake names again. Jon's attitude increased his own uneasiness tenfold.

"No," Mikelo answered quickly. "And I should be down there, in case. I thought Junei was a gavaro spying on us."

"She is a spy," Jon agreed. "But I hope she's not spying on us. Come on then. Junei, you stay here with Miranda." Miranda looked like she was going to come out of her skin, but Jon didn't seem happy with her either. Both he and Miranda looked like they wanted to hurl daggers at each other.

"I need to look for my boys," Miranda said.

"You're the one who took an unnecessary risk!" Jon exploded. "Working for Cassis? Junei was my spy, not you!"

"And everyone in that army knew Junei worked for you, didn't they? Captain Lobardin certainly did!"

Captain Lobardin?

Junei huffed and crossed her arms. "What we do on our own time is our business."

"You're sleeping with him, Junei?" Jon said with astonishment. "You know what that man is like."

"I do know what he's like, but he trusts me enough to use me as a liaison."

"So, you see," Miranda said, her voice tight and shaking with barely controlled fury, "*I* was your spy. I was the one giving you all the information. No one ever suspects the woman who does the laundry, they never even *see* her. I welcomed you all into my house, helped you heal—"

Jon's voice hardened, which didn't seem like what needed to happen at this point, but what did Mikelo know about relationships? "Thank you. For the information and for the house. I promise you, Miranda, I will find your boys. We can't jump to conclusions. If there was no sign of a struggle, maybe they left on their own. They're boys."

Miranda's eyes snapped. "And they've grown up in war. They know how dangerous the forest and road can be. Do you think I'd leave them without teaching them to take care of themselves? They know what they're part of. They know they're carrying on their father's legacy!"

"And they won't be boys forever. They've had to grow up too fast and maybe they decided this was a time to act like men." Jon put his hand up to stop Miranda's objections. "No, I know. It might have been a foolish decision. But huddling in a house being frightened can take its toll."

Mikelo winced before he could help himself. Was that what he had been doing? He'd even started avoiding the sheen of coffee in his coffee cup because he didn't want to see a reflection in it.

Mikelo, you need to wake up. This is not who you are.

"Mikelo, Silva," Jon said. "With me."

Mikelo looked up nervously at Silva. It felt strange seeing him after the mirror vision. Silva eyed him curiously as Jon strode far ahead of them. "What's wrong, Mikelo?" he murmured.

"Nothing, I—"

"You're a bad liar. What's going on? I set off like Jon wanted me to and halfway back to the house the earth split in half. And a mist came out of it..." He shuddered. "Jon ran up and dragged me away, then we found Miranda on the road. Her horse had stepped in a pit...Jon had to put it out of its misery. Where's Kyrra?"

"I don't know, but—"

Suddenly there was an explosion. Not the earth splitting with magic.

The unmistakable sound of gunpowder.

CHAPTER 53

ARSENAULT

"Kyrra!"

Nothing answered, except more tearing earth. A chasm ripped open right in front of him and he jumped, teetering on the crumbling edge with that hot and hateful substance bubbling right beneath his heels. Not lava, which he might have expected if Cassis had exploded a few kegs of gunpowder in a hidden vent. This felt like a passage had been opened to the underworld, like a chorus of voices echoing in the fathomless blackness, infinitely in pain and yet infinitely familiar...as if every fear and regret he'd ever felt at the end—so godsdamned *many* of them—were crying out to him. It felt like death, but not death in a general sense. *His* deaths, specifically.

He stumbled back from the abyss, shaken. Steaming pits had turned the courtyard into a maze. Mist curled from them in tentacles and charred the landscape everywhere it touched.

But the chimney of the forge was cloaked in a different haze.

What the hells, is that smoke?

Dammit, he should have paid more attention to Kyrra's Sight the day he'd discovered the leak in the roof and Kyrra had stared into the drizzly sky and asked, *Is that smoke?* But how could he have predicted *this* nightmare?

It *was* smoke. Somebody was in the forge.

He pushed his knife back into its boot sheath and pulled his sword instead. All the runes lit up, shining bright white in the mist. He walked carefully toward the forge, testing each square of ground before he stepped onto it. He cautiously tried opening himself to his magic, but the magic was such a swirling, burning mess it would be dangerous to use it. More mist brushed his arm—

He lay beneath the dirt. Mouth and nose full of crumbly earth, colder than he had ever been, colder than he thought it possible to be—

Arsenault jerked his arm back with a cry. Frost coated his sleeve, burning a black gash through the fabric as it melted. He shook off the remainder and tried to slow his panicked breathing. *Focus on facts.* Somebody had built a fire in the forge—for protection?

He ran the last few yards and threw himself at the door as a long finger of mist slid by him. The magic had fouled the runes he'd laid around the building to keep the dragon limb safe; everything was a mass of confusion. He cleared them away with a swipe of his hand, held his sword at guard, and shoved the door open with his other arm.

A person on the other side surged forward to meet him. A brief flash of snarled yellow hair and the flap of a brown cloak, and then his sword clanged down against the head of a hammer, right under his chin. The person cursed and dropped the hammer, precariously close to his foot. Startled, pained blue eyes looked up at him.

"Kyrra!" he exclaimed and slammed his sword back into its scabbard.

"Finally," Kyrra breathed.

He grabbed her with both hands and kissed her, joyful with relief.

She pulled away too soon with a crooked, embarrassed hook to her mouth. "I was wondering what kept you."

"You took a fall?" He gingerly touched the scrape marring her cheek. She was a mess. Leaves and sticks tangled in her hair; dirt smeared over her jaw.

"I'm all right. But I'm not the only one here."

He raised his head. Two boys huddled near the hearth. *Fillipo, Hani*, his startled brain registered, and then—

"Fucking gods," he swore. "The dragon!"

The gratitude in Kyrra's eyes snapped to anger in a heartbeat. "You told me you got rid of it."

He'd known he was putting it off too long. That he was flirting with disaster. But if he'd just had a little more time to discover what was at the dragon's heart...

"I wanted to make sure it was safe to put in your arm. It was the only source of tiaannamir I had, but there was something about it... Fuck. Kyrra. It's all my fault."

"I'm not angry at you for not getting rid of it. I'm angry you lied to me about what you did with it. You should have told me. It should be different than it was."

"What should be different?"

She hit him on the chest with her closed fist. "You! You should be different. We should be different. You should trust me!"

"I trust you fine. Everything I found, I wrote down for you! I don't —I don't—"

I don't trust myself. I was ashamed that I still wanted to see what I Saw in the metal. That I still wanted to look for Sella after all these years.

Gods. There wasn't time to break this down. He'd have to explain later. He *would* explain later. "I didn't trust the magic," he finished lamely. "I should have just buried the damn thing, like Jon said."

Some of the anger leaked away from her expression, leaving her looking conflicted. She turned to watch the dragon over her shoulder. It was damn disconcerting seeing the ghost of a dragon hunched atop his workbench. Silver mist, golden eyes. Watching. Stretching out its claws like a cat and adjusting its wings.

"I can't tell if it's dangerous or not," Kyrra said slowly. "We've been sitting by the fire, just in case."

Arsenault looked around the room for the first time. "My shelves," he said helplessly.

She flashed him a guilty glance. "We had to chase off the mist."

"No, of course. It was silly of me to think of it as my workshop anyway." He picked up a piece of paper lying on the floor. His sketch of their marriage bed. He'd found a seasoned piece of linden, started carving... He looked around for it wildly. Thankfully it was still propped against the wall where he'd left it. It was just a piece of wood. He'd rather Kyrra used it to keep her and the boys safe; he could always start over again on a new piece. But still.

He folded the paper carefully and slid it inside his tunic, aware the dragon was watching his every move.

"How long do we have to stay here, ser?" Fillipo asked.

"I have no idea," Arsenault replied. "I left Mikelo out there, but your idea of warding off the mist with the fire was good. We should get Mikelo in here, not the other way round."

"But the dragon," Hani said.

"Mmmm." Arsenault eyed it. "It's not a real dragon, is it? Just a memory of a dragon. An illusion, like a phantom limb. Everything was so tangled in the metal, I couldn't make out where it came from, what it had absorbed, just that—"

He bit down on what he'd been going to say.

"What, Arsenault?" Kyrra sounded frustrated.

"It shared a lot of memories with me," he admitted. "However it came to be underneath the Aliente lodge, it had once seen Tule. I'm afraid to See into it now, though. I don't want to set it off."

"So, it's not a friendly dragon," Hani said. "It's one of the dangerous kind?"

"We were hoping," Fillipo added, "that since it hadn't attacked…"

"And it seems rather small…"

As if it understood, the dragon uncurled. It raised its long, sinuous neck higher and higher until it smashed its head along the ceiling and turned to look at them backwards, coiling like a serpent. It wasn't small at all.

It stretched one wing toward them. Mist swirled dangerously close.

Arsenault grabbed Kyrra and yanked them both closer to the fire. All four of them were wedged into a small corner of the room now while the ghost-dragon grew to fill most of the space.

"It's going to smother us," Hani said.

"Close your eyes," Arsenault said quickly. "All of you. It's growing on fear. If you control your fear—"

"Will that dispel it?" Kyrra asked. "I have a theory…"

Arsenault put his hand on Hani's shoulder and the boy shakily fought his eyes closed. His muscles were still strung taut, but at least the dragon ceased to grow. Now maybe it was just feeding on his uncertainty and Kyrra's.

"What kind of theory?" he asked, keeping an eye on the dragon.

"My theory is that the gods—the new gods—abused the magic somehow. Poisoned it. Then they shackled it under their control, like a slave. Attrasca tried to free it, but it was too late and the magic we've been handed is traumatized. Ires was supposed to be its defender, but in defending it, he must have done something monstrous. And now, the collapse of the lodge has let out *something*, magic that's been trapped for gods know how long, and it's frightened and hateful and maybe it even wants revenge."

"Revenge," Arsenault repeated. "Who does it want revenge on?"

"If my theory is correct, then I would assume it doesn't care. It just wants to vent its fear as it runs away."

"*It*, we always say," Arsenault muttered.

"*Them*, I think," Kyrra said. "There are a lot of voices."

Everything she said made sense. And yet, his memories, his thoughts, had always been so fragmented he'd never put it together.

He *should* have put it together. Maybe he had at one point, but Erelf—

The dragon growled, deep in its throat, and took a step with the tiaannamir claw. It clinked against a piece of metal embedded in the floor. Arsenault drew Kyrra and the boys further against the wall. Hani made a frightened whimper in his throat, then swallowed and bobbed his head.

"I'm not afraid," he said. "I'm not afraid, I'm not afraid..."

"Good lad," Arsenault murmured and squeezed his shoulder. He caught Kyrra's gaze over the boys' heads.

"I'll bait it," she said. "And you can get the boys out."

"That's a terrible plan."

"Do you have a better one?"

"*I'll* bait it and *you* get the boys out."

"That's hardly—Arsenault!"

He started moving as soon as she began to speak, shifting to give himself space to draw his sword. It was close quarters, but his knives wouldn't be as effective against magic. The firelight edged the blade with a bloody glow. "Dragon," he said softly. "Why don't you tell me where you come from, why you're here?"

The dragon drew its neck back to follow him with its gaze. He moved closer to the door.

"Boys," Kyrra said, voice tense. "Get ready to run. Fillipo, we need the gun."

Damn, he'd forgotten the gun. And Fillipo had it with him?

"What are you planning, Kyrra?" he asked in a quiet, calm voice as he took another sidestep to the door.

"At least bring the powder. Light a taper. An explosion ought to dispel the ghost, shouldn't it?"

"It doesn't have a body."

"But it's made of *mist*, and we can burn that away."

"All right, yes. But don't blow me up. I don't know if I'll come back."

He'd meant it as a joke. But darting a glance at Kyrra, he could see she didn't think it was a joke at all. She was realizing the same thing he was: If he was on reprieve, *would* he come back? Or would he, after all these years, finally achieve what he had wanted for centuries—to actually cross over.

Time had suddenly become valuable again.

He swallowed dryly. One more step and he put his hand on the door.

The dragon continued to watch him. Maybe it was just a harmless illusion after all, a ghost that bore them no ill will—a weird manifestation of the magic. He pushed on the door—and then the dragon struck.

It shot its head out with lightning speed. For a ghost, it bore a surprising density. Its muzzle struck the door with blunt force as Arsenault hurled himself through it. He sliced his sword down on its head hard, but the blade passed through like it was...mist.

At the same time, he felt as if he'd driven the blade through the flesh of someone he loved. It felt like murder and betrayal, fear and shame, every black deed he'd ever done. It felt like blood should be gushing over his hands.

Good gods, it feels like staring at my darkest reflection in the Ice.

"Haven't I paid enough?" he shouted at it, driven to sudden, irrational anger. "Godsdamn you, haven't I done enough penance?"

For a moment, the dragon's eyes looked horribly, inexplicably sad. Then the sadness fled and it lashed out with the tiaannamir claw.

He barely threw himself out of the way. The claws tore through his shirt, narrowly missing his skin. He stumbled to his feet, swinging the blade in a drunken arc that again cut through nothing but air. The dragon took the sword in its teeth, bit *through* the blade, then tossed it carelessly away. In desperation, Arsenault grasped for his magic, but the magic refused control, raging over him like he was a tiny piece of flotsam caught in a violent flood.

He clawed for the surface like he was physically drowning. The magic burned and roiled, battering and searing him inside and out. He fought out of it, gasping, and found himself staring straight into the incomprehensible eyes of the dragon.

By all the gods, it *did* know him. It knew who he was on the inside, all his history—who he *really* was.

Not Arsenault.

Ari.

He had always, forever, been Ari.

Its head flashed out, striking at his face with teeth the size of daggers. He jerked back, but not fast enough, not—

A body rushed in front of him, knocking him to the ground. Instead of slashing his face, the dragon's teeth clanged loudly on metal.

Arsenault looked up in horror.

Wicked incisors the size of dagger blades sank into the metal of

Kyrra's arm, tearing through it the same way they had destroyed his sword.

The dragon worried her arm like a dog with a bone. Kyrra gritted her teeth, her face sick and pale, as Arsenault lurched for his broken sword. He thrust it between the dragon's jaws like a lever, but the dragon only bit down harder.

Kyrra made a helpless noise and squeezed her eyes shut.

"Ser!" one of the boys yelled. "What do we do?"

They stood behind the dragon. Hani held a pot of powder and a lighted taper foolishly close, Fillipo feverishly wound back the lock on the gun—

"Throw the powder in that pit!" Arsenault shouted, still struggling to prise open the dragon's jaws. "Blow the ground behind the dragon! Kyrra, hold on…"

Hani hurled the pot and Arsenault let go of his sword for an instant to draw the Sanctuary rune, hoping with all his might that this would be enough to drive the dragon backward. The remaining metal of the blade flashed bright white as Hani threw a lit taper into the pit with the powder.

The explosion reverberated with a heavy, vibrating thud. Chips of stone and dirt poured down like rain. The dragon screeched and twisted backward, ripping its teeth through Kyrra's arm as it let go of her. She screamed in pain and Arsenault dropped his sword to catch her when she fell, curling his body over hers to take the brunt of the debris.

The dragon had torn a chunk from her arm. The fabric of the sling was in tatters, the already mangled metal pitted with acidic saliva and missing—gods, part of her bicep was just *missing*. He dragged her away from the expanding edge of the pit, now bubbling with black sludge. It flowed over the dragon's claw, eating away at the misty image of the dragon, then slid over the end of his blade.

"Arsenault," Kyrra gasped. "Your sword!"

The magic was eating what was left of it, turning it back into the ghost of the being the metal had been part of when it was alive. The plaintive, ghostly howl of a giant wolf reverberated through the air. Arsenault grabbed it before the sludge reached the hilt. He wiped the sludge onto the grass, which immediately charred black.

The blade had been ragged before, but now the runes were distorted and dull, too. The metal itself was completely ruined. Something had been taken out of it.

The sludge is the opposite of life.

The earth stopped trembling and the mist cleared as the sludge flowed on down the hill. The boys stood safe, staring around them bewildered.

Kyrra looked up at him, trembling, clammy and sweating with shock.

"You won't be able to leave this wound alone, will you?" she said, her voice shaking. "You'll have to Fix my arm now no matter what it does to me. We waited too long."

CHAPTER 54

KYRRA

Memories clawed at me like vicious ghosts.

The axe. The chopping block. My severed arm lying there as if I was an animal being butchered... I felt like I was drowning in a flood of deep, burgundy blood.

But there was no blood in metal. Was it new pain or old pain that made me feel like screaming? Had the metal frozen it, like an insect trapped in amber? And now that the metal was gone...

"Just breathe, Kyrra. Keep breathing, that's it."

Arsenault. He'd stripped his tunic and wrapped it around me, but I still couldn't stop shivering. I fought to keep my eyes on his face. If I was looking at him, I couldn't see my memories. Over his shoulder, more worried, frightened faces watched me—not, thank the gods, the cold, hard faces of the Circle, which kept trying to push their way into my mind. New faces. Mikelo leaned past Arsenault, and on his other side, that conjure woman who owned the farmhouse—*Miranda*—Jon, Silva, a Tiresian woman I was sure I'd seen at Jon's house, who said, startled, "Kyris!"

When had she come? *Why* had she come? The oddity fanned my anxiety and blackness overwhelmed me again.

"But we didn't know if we could trust the messenger, Mama. So we took the letter. Everything was fine until the earth started splitting, but we'd found the mes—Kyris by then."

The boys.

I tried to wave my good hand to get Miranda's attention. "C-clever boys," I said. "They brought your letter, a gun—"

"They killed the dragon," Arsenault told her. "You should be proud. I don't know what we'd have done without them."

"Any c-captain would be h-happy to have them," I said.

"This one was," Arsenault said. His voice was matter of fact, but I thought I also caught a chastised tone in it. *He's calling himself a captain again.* Maybe it was just for the boys, who beamed with pride. Maybe it was so he could take all the fault for what had happened. He probably hadn't listened to me at all. I would have kept the godsdamned dragon limb, too. I would even have let him put it in my arm.

I struggled to sit. Fresh pain and shivering assaulted me. Hands caught me. I lost time again.

"I can't heal this, Arsenault," Mikelo said. "How—"

"I don't know. It was just as you said. The black liquid was like the opposite of life, so it stole the tiaannamir. Pulled it all into oblivion, like it had never existed." Arsenault paused and when he spoke again, he sounded frustrated, angry. "I saw something similar long ago, but I'd forgotten. It happened on Tule. All the natural magic pulled out of the land and fouled."

"This place is evil," Miranda said in a low, passionate voice. "It's forever tainted."

"Whatever was underground, it was always tainted." I grimaced as I tried to breathe through the pain. "The gods did something to it, long ago. The longer it stayed trapped, the worse it got."

Miranda's expression grew more thoughtful, in a troubled way. "Maybe this is what is happening to women."

Her statement startled me. "What?"

"Every conjure woman knows it's becoming harder and harder to find the life source here in Liera. I've been writing to other conjure women in other countries and it's not as difficult in those places, but even there it's becoming darker, harder. Women stop bearing even when they want to have children. Babies are born stillborn. Men stop fathering children. Isn't that why they instituted the new laws, so men could marry more than one woman? And now it's younger and younger women, just to have one or two children to keep their House going."

"Some men *should* be stopped from fathering children," I said. "If they're not going to keep it in their pants."

She snorted, then glanced up at her boys. I would have blushed if I could have. "S-sorry," I said. "But conjure women use this force, too, don't they? To stop women from bearing. Voluntarily."

"Did you have that done to you?"

I nodded jerkily. I didn't know where the men had gone; they seemed to have left me alone with Miranda, even Arsenault. Jon had Junei off to the side, getting a report; he wouldn't want her to know who I was. I'd met her in passing a few times, always as the gavaro Kyris. If Jon was keeping my secrets, I was grateful to him.

Miranda frowned. "By your consent or against your will?"

"I asked for it. Isia told me it might last forever, or it might not last at all."

"It depends on how capable you are of pushing it out, what your true desires are. Or if you're truly conflicted. It's not really the same, Kyrra, but it's better not to have that magic in your body. There are other methods kinder to you and to the wild magic itself."

I didn't want Arsenault to overhear this conversation. I knew how much he wanted a family, and here we were in an evil mess of oblivion and part of my arm was gone, and maybe that was why I was suddenly determined not to let go of this strange opportunity I had to ask the question I had been worrying about for days. For weeks.

"Is it still working? Can you tell?"

She looked like I'd surprised her. "You want me to tell you...now?"

"We're in the middle of a new war. I... I need to know if I'm fertile."

"In case healing your arm is hard on you?" she asked, still confused.

"Yes," I lied. It was a lie but also the truth. By all the gods, if I was pregnant *now*...

The thought ended in blackness. I couldn't think about it.

"You're worried about telling Arsenault," Miranda breathed, as if finally understanding.

I *was* worried about telling Arsenault, but I wasn't sure which news I didn't want to give him. I wasn't sure what *I* wanted. I tensed and my arm hurt so much I must have blacked out.

"Shh," Miranda said, her hands on my shoulders keeping me upright again. "If it's that important, then—"

Her magic flooded me. It was warm and bright, the opposite of the blackness and the mist. It lit me up—but it also hurt. I wasn't sure I was ready to be that bright inside.

When the light dimmed, I was cold again, but more comfortable. I could breathe.

"I wish I could tell you something firmer," she said. "You're not pregnant, but with all that magic doing battle inside you, everything is in flux. You're not barren, but I can't say you're fertile either. What your other conjure woman told you still holds, I think. It's going to be up to you, what you *really* want, deep inside. You may not even know —and certainly not *now,* love. Give it some time before you start thinking about it. And bring him into the conversation."

She twitched her head as Arsenault knelt beside her. "What conversation?" he asked.

I looked at him—really looked at him. The slash marks in his shirt. The dirt and black powder smeared over the scar I barely noticed anymore. The silver-white streak in his hair showed up in stark relief against the mass of thick, wind-tossed black. He tried, briefly, to smile for me, but it couldn't erase the fear in his eyes. I'd been angry he hadn't told me about the dragon, but now all I wanted was not to lose him again. When I'd killed Geoffre, I'd thought our journey was over, but really it was just beginning.

He picked up my good hand. "Kyrra. I'm sorry about the dragon. Sorry for keeping it and sorry I didn't tell you what I was finding or where I put it. Stupid to apologize now, I know, but—just stupid, I guess. I shouldn't have tried to hide my guilt, and I should have realized sooner the limb was trying to draw me out. I played right into their hands and you paid the price."

I was having trouble following his logic. "How is it about you?"

"The dragon knew me. Which means Cassis's scholar..."

"You think he knew who you were, too?" I moved too quickly and pain burned my arm. I sucked in my breath and started shaking again. "Dammit."

Arsenault let me squeeze his hand until it passed. "I think it's likely," he answered softly. At least he didn't tell me to hush, that we'd talk about it when I was better. I kept on not getting better, but I always needed information now.

"Did Cassis tell him? But then, why go to all this mystery with the dragon limb?"

He gently moved my metal arm and used his tunic to fashion a new sling. The support combined with Miranda's magic made it feel better but still not good. "You'll have to walk out. The others are scouting the best path, so we don't accidentally fall in any pits."

"Good idea," I rasped as he lifted me to my feet. I swayed when I was up, overwhelmed with dizziness. Arsenault slid his arm around my waist and nudged his shoulder under my left arm, though he had to stoop to do it.

"What conversation were you supposed to bring me into?" he said.

"I'll tell you at the house," I promised.

❧

I HAD MADE MY SHARE OF LONG, WOUNDED WALKS THROUGH ROUGH terrain, but this was one of the worst. After falling off a cliff, rolling down a mountainside, and being bitten by a ghost dragon, I was in no shape to walk anywhere. The poison continued to burn in the metal as if it was eating holes into my flesh. I drifted in and out, trying to put one foot in front of the other. Arsenault kept encouraging me onward. Mikelo and Silva spoke to me. Jon, too, but I have no idea what anyone said.

It seemed to take an eternal amount of time. Then I was on a couch. The couch in the common room.

Early in my recovery, this couch had seemed wonderful—a victory I had won, territory I had conquered. Notwithstanding my earlier memories of sharing the couch with Arsenault, I was beginning to detest it a little. It seemed like an anchor from which I couldn't break free.

Mikelo's now-familiar magic swept through me as Arsenault pulled off my cloak and unwrapped my arm. It took only a moment and then he let me go and sat back on his heels.

"All I can feel are bruises. Deep bruises, but nothing broken."

"That's a relief." *Arsenault*. My cheek stung as something wet touched it. I opened my eyes, not realizing I had closed them. The room spun before it came into focus. Arsenault was cleaning the scrape on my cheek with a wet cloth that smelled of imya.

I lay against the arm with the hole in the upholstery, where the burgundy silk beneath showed through. I lifted my head and frowned at it.

"Whatever the dragon injected her with, it's still there," Mikelo said. "I can't Fix her arm, but I can feel the spots of—it feels like it should have a name. In the books I was reading by Oji la Kaif, he describes a lot of magical formations, but he keeps mentioning something called *antivita* and—"

"That's it," I said, pushing myself up too fast and paying for it in dizziness. My voice sounded raspy and strange; perhaps I was slurring my words. "That's the word the author of *Dance of the Heavens* uses in the description." The one copied by the man who'd sold Arsenault the metal for my arm and notated *Ask Arsenault*. It seemed an eternity ago I'd been thinking about that. The mysterious man named *Bruzzia*.

"Which description, Kyrra?"

"About the Gods' War. *And magic, once bright and golden, now streams along the ground/Black and hot/Like blood from the weeping Earth.*"

"You're really reciting poetry now."

"Fuck you, Mikelo. It matters. *Antivita.* That's the word in the original my tutor made me memorize. I asked him what antivita was and he said scholars had searched for the meaning for years. Then he started talking about theories and I lost interest. But Bruzzia—the man who copied out the manuscript Jon owns—translated it. He didn't write down *antivita*, he wrote down *magic*. I didn't even notice because it was so natural. But that's what let me make the connection between my vision and the disaster Lobardin unleashed on the whole fucking countryside. Ow, Arsenault, what are you doing?"

"Keep talking," he said grimly, adjusting my metal elbow to get a better look at it. "If it keeps you distracted."

"We have to work on your bedside manner," I said nervously.

"Mmmm," he answered. His magic touched me and I shivered. It seemed more hesitant than usual. Mikelo's touch had been gentle as well. Had they been so spooked by the magic that had broken through the earth? Had something gone wrong with their magic, too?

Or were they just afraid of touching me?

A lot of thoughts spun around my mind. I sniffed the air.

"You're burning kacin," I said.

Arsenault looked up from my arm for an instant. "You weren't conscious enough to drink it. But it would be nice if we could switch you to tea, because I think I've breathed in enough myself."

"Oh, all right," I said tetchily. Now I could tell I'd had kacin. Words kept wanting to fall out of my mouth.

Arsenault nodded to someone I couldn't see. Fabric rustled, like somebody moving, but both he and Mikelo stayed with me.

"The man who copied the manuscript," I went on, "was an Empirist. *And* he shared a name with the man Arsenault said sold the metal for my arm. Bruzzia. A freeholder name, not a House name. It seems a strange coincidence."

Mikelo looked at me with a faint smile. "You're the only person in the world who manages pain by solving mysteries."

"That's not true. I've gotten a lot of men through injuries by asking them questions. They talk or they get annoyed at me and they don't think about how much it hurts. Besides, you're the ones who made me breathe kacin."

Arsenault grimaced, but I didn't feel him doing anything—which didn't seem hopeful. "I know you don't like kacin, Kyrra. But this will hurt. I hope your body is well enough to handle it, but—"

"What are you going to use to fill the hole?" I asked.

He frowned, which also didn't seem hopeful. "I'm not sure."

"You're not going to cut it off and recast it, are you?"

He let his breath out heavily. "We've been through this already, but..." He raised his gaze to mine. I didn't like the way his expression seemed to weigh on him. "The best course might be to amputate all the metal and let Mikelo heal the stump. Full recasting would have to be done in two steps—take the arm off, put a new one on. It would be too hard on you and I don't have enough metal for it anyway. It might be possible to recast the original by Fixing it while it's a part of you, but the metal remains the issue. I was hoping to use the dragon limb, but it's probably best we lost that."

He shifted his gaze and I let my head roll to the side to see what he was looking at. His sword lay on the stones of the hearth, like a fallen warrior laid out on a pyre. It made me sick to see it. It was *my* sword, too. My faithful companion. And now...

The blade was nothing but ragged splinters jutting up from the hilt. Antivita had eaten deep runnels into it, leaving the bright, gleaming metal dead and black. It looked as if it would shatter any moment.

"That's what my arm looks like?" I asked.

Arsenault rubbed his brow and I knew the answer was *yes*. "You might be better off without the arm. It would be like when you lived in the barracks. You could work, fight one handed, do anything you wanted, really."

I thought about it. It was all true and, moreover, it was exactly what I had told Razi before the chirurgeon had amputated *his* arm. I would just have to work harder and differently than people with two arms. Loading a gun would be difficult in the stress of a battlefield, if not impossible. I wouldn't be able to use a two-handed sword. And I wouldn't be able to queue my hair myself, so I'd have to cut it short. But in the end, the metal wasn't worth my life. For that matter, it wasn't even *my* arm. It was just one solution to a problem that was never going away.

And yet, an arm was not like a hammer or a knife, a tool you could discard when it broke. It was a part of my body. Of my identity and my trade. After I'd learned to use it, I'd felt strong again. The thought of having my arm severed a *second* time, having to fight through the fear and the blood and the pain *again*...

I couldn't do it.

"No," I said. "That's a last resort. There must be another way."

And then I remembered.

"We do have another source of tiaannamir. Upstairs. Under Mikelo's bed. *The Prinze sword.*"

CHAPTER 55

KYRRA

For a moment, shocked silence filled the room. Then Arsenault shoved himself to his feet. "No. There has to be another way."

Mikelo looked dazed. "My relatives are already fighting over the succession. If you put the symbol of Prinze authority in your *arm*..."

Arsenault scowled. "I don't give a rat's ass about the Prinze succession. Using the sword will put you in danger. From the rest of the family, true, but—think of all the blood on its blade, Kyrra. Aliente blood, *your* blood. We talked about this!"

I stared him in the eye. "So, the only choice is to cut off my arm again?"

Arsenault held my gaze, meeting my challenge, but then his jaw twitched. "No, it's not. Dammit!"

He sat on the couch suddenly and leaned toward me, speaking urgently. "That sword is called Kinstealer for a reason. When Geoffre was preparing for his Empirist meetings, he used to make me hold it. By the time I realized the point wasn't the stupid artistic flourishes he wanted me to Fix on his mask but the repulsion and fear I felt when I held that blade, he'd beaten me so low the only thing I could hold on to was Jon's plan. It was the only thing that kept me from killing myself and walking away from it all. Then again, none of my attempts at escape ever worked. They just left me in more pain."

He'd wiped the grime from his face, but he still looked battered—like a captain contemplating the possibility of surrender. I shoved aside the desire to kill Geoffre again. It seemed like I had to do that every few days, even now.

"Geoffre was an Empirist?" I asked instead. I felt like my mind was being too clumsy, that there was something important to grasp, but I didn't know what it was yet. "The Empirists in the cafes were mostly old men who went on and on about the glory days of Attrasca."

Arsenault looked supremely frustrated at me. I felt like the next words out of his mouth would be, *dammit, Kyrra*. Instead, he said, "That's not the point. Geoffre used that sword in battle against your House, your relatives—*men you knew*. He used it when he was possessed by the god. It gave you all those scars!"

For once I kept my mouth shut and just stared back at him. Did he think I didn't know all those things?

He didn't back down, but he switched tacks. Some of the strained patience I remembered from our days at the Villa laced his voice. "I've finally put together all my notes about your arm. The ingots I used came from guardians. It wasn't exactly *safe*, but guardians in the Old World had integrity, they took their promises to a place and a people seriously. And even though I used only honorable metal, you've *still* had problems with the arm."

He jumped up again to pace and ran a hand through his hair in that way he did when his thoughts were restless. His hair was already a mess; it must not have been the first time he'd attacked it while he thought. "I didn't know how wrong things had grown inside the magic because I'd been banned from it for so long. The ghosts of the guardians in your arm must have faced a paradox: They couldn't protect you against poison if it was also a part of them. The only thing they could do was destroy themselves. But if I introduce *the Prinze blade* into the mix, what will happen then?"

Guardians. Despite Arsenault's doomsaying, knowing my arm hadn't been part of an evil monster rampaging villages made me feel better. Although some of the guardians of ancient legend were hardly better. Giant three-headed dogs. Enormous, serpent-like dragons. Whatever lurked at the bottom of the Maelstrom and ate ships as they tried to sail around Thunder Cape.

I suppressed a shudder. "Whatever's wrong with the magic, it affects everyone, doesn't it? Not just me with my arm but you and Mikelo, the conjure women—even people with no magic at all. That was Ires's point, when he told me to look for the Prinze sword. We've made him out to be mad, a destroyer. But he calls himself a guardian, *the* Guardian. Maybe that's why he came to me—because I have an arm cast out of the skeletons of guardians. But how in all the hells will I be able to guard anyone if I can't use my fucking arm?"

"You don't have to guard anybody!" Arsenault shouted. He snapped his mouth shut when I recoiled and took a deep breath. "Kyrra. Forgive me. I can't lose you. Not again."

"This isn't about me, Arsenault," I whispered. "The dragon wasn't trying to kill *me*. It wanted *you*. And..."

I took my own deep breath and looked at the burgundy silk peeking through the hole in the couch's upholstery.

I slid the fingers of my good hand into it and tugged as hard as I could. Arsenault and Mikelo both jerked in surprise at the sound of tearing fabric, but the tawdry blue satin was hardly tacked down. It ripped easily, revealing the unmistakable rich tones of high-quality burgundy silk beneath it. Faint roses formed a pattern on the arm; the dark wood that ran along the back of the couch was carved with a hunt scene, hounds chasing a wolf. I recognized it now, almost as if my Sight had carried me back to my father's office that hot, dusty afternoon I'd snuck in to serve Cassis water with my two hands of flesh.

When I looked up, Jon was standing in front of me, holding a teacup on a saucer, and the boys were standing behind him.

Two *Aliente* boys. I had finally pieced it all together.

Now I realized why I hated kacin tea so much. It wasn't the kacin. It was because drinking it reminded me of the tea my mother had sent me before I was hanged. I'd thought I could redeem myself for condemning my House by sacrificing my life for it. Was putting the Prinze sword in my arm an equally doomed act of self-sacrifice? Or was it our only chance to turn this mess into something good?

I took a ragged breath. "I think I do have someone to protect. This couch is from my father's study at the Villa. So perhaps you'd better explain."

Arsenault stared at the exposed arm of the couch like he, too, was surprised. "Kyrra, I'm not hiding anything else. I don't know how the damn couch ended up here. I shipped it off to Jon. I couldn't stand to see it all burn. Your mother would have given the Prinze bare, black earth if she'd been in charge. Sometimes I think she should have been captain."

Jon handed me the teacup and ignored the bewildered glare Arsenault shot him as he settled himself in a chair. He'd cleaned up a little but only to get rid of his dirty tunic and boots. "We ran what we could through the same channels we used to smuggle guns and powder.

Some of it ended up in Rojornick, some scattered here and there in the foothills, in safe houses like this one. Anything valuable Arsenault wanted out. Miranda and her husband were at the center of a network, well-respected, trusted—and also isolated."

"But the furniture?" I asked, dazed.

"What we could save. Tapestries. Art. The household gods."

I looked up at the little wooden votas on the mantle. I'd thought they seemed familiar, but I had never really *looked* at them. As I studied them now, I recognized them, too. The small gods had resided over the central hearth of the Villa, where the fire was never allowed to burn out, just as the fire burned in this hearth day and night. It was an old Eterean tradition left over from the Old World and the old gods, which made a house feel like home. I hadn't seen these little gods since my titles had been stripped nine long years ago. But now here they were, watching over me again. Their familiar, nameless faces forming a connection to the past I'd thought dead and buried.

"I didn't know where Jon hid anything," Arsenault said. "Or where your family members hid anything. That was on purpose. But we tried to save what Carolla didn't throw in Geoffre's face. Isia, the conjure woman, came around a few times to remind me, *You vowed to protect Carolla's children, that's more important than the furniture.* As if I had to be reminded why I was fighting the godsdamned war."

Mikelo had been sitting in another chair, following the conversation with a brooding expression the way he did sometimes—as if he'd become again the hostage I'd taken, trying to hide in the background. Now he interrupted, confused. "I thought you were an only child, Kyrra. How could Arsenault protect your mother's *children?*"

I'd asked myself the same question, with no satisfactory answer. But Arsenault answered before I could.

"I runed your brother's grave," he said. He sounded so *tired*, bone-weary. "I thought maybe that was what she meant. We took down the headstone and buried it, too, and then we planted a wisteria vine that would climb into the tree and mark the place. I didn't trust Geoffre not to desecrate the grave."

It was one of the worst crimes a Lieran could commit—to disrespect the dead, to pull them out of the underworld and condemn them to an eternity of wandering.

The kacin loosened my lips. "I think he was Geoffre's son. Surely Geoffre wouldn't have done that to his own son?"

I only realized how loose my lips were when everyone stopped and stared at me. Arsenault. Jon. Silva walking into the room with a whole pot of tea held in mitts. Mikelo, especially. Miranda put her hands protectively on her boys' shoulders.

Aliente boys.

I had forgotten that no one had put the pieces of that puzzle together the way I had. I was the only one who had figured out the mystery of my brother's parentage.

"How—" Mikelo began, stunned.

"Because Geoffre loved my mother, even though she was Caprine, and he lost her to my father. He visited us the year my brother was born, dead. I was only six years old. I had no idea what was going on. But when I look back now, the way they all acted, Geoffre, my mother, my father... The way my mother reacted when Cassis and I..." I had to stop and take a drink of tea. "It just seems obvious."

Silva set the tea pot down and began stripping off the hot mitts he was wearing. "That would make him about the same age as you, wouldn't it, Mikelo?"

Mikelo's face darkened. "You think Geoffre wanted me as a replacement?" he snapped. "For the son he'd lost but could never have?"

Silva recoiled. "I wasn't saying anything, Mikelo, just trying to set everything in time."

I wondered why Mikelo was so angry, so sensitive. But, of course, he was the bastard son of the line. Even more of a bastard son than my brother would have been, because my father would have raised my brother as his own. Even made him Heir, if he'd lived. Had my mother looked ahead to the possibility of a Prinze inheriting the House d'Aliente when she found herself with child?

The thought left me—somewhere beyond cold, in spite of the kacin.

"Geoffre wanted to blame me for the war because I was a convenient scapegoat," I said. "But he had been waging war against us for a long time."

In Rojornick, I'd had Sight dreams of my mother, her face smeared with ash, hurling a chair out the window to be consumed by a raging bonfire underneath, trying to keep everything we owned out of Geoffre's possession. I touched the burgundy silk on the couch arm again, as if by touching it I might again feel my mother's hand. In all the time I had been back in Liera, I had never come face to face with the life I'd lost like this. I had never been able to feel it, to run my fingers over its smooth, well-worn surface, so familiar and yet so startlingly, painfully new.

"So it *is* true," I said to the boys, finally. "You *are* Aliente. And not just from a distant, minor branch?"

Slowly they nodded. Hani looked like he might want to run away —a boy who had devised a way to carry a secret message through an enemy line and then exploded a ghost dragon, as if my grief were more terrifying. Maybe it was. It was also his grief—our grief.

I had never used those words before—*our grief.*

Fillipo squared his shoulders. "Our father was Aliente from one of the younger sons of the main branch. This whole area was our land— the house, the village, it was all Aliente once. Our father rode as a messenger in the war. He carried codes and our mother distributed the letters. That's what I meant by our legacy."

I didn't know what to do with this feeling that suddenly overwhelmed me. Maybe the Aliente "sympathizers" in Liera were a bunch of useless pricks drinking themselves into debt, but these boys were *real*. Should I hug them? Continue to stare? I had a House again, even if it was only me and these two boys. I knew I couldn't be a member of that House anymore—definitely not Heir—but I felt like I was responsible for the whole world. It was exciting and joyful and—

Utterly terrifying.

"Tell me about the Empirists," I said.

Mikelo surprised me by answering instead of Arsenault or Jon. "The Empirists became a minor party during the wars. They backed the Prinze because my uncle's admiration for Attrasca was no secret and his desire to be a new Attrasca uniting the peninsula was no secret either. All the Empirists wore masks and hid their House colors at meetings. A small group of those who knew and shared his views visited him privately, but I wasn't allowed in the room with them for very long. One woman attended as a swan. Another man always dressed as a lynx."

"What did Geoffre wear?"

Arsenault answered curtly, but he looked like he was interested in where I was going. "Serpent. Dragon."

It was so godsdamned hard to pull all these threads together, as thick as my mind had begun to feel. The kacin dulled the pain, but it felt like all my thoughts were stuck in honey.

Masks. Disguises. False identities.

"Did they have codenames?" I asked.

"Felix," Mikelo answered, "was the cat."

"What was the name of Cassis's Empirist scholar?"

"Lupa," Jon answered. "Junei and Miranda have just finished telling me about Ser Lupa and his Dakkaran secretary, who wears the gold of a Hidden Blade. This Lupa seems to have quite a bit of ancient knowledge. Junei says he's moving antiquities. At least that was the information Lobardin got out of Tomas—the secretary—and passed along. Lupa went with Cassis to Liera to deal with his plundered ship, but Lobardin was able to evacuate the lodge and blow it because of Tomas's knowledge of the tunnels beneath the lodge—taken from Lupa's maps."

"There are maps of the tunnels?"

"Junei and Miranda both say so. They don't know if Lobardin and Tomas got out, but everyone else did. Lobardin apparently used our ghost as an inspiration for his strategy. He said Tomas seemed especially curious when he mentioned Arsenault."

Arsenault looked troubled. "So, there's a Dakkaran connection. That dragon, the one the metal limb had in its memory, it *knew* me. Not Arsenault, but *Ari*. Maybe because it's from Tule, but how did Lupa know to give it to Cassis? It seems a huge coincidence unless he knew Cassis would bring it here and involve me. But why? Do you know this Blade, this Tomas?"

"I used to know a pirate boy named Tomas," Jon said carefully. "It's been a long time, though. I've mostly been north since then. If it's the same Tomas..." Jon shrugged. "I don't know. The reach of the Blades has spread farther and thinner since Geoffre helped the Arak take my father's throne."

"Could Lupa have been at the Empirist meetings?" I asked. "Perhaps wearing a wolf mask?"

"Lupa," Mikelo breathed. "*Wolf*."

"I wasn't at my best at those times," Arsenault admitted. "I don't remember a wolf—but that doesn't mean there wasn't one."

I didn't want to put the Prinze sword into my arm. It repulsed me. I knew all the crimes it had committed. I didn't want to marry Cassis and I didn't want to tell Arsenault about it either. When Cassis had first said the words to me, I had dismissed them as ridiculous. But now, with all these connections swirling around and Aliente still alive...

I'd been a fool.

Trust for Arsenault and me was a rickety bridge in need of repair. I wasn't sure which of us was at fault or if both of us being this way meant we would be like this forever. This, I knew, was going to be worse than a hidden dragon limb. But I couldn't keep on hiding like a coward just because I didn't want to face the shame and fear Cassis's words had stirred in me.

"The day Cassis brought the dragon, he floated me a proposal," I said. "He told me Lupa had suggested it. Cassis thought he could circumvent Devid and unite the city if he made the Empirists and the 'Aliente sympathizers' happy by showing how noble he was—pardoning me, giving me back all my titles, and...marrying me."

The room went so silent it felt as if even the fire paused to digest my words.

Arsenault turned white. I thought he was going to pass out. "He...*what?*"

I took a big drink of the tea, even though I hated it.

"He's putting off Camile, his second wife is dead, he wants to marry Driese, and he told me he had an open slot. I told him to fuck himself. He told me I was going to be responsible for another war."

"That godsdamned fucking *bastard*," Arsenault seethed. "Why didn't you tell me? I would have taken care of him right then!"

"He said to ask you about Viela."

"He would. Gods." Arsenault scrubbed a hand through his beard helplessly. "All right. So, we're going to do this now? When I came back into Cassis's household and he discovered who I really was, he took his revenge on me by using me in his wastrel act. I was his best smoke screen for Geoffre and he knew that since I was working for Jon, I'd go along with whatever he wanted me to do. One day—"

Arsenault stopped. His expression told me everything I needed to know about that day, but he cleared his throat and kept going.

"Well. I was living down in the dirt, but apparently, I still had a line. Anyway, I stumbled my way out of the party and went up to the roof. Made it halfway to throwing myself off into the canal. I hate drowning, but I figured I'd wash out into the lagoon and at least I'd forget everything."

He paused, sighing heavily. "I was drunk. Really drunk. Viela found me and talked me back. We developed...a relationship. She had a lot of lovers because she thought she could get away with it—she was a Garonze trying to manipulate the Prinze for her family's benefit—but mostly we were friends. Then she found herself with child and Geoffre killed her. I would have protected her, but she was married to Cassis. I couldn't help her escape that, and in the end, I couldn't protect her against poison either."

The kacin was doing its work, blunting my emotions so I could hear that damn story without—I wasn't sure what I would have done if I was sober. How could Cassis ask me to ignore not only what he had done to me, but what he had done to Arsenault? As if *Cassis* was the one who had been hurt?

"Was the child yours?" I asked, feeling like the question had to be dragged out of me.

"I don't know. I doubt it. Gods, I was a horrible man. It was all horrible."

"Arsenault," Jon said, as if Arsenault's admission had stunned him. "Why didn't you tell me? I knew about Cassis's parties, I knew he was cruel, but—"

Arsenault waved his hand. "It doesn't matter now. It didn't matter then. I didn't have anything to live for. I could have left to start another life, but what was the point? You don't understand how long time is. It just goes on and on, one life after the other. After a while, they're all the same."

This is why I fought Geoffre, I thought. *If I agree to Cassis's proposal to save the city, this is what I will condemn him to again.*

"My brother," Jon said, his voice rough, "you have never known what pain you cause us because you can't see your own worth. That's why I told you to get rid of that damn dragon. I knew it would bring danger to you, because all the metal we found from your ship and all the others—it was all cursed. And it didn't get you any closer to Guin, did it? It just brought grief. To *you*, most of all."

Arsenault frowned as he absorbed this. I could see him trying to formulate questions, but he likely didn't even know what to ask. I didn't, either.

Jon looked more agitated than I had ever seen him, as if he wanted to say more or do more but couldn't. Instead, he practically leapt out of his chair, reaching out to take my empty teacup. "I'm leaving for Liera tomorrow with Junei, Miranda, and the boys. I was wrong to push them away; they'll be safer with me. It's time to stop dancing around the edges of these Empirists. Mikelo, you had better decide what to do with that sword and what you want to do about your family."

Mikelo stood. "I'm going with you. I thought if I brought the sword into the Council, it would be a first step toward peace, but I don't think so anymore. My family's determined to have war. Take the sword if you want, Kyrra. Let it do some good for once. I refuse to play by their rules."

Everyone's eyes were on me. But my decision hadn't wavered. "If

Cassis thinks I'm a tool he can use, then let me be a sword. Put it in my arm, Arsenault."

Arsenault stared at me in bewilderment. "After all those stories, you still don't see how dangerous it is?"

"I have to protect my House. And wherever Geoffre is, I hope he knows the symbol of *his* House is now part of the Aliente whore he tried to destroy."

Jon smiled bleakly. "In that case, I have an idea..."

PART IV

Sometimes the traveler will find himself in need of rest. Even the camel requires water on its long journeys across the drylands. But if the camel finds no water? If the traveler finds no rest? Adventures once eagerly anticipated become instead bitter trials. The traveler shreds the soles of his sandals on a rocky road and lies down in the brush only to find brigands have stolen his cloak. In those times, it is the wise traveler who humbles himself to walk barefoot beneath the light of the Magnificent Sun, which shines on all men, the evil and the good, and the lucky traveler who has found a companion to share his travails.

—Oji la Kaif
   The Path of Adventure

CHAPTER 56

ARSENAULT

KYRRA,

I remember the day the stars fell.

I remember my wedding.

I remember the day the dragon died in the harbor.

I never had the heart to tell you I chose Longest Night as my nameday because I couldn't remember what my nameday was.

Here I am staring at this sword with its blue sapphire eyes and wondering...

What will I do if I lose you?

How will I stand the pain of remembering forever?

CHAPTER 57

ARSENAULT

THE OVENS, TWENTY YEARS AGO

JON WOKE HIM IN THE MORNING. A DOWNPOUR POUNDED ON THE roof and splashed off onto the ground.

"Here, ghost." Jon pushed a man forward. "I've brought you a friend."

Arsenault looked up blearily, still half-caught in a restless nightmare of Sella calling to him as she was tossed about in a boat sailing on an ocean of molten silver magic. The man returned his look and smiled weakly.

"Renzo?" Arsenault asked in confusion. He didn't know whether to be relieved or angry. It was probably irrational to blame Renzo for being used by Promethi.

Renzo grinned weakly. "So nice to see you again, Arsenault."

In addition to bringing Renzo, Jon had also brought breakfast, which he laid out on a cloth on the bench. He propped the door open with a rock to allow in the coolness of the rain, making the hut marginally bearable.

He didn't waste time on small talk. "There are only six people in all of Dakkar who know Edo is alive," he said abruptly.

"Six?" Arsenault said around a bite of millet cake. He licked the honey from his fingers and used them to tick off possibilities. "You, me, Adayze, Chayma..."

"Haq, Renzo." Jon speared a fried plantain on the end of his knife and waved it at him. "We will use this to our advantage."

Arsenault glanced warily at Renzo. "Why did you tell him?"

"I appreciate the vote of confidence," Renzo said with a wry look, then winced. He was moving stiffly this morning, as if he hadn't escaped either the sphinx's wrath or Neyane's.

"Believe me, I'd have kept it from him if Adayze had let me," Jon replied. "But after she finally did the truthtelling, she thought it would be better for him to know what he was working for. I trust she knows what she's talking about."

Arsenault turned to Renzo. "So, you *were* telling the truth after all? About everything?"

Renzo looked cagey for an instant. Jon jumped in before he could answer. "At least enough that Adayze roped him into her scheme. I don't know what questions she asked. He was going to be tortured today, then executed. Adayze wants to have him pardoned, but there are conditions."

Renzo sighed as he peeled his egg. "I'm offended you'd think I'd want to feed your heirs to Promethi's sphinx."

"Your families poison each other, don't they?" Jon said.

"I happen to be rather clumsy at intrigue. Witness how my brother has maneuvered me into these distant lands, well away from any chance to seize power at home."

"Didn't you say your brother thought the key to the peninsula was trade with Dakkar?" Arsenault prompted.

Renzo let the last pieces of eggshell fall into the straw, then pushed them away with his foot. "The Chair wasn't always the most important thing in his life, but our father taught him his lessons well. Now his ambition doesn't leave space for anyone else. He'll use anything to bolster *his* power. I cooperated completely with the Lady Adayze."

Jon looked skeptical. "Well, whatever she discovered, she believes you had nothing to do with Edo, and she believes you too, ghost, about Promethi. I don't know what happened, but when she returned, she was shaking like a leaf. She poured herself a big glass of rum and after she drank that, she came out with this plan."

Gods, Arsenault hoped he hadn't just turned red like a teenager. He tipped up a flagon of beer and drank, probably more than he should have, then wiped the foam out of his beard with the back of his sleeve—slowly, deliberately, trying to compose himself. "There were ghosts," he said finally.

"That's one bonus," Renzo said. "The ghosts stayed away from me."

They damn well should have. After I made the effort to protect you. But Arsenault wasn't sure how Jon would react to the idea that his illegal use of magic in protecting Renzo had assuredly factored into the gods stealing his voice after he'd hidden Edo. So, he just ate another millet ball.

"Here is what we're going to do," Jon went on. "The six of us will keep Edo a secret. Adayze is sending him away. Where they're going *is* to be a secret, a real one. None of us will know his destination. We're going to pretend he's dead."

"Dead?" Arsenault said, startled. "But why—"

Jon turned a hard, solemn gaze on him. "Because you killed him, ghost."

The air in Arsenault's lungs stopped. He felt like somebody had punched him in the chest. "But why would anybody believe I killed him? Just because of what Promethi said?"

Jon looked uncomfortable. "Not just because of Promethi. Adayze said people would believe it...because she refused to help you with your fellow galleymen...and also..."

Jon paused and stabbed his knife into another piece of plantain.

"Because she did not want another husband and refused to bring you into her bed."

⚜

JON EXPLAINED THE PLAN WHILE ARSENAULT TRIED TO RECOVER. He hoped Jon didn't notice how his hands shook. The whole thing turned on faking his death—which, damn them, *of course* it did—then showing up in disguise on a riverboat to Arak lands, with Adayze pretending to visit Dirik and Promethi on a courting trip, considering that her husband *and* her Heir were both "dead." They would put it about that Promethi had been right about Arsenault being in league with the pirates and that *he* had been part of the group that had manipulated Renzo. The papers Jon had been keeping about his crimes were given in evidence.

Jon was taking a demotion from the Ibuu over it, Renzo would be painted as a complete innocent, and Arsenault... He was to be the epitome of evil, a monster dressed in hero's clothing. Luckily, he wouldn't have to endure knowing how easily people could change their opinion of him, the crimes they would too easily believe he had committed, because he would be "killed" in a matter of days.

He was still chewing over how much could go wrong with this plan when the creak of the door made him look up.

It was Adayze.

She wore an oilskin, hood up and dripping water, and though she was probably dry underneath, she still looked miserable. He scrambled to his feet. The chain had wrapped around his ankle and almost tripped him. Biting down on the urge to curse, he kicked it out.

When he looked up at Adayze again, she was smiling a little, uncertain. She pushed her hood down. Her hair was wrapped in a crimson headscarf as extra protection from the rain. "I'm sorry I can't make you more comfortable, Arsenault."

"It's...not a problem. Jon brought breakfast."

"He told you what I have planned?"

"It's a great risk. What will you do when you reach Dirik's hold?"

"Find out what's going on. How did they acquire those machines? What are they doing with your people? Are they plotting anything against my father and why? And then, when I have learned everything I need to, I will destroy them in their own house, on their own lands."

"I should tell you... There are some complications when I die."

"I'm not really having you killed."

"Wouldn't that be more convincing? I'd prefer to keep my head, if it's all the same to you, and hanging is rotten if the rope isn't new. A clean thrust with the sword—"

"*I'm not going to have you killed,*" she said in an anguished voice and stepped forward until she was almost close enough to touch him. The space between them was excruciating, so close and yet so far.

"It's a ruse, Arsenault. All the things I am saying. Did you think any of it was true?"

"I...didn't know. Not after you left."

"You understand *why* I left, though?"

He wanted to touch her, but he forced his hands to remain at his sides and just nodded.

Her shoulders lowered. She breathed easier. "I know it's hard to understand. I am allowed more than one husband. Even concubines. The lineage is always clear for me since I'm the one bearing the heirs. But conferring that status on you, Arsenault... I don't know how well you would do as a concubine. Or even a co-husband."

He laughed softly and shook his head. "No," he said. "You're right."

"You should be free to choose on your own."

He glanced down at the shackles around his ankle. "Seems ironic to say so now."

She dipped her head. "True. I love Isa, Arsenault. I don't want to admit he's dead. And if he is dead—" Her voice cracked. "Just...not...

not yet. No one else knows this, but...I promised when we wed that he would be my only husband, that we would do things differently. I can't go back on that kind of promise, even if I *know* I need to bear a second child. A child deserves to be more than a duty his mother is doing, doesn't he?"

The pain in her voice broke him. He drove his fingernails into his palms to keep from reaching out to her.

"I *do* understand," he said raggedly. "I still miss my wife. I didn't want to share her either."

"You didn't or you wouldn't?"

"Didn't. She had an affair. It's a long story and the ending is about as bad as an ending can be, but there's more to it than Fariq's papers make it seem. Not a day passes that I don't wish I could beat some sense into my younger self's head. I'd rather not be on the other side of things."

Adayze looked troubled. "I suppose you were right when you said I wasn't soft. I should let you go now. Instead, I'm going to keep using you. I hope you'll forgive me."

"There's very little I could hold against you, Adayze. If you do kill me..."

"I told you, Arsenault—"

"Things go wrong." Adayze started to protest again and he went on quickly, "If you *do* kill me, give me a book to write in first. To write down my memories. This last time, the gods left me just enough to know how badly I failed Guin. I don't want to forget him—or you—if something goes wrong."

"The gods take your memories? All of them?"

"Sometimes. It depends."

"I'll tell you again, Arsenault: I'm not going to kill you. My father and I will work out your sentence as soon as we can. Chayma will give you a potion to drink that will make it seem as if you're dead. Jon will be responsible for the execution itself. Justice is swift for the B'ara. You won't have to wait long, but I can't announce my intention to travel with Promethi until my seven days of formal mourning are done for Edo. It makes me sick to even pretend to go on this voyage, but... it will be expected. I'll need to be seen doing my duty to the B'ara and Dakkar."

Arsenault sighed, wishing he could do something to ease the bitterness in her voice. "All right. Will you get me a book to write in? Just in case?"

"It would be evidence, Arsenault. I can't take the risk."

He rubbed his brow wearily. "I suppose you're right."

"Arsenault... I *am* sorry. For all of this. I'm sorry that pirate raided your village and took you away from your peaceful life. I'm sorry I need to use you in this way. I'm sorry I slipped in a moment of loneliness and made you think there was an opportunity I can't give you."

He stared at the straw at his feet. The peel of Renzo's egg sprinkled it like salt. *That will probably draw rats.* His mind was a blank. It was too hard to think, to feel.

He forced himself to deal with the matter at hand. "None of that is your fault, Adayze. Sometimes when there's a hole in your life, you can't fill it, no matter what you do or don't do. Hope isn't a thing to let go of."

"And yet...there will come a time when it won't be a ruse. Isn't that true? My life is a little like a shipwreck right now. Some day I'll have to let go of the wreckage and swim to shore."

"If you've realized that, Adayze, it means you're already part way there."

"One day you'll find solid ground again, too, Arsenault. You don't live like a man who's abandoned hope."

CHAPTER 58

ARSENAULT

HOPE SEEMED TO RETREAT EVER FARTHER OVER THE NEXT FEW DAYS.
Verisimilitude was the art of making things seem real, and his imprisonment in the Ovens felt real even though it was supposed to be a ruse. The godsdamned heat. The ghosts. The waiting.

Then one morning the door creaked open.

"Get up, murderer. Time to meet your fate."

He moved too slowly and earned one kick and then another before two guards he thought he recognized locked his hands behind his back and dragged him into the fuzzy dawn light. The heat had left him weak, but he stumbled up the path between them to the armory. The path was surrounded by people whose faces all became a blur until they reached the courtyard where the Ibuu sat in an ornately carved mahogany chair, flanked by Adayze and Neyane. Jon stood near him holding a coil of rope. He caught Arsenault's gaze once but looked away. The stone armory loomed over them hard and stern, like a judge.

Executions never got easier. If anything, they'd grown harder. Each one was exactly the same. The humiliation. The shame, the anger and helplessness, especially if he was innocent—the pain and fear of *waiting*. It all called up too many memories of his very first trial.

The guards shoved him onto his knees in the mud in front of the Ibuu. He tried to will himself to be calm, to look like the kind of unfeeling monster who could commit the crimes Adayze had accused him of.

"I have reviewed the evidence," the Ibuu said in a hard voice. "It all tells me you murdered my grandson, the Heir after my Heir. Do you have anything to say for yourself?"

Arsenault had been coached on how this would go. The words tasted foul in his mouth, but he said them. "You seem to have discovered everything, my lord Ibuu."

"Are you admitting you killed Edo dom B'ara?"

The lie stuck in his craw. *Yes* wouldn't come out. He'd failed his own children, but he didn't want anything on the record that could be twisted against him when this story was later told to Edo. That was the nature of stories. You never knew who would do the telling. If this worked, it would be far too easy for the lie to be told as truth. Better to tell the truth and let them hear what they wanted.

"I admit to trying to save my men. I admit to desiring the Lady Adayze."

A gasp rippled through the crowd. Arsenault didn't bring his eyes up because he didn't want to have to look at Adayze.

"My daughter gave you a position in the Guard. She raised you up from the dirt and rescued you from poverty and disease. And this is how you repay her?"

"I am loyal to my promises," he said.

The Ibuu stood. "Then my course is clear. I sentence you to die here before me and all the B'ara. Our retribution is swift and sure. Let it be done."

The waiting crowd echoed the Ibuu's last words.

"Do you have a last request, dead man?"

"A drink of wine, my lord. Let me cross to the gods with the knowledge of the happiness I threw away."

"Bring this villain some wine," the Ibuu ordered. "Not because he wants it. Because *I* am merciful."

So far things were going the way Jon had told him they would. The wait was only a few moments, but with all the hate of the B'ara directed at him, it might as well have been hours. Haq returned with the wine Chayma had doctored and tipped it up for him to drink. Chayma had tried to hide the taste of her herbs and magic with sugar, but it didn't do much good; a harsh, hot bitterness lingered beneath the sweetness. Maybe everything was under control. He couldn't say he was beginning to relax, but maybe—

Jon moved forward, but the Ibuu suddenly rose from his chair. "No. I'll take care of this man myself."

Damn.

Jon bowed before his father, while Arsenault tried to swallow the fear that always overtook him before an execution. "Why soil your hands with this traitor, my lord Ibuu? It will be my honor to take care of it."

"Because it's my duty as Ibuu and my right as a father and grandfather to see this justice done. *Myself.*"

Arsenault could only imagine the pain the man was in, believing Edo had been murdered, but he didn't want that pain taken out on him. He didn't doubt for a moment the Ibuu would actually kill him.

"Lord Ibuu, let me do it. Surely, *I* deserve the vengeance!" Adayze interjected viciously.

The Ibuu was walking toward Arsenault but turned to face her. "He has done you enough evil, daughter. I should never have allowed Jon to give him a place in the guard close to you."

Jon flinched.

Nervousness and anticipation from the crowd vibrated around him. The Ibuu was a big man and the muscles of his arms and shoulders were still well-defined and hard. He took the rope from Jon and stood in front of Arsenault. Kneeling in the mud, all Arsenault could see were his boots—not shiny and fashionable, but plain and well-worn.

And the Ibuu's big hands with their nicked-up knuckles uncurling the rope.

It didn't surprise him that something had gone wrong. Something always went wrong. He hated dying by rope, but for the gods' sake, he wished they'd just get it over with.

As if the gods would grant any wish he made for mercy. Instead, there was a commotion at the gate, yet another delay.

"My lord Ibuu," Neyane said. "The box is here for his body."

Box...

Oh, by all the hells, no. It was a coffin.

Just big enough to wedge his body into, carved all over with protective magic signs to keep him from escaping it.

He made a harsh sound through his teeth.

"Our people are given freely to the sea, but we wish to foul neither sea nor soil with your body," Neyane said. "So, we also condemn you to this box. We will take the box out of the harbor and dump you into the sea, where you will sink like a stone to the bottom. And there you will stay until your gods decide to take you back."

Had Jon or Adayze told her his secret? There were too many fucking coincidences for any of them to actually be a coincidence.

He looked around wildly, unable to keep his calm façade in the face of being trapped in a coffin. Neyane's voice dripped with venom as she finished her speech. Was it because she believed he'd hurt Adayze and Edo, or was she really bent on getting rid of him for some other reason?

What if he broke and told the truth?

No, he couldn't do that. The whole purpose of this ruse was to keep Edo *safe*. To uncover Promethi's duplicity, to find Guin, to help Adayze...

He was sweating as the Ibuu looped the rope around his neck. His fingers and toes had begun to feel alarmingly distant, as if death was creeping up on him. He tried not to fight it as the cold climbed his arms and legs. His body felt like lead. He tried to move and couldn't and his heart raced with fear.

It's Chayma's potion, idiot. Let it work. You're going to be killed anyway; what does it matter if you can't move your arm?

What would it be like to be paralyzed inside that coffin? Would he still be aware? Would Adayze let them dump him into the ocean, dead or not?

Calm down. Remember why you're doing this, who you're doing it for. Stand firm, gods damn you.

The Ibuu stood behind him, the ends of the rope crossed in an X to tighten around his throat. A cold heaviness had begun to creep into his chest. He was having trouble breathing and the Ibuu hadn't yet pulled the rope; his heartbeat, which had been too fast, skipped and slowed and paused. He tried to gulp in air, feeling like he was suffocating already.

At that moment, the Ibuu yanked the rope taut.

Panic slammed into him, black and heavy. He tried to get his arms around to claw at the rope, but he couldn't even make them twitch. He knew Erelf would never let him forget the unforgiving expression on the Ibuu's face as the Ibuu dragged his body backward and choked him against his boots. But he didn't know if it was Erelf or Chayma's potion that left him aware, trapped in his own body, as the Ibuu dropped him into the mud and two men stuffed him into the tight wooden box. He could see the sky for a moment—silver as metal.

Then they dropped the lid on top of him and the airless dark swallowed him up.

ARSENAULT

IT SEEMED LIKE HE WAS FROZEN AND TRAPPED IN THAT BLACKNESS for an infinite time. Then slowly he began to feel again. At first he was sure it was his imagination, but as the feeling persisted and grew, he realized—the drug was wearing off.

Arsenault wanted to laugh, in a crazy way. The magic bans the coffinmaker had carved into the wood must have negated the magic of Chayma's potion. So, now he was going to be *aware* that he was trapped in a coffin when it sank to the bottom of the sea.

Great fucking gods.

He twitched his fingers to assure himself he could move. The drug must have still retained its effectiveness as a sedative or Arsenault knew he'd be clawing at the lid and shouting to be let out. As it was, it felt like a dream. The terror of the small space was muted—

But not enough. Arsenault wanted to close his eyes to get hold of himself, but closing his eyes made everything seem smaller, tighter, darker, like he was running out of air—

All the drug was doing was making it hard to *think*.

Slow breaths. The boards aren't airtight. There's a gap at the corner; they built the coffin too fast...

He and Guin had built a few coffins. Guin even dove-tailed the joints, as if he were making a bridal chest and not a box to hold a corpse. *The dead also deserve my best,* he'd said. This coffinmaker had thought Arsenault had deserved his worst *and* he'd been in a hurry. The magic bans were carved with care; Arsenault could feel them crawling around him. But with every bounce and rattle of the cart, the boards vibrated a little farther apart.

Arsenault tried to work his toe into the gap. Each movement threatened to make the panic worse; the only way around it was to narrow his focus to *doing* the action instead of worrying about the outcome. *Where are your feet?* he asked himself, but they wouldn't move enough, he couldn't quite get his toe in, and every fucking bump rattled him—

Use the bumps!

He started shoving on the boards at the end of the coffin with both feet every time they hit a bump. The dim light inside grew a little brighter, the air in the coffin—so hot it stole what breath he had—began to move a little more. He tried to take a big breath and his throat throbbed; being trapped in the coffin had almost made him forget he'd just been strangled.

He wasn't supposed to cough, dammit. He was supposed to be dead. He bit his lip on the sound.

"Ho!" someone called—a man's voice; no one he recognized. Probably a servant, somebody to take out the trash. "Did you hear a noise?"

"Corpses make noise sometimes."

"Has he been dead long enough?"

"Magic on the lid to keep him in if the Ibuu didn't finish."

The magic on the lid would probably be enough to keep the lid on. It would also prevent him from Fixing the nails—the gods would have come down hard on him for that anyway—but fortunately, it didn't keep him from using his completely human muscles on the side boards. Good for him that Promethi had built him into a mythical creature reliant on magic or else they might have built the box to contain him tighter in addition to warding it.

The cart stopped. Arsenault forced himself to lie still while rivulets of sweat dripped from his forehead down the back of his neck. Then the sickening sensation of being lifted carelessly in the air, dipping, swaying—

The coffin fell. Or they dropped it. His head snapped up and back and cracked on the bottom. The impact jarred through his whole body. He bit his lip hard to keep from crying out, and another wave of panic hit him. Fear always seemed to draw on an inexhaustible well. He breathed through his nose until the feeling ebbed.

On the ship, he couldn't risk making noise. His tiny movements might have helped nothing but his state of mind. It seemed like it took forever but also like it was only a moment before the coffin was lifted again.

This time—*shit*—going over the side...

The feeling of being suspended in the air, even for a moment, was strange. His stomach lurched as the coffin began to tip—headfirst—

And then it hit the water with a crash.

The impact was just as bad as when they'd dropped the coffin on the ship's deck. His head snapped against the boards and then the rest of his body, with nowhere to move, simply absorbed the force. It took his breath and he missed the chance to prepare for the water rushing into the gap he'd made bigger by kicking. It swirled around his bare feet as he tried to kick the board again. The coffin continued to tumble and sink, except for another jarring impact that drove his head, hard, against the end of the coffin.

What the hell was he hitting? Rocks, reef, what?

The gap at the end split wide open. The boards wrenched apart and the water—to his knees now—gushed in. He gulped in a deep breath just before the water filled his air space, then slammed his feet into the end board of the coffin.

The wood splintered and the coffin fell apart, leaving him suddenly floating in a mess of spinning boards. One hit him in the head, and a cloud of blood bloomed around him as he shoved the board away. He clawed out from under the lid and tried to get his bearings in the murky water. Pulled himself forward and hit more timber—

Great gods. An Eterean ship.

A monster—a dragon or a serpent—was painted on the hull, still visible through all the crusted barnacles and coral that had grown over the wreck. Silver glimmered through the cracked planking of the deck. The hold was full of it.

Arsenault grabbed a post and turned himself over, searching frantically for the light of the surface impossibly far above. He didn't have enough air to reach it, let alone search the wreck. Chayma's magic was creeping in again. His calves began to cramp as he hauled himself up the mast.

The shadow of something big moved in the corner of his eye. *Damn, the blood...* He was not going to be eaten by a fucking shark, not after he'd escaped a coffin. The shape darted toward him; he kicked off the wreck as hard as he could—

Suddenly the surface cracked above him. Something long and sharp hurtled through the water—

A spear hit the shark in the side. It thrashed, whipping into him with its tail, casting him down, farther from the surface. In desperation, Arsenault glimpsed a rope snaking down from the shadow on the surface and lurched for it. He wrapped it around his hand, just as the potion pushed through him again, freezing his limbs. All that effort and he was going to drown anyway. Would the potion keep him from needing air? The burning darkness was taking him over.

The rope quivered. He thought he felt himself being pulled upward. And then—

Maybe it was a dream. Hazy sky. Air. Sunlight. A boat, a fisherman draped in an abaganda, shaded by an enormous hat.

Jon. Jon had come back for him.

CHAPTER 60

ARSENAULT

SERAPO RIVER, TWENTY YEARS AGO

Arsenault! Arsenault!

Whose voice, calling him?

No, rub his arms, they're too cold. Is he breathing? Use the mirror!

We're supposed to pound his chest if he takes too long.

Dammit, it's been eight days. What if he's really dead?

A fist slammed down on his chest above his heart, like he was a blade being hammered by a smith. Another blow rained down on him and it felt as if molten steel were rolling through his veins.

He forced his eyes open before they could hit him again.

"Thank all the powers," a woman's voice whispered. "He's alive."

"Stop hitting me, for the gods' sake," he croaked, his voice thick and distant in his own ears.

"If you start breathing on your own, we will. It's damned unnerving to see you lying there so still."

Did he know that voice? It wasn't Adayze, but it sounded familiar...

He opened his eyes again. This time he moved his head, too, so he could look up and around.

"Etranée?"

She smiled that twist of a smile he remembered, then laughed weakly and hung her head in relief. A few strands of chestnut hair spilled out of her headcloth and brushed his cheek. Beside her stood her first mate Koji, scowling, and on the other side of the bed—Seely, the big quartermaster with the scars.

Seely cracked his knuckles and grinned. "Too bad he's awake, Captain. I might have liked getting in a few more blows."

"Maybe later, Seely," Etranée said. "Wouldn't want to forfeit all that gold Jon paid us, would we?"

"Jon...paid you?" Arsenault rasped.

"To ship you on board, although you were nearly as cold as a corpse and soaking wet, like he'd hauled you up with the latest catch. He said to give you eight days and then make sure we could wake you. And that you remembered our names. Do you?"

Arsenault looked them over, making sure he remembered the events they'd been party to as well. He found he remembered Etranée's dusky skin and ale-colored eyes too well. Relief flooded him.

"I didn't die after all," he said in wonder.

"Apparently not. But just say our names so I can report to Jon you're all right."

"Etranée, Seely... Koji. Hello."

Koji folded her arms over her chest and glared at him. He found it so familiar he wanted to leap out of bed and dance her around the room so she'd scowl at him more. Thankfully, his body hadn't quite caught up to his brain.

"Well," Etranée said. "I suppose this is as good a time as any to welcome you back to the crew...and let you know that if you make a step out of line this time, I'll run you through myself."

⚜

"You didn't tell Jon the whole story, did you?"

Time had run away from him in all sorts of ways, but now he was finally able to sit up in bed. Etranée leaned against a table, interrogating him while he ate.

He wasn't on the *Good Fortune*. The table Etranée was leaning against was not the same table. It was an exquisitely carved piece of teak bolted to the floor. But that was all he knew.

"The whole story of what?" he asked, reaching for a third piece of bread. He'd already finished a bowl of soup, a rack of tiny smoked fish, and a dish of fried yams and plantains. Etranée had allowed him water and tea, but no beer or wine. He was a little disappointed, but even water and tea seemed celebratory now.

"The whole story of you on my boat. Jon wouldn't have been so sure of himself if he'd known that code you signed obligated me to kill you on sight."

"So, why am I still alive?"

"Well, for one thing, you looked like you might already be dead. And for another, Jon paid me well. In addition, you have my information about Fariq, don't you? You must have gotten it before you drowned his mate."

"If he hadn't attacked me, the boat would never have turned turtle in the first place."

"That's a split hair, Arsenault."

"*Splitting hairs* is the term, I believe, Etranée."

She waved his words away, folded her arms over her chest, and walked closer to him. It was more like a sashay. He had to force his gaze away from her hips. Damn the woman anyway.

She leaned on the bed. "In any case, imagine my surprise when I received a note from Jon telling me he knew about my connections to Neyane dom B'ara, and if I didn't want them exposed, I'd meet him to see about a job."

What was Jon doing? Did he trust his aunt or was he trying to ferret out more information about her through Etranée?

"I wonder how he knew about Neyane," Arsenault said innocently.

Etranée arched an eyebrow and her mouth quirked. "I wonder. What in the name of all the gods is going on, Arsenault?"

"How long have I been lying here in your bedroom?"

"Almost nine days now. When Jon brought you down, you looked ghastly. White as a corpse, lips tinged blue, big purple bruise around your neck as if you'd been hanged, except your face wasn't black. And then the smell of fish and saltwater." She sat on the edge of the bed and stole one of the small, fried balls of puff from his plate. "Strange he brought you down the day after we heard the Ibuu executed a magician for the murder of his grandson and the attempted rape of his daughter."

Arsenault gave her a sharp glance. "Do you really believe I'd do those things?"

"Considering you knifed two men in cold blood before anyone had a *single clue* what you intended? I think you're capable of extreme violence."

"But a child? And rape?"

"Oh, don't look at me that way. No, I didn't believe it. I had a hard time matching that man to the man who'd seemed so *chivalrous* when it came to seeing to my needs before he satisfied his own."

She gave him an enigmatic smile and slid the puff into her mouth.

He lay back into the pillows, trying to ignore the memories of her he had definitely not lost. "I was a proper knight in shining armor, was I?"

"Well, maybe not. But I didn't think you were the sort of man who'd take a woman by force. It also seemed strange that Jon would rescue such a man and put him on the same boat with the Heir. Unless Jon was behind the assassination attempt and wanted Lady Adayze dead, too?"

"No. I did not kill Edo and I would never lay a hand on Adayze. And neither would Jon. Are you satisfied?"

"I also want to know how you got your hands on a Dininga death drug and the magic needed to activate it."

"Is that what it was?"

"You took it without even knowing anything about it?"

"I didn't have much of a choice."

"And you used not a single honorific when you spoke of the Heir. You and Jon are in the royal household, aren't you?"

If only Jon had given him more instructions.

"I'm on your side, Etranée. I'm still trying to find the man Fariq sold to Dirik dom Arak. That hasn't changed. Adayze's interests align with mine in this case. And probably yours. Promethi dom Arak was involved in the business with Edo and is almost assuredly in league with Fariq, but we need proof." He hesitated, then decided to take the risk full on. "There's something going on at the palace. I'm not privy to everything Jon knows or everything he's doing. But Neyane may be involved."

Etranée sat back in surprise. "You think Neyane's in league with Fariq? Is that what you're trying to say?"

"She was awfully keen to get rid of me. And she'd warned me a long time ago not to stick my nose in. There's a sunken ship in the bay that looked as if it might have a lot of Eterean metal in it, but I...I wasn't able to investigate."

"There are a lot of sunken ships in the bay, Arsenault. Mdembu's been the most important harbor on the east coast for centuries, probably since before the Gods' War. Some of those ships might have belonged to Tekus himself. You're accusing Neyane of plundering the wrecks for magic metal?"

"You heard about the sphinx."

"You think *Neyane* had something to do with the sphinx that killed her own nephew?

"I don't know." Arsenault rubbed his forehead, where his cut was still scabbed up. "You honestly think there could be wrecks from the fleet of the gods down there? Or were you just joking?"

"The legends say so. But it's difficult to separate fact from propaganda in the old compendiums. Every merchant in the Old World wanted to advertise that they did business with the gods, because the gods paid in magic. My father spent countless hours poring over those manuscripts, trying to discover what that *actually* meant in those days. Was it Fixing magic, Sight, or something else we've lost? How did the gods grant mortals magic that wasn't permanent? Or *was* it permanent, given after a certain amount of service? The writers couched so much of their relationship with the gods in metaphor and hyperbole, probably to keep their competition away. My father finally came to believe the gods paid mortals with a sort of magical elixir that temporarily granted them the Talents we associate with magic today. The perk of doing the gods' business was being able to feel like they *were* gods. What my father wanted to know—theologically—was what changed in the Gods' War for the gods themselves. He thought the legends seemed to indicate that before the war, even the gods could die. Erelf killed his brother and there's that story of Erelf's daughter—"

"I know it," Arsenault cut her off brusquely. She blinked at him, surprised, and he tried to smooth his tone. "There are a lot of stories of the old times. What bothers me most is that someone seems to be trying to bring them back—or at least to use their remains."

Etranée regarded him curiously. "You're not a treasure hunter, are you, Arsenault? Searching in vain for the Legacy of Attrasca?"

He picked up his cup of tea. "If I was a treasure hunter, would I tell you about that wreck?"

"I do wonder at how many ancient authors you've read. In your life as a mercenary and a galleyman. Oji la Kaif didn't seem to think the Legacy of Attrasca was an artifact, you know. Some people say Oji must have been granted some of the old magic himself, the way the gods rewarded their favorites in the old times. He produced an enormous number of manuscripts over his lifetime and if you add up the dates, they don't quite make sense."

Arsenault sipped his tea and frowned. "Could be mistakes in copying."

"My father didn't think so. That was the whole reason we came south. My father wanted to pursue his ideas about magic, how it worked, where it came from. He didn't have any magic himself, but he was endlessly fascinated by it. And then..." She broke off with a bitter, mirthless laugh and looked away from him, smoothing her skirts over her knee. "You know, he would have found it somewhat ironic that his search for immortality killed him. But in essence that's how it went. Anyway, what happened to my father is neither here nor there."

Arsenault tried to absorb what she'd told him. He wanted to ask more questions, like how the daughter of a scholar had become a privateer and if her father's death had anything to do with it. But immortality was a topic he didn't like to ponder too long. He still held out hope his life would really end one day. And he sure as all the hells felt as mortal as anyone else. He rubbed the bruise on his neck that had turned yellow and ugly.

Curious about Oji, though.

"So, you don't know why Neyane would want the metal. Or what kinds of dealings she might have with Dirik or Promethi," he said.

"We work on a need-to-know basis. I can infer a few things. She's involved in the manufacture of guns and cannon, and she has channels for moving them that operate outside the Ibuu's official gunsmiths— or else we wouldn't have guns. She gives me names to hit, mostly of known pirates.

"But not always?"

Etranée looked troubled. "There are a few targets I've regretted hitting based on later information. But it does help our cover; the underworld doesn't think we're *too* good. I've never questioned that Neyane was loyal to the Ibuu, though. The rumors that sift through the back channels paint her as a ruthless woman, but it's not so different from what people say about me. Neyane just keeps her private life more discreet. She *is* the Ibuu's Dagger. She's been trained from childhood to work in the shadows."

"I'm just trying to figure out why Jon roped you into this plot. Are you going to let me stay or not?"

"Of course I'll let you stay. Jon paid for all the repairs to my ship and gave me this beautiful riverboat, too. But we're going to have a little trouble with the crew. I couldn't get you in here all by myself, so various people know who you are. They'll expect me to adhere to the code. If I allow an exception to a man they know I was bedding, then..."

Damn Jon, why couldn't he have found anyone other than Etranée to chase Promethi? Was this his idea of a joke?

He sighed. "Fine. I was just strangled mostly to death, put in a coffin, and almost drowned, what's a few lashes on top of that?"

"I'm not going to lash you. You're going to fight Seely on deck for a right to a berth."

CHAPTER 61

ARSENAULT

"It'll be easiest to give you a Qalfan story, so you can veil. Your Qalfan is antique, but it will do. Where did you learn it?" Etranée asked as her navigator, Sandro, sorted a bundle of white linen that turned out to be an urqa and allaq.

"From a friend. A long time ago." Arsenault grabbed his shirt and pulled it off over his head. He was sure it had been a friend, but he didn't know how he knew. "I've worn robes before; you don't have to teach me."

Etranée gave him a lingering, appreciative glance. "Good. Unfortunately, I think this is my signal to leave."

"You told me I was allowed my own hammock," he called jokingly after her.

"Keep going and I'll tell Jon I've decided to lock you in my room and make you my personal slave."

"Hey," Sandro said. "There's no mixing business and pleasure. Isn't that what you tell us all the time?"

She shot them a blinding smile over her shoulder. "Good for me pleasure and business cross sometimes, isn't it?" Then she pulled the door shut firmly behind her.

As soon as she was gone, the humor leaked from Sandro's eyes. "You know, she's more than a joke and a quick tumble in the bed."

Arsenault paused in the process of pulling on the allaq over his trousers.

"People look at her and see the Spider," Sandro went on. "The Scourge of Alabad. But she's a woman, too."

"I'd figured that out."

"You take advantage of her generosity again, and I don't care if you're working for the Magnificent Sun himself, we'll gut you and heave your body overboard."

Arsenault straightened the allaq down his legs. "Generosity? I watched her maneuver a man into dying by choking on his own hat, for the gods' sake."

"She ripped up your writ, didn't she? The same way she ripped up all of ours."

Oh.

It all made sense now.

"You're all former indentures," he said. "Or slaves? Her whole crew?"

Sandro eyed him curiously. "You didn't know?"

"Etranée, too?"

"We escaped together, Koji, Seely, Yeo, Etranée, me, because we knew our way around ships. We thought we'd be able to take more ships by surprise if our captain was a woman. Etranée and Koji sorted their roles together. You thank your gods you never had to deal with the Sugar Kingdom."

Arsenault put two fingers to the fading bruise left by the Ibuu's rope. "Instead, I got this. So much better."

"Hey, you had a choice. You chose the noose. That's all on you. But if you think we're going to let you endanger our ship or our captain for any amount of money from Jon, you'd better think again. We'll be watching, even if you beat Seely into the deck." Sandro grinned. "I'd like to see you try, though."

Arsenault returned the grin weakly, then belted the allaq. When he had pulled it snug on his hips, he lifted the hem, tucking it into the belt he'd created. After that he wrapped the urqa around his head and face, leaving a gap for his eyes and making sure it wasn't too tight to pull below his chin.

Sandro watched him with a troubled gaze. "Was your friend Nezari? You wear those robes Nezar style."

Arsenault had to think for a moment to remember what a Nezar was. The elite guard employed by the Emperor? No, maybe there were more Nezari now. He shrugged wordlessly.

Sandro eyed him critically, then rewrapped his own urqa. "It'll do. Hides your scar and your hair. But let the allaq down. If any real Nezari saw you, we'd be in trouble."

"All right," Arsenault said. He didn't like the fabric swishing around his calves, but he could deal with it. "Have you created a story for me, or am I to invent one myself?"

Sandro turned to the cabinet built into the far wall and opened the door. A row of swords and knives gleamed in the morning light—weapons for him to choose, finally. "With your looks, I'd say you're the son of a guard who tired of protecting his master's wares from bandits down through the Wastes. Now you want to fight for your own profit. That cover it?"

Arsenault raised a brow. "I'll make it work."

৩৶৯

WHEN ARSENAULT ARRIVED UP TOP, AN AUDIENCE HAD ALREADY gathered around Seely, who had stripped to the waist and was stretching his arms. The scars on the big man's face had their counterparts on his back and chest; he'd been flogged in the past, probably more than once, and the history of it stood out in thick, silvery-white ridges.

Arsenault remembered Etranée insisting on feeling his back before they made love. The way she moved sometimes, stiffly, as if she were in pain. He'd thought that the remnant of an injury taken as a pirate, but maybe it wasn't. Her words came back to him— *Anyway, what happened to my father is neither here nor there.* But maybe it was always here, always with her.

Unease touched him briefly, like a cold hand on his neck.

She stood between them, cutlass out. She wore a smart blue silk tunic, a matching Tiresian split skirt, a royal blue headscarf to hold back her hair. The rings on her fingers flashed in the sun. She looked confident—piratical. But it was just a disguise, wasn't it? She was beginning to make sense inside her glass bowl, the way she said you could make sense of anybody if you looked at them inside themselves. Arsenault wasn't sure he wanted to feel this close to her. It was different than being close to her body.

"Drop your weapons," she told him. "This is to be a fight with your hands only. And take off your boots."

"My boots?" he asked in surprise.

"Bare feet, bare hands. Those are the rules."

Seely, standing across from him, wriggled his bare toes and grinned. The crew were all there, hoping to see Seely wipe the deck with him—everyone who had a vote and knew about him and everyone who didn't. Yeo looked up at him with a knowing smirk as she held out her hands for Arsenault's swordbelt.

"Still want to earn a berth, my dear?" Seely asked as he settled into his fighting stance.

Arsenault raised his hands. "Whenever you're ready."

Fighting was like dancing in a way; they began to walk their wary circle together, sizing each other up. The crew on the sidelines catcalled, hooting and hollering, like a crowd urging the dancers on. He wished he could take off the damn robes; he wasn't used to seeing around the fabric of the urqa.

Focus on Seely's midsection...

Seely twitched to the right.

Arsenault blocked the blow, but Seely immediately followed it with a round kick to his side. He barely managed to dodge the full force; Seely's foot still drove hard into the soft part of his midsection. He fought for breath, snatched at Seely's ankle before the big man could put his leg back on the desk, fought the claustrophobic feeling the robes gave him in this humid heat, and wrenched Seely toward him. The man slipped and fell backwards but caught himself on the mast. Arsenault tried to follow up his advantage with an elbow to the face, but Seely drove his fist into Arsenault's stomach.

"Gods*dammit*," he gasped as he doubled over. Seely's body flashed in front of him. He lurched out of the way purely by instinct and made a flailing grab for Seely's braid as it twitched out behind him like a rope. Arsenault yanked down on it as hard as he could.

Seely careened into Arsenault with a howl, but Arsenault pressed his advantage—wound the other man's hair around one hand and drove the flat of the other up into Seely's nose. But Seely jerked backward into Arsenault's hold, putting them both off balance, and Arsenault missed and loosened his grip on the man's braid.

He wished his swordmaster had been less worried about honor and more worried about teaching him back-alley brawling. Every fist fight was fucking chaos.

Seely pummeled his own fist into Arsenault's ribs, pounding the air out of him again and again like his fist was a bilge pump. Arsenault let go of Seely's braid and staggered backward. Seely followed, catching him under the jaw with an uppercut followed by a blow to the side of his face.

"*Fuck*," he cursed. His voice sounded slushy, distant. Pain rang round his head as he fell backward into a body. *Yeo.*

She flashed him a grin and shoved him back at Seely. "Keep going! You're doing well!"

"Fucking hell," he muttered and barely got his arm up to block another punch Seely threw at him.

He threw his own punch underneath the block. It caught Seely in the chin and felt like he broke every one of his godsdamned knuckles doing it.

This is insane. How long was Etranée going to let this go on? Seely kept hammering him with body blows in places already aching from being hit. He had to use his arms not to hit but to protect—

"Had enough?" Seely panted, pausing for an instant.

He's tired, too. "No," Arsenault gasped and launched himself at the man. The only chance he had was to turn the fight into a wrestling match, pin Seely's fists so he couldn't use them, but Seely dodged and —there! Another chance at his braid.

He wrapped Seely's hair around his hand, threw him down on the deck, then kicked the big man in the face. Blood erupted from Seely's nose. He drew his foot back to kick Seely again but the big man grabbed his ankles and brought him crashing down, too.

He barely managed to avoid cracking his head. This was fucking it, he was ending this *now.* He snarled and drove his foot into the underside of Seely's jaw as hard as he could. Seely's head snapped back and hit the mast.

Arsenault drew his foot back for another kick but suddenly something thwacked against his chest and the pain in his bruised ribs somehow cut through the haze of fight that had taken him over.

Panting, dripping blood and sweat inside the urqa, which made him feel like his own body was trying to drown him, he stopped kicking Seely and looked up in confusion. Koji stood over him with a staff.

"That's enough. Captain called it a draw."

"A draw?" Seely dragged himself into a sitting position. Blood dripped from the end of his nose until he wiped it away with the back of his forearm. "I was winning most of that."

"It's only the end that matters." Arsenault struggled up. He reached inside his urqa and put a hand to his mouth and then his nose. Both were tender. Everything was tender; he couldn't tell where the blood was coming from. He wanted to wrench the urqa off, but instead he used it to mop his face. At least it was loose now, so he could breathe better.

"Captain's word is what matters," Seely said. "That's what you'll find. If you'll stick around for a rematch."

"Give me a few days to recover. I'm not as young as I used to be."

Seely chuckled. "Nor are any of us, mate." He stretched out a hand. "It was well-fought."

Arsenault took it.

Etranée stood a few feet away with her arms crossed and feet spread wide. She looked a little pale, but she covered it quickly with a twitch of her head.

"You stood up to Seely, so I suppose you've earned your berth. What's your name then? Some awful Dagmari concoction? *Kenute*, perhaps?"

He chuckled behind the urqa and wiped more blood off his face. Then he looked up and over the railing. A large party of well-dressed Dakkarans waited on the dock, Adayze in front, accompanied by two chambermaids holding parasols. She was dressed in a high-necked, tight-fitting white silk dress, her hair tied up in a white headcloth, no jewelry on her wrists and ankles, which made her look as if she had prepared her own body for death. Jon stood behind her, dressed in the uniform of the palace guard, and at her side was Promethi, flanked by Renzo, clad once again in his sky-blue silk tunic and Lieran shirt.

Arsenault's laughter faded. He turned back to Etranée.

"Ari is my name," he said, loud enough for Adayze and Jon to hear. "The one my mother gave me."

A strange expression flickered over Etranée's face. "All right. *Ari*. Get down in the hold and Yeo will see to you."

She turned to the rest of her crew and raised her voice.

"Look lively, you lot! Passengers coming on board! We're shipping when the sun's quarter high!"

CHAPTER 62

CASSIS

THE ROAD NORTH, PRESENT

IT TOOK A SURPRISINGLY SHORT TIME TO REDUCE A BUILDING THE size of a fortress to a pile of rocks.

Cassis hadn't thought things could get worse until they did. Not only had he lost his marriage, his money, his ship, his guns, his supplies, his freedom, and his pride, but now he had to watch as his sole remaining possession crumbled to dust: the Aliente hunting lodge.

He and Lupa were on the eastern road, taking a roundabout route to avoid Devid's gavaros, when the lodge blew. The Empirists had "loaned" him an escort of fifteen men who didn't wear armbands; instead, they wore wolf's head badges to represent the Imperium, which Cassis thought was a bit pretentious.

Saying the explosion took them by surprise was like saying it was a "surprise" to see Liera sink into the lagoon on a bright spring day. Lupa whipped out his spyglass when the first loud crack of stone split the air and kept it as the roar of the collapsing building shook the ground beneath them. The horses plunged and reared, and Cassis had a hell of a time getting his mount under control. By then, the whole building lay in rubble. When Lupa finally did hand him the spyglass, Cassis couldn't keep it steady enough to look through properly. Could anyone inside have survived that disaster? And then Vokavik's army swarmed over the rocks like ants invading a carcass.

He handed the glass back to Lupa, feeling sick. "I think I've seen enough."

Lupa sighed. "Who knows what treasures have been lost beneath the rubble."

"I don't really care about treasures right now, Ser Lupa. I'm thinking about my men." Was there anything he could do, though, even if there were survivors? The Empirist "escort" was really a guard to make sure he didn't escape Empirist control. He was being treated like a hostage, not an ally. "Let's get this over with before I lose the stomach for it."

Lupa eyed him curiously over his spectacles. "I've never heard about Kyrra d'Aliente being homely, mestere, just ill-tempered."

"It's not—oh, never mind. You wouldn't understand. But I have to warn you—"

Cassis paused. The collapse of the lodge left him too shocked and numb to think properly. He kept seeing that cloud of dust and Vokavik's army swarming through it, over and over again. Had he really lost not only the building, but his entire army? All those men...

He didn't need to tell Lupa about Arsenault. If this marriage with Kyrra would really help keep the peace in Liera—if it would help him avoid more disasters like *this* one—then he wanted it to work in its upside-down diabolical fashion. But he'd rather have a knife up his sleeve in case the Empirists wanted to stab him in the back. Which he was reasonably sure they did.

"Mestere?" Lupa prompted politely.

"I have to warn you that Kyrra *is* ill-tempered. You may change your mind about her political expediency. If what you say is true and she is alive."

They traveled on in ridiculous silence for a while. Who in all the hells just *rode away* from such a disaster without stopping to investigate or help or even to cope with the enormity of it all—a whole building!—as if it was something that happened every day? Cassis didn't know if it made him angry, or if, by this point, he was just numb.

Finally, Lupa said, "I am curious as to what Kyrra d'Aliente has been doing in a country farm so far north."

"Yes, well, I'd like to know that, too." Under his breath he muttered to himself, "And I'm sure she'll tell us if we ask nicely."

"What was that, mestere?"

"Nothing," Cassis said. "My latest intelligence was that someone who *might* be her had taken up residence there with a few of her supporters."

"This champion, perhaps, who murdered your father?"

"Perhaps," Cassis hedged. "It'll be best if we leave the men at the bottom of the road when we approach the house, to avoid signaling we're a threat. I'm...I'm not sure how many supporters she would have with her. If it's really Kyrra in the first place."

He wasn't sure how long he should uphold this fiction that he didn't know she was alive. It had become less about Kyrra and more about protecting himself now.

"You speak as if you know the terrain?"

"This whole area was riddled with Aliente fighters during the war. A few of these places belonged to men my father executed. This house is one of them."

"According to the accounts I've pieced together, there were others involved in the final battle with Geoffre di Prinze." Lupa ticked them off on his fingers. "The Dakkaran merchant Jon Barra, whom you accused my secretary of having ties to; Mikelo di Prinze, whom you took prisoner but allowed to escape; and a gavaro named *Andris*."

"Mikelo is no threat," Cassis said. "He doesn't even want the Chair. His father Renzo is the real problem."

"What about this gavaro, Andris? Is he one of these supporters you mentioned? Your father used to bring him to Empirist meetings, according to my compatriots. He was privy to much of what they spoke about. He was also a Fixer, I believe. But he betrayed you, didn't he?"

Cassis tried to make his voice bland. "How so?"

"Well, he was your gavaro, wasn't he? According to some of the men I talked to in Devid's camp, he gave away all your positions to Geoffre. Before or after he was tortured, but I'm not sure it matters. What I don't know is whether he died in the battle."

"Why are you so interested in a gavaro? So my father brought him to Empirist meetings. My father's Talent lay in using the Talents of others. I'm sure he was using Andris, the way he did all the Fixers he collected. He *liked* to use people."

"I'm just wondering if we'll be facing this Andris when we get to this house. You don't think Kyrra d'Aliente will see reason? That we'll have to use force?"

"You know it won't look at all *noble* if we kidnap her."

"It will be her word against ours, won't it?"

"I suppose so," Cassis muttered through gritted teeth.

"It would be a pity if Andris had died, mestere. I believe he could also be an asset for us. If Geoffre brought him to the Empirist meetings, it was because he had a particular kind of magic or knowledge. Are you quite sure he died in the battle?"

While Lupa spoke, he reached into his pocket and pulled out something metal that glittered in the light. It wasn't Kyrra's wolf, because he carried that in his other pocket. This was smaller, made of gold. As Lupa turned it in his gloved hand, Cassis caught a glimpse of something that looked like a flower—a daisy. Thank the gods Lupa seemed distracted because Cassis had to fight not to respond. *Did Lupa know Arsenault couldn't die?*

He decided to play it safe. "I didn't witness exactly what happened to him. But the way my men told it, my father was trying to have him drawn and quartered."

How had he come to the point where he was protecting Arsenault? He didn't know what he wanted anymore, except to get free of this trap. And to not die doing it.

The darkness of night as they'd camped beside the road had allowed him some time for thought. The Empirists had killed Devid's guards and smuggled him out of the prison by staging a riot that demonstrated everything they'd told him was true: The people hated what Geoffre di Prinze had put them through. Marriage to Kyrra wasn't a bad idea, politically, but how the hell was he going to get out from under the Empirists' thumb? He had no objections to them if they'd support him as subjects of the city, but that was antithetical to their whole reason for being. *Unless* he could convince them that he was interested in and capable of being a new Attrasca.

Kyrra would laugh in his face. The new Arsenault would kill him.

If Kyrra would just play along long enough, if he could convince Arsenault it was a ruse, maybe he could earn Jon Barra's support by promising Jon he'd reinstate the Barra to the Ibuu's Throne. If he climbed to power on the back of the Empirists... If he promised to settle Kyrra on her own lands as soon as he'd gained the power to root out the Empirists... If he kept Jon and Arsenault in his pocket... If he portrayed himself as a patriotic and democratic Lieran faithful to the Council...

It might work.

It would take years, but it might work.

A rustle in the trees at the side of the road caught his attention. Lupa put up his hand to stop. The men reined in their horses and formed a protective ring around them. Guns and swords came out. The brush rustled again, but this time, a man stepped out of it.

Clothes torn and filthy, Tiresian beads clacking against each other in his long braids...

"Tomas!" Lupa exclaimed.

"Ser Lupa! I-I wasn't expecting to see you on this road."

So Lupa's secretary survived but not—

A figure moved behind Tomas. A dirt-smeared white sleeve fluttered in the wind, shoving aside a branch...

Lobardin grinned at him. "Well, mestere, so we both managed to stay alive!"

CHAPTER 63

LOBARDIN

*A*LIVE.

That was the strangest thing. Lobardin had expected to be dead. He'd even prepared himself for the likelihood. Thrown a vota into the well, said some very heartfelt prayers to Ekyra, resisted the urge to get roaring drunk with Tomas in the empty, already crumbling lodge after everyone else had escaped through the tunnels. Alone, they packed their little remaining powder into the holes he and his men had drilled into the weak points of the cellars and caves.

They use gunpowder to quarry rock in Dakkar, Tomas had told him. *We don't have Fixed powder, but the method is the same. If you blow a keg of gunpowder, its force is large, but the blast is only focused in one area, yes? If you spread the explosion out into lots of smaller explosions, you spread out the area the powder affects. If you use the powder to take away the stone of the lodge's foundation...*

It will fall into the caves! Lobardin had exclaimed happily. Then—*No, wait, Tomas, how do we get out?*

Tomas had looked very serious. *We hope we have enough rope.*

But there had been enough rope, plenty of rope, or well, maybe not *plenty* because the rope had burned a lot damned faster than he and Tomas had speculated it would. The first explosion had gone off when they were barely halfway down the passage. They'd run like hell, with bombs exploding behind them and the rumbling...

Lobardin never wanted to hear that sound again. He knew he would hear it in his sleep, in thunderstorms, in drums, at odd, terri-fying moments, the way he also heard gunfire and cannons, but by all the gods, they had outrun it. They had outrun the trembling ceiling of the passage, the millions of tons of rock cascading down behind them, plummeting maybe even to the center of the earth, and the runnels of black *stuff* that had begun pouring out of the cracks in the walls. The substance had eaten a giant red weal down his arm and burned Tomas's binding mark into his skin like a brand, but they had *made* it. Out of the collapsing darkness, down the passage that felt like it would never end, and finally into the light.

Lobardin had almost forgotten that light existed when they'd pulled themselves out of the ground. Shafts of white sunlight falling between still leafless branches had blinded them both and they had thrown themselves on the ground, cold and muddy as it was, and looked up at the blue sky and the clouds and laughed like lunatics.

Alive, by all the gods.

But now...Lupa and Cassis. And a lot of armed men. Not men he recognized.

Lobardin fixed his grin in place as he quickly counted the men—what was that, a fucking wolf's head? So, they weren't Cassis's. And what was Cassis doing riding *past* the lodge with Lupa? Something—a lot of somethings—didn't add up.

"Lobardin—Captain," Cassis said, as if trying to recover both his composure and his sense of command. "Can you tell me what happened to my fortress?"

"Ah. Yes, mestere." Lobardin bowed. Erased the grin and replaced it with a more military visage. Tried not to panic. This was the moment that had worried him most—even more than escaping a falling building, which made not a lick of sense. But now that it was here, he found it wasn't the sort of moment he'd been envisioning at all.

When he came back up from his bow, he clasped his hands behind his back and prepared to report. Lupa watched him inscrutably from behind his spectacles. He sat his horse very easily—too easily. Meanwhile, Tomas had tensed.

"Vokavik's cannons were going to destroy the wall," Lobardin said. "I had to decide between the lodge and the men, and I chose to save the men. We got everyone out through the passageways."

Cassis cast a quick glance sideways at Lupa. "I assume you gave them a rendezvous point."

"Yes, mestere. I ordered them to Padera." Actually, Lobardin had ordered his men to disperse by squadron and send word to him in Padera giving their location so he could contact them. Men couldn't be expected to fight without coin or food. Treating them with respect would go a long way toward keeping their loyalty when it came time to fight again, with Vokavik now firmly fixed in their mind as an enemy—and by extension, Devid. But he didn't want to blab all that in front of Lupa. Not after what Tomas had told him, and not until he got a better handle on *this* situation.

"And so—do I have this clear—you *let* Vokavik destroy the lodge?"

"His cannons must have finally hit a weak point," Lobardin lied. "All those passages and caves underneath… It stood against ancient warfare, but not with our modern methods."

Tomas, gods bless him, remained silent. Lobardin still had no idea where the man's loyalty ultimately lay, but it didn't seem to lie entirely with Lupa.

Lupa leaned forward on his horse. "And did the collapse…release anything? Turn up any artifacts?"

"I'd imagine any artifacts are pulverized, ser."

"Hmm. Were you injured? That looks like a burn."

"Arquebus misfire."

Lupa didn't look satisfied with his answer. Had Lupa known about the black acidic substance, too?

Cassis turned to Lupa. "Let these men have horses and order two of your men to walk."

Two of *your* men?

Oh, this was bad. This was not what he had expected at all.

"Very well." Lupa gestured at the two men closest to him. "Give your horse to Mestere di Prinze's man, and of course my secretary will need one. You two bring up the rear. Watch out for any complications caused by Captain Lobardin's military strategy."

"Where are we going?" Lobardin asked.

Cassis turned wan. He wasn't even doing a good job of *looking* like he was in charge.

"To find Kyrra," Cassis said. "And present her with marriage papers."

CHAPTER 64

ARSENAULT

FARMHOUSE, PRESENT

THE HOUSE SEEMED EMPTY WITH ONLY HIM AND KYRRA IN IT.

The others had left before dawn. Kyrra had slept fitfully all night but woke to see them off. So far, a mixture of Miranda's herbs, magic, and kacin had kept her functional. Now, she was sleeping on her father's couch in front of the fire, wrapped up in one of Miranda's blankets. The reflection of the couch's exposed burgundy silk glimmered on her arm, as if the very metal was bleeding, and the house was too quiet. Like all good-byes.

Arsenault didn't often have the luxury of good-byes, but even if there was space for them, he preferred not to. It was a fiction he upheld for himself that farewells wouldn't be final. He moved through the lives of others; some people grieved him, some cursed him. Then he went on to the next place, all the people he'd forgotten like a feeling lying just under his skin in a forever present he could never access but that remained with him nonetheless.

It was so quiet he found it hard to focus on his task—dismantling Kinstealer. They'd already borrowed an extra day from Kyrra so he could make what Jon needed for his idea. Arsenault wasn't sure it would work, but Kyrra had agreed it was worth a try. And setting the forge to rights and pounding out his fears and worries on a blade amid all the destruction had helped him reorient himself. Now he was trying to remove the hilt and pommel from the Prinze sword in the hopes he wouldn't have to use the blade at all. Maybe the hilt would contain all the metal they needed. But the peg that fastened the tang to the hilt felt like it was welded in, not merely hammered. The artisan in him forced him to take care instead of reducing the damn thing to slag the way it deserved.

Someone of exceptional Talent had forged that serpent. Even the serpent's eye sockets had been crafted with extreme artistry, which he'd discovered when he'd popped out its sapphire eyes and felt as if he'd blinded a living creature. The metal had been formed from the corpse of a true serpent, he was sure of it; it had devoured the flesh of its loved ones; it had been overtaken by anger and wept—

He shook himself out of the grip of the metal and picked up his small hammer again. He tapped the peg with the hammer, then hit it harder in frustration when it wouldn't budge—a little too hard. The peg suddenly popped free, releasing the tang of the blade, which slipped and sliced his thumb. Blood welled up and dripped onto the cloth he'd spread on the table to protect it.

"Godsdammit," he muttered. He sucked the cut on his thumb. Now the blade had *his* blood on it. He watched as it spread from the edge toward the center, where it soaked into two nearly invisible markings in the watered pattern of the metal. He squinted. They looked like runes.

"Arsenault? What happened?"

Arsenault looked up, startled. Kyrra stood next to him in her chemise and bare feet. Dammit, he'd gotten lost in the metal again— or she moved quieter than a ghost. "I thought you were asleep," he said.

She put a hand on his shoulder, then frowned at the blood on the blade and the cloth. "Can't sleep. My arm... I heard you swear. You cut yourself?"

He sliced off a strip of cloth with the blade's edge and wound it tightly around his thumb. The thin, makeshift bandage soaked through almost immediately; cuts on fingers bled so much.

"I was being careless. But it showed me something. See, here." He tucked his bloody thumb against his palm and gestured with his knuckles.

"What do they say?"

He started to answer but when she leaned over to look at the blade, her chemise fell open to reveal her breasts, which was very distracting.

"Ah..." he said.

She looked up. Her mouth quirked knowingly. "I'm beginning to think you find injuries attractive."

"I find *you* attractive. You just happen to keep injuring yourself. You attract trouble like a lodestone."

Kyrra rubbed her brow. "An old failing."

Arsenault sighed. He cut another bandage and put more pressure on his thumb; it was still bleeding. "You always assume I mean there's something defective about you. What happens when you bring a bright light into a room full of sick men and hungover drunks?"

She frowned. "They try to put it out."

"Exactly. It's the same thing."

"It isn't. I'm always poking my nose in where it doesn't belong and acting before I think. Mouthing off especially."

"All right, point. But mouthing off doesn't account for all of it."

Her face twisted. "Point," she allowed. "So, what are the runes and why are they hidden on the tang? Did you hide runes on your sword, too?"

"I forged that sword before I had any battlefield experience. I didn't think of the disadvantages of not hiding them."

"So, whoever made this sword..."

"Was either more experienced or had more to hide. And was also exceptionally Talented."

"You say that like it's a crime."

"I don't really want to respect the godsdamned thing. It would be easier to be repulsed by something that wasn't a work of art."

"And the runes?"

"Hard to read, but you can see the slash mark there. Similar to the runes Qalfans use to bind men. Strange to find it on a blade."

"If the sword is tiaannamir, does the rune bind the spirit of the thing into it?"

"There's no need. Spirit and metal aren't separate entities. It *is* the thing. It's not like the spirit can escape."

"Then what is the rune binding?"

"That's a good question." He checked his thumb again. It had finally stopped bleeding. The blood that outlined the odd runes on the blade had begun to thicken and blacken, making them stand out more. "The second rune, here, is a variation on Sanctuary, which I wouldn't have expected to find on this blade either. Destruction, Vengeance, Strength—those would make sense. Even Repulsion, considering how it makes me feel. It's not like this sword has been used to create a haven for anyone."

Kyrra sat beside him, wincing as she gingerly maneuvered her arm. "Geoffre wanted to make his House unassailable."

"There's a difference, trust me. But this is an old version of the rune. It looks a little like how my teacher used to draw it."

"Does the meaning change if you draw it differently? Or does everyone have their own...runestyle, the same way people have different handwriting?"

"To some extent. Sometimes the differences are subtle. Every Fixer has their own personal relationship with the magic, too. So, I suppose the answer is both." He reached for his book, which lay open beside the cloth. Gripping the stylus clumsily because of his thumb, he started trying to copy the rune.

"In the Old World," he said, "someone would have used this rune to hide something, not to keep the wielder of the sword safe."

"The Prinze have never acted like they have anything to hide."

"Maybe whoever wrote the rune was trying to hide something inside the blade and the best way to do that was to give it to a House with a lot of bluster."

Kyrra looked thoughtful. "I always heard that Attrasca gifted the sword to the founder of the Prinze. Maybe Attrasca had the runes drawn into the blade?"

Arsenault concentrated on copying the style of the rune as closely as he could. It did look familiar. "Maybe..."

"Maybe Ires put them in the sword and Attrasca had the sword from him in the first place," Kyrra went on impatiently. "Maybe that's why Ires wanted me to find it. I suppose it's not his fault he can only speak in riddles. He has a sentence with terms he can get around and some he can't, like you."

Like me. Arsenault took a deep breath and put his stylus down.

"Sometimes I forget I'm not under terms anymore," he said.

She frowned and lifted her gaze to his face. The scrape, the flush, the glaze in her eyes—it all made his heart hurt. He stretched out his good hand to touch her, wishing he had Mikelo's Talent to heal it all. "What do you mean?" she asked.

"The dragon. Sneaking about. I didn't lie to you exactly; I just didn't tell you the truth."

She stared at the pieces of the sword in silence.

"Would you marry Cassis?" he went on. "To save the city, your House? In the Circle, our scars would only count as a gavaro love oath. Not the same legally as a householder contract."

She made a noise and wrapped her good arm around herself as if she were cold. A ball of dread began to form in his stomach.

"I don't know why I didn't tell you what he said. Maybe I was trying to pretend he didn't say it. I kept *meaning* to tell you, but there never seemed to be a good time."

"You didn't answer the question, Kyrra."

"I told him it was a ridiculous proposal."

"Are you still using conjure magic?"

"I—"

"Kyrra. It would be ridiculous and hypocritical for me to be angry about you having lovers while we were apart, considering the things I did. I mean—it *would* be ridiculous, but I can't pretend I wouldn't also feel like punching in their teeth if I met them in a tavern."

She snorted. Almost a laugh. "Now you know how I feel about Madame Triente. Even though I know she used you because it made her feel important to have a big strong man for a whore. That just gives me a second reason to want to punch her."

He flinched. But of course, it was true.

"Sorry," Kyrra said. "Mouthing off again." She paused. "There weren't any lovers, Arsenault. There were a couple of men—friends— who tempted me, a few close calls when I had to visit a bathhouse or Pana's...but no. Marking the vow on my hand was just a formality. I've been living that promise for years. The only conjure magic working inside me is the magic Isia gave me all those years ago. Miranda says it's in flux."

"You asked Miranda?"

"When the lodge blew, the first thing I thought was that Cassis was right and everything he had warned me about—all the destruction in my visions—was going to come true. I'd been worrying for days because I hadn't bled, and what if I was pregnant, and—that's what set me off, I think. Memories. But there is no child. I'm not pregnant. Miranda says I'm not barren either."

"Oh," he said.

Her words felt as if they should have triggered a cascade of emotions inside him. She wasn't barren so he should be happy, because even the *possibility* of having children was more than he'd ever felt he deserved, and yet the prospect also terrified him. And she wasn't pregnant, which relieved him, because her health couldn't support a child now, and disappointed him simultaneously, because it meant there would be no child to love. But what it came down to...

If she was fertile, there was nothing to prevent her being married to Cassis di Prinze for political reasons. Nothing to stop Cassis. And nothing to stop her from thinking that marrying someone so hateful could actually do good.

Cassis fucking di Prinze.

Did he feel angry or hurt? He *thought* it was both. He *thought* he wanted to strangle Cassis di Prinze. But he was also terrified of being angry. He didn't want to allow himself to feel anything. Why hadn't she told him?

"Arsenault. I told Cassis it was ridiculous."

He took another deep breath, tried to center himself. "But that isn't yes or no. Would you marry Cassis now that you know there *are* Aliente to look out for? Would you want your titles back? To become your father's Heir in name and reality? Do you believe marrying Cassis would save the city?"

She frowned, which wasn't quite the response he wanted. He wanted passionate Kyrra, angry Kyrra, Kyrra with that stormy look in her eyes who would say, *How in all the fucking hells do you think I could say yes?*

What he got was a Kyrra who looked older, drained, and hollowed out. He hoped to all the gods it was just the pain because it scared him. It scared him even more when she turned her hand over to look at the scar on her palm.

He couldn't stay sitting down. He pushed himself away from the table, stood, gripped the back of the chair. He needed something to hold on to. Anything.

"It was a fool's promise," he said without turning around. "But I meant it. Even if it means I'm just your captain."

"I don't need a captain!" she snapped. The anger in her voice released a rush of relief in him. He struggled not to feel it too much, because it still wasn't *no*.

"Arsenault. Gods. I don't know what to do. I don't know what the right thing is. I'd still put a bullet in Cassis's brain if I thought it would help. But maybe I've just seen too much killing. Too much destruction." She sighed and rested her chin in her good hand. "You're right. Maybe it was a fool's promise."

It wasn't. It was the best promise I'll ever make. I should have done it far, far sooner. Don't throw it away, Kyrra, please.

"But it was a fool's promise because I'm a fool. And how will things change if we keep trapping ourselves in the same old unhappy politics? Will it save anyone if I crawl back to the man who seduced me so his family could steal everything from me? How will a fake image of nobility make one single thing truly better—even if it does stop the fighting for half a moment?" She shook her head fiercely. "I don't know, Arsenault. *I don't know*."

He crossed the room in two steps to kneel in front of her. He took her hand and kissed the scar on her palm. "I made a vow that your honor would be my honor, Kyrra. It's enough."

"Is it? Because I'm not sure it should be." She looked at him intently. "If we found that Sella was still alive, what would you do?"

Taken by surprise, he stopped. She studied his face, waiting for an answer. He couldn't look away, but he couldn't answer the question either. His voice felt like it was stuck in his throat.

"Arsenault. I told you the truth. Now you tell me."

"I...I don't know. I made her a promise, too."

Kyrra's face fell. Her eyes looked suddenly like two open wounds, until she turned and hid them. He caught her by the good arm so she would look at him again.

"You're not listening. I don't know because I made a promise. She was my wife. But I meant the promise I made to you. I made *two* promises and I don't know what that means."

"*Arsenault.* I just want to know what you *want*."

He put his hands on her face and pulled her to him. "I want you," he said roughly. "Nothing but you. I'll take you however I can have you—whatever I have to do."

She grabbed his shirt and laughed—the kind of wild, desperate sound soldiers made before a suicide charge. "Then I want you here and now, before you put that godsdamned sword in my arm—or before your goddess wife walks in or this moment changes."

"But Kyrra—your wounds—"

"I told you once I don't care about that, not if I'm *asking*. Now take me, dammit, since you offered."

Thank the gods, there was passion in her voice. This was *his* Kyrra. She was still with him after all.

❧

He didn't have to be asked again.

As soon as her lips touched his, it was as if she set a torch to the worry and fear that had filled him for days, burning it up in a bonfire of desire. Desperation hit him like a drug. The rest of the world disappeared, nothing left but her locked together here with him, her lips on his, his hands in her hair, her body pressed against him.

He barely realized how far he'd leaned forward until the chair tipped into the table with a clatter. She gasped a little.

"Did I hurt you?" he asked breathlessly.

"Gods, no. Don't stop." She twisted his shirt in her fist and forcefully drew him back to her—kissed his neck with her teeth. He had to take a breath to slow down so he didn't jerk her closer and hurt her, as if they could ever be close enough to satisfy his need to be with her. He wanted to touch her everywhere, as if the mere act of touching could Fix her here with him forever, in all his remaining lives until eternity.

The Prinze sword glimmered in the light, catching his eye.

This wasn't right. He wasn't averse to taking her right here in this chair, but if everything changed after this moment...

He straightened. She looked up at him, startled, as he hefted her out of the chair and into his arms.

She gripped the back of his neck with her good hand. The way her nails dug into his skin made him shiver, and his shiver made her tighten her grip. "You're always carrying me. Why?"

"It's what a man's supposed to do with his wife on his honeymoon, isn't it?"

"I think we're far past the honeymoon now, Arsenault."

"I like taking care of you." He brought her into the bedroom and laid her down. She stretched her limbs like he'd poured her out, the injured metal arm snug in its sling against her stomach. Then she bunched his shirt in her fingers and pulled him down with her. He wanted to feel her body beneath him, her breasts crushed against his chest, the strong muscles of her legs wrapped around his, but he *was* worried about her so he propped himself above her, leaving a space that crackled between them like a stoked fire. *These godsdamned clothes.* He put a hand on her waist, ran it over her hip, down and around her thigh, then clambered off the bed.

Kyrra tried to push herself up on her elbow—mussed, hazy. "What—"

He stripped his shirt and trousers. "Hush. Just lay back."

She did, her blue eyes dark as a flame as she swept her gaze up and down his body. Everywhere it lingered left an imprint of heat, as if she'd walked over his skin with her fingers. He let himself look at her a moment, too, the way she sprawled on the pillows, the skirt of her chemise rucked up past her knees. It had pulled off her shoulder, exposing the line of her neck, the curve of her breast. She could change from men's clothes to women's, but clothes meant so little. She was always *Kyrra*, no matter what she wore. It was the fire inside her he craved, the way she burned so brightly and always had.

He wished suddenly he could draw her looking just the way she did now, with the passion smoldering in her deep blue eyes—the longing, the love. He knew he could never do her justice, but if he could find a way to freeze the moment forever and hide it from the gods so they could never, ever steal it...

That one, blond brow crept suggestively upward.

"You're not going to make me wait all day, are you?"

Gods, the woman. He growled deep in his throat and had to restrain himself from throwing himself on the bed and just taking her. Instead, he climbed onto the bed like a civilized man...

A civilized man about to thoroughly make love to his wife.

He pushed her chemise up slowly and swiped up a handful of glistening ointment from one of the pots of salve Miranda had left on the nightstand. He smoothed it over the curve of her calf, then began rubbing it into the muscles of her thigh in slow, deep circles. She made a small gasp as he brushed the cleft between her legs. He wanted her immediately, but he also wanted to make this last forever, so time itself would stop and he wouldn't have to put the sword in her arm, so Cassis di Prinze would cease to exist and they could stay in this bed together, forever.

He worked his hands up over her hips, then pulled the neck of the chemise lower to expose her breasts. He wanted to memorize her like this, too, and if he could have erased the scars from her body and the pain that had caused them the way he could take lines out of a drawing, he would have. She bit her lip and watched him, catching her breath as he slowly traced the skin between her breasts. When he took her breast in his hand, she arched her back, lifting herself up off the bed.

"You're teasing me on purpose," she gasped.

He chuckled darkly, relishing the pleasure evident in her mouth, her eyes. "I like making you squirm."

"Bastard."

She grabbed his braid and tugged him forcefully down to kiss him again. He tried to be careful of his weight on her, but damn, he liked the way his body slid against her skin, slick with the ointment that smelled like sandalwood. He liked the tease of her warmth so close to his cock and the way her pelvis rubbed against him. The little frisson of pain and danger that came from her grip on his hair, the thrill of knowing he was right where she wanted him. He moved his hand between her legs and she bucked up into it with a breathy growl.

He couldn't help but watch her as she melted into the pleasure he was giving her— her lips bruised not by blows but kisses, her golden hair spread out over the pillow like streams of sunlight…

How could he lose her? How could he let Cassis di Prinze do to her what Cassis had done to him?

He couldn't. He *wouldn't*. He wanted to be gentle, but his fear made him rough. She wrapped his braid around her hand and pulled him down onto her even harder. Her breath fluttered hot in his beard as he leaned in to kiss her.

"Tell me we're both fools," she gasped.

"As we've always been," he answered, and then she let go of his hair to push him into her and he groaned at her tight warmth.

He wrapped his arm around her from underneath, trying to keep her as close as he could without hurting her arm, so no one would ever take her away. Her muscles tightened around him; she moved him as much as he moved her, their hips locking together…

"Gods!" she cried out. She sank her fingernails into his back as she clenched and shuddered around him, bringing him so close to his own edge. He drove in deeper, harder, until she came again with another, longer cry, and then he surrendered to his own need and thrust into her one last time. His release rocked through him, powerful and hot, and she surprised him by shoving herself down on him once more, and they rode the crescendo together until everything grew warm and languid and quiet.

He shifted to lie next to her. She stroked his beard and looked into his eyes, so close he could see the gray flecks in the blue, like the cooling blade of a sword.

"Kyrra," he said. "You've never known how much I love you. How much I need you."

"I loved you from the moment you cut my hair," she whispered, "when you invited me up out of the dirt. I don't want to spend my life with anyone else."

He held her as long as he dared, so tightly he was afraid he'd hurt her. Then he tucked a strand of golden curls behind her ear and kissed her before he pushed himself off the bed. Because it was time. She needed the blade. He put on his clothes and went to get the metal.

CHAPTER 65

ARSENAULT

His dried blood in that rune bothered him. What was locked inside this sword? It took time to tease apart a rune done by another Fixer, time he didn't have. Feeling uneasy, he wiped the rune out with a towel, filled a pot to measure roughly how much tiaannamir was in the serpent hilt by how much water it displaced. It wasn't anything exact, but it was better than nothing. He did the same with the blade in the washbasin. He could only guess how much metal Kyrra's arm would require, but he'd wager using only the serpent would cut it very close. He dried everything, then went to the pump for more water; he was going to be using a lot of heat and didn't want to catch anything on fire.

When he came back in, he stood in the kitchen a moment, running through his mental checklist. Silva had left a stew simmering in the kettle all night, there was bread in the pantry, wine, kacin for Kyrra... She'd be hurting when they finished, even if everything went well, and he'd be hungry, exhausted.

Everything was in order. He shoved his book into his pocket, wrapped the parts of the sword in the cloth, grabbed a jug of grappa from the counter, and carried everything into the bedroom.

Kyrra was sitting up in bed. He put the sword on the hearth rug, then came to the bed to kiss her. She smiled at him nervously.

"Surely this won't be as bad as getting the arm in the first place?"

"I hope not. It will hurt, but if anything feels really wrong, stop me."

"When you gave me the arm, it was all fire. I couldn't have stopped you if I'd tried."

"I'm hoping nothing will go wrong. But if I have to use the blade and whatever is bound to the blade unfolds before I can cut it off—"

"Cut off my arm?"

He thought she was joking, but he wasn't sure. "Figure of speech. I should be able to shield you from the binding inside the magic. But nothing is one hundred percent certain, Kyrra. I still think it's a bad idea. If something goes wrong, reach out for me."

She sighed. "Just get it over with."

He handed her the jug of grappa. "Drink. I don't want you drifting like you do with kacin."

"Si, Captain. If that's an order." She raised the bottle in salute and took a long drink, grimacing as she lowered it. "Gods, that's strong. The grapes they grow up here are different."

"Another one," he instructed. "Then at least one more."

She cocked an eyebrow but obeyed. When she put the bottle down, he took her by her good arm.

"Down here by the hearth." When she looked at him questioningly, he added by way of explanation, "Hot metal. Don't want to start a fire."

A sickly gray tinge washed over her skin. But she shifted slowly out of bed and lowered herself to the floor in front of the stone hearth. After she arranged her legs on the rug, he sat with her and stretched her metal arm out in his lap as straight as he could bend it. She shivered as he ran his fingertips up the inside of her forearm.

"That's a good sign," he said to distract her. "If you feel something more than pain from the antivita."

She bit her lip and nodded. The obvious pain on her face made him want to give up this terrible idea right now. Except it really was the only option, short of severing her arm again. The ragged hole in her metal bicep made him sick. Inside the wound there was only yawning emptiness, with runnels of darkness shooting down to her elbow and up toward the flesh of her shoulder.

She twisted her head to look at the wound with him. "I saw what happened when the antivita swallowed a man. Will that happen to my flesh when the poison spreads far enough?"

"I don't know if the antivita is as strong as it was," he said, though he didn't know any such thing. He retrieved his book from his pocket to look at the measurements he'd made of her arm and all the wounds, comparing them in his head with the rough volume of the serpent hilt and blade. Working with numbers calmed him, helped him think of what he had to do as a challenge of craft instead of *Kyrra*. This was why chirurgeons didn't perform surgeries on their loved ones.

"I'll try to stretch out your arm first," he said. "It will be like putting in a dislocated joint. Then I'll do these dents here. Once that's done, I'll let you rest a moment before I put the Prinze metal in. Take another drink of grappa."

"If I drink too much, I'll throw up."

"Just take another drink."

She sighed but reached for the jug. While she was distracted, before she had a chance to tense up, he let his hand sink into her arm.

A discordant clangor immediately rose around him, drowning out her curses. Kyrra's heartbeat drummed faintly through the twisted, damaged metal, proof her body wanted the arm. He just wished it was stronger.

Shh, he told her inside the magic, pausing to allow her to adjust. The heartbeat slowed slightly, but damn, he had to strain to sense it. Everything in this metal was *wrong*. His magic pushed at him, eager to put it to rights.

Yes, he told it. *Mend what's broken. Purify what's poisoned. I set you free with my intention.*

The old formal words released his magic in a bright, hot flood. He wanted her whole, he wanted her well, he wanted this metal and magic put to rights—not to hate and destruction, but to beauty and will and order. He wanted fingers that could touch and love and grip a stylus or needle as well as a spear. An arm that could hold and hug and lift as well as it could fight, to match the iron core in her that wasn't about killing but about continually picking herself up—an arm as good in peace as it was in war.

The magic burned so brightly it felt like the sun was balled in the crook of her elbow. Arsenault gripped her shoulder with one hand and took her metal hand in his other, allowing the ball of light to stretch and spread as he pulled her arm straight. The mangled dents and twists, the little pits, erased and her forearm began to look healthy and whole, covered in smooth metal skin. But it glowed hot—red to orange to white—seething and flowing to remake itself into its original shape.

Distantly, he heard her crying out. No, she couldn't have stood this at first. Her body had had to heal to take this. And the divot and the hole remained.

He tried to send out a rush of reassurance and hoped she felt it. "Hold on, Kyrra. Not too much longer..."

The fierce white light hit the dead, black streaks of antivita and the metal screamed. The light rushed up the runnels the black acid had left, burning all of it. Kyrra gasped and twisted, but it looked as if the magic was going to win...

Dammit. The light kept leaking out the holes in her arm. He needed actual, physical substance to stop it. Nauseated, he reached for the serpent. The magic in his hand turned it into a molten mass of silver, curiously cool and distant. He poured it from his palm into the hole in Kyrra's metal bicep before he could lose his nerve. It flowed in, thick and easy. Maybe it would be enough...

"Come on," he muttered. "Come *on*..."

It stopped flowing. Short.

He'd have to use the blade after all.

Fighting his fears, he squeezed off the tang and layered its molten mass on top of the serpent metal.

Immediately, the black streaks exploded into black spiderwebs, trying to shoot back into the glowing mass of Kyrra's arm. Kyrra looked down at it, her eyes wide in horror.

Why didn't I give her kacin? No one should have to *see* this happening to their body; it was bad enough he had to have her conscious at all. What in all the hells was the the antivita, really? He turned his Sight on it.

His magic fought him. It didn't want to let him See into the spreading dead, black rivulets. It was battling them, trying to send them backward, but—

The magic was doing battle against itself.

It was trying to remake the metal, but the metal wasn't the problem; the problem was the paradox—the magic saving her and killing her at the same time. It was fighting a secret that lay at the core of itself, a lie it was supposed to accept as truth—a twisting feat of anti-logic that kept it perpetually in shackles while it slowly killed the creative force animating it. So, it raged and lashed out, tried to escape, uselessly...

Kyrra was going to die before he wrestled out the truth. But that's what he needed to battle back the darkness—a *Truth*.

"Kyrra," he said raggedly. "Give me something true to contradict the lies, something you can hold in your mind—"

"What do you mean?" she said weakly through gritted teeth. "It hurts, that's the godsdamned truth!"

"The poison that's eating you—whatever the gods did, whatever they've been hiding, it's killing the magic. Give me a truth, Kyrra, so I can Fix it in place and beat back the secrets, the lies. Don't tell it to me, just let me See the Shape of it. Dammit, Kyrra, *I need a Truth or you're going to die!*"

She made a noise—a whimper, a cry—but then...a Truth did take Shape, faintly at first, and then suddenly, solid.

In poetry, Truth was a bright and shining light. But not all truths shone brightly. Some truths were dark and painful. They throbbed like a splinter no one could see, buried deep within bone and flesh. Some were self-inflicted wounds, but how often were such truths burdens forced on a person by another who had created it but refused to carry it—who lashed their darkness to someone else, making them believe it was their own.

In his Sight, Kyrra's Truth looked like a bloody, beating heart. As if it had been cut straight from her chest.

It made him want to weep.

I don't want to Shape that into your arm, he thought.

Her eyes were wide and frightened blue wells as she looked back at him—the eyes of a woman who had spent too much of her life being used by others. He hated it, but this *was* her Truth. It would beat back the darkness of lies.

He grabbed it in his fist before he could lose his courage. In his Sight, blood seeped between his fingers. He smashed it down, right over the hidden rune, in the middle of all the creeping darkness.

Red light flashed, swallowing him whole.

❦

HE WAS WALKING DOWN A HALLWAY.

Startled, he stopped and looked around. A vision, now? What in all the hells was this?

The rune.

This was what was hidden inside the sword. The Truth he'd Fixed on top of it had unbound it, but why had he fallen into it?

The hallway looked familiar.

Whitewashed stone walls. A stairway. The ghost of children's laughter, nearly forgotten, drifting past outside. The house itself was dim, barely lit. The only light came from up the stairs.

Why did the stairs raise so much dread in him? And yet, he couldn't ignore this; he had to see what he'd just put into Kyrra's arm.

He put his hand on the cool stone wall, began climbing, counting risers—one, two—

Somehow, he knew there would be twelve.

When he reached the landing at the top, he stopped and stared at the golden light spilling out from under the door of the room ahead of him. He felt sick, cold, afraid—why was he afraid of light?

He pushed the door open.

Sitting in the middle of the room was a battered chest. He gave a violent start. He knew that chest. It was Sella's, the only thing she had brought with her when they'd married. Inside, there had been...

He ran to it, fell on his knees, fumbled the latch with shaking hands. It didn't want to open, so he heated it, smashed it, cast it aside. He shoved the lid up and light flared, blinding him.

He knew what had been in this chest, but he had forgotten. Metal, pieces, parts—dragon bits, griffin bits, pieces of serpent and sphinx. A collection of relics, the corpses of monsters. They were all there—oh gods, the *limb*—why hadn't he remembered, why had he kept it?

But the piece on top, that was new. Sella hadn't brought that with her.

It was the knife that had killed her, her blood still on the blade.

⚜

"No!" he shouted, ragged, shaking.

He came out of the vision in a frantic rush to find Kyrra lying on the floor, unconscious, the metal hardening in her arm.

"Oh, gods, no," he whispered. He needed to get the metal out of her, take it back—

The Prinze sword had been forged from *the knife that had killed Sella*.

But he didn't have any other metal, there wasn't anything else to use, and he couldn't rip it back out, the shock might kill her.

He lifted her up off the floor. "*Kyrra*. Say something, please."

Her head sank onto his shoulder and the metal of her bicep, now whole and unmarred, shone red in the firelight, the color of blood.

"Dammit, a Truth—a Truth—"

What Truth could he use to counteract what had been hidden? The kind of vengeance that would allow Erelf to use that sword just to possess a piece of something that had stolen his daughter from him?

At the edge of his mind, he felt a rune on the road trip.

He froze for an instant. He couldn't divide his magic. He was using too much for Kyrra's arm to focus it on any outside threats. He had to let the defensive runes go for the moment, hoping they had enough residual intent in them to divert whatever or whoever was coming up the road.

He couldn't take the metal out of her. His only choice was to finish the job as best he could.

He let his Sight fill him. Before her arm could cool completely, he wrenched the metal he'd always Seen inside her to the surface.

She jerked awake as if he'd punched her. The metal vertebra he'd made to save her when he'd freed her from the noose, long ago, vibrated like a tuning fork, and she writhed with it, crying out. He pushed all the determination and strength and bravery that existed inside her into the pool of gleaming foreign metal until the two became indistinguishable. Then he redrew the runes he had put there to keep her safe, hoping they would protect her from the evil the Prinze sword carried. It took all his strength to stop his finger shaking enough to write them.

Strength. Endurance. Agility.

Courage. Integrity.

Sanctuary.

He drew the last more deeply than the others and wished her safe with everything inside him.

Magic pooled in the lines, flashing brilliant white. In the light, he thought he saw teeth and flashing eyes—something dangerous and wild. He sat back as the silver sheen of metal disappeared from his fingertips.

What kind of monster did I put into her arm?

What kind of monster could be worse than the monster I was?

CHAPTER 66

ARSENAULT

ARSENAULT LAY IN A STATE OF EXHAUSTION BETWEEN SLEEP AND wakefulness after the magic subsided—for how long, he didn't know. An image formed in his mind, a knot in a rope slipping free.

Sanctuary?

Someone was untying his rune.

Arsenault shoved himself upright—too fast. The world spun around him. Using that much magic had worn him dangerously thin. Kyrra rolled her head to the side.

"It's done?" she murmured. Her voice was raw, like her throat had been burned.

"Almost. There's one more step—"

The slip of another string through the knot.

How in all the hells was someone untying his rune?

"Fuck." He shoved himself onto his knees. The world did not stop spinning and he was suddenly, ravenously, nauseously hungry, but he managed to crawl to his boots. He sprawled on the floor, trying to tug them on. When he finally finished, he lurched to his feet and drew one of his knives from the boot sheath.

"Arsenault?" Kyrra had picked up on his alarm. She flailed out a hand weakly for the hearth ledge.

"Runes tripped," he muttered, no idea which language he used. Too hard to sort languages now. "Fixer."

"Arsenault!"

He opened the door and staggered into the hallway. His legs felt about as strong as paper. He had to lean on the wall as he walked into the common room. Late afternoon light filtered in through the shutters; hours had passed since they'd begun. The fire had burned down, leaving the house too cool.

Another string slipped free.

It was almost as if the Fixer *knew* his runes, so he didn't have to puzzle out how to undo them. But that would mean someone knew who he was—knew his magic, too. And that he was *here*, with Kyrra.

Fuck. It had to be Cassis's scholar.

Lupa. *Bruzzia.*

Arsenault had never met the man who'd sold the ingots that went into making Kyrra's arm, but he'd collected a lot of notes trying to run him down. From all accounts, Bruzzia-Lupa was a fair copyist, a middling scholar, and a lucky antiquities dealer who'd fallen into a treasure trove of artifacts. Most of the vendors thought Bruzzia had allowed this luck to go to his head. They'd ridiculed his plan to sail to Tule. Bruzzia had hired a ship, a Dagmari captain and crew, but all the Dagmari gavaros Arsenault consulted had laughed it off—the captain was in desperate straights, the crew bottom-of-the barrel sailors, the cheapest he could find, and no one expected the expedition to make it past the tip of southern Vençal.

Which, coincidentally, was where Orienne lay. Arsenault hadn't thought much of it at the time, but...

If Lupa and Bruzzia really were the same person, if he had found himself stranded in southern Vençal with time on his hands and the vineyards of Orienne to explore? He wouldn't have had to make it all the way to Tule to discover Arsenault's past—if not as Ari Gunnarsson, then at least as a man who'd shown up in too much history to be explained logically. Or perhaps the scholar had foundered in the Outer Isles and heard stories about a man named *Arsenault* kidnapped to a galley twenty years before, then made the connection back home in Liera where *Arsenault* was the dead Aliente captain. If he'd also found a Dakkaran gavaro who could fill in more blanks—blanks Arsenault still hadn't filled in himself—

But nothing anyone had told him indicated that Bruzzia was a powerful Fixer. Certainly not one with the ability to undo Arsenault's Sanctuary knot, one of the most elemental and personal runes any Fixer possessed.

The last strand slipped free.

Shit. Arsenault grabbed Miranda's distaff from the corner. Gripping it tightly, he edged over to the front window. The shutters were bolted, but he knocked the bolt back with the end of the distaff and used it to slowly pry open the shutter just enough to peer outside.

Footsteps shuffled behind him. *Kyrra.* "Are you well enough to be up?" he asked in a low voice as she stumbled up to join him.

She leaned against him to see out the window. The hard iron fire poker nudged the back of his leg and her knuckles pressed against his thigh as she shifted her grip on it. "No. I feel strange."

He took a quick look at her over his shoulder. At least she was standing. Sweat darkened her hair and her normally golden olive skin was green-tinged, almost translucent. Her right shoulder was an angry red where it met the new metal, but the metal itself seemed to be holding—no black streaks, the musculature smooth and well-defined, mirroring her flesh arm.

He caught her up. "Someone's undoing my runes. I don't know how. I'm too worn out to fight him with magic. Can you make it to the barn? Maybe we could escape out the back—"

Men on horseback circled around the house. Damn. The back exit was cut off, too.

"No armbands," Kyrra murmured. "What are those insignia? Wolf? Who do they think they are, the fucking Imperium? Oh, gods, *wolf.* Lupa. *Cassis.*"

She stumbled against him. He fumbled his arm around her shoulders to hold her up. When he touched the metal, it felt different. For an instant, he panicked, afraid it would repulse him just as the Prinze sword had. But the metal just seemed to be deciding what it was going to be. She looked up at him in surprise.

"I can feel your hand," she whispered.

"It will take eight days for the magic to settle. We don't have a chance against that many men in a straight fight."

"They're coming up the walk. Cassis, Lobardin, that must be the gavaro—is he Dakkaran or Tiresian? And—is that Lupa with the spectacles?"

Tall man, carrying a satchel, dark cinnamon-colored hair tied back haphazardly, but he carried himself with an easy confidence that spoke of physical competence and authority. The scholarly trappings were deceptive. The tattered ink green coat, the worn brown boots, even the spectacles he was looking over, not through—they didn't seem to fit.

Something gold glinted in the man's hands as he gestured for his gavaro to walk ahead of him.

"Those beads aren't right," Kyrra muttered. "It's like he bought them all in the same batch. Nibas finds each of his beads special, to weave them into his history."

"Two rings in his ear," Arsenault muttered.

If it was a disguise, why would Lupa's gavaro need to *pretend* he was a Blade? Had it been supposed to get him in with Jon, except Jon wasn't in the right place for it because he had been here with them?

The gavaro banged on the door.

"Are we going to talk to them?" Kyrra asked.

"I want to know what Lupa has in his hand first."

"No answer," the gavaro called, his voice muffled by the wall. Behind him Lobardin and Cassis shifted. Cassis looked damn tense and Lobardin—

"Lobardin's seen us," Kyrra whispered as Arsenault pulled back from the shutter. "But he's not saying anything. Why would he look the other way?"

"There's smoke in the chimney," Lupa called back to his gavaro. "Try the door."

"Is he in charge?" Kyrra whispered.

Arsenault had bolted the door before he'd started working with the sword. The gavaro rattled it, there were words, then Lupa shoved him aside and Arsenault caught a glimpse of what Lupa was holding.

"Daisies," he said, stunned. "They're...Pippa's daisies, the ones I Fixed..."

He suddenly felt as if the whole world had been pulled out from under him.

"But how did he find them? How did he figure you out?" Kyrra asked.

"We need to be in the safe room. The runes tripped because they Saw him as a threat; to get in he had to take the runes apart...."

Magic flared on the metal doorpull, twisting it—

"Dammit, he's a Smith!" Arsenault yanked Kyrra down the hallway, into the bedroom. The door to the heart room was open, the manuscripts tucked into their places. Kyrra tumbled in, still gripping the poker. He tossed the distaff and the knife in, then threw the bolt on the bedroom door, ran to his war chest for his axe.

Boots clattered in the common room as he hurled himself inside the heart room with Kyrra. He called on every ounce of strength left in his body to close the fucking wall. The heavy, magic-traced door ground shut just as he heard the metal on the bedroom door start to groan. *A little more magic, just a little more...* Something to hide behind... Sanctuary wouldn't work if Lupa knew how to take it apart—

"Blank your mind," he panted to Kyrra. "Try to think of absolutely nothing. A void."

He couldn't see her in the darkness but felt her hair scrub his shoulder as she turned toward him. The little room was so dark and close and musty, they could barely wedge between the books and scrolls.

If he couldn't create a Sanctuary, maybe they could hide in emptiness.

In desperation, he wrote the rune for Absence in the air. The magic groaned out of him, feeling as if it had been tugged from his very bones. But it was such a small rune, maybe it would work. He tried hard to push aside the fear, the anger, the exhaustion, to feel nothing, to need nothing, to *be* nothing. Just as he'd attempted to spend most of his lives hiding inside his own heart room.

It was so difficult to find that space again with Kyrra standing beside him.

The stone muffled the sound of voices and the ring of hobnailed boots on the stone floor. Gradually, it grew quiet.

Arsenault wanted to hope they'd gone, but—*No! Think of nothing!*

"Oh." Was that Lupa's voice? "That's ingenious. That's really very clever."

The stone in front of them began to glow.

"Fuck," Kyrra breathed. He felt her tense. If there was any time he'd ever wanted Ires at his back, it was now.

The door slid back, revealing a room full of soldiers. And Lupa, who grinned at him.

"Hello, Ari," he said. Then to his gavaros, "Take her. But kill him."

CHAPTER 67

KYRRA

"Cassis! What the hell are you doing?"

I shoved myself between Arsenault and Lupa. Arsenault's axe wedged hard against my shoulder blades. I didn't want to block his weapon, but at least they'd have to go through me to kill him. It sounded as if they wanted me alive; I didn't want to think about what for.

I didn't feel very alive. Danger was the only thing keeping me in motion, dampening the new presence slithering around in my arm. Fighting our way out seemed doomed to failure. I had never developed the skill of negotiation, but it looked as if I would have to rely on it now.

Lupa blinked down at me in surprise. His eyes were the color of a bronze statue before it was touched with green, but the green was there—in the flecks around his pupil, creeping inexorably into the golden brown.

Everything Arsenault had done to my arm left me feeling so strange. Colors, feelings, scents, images—they all seemed to take on greater significance. It was like the beginning of a kacin high. The light spilling in through the cracks in the shutters refracted off Lupa's lenses, awakening a bright, sharp pain in my head. Lupa continued to watch me and I realized it was because I was still only wearing my chemise; Cassis and Lobardin were staring at me, too. I brandished the poker at Lupa and he stepped back.

"Your arm, messera," he said. "I'd heard rumors it was metal, but I didn't realize—"

He put his hand out like he was going to touch me. I thrust the poker forward, up, into his chest.

Or that was what I hoped to do. But he was too fast, or I was too slow and clumsy; he grabbed the poker before it could do more than press against his sternum. In an instant, the poker softened to black slag that dripped in sizzling globs to the floor. I flung it off my hand and jerked backward into Arsenault, drawing my bare feet away as it fell, hissing, onto the tiles where I had been standing. Arsenault laid a hand protectively on my shoulder. His fingers dug into my collarbone.

"Don't touch her," he said in a quiet, hard voice that made me shiver. "Cassis, you promised to leave us alone."

Cassis moved out from the group of soldiers, Lobardin flanking him. I couldn't read Lobardin, but Cassis looked nervous and afraid. "I'm sorry, Kyrra, but you don't know what it's like in Liera. Kinless and freeholders are rioting, backed by Caprine. Devid arrested me. He's bringing in Qalfan troops to keep the peace, making agreements with Amora, Vençal—I had to sign the papers."

"What papers?" I asked, feeling suddenly nauseous.

Lupa dug in his satchel and held up a sheaf of parchment. "These."

Warily, I took them. *I, Cassis di Prinze, do pardon Kyrra d'Aliente her crime and return to her all titles due a woman of the House d'Aliente as I seal the bonds of matrimony—*

The words wavered before me.

"Those are marriage papers," Arsenault said in disbelief, reading over my shoulder. "You signed *marriage papers* without her consent?"

"*Devid was going to kill me,*" Cassis said, like Arsenault should understand—and by extension that I should, too.

I thrust my arm toward the hearth. "If I drop these in the fire, they never happened."

Cassis turned to Lupa. "Ser Lupa, you didn't tell me you wanted Andris dead."

So, he thought he could use Arsenault as a bargaining chip, did he? It made me furious that he was right, at least at this moment.

"I think we can drop the little fiction of *Andris,*" Lupa said. "I know who he is, I just never thought I'd meet him. All those old stories, that ridiculous epic about Ari the Smith in search of Truth... But here you are, in the flesh. And Kyrra d'Aliente. In the flesh, too, it appears."

Lupa frowned, then reached toward my arm again as if his fingers were drawn there by a lodestone. The fingers that had recently turned an iron rod to smoking puddles.

I twisted away from him. "Don't fucking touch me!" His fingers brushed me anyway and some of his magic passed through my arm before Arsenault jerked me against his chest. The new metal in me writhed. I gasped in pain and Arsenault's grip on me tightened.

"What have you been doing, Ari?" Lupa murmured, like he was surprised.

"If you just want to kill me to get at Kyrra, why does it even matter who I am?" Arsenault replied roughly.

"Well." Lupa pushed his spectacles up to the bridge of his nose in a way that made him look much more harmless than the man who'd snatched and melted an iron poker. "If only to confirm the evidence I've tracked down. The most interesting books of all were in a villa in Orienne. Like"—he dug in his bag again—"this one, which I discovered when our ship was forced to put in for repairs from a storm. Fortuitously, I was stuck there quite a while. I had plenty of time to map out *exactly* where to look for treasure when I finally arrived in Tule.

"But when we sailed into harbor, we discovered that Tule is just a giant black rock in the middle of the ocean. All its people have left for more hospitable places, its riches and magic plundered, its life...gone. The ship's crew laughed at me and then they were angry because they'd been promised wealth beyond their imagining and there wasn't even a way to replenish their stores. Nothing to eat except auks' eggs and decaying whale meat on the beach. I thought I would die there— alone, bankrupt, unknown to history. The only find I made was the old metal dragon limb—extraordinary, but useless without a market to turn it into coin. And then..."

I couldn't help but be fascinated. This was the man who'd found the metal that made my arm? I wondered if the time Lupa had spent marooned had driven him mad; he looked like he wanted to pace, there was something not right in his eyes, and the touch of his magic felt like something furious bound just beneath the surface.

Though Arsenault had tensed when Lupa revealed the fate of his homeland, he'd been shifting in tiny increments that would allow him space to swing his axe. I thought I could grab a sword from Lupa's gavaro if Lupa kept everybody distracted. I would throw the papers still clenched in my fist into the fire first. I didn't have the strength to swing a sword, but I could fall on someone with it.

"I must admit I was growing both desperate and hungry," Lupa continued. "My only escape seemed to be suicide. Luckily, I had an entire ocean in which to drown myself. The dragon limb was heavy—

what have you done with it, by the way?—but it became my salvation, the reason the goddess sent me that seal boat! It brought me back to Dagmar, and I still had the limb, my proof. Your House conflicts are so petty and worthless. What we need is an empire of magic, like the Old World, where the gods can again live among us. The first step is to put the Prinze and the Aliente back together."

Goddess. I wondered what goddess he was talking about. Which goddess would have a dragon limb? I was afraid to find out.

"What's the next step?" I asked, moving the last bit Arsenault would need.

"Proving Ari Gunnarsson is standing behind you."

Lupa whipped out a gun. A fucking gun.

The room erupted into chaos. Arsenault swung his axe toward Lupa, Lupa dodged backward violently, the gun jerked upward toward the ceiling as he was pulling the trigger. The *crack!* reverberated in the small room, smoke roiled up around us, and sparks rained down on my right arm. Pain seared through the metal, but I tossed the marriage papers in the face of a soldier coming for Arsenault, then lunged for the nearest man.

Which happened, damn it all, to be Cassis. We tumbled into a heap on the floor.

"You didn't even ask!" I shouted at him, praying for Ires to take me, for the battle magic to take over; but no, it was just *me.* What was the use of a god if he wasn't there when you really needed him?

Cassis grabbed my metal arm, tried to drag me back as I scrambled up. "Kyrra, I had no choice—"

"You always have a fucking choice!"

Lupa was trying to load his gun again. Arsenault cleaved a man straight through the chest with his axe and the blood sprayed me and Cassis. Cassis recoiled and tried to wipe it off his cheek, and I seized his hesitation and drove my knee into his face. As I staggered over him, I looked up expecting to see Arsenault already out the door, but he had paused, waiting on me, and—

"Arsenault!" I shouted.

Lupa's gavaro Tomas punched the hilt of his sword straight at Arsenault's head.

The heavy hilt smashed into Arsenault's skull with a sickening thud and blood erupted, pouring down his face. The axe fell from his fingers and clanged onto the stone floor, then his legs went out from under him and he collapsed like a rag doll.

I felt like my heart stopped. Like I had entered one of my dreams.

Then time started up again.

I lunged for Tomas, spewing curses, not knowing what I was saying. Sounds just fell from my mouth. Hands grabbed me from behind, fighting me backward. Lobardin brushed past me quickly to kneel at Arsenault's side.

"Let me go!" I shouted.

"Kyrra," Cassis whispered in my ear as I fought him. "Everything is not as it seems."

I stopped, brought up short for an instant.

Lobardin blocked Arsenault's face with his body as he leaned over him, feeling Arsenault's neck for a pulse. He slid his hand over Arsenault's mouth as if to feel for breath—but did he slip something into it? Gods, I was probably seeing things.

Lobardin finally leaned back. "It looks as if you got your wish. He's dead, ser."

I opened my mouth to...cry, scream, I didn't know what. But nothing came out and Cassis gripped my left wrist so tight his fingernails sank into my skin. Blood dripped from Cassis's nose onto my shoulder. I tried to turn, to punch him. I knew it was useless, but I had to do *something*. I had to get to Arsenault on the floor.

Would he wake again and forget me?

Or—since he was on reprieve—was he truly dead this time?

My stomach revolted, from fear and grief and the smell of blood, but there wasn't anything in it to vomit. I heaved against Cassis's side, trying to stop as tears pricked my eyes.

This couldn't be happening. Not so *soon*. Not when I had fought so hard to stop it.

"Kyrra," Cassis whispered again. When I lifted my head, Lobardin was staring at me like his black eyes could bore a hole into my brain. I was shaking. My legs wouldn't hold me up. Cassis was holding me. Cassis had prevented me from reaching Arsenault in time.

Cassis.

I tried again to pull away from him. *Wait*, he mouthed to me.

Wait. What did that fucking mean? Anger boiled up inside me, but Cassis's grip was iron.

Lupa unwound his pistol and tucked it back inside his coat. He looked in distaste at the dead men on the floor sprawled beside Arsenault. Arsenault had killed four of them, and axe blows were not kind. Blood soaked into the tiles, splattered the quilt on the bed, the walls, my chemise. Nameless men I had never encountered until this moment, now forever bound by violent death to this room where

Arsenault and I had loved each other. It felt despicable, the worst kind of violation.

And Arsenault...

Wait.

Wait because he would come back?

Or wait because he wasn't really dead? I wanted desperately to grasp for any kind of hope, no matter how pathetically small. I forced myself to think. Head wounds bled a ridiculous amount for the smallest cut. Arsenault hadn't been hit with the edge of the blade, but the hilt. I had killed innumerable men with a blow from the hilt of Arsenault's sword, but if Lupa's gavaro hadn't gotten enough force behind it... He *could* have survived the blow. I didn't know why Lobardin would lie, but what if he had?

Arsenault still wasn't moving.

"You—get these bodies out of here," Lupa directed the other gavaros still standing in the room. "Tomas—with me. Mestere, I assume you'll want to handle your wife."

Your wife.

I stared at Cassis. Blood slicked the stubble lining his cheeks and jaw. He stared back at me out of the deep brown eyes I had once prayed to look into as someone spoke those words—*your wife*. Now I hated him even more than I had before. What new game had we been bound into as pawns?

"Of course," he rasped.

"That leaves me to deal with Arsenault?" Lobardin asked solemnly from the floor.

"I suppose," Lupa answered absently. "Lay him out on the bed if you want. Otherwise, just leave him there on the floor. We'll have to wait to see if my theory is correct. Come on, Tomas."

They left. The soldiers picked up their fallen men. Arsenault continued to lie still—not even a twitch. I had to stay with Cassis until the men were gone. As soon as they left, I hit him in the face. He didn't even try to stop me.

"Your *wife*?" I was too angry to even curse him. There were no curses meaningful enough to express my hate for him in this moment.

He rubbed his jaw and looked shamefaced, which only made me loathe him more. "I'll tell you the whole story, Kyrra, I promise."

I left him and stumbled over to Arsenault's body. My metal arm clanged on the stones beside him as I knelt. I reached out to put my hand on his chest and Lobardin caught it before I could lay it down.

"Don't fuck this up, Kyrra. Please," he whispered. "So we can all get out of here."

"Don't *fuck this up*?" I seethed.

He raised his voice. "Best take her out into the other room, mestere."

Cassis walked over to pull me to my feet, but I resisted. I looked down at Arsenault lying still on the stones. The blood still trickling from the wound in his head.

Still trickling…

I moved to stand, struggling a little so my metal arm passed over Arsenault's mouth. A brief, impossibly thin film of condensation formed on my elbow, then disappeared as I stood.

Lobardin *had* been lying.

Arsenault was alive.

CHAPTER 68

MIKELO

LIERA, PRESENT

"WILL YOU EVER TELL ME WHAT THEY DO AT THESE EMPIRIST meetings?" Silva asked, looking like he was more interested in choosing one of the small bites off the plate in front of them. The food wasn't bad for a rundown dockside tavern like The Lady and the Vine. Returning to Liera made Mikelo realize how much of the city he'd never seen—how much of a prisoner his uncle had made him in truth, if not in name.

Everywhere he'd looked as they rode into the city, Mikelo had seen Geoffre. The private Geoffre, lurking in shadows and alleys, the public Geoffre shining in the alabaster buildings that towered over the ramshackle, crumbling ruins the war had made of most of the city. Down here at the far end of the docks, beyond the patrol of Prinze customs agents, he had finally—blessedly—moved away from Geoffre's visible influence. But Geoffre's presence still haunted him as he tried to focus on the task at hand.

It wasn't that Mikelo didn't *want* to do the job Jon had set before him. It had, in fact, been his idea, and Jon had been the one to protest it. But it had seemed so much simpler sitting at Jon's table, drinking Jon's wine, eating Jon's food, and stretching out his feet in front of Jon's fire while Jon's people patrolled outside and kept them safe.

If you want to draw the Empirists out, why not dangle me in front of them like bait? I can get into their meetings and tell you everything I learn.

It makes sense, Jon had said about his plan, *but I'm not sure I like it. It puts you in danger and risks giving away too much to our enemies.*

So does faking the Prinze sword, but that's part of your plan, too, isn't it?

The sword Arsenault had made them by magic looked *almost* like Kinstealer if you didn't examine it too closely. Arsenault had used the sapphire eyes of the original, but he hadn't had time to make an exact replica. *Don't try to use it,* he'd said. *It's mostly illusion.* The fake sword—and the idea of the real one going into Kyrra's arm—had made Mikelo far more nervous than the idea of taking a boat to the Lady and putting it around to the Empirists that he would like an invite.

Until, that is, he and Silva walked inside.

According to Jon, The Lady and the Vine was a notorious hub for smugglers, spies, and gavaros looking to pick up jobs off the Talos. Mikelo felt uncomfortably out of place in a room crowded with men wearing swords and armbands, while male and female courtesans prowled for customers, though it was only midday. Maybe it was his imagination, but too many gazes seemed to be crawling up his back. Kyrra's alter-ego Kyris had been a regular here and there were wanted posters all over Liera featuring likenesses of both of them. He wondered what this clientele would think if they discovered the letter from Kyrra hidden in his pocket, which he was supposed to deliver to a friend of Kyris. He knew if it had been *seriously* stupid, Jon wouldn't have let him out of the house, but he was beginning to think Jon's reluctance had been smarter than his own desire to prove himself.

"Mikelo." Silva offered him a fried meatball on a stick. "These are fantastic. You should look at least like you're trying to belong."

"I thought I was supposed to stand out."

"Trust me, you'll stand out either way. Have you had the toast with sardines? How about a rice ball?"

"I think you're enjoying yourself too much, Silva."

"I've never been to a tavern just to *eat*. At the Youth, if we were lucky, a man would buy us a meal and a few glasses of wine, but—" Silva stopped. "What is it? Have I said something?"

"No, no, I just—" Mikelo picked up a rice ball, though he didn't have much appetite. "What were you saying about the Empirists?"

"I was asking what happens in the meetings. The barmaid said more people here on the docks are identifying themselves with the Empirists. Sometimes they get belligerent with the householders and freeholders. But actual meetings are rumored to be very secret. It's a high honor to be invited."

Mikelo took the meatball Silva proffered and darted a glance around before answering in a low voice. "The meetings always struck me as silly on the surface. They talk about old, dusty books. Drag out stories of how life used to be. Throw metals into cauldrons and melt them down to make Eterean magic." He added reluctantly, "And they do experiments."

Silva poured them both a glass of wine from the bottle on the table. "What kind of experiments?" he asked, leaning closer.

The smell of meat suddenly made Mikelo nauseous. He put the meatball down on his plate without touching it. The experiments hadn't seemed silly to him at all.

"The Empirists want to know how *everything* works. Metal, machines—the insides of living things. It's how my uncle discovered my Talent. I was at a meeting one night and they had a cat. They thought it was dead. But when they laid it out on the table and readied their knives, I felt it breathing. Not with my hands."

Silva looked at him in horror. "They were going to cut open a cat? For no reason?"

"They did have a reason; they wanted to see what it looked like inside. But I knew it was alive. So, I...healed it. None of the other Empirists had any magic at all, so they had no idea it was me. When it yowled and ran away, it shocked them, but then they laughed. My uncle, though... He knew."

That night remained burned in Mikelo's memory. The way Geoffre had rested a hand on his shoulder while he stared at the scruffy tabby on the marble-topped table. The sick feeling in the pit of his stomach as the men laid out their scalpels in a line below the cat's paws. And then...

The world had lurched as he realized he wasn't looking *outside* the cat anymore, but *inside* it, into the warm, hot tangle of blood vessels, the dark, wet clump of meat the size of a walnut that formed its heart, contracting faster than his own but in a sense ever so slowly. Without thinking he had simply *wanted* it to speed up.

And then the cat had jumped to its feet, claws out and spitting, and darted away through the crowd.

Mikelo took a long drink of wine.

"It's how I met Arsenault. I passed out after healing the cat and eight days later, I woke up in my room and he was standing guard at my door. I'd never seen him before. I met Jon through him."

"Funny how Fortune works," Silva murmured, raising his brows as he sipped his own wine. It was almost like a toast, which Mikelo would have found darkly funny if so many people weren't *staring* at him. He knew the point was to stand out like a worm on a hook, but he was beginning to feel a lot of sympathy for the worm.

"Do you think Fortune is really in control? I know it's blasphemy, denying that the gods guide events—that the fatespinners don't manage the warp and weft. But is there a real reason I was born *me* and you were born a shepherd?"

"If you don't mind me saying so, mestere," a female voice said from behind him, "that's a bit more philosophy than I'm used to hearing when I eavesdrop in a place like this."

Mikelo jerked around. The woman sitting behind him was wearing a hat like he was—well, not a gavaro's hat, but a jaunty, rakish, feminine hat with a green heron feather stuck in the band. The shadow of its brim and the angle at which she was sitting made it hard to see her face, backlit by the sun as she was. But her dress was a deep Caprine green and the Qalfan man sitting with her wore a sash of the same shade across his allaq in lieu of an armband. Only his dark eyes showed through the slit in his tightly wrapped urqa as he studied Mikelo. Could either of them tell he was Prinze even though he wasn't wearing House colors?

"Have you been listening to our whole conversation?" he asked.

"Enough of it. I heard you mention the Empirists."

"I'm back in the city after being away several weeks," Mikelo said carefully. "It's surprising how much things have changed."

"I've been away for a while myself. The peace seems to have been more of a ceasefire. Am I correct in calling you mestere and not ser?"

"Yes," he answered, in an equally polite voice, though he was trying hard not to fidget. There was a lot of green and Imisi yellow in this tavern. No blue that he could see. He fought the urge to take a deep breath while Silva watched over the rim of his wineglass, as if waiting for Mikelo to give him his lead. "In a situation like this, where one House is bent on destroying itself and everyone else incidentally, I'm beginning to see the appeal of Empirism. I'd like to attend a meeting, see for myself why they've become so powerful overnight. Maybe we will have another Attrasca. I'd like to be on the right side of things."

The woman sighed theatrically. "And here I thought you were interesting."

"I beg your pardon, lady?"

"Not just another householder scheming to be on the right side of things."

"Pardon, messera," Silva interjected. "Speaking from a lower perspective, I think it is important to be on the right side of things. The wars have caused a lot of misery because some of the Houses were on the *wrong* side of things—the side of war."

The woman raised an eyebrow. "I see you've brought an interesting companion at least. Are you a courtesan climbing the ranks?"

She was very blunt for a woman. Then again, what respectable householder maid or matron frequented a tavern like The Lady and the Vine?

Silva shrugged. "War might not be bad for business, but when I get enough coin, I'll be leaving for a more peaceful city."

Silva's words gave Mikelo an unexpected jolt in the heart. The antivita vision returned to haunt him, not for the first time. *No one is allowed to leave unless I give them permission!* He knew Silva was putting on a role for the moment, but he didn't like the way it made him feel. He'd had enough problems adjusting to sleeping alone in his own room after sharing the loft with Silva these past weeks. The bed felt empty and cold and Geoffre's voice was too loud in the darkness.

He tried to appear nonchalant by pouring himself another glass of wine. When had he grown so attached to Silva anyway? "I'm just curious. What do the Empirists really want? To bring back the order of the Empire, make it safer for travel and trade, for residents of the cities to do their work? Will they stop the fighting? Or are they only about power? I've heard they're buying up guns."

"Have you?" The woman held out her own empty wine glass and he obliged her by filling it. Her eye gleamed curiously beneath the brim of her hat, but she turned too fast for him to get more than a cursory look at her features. Then again, he wasn't Kyrra, who had grown up in the tangled pre-war world of Lieran householders. He wouldn't recognize a Caprine.

"I heard Renzo di Prinze hit his nephew Cassis's ship, stole all the guns, and sold some to the Empirists. Strange, unless the Empirists are supporting him."

"You think he'll step into Geoffre di Prinze's shoes? That the Empirists are really Prinze backers in disguise?"

"I don't know. That's what I want to find out."

"You know, mestere... You look an awful lot like the man who killed the smuggler in the Night Market."

Mikelo blinked. He'd been bracing himself to hear *you look a lot like Mikelo di Prinze,* but instead she thought he looked like *Kyris?* "That's—"

A barmaid pushed her way in to take their empty plates. "If you don't mind my saying so, mestere, you do have the look of Kyris about you. But you're taller and he has a lot more...swagger."

Her mouth curved upward at the corner, then the smile disappeared as she adjusted the plates on the stack on her tray.

"I'll lay odds as high as you want Kyris was just convenient and they're covering up the real murderer. Nibas and Razi said the same, said somebody was after Kyris and it was likely him that killed Vadz, the same man as shot Razi in the arm. Then I saw the wanted posters and damn if the Prinze aren't trying to say Kyris kidnapped Mikelo di Prinze, too. I don't know what Kyris got himself wrapped up in, but he was always good to me. Now *he's* missing—probably dead—and it's a damn mess. So, if these Empirists or whoever they are can sort things out, I'm for it. You want anything else to eat, Silva? Another bottle for your mestere and the realdo cheese maybe?"

When had she learned Silva's name? Mikelo was still struggling to keep up with all the information, but Silva gave the barmaid a bright smile Mikelo would have killed to receive. "Thank you, Mari. And maybe I'll have some questions for you about this Kyris later, if my mestere's going to be mistaken for him all the time."

He wished Silva would stop calling him *my mestere*. He shifted too much trying to hide his blush and knocked his elbow against the Caprine woman's chair. The woman came out of her seat and frowned down at her bodice. A stain had begun to spread as if she'd spilled her wine. Her movement distracted Mikelo into looking; even her modest neckline couldn't hide her generous breasts. Now he did blush and reached for a napkin.

"Here, messera, I'm sorry if I caused a spill—"

"No!" she exclaimed, leaping to her feet as she snatched the napkin from his hand. "No, it's all right. It's time I moved along anyway." She reached into her purse and handed Mikelo a coin. It was an Imperial coin, stamped with Attrasca's face. "If you're still open to being maneuvered by Fortune, there will be a meeting tonight at the Paupers' Tombs. It should be interesting for someone with the right connections."

She gave him a tight smile, then moved off quickly, followed by her gavaro.

The barmaid tucked her tray against her hip and shook her head. "She's got a little one she needs to attend to."

"What?" Mikelo asked in confusion.

"Her milk. Came in too fast. Stained her dress. Guess she'd be trying to hide it."

"Why do you say that?"

"I think that was Driese di Caprine. Last I heard, she wasn't married."

⚜

SHE WAS GONE BY THE TIME HE AND SILVA MADE IT OUTSIDE.

"Damn," Mikelo said. "Damn!"

"Do you think she's really an Empirist, or is she trying to trick you into a dangerous and out of the way location?" Silva asked. "The Paupers' Tombs... Where is that?"

"It's an island in the lagoon where they bury the kinless. No one wants their ghosts wandering the streets. It does seem like the kind of place the Empirists would meet. But does she know who I am? Would she want to get rid of me as a favor for Cassis?"

"My question is, why is she spending her time in a place like The Lady and the Vine when she needs to nurse her child? Is she not having a wet nurse do it for her? How long ago was the child born? She looked as if she was laced up pretty tight."

"That matters?"

"I worked in a brothel, Mikelo. Conjure magic sometimes fails. After a woman has a baby, it takes a while to heal and regain shape. Some of the men who came to the Youth liked that in a woman— heavier breasts and hips—so our girls got to keep their babies."

"Girls in other houses didn't?" Mikelo asked, aghast. What would have happened to him if his mother hadn't kept him? Would he have been exposed on the street, thrown out with the trash as he'd heard happened to unwanted kinless children their mothers couldn't feed?

"No," Silva said. "It's considered good luck to adopt a baby from Karansis. A householder family takes the baby home, raises it as their own, and no one's the wiser. Except the mother who had to give the baby up, of course." He tugged at his queue as he squinted into the distance. He looked hardly flustered while Mikelo felt like he must look like a wild, too innocent householder who'd just lost his purse to thieves.

"Of-of course." Why did this whole encounter disturb him so much? From being taken for Kyrra in her male disguise to discovering that he was talking to Driese di Caprine who was an Empirist, and now somehow thinking about mothers and babies and bastards—

Of course. The baby they were talking about was Cassis's *bastard.* Another Prinze child conceived and born out of wedlock, just as he had been. *Of course* he couldn't help layering his whole life onto that tiny little imagined child.

Where are your feet, he heard Arsenault say in his mind as he tried to settle himself. He hoped the procedure Arsenault had attempted with Kyrra's arm had gone well.

More voices seemed to whisper at him from the back alley.

Are you sure the herbs didn't really kill him?

With our luck, it won't keep him down long enough, mestere. I'm doing my best.

Are we really going to put him in the ground?

It's our only option. Don't worry; we'll dig him back up.

Mikelo whirled around, but nobody was there but Silva.

"Mikelo?" Silva laid a hand on his shoulder in concern. For once he was too distracted to be sensitive.

"Did you hear voices?"

"We're the only ones here."

"It sounded like Lobardin and Cassis," Mikelo realized. "Now I'm going mad." He rubbed his eyes to rid them of the reflection from the water of the canal.

A man lay very still on the ground. Dried blood painted dark flowers on the cream-colored fabric of his shirt. The long white-silver streak in his black hair was stained pink and clotted against his temple.

Arsenault?

Dead as a doornail, Geoffre said, leaning over him. *I think they will put him in the ground.*

Mikelo drove his fists into his eyes and gradually came back to the sounds of water and people—Liera.

"Mikelo, are you all right?"

"It's nothing." Just his uncle trying to trick him again. It kept happening in these stressful situations. Made it hard to know what was Sight and what was his own worried imagining. Not that he could do anything about either right now.

He sucked in a deep breath. *My feet are in wool socks that are too hot, inside worn-out boots, standing on the cobblestones.* "Go tell Jon about Driese and the meeting tonight. I'll deliver Kyrra's letter, then head back after you."

"I don't know if that's a good idea, Mikelo..."

"Jon needs time to prepare, and I promised Kyrra. Go. I'll catch up. I know my way around." He gave Silva some coins. "Hire a boat, the same as we did coming down."

Silva looked skeptical and Mikelo dragged out a smile. "Things are coming together. I just need some time to sort them out. By myself. It's not a far trip and it will do me good. I'm armed. Sword, magic. If I run into Driese di Caprine again, maybe she'll be more forthcoming if I'm alone."

"If you say so, mestere."

"What's that supposed to mean?"

"It means I don't think this is smart, but I don't think I can talk you out of it either. People thinking you're Kyris, and Devid and Renzo out there, both probably wanting you dead."

"Sword. Magic. I'm better armed than you on these streets, Silva."

"Right." Silva gave Mikelo a look that was at once both troubled and hurt, then turned and started walking back toward the Lady.

<h1 style="text-align:center">CHAPTER 69</h1>

<h1 style="text-align:center">MIKELO</h1>

MIKELO WALKED THE DOCKS AND ALLEYS AS FAR AS HE COULD. BY the time he couldn't avoid hiring a boat, he'd shoved the vision and Driese di Caprine to the back of his mind. Instead, he found all his thoughts taken up by the state of the city.

It was one of those unseasonably warm Lieran spring days that warned of hotter and more humid days to come, but could just as easily turn to cold, days-long rain. After spending the past weeks in the mountains, it felt nothing but hot. Sweat trickled down his neck and left big stains at his armpits, almost as if he found himself in the grip of a fever. Trash slopped up on the edges of the canals and black flies rose from it in big clouds. It smelled bad, like something dead. The gutters were full of water and decomposing vegetation.

Mikelo choked and pulled a handkerchief out of his pocket. He wrapped it quickly around his nose and mouth. Mosquitoes landed on his forehead and hands, the only exposed parts of him. He brushed them away and gnats mobbed him. Quarantine notices glared from the windows of buildings, the big swooping black and green symbols of water fevers. Already, and the season was just beginning.

How much magic would it take to cure them all? Could it even be done?

Maybe the Empirists had the right of it in some ways—studying the insides of animals, trying to get a sense of how bodies worked. He'd been grateful for that knowledge when he'd healed Arsenault and Kyrra; otherwise the inside of a body was a dark, hopeless mess. He wished he could continue his study of herbs so he could do real healing, not just desperately patching up holes.

He docked his boat, paid the poler, and hopped out on the sidewalk in front of a tall, skinny building clear of trash, decorated with red geraniums in wooden window boxes. The building next door was half-rubble, though the roof had partially held. A handful of scruffy children exited while he watched, chewing on pieces of bread and joking with each other until they saw him.

Mikelo pulled the handkerchief down and raised his open hands. "I'm looking for a woman named Aleya. Is this her house?"

"Why do you want Aleya?" one of the children asked.

"I have a message to deliver. From a friend."

Another of the children straightened. "You leave your swords out here, then, ser."

Mikelo pulled his sword and carefully laid it on the step. "Is that better?"

"It's not far enough away from you, ser."

"How far away does it have to be for you to let me in?"

Before the child could answer, the door creaked open. A woman dressed in red Qalfan robes stood in the doorway, hands on her hips. Her thick braid—black but for a few twisty strands of gray—flopped over her shoulder as she leaned forward.

"I see my bodyguards are doing their work."

"Yes," Mikelo answered solemnly. "Very good work. But I assure you I mean no harm. A friend of mine sent me with a message. I told h-him I'd deliver it when I was in the city."

The woman raised one perfectly curved black brow. "Do you stutter?"

"N-no." Mikelo cleared his throat. "Sera. Your name is Aleya, isn't it? The healer?"

"Chirurgeon," she corrected.

"Oh!" His interest piqued. Kyrra had made it clear he wasn't to involve Aleya in any of Jon's schemes, but he had so many questions he needed to ask about medicine. "Can I come in at least?"

"You haven't told me who your message is from yet. People mostly come in and out of here to be healed. We keep the weapons on the step."

"Right." Mikelo moved his sword further away from him with the toe of his boot. "The message is from a friend of mine. A gavaro named Kyris."

The woman's face suddenly turned the color of old parchment. "*Kyris?*"

She grabbed him and pulled him up the steps.

❧

"THE LETTER," SHE SAID WHEN THEY WERE INSIDE. "GIVE ME THE letter!"

Mikelo complied with shaking hands and a deep, sinking feeling. All Kyrra had told him was that Aleya was the wife of a friend, a smuggler she'd known.

Known. Why hadn't he picked up on the past tense? What had happened to this smuggler?

Aleya lowered the letter and stared at the wall for the moment, pressing it against her breast. Then she seemed to realize again that Mikelo was in the room with her.

"I'm sorry. Here, sit. I'll make you coffee and you can drink while I write something in return."

"I probably won't be going back that way for a while," Mikelo said carefully. "And I'm not sure when Kyris will be coming to Liera. But I'd be happy to carry a letter for you."

"How is Kyris these days?"

"Kyris ran into some trouble. H-he's been laid up for a while, recovering."

Aleya studied him intently. "So...you're a friend? Cousin? Or... brother? You've a similar look about you. In the eyes, I think."

Two people in one day? Was this going to happen whenever he ran into people who knew Kyrra? It must be the wild blond hair. He stifled a sigh. "Just a friend. I think Kyris would be insulted to hear you suggest we were related."

Aleya continued to look skeptical. "Kyris had a lot of secrets, like many gavaros. But I think Kyris had more than most. Hmmm?"

Mikelo froze. "Sera, I'm not sure what you mean..."

Aleya laughed. "I think you know exactly what I mean, gavaro. You've stuttered so many times on which pronoun to use that I would have figured it out by the end of our conversation. Lucky for Kyris, it's nothing I hadn't already figured out for myself. I wonder how *you* know, though. Are you lovers?"

The suggestion startled him so much he laughed out loud. "Dear gods. I don't think I'm quite Kyris's type."

Aleya chuckled. "Forgive me, but I'm not sure I have a clear idea of what Kyris's 'type' is. He seemed lonely, but he turned down all offers, women and men. We had a lodger once who seemed very enamored of him. Vadz teased him about it." Suddenly, the humor went out of her. She sighed heavily as she set out coffee cups, sieve, and kettle. "For a smuggler, Vadz could be a bit blind. Which was probably what did him in, in the end."

Mikelo's good humor died, too. "Your husband was the man killed in the Night Market?"

Aleya looked up at him sharply. "The broadsheets say Kyris killed him. Kyris thinks I blame him. That's what that letter was about. And to make sure I got my money." She adjusted her robes over her shoulder. "You can tell Kyris I don't blame him and I did get my money and thank him for the refugees and kinless who've profited from it already. I'd rather have my husband back, but at least the work gives me something to do. It's more money than the Prinze ever put in the coffers, that's sure."

She looked angrily out the window toward the canal, where the children who'd confronted him at the door sat on chunks of masonry, throwing rocks into the water.

"This summer will be even worse than the last. After the war ended, it was serfs uprooted from their land flooding Liera. Now it's gavaros answering Devid di Prinze's call to arms. The city's like a barrel of gunpowder. Drop a spark on it and watch it explode."

She set a cup of coffee in front of him, then collected an armful of writing implements and paper from a cabinet in the corner and sat facing him. Mikelo bent his head to take a sip while she began writing. The coffee was bitter, thick, and hot. Something like the day.

"That's probably what you're here for, too, eh?" she asked without looking up from the paper.

He shook his head. "I'm working for an acquaintance of Kyris's."

Aleya snorted as she blotted the ink with a scattering of sand from a small pot. "Better be careful then. Kyris seems to attract trouble."

Mikelo put his cup down and mustered his courage. He needed to know what had happened in that dream of Arsenault—if it was a Sight dream or not. Surely a chirurgeon would have some idea... "Speaking of trouble, I wondered if you could answer a question for me. Actually, a couple of questions."

"I won't answer anything that will put my patients in danger."

"No, nothing like that. I just wanted to know, is there something you could give a man that would make him seem like he was dead? Not to kill him, but just to...look like it."

Aleya darted a sharp glance at him. "As if I'll answer such a question. Why don't you talk to the Amoran apothecary down the street?"

"No, sorry—" Mikelo laughed hesitantly. "I'm not going to *give* it to anyone. I just want to know if such a thing exists. Outside of magic."

"I'm not sure if it exists inside of magic. To appear dead, a person would have to have an incredibly slow heart rate. Respiration would need to nearly stop. To look as if you were dead, you would need to almost *be* dead."

"So, there's nothing that would accomplish such a feat? Not even a"—he wanted to say *rune*, but he didn't know how much she knew about magic—"magic spell?"

"Who knows what those Fixers down at Erelf's temple do? I stay away from them, and you should, too. All Liera needs is to have magic involved on top of guns and cannons. They're trying to learn to Fix guns now, like the Dakkarans used to do. You're probably too young to know what kinds of wounds we saw at the beginning of the wars, but I don't want anything to do with that again." She started writing at a more furious pace. "Kyris asked me about the gavaro he knew down at the Lady. That Nezar, Razi was his name. Had his arm blown off by a Prinze pistol the same seven-day Vadz died."

"Is he still alive? I asked around for Kyris, but no one had seen him or his friend. Nibas, I think he's called?"

Aleya made a hard dot and ink spread out from the end of the quill like a black flower. "Razi had his dark moments, by all accounts, but he survived the amputation." She shook her head fondly. "He also charmed a few of the nurses and one of the gavaros convalescing next to him. I haven't heard of him since. Somebody told me the Nezari let Razi go and Nibas was taking him out of Lieran territory. North."

"Kyris will be happy to know he survived."

"Good," she said. "What was your second question?"

"I wondered if you still had any dealings with gun smugglers."

Aleya's quill stopped mid-sentence and she leaned back in her chair, looking at him. "I don't run guns. I heal gunshot wounds."

"I don't want a gun. I want to know if there have been guns moved on the docks in the past few weeks, and if so, where they went."

"And you're asking...why? Are you a Prinze agent?"

"If Devid knew I was here asking you questions, he'd have me shot on the spot. I just want to know where they're going. I'm not planning on using them."

She gave him a hard, appraising look. He didn't think she had

Sight, but she studied him the same way. He shifted uncomfortably in his seat.

She turned abruptly back to her paper and folded it carefully into thirds. "I suppose if Kyris trusts you, then you might as well know there's a man out there who can probably answer your questions better than I can."

With a jerk, Mikelo shoved himself up from the table and strode over to the window, almost knocking over his chair in the process. "Now? Where?"

"I'm not saying what he knows and what he doesn't," Aleya cautioned. "Don't go jumping to any conclusions. His cabin boy has a festering cut I'm treating."

"He's in the building next door?"

Aleya held the letter out to him. "Don't forget this. And if you're talking to gun smugglers, you probably ought to be more careful. They won't all invite you in and serve you coffee."

CHAPTER 70

MIKELO

Aleya had used Kyrra's money to turn the building next door into a hospital.

It was crowded with cots and people. Despite the sheer volume of human misery, the run-down building was clean, well lit, and all the cots were wrapped in laundered linen sheets. Two women and a man moved among the beds, changing dressings, giving water or a kind word. The man, who wore a white urqa pulled down to his chin, noticed Mikelo standing in the doorway and rapidly walked over to greet him.

"Can I help you? Are you injured? Sick?"

Mikelo shook his head forcefully, too stunned to speak. Instead of fighting over the Householder's chair or control of the peninsula, cutting up cats to see how the Etereans used their magic, why not put their efforts and their coin into something like this? Why were Lierans content to have all their medical concerns taken care of in the Qalfan Quarter?

You could do this if you took the power for yourself, Geoffre's voice ghosted through his mind. *And so much more. These only use plants and needles to heal, but you could use magic, a whole army of Fixers—*

"Ser? Did you hear me? I asked how I could help?"

"Yes." Mikelo cleared his throat, tearing himself violently away from Geoffre's temptations. "Aleya. Told me there was a captain here. With his ship boy?"

"Ah." The man nodded. "They're in the other room. If you'll follow me?"

He led Mikelo on a winding path through the cots. Mikelo pulled his handkerchief up over his mouth and nose. He tried to keep his gaze on the other man's back, but he couldn't help looking down at the beds he passed. A man with half his face swollen black and blue, the tiny girl whose mother kept swatting the flies from the corners of her eyes, the old woman whose hand rested lightly between her husband's as he hunched on a chair at her side.

There was so much pain in this place, it was like a giant block of stone weighing down his shoulders. Even with the coin Kyrra had provided—even if Mikelo were to use his magic to help today— Aleya's hospital was already full, with more people waiting outside. When he'd lived in the Prinze compound, he'd turned a blind eye to all this suffering. How did Aleya keep working day to day *seeing* it and knowing how small a contribution one person could make? Knowing that no matter what she did, there would always be that line at the door?

And yet, Kyrra had taken her blood money and given it to Aleya to make a difference. Maybe that was the answer. But if good continuously had to come from vengeance redistributed, would the cycle ever end?

The Qalfan man stopped and extended his hand toward a small, dim room. Mikelo almost bumped into him. "In here, ser."

He grabbed his hat off his head, nodded jerkily in thanks, and strode into the room before his attention could wander again. The man shut the door after him.

It took a moment for his eyes to adjust to the deep shadows. The curtains were drawn over the narrow window on the far wall. A small, dark-haired form lay on the cot, a wet cloth draped over his eyes. At the boy's side, a man sat in a chair, adjusting the rag, murmuring to him in a comforting voice.

What did gun smugglers look like? The most impressive thing about this man was the big roll-brimmed hat he wore the way sea captains did. He had an unassuming medium build and a loose tail of dark, curly hair that fell casually down his back. Completing the sea captain image, large gold loops dangled from each ear and he wore both sword and holster at his hip. He turned to look at Mikelo over his shoulder, revealing salt-and-pepper sideburns that faded into a hidden beard and startlingly blue eyes. The lower part of his face was obscured by a cloth just like Mikelo's.

The hat tilted as the man looked him up and down. His gaze settled on Mikelo's sword belt. "I'm thinking you don't work for

Aleya," he said, his voice muffled by the rag tied around his nose and mouth.

Mikelo tightened his grip on his hat. "No. She told me to ask you some questions."

"Did she now?" The man shifted in his seat, facing Mikelo. His accent was strange. Eterean laced with a faint Dakkaran lilt. Not unlike his own when he got tired or forgot to maintain the cadences his uncle had insisted upon.

Mikelo stared at him, confused. "Pardon me for asking, but have you spent time in Dakkar?"

"You have me at a disadvantage. I'm stuck caring for my boy here, and you're free to barge in and out asking questions. Who are you?"

"My name is Mikelo, but I guess that doesn't really matter. I need to know about some missing guns and Aleya told me you might know where they'd gone."

Again, the tilt of the hat. "Aleya told you no such thing. She keeps her mouth shut."

"A friend of mine paid for this hospital. Aleya thinks well of her friend's judgment. That's why she sent me in here."

"Trust by association?" Amusement laced the man's voice. He reclined in his seat, folded his arms across his chest, and stretched out his legs. In that moment, with the gray sweeping back from his temple, he reminded Mikelo too much of Arsenault. But even in the dim light Mikelo could see the lines stamped at the corners of his eyes, lines Arsenault didn't have.

"You've a glib tongue, boy," the captain said. "What makes you think I'm just going to start spilling everything I know about guns? I'll tell you this. They're illegal. I've no wish to get pulled in by a Prinze agent."

Mikelo dug his fingernails into his hat. "I am *not* a Prinze agent," he said between his teeth. And then, because he was tired of talking, he grabbed hold of his Sight and turned it on the man.

Mikelo! Be careful!

Sight was the first thing Arsenault had taught him. *There's hardly ever a person who won't show you something beautiful when you strip them like that,* Arsenault had said, *but there's hardly ever a person who won't show you something ugly, too. You have to keep a handle on the magic or else you'll See everything. People ought to be able to keep some secrets. Leave them some dignity.*

Too late.

In his eagerness, he stripped away too much.

The captain sitting before him was a different man inside than he was on the outside. On the outside, he was a pirate, an outlaw, a gunrunner. A lawless, dangerous man, with a sword at his side and a gun hidden at his hip. On the inside, he was more like a wolfhound, faithful and loyal.

But loyal to whom?

Who are you, Mikelo thought, but maybe he said it aloud. The man jerked up straight, staring at him, and a name floated into Mikelo's head.

"You're Renzo di Prinze," Mikelo whispered.

❧

As soon as he said it, Mikelo knew he should have kept the knowledge to himself.

Renzo's eyes widened. He stood, then took the two steps between them and ripped the handkerchief off Mikelo's face. Mikelo felt like his feet had been frozen to the ground. Renzo's eyes—Prinze blue, but so much brighter than Devid's or even Geoffre's—roved over him. Mikelo was startled to realize he was taller than Renzo. It didn't seem right.

"Are you Geoffre's?" Renzo asked.

Mikelo shook his head. "Yours."

The word felt like it was choked out of him.

"Both my sons have dark hair. You don't look anything like them."

"My name is Mikelo. My mother wasn't your wife."

"You think you're my *bastard?*" Renzo said in disbelief.

Mikelo flinched. The word felt like a punch to the gut. "Yes." He knew his voice was coming out stiff, but it felt like someone else was talking. "Your bastard."

"I suppose there might have been a couple of nights I don't remember, but... How old are you?"

"Twenty."

Renzo laughed softly and shook his head. "Twenty years ago, I was a captive of the Ibuu of Dakkar. I think I'd remember if I'd had a liaison with any of my prison guards. Of course, they were all Dakkaran and you're obviously not, so..."

Renzo held out his hands in a gesture of helplessness.

Something inside Mikelo snapped. "Well, you would say that, wouldn't you? You've been hiding for the past twenty years, shirking your duty to your House while your brother pushed it through all six hells! And *now* you show up, just a common pirate, running guns to a group of men bent on grabbing power over the whole peninsula at any cost! You're a liar and a cheat!"

He slammed his hat down on the floor.

Renzo watched him silently for a moment. "Been saving that up a while, have you?"

"Yes," Mikelo growled. He bent to pick up his hat.

"Well. In the first place, I never shirked my duty to my House."

"Oh, *gods*—"

"I saw what Geoffre was doing to the Prinze and didn't want to be a part of it. I gave up my life to work against it."

"By running away to become a pirate?"

"And a liar and a cheat. My brother, I assume, was supposed to be the honorable one. Was he?"

Mikelo pressed his mouth closed.

"If I'm a liar and a cheat, at least I'm lying for the right side. Now you tell me. How do you know about the gunrunning? I thought you wanted to *ask* me some questions, not tell me what I was doing."

Damn.

He was clenching his teeth so hard he felt like he was going to chew off the crowns.

"I know Jon Barra," he said finally.

"Ah." Renzo rocked back on his heels the way gavaros did and stuck his thumbs in his swordbelt. "Well, that changes things a bit, doesn't it, Mikelo...di Prinze? Or didn't my brother allow you the family name when you came seeking it?"

"I didn't come seeking it," Mikelo said through his teeth. "I always had it."

"That's interesting. Now that we've established our mutual acquaintance, maybe we'd better retire to the ship to talk about it, eh?"

The ship...

"No," Mikelo said. "I'm afraid I have an appointment later on..."

"Oh, so now you're going to be civil?" Renzo laughed. "Well, I think you'll have to miss your appointment. Family's more important, isn't it?"

"What do you care about family? You left your wife and your children. Just like..."

You left me.

Dammit, the words wouldn't even come out.

"Whoever's convinced you I'm your father deserves to be strung up as a coward and shot, but I'm willing to bet he's already dead. It was Geoffre who told you that, wasn't it?"

"It was my mother."

Renzo held his gaze for what felt like a long time. Then he gave his hat a tug and settled his hand on the hip that didn't have a scabbard.

The gun. Mikelo's skin prickled with cold despite the heat.

"This is all very interesting, Mikelo. As I said before, I believe we can talk about it better on ship." He pulled the dikkarro from its holster and gestured at the door, smiling tightly. "After you, mestere."

This ridiculous fucking family. Mikelo returned Renzo's fake smile with one of his own, plus a small bow.

"As you wish. Father."

CHAPTER 71

MIKELO

LIERA LAGOON

MIKELO THOUGHT ABOUT MAKING A RUN FOR IT ONCE THEY WERE outside the building, canal-side, but once again, his need to know got the better of him. Renzo untied a canal boat and gestured him inside with the gun, then made him pole the boat to the Mera di Capria and out into the lagoon.

"Tie up here," Renzo said when they reached the columns marking the lagoon's entrance. It spread out before them, a wide, green expanse of water hemmed in by a curve of land shimmering in the afternoon heat. Half-finished buildings rose from the barrier island like seedlings popping out of the ground. Tall wooden cranes swung blocks of stone into place, their pulleys winched by hundreds of men and oxen on the ground. On the near side of the island, the skeletons of ships took form and the sound of banging hammers echoed across the water in volleys, like gunfire.

Devid was building a fleet.

"There's Qalfan money at work there," Renzo murmured. "Come on. Onto the dock with you. I'm right behind you if you get the notion to run. Aim's good at this distance."

"Not the first time I've been on the wrong end of a gun," Mikelo mumbled as he hauled himself out of the flat-bottomed wicker boat onto the dock ladder.

"You've prior experience as a hostage?"

"You could say that," Mikelo sighed.

"Down the dock to the second rowboat. Hey, Seely!" Renzo called and the man sleeping in the bow tilted his hat upward off his forehead.

Mikelo blinked in surprise. The man's face was all over scars, his blocky chin and massive arms testimony to a life of hand-to-hand combat. Green yarn threaded through the long braid that hung down his back—a mix of black and gray that made it look like tarnished silver.

"Bringing us some fresh blood?"

Renzo waved the gun at Mikelo's back. "Says he's my son. Wants to know about guns. And Jon Barra."

"Does he now. Captain will find that...interesting."

"Get in the boat, Mikelo. Seely only bites if you provoke him."

The man named Seely grinned like a shark.

"I thought you were the captain," Mikelo said as he stepped in.

"Alas, I'm only the mate."

Seely guffawed into his shoulder as he turned the oars and propelled them out into the lagoon. Mikelo wondered if he was going to be let in on the joke.

"Where are we going?" he asked.

"See that ship anchored by your new armory there?" Renzo said. "That's where we're going."

It was a big caravel, sleek in its lines like the Qalfan ships Mikelo had seen in Mdembu's harbor. Its sails were reefed and it bobbed on the languorous rippling waves of the lagoon. As they drew closer, Mikelo could make out the figurehead in more detail.

A woman, her hair blowing over the bow, bloody dagger in one hand, coins in the other. She wore a dress of deep azure and her wooden hair glinted with gold gilt, just like the name of the ship, written in big, swooping letters below: *Good Fortune*.

"Oh, gods," Mikelo said. "She's Ekyra's ship."

"Gotten on the wrong side of Fortune lately?" Renzo asked mildly.

"I hope not. I thought I was doing the right thing coming here. I even asked if *she* thought I was doing the right thing and she told me they could take care of themselves..."

For some reason, the sight of Ekyra had made him run at the mouth.

"Who could take care of themselves?" Renzo asked. "You asked the goddess for advice, did you? And got a reply?"

Mikelo tore his attention away from the ship and focused on Renzo again. "Not the goddess. Just...one of her chosen."

Renzo traded glances with Seely. "Ah. Well. She's been a good patron to us all these years. Though perhaps not to everyone we've shipped with."

Seely grunted his assent and they both looked somber for a moment. With a few more strokes Seely pulled parallel with the ship. Renzo called for assistance and a couple of hands appeared at the rail, then threw a rope ladder over the side.

"Weapons out!" he called to the men standing above them.

"Aye," they called back without question, and by the time Mikelo reached the deck, a greeting party had gathered, swords and guns drawn.

"I'm flattered you think I need this much protection," Mikelo said.

"I think there's only one man who could be your father, Mikelo, and it's not me. I'll keep weapons on you, if it's all the same."

"You're trying to put me off on Geoffre?" Mikelo said in disbelief. "Can't you just own up to your mistakes?"

Renzo ignored him and turned to a tall, middle-aged Dakkaran woman wearing two curved swords at her hips and a sleeveless vest that showed off her wiry muscles. "Where's Herself?"

The woman gestured at a stairwell. "In the cabin."

Renzo sighed. "I suppose there's nothing for it but to sort this out as one big happy family."

"Is that what you've been doing?" Mikelo snapped. "Fighting with Cassis and Devid like one big happy family?"

The woman grunted. "Your family is a pain in the arse, Renzo. Always making some new complication for us."

"Now you know how I feel," Renzo replied. "Seely, with me." He pressed the gun into Mikelo's back. "All right, on with you. I think we're committed to this conversation. Down the steps and to the right."

Mikelo glared indiscriminately. The stairs were so narrow Mikelo wondered how Seely fit, but somehow the big man managed, thumping down behind him.

Geoffre's master cabin had reflected his personality—severe but luxurious, all the furniture carved of expensive, heavy, dark wood— but this cabin looked more like someone lived in it. Not that it was worn or untidy, but there were little touches here and there—a whale that looked as if it had been carved by a child, a somewhat more skilled metal sculpture of a mermaid, a tapestry with a lion stitched into it and a splash of burgundy. A table that looked as if it had seen fighting.

Sitting at the table with a quill and parchment was a woman. *Herself*, Mikelo supposed. Was *she* the captain?

A cane leaned against her chair, but she didn't look old enough to require one—the hair that spilled out of her bright blue scarf was mostly golden brown, with a few threads that might be silver or might be a trick of the light. She was smaller than he imagined a pirate captain should be, but she looked up with an air of authority. Her brows lifted in surprise.

"What have you brought me now, Renzo? Is this a stray or have you finally found someone with information we can use?"

"Possibly both. He's a Prinze. The one we heard Geoffre was grooming. Used Sight on me to learn who I was. I think he's my nephew, Etranée."

"I'm his son!" Mikelo blurted out, unable to help himself.

Etranée's brows lifted higher and her mouth curved upward in amusement or irony. "Well, which is it? Son or nephew? If you tell me it's both, I'm going to need to hear that story, Renzo, posthaste."

"*Nephew*," Renzo said, with an air of exasperation.

"Gods—" Mikelo began, but Renzo swept off his hat and tugged off the rag that hid his lower face.

"Look at me, Mikelo. Do I look like you?"

"I—a little!"

"What color hair did your mother have?"

Mikelo glared at him. "Black. But that doesn't really matter!"

"No one in our family is blond, as far as I know, back into antiquity. Do you know why?"

"It seems unlikely that *none* of our ancestors had blond hair. Should I know why?"

"It's because the Caprine have blond hair. *Farmers* have blond hair. The Houses that live in the north and have branches of their genealogy no one talks about because they came from Eterean *slaves*, raided from places like Dagmar and sold to the nobles. The Prinze and the Caprine haven't mixed for a long, long time."

"But my mother could have had blond hair somewhere in her family tree. She certainly wasn't a householder, she was just a—"

Whore, he was going to say, but the word didn't want to come out. It was true that his mother hadn't cared for him so much as he had cared for himself *and* for her when she'd been floating on her kacin dreams, but he'd loved her anyway and she'd loved him, too, in her own way. She'd—

He didn't know what love was really, except that abandoning a woman with child wasn't it.

Renzo was staring at him intently.

"She wasn't a householder," he finished lamely. "She wasn't Prinze or Caprine, so the rules don't apply to her."

"Was she Eterean?"

"She, yes—she—"

Gods. His mother looked *nothing* like him. She had the dark olive skin, black hair, and brown eyes of a native Onzarran. But he didn't want to admit it to Renzo, who looked exactly like his portrait in the Villa di Prinze, just older, and also like a handful of the other portraits of his ancestors, with his dark hair and blue eyes. Mikelo had always felt even more of an outsider when he'd stood in the Hall of Portraits.

"Well?" Renzo said.

Mikelo forced himself to admit the truth. It was no use keeping it back, not if he wanted Renzo to confess. His mother's life had gone so badly. "My mother's name was Ina. I think she was from Onzarro, but she didn't really say. She told stories of growing up on ship and on the caravans, but by the time I was old enough to remember, she was working as a whore and we were living in Baleria. She had black hair and eyes and she used to say that she'd once been offered a cloak made of seasilk from a siren who'd lost her voice and wanted to trade for hers, but she said no and the siren cursed her and that was why she couldn't carry a tune. She told that story so many times, I could probably repeat it word for word. Does it jog your memory?"

"She sounds like an interesting woman, but sadly...no, Mikelo. And you know you don't look a thing like an Onzarran, or anyone else from the southern peninsula. Onzarro's more than halfway to Tiresia. Were you her only child?"

"She used conjure magic."

"If the magic worked so well, why did it break down only for you?"

"But it doesn't make sense! Why would my mother claim *you* were my father in the first place? Wouldn't she have *known* which brother she slept with?" He stared at Renzo, aghast, as something else occurred to him. "She didn't sleep with *both* of you and just...pick the one she liked best?"

Renzo drew back in horror. "No!"

"Why would Geoffre pawn me off on you, then? Just because I don't look exactly like my mother, doesn't mean *you* can't be my father!"

"It also doesn't mean she's really your mother. Maybe your birth mother asked someone else to care for you—a friend or a servant. And if that woman wanted to take advantage of the rich Prinze, why wouldn't she claim you as her own? Wouldn't it have been convenient to claim me as your father if I wasn't alive to disprove the story?"

"This is all just conjecture!"

"Mikelo. I'm going to ask you again, for the last time... *Where did the blond hair come from?*"

All the blood rushed away from his head. "Are you telling me you think my mother was a Caprine? That *Geoffre* had an affair with a Caprine daughter? That's insane. He hated the Caprine!"

"What I'm telling you, Mikelo, is that I had an agreement with my wife. Our marriage was as much a convenience as any other householder's, but we promised each other we would make it as real as we could. She didn't want me to sleep with women when I was away on my long trips. I honored that agreement, at least until it became impossible for me to go back home and I was dead and she remarried. Which was *after* you would have been conceived. So, there is *no way* you could be my son."

The words were only a jumble of sounds.

"You're lying," he heard himself saying.

Why did it feel as if it would be better for him if his mother had been a common whore? Even if Geoffre *was* his father?

Gods. *Geoffre.*

"Geoffre fell in love with a Caprine girl before he got married. He knew he couldn't marry her, but don't you think it's possible he had an affair with *her*? Doesn't it make more sense?"

Now. This was it. This was why the whole story felt like splinters being driven into his flesh.

"But that Caprine girl was Kyrra's mother," Mikelo whispered.

Renzo looked hopelessly confused. "Who?"

Mikelo's mouth suddenly felt too dry to speak. He forced himself to say the words rationally, coolly. They came out of him as if they weren't part of him at all.

"The woman Geoffre fell in love with was Kyrra d'Aliente's mother. Kyrra said she was her mother's only child, except her mother had a stillborn boy." He took a step toward Renzo as if he was drawn forward. He knew the gun was there, knew Seely was watching his back with a sword and those big fists, but his entire world had ceased to make sense. If he wasn't who he'd always thought he was, then who was he?

More importantly, what chain of events had led to him becoming Mikelo di Prinze?

Geoffre and Carolla d'Aliente... They wouldn't have killed someone else's baby to hide him.

Would they?

Gods, *would they?*

He grabbed Renzo by the shoulders and leaned in close to his face. The captain's chair clattered as the captain leapt to her feet and Seely grabbed his arm. He didn't care.

"I am not Kyrra's brother," he said. "*That baby was born dead.*"

Renzo pulled away from Mikelo and waved Seely and the captain back. "You talk about Kyrra d'Aliente as if you know her. I thought she was dead. She was the girl Geoffre blamed the war on, wasn't she? He had her arm severed? That was the news we got." Renzo tilted his head, watching him. "You do know her. She isn't dead at all, is she?"

"She killed Geoffre," Mikelo said. "I was there."

It seemed unimportant now, hiding that information from Renzo. He felt like he was going to be sick. "She knew her mother had an affair with Geoffre. She told me the baby was Geoffre's son, not her father's. And Arsenault said he knew you, but did he know I couldn't be your son? Is that why he never told me about you? Why have you all been hiding so many secrets from me!"

Renzo's eyes grew wide. Big hands wrestled Mikelo backward, wrenched his arms behind his back.

Renzo pressed the muzzle of the gun hard into Mikelo's sternum. "You said a name. Arsenault."

"That's impossible, Renzo." Seely's voice was strained with effort. Mikelo's muscles burned and he twisted, but Seely's arms held him like iron bands. "Arsenault's dead. It must be someone else."

"Did you see him die?" Renzo interjected. "I didn't."

The captain's cane thumped as she circled around to stand beside Renzo. "Did the Prinze send you here looking for guns? Or have they finally figured out Renzo is hiding in their own harbor?"

"Jon Barra wants to trace the guns that have gone to the Empirists," Mikelo said. "Did you hit Cassis di Prinze's ship?"

"If I said yes, what would you say?" the captain asked.

"I'd say that seems proof you're in league with Jon, even though he wouldn't admit it, which means he *could* have told me my father was alive, but he didn't. For whatever it's worth, I've thrown in my lot with Jon and the Aliente—what's left of them. But I'm here on this ship because I thought *Renzo* was my father. And the evidence that he's not is just...wildly speculative. Am I supposed to believe you honored an agreement with your wife until you *abandoned* her and then sailed off with your lover?"

Renzo and the captain traded a brief glance. "She wasn't my lover when I sailed away with her. If there had been any way possible for me to return home, I would have. But Geoffre would have had me killed as soon as I stepped off the boat. Maybe Etranée and I were both in mourning a little. You don't know anything about those events."

"That's right. Because Arsenault didn't fucking tell me anything!"

For a moment, the three pirates in the cabin seemed to hold their breath.

He glared back, trying to stem the red haze that lay over his vision, to beat back the voices that urged him to let his magic take over.

Your feet, Mikelo!

The woman's cane whipped up toward him. He jerked backward into Seely's chest, but he couldn't entirely avoid the six-inch blade that popped out the end of the cane and settled against his collarbone.

"Now listen," she said in a quiet, level voice. "I'm the captain of this ship. You're going to tell me everything you know, right now, *politely*, and especially anything you know about Arsenault, or you'll be trying to breathe out of a hole in your neck. Do you understand?"

"Etranée. He's my nephew," Renzo said.

"I don't care if he's the god of magic himself. He's going to talk, or I will use this blade. Do you think I'm bluffing?"

Mikelo stared back at her. Her eyes were as hard as amber.

"No," he said. What would Arsenault or Kyrra do to get out of this situation? His body seemed to have taken over completely. Every beat of his heart distracted him. He didn't know where his feet were, but by all the gods, they were going to get him out of here, *now*.

"Good," she said. "Then start talking, chiré."

He took a deep breath...and swirled down the rabbit hole of his magic.

Etranée's cane became a twisting vine, as alive as a snake. It wrapped itself around her arm and she cried out and jerked backwards. The blade sliced down his collarbone and over his chest before the now-living cane devoured the metal in its green maw. The metal-edged plant fell to the deck and sprouted heads like a hydra.

Seely yelled and let go of him. Renzo's shout joined the clamor. Renzo shot the thing with an enormous *crack* and a noxious cloud of thick white smoke. Pieces of green vine splattered in all directions.

Mikelo bolted for the door, shoved it open, and leapt up the stairs, taking them two and three at a time.

"Dammit!" Etranée shouted behind him. "Arsenault did teach you, didn't he?"

She was the only one who'd reacted to him, not the vine. She clattered up the steps right behind him. He emerged into the blinding sun of the upper deck and a group of surprised pirates. He elbowed one out of the way and ran for the quarterdeck.

"Koji!" Etranée bellowed. "Catch him!"

The tall, muscled Dakkaran woman spun toward him and he pushed the magic out in a desperate wave. The gunwale sprouted branches like arms. They thrust into Koji's face, shoving her backward, then gripped him and threw him overboard.

His feet bounced on the spar and then he was falling, feet first, into the green waters of the lagoon.

As soon as he crashed through, all the sounds of the upper world dissolved. His jump put him down deep, all the way to the bottom of the shallow lagoon. He shoved off, blood lifting from his chest like a spill of ink, panic—a memory of being trapped under the mountain stream—gripping his thudding heart. He fought against it, stretching for the surface. Then he broke into daylight, gasping for air.

"There he is!" someone shouted and immediately shots cracked in the air. Lead balls splashed into the water around him. He sucked in as much air as he could and dove again, striking out underwater for the island where Devid was building a fleet.

When he came up again for air, Renzo was shouting, "No, dammit, don't kill him!"

The shooting stopped. The sounds of creaking ropes and pulleys reached him; they were winching a boat down.

Mikelo swam as fast as he could for the shore of the island and the glut of small boats docked there. He reached one just as their boat splashed into the water. Instead of heaving himself inside he ducked under it and continued on to the next and the next, until finally he reached the corner of one of the unfinished buildings. The water here was brown, not green, full of garbage the workmen had discarded. It smelled like a cesspit.

His stomach heaved, but he forced himself to tread water beside one of the boats, making sure that only the top of his head poked above the filthy water. As slowly and quietly as he could, he lifted his hand and traced the sign for Sanctuary.

Use your desire to be loved, Mikelo. Your hope for a better world. And throw it in the face of the darkness.

Instead, he used his fear. His fear that Renzo was right and Geoffre was his father. His desire to never, ever hear anything else on the subject. His conviction that Renzo *had* to be wrong. Not because he *was* wrong, but because he *had* to be.

The rune flashed briefly silver, then dissolved as Mikelo waited for the pirates to stop searching for him. As they rattled the boats he was hiding among, he ducked under the sludgy water and closed his eyes, trying to blank everything from his mind. Anything that might give away that he existed. Anything that might confirm it to himself.

When he resurfaced, the pirates were headed back to their ship. He waited until he was sure they'd all made it, then dragged himself up onto a cement piling.

He made his way into the half-constructed building and from there to the rickety wooden bridge that led back to the city. A group of craftsmen was walking across it. They gave him a wide berth but hid him well enough he wasn't afraid he'd be seen.

Finally back in Liera, he looked at the ship across the harbor. On its deck, a man wearing a hat paced.

Mikelo turned around and began to run.

ARSENAULT

FARMHOUSE, PRESENT

Ghost.

Jon, calling him. Jon was gone, wasn't he? Back to Liera, leaving him and Kyrra alone. Something had happened, he couldn't quite recall... He felt like he was suffocating, like his breath or something even more precious had been stolen from him.

In his dream, Arsenault saw himself wedged in an alley that intersected a dark canal. Filthy water lapped the bricks, washing up piles of soggy powder twists, play bills, old newspapers. Shards of green glass littered the ground around him. His dark, dirty clothes and scruffy beard made him look like a pile of cast-offs. The only indication he was alive at all came from the gleam of his eyes behind the matted tangle of his hair.

He knew this night. It was the night he'd tried to kill himself.

It had been a stupid thing to do. In the first place, he'd been too drunk to do it right. He'd shattered a bottle on the bricks of the alley and tried to slit his wrist with a shard of glass. Instead, he'd sliced into his forearm, just deep enough to soak his sleeve with blood and open his skin to fester.

In the second place, if he'd been sober, he would have realized Erelf would never let him forget the pain he was running from.

"*Arsenault,*" Jon said in horror. "That is you, isn't it? Underneath all that dirt?"

"Go away," the Arsenault sitting in the alley replied. "I'm trying to die."

"I'm not sure you can call this living, but I think you've failed."

The Arsenault in the alley laughed wearily and pushed his sleeve up. "Shit. Is it still bleeding?"

"It could use some stitching," Jon said softly. "Up with you. I'll take you to the Quarter."

"No coffins, all right? Just dump my body in the canal."

"And no graveclothes, either. I understand. But you're not dying. Just drunk as hell." He slid his arm around Arsenault, grunting as he took his weight.

In Arsenault's memory, that moment was a whirl of light; the sweat sheen on Jon's skin and the clean, fresh scent of the oil he used in his hair. "Did I know you?" the other Arsenault asked in confusion. "In the wars?"

"You made me leave in the wars. To keep an eye on someone."

"They're all dead now. Nobody to keep an eye on anymore. Who did you say you were?"

"Your friend, Arsenault. I'll explain later."

But you didn't, did you? You let me think Kyrra was dead. Did Adayze tell you to keep Kyrra away from me? I could have had more time!

Jon caught the dreaming Arsenault's eye. "Hey. Don't think I can't tell you're watching this from somewhere."

Arsenault the dreamer took a step backward in surprise. Then he recovered angrily. "I died *three times* for you, Jon."

"You died three times for Adayze, even if you didn't know you were doing it. The fila watch out for you, but I can't be there to save you all the time. You need to wake up, ghost. Stop letting the world move you and start moving it, even for a single step. Erelf didn't even have to put shackles on you this time—you kept them on yourself."

Fucking dream. He was sure he was having this argument with himself and Jon was just a convenient mouthpiece for it. It wasn't a Sight dream, was it?

Was it?

Something was terribly wrong.

"Are you the victim or the villain in your own life, do you think, Ari?"

A woman's voice, too achingly familiar.

Sella.

She stood behind him, her hair curled around her face like a low-banked fire. She was wearing the last thing he'd seen her in, the emerald gown he'd brought back from Dagmar. The laces of its bodice hung undone and her chemise showed through underneath, soaked a deep burgundy with blood.

She smiled at him, if you could call it a smile. Her mouth twisted up at the corner where there was just the slightest nick, a reminder of their childhood, when she had chased him in the woods on the mountain and he had let a branch whip back into her face. He'd lingered on that scar when they were older, brushing it with his lips, apologizing for an indifferent childhood with kisses while his hands worked lower, pulling on laces that now hung loose because his brother had mapped her body the same way.

She was not, for the moment, wearing her winged form.

He began, uncontrollably, to tremble.

The curve of her mouth flattened. "What's done is done. Why can't you let me go? You hardly tried to hold on to me when I was alive!"

"I didn't think it was my place! I thought you'd always be there, that you were immortal—"

"Ari. We both know we were living in the same space but absent from each other. I left long before the moment you found me with Tavi, and yet you still can't let go of me."

"Because you're my wife!"

"I *was* your wife. Has another taken my place? Or do you think you can have both of us at the same time? That role only has room for one."

Her words stung as if she'd slapped him. "You gave up your place. You didn't want my promise, you didn't want your children. You wanted Tavi and his false worship. How am *I* responsible for letting go when your father is the one making sure we'll be tangled for all eternity?"

"And yet, you couldn't just *bury* that dragon, could you, like your friend told you to?"

Her furious green eyes, with the gold flecks that glowed like stars, pinned him. He wanted to shout at her, to marshal some kind of defense. But she was the goddess of Sight and he knew she would See the Truth in him. He was unable, now, to avoid Seeing it in himself.

All those excuses, the rationalizations, he'd made for keeping that limb... That he needed to discover what Cassis was up to, to make sure the limb was safe to use as a source of tiaannamir for Kyrra's arm... He hadn't wanted to admit that he wanted Kyrra to be right. He'd been hoping Sella *was* still alive, even just a tiny piece of her, and he couldn't help searching for her. *That* was the shameful secret he hadn't wanted to share with Kyrra.

Gods. What a fool he was.

He'd promised Kyrra everything and yet he hadn't given it. He'd self-ishly guarded his past, his guilt, the love and hate he'd felt for a goddess who should have been above all their petty human dramas—or at least immortal—but in the end was just as heartbreakingly imperfect and mortal as his own brother—or, for that matter, him. After so many years, so many lives, his emotions had grown so thorny and complex, he wasn't even sure how to name them anymore. It had felt like a terrible sin to admit that his anger at Sella—for abandoning her children, for betraying him—had any sort of justification. Instead, he'd swallowed it all. It was so much easier to hate himself than it was to take true respon-sibility for his actions and then to move *on*, at least as well as he could.

"I'm not sure what letting go of you looks like," he said finally. "I'm not even sure what I'm holding."

"Let me show you, Ari."

She put her hand on his cheek and he drew in his breath sharply. She was looking at him the way she used to, with her head tipped back and that warm gleam in her green eyes that had always made him feel like a summer night.

"This is a dream," she whispered. "But here is reality."

Black lines shot through the flesh of her cheeks like the cracks the antivita had torn into the earth. He struggled backward. "No, Sella—"

The blackness spread, eating holes into the meat down to the bone. The flesh dripped away from her face like candle wax. Until bone was all that remained, a skeleton in a dress that gripped his tunic and pressed itself against him...

"No!" he shouted, trying to tear himself away. He felt like he was drowning. Something filled his mouth, someone was holding him down, pressing on his chest... He couldn't breathe...

"*NO!*" he yelled.

He woke up, choking on a mouthful of dirt. Lobardin and Cassis stood above him, holding shovels.

❧

"LOBARDIN! CASSIS!" HE SHOUTED, NAMING THEM IN RELIEF that quickly turned to fury. He dug his fingernails into the soil and shoved himself out of the shallow grave. His legs gave way before he half-stood. He fell onto one knee, then launched himself at Lobardin.

"Arsenault!" Lobardin cried. He came down hard on his hip and Arsenault bunched Lobardin's trousers in his fist and dragged him close enough to punch him in the jaw. Lobardin tried to block it with the handle of the shovel, but Arsenault smacked the handle back into Lobardin's face.

Lobardin cursed as blood erupted from his nose and swung the shovel grip at Arsenault's head. Arsenault saw it coming but couldn't duck fast enough. The metal grip clipped him.

Pain, far too great for the hit he'd just received, rocked through him. He rolled off Lobardin onto his back and brought his hands up to his head.

"Oh, damn..." His stomach rebelled and he barely shifted to his side before he was vomiting bile and dirt.

"Arsenault, let us explain!" Cassis shouted.

Arsenault squinted at him through watering eyes, then grabbed him by the shirt and dragged him down, too. "You son of a bitch. Where is she? Where is Kyrra?"

❧

He had never felt this bad coming back from death before.

Daylight knifed his eyes. When he tried to stand, pain slammed him and he fell. He couldn't walk without staggering and Cassis and Lobardin had to help him back to the house—Lobardin bleeding and cursing. He paused to throw up at least twice more. Trails of red and blue spun in his vision like Longest Night fireworks.

Then he was sure he saw Kyrra standing in the doorway to the farmhouse. The afternoon sun flashed off her metal arm, sparking a nimbus of light around her head. He tore himself away from Lobardin and Cassis, tripped on the steps, and slammed against the door with his shoulder.

Kyrra was *not* there. It was only a hallucination. Lobardin shoved the door open and Arsenault fell full-length into the entry. His knees smacked the stone floor of the kitchen with an impact that cracked through his whole body. He spread his arms out to hold on to the floor. The stone was blessedly solid and cool against his face.

"I don't remember standing before the Tribunal," he rasped. "What happened?"

"You mean the Tribunal of the Gods?" Cassis asked incredulously. "Is that what happens when you die?"

If he kept his eyes closed, he could almost think. "Cassis. When I can stand up, I'm going to beat the shit out of you. Just tell me what happened and where Kyrra is." His mouth went suddenly, unbearably dry. "And get me something to drink."

"Won't you just throw it up again?"

He growled.

Lobardin snuffled as he swiped more blood away from his nose with his sleeve. "It's an effect of the poison. Lupa spent half the ride up here plotting ways to kill you. In the off chance he didn't succeed, we thought we could play a ruse on him. It seemed our only chance, beyond hoping you were resurrected. I snuck away to look for the herbs I'd need under the guise of scouting. I don't know if Tomas didn't kill you on purpose or by accident, and I never thought I'd say this, Arsenault, but...I'm glad he didn't. We figured if you actually died, then..." Lobardin shrugged. "It wouldn't be such a big mistake."

"You bastard. I'm still on reprieve. I might really have died. I don't know what the rules are anymore."

"Lupa seemed to regard your death an acceptable experimental outcome. It was tricky making him believe you were really dead, though. Sadly, putting you in the ground was our only option."

Arsenault fought back the overpowering urge to pull Lobardin down by the ankles to punch him in the face again. "Kyrra, though. Where is she? Where's Lupa? Did you get rid of him finally?"

"Ah..."

Lobardin's tone of voice told him everything he needed to know. Arsenault pushed himself up on his elbows. "You let that son of a bitch take her."

"Before you do something you'll regret," Cassis interjected, "you should know Kyrra knew what we were doing."

"She—what?" The room was spinning again. Arsenault pushed himself up onto his knees. Slowly. "She knew you were poisoning me?"

"She knew it was the only way to keep you alive. It took her no time at all to figure out how much I needed you, as much as I hated to admit it. It wasn't my idea to sign those papers, Arsenault; Devid was going to hang me. Signing was the Empirists' condition for my rescue. When I got out of the prison, I realized I was just as much their hostage as I had been Devid's prisoner. But I *thought* we were only going to bring Kyrra back to Liera, I *thought* maybe you'd stand in Lupa's way—not with an *axe*, of course—and we'd all get out of this godsdamned mess. But then suddenly Lupa was an extraordinarily powerful Fixer who knew who you were. And he seemed very agitated about Kyrra's arm. So agitated he changed all the plans."

"The plans," Arsenault repeated dumbly.

"The *plan* was that Kyrra would see reason and let me take her back to Liera, where we could make a show of uniting the Prinze and the Aliente—too public for Devid to do anything. If the Circle wanted proof of consummation—"

Arsenault lurched to his feet and tried to grab Cassis by the tunic. Instead, he crashed into him. Their combined weight shoved the table backwards with a screech, knocking chairs over, until finally it hit the wall and stopped.

Lobardin grabbed him by the shoulder and yanked him backwards. Arsenault's feet tangled together and he fell into Lobardin, who righted a chair, shoved him down into it, then handed him a cup full of thick black liquid that smelled like cooked beans.

"Stop acting like a godsdamned stag in rut and drink the antidote, would you?"

"You can both fuck the hells off. *You let her go.*" He took a big drink of the thick, sludgy liquid and nearly threw up again. It tasted overpoweringly like a Dakkaran bean cake laced with bitter herbs—not anything one expected to drink from a cup. This was worse than a Dininga death drug. "Gods, Lobardin. You're sure you're not actually trying to kill me?"

"Not intentionally. But if I've forgotten the ratios for the antidote, I apologize, because it *will* kill you very quickly."

"Fine. How long does it take to work? How long ago did Lupa take Kyrra? What was her state? How long has it been since I—"

"How about you sit there and let us tell you?" Lobardin flicked a glance at Cassis. "Mestere?"

Cassis adjusted his tunic before he replied. "Lupa stayed for five days. We kept you dosed as well as we could, but we had to put you in the ground or Lupa would have known something wasn't right. We kept dosing you while you were buried, but we let it wear off when it became clear Lupa had a timeline in mind for you and we were getting past it."

So, he'd been buried for five days. Dear gods, *five days*. Arsenault ran a shaky hand through his hair, raking more dirt onto his shoulders and the floor. Cassis and Lobardin both watched him like they expected him to object to his treatment, but he didn't give them the satisfaction. "Go on," he said.

"I still thought we were going to adhere to the plan of taking Kyrra back to Liera once Lupa gave up on you. But the whole situation seemed to unhinge him. Thank the gods he left me alone with Kyrra once. Perhaps that was his attempt at a 'wedding night.'

Kyrra broke a wine bottle and threatened me with the broken glass."

"You're still here, so I'm guessing she didn't stab you?"

Cassis gave him a surly glare. "She needed to know what we were doing with you. And then, well, she didn't like it any more than I do, but we had to conclude a ceasefire, didn't we? Arsenault, I swear I didn't know you were married. Whatever love affair you'd had, I didn't know you'd made a *marriage* vow."

"Would it have stopped you if you had?"

At least Cassis had the decency to look uncomfortable. "No. And I think Lupa left a copy of those papers in Liera with the Empirists. But I would have prepared differently."

Damn. So even if they'd destroyed the papers, there was probably another set. Arsenault made a noise to indicate he'd heard. It was all he could do.

Cassis went on. "I told her everything. She wasn't well—if she had been, I think everything would have gone differently—but she agreed to go along with it."

"When you say she wasn't well..."

Lobardin looked troubled. "It was like she was walking around in between worlds, not completely in one or the other. She was struggling to stay in this one. Whatever it was, Lupa could feel it. Her arm looked better, though, and she was breathing clearly."

Her body might be trying to reject the metal. Godsdammit. "You had the worst timing. I was Fixing her arm. I put—" He remembered who he was talking to and shut his mouth. "She's probably having trouble because I didn't *quite* finish. There's one more step. But why didn't Lupa take her to Liera? It seems like he's just thwarted all his carefully laid plans. And why leave you without a guard?"

Cassis and Lobardin glanced at each other, both pale. Cassis spoke. "Lupa said the metal in her arm made her too valuable to leave with me and that she would need to be 'dedicated' for a higher purpose. He wanted me to deliver a message to the Empirists. That if they trusted him, this discovery could change the course of 'the war.' I'm not sure which war he meant. The guards protested, but Lupa killed them."

"What? All of them? Himself?"

"He pulled out a mirror—" Cassis began.

"Get me some water first," Arsenault interrupted. "Or some imya maybe, something to kill this headache." Too many things about

Lupa's words were troubling but capping it off with a story that began with a mirror needed something stronger than water.

"Oh, si, mestere," Lobardin said. "Whatever you want, mestere. You know you're going to have to drink more antidote tomorrow." But he pulled out another cup.

Cassis turned back to Arsenault. "The captain of the guard looked into the mirror and started screaming. And then...something came out of it."

"A mist." Lobardin set the water in front of Arsenault, then sat himself. "It wasn't anything like what happened when Geoffre..." He thumped his thumb on the table nervously. "Arsenault. You know what I'm talking about."

"It wasn't like your Scrying, you mean."

"All I saw then was myself in the mirror, the terrible things—"

"So, Lupa opened a window into the magic itself?" Arsenault cut him off and Lobardin shot him a grateful look.

"That would make sense. The mist wrapped itself around the men. There might have been faces in it... I-I don't know. But whatever it was..."

"It ate them," Cassis said. "That's all you can call it. Swallowed them up and melted the flesh from their bodies."

"Just like the antivita," Arsenault murmured. "Lupa opened a window into the magic, and the magic was poisoned. Damn."

That was Old World magic. Lupa had known both sides of the equation and used its failure as a weapon.

Arsenault stared at the shimmering water in the earthen cup. Behind the outline of his own reflection another began to take shape. "And Kyrra was there when he did this?"

"Sitting on the bed," Lobardin confirmed, his tone growing curious. Maybe he'd realized what Arsenault was doing. "He bound her with metal."

"Lupa's a Smith. He could alter her arm."

"He didn't," Cassis said. "Arsenault, you're beginning to look queer. Did Lobardin make a mistake?"

"Thank you for the confidence, mestere," Lobardin mumbled under his breath.

Arsenault tried to hold back a little longer, keeping the image he wanted frozen in the water, like a sketch with the ink still wet. "Kyrra's been mostly put together with magic. How did she react when Lupa brought out the mirror?"

"As you might imagine," Lobardin said with a sigh. "She threw herself off the bed, right at it. We were all standing around like idiots, focused on the mist dissolving nine men, and Kyrra tackled Lupa and broke the mirror. It fell out of his hands and shattered on the floor."

"What then?" Arsenault asked.

"A thousand shards reflecting a burst of light, all around the room. It was like a gunpowder explosion, in a way. The way it makes you blind and deaf for an instant? Then all you want to do is get the hell out of there."

"And she made it through that?"

"Writhing on the floor," Cassis said. "But yes. Lupa had Tomas haul her up and throw her on the bed again. Then he tied her down and left her there, took Lobardin and me out into the other room, and jammed the bedroom door locked from the other side. He'd already locked the window."

Arsenault wasn't sure what to call the emotion that rumbled through him. It was far more complex than mere anger. After all those years of war and insanity, it didn't seem fair that she should be rewarded by *this*. All because of his inability to give up the past and commit, regardless of what he had *said* when he'd made his promise to her.

He traced the scar on his palm with his fingertip and stared at the hazy outlines of Kyrra's image in the water.

I'm not sure what letting go looks like, he'd told Sella.

Had he always been looking at it wrong, though? Maybe the past didn't have to disappear for him to keep walking forward out of it. Maybe it didn't have to be washed of its dirt and blood for him to just let it be.

He could commit to the present even if he didn't control it, couldn't he? Like sitting helplessly by Kyrra's side hour after hour, unable to do more than keep a wet rag on her fevered forehead. Watching her pull apart like a clumsily placed stitch, not knowing if she could resew her own pattern—if she would always, irrevocably, be someone different than he remembered. This constant, gnawing terror that he would fail her and she would leave.

What if letting go didn't happen all at once, but in little, ordinary moments, the way days were made? What if it was something that kept happening, the way you built a promise not by making it once but by coming back to it, over and over again?

Maybe letting go was simply the continual process of reaching out for something else. Something better.

The magic swept him under like a whirlpool. It spit him out into a conifer forest straggling up a rocky slope. A dusty, clap-trap coach rattled along a bumpy road. The man who drove it wore spectacles, his curly dark hair flying free from his braid.

Arsenault recognized the coach in relief; it was the one that had been stored in Miranda's barn.

The magic drew him in closer until he could see inside the coach. The interior was dim with the doors and windows closed. A lot of blankets were stacked on the bench, and then a cascade of Jon's folios and scrollcases. Jon would be furious. His own books also formed a stack, and there was his broken sword and the wolf he'd let Kyrra take from him so long ago, in an act of denial that was also his first act of trying to maintain a connection that would last longer than a lifetime he expected to be short.

A man sat in the corner, brown braids gathered at the nape of his neck, glass beads clicking against each other with the motion of the cart. The bars of light falling through the shutters illuminated the binding mark on his chest, the gold in his ear, his light eyes—blue or gray. The muscles of his jaw were corded with tension and the tendons of his hands stood out from gripping the sword he held across his knees.

That's the sword he hit me with, Arsenault realized. He studied it briefly—two-handed, not Dakkaran-style. The wrap on the hilt looked barely worn and the design could have been copied from an old book about the Empire—in fact, it looked a lot like his own sword, lying on the floor, dead and useless.

Curious.

The gavaro was an enigma and Arsenault didn't like enigmas. He wanted someone whose motivations he could predict.

Kyrra sat across from him, propped against the frame of the coach.

Her eyes were closed. She was wearing one of Miranda's dresses, with crimson skirts that seemed too cheery for the situation. Her arms were folded across her chest and secured with bright silver bonds. Every time the cart hit a bump, her body raised up and fell again with a heavy thump as her metal elbow hit the wood. She opened her eyes briefly and flexed her metal fingers.

By all the gods, she had *movement*.

Seeing her like this and being unable to help made him feel exactly like he had during all those godsdamned dreams the magic had dragged him into when she'd been fighting in Rojornick. He'd been under his proscription then, suffering for the transgression of giving her the arm, so he couldn't scry for her on purpose. But wild magic obeyed few rules and it had often and unpredictably swirled them together in sleep. That had hurt more than he'd ever admitted, being able to see her, sometimes even touch her, but knowing he couldn't do a damn thing about whatever pain or danger she'd found herself in.

Kyrra looked around as if she sensed him. Flexed her fingers again.

Five days, Lobardin and Cassis said. Four more and the time for blood would be past. She should have some use of the arm, but not full integration. That might be for the best, not to wake the slumbering blade of betrayal he'd grafted into her. She bore the scars of enough betrayals already.

She looked at him directly. Surprise and relief, which she quickly schooled, washed over her face. *Where*, he mouthed silently, trying not to give away his presence to Lupa or the gavaro sitting in the back of the cart with her.

She glanced at the gavaro.

"Tomas." Her voice sounded thick. "We're traveling uphill. Are we headed to Rojornick? Kavo?"

"I can't tell you, messera."

"At least tell me where I'm going if I'm to be a figurehead. What language will I have to speak? What god am I to be dedicated to?"

"We're going uphill. You can feel that."

"But which direction? I'm not even sure where we started from. I know the roads from the hunting lodge, but where is that farmhouse? I've no idea."

"North," Tomas said curtly.

"Ah." Kyrra looked up at the roof of the coach and began musing out loud for Arsenault's benefit. "So, if we're going uphill, that means we'll be headed straight to Rojornick. The question is, will we stay in Rojornick or push through? Rojornick has its share of ruined temples, but Lupa is Eterean so maybe we'll be headed across, toward Consel or Vençal—or even Dagmar. Or perhaps we'll be attacked by highwaymen at the first pass on the Spice Road. Have you ever been this way, Tomas?"

"I have not," Tomas replied flatly. He flipped up a slat covering the window to look outside.

"It would have been easier to take a boat to Kavo; the High Peaks will still be hell this time of year. A coach stuck in the snow is easy pickings for bandits. The road squeezes through a chasm, then leads immediately onto a bridge. Makes it easy for bandits to hide, hard for anyone on the road to see them. But there's no other way around."

North Road, First Pass, bandit raid. *Got it*, he mouthed. Then, *I love you*. Her eyes lit with a deep yearning that hurt him. He had a desperate urge to kiss her. He wanted to trace the Sanctuary rune on her forehead to keep her safe until he caught up. But even thinking about it lit the runes on her arm with a soft, white light. In horror, he tore himself away, pulling for the surface like a man about to drown. He came up gasping, knocked the cup, and spilled water in long, glimmering fingers across the table.

Cassis and Lobardin had both been leaning over him. They jerked back, startled.

"I thought maybe I did misremember the ratios in that antidote," Lobardin said with a shaky laugh as he grabbed a towel to wipe up the water. "But you're back."

"She's on the north road to Rojornick." Arsenault shoved himself up from the wet table. "We don't have much time."

Cassis picked up a bundle of clothes from another chair and threw it at him. He barely caught it. Trousers, shirt, stockings.

"Do us a favor and change your clothes. We couldn't figure out how to stop you pissing yourself as the poison wore off."

ARSENAULT

SERAPO RIVER, TWENTY YEARS AGO

AS THE JOURNEY DOWN THE SERAPO CONTINUED, ARSENAULT sometimes peered into the reflective surface of the river with the same disconcerting feeling he'd had when he'd looked into mirrors in the palace; he was sure someone was watching from the other side. He worried it was Promethi—or worse, Tavi—but the presence didn't feel malevolent. Now and then, he caught a glimpse of a face in profile—fine-boned, with light hair queued like a soldier's and a sensual, mobile mouth that turned his head. The image always blurred and disappeared before he could see more, no matter how hard he tried to study it. During the lonely night watches, he found himself treating it as a companion, holding whole conversations with a phantom in the water. Then something would distract him or Koji would yell, "Ari! Jump to!" and he did jump, because hearing that name was like being prodded with a hot brand.

Adayze said nothing to him in her daily promenades on deck, though she spoke to many of the other sailors. Her fear for Edo was etched on her face, along with the misery at having to allow someone else to care for him; it was easy to mistake both emotions for grief.

This night was quiet and clear, with a bare sliver of moon. A stiff wind breathed relief into the still-hot air. He'd just finished repairing a hook someone had knocked loose and was rewinding the rope hanging from it. The crew worked him hard, but at least it wasn't a galley.

"Copper for your thoughts," Etranée said as she came to lean on the gunwale beside him.

Sharing his thoughts with Etranée was more complicated than sharing with the presence in the water. "Stargazing," he answered.

Etranée tipped her head back to study the sky. "I watched the stars all the way from Vençal," she mused. "We went by ship part way, then caravan. Their positions changed in small increments until suddenly they were totally unfamiliar. My father helped me keep track. I suppose it was more dramatic for you."

"When Fariq dragged me up on deck, it wasn't to stargaze," he agreed.

"I was taken in the Wastes. Ambushed by bandits. My father and brother died, but I'm a survivor, I guess. They sold me to a Sugar Kingdom noble. I was small and young and pretty. His wife treated me like a doll. He did not." She gave a short, embarrassed laugh that contained a great deal of pain, which she was obviously trying to hide. "I'm sorry, Arsenault. You were having a quiet moment and I've spoiled it."

He carefully hung the rope wound between his hand and elbow back on its hook.

"Permission to stand beside you, Captain?" he asked in a soft voice.

She gave him a bemused look. He leaned on the railing next to her and pulled his urqa down to his chin.

"In the north, great washes of color dance across the sky. Only on clear nights."

"What causes them?"

"Who knows. They're said to be ghosts of the old gods. The trails of their loneliness and sorrow; all that's left, burned into the darkness."

"That's a lovely, sad story, Arsenault. You Tulans are so cheerful." She gave him a wry, sardonic smile, then fell silent for a moment. "Do you miss it?"

Arsenault squinted out at the night. "It's been a long time. Sometimes you can see the lights from the Outer Islands, but not very often."

"You didn't answer my question."

Did he miss it? He hardly knew how to untangle those feelings. "By now I barely remember what it was like. But there's something to be said for the moon on a night like this and not freezing my arse off."

"I don't even remember what it's like to freeze my arse off. Likely my definition and your definition are different anyway."

He smiled, looking down at her. "Likely."

She touched his chest hesitantly. He flinched at first, but then she let her fingertips run along the edge of the V the allaq made, pausing to rub the place where the two sides overlapped with her thumb. He thought about Adayze in her cabin, lonely and pretending her son was dead. It didn't seem fair that he got to be out here in the moonlight and the breeze. And on the other hand, all he wanted was to be allowed inside that cabin with Adayze—a thing that could never happen, or most certainly wouldn't.

For a moment, Etranée stood watching him, like she was giving him the choice to move. They both knew this was a line they shouldn't cross again. He could have pulled away, but he didn't. Sometimes it was damn hard knowing what the right thing was and sometimes he didn't care. Sometimes he felt like he should be reduced to a wash of color in the night sky, too, just a twisting fire of loneliness.

Etranée tightened her hand on the allaq, tugging him down to kiss her. He followed willingly, sliding his fingers inside her headscarf to feel the silky warmth of her hair, trying to linger in a moment he knew wouldn't—and shouldn't—last.

She pulled away from him finally and stood a moment, eyes closed, unmoving between his hands. Then she opened her eyes and sighed. It sounded like a prelude to an ending.

It wasn't as if he hadn't expected it, but it still took hold of him somewhere inside and squeezed. Etranée spread her hand out flat on his chest, over his heart. "Some day, Arsenault, you'll find someone who refuses to give you up, no matter where you find yourself."

He withdrew, laughing bitterly. "My chance at finding anyone like that died a long time ago. If I ever deserved it."

If Sella ever was that kind of companion, he thought, barely catching himself before he recoiled from the words. It felt like an extra betrayal, and yet he knew it was true. What kind of idiot expected human constancy from a goddess? Their marriage had been doomed from the beginning, but it hadn't needed to end so violently.

"You don't think you deserve someone who loves you?"

"The kind of commitment you're talking about is different. Making that kind of promise to a man like me would be too hard on anyone. It's like the moon and the colors, isn't it? I should be satisfied with what I've got."

A noise came from the darkness beside the main mast. Arsenault whipped his head around, jerking his urqa up over his nose as he did so, and Etranée straightened, her hand going to the hilt at her side.

A figure stepped out of the shadows, dressed in dark-colored silk, which caught the moonlight in small pools in its folds. It took a moment for him to recognize Adayze. She was covering her mouth with her hand.

Etranée leaned lazily against the hull. "Can I help you, Lady Adayze? If you're in need of something, I'm sure Yeo can see to it."

Adayze strode toward them, holding the knife hilt that jutted up through the gold sash at her hip. "I see you've wasted no time, Ar—Ari."

He cringed, especially hearing the old name, but then, like the ricochet of a lead shot, the guilt turned to anger—which he throttled, mercilessly. "Lady Adayze. You've made the kind of commitment Etranée was talking about, and it's not to me." His words came out cold and brittle, and the bow he meant to seem polite only felt like he was mocking her. But he couldn't call it back now.

Adayze strode forward purposefully, grabbed his right hand, and turned it over. The scar she'd sliced into his palm didn't show in the moonlight, but when she traced it, hard, with her fingertip, she knew exactly where it was.

"That's a commitment," she whispered viciously. "Right there, visible forever on your skin."

"I agreed to die for you, wasn't that enough?"

Adayze's glare pulsated in the darkness before him like it was a palpable thing.

Etranée's cynical laughter cut through the tension. "Oh, Arsenault, I get it now. You were *sleeping* with the Lady Adayze. How does Jon figure into this? Do you know you have a Blade in your retinue, Lady Adayze?"

Now it was Arsenault's turn to glare at Etranée. "I was never Adayze's lover. I told you my story, how I came to be on this boat."

Etranée looked Adayze over. Adayze's jaw tightened, though she was trying to appear unaffected.

"Oh, dear gods," Adayze muttered. "I can't believe we're having this conversation." She smoothed her tunic. "I apologize, Captain. I was taken by surprise. Of course there's nothing between Ari and me."

That name. It made her words hurt much worse. *Of course there's nothing between Ari and me.*

"I still have questions." Etranée's lips twisted into her terrifying smile. "Perhaps we might even have a threesome if we were on better terms."

Arsenault had never been more grateful he was wearing the urqa. He flushed so hot he was certain it would blaze through the fabric.

"You're a scandalous woman," Adayze said in a strained voice. "You're speaking to the Heir."

Etranée folded her arms across her chest like a man. "Lady Adayze, let's stop dancing around the truth. I am indeed a scandalous woman. And I must say that in the right circumstances, I would not object to inviting both of you to my cabin. But I want to know what your guard was up to when he walked into that card game and then into my bed. Care to tell me, Arsenault? What information are you after? Did Jon put you up to everything—even this, tonight? Don't worry about being overheard; the only person near us is Koji and she'd put a knife in anyone who tried to listen. *She* definitely doesn't want to hear about my romantic escapades."

"What game is she talking about?" Adayze asked in a dangerous voice.

"The—there was a game of indij. Look, Adayze, it's not important now—"

"Jon lost him in a card game," Etranée said. "To me. But he did seem to enjoy the attention I gave him." She looked at Arsenault with that crocodile smile again. Arsenault's hands began to shake. Why was she being this way? Just to get information? Or had she let down her guard too much with him, the way he had let his guard down too much since...gods, since he came out of the mountains.

"When was this?" Adayze asked, frowning.

"Alabad," Etranée said. "Ari played quite a role."

Adayze swung around to look at him directly. Anger rolled off in waves. "You are not supposed to keep me in the dark about events as important as that! Neither you nor Jon!"

"Etranée destroyed Alabad. I had nothing to do with it."

"You just destroyed Fariq's first mate." Etranée leaned against the railing and crossed her arms again.

"So, before you came back...before the sphinx...you shared this woman's bed?"

What could he say to that except... "Yes."

"I'm not sure what kind of information you wanted out of me tonight," Etranée said. "But Lady Adayze, I hope you got what you needed after he returned from Alabad."

That was the last straw.

"Gods' balls, Etranée," Arsenault exploded. "You're no innocent. I woke up in the morning tied to your bed! You had your own agenda!"

"Such a victim, Arsenault."

"You're not—ah. *Dammit.*" Arsenault put his hands to his head to rake his hands through his hair and gripped the urqa instead.

Etranée drove her finger into his chest. "You didn't have to go back. I tore up your writ. Were you just using me to get to Neyane? *What are you doing, Arsenault?*"

"To get to Neyane?" Adayze said in surprise before he could answer. "Why—"

"Ship!" a loud shout came down from the crow's nest. "Coming up behind, fast!"

Etranée was instantly all business. She pushed herself away from the gunwale and called up to the lookout. "Are there lights? Colors? Who does she belong to?"

"Lights being hung now. I can't—"

Fire belched into the night with a loud boom and a cloud of billowing smoke.

Arsenault and Etranée reacted simultaneously. Arsenault threw himself at Adayze, while Etranée ran for the helm, shouting, "KOJI! BEAT TO QUARTERS!" But not before Koji had already begun to ring the alarm bell, yelling, "BEAT TO QUARTERS, BEAT TO—"

Arsenault and Adayze hit the deck as the cannonball crashed into the main mast. Everything happened too quickly for anything but instinctive terror. The mast sheared away in a rain of splinters and toppled downward like a giant bird, the white sail its outstretched wings. Arsenault rolled Adayze away from the yardarm as it smashed through the deck planking into the hold. They both began to slide until Adayze pulled her knife and drove it into the wood.

Arsenault grabbed it and hung on, his hand over hers. Wooden splinters had driven into his cheek; blood leaked warm and wet from the cuts.

He looked wildly into Adayze's face. She was staring back at him the same way.

"Adayze. Are you all right?"

"Fine," she said. "Come on."

She began to climb back up onto the level deck and he followed her. Etranée was shouting commands and before they could find their footing, a loud explosion rattled the hold below them, followed immediately by a second. The whole ship shuddered with the force of their own cannons. Smoke billowed up from the stern. And then—a splash and the splintering of wood as only one of the cannonballs hit.

"Damn!" Seely shouted.

"It's Fariq's ship!" someone else yelled.

"The pirate who captured you?" Adayze said in surprise. "Did he know we were on this ship?"

"Looks that way," Arsenault rasped as he hoisted Adayze up by the elbow.

The mast had crushed more than one of Etranée's men and their howls punctuated the shouted orders from Etranée and Koji. The pop of gunfire came from the other ship, followed by the closer cracks of arquebuses as Yeo and Sandro fired back. Smaller boats swarmed alongside them, full of men with swords and grappling hooks. Arsenault drew his own sword and ran to the side of the ship, slicing through a series of ropes. The men climbing them crashed back down into the boats and the water. A pirate standing in one of the boats fired a pistol; Arsenault shoved Adayze out of the way and the lead ball screamed past him.

"We need to get you safe," he said.

She pulled her big knife. "I can defend myself, Arsenault."

"You don't have any say in it. You've a responsibility to your people and to Edo not to put yourself in danger, and I made a vow to protect you. Come on."

He grabbed her by the arm and dragged her across the deck, through the chaos of gunpowder smoke, the wreckage of the mast, and Etranée's men, coming now to repel the boarders. The big guns went off again as he shoved her down the hatch. The whole ship swayed, knocking them against the narrow walls.

The hold was a haze of smoke and heat billowing out of the gunnery deck. Seely was swearing. "Get that shot in there, damn you! Faster! Aim for the helm!"

"The gunner's closet! The lady's hole!" Arsenault called to Adayze.

"If it's called the godsdamned lady's hole, won't they expect me to be there?"

"Safest place on the ship," he said, breathing hard as he wrenched the door open and pushed her inside. "Lock it from the inside, bar it with the supply crates. They're full of flint and steel, extra fuses."

"Damn you, Arsenault, I'm not—"

He slammed the door closed and threw the bolt, then ran down the passageway.

It was finally time to take Fariq.

CHAPTER 74

ARSENAULT

Arsenault clambered back on deck into chaos. The cannons thundered and smoke choked the air. Fariq's men were already throwing themselves over the rail. Jon sliced two nearly in half and Etranée shot a man coming over the rail of the quarterdeck in the face with a pistol. In her other hand, she held a cutlass, and she bashed a pirate in the skull with the hilt, leaving a bloody dent in his head. Renzo was there, too, swinging a jagged piece of mast since Adayze hadn't allowed him a weapon.

Arsenault looked around wildly, trying to make out the faces of Fariq's pirates through the smoke. The riverboat wouldn't need as many rowers as the *Gannet;* Fariq might be using galleymen to board, like throwing meat in a grinder. Arsenault's greatest fear was that he would kill Guin by accident, unable to remember his face.

No. Think. It's more likely his writ was sold to Dirik or he's still rowing on the riverboat. He has no experience with weapons.

Sword in one hand and knife in the other, Arsenault ran for the rail where a row of grappling hooks dug into the wood. He chopped his sword down on men's hands, hacking through fingers and sending the men screaming into the water below. One of them still managed to hurl himself onto the deck. Arsenault stabbed him in the side and kicked him away.

"Ghost!" Jon shouted. "Where is Adayze?"

"Safe!" Arsenault wiped his sword and knife clean on his robes, then shoved them both in their scabbards. He hooked his robes in his belt Nezar-style and threw his leg over the railing.

"What in the hells are you doing?"

Arsenault grabbed Jon's tunic and pulled him close. "Adayze is in the gunner's closet," he said into Jon's ear. "I'm getting Fariq. Promethi must have tipped him off."

"Disable their cannons," Jon ordered breathlessly. "We'll have half a chance then. Adayze sent soldiers ahead of us, so we won't be totally undone if this goes to shit." Jon slapped a hand down on his shoulder. "May Fortune follow you, ghost."

Fortune follows me too godsdamned close. Arsenault grabbed one of the ropes and let himself over the side of the ship.

The men in the boat below shouted and raised their weapons. Arsenault kicked himself outward and drove his iron-shod boots toward the pirates' heads.

He clipped one in the shoulder, but the other avoided him entirely. Arsenault flicked the knife from his wrist sheath into his left hand as he dropped into the boat. The knife gave him just enough time to counter the strike that came at him before he drew his sword with his right hand. He ripped the knife down the other man's sleeve and blood bloomed in its wake. The man came back at him with a wild swing of his cutlass, but Arsenault got his sword in the way of it. The blades clanged together. Arsenault used the bind to shove him off, then thrust the knife into his gut.

Fariq employed the least common denominator. He didn't hire swordsmen.

By this time the first man had recovered. Arsenault jerked the knife, slick with blood, out of the second man's belly. The man staggered backward, dropped his sword, and rocked the boat. The railing caught him in the back of the legs and he went overboard with a heavy splash, rocking the boat even more wildly.

Godsdammit, this was Boucher and the skiff all over again, except worse—the other pirate came at Arsenault with a long Qalfan knife in an upward thrust.

Don't panic now, damn you. Arsenault swept his sword around and caught the man's hand with his blade. Etranée made sure her crew had fine weapons; the blade cleaved straight through the man's wrist. His hand still gripped the knife when it fell into the bottom of the boat. Blood fountained from the stump; the man screamed, clutching it with his other hand, and Arsenault kicked him overboard.

Time to get to Fariq's ship, quickly. He sheathed his weapons and grabbed the oars, flipped the hand and the knife into the water, and tried not to think about what he was doing. The man who'd lost the hand bobbed up in the water and grabbed weakly at the oar with his other. Arsenault whacked him hard across the face with the oar, and the man sank back under the black surface again with a cry.

Gods. He was going to see that in nightmares. No time to dwell on it now. He struck out grimly for the *Gannet* under a cloak of gunsmoke.

Arsenault hunched down in the boat as he came close to the *Gannet*'s hull. He stowed his oars before climbing the rope ladder that hung over the side. Etranée's guns had blown a hole straight through the quarterdeck, but the helm was still intact. In the weird glow of lantern and gunfire, Arsenault made out Fariq, sword drawn, snapping orders at his crew. He counted five men in total, including Fariq, plus two snipers up in the rigging, which would leave a couple of gunners and powder monkeys on the gundeck. Most of Fariq's fighting men had gone out in the boarding boats.

Not great odds, but it could be worse.

Arsenault lifted himself quickly over the rail and landed as softly as he could on the deck, then ran toward the hatch in a crouch. The cannons boomed again, followed by the sound of splintering wood. Fariq laughed as the shots hit and lowered his spyglass.

"Another few like that and they'll be begging us to accept their surrender. Lord Promethi did say the ship should be completely disabled."

Confirmation of what Arsenault had already guessed, but hearing it was like a kick in the gut. Fariq must have already been on his way down the Serapo to get Promethi's message so quickly, or maybe Boucher had lied, the bastard. Arsenault lifted the hatch and let himself down the ladder.

The passage to the gundeck was choked with smoke. "Pack it in!" the gunner was shouting. "We'll give 'em another round, quick!"

The lead gunner had his back turned and the second gunner bent to hoist a ball from the floor. A couple of whip-thin boys held cloth bags of gunpowder at the ready as they hunkered over the big guns. The taller one impatiently twitched a shock of cinder-black hair out of his face.

Zim. The cabin boy.

He searched the benches frantically for Guin. The light was too dim to make out all the rowers. He wished he remembered names, but all the men remained swipes of memory from nights like this one, blood and fighting, chains clanking in the dark, oars creaking, men crying out. His stomach sank. When he'd recognized Zim, his hopes had risen too much.

Get your arse back in order, he told himself gruffly; if he didn't get rid of the gunners, nothing else would matter. Arsenault pulled his boot knives. It was risky, throwing knives—didn't work most of the time—but Fortune smiled upon him for once. One blade buried itself to the hilt in a gunner's back with a satisfying thunk, but the other blade hit in the shoulder. The man with the knife in his back seized up and collapsed to the floor, gasping like a fish out of water. The other man whirled, cursing. Then he grabbed the knife and wrenched it out of his own shoulder.

Fuck.

Arsenault drew his sword and ducked out of the way as the gunner threw his knife back at him. It was a wild throw and the blade buried itself in the timbers, but it gave the man enough time to grab the ramrod from his dying compatriot and wield it like a sword. It clanged off Arsenault's blade in a blow that vibrated into his teeth—probably damaged the fucking blade, too—but the man was hurting, swinging the heavy rod one-handed because his other arm was useless; Arsenault danced back from another wild swipe and came up under it to drive his blade into the man's stomach.

The stink of guts spilled into the air along with blood as Arsenault drew his blade out. The man cried out like he was surprised—death was always a surprise, even when you saw it coming—and put his hands to his stomach like he was trying to shove his guts back in. Arsenault did him the mercy of stabbing him through the heart to put him quickly out of his misery.

The two boys stared at Arsenault in fright. He swept off his urqa and let it fall to his shoulders.

"Arsenault!" the tall Qalfan boy said in surprise.

Thank the gods I remembered right. Then again... If Erelf allowed him to remember Zim, even in this vague way, what torment did the god have in mind because of it?

Quit being so fucking paranoid.

He sheathed his sword and hastily knelt to search the dead men for keys. "You need to get out of here, now. There's a boat stowed on the starboard side. If you run up quick..."

"Zim!" the other boy exclaimed. "Captain's going to wonder why the guns have stopped. He'll see us!"

Arsenault crossed the room. "Where are the godsdamned keys?"

"I don't know!" Zim said. "What are you doing? You looked like you were going to die when I saw you last!"

Arsenault turned to the rowers. "Keys!"

One of them pointed a shaky finger at the hull.

Gods, they looked bad. Skin and bones, tattered clothes—was that what he'd looked like? He grabbed the keyring off the hook fastened on the hull. Zim and the other boy watched mutely as he unlocked the first rower. He ignored them for the moment.

"Guin," he said urgently. "You know who I'm talking about? Brown hair, from the Isles—"

"Don't know names. Who are you?"

Dammit. They must be new. If Guin had gone to Dirik... Now Promethi had fucked everything up. What was Promethi's plan? He was getting what he wanted; Adayze had come to him. Why have Fariq attack?

Unless Promethi knew about the troops Adayze had sent into Arak territory and it was a ruse to take Adayze hostage.

Arsenault stifled a groan. No wonder Adayze had been so upset when Etranée had mentioned Neyane. She must have spoken to *Neyane* about what she was doing, trusting her aunt. Promethi's actions only made sense if Neyane was involved. Promethi's betrayal of Renzo fell into place, too; it would take the eyes off the illegal gun trade Neyane was running using her identity as the Ibuu's Dagger.

Was she also involved in the trade of metal and galleymen for "experiments"? The Dagger had a lot of leeway. Who was to say whether any activity they were involved in was truly criminal. But where was the line?

Arsenault threw the keys to the man after he unlocked the shackles. "Free the rest of them and get the hell out as quick as you can."

"I asked you to go to the Qalfan legation in Mdembu. Did you do that?" Zim asked.

"I went to the Ibuu's daughter. But there's been a slight...complication."

The rowers gathered behind him in a ghostly group. "Get out," he said. "Now."

"But the deck—"

"Most of the men are boarding the other ship. You have a chance at taking this one, but not if you stay down here. At least you can escape."

Arsenault picked up the most lopsided ball he could find in the box of shot and dropped it into the furnace beside the second gun as the rowers scrambled to follow his directive. The door to that gun was open, the barrel empty. He pulled the shot out with the tongs and rolled it down the barrel. Then he grabbed the bag of powder from the other boy, who was clutching it to his chest, dumped it in after the ball, and shoved the wadding in.

"Why didn't you write about Guin?" he asked Zim again. "I know I asked you to. Was there a reason you wanted me to forget him?"

"Is that what you think?"

Arsenault struck flint and steel to light the fuse, first one gun, then the other. He swung the bronze doors closed but didn't seal them all the way.

"We'll talk about it later." He grabbed both boys and shoved them toward the door.

"But—gods! That will—" the other boy said, looking back over his shoulder as Arsenault pushed him out into the hall.

"Come on!" Arsenault shouted. He only hoped all the galleymen had gotten out, too.

Behind them the guns went off in a staggered crescendo. As Arsenault had planned, the explosion didn't send the ball out the front. Instead, it exploded out the back, blowing half the cannon to pieces and sending the shot careening into the gundeck. Metal shrapnel fell in a deadly rain. A sliver sliced Arsenault's cheek and flames roared up behind them.

"But there's powder in that room!" the second boy exclaimed.

"Up the ladder now, there's a good lad." Arsenault all but hurled him up the ladder toward the deck. The gundeck was going to blow any second.

He grabbed Zim and threw him at the ladder, but Zim stopped himself with a hand on Arsenault's shoulder.

"Arsenault, you don't understand, my father—"

"*Get on deck*." Arsenault shoved Zim at the ladder just as the fire caught the powder barrel in the room.

The explosion tore through the gundeck. The concussion slammed Arsenault against the narrow passageway and fire boiled through the wooden skeleton of the ship right behind him. Heat licked his back and jagged pieces of wood rained down on him. Deaf and in pain, he hauled himself up the ladder with a desperate last-ditch pull and lurched out into the smoky night air.

He collapsed on the deck, ears still ringing, then stumbled to his feet behind Zim and the other powder monkey, who was shaking, eyes glazed with fear.

"I'll get you out in a boat," he said. He felt like he was speaking faraway and underwater. "Wait for me."

"What are you going to do?"

"Take Fariq."

He threw his urqa over his head and moved toward the quarter-deck, which had dissolved into chaos. He expected Zim to obey, considering the flames shooting up through the deck, but instead Zim shouted, "*Captain!*"

Fariq whipped around.

Zim yanked the urqa from Arsenault's head. "Captain! It's him! He's coming for you!"

Fariq stared at him for a bare instant, then roared at his men, "Take him now!"

Arsenault didn't even have time to curse. Three men ran at him and Zim was standing in the way. He moved back to raise his sword, but the other men pressed in around him, using their hilts, not their blades, and he no longer had the advantage of reach. He ducked a blow aimed at his head, punched his hilt into a man's ribs, then stepped forward only to meet fist and metal with his jaw.

He reeled backward and sliced a pirate in the side thanks to nothing but reflex.

"Captain! You'll tell me where you have my father now?" Zim called.

"He's dead!" Arsenault bellowed. "Boucher killed him!"

Fariq pulled a pistol and shot him.

CHAPTER 75

ARSENAULT

He came to in a great deal of pain.

His jaw ached. Maybe something was broken. And his foot felt like it was on fire.

Groaning, he opened his eyes.

He was on the deck of a ship. He tried to move and discovered he was sitting upright and tied to the mast. It was daylight. Mist lifted off the river in gauzy white curtains. His legs stretched out in front of him, but he was missing one of his boots. That foot was wrapped in a bandage stained red with blood.

"Bastard shot me in the foot," he muttered.

"Could have been worse."

Arsenault lifted his head with difficulty. Jon was bound to the mast, too, facing port. His shoulder pressed against Arsenault's. Arsenault was facing the stern.

Fariq's ship listed in the middle of the river as if it had become a new island. The masts had collapsed like burned-up, lightning-struck trees. Eagles roosted in their remains. Every now and then one plunged into the water and emerged holding a chunk of flesh in its beak. On the bank, a band of slate-colored jackals edged closer to the water, only to awaken a massive splash as a crocodile lunged at them with teeth the size of penknives. In the rolling waves something colored a dirt-streaked white heaved upward and remained bobbing for a moment before a crocodile caught it in its jaws and dragged it under again.

Only after the crocodile disappeared did Arsenault realize the 'something' had been a dead man.

"Gods." He retched up a thin trickle of yellowish bile that dripped off his chin when he was done.

"I think you've just made it worse, ghost."

"Sorry," Arsenault rasped. "What the hells happened? I remember blowing those guns on Fariq's ship. I got Zim up…"

"Zim," Jon interrupted.

"The cabin boy. The one who wrote the note you found in my pockets. But this time he sounded an alert. Last thing I remember a bunch of hilts came at my face and the gun went off."

Jon let out a breath that wasn't quite a sigh. "Like I said, could have been worse. We still have our rudder, for what it's worth, but we lost a fair portion of the crew and the guardsmen. Mast is down. Fariq brought you over in a rowboat and hauled you up on deck, dripping blood. Kicked you a few times to see if that would wake you. The Saien woman on Etranée's crew tended your foot. Dug the ball and splinters out, but it doesn't look good."

"Don't cut it off. I don't know if it'll grow back."

"I'll remember that."

"And no graveclothes."

"Any other instructions? I'll try to remember them as I'm waiting to die beside you."

"Are you hurt?"

"Fine for the most part. Just cuts and bruises."

"Adayze? Etranée? What about them?"

"Alive."

There was something off in Jon's tone, like maybe "alive" didn't cover everything, but he couldn't parse it. Arsenault's shoulders slumped. "Good. Where are they?"

"I'm over here, Arsenault." Etranée's voice came from beside him, not far away. She wasn't bound, but she looked bad—covered in soot and powder, dried blood and bruises, her jacket and skirts ripped and tattered. She smiled that familiar sarcastic half-smile, which, oddly, made him feel better—but why had Fariq left her free? She looked over her shoulder at Koji, who was still armed with her knives. Of course, they were survivors, Etranée would have done what she needed to save her crew, but… What the hell was going on?

Etranée knelt in front of him. "I have to say, that was a strange conversation you were having with Jon."

"Magic," he mumbled. "And Adayze?"

Etranée laid a finger on his lips briefly. He looked up, startled. She shook her head imperceptibly.

"We'll talk later, ghost," Jon murmured and Arsenault became aware of the sound of bootheels behind him—more than one pair. He struggled to look over his shoulder, but sick waves of pain and dizziness washed over him, enough to make him close his eyes.

Broken nose? Or maybe it was his cheekbone.

Something wasn't right.

When he opened his eyes, Promethi was smiling at him blandly.

"Ah, you are alive. Last night, I wondered if Fariq had thrown your miraculously preserved corpse at my feet. But it is you." In Tulan, he gave an old proverb, "*You tied a scarf around my eyes, but the weather has warmed.*"

"Fools see what they want."

"I suppose that's true." He rose and Arsenault followed him with his gaze. "I'm a bit tired of looking like a fool, though. I wondered why Lady Adayze would propose such a trip when she was clearly dealing with terrible grief. I couldn't tell, was she mourning more for her child or for you? I would have expected more viciousness from her at your execution."

"Maybe she just knew you were lying."

"Well. It's now evident *she* was lying, so at least we have that ruse cleared up, don't we?"

Damn. Nothing had gone right. He'd blown Fariq's ship, but he'd also blown their cover.

"Pay attention, Arsenault," Promethi said. "I'm not done with you yet."

"Do you know how many words there are for *fuck you* in my language?"

"I'm sure you know a good many of them. But try to attend. I'm curious why you attempted to rescue Fariq's cabin boy instead of simply sabotaging the cannons?"

"He asked me for help a long time ago."

"The boy did? Not his father?"

"His father is dead. I don't understand why Fariq would be faking that. What the hell's so valuable about a cabin boy you need to lie to him about his father to keep him in line?"

"You...are you being honest with me? You honestly didn't know who his father was?"

Arsenault frowned. He had the feeling he'd just made a blunder—a big one. He tried to call up a memory of the doctor's face, or even his

name, but all he could remember was what Etranée had told him...
Miha la Hallad. The artificer. And that feeling of betrayal—had the
doctor betrayed him just like his son? Then why had Zim helped him
at all?

"Was he a Fixer?" Arsenault said, coming to the sort of conclusion
he was aware sounded slow. The pain in his jaw had turned his words
to slush.

Dear gods, had he helped anyone at all?

"Arsenault. I said pay attention."

He squinted in the sunlight. Promethi was leaning over him again,
watching him with those large russet-colored eyes. His locs spilled
out of his head scarf to form a dark corona in the backlight from
the sun.

"I would like to know if you knew the cabin boy's father.
Truthfully."

"I was sick with fever. I wouldn't have known my own mother."

"How did you know he died?"

"You get to know what killing sounds like, after a while."

"Arsenault. What is your true goal here?"

His head dipped. He felt strange. The pain had lessened. Had they
drugged him, maybe? Or... No.

He pulled against his ropes, trying to awaken the pain again—use
it to concentrate. Promethi's magic knocked at his defenses, trying to
find a way in. "This is a different kind of truthtelling, isn't it? I just
can't... I can't tell exactly what it is..."

"You're talking about Miha la Hallad," Etranée interrupted
suddenly in a worried voice. "The cabin boy's father. Were you using
that boy as bait to trap Arsenault?"

Promethi straightened. Something let go of him and Arsenault
slumped in relief.

"Ghost," Jon whispered. "Are you all right?"

Arsenault forced himself to make a noise. He wasn't in any condition to marshal magic, even in self-defense. If Promethi tried to wade
in against him again, he wouldn't be able to fight him off.

Promethi smiled tightly at Etranée. "Well, having him will
certainly help. The boy's life was useful to us for a different reason.
But it was helpful for the boy to think he had a reason to stay, too.
Easier to keep him in line that way. And his father."

"You have his father?" Etranée asked.

"Let's say I know where he is. He told us some interesting things
about Arsenault. But as time went on, it seemed we might be wrong.

Arsenault did appear to be very dead after that execution. Then again, the Dakkar have always been tricksters."

"And the Arak have always been liars," Jon spoke up. "Lady Adayze thought your advances were made in good faith, until your machine began hunting her son."

"Yes, let's talk about him, shall we? I assume he's not dead either? If Arsenault's execution was a fake, then the murder he was sentenced for was surely a fake, too."

Arsenault stirred uneasily. His foot throbbed in pain. "You knew I didn't kill him. Or you never would have tried to frame me. You wanted him dead."

"Do you know where he is?"

"I can think of five right now."

"Excuse me?"

"Ways to say *fuck you*. In my language. Give me some time and I'll think of more."

Calmly, Promethi settled his foot on top of Arsenault's wounded one and leaned forward, putting all his weight on it.

Pain shot through him like a sword thrust. He cried out, but it sounded like a wounded animal, howling. When Promethi took the weight off and Arsenault blinked away the sweat and pain tears, he had a brief impression of Etranée and her crew looking ashen and sick, but then Promethi was in his face again.

"Arsenault. We both know I could cut off your foot and you wouldn't tell me anything. I've Seen enough of you to know that. But right now I need your help finding the Lady Adayze. She seems to have been misplaced."

CHAPTER 76

ARSENAULT

Promethi's cabin was both fastidious and opulent, a mix Arsenault might have predicted had the ship not been bombarded with cannonfire the night before. It seemed strange someone had taken pains to re-establish this kind of order when the search for Adayze must have been a priority. But several servants scurried around them in tattered clothing, heads down, arms crossed over their chests as they backed out the door. While Fariq's men bound Arsenault to a chair, he looked around the room.

A few chests, a writing desk with a stack of books in a wooden crate beside it, silk coverlet and pillows on the bed... Renzo and Fariq sat at a table, drinking coffee from delicate demitasse cups and eating mango slices speared on small silver forks.

A brief frown twitched over Renzo's lips. He made a show of setting the cup down and letting his brows rise in surprise.

"It's true? He really is alive?"

"I'm afraid so, Mestere di Prinze. Though maybe not for long."

Fariq put his coffee down, too, and looked at Arsenault's foot. "The Ibuu's new pistols do quite a bit of damage."

"As do the cannons," Promethi added appreciatively. "The battle was a rather impressive display of firepower. How much damage did he do to them?"

Fariq glared at Arsenault. "Irreparable."

"I imagine Miha will have something to say about it."

The shame of being duped burned inside Arsenault so brightly he wasn't paying attention when Promethi put a hand on his shoulder.

That brought him back to the moment, quick. He tried to pull away, but there was nowhere to go.

"Captain. Mestere. I'm afraid I'll have to ask you to step out for a moment. I have some questions to ask Arsenault about the Lady Adayze."

Renzo fiddled with the silver filigree of the coffee cup. "This is all very distressing, my lord." Had Renzo also duped him or was Renzo just playing along, trying to survive, like Etranée? His foot hurt too much to figure it out. "You don't think he survived the execution only to complete his vengeance against the lady, do you? Perhaps he took advantage of the chaos to get rid of her?"

Promethi's mouth hooked. "Well, perhaps he got rid of her, but I doubt it was in the fashion you're thinking of, mestere. Isn't that true, Arsenault?"

"I don't know where she is," Arsenault replied.

"Well..." Promethi sighed. "It would have been easier if I thought I could torture the information out of you. But I think you're telling me the truth. Pity. I'd rather keep things neat and simple. Now we'll have to do something complicated. I dislike allowing that much opportunity for error." He turned to Fariq. "Have your men take the crew off the boat and leave them in the bush. Not Jon, though. Just the pirates. They were working for Neyane, but I'm not sure I trust them to sail with us. If you set them off, they'll get back to her, let her know what happened, but they won't interfere with us."

"As you wish, my lord," Fariq said, rising. "And the Lieran?"

"Take him with you. I want you to keep an eye on him."

Renzo swallowed and stood. He caught Arsenault's gaze helplessly, then turned away. "I assure you, my lord, I have no opinions in this matter."

Don't do this to me, Renzo! I saved you! But Renzo left quietly with Fariq, not even sparing him a backward glance.

"So," Promethi said when they had gone. "Now it's just you and me, yes? And we can discard this veneer of nicety."

Renzo's denial had rattled him. He tried to pretend it hadn't. "Have we been functioning under a veneer of nicety? I couldn't tell."

"I want Adayze, Arsenault. But first I need to know a little more about you."

"There isn't any information there for you to See—" Arsenault began, but his words choked off as the other man's power slammed into him. He tried to marshal his own in defense, but Promethi rammed his way through as if it were mist. In desperation, Arsenault fell back on his instinctive Talent, manipulating the metal inside him, trying to deflect Promethi away from the most sensitive information...

But Promethi slid off that metal as if he hadn't been looking for the secrets it hid at all. Instead, he directed his magic like a pick prying meat from a nut. It went straight for the softest parts of him.

He began to churn up images, memories Arsenault had lost or perhaps nightmares, as if there was a difference anymore... Blood, pain, monsters he'd feared as a child, monstrous things he'd done. And then...

A figure with a scar and a black hat, a raven on his arm—

Erelf.

"No—"

—a flame-haired woman with green eyes—*Sella*—

—a dark-haired man who looked so much like him—*Tavi*—

And at the very bottom...

"Oh," Promethi breathed. "I see now. How fortuitous this is."

Arsenault made one last feeble attempt to kick him out. But it became clear—in one glaring instant before he lost his awareness entirely—what Promethi's Talent was.

He Shaped fear.

And what do you fear most, Arsenault?

The answer was easy.

What he feared most was himself.

⁂

It was like looking at himself in a mirror. Except he was sitting in a chair with a bruised jaw and a swollen face and the other him bent in front of him, nose almost touching his—no scar marring his temple, no metal streak in his hair. Wearing the dark green tunic Sella had embroidered with golden stags. The high brown boots. The brown trousers with the small hole she'd mended for him.

It was him, as he'd looked so long ago, the day he'd torn his world apart.

"No," Promethi muttered. "That's not quite right."

While Arsenault watched, the scar rippled down his temple into his beard and the light streak shot through his hair. It aged him years in an instant, turned him from a young man to a hardened veteran. He'd been barely a day older when both marks had appeared, but in his mind the scar represented a million years of experience. It was the dividing line between innocence and knowledge, pride and humility, joy and sorrow.

"Now, the clothes."

The tunic became a plain white shirt, open in a V at the throat. Boots changed in style, turned darker, lost the fur edge that poked over the uppers, and gained a rolled cuff. A leather sword belt hung carelessly on his hips. A battered scabbard swung against his thigh. The scabbard he'd worn before he'd killed Sella and Tavi had never looked that used.

"Perfect," Promethi said. "Have you ever seen a more intricately rendered simulacrum, Arsenault? Who would ever recognize that it isn't really you?"

The mirror-image straightened, a person physically standing in the room before him, flesh and blood, or whatever the hell Promethi had Shaped as a substitute. A body made completely of all the habits and impulses and flaws Arsenault was most afraid of. The simulacrum looked down at the real him, tied up in the chair, covered in dried blood and black powder, and smiled.

Surely that dangerous, cruel hook wasn't his smile. Surely his eyes weren't that flat, unflinching, emotionless...gray and hard as stone.

Surely he didn't look that much like Tavi.

"He has all your knowledge, Arsenault. All your abilities. Adayze will come running, I'm sure."

Arsenault made a noise. Pulled at the ropes. Useless. The bruise bloomed on his simulacrum's face, so it really did feel like looking in a mirror... Like the day his teacher brought him to the glacier and forced him to peer into all his dark corners.

That's who this Ari was. This Arsenault.

He was the man in the Ice. The reflection of all his darkness.

CHAPTER 77

MIKELO

LIERA, PRESENT

MIKELO DIDN'T STAGGER BACK TO JON'S SAFE HOUSE UNTIL AFTER sunset. The crowds on the Talos had formed small groups playing indij and drinking. The air smelled like roast lamb and horseshit.

Jon's back door was locked so he pounded on it and nearly fell inside when Silva jerked it open.

"Where in all the hells were you? You said you wouldn't be long!" In the guttering candlelight, Silva's eyes glowered—dark, angry, and worried. He was already dressed for the evening, in sienna and gold livery.

Mikelo brushed past him, trying to keep from touching Silva's silks with his dirty, smelly clothes. They'd dried stiff with salt and blood and filth. The skin of his arms and thighs had chafed raw from running in them. He tried to keep his feet, but his legs buckled as soon as he made it to a chair. He fell into it, almost tipping the chair over.

"Mikelo!" Silva exclaimed.

"Can I have something to drink?"

Jon appeared from the shadows in the other part of the house. "Did I hear Mikelo come in, finally?" He caught sight of Mikelo and swore. "So, you were running an errand for Kyrra, were you?"

"I had to deliver a letter. But then I turned up a lead to those stolen guns. I followed it and..."

"And?" Jon said.

"And it turned out to be Renzo di Prinze."

Silva had been leaning forward to study Mikelo's chest. The brown tunic hid some of the bloodstains, but the fabric flapped open below his collarbone, revealing the long gash. Now he looked up, startled. "You met your father and he pulled a sword on you?"

"It was a cane. It-it wasn't his. I need to take these clothes off." Mikelo pushed himself up, but his legs suddenly turned wobbly as a marionette's. Silva caught him by the shoulders.

"Jon, I think we need some tea. And water to wash. Mikelo, did you bring anything in that pack of yours to use on this cut?"

"Yarrow salve. I'm all right. I just need to catch my breath."

Jon watched him inscrutably. That was somehow worse than anger from Jon.

"Take him in the back room and help him change. I'll bring you water for a bath. Throw the clothes in the yard when you're done and we'll burn them. I'm not sure we'll be able to wash the stink out of them. Perhaps we should cancel that meeting tonight."

"If invitations are so hard to come by, I might not get another. They won't take me seriously. I'm fine. I just need to change—"

Silva took Mikelo's arm. "You can't even walk into the back room by yourself. How are you going to—"

"I said, I'm fine!" Mikelo shouted at him.

Silva winced.

Mikelo drew a shaking hand over his brow. Even Jon seemed disturbed by his outburst. "S-Sorry. I'll *be* fine. Just let me change and eat."

He expected Silva to leave him alone. Instead, Silva pressed his mouth grimly shut and remained at his arm as he made his way into the back room.

Silva let him go to light the candle. Mikelo fumbled at the buckle of his swordbelt, got it undone, but lost his grip as it came loose. Silva caught the belt as it fell and silently hung it on a hook. Mikelo tried to lift his tunic off over his head, but the motion tugged at the barely-closed wound and he hissed in pain.

"You idiot," Silva said. "Wait and I'll help."

"But..."

Silva bent to ease the sleeve off Mikelo's arm. Allowing Silva to help him while wearing that livery, even though it was House neutral, made him uncomfortably aware of their different positions here in Liera. If only they could have remained in the mountain house forever. Then he might never have discovered any of these horrible secrets.

He felt like the gangly thirteen-year-old Geoffre had ushered onto his ship in Mdembu's broken harbor. Mikelo had always dressed himself, but Geoffre had required him to allow the servants to dress him. The servants hated submitting themselves to a bastard, the son of a whore, and the way they had attacked the unfamiliar buttons and laces of trousers and tunic could only be described as violence. The servants had waged war on his long, braided curls, too, wielding oil and combs and scissors like weapons. After many painful hours, a stranger had stared back at him out of the metal mirror, a thin and hollow boy with short hair he didn't recognize.

Silva's hands were kind, his touch firm but gentle. Mikelo wondered how many men they had undressed, not because they wanted to but because it was Silva's job. He caught Silva's arm as he drew away, holding the dirty, foul-smelling tunic. Silva looked at him in surprise.

"Thank you," Mikelo said. "You didn't have to help. I could have managed it myself."

Silva seemed flustered for a moment. Then he snorted and pulled out of Mikelo's grasp. "And I'm the Alissar of Tiresia. I'm taking these clothes out to be burned. Can you manage your trousers on your own?"

Mikelo's cheeks flamed. He ducked his head and hoped Silva hadn't noticed. "Yes. Perfectly capable of managing my own trousers."

Jon dragged in a tub. It took some time to cart in enough water to fill it. "Towels in the wardrobe. Drop some herbs in that water, too; you smell bad, Mikelo. If what you said about that meeting didn't make sense, I would lock you in this room, but you can tell me what happened after you're done. Give me your trousers now and I'll throw them in the burn pile, too."

Mikelo wasn't sure what the noise that came out of his mouth actually meant, but he fumbled the laces of his trousers free and forced himself to push them down. He had to hold on to the rim of the tub for balance while he pried the trousers off.

When he was done, Jon gave him a strange look, then made a *hmmph* sound, scooped up the old clothes, and left him alone with Silva.

They stared at each other for a moment.

"If you start thinking of me as your actual valet," Silva said, making a joke out of it, "I'll leave you here to trip on the rim of this tub and break your leg. Anybody who decides to roll around a latrine—"

"It was the lagoon. Near the new armory and shipyard."

"How did you end up there?" Silva took Mikelo's elbow and helped him to the tub, and Mikelo was too tired to protest. The water was warm enough not to be a shock, cool enough to be a relief. Mikelo sank under it, rinsing the filthy, dried seawater from his hair. He surfaced in a moment, pushing his hair back from his face, and Silva handed him a cloth and a bar of soap. Mikelo gingerly swabbed his cut with it. He couldn't see well enough to tell how deep it was.

"Mikelo. Which of this stuff do you need?"

Mikelo looked up. Silva had the kit from his pack spread out on the bed.

"The ointment. You'll have to tell me how bad the wound is. Jon might have to stitch it."

"Can't you heal yourself?"

Mikelo switched to scrubbing his arms and legs, then his stomach and what he could reach of his back. "It takes a lot of energy to heal. Don't know if it would work anyway."

Silva walked over to the tub, ointment in hand, and wrinkled his face up at the cut on Mikelo's chest. "Looks shallow. Here, you can see yourself..."

He stretched for something he'd left on the bed. Before Mikelo realized it, Silva was holding up a polished metal mirror to reflect the wound. An absurd rush of fear overtook him and he smacked the mirror out of Silva's hands. It tumbled into the water and immediately sunk to the bottom.

Silva stared at him, dumbfounded.

Suddenly the water didn't feel as warm. "S-sorry, I just—I—"

"It's a magic thing, isn't it?" Silva rolled up his sleeve and fished in the water for the mirror. It was a huge relief not to have to touch the mirror himself, but also the most excruciatingly awkward moment Mikelo had ever endured.

"Yes." He tried to crunch himself into a ball in the corner of the tub, a physically impossible feat, given the length of his legs and the size of the tub. Silva's forearm slid by his calf. Finally, Silva pulled out the mirror, shook the water off, and laid it on the bed out of Mikelo's sight.

Mikelo finally relaxed, until Silva returned to sit on the rim of the tub. When he leaned over to smear ointment on the cut, Mikelo flinched.

Silva paused. "Not another magic thing, surely?"

Mikelo sighed. "I...just don't like to be touched. I need a moment."

"Only one?"

"Hah." Mikelo gripped the sides of the tub and forced himself to sit still. Silva touched him hesitantly. How could he explain how Silva's light touch made him feel? He dared not look Silva in the eye, but fortunately, all Silva's attention seemed to be on rubbing the ointment into his chest. Still, the deep pressure of his fingers...

"Healing myself would be just like what Cassis made me do," he said, to take his mind off Silva. "When he forced me to See myself. Arsenault says you have to be able to face up to what you See in the mirror, but I don't know what happens if you fail. I don't want to go through it again."

I've been avoiding it for weeks.

"What if people needed you? Would you try to heal yourself then?"

"That's a slippery slope, isn't it? Too easy to keep grabbing at eternity. Ow." He winced, more genuinely this time, when Silva pressed too hard on the end of the cut.

Silva drew his hand back and rinsed it in the water, then stood. "Here, mestere, I'll help you wash all that filth out of your hair and then we'll queue it up. You can't be carving up cats when you look like that."

"What? No, Silva, you *aren't* my valet—"

"If I'm to pass as your valet tonight, I might as well practice now. You'd struggle with this for ages and still look poorly when you were done. Can't have that when we're meeting the Dead Cat Society."

"The Dead Cat Society?"

"Allied to rid the streets of strays."

Mikelo snickered and bent his head while Silva worked the soap into his hair with his long fingers, patiently drawing out the strands, soaping them again and again until the tangles began to loosen. It was obscenely relaxing. The warmth of the water, the circles Silva's fingers massaged over his scalp, the way he drew his fingers down into the curls—not like a valet at all, more like a caress. What would it be like to catch those fingers in his own, to draw Silva down close to him—

Someone was talking in the other room.

"You know somebody could have followed you," Jon said.

"Nobody followed us. We've got Seely trailing to make sure."

Mikelo stiffened and Silva stopped combing. "What's wrong?"

"That's Renzo's voice. Let me up. Help me dress."

"Your father Renzo?" Silva exclaimed. "Here?"

Mikelo clambered out of the tub, shedding water onto the rug and Silva, who was slow getting out of the way. Silva handed him a towel and he dried himself vigorously, making a mess of his hair again.

Another voice filtered in from outside. "We're not amateurs, Jon. I know you don't want us to meet you here, but you don't think I'd let anyone put us together, do you?"

"A woman?" Silva murmured, holding Mikelo's shirt out to him.

"The captain of the pirate ship. She's the one who cut me." Mikelo grabbed the shirt from Silva and tried to pull it on as he walked toward the door, but pain stopped him as soon as he tried to raise his arm. "Damn."

Silva took the shirt out of his hands and helped him work it over his head. Mikelo laced his shirt, then Silva handed him his trousers. The silk clung to his damp thighs. "I dropped Arsenault's name, and I guess she knew him, too. Threatened to stab me if I didn't tell her about him."

"Why didn't you?"

"She thinks he's dead. And I just had to get out of there."

"You want me to go out and listen?" Silva said. "We're only getting snatches through this door."

"They'll never talk when they see you. Just stay here."

"I'll trim your beard then."

"I don't have a beard—"

Silva pushed his fingers through the hair on Mikelo's cheek, letting them linger. "You don't look at yourself anymore, do you?" he said, his voice pitched low and heavy with emotion.

What made him feel more trapped—Silva's touch or his words? For a moment, Mikelo couldn't breathe. He stood staring at Silva staring back at him, mouths so close they could almost touch, Silva's breath brushing warm over his lips and Silva's fingers tangled in the curly hair of the beard Mikelo had been denying he had.

It was too much. Too much touch, too much emotion, too much compassion Mikelo was sure he didn't deserve. His feelings wouldn't stay locked up anymore. His heart beat wildly as he leaned forward a fraction of an inch and pressed his lips against Silva's. Silva made a noise against his mouth, then slid his hand from Mikelo's cheek into his wet hair, holding him tightly against him—chest to chest, hip to hip, as if he'd been impatiently waiting for this moment, too. Something let go inside Mikelo, something that had held him bound for far too long—much longer than the time he'd known Silva. He kissed Silva hungrily, as if he had been starved of far more than food.

Eventually he had to breathe. Silva grinned at him crookedly with lips that looked red and bruised. "I thought you'd never figure it out.

Or that maybe you didn't like men. I thought you might not want a courtesan—"

"I thought since you'd been a courtesan, you probably didn't want an oaf like me," Mikelo said.

"An *oaf?* Mikelo, you're the least oafish—"

Mikelo took Silva's face in his hands and cut him short by kissing him again. There was so much pent-up heat and desire inside him he thought he might explode.

Another break, both of them breathless, and Silva's eyes shining in the dim light. Mikelo reached for him again, but then more voices filtered through the door and he stopped.

"If you're worried about people giving you away," the woman was saying, "maybe you should have taken more care with who you've been recruiting in Liera. Letting that one run around unsupervised is like arming a child with a cannon and telling him to go play."

"How was he supposed to react when you took him on board like a prisoner? And then you cut him?" Jon retorted.

"I didn't cut him on purpose. Dammit, he ruined my cane! He turned it into... I don't know what. Some kind of demon vine."

Silva raised a brow at Mikelo.

"I had to get away," Mikelo whispered.

"I'll help you with your tunic," Silva replied in a low voice.

Silva turned to pick up a tunic made of rich sienna silk. It matched Silva's livery, but it was much finer and more ornate, embroidered with leaping stags on the sleeves and hunters around the hem. A fantastic mask of silk and feathers made to resemble the head of a stag lay on the bed. The artist had used real antlers.

How in all the hells was he supposed to walk through a door wearing *that?* And where had Jon found it on such short notice?

Suddenly the euphoria of kissing Silva evaporated. He felt like he was coming apart at the seams again. He tried not to tremble as Silva slid the tunic over his head.

Silva eyed him critically, then chewed his lip as he glanced down at the mask on the bed. "On second thought... I'm not going to trim your beard. Or queue your hair."

"Why not?"

"Let them see you're more dangerous than they think you are."

He didn't feel dangerous. The thought of facing Renzo again, of Silva learning he was actually the *son* of the man who had destroyed Silva's family, undid him. And then if he also learned that Jon had known this secret, too, or that *Arsenault* had known and hadn't told him—although why would Arsenault have gone to such lengths to protect a dead baby's grave *as if* it were his? And why would Jon encourage Renzo to fight for the Chair if he knew Mikelo wasn't really in his succession, but in Geoffre's?

In Geoffre's line of succession with Devid and Cassis. His *brothers*.

No. He couldn't face this *and* still go to the Empirist meeting. He needed his wits about him, and the more he thought about all these family secrets, the more he felt like he was disintegrating, losing whatever tenuous sense of self he'd been able to maintain in the face of his uncle's attempts to control him.

His *father's* attempts to control him.

"Grab those cloaks," he told Silva abruptly. "And my swordbelt. Wrap the hilt of the fake sword like we talked about. This will be the perfect opportunity to let people catch a glimpse of it, to let them know *I* have it, not Devid or Cassis. No one will be able to challenge me at a meeting where everyone wears a mask. We're going now."

"Right past Jon and Renzo?"

"No. I learned a few things from Kyrra. We're going out the window."

CHAPTER 78

CASSIS

IRONDEL MOUNTAINS, PRESENT

Cassis shook Arsenault by the shoulder. It took a good long moment before Arsenault jerked awake and stopped swaying in the saddle. Most of the trip had been like this—Arsenault trying to push himself past his limits on a difficult road made more treacherous by yawning pits of what Arsenault called *tainted magic*. Lobardin had tried to explain that the poison's effects would linger indefinitely, but Cassis had thought that would be Arsenault's problem. He'd assumed he and Lobardin and Lupa would be back to Liera by now. *With* Kyrra.

Arsenault rubbed his eyes. "We're still going uphill."

"And will be for some time," Lobardin answered. "It's a long, rough road and we're not making good speed with you falling off your horse." He pulled a stained and crumpled roll of paper out of his tunic —a map of the area, hastily drawn. The moon was bright tonight, but not bright enough to see much detail.

"That last fork would have been too hard to take with a coach," Lobardin said. "I think it's a new route hacked into the forest, probably by gavaro scouts. According to the stars, we're still headed north. That other fork would curve around to the west and then south again. The north road is the only way to Rojornick. It continues above the tree line until it joins the Spice Road, then descends on the other side of the High Peaks into Rojornicki territory."

"You've ridden it before?" Arsenault asked.

"Not this road. When I ran from Amora, my father expected me to go straight to Liera, so to fool him I took this road here"—he put his finger on a spot that looked vaguely like Amora, then dragged it across the map—"up to where it joins the Spice Road. Hired on a caravan through Rojornick and down to Consel, then made my way back across to Liera. The Spice Road takes the easiest pass across the High Peaks, but crossing is a bitch no matter where you do it. Don't tell me you've never ridden through the Irondels, Arsenault. Not even once?"

Arsenault squinted at the map, then shook his head too hard, as if clearing water out of his ear.

"Still having problems with that poison, are you?"

"Not sure. My returning memories give me problems, too. I rode the Spice Road at least once, long ago. Don't know if anything I remember is accurate."

"Where did you get this map, Lobardin? Is *it* accurate?" Cassis asked. He didn't like this forest. Or riding with Arsenault at his side, the way he had before Arsenault had betrayed him. Now that they'd dug him out of the ground, Arsenault was trying to take control again.

Maybe it would have been better to have let Lupa kill him for real. A part of him wished he could just ride off into the darkness away from Liera and all his responsibilities forever. That it had suddenly become a real possibility left him giddy. At the same time he knew he would never do it. His emotions were like a ship on heavy seas—one moment at the top of a crest, the next deep in a trough.

Lobardin rolled up the map and tucked it away. "To the best of my knowledge, it's good. A friend drew it the night I received word my father had issued a warrant for my arrest. Rafelo was a surveyor. He knew the roads, and I trust that... Well, we grew up together. He came from a minor House, but his father worked in the palace. I taught him to steal fig cakes from the palace kitchen." Lobardin snorted bitter laughter. "He was such an innocent soul until he met me."

"You got caught stealing the fig cakes, I assume," Arsenault said.

"Rafelo would lift information, pass it on to me, and I'd do the necessary work of throwing my name around. Then we'd split the profits. Until the fig cakes grew too big for my father to ignore. I hoped I'd taken the fall, but later, I heard the Polici came for him. I don't know if they hanged him or just threw him in the Pit, but it doesn't matter—they're both different paths to the same end."

"Why didn't he come with you?" Cassis asked.

"He had a crippled leg. Thought he'd slow me down too much. I protested, but thank the gods he was so fucking heroic. Better he died in the Pit than to suffer with Geoffre. I'd never have forgiven myself."

Every terrible thing always comes back to Geoffre.

"We should stop," Cassis said suddenly. "There's not enough moon to keep going. One of the horses will put its foot in a hole."

"As long as the road stays like this, there is enough light," Arsenault said. "Gods hope Lupa stops, though, so we can make up some time."

"You don't think Kyrra can handle him?" Lobardin asked.

Arsenault put a hand to his tunic, where paper crinkled beneath his fingers. It was funny what a life came down to sometimes, how precious a single piece of paper could be—Lobardin's map, the marriage agreement Cassis had signed, the sketch Cassis had watched Arsenault tuck away before they'd left the farmhouse; plans for a bed, its headboard carved with orchids.

Arsenault pushed the paper back securely over his heart. "I'm going to get my *wife*," he answered roughly.

"Technically, she's my wife," Cassis muttered.

"Mestere?" Arsenault asked in a dangerous voice, and even Lobardin looked at him, surprise evident in the way the brim of his hat tipped upward.

Cassis rubbed his own eyes with the back of his arm. Might as well plunge into the issue; they would have to deal with it eventually. After all, this was the whole reason for the ruse—the whole reason he was on this godsdamned road in the first place.

"I signed the papers, so officially she's my wife. I...I've been thinking, the Empirists are right—the marriage would heal a lot of the city's wounds. Especially if I married both Driese and Kyrra. Then all our Houses would be linked. And I mean it, Arsenault. I'd take the Villa D'Aliente from the Forza, give them something else to keep them happy, and let you and Kyrra run it just as if she was Heir."

"You're so gracious, mestere." Contempt dripped from Arsenault's voice.

Cassis shot him a spiteful look. "You'd bring the city down just because you don't want to share?"

"I'd bring the city down in respect for a woman's desires. If you think you're going to force Kyrra to go along with your scheme, you'll be eating my sword, and your city can burn for all I care."

Cassis grabbed the bridle of Arsenault's horse and yanked it to a stop. The moonlight picked out the wild glare Arsenault directed at him. On the other side of Arsenault, Lobardin slowed to a stop. Cassis realized he didn't know where Lobardin's loyalty ultimately lay—if he would come down on Cassis's side or Kyrra's now that the world had changed. He needed to take command. Demonstrate to Lobardin that he'd held on to his authority, no matter what had happened with the Empirists. Make a generous gesture to Arsenault, convince him this alliance could work. They all needed to be on the same side.

"I didn't say I'd force her, Arsenault. I feel like I owe her a debt. What my father did was never what I wanted."

Arsenault regarded him warily, which Cassis took as encouragement.

"If I'm being honest, a part of me was relieved when I heard about Kyrra's child. I was young. I didn't want the responsibility, even a bastard I would feel beholden to provide for. I had lit so many candles to Ekyra praying Kyrra would be infertile, that my father would forget about her—but Ekyra laughed at me. And then, after Kyrra lost her arm and I had done every horrible thing my father wanted, and it *still* wasn't enough to satisfy him, I was *furious*. At my father, at Kyrra's parents, at every fucking householder who had ever lived. I went to those ridiculous courting parties, but I could see it in all the girls' eyes —they were *afraid* of me. I was so...*angry* at Kyrra. For being like she was. For taking that godsdamned potion. For making me into a monster."

He took a big, ragged breath. "Dammit, Arsenault. You don't want to hear this, but I *would* have married her—as my first wife. She wasn't like the proper householder girls who made polite conversation and nibbled on confections like food was beneath them. I once watched Kyrra eat an entire lemon cake and lick her fingers when she finished. And after, we sat in the salon and she kicked off her *shoes*."

"I think you had probably better be finished, too, mestere," Lobardin murmured.

"We'll stop," Arsenault said, suddenly throwing his leg over his horse and dismounting in a quick, ungainly motion, like he really was falling off the horse. "Only for a few hours. I'll sleep. Lobardin, you take first watch."

Lobardin gave Arsenault an ironic salute and slid off his horse, too. "Si, Captain."

Captain? No, dammit, that was not going to happen. Arsenault was not going to be in charge simply because he didn't want to hear what Cassis was telling him. That was not what this was supposed to be about.

Cassis caught Arsenault by the shirt, jerking the bigger man to a stop and forcing Arsenault to look at him in surprise. "By all the gods, Arsenault, you're going to listen to me while I explain."

Something snapped in Arsenault's eyes and Cassis realized, too late, that he had still been thinking of Arsenault as Andris. Suddenly he realized why he'd pushed Andris so hard. Even at his most abject and deplorable, it was evident Arsenault had *chosen* to give up, and how that had enraged him—how *dare* the man continue to take responsibility for his actions, how dare he maintain his sense of control, when Cassis felt like he had never been in control of a damn thing his entire life.

But now—Arsenault had Kyrra. And he had no reason to be Andris anymore.

Cassis tried to pull his horse back, but Arsenault caught him by the collar and jerked him off the saddle. Cassis hit the ground, struggling, but Arsenault's fist closed around his neck and pressed, hard, into the apple of his throat.

He choked and scrabbled at Arsenault's fingers, overwhelmed by panic. In the next instant, a hard metal blade dug into his ribs.

"Lobardin!" he gasped.

Lobardin, damn the man, just pushed up the brim of his hat like he wanted a better view of the spectacle.

"It wasn't Kyrra's fault," Arsenault said, still gripping Cassis's throat as if his fingers were made of steel. "Say it."

"What?"

"Say, *it wasn't Kyrra's fault*."

"It wasn't Kyrra's fault," he choked. Just say what the man wanted, he was clearly insane.

"Say, *it was all my fault*."

"Arsenault—" Lobardin tried to interrupt, but Arsenault jammed the knife into Cassis's ribs harder and Lobardin put up his hands and stood still.

"Say it!"

Arsenault shook Cassis so hard his vision went black. The blade pressed deep enough into his side to bring a bright pain and a trickle of blood, and when Cassis could see again, Arsenault's eyes gleamed a bright and terrible silver. All around them silver cracks spread through the ground as if the soil was a crust over a pit of light.

"It was my fault, my fault!" Cassis cried out.

Arsenault loosened his grip enough for Cassis to suck in a few breaths. "You still think you've got me by the balls. But you betray us, and I'll have this knife in your ribs quicker than you can flick your pretty fingers. And don't think you can kill me first, because I will come back and I will find you. You'll never be safe. The only reason I'm leaving you alive is because three against two is better odds."

"You bastard," Cassis gasped, suddenly blinded by anger instead of fear. Something snapped inside him, too, and he didn't care anymore. "Don't you think I had a right to be angry? Just because I thought I didn't want a child doesn't mean it didn't hurt. *It was my child, too.*"

Arsenault swept his gaze, still bright as a sword blade, over Cassis's face. For some reason, that was more frightening than the knife—as if Arsenault could see through him.

Oh gods, he's using his Sight!

Arsenault let go of him. Cassis tried to stumble out of his way, but Arsenault lunged and caught his arm. This time Lobardin did try to intervene.

"Arsenault, let him go. You'll both fall to your deaths. This isn't getting us any closer to our goal."

The unnatural glow still lit Arsenault's eyes, as if moonlight had lodged in them like slivers of metal.

"He needs to see the Truth," Arsenault said through clenched teeth. The same way his father had said Truth with a capital letter, as in *twisting the Truth out of that man.*

"You're talking about the mirror, aren't you?" Cassis said in horror.

"By all the gods, Arsenault!" Lobardin exclaimed, *finally,* thank the gods, going for his sword. "Surely you won't—"

Arsenault did something—a twitch of his gaze, of his fingers, *magic* —and Lobardin cursed and dropped the sword like it was hot.

"He needs to see Truth," Arsenault repeated doggedly. "No, don't look in that pit, all that will show you is evil. Here, damn you. Look *here.*"

Arsenault took the knife out of his side and held it up to the moonlight in front of Cassis's face.

Cassis cried out before he could help himself and threw up his hands to cover his eyes, but Arsenault pinned one arm tight against his body and wrenched the other behind his back. He squeezed his eyes shut and Arsenault stamped on his foot, hard, with the heel of his hob-nailed boot.

His eyes flew open out of reflex.

He expected whatever horror had made Mikelo scream and try to claw his way out of the stable stall—something Cassis had not been prepared for—but encapsulated in the metal of the knife blade was an image of the Villa d'Aliente. Not burned and broken like an Eterean ruin, but draped in climbing roses and jasmine vines, whole and shining the way it had been the first time he'd seen it. A much younger version of himself stood in the room Pallo d'Aliente had provided him, examining his reflection in the mirror. Or so it would have seemed to an observer. Inside the mirror, though, the blurred image of his father moved as Geoffre kept an eye on him.

An emotion deeper than panic made him tremble. "Gods, not Geoffre," he said, half a whisper.

Have you spent time with the girl yet, Cassis?

Not yet, Father. She seems to think I'm going to propose a marriage contract.

Silly girls, thinking love means anything without a signature. Are you upset about this, boy? You know why I'm asking you to do it, don't you?

But she's the Heir to Aliente lands. If I married her—

And give the Aliente a legitimate claim on our fortune? Hand the Caprine the means to destroy us? I didn't raise you to be stupid, Cassis. It's bad enough you were born without Prinze magic, you can at least put your looks to work for your House. I knew I shouldn't have let your mother fill your head with all those frivolous ideas—

Chivalry isn't frivolous, Father, the Etereans thought—

The Etereans invented chivalry to keep Vençalan nobles busy while they went about the business of crushing their enemies. You embarrass me, Cassis. I know you're secondborn, but how strong is a wall with one stone missing? If you want to walk away, fine. But see how well you do outside this House, knowing you failed your family.

Reliving his father's words in his father's voice, remembering his fear that a servant would enter the room and hear them, too... The memory flooded him with the same shame he'd felt at the time, a hot, viscous feeling that burned in his chest, tarry and black as the bubbling, tainted magic in the pits that lined the road.

In the knife blade, he looked through the mirror at his younger self looking back. The ugly flush on his neck, the puffy red eyes and humiliating tears that proved everything his father had said, this flaw inside him.

Weak, his younger self whispered viciously at the mirror. *Always so fucking weak. She is a stupid, silly girl and you're an idiot, just like he says.*

The younger Cassis pointed his finger at the mirror like he was having an argument with himself. *But—but! He's using you like a whore. Surely the secondborn son of a House as important as the Prinze merits better treatment?*

The scene changed. Now, the Villa di Prinze, the dark halls, the house as it had been when he was a child. What would the damn knife show him now? If the magic was determined to show Geoffre being awful, there were so many scenes to choose from. The cupboard? Geoffre upbraiding him in front of the servants? That had happened so often, it had grown boring. Or perhaps the time Geoffre had locked Cassis's mother in her room for a week until Frieda pounded on the door and begged to be let out? His father had never committed physical violence against any of them, but Cassis's stomach was twisted just as tight with dread as if he were facing an army on the battlefield.

"Arsenault, stop, this is enough. I don't need to—"

Pretty boys like you are usually only good for one thing, Cassis. I'm giving you the chance to elevate your mind over your body, to learn how to be a warrior, a statesman, and what are you doing? Throwing away all my teaching for a mangy, stray dog?

Oh. The dog.

The dog.

"Don't make me watch this again, Arsenault, *please*."

He'd found a hurt, stray puppy in the back alley, a runt. Someone had obviously not thought it worth caring for; the poor creature was eaten by fleas, lice, and mange, mostly a skeleton, and ugly, too, a ball of scraggly gray fur and scabbed pink flesh. The groom had told him it would likely die even if they cared for it and had wanted to put it out of its misery. But ten-year-old Cassis had begged to be allowed to *try* to heal the dog, unable to bear the thought of having to watch it die. They'd made a bed from an old wooden box and Cassis had taken an old blanket from the linen closets when the maids weren't looking. He bathed the dog with a cake of soap from the house, fed it goat milk from a bottle with a nipple of sorts he'd fashioned himself of twisted cloth.

He even gave the dog a name, trying to strengthen it with his belief in its future—a brave name, *Wolfeater*. He sat in the stall and whispered stories to the puppy while he picked nits from its fur. The stories his mother read to him from ancient epics were about heroes and gods and beautiful princesses and monsters that always died horrible deaths in the end, slain by noble warriors. In his experience, monsters never died, they just grew stronger, and it was comforting to think a world existed where a brave man could chop a dragon into pieces with his sword and vanquish it for all eternity, never to bother anyone again.

You'll be my faithful companion, he'd whispered to the puppy, which had always been on the verge of death. He knew that now. *We'll kill dragons and the bards will write your name into a song. Wolfeater.*

His older self braced for what he knew would come next.

Geoffre dumped the limp body of the puppy on his writing desk where he was copying out a piece of ancient Eter for his tutor. It fell right onto the paper with its carefully done letters, something Cassis had struggled over for hours, trying to make them absolutely perfect. Geoffre's lip curled in contempt while Cassis stared, frozen in horror and panic. The sightless eyes of the dog reflected in the glass of his ink pot, the tips of its fur smearing his writing—

Father? You killed Wolfeater?

Wolfeater? Geoffre didn't even have the decency to shout. Instead, he laughed. That was the worst thing. Cassis felt like he could have dealt with physical pain and had sometimes *begged* his father to hit him and be done with it. He needed a bruise, a wound to point to, so he could say *this is real*. But contempt cut like a sword and left no outward traces to prove any harm had been done, though it left his heart bleeding and in pieces.

What a ridiculous name for a bitch runt. You should have drowned her when you found her. It's for your own good, Cassis. Pretty, soft boys go nowhere because they're too weak to do what's necessary. I'm afraid you'll never make a real Prinze, but we'll keep working on it, won't we? Patience—that will forge you into someone who'll keep my legacy after I'm gone.

Gods, Cassis had forgotten about the godsdamned *legacy*. Geoffre wouldn't let go of him even in the grave.

"Isn't it enough I've had to live this, Arsenault? I don't need to see more!"

"The magic thinks you need to See it, so by all the gods you're going to watch."

"But I already know my father was awful! He tortured all of us, I hated him—gods, I *hated* him, all his ridiculous insults and exhortations. *Nothing* I did could ever make me into the son he wanted. Kyrra cheated me by killing him! That was supposed to be *my* revenge! She *stole* it from me, just like she stole any chance I had to live up to what my father wanted from me when she...when..."

The scene in the knife changed again. Now he was in the garden with Kyrra. Fumbling at her dress with fingers that felt numb, trembling not with passion but with fear, hoping Kyrra didn't notice. What if he failed, what if he *was* only pretty and soft—

No, he'd show his father. He was a stone in the Prinze wall. Strong and unfeeling. Inhuman. Everything he'd thought he felt for Kyrra had been silly infatuation. He was above it now. Only why couldn't Kyrra *see* what he was doing? She *was* just another stupid, silly girl like all the rest of them, and his father was right—she deserved it. And her father deserved it for the way he coddled her, letting her run wild.

It wasn't like Cassis had a choice, in any case. *Choices* were for minor Houses and extra sons and freeholders and farmers, not important men of important Houses like Cassis—

His anger carried him through fucking her that first time and drove the last nail into the casket of the boy who'd once thought he could be a hero and instead had discovered the only story available to him was the villain's.

All because of his *father*.

He'd never understood why Kyrra had come back. He'd thought, when it had been done with blood and tears, *thank the gods she'll be through with me*—but Kyrra had always been a mystery to him. The way she'd been driven to their dangerous liaisons had led to a relationship not with each other, but with their own anger and rebellion.

The magic was as merciless as his father had been, making him witness not only the severing of her arm—which was horrible enough—but also—

"No, Arsenault, not the hanging, not—"

How could she just *stand* there, ready to die for her House? How had the simple act of dancing with a pretty girl condemned her to a scaffold and a noose? How had something so innocent transformed him into a monster so guilty?

Watching it again in the knife blade, he panicked. When the trapdoor beneath her feet snapped open, he cried out, struggled to turn away, but everything happened the way it always happened, in his memories, his nightmares—the noose caught her around the neck and he had to have imagined hearing it *snap*—

—and was he imagining that it was *his* gavaro with the terrible, silver eyes who thank the gods saved her and damn all the gods saved her—betraying him, condemning him to a further life of hell, helplessness, and war...

"No!" he cried out, trying to cover his eyes, and this time Arsenault let go of him. He got his arms over his eyes to block out the memories and fell on his knees in the dirt.

He didn't know how long he stayed there like that. Trembling. Afraid of the tears. Tears for himself, for Kyrra, for a history that Geoffre had twisted, that shouldn't have happened the way it had.

"Mestere," Lobardin said softly. Thank the gods Lobardin didn't touch him. He couldn't have borne that. "It's done now. You can get up."

"What is the purpose of getting up? What is the purpose of doing anything?"

Silence.

Darkness.

This cold, hard ground.

"Cassis." Arsenault's voice. Not angry anymore, but he didn't want to listen. He especially didn't want to listen if Arsenault was going to pity him. He should have been stronger. Why had it taken him so long to stand up to Geoffre? It was because Geoffre had been right. He *was* weak.

"Your father was a monster. That doesn't mean you have to be a monster, too."

"Was this your version of torture? Revenge for all I did to you?"

"No. I thought I wanted revenge, at first. Truth isn't always kind, but it's better in the end. I can't fight a war on two fronts. You and Kyrra should be allies, not enemies."

Cassis looked up at him blearily. "I'm confused. Does that mean you'll support the marriage?"

"I'll support Kyrra's decision. But let's have one thing clear: I made her a promise and I meant it. She's my wife and I'll fight like hell for a world where she doesn't *have* to make such a decision. All I'm saying is that Geoffre's dead and you have nothing to lose. You can make something different, something better. But if we're going to fight Lupa and the Empirists, we need to stop fighting each other."

Arsenault put out his hand.

Cassis stared at it for a while. Then he reached out and took it.

MIKELO

PAUPERS' TOMBS, PRESENT

"When that woman said the meeting would be at the cemetery, I didn't know she meant *in* the cemetery."

Silva stood nervously at Mikelo's shoulder, like a gavaro protecting his back. The Empirists always held their meetings after dark in varied locations. Tonight, they'd transformed the Paupers' Tombs into a decadent householder soiree.

Red velvet carpets hid the marshgrass growing on the pathways between the trenches where kinless bodies lay unremarked and unremembered. The meeting was being held in the newest kinless burial ground, opened at the end of the war on the outermost island. Some of these islands had been used as boneyards since the Old World, but the only traces of those populations were the strange half-animal, half-human figures painted on the crumbling walls of old temples and the odd black stone obelisks that warned of ghosts.

Garlands of spring flowers festooned the murder markers and servants navigated the maze of shattered ruins to pour wine and offer thin slivers of kacin, which many of the guests had sampled, judging by the acrid odor lacing the air.

"Shh," Mikelo said. "We're supposed to be cynical householders, not superstitious farmers."

"You be the cynical householder," Silva grumbled. "I'll continue to be sane, thank you. And I'm not a farmer, I'm a shepherd."

Silva didn't look like a farmer or a shepherd, but then he never did. With his long hair clasped at the nape of his neck, a curl escaping artfully or accidentally past his temple, the simple swipe of leather he wore as a mask lent him an ethereal quality, as if he were a night spirit who belonged on this foggy island of the dead. Mikelo was relieved that underneath he remained the northerner who hadn't wanted him to bleed on a grave in the woods.

"Just pretend you've seen it all, whatever you decide you are."

"I've seen too much already. But all right." Silva lifted two fig cakes from a servant's tray. He took a bite of one and extended the other to Mikelo. "At least the food is good."

Mikelo accepted it gratefully and tried not to pop the entire thing in his mouth at once. He'd eaten nothing since his half-hearted meal— if you could call it a meal—at The Lady and the Vine. He and Silva had crawled out Jon's window and snuck through the Talos aided by a hasty but heartfelt Sanctuary rune. Stopping to eat had seemed like tempting the fatespinners too much. He was sure Jon had sent someone to track him down, since Silva had told him earlier exactly where the Empirist meeting was being held, but at least his father —*Renzo*—probably wouldn't come.

The fig cake suddenly tasted like dry crumbs. He forced himself to swallow, though the tight hunger pangs in his stomach brought back too many memories and ignited the irrational desire to run down one of the servers and eat everything off his tray before it disappeared—or before he disappeared.

"How do you tell who anyone is?" Silva asked, handing him a glass of wine, which Mikelo also accepted gratefully. "I feel lost. What are we supposed to be doing again?"

"Look for masks that look familiar and...mingle."

"Because you're so good at that."

"Just follow me around like we belong. They're a bunch of over-confident, bored householders and overambitious, social-climbing freeholders with too much time and coin on their hands. See that table where people are gathering? That will be whatever the point of the meeting is."

"The cat?"

"Sometimes it's experiments with metals...or chemicals...or..."

"We're in a *cemetery*, Mikelo. Full of kinless bodies."

"I'm sure we'll be able to handle it," Mikelo said with more confidence than he felt.

He set his wine glass on a broken pillar and edged his way through the men standing around the outer graves until he reached the group thronging the center table. This meeting seemed *more* than other meetings in the past—more people, more money, more extravagance.

But it felt strange, recognizing masks without Geoffre at his shoulder guiding him in his interactions. If he listened hard to the wind, he could almost hear Geoffre's voice on it. He shivered despite himself. Thank the gods Geoffre's body was interred in the Prinze crypt on the other side of the city.

"Mikelo?" Silva asked.

"It's nothing, I—"

Turning to look at Silva, he bumped into someone standing next to him, as if the person had been following him. The figure was dressed in dramatic silks the same color as the night and wore a mask with a long, white, swordlike beak, dripping with iridescent black feathers. The feathers glimmered against alabaster hair, which startled him until he realized it must be a wig.

"You're a night heron!" he exclaimed.

"You're more observant than many of the others here, mestere. Or at least more knowledgeable about birds."

Mikelo flushed. "The footing is more treacherous than I thought."

"No harm done," the person replied in amusement. "A heron is at home in the lagoon." Their eyes—dark, with a hint of amber gold when the torchlight caught them—lifted upward, following the line of his antlers. "A stag—probably not. Are you a devotee of Adalus?"

"If Adalus wants to claim me. I've recently stepped into my inheritance and feel I've earned the right to dress as a buck."

Silva darted a curious glance at him. Mikelo ignored him and smiled at the heron. *If only I could always wear a mask, perhaps I could always be this brave.*

The heron laughed. "Well, then, Mestere Buck, it seems you have me at a disadvantage. This is only my first meeting."

"I didn't think I recognized your mask."

"No, I'm here with—what do you call the person who invites you?"

"Your sponsor."

"Ah, yes. So secret. My sponsor. Over there. The swan mask."

She pointed to a woman standing in the center of a glut of men. Her shimmering pewter silk gown caught the candlelight in every curve, and her hair formed an intricate dark crown of braids behind the white and indigo feathers of her mask.

The swan who used to visit Geoffre.

Mikelo tried not to tense. "I've seen her before. Shall I assume you and your sponsor share common interests? If I recall, hers lay in the preservation of old Eterean trade routes."

He'd learned from observation that one couldn't come right out and *ask* in these meetings, even if one was reasonably sure of filial attachments. He'd always been fairly certain the indigo feathers indicated the swan was Sere, but he didn't *know*. The masks made it hard not only to recognize features but also voices.

But there was something familiar about the way the heron spoke, and the cut of those clothes was rather more generous in the chest than the style for men these days. His experience with Kyrra made him look twice. Was the heron Driese di Caprine in disguise? He couldn't be sure. She'd obscured almost every detail he might have recognized from the tavern. He didn't want to use his Sight in this company if he didn't have to.

"To be honest," the heron said, "I'm only here because my sponsor doesn't want to let me out of her sight."

"And what have you done to deserve such a fate?"

"You say that as if this party were a punishment."

"Isn't it a bit? Who holds a feast in a cemetery?"

"Well, I think that should be evident. They want to call ghosts, don't they?"

Mikelo froze. Silva scowled and moved closer, bumping his elbow.

"Whose ghost?" Mikelo asked shakily.

The heron laughed, eyes glinting merrily. "Oh, I wasn't serious. It's just another tiresome Lieran attempt at shock, isn't it? Let's see how decadent we can be, holding a party in a kinless graveyard, getting drunk and rutting among the graves. We'll put a respectable seal on it, though, by talking about Attrasca." She rolled her eyes and sipped at her wine. "Perhaps they'll try to raise him from the dead next."

"I…think he's buried in the Doge's Palace? Under the Dome of the Gods?"

"Good thing then." The heron's gaze roved the graveyard before it settled on Mikelo and Silva again. "Oh, dear, I've shocked you, haven't I? That's probably why my sponsor thinks I should be kept at her elbow all night. Or within sight of her gavaros at least."

The heron nodded toward the shadows. Two men in plain leather masks stood in the shelter of the ruins amid a tumble of sunken grave markers. "They're for our protection, of course. But don't worry. They've had their tongues cut out. If they hear anything, they can't repeat it."

Silva glanced at Mikelo in alarm. "Are you trying to say you're a prisoner?" Mikelo asked in a low voice.

"Not exactly a prisoner. More of a pawn. And yourself?"

The heron smiled brightly.

Dear gods.

"Well. Once, I found myself in a similar situation. But fate conspired to give me the opportunity to play my own cards. Now I strive to be the one who plays the game, not the one being played."

The dark eyes behind the mask glinted shrewdly. "You'll have to tell me how you've succeeded in that, mestere. For now, it looks as if our main entertainment is about to begin."

Silva bumped Mikelo's shoulder on the other side and leaned in close. "Maybe the heron is right about the ghosts," he murmured.

Two men were pulling a cart through the crowd toward the table in the center. On the cart lay a long, bulky object wrapped in white rags.

A body.

CHAPTER 80

ARSENAULT

ARAK STRONGHOLD, TWENTY YEARS AGO

ARSENAULT DIDN'T KNOW HOW LONG HE'D BEEN IN PROMETHI'S cabin when Promethi finally dragged him up on deck. It was like emerging from the galley hold, although that felt as if it had happened in ancient times. The light hurt his eyes as he looked up at the mountain rising above a sea of green trees and gray mist. The fortress built into its side loomed over the river the way Promethi loomed over Arsenault when he spiraled back down into his dreams.

Kacin, magic, pain, and fever. It all became a blurry tangle until he wasn't sure what was imagination and what was Sight. He felt like he'd been unraveled, all the strands of him spun gossamer thin as a spider web.

"I'm so thirsty," he said.

"What are you dreaming about? Tell me."

The voice was soft. But there was something about it he didn't like. He closed his eyes, tried to ignore it.

"Tell me what you see and I'll get you some water."

The fake him looked off into the distance. A Dakkaran woman was trying to climb a red clay riverbank in the pouring rain; her feet kept slipping in the sticky, runny clay and her legs were streaked bright orange-red from falling. The clay clung to her fingers and the palms of her hands. When she finally pulled herself into the undergrowth, she sat, catching her breath and watching the gray sheets of rain sweep across the river, hiding the broken hulls that lay in the distance like dying monsters. Then she pushed herself to her feet and fought her way into the forest, pulling aside vines and stomping into the undergrowth. Eventually, she emerged on a road.

It was little more than a wide path cut into the jungle, a stream of red mud. Through the pat-pat-pat of the slowing raindrops came a creaking and a cursing.

An old man and a boy were trying to free their cart from the muck. A large ox pulled it, straining in its yoke as the back wheels sank. The boy stood beside the ox's head with a small switch while the old man pushed from the back. Finally, the wheels popped out and the ox lurched forward.

Adayze stepped into the road in front of them, putting her hands out, palm up, in the Dakkaran gesture of supplication.

We have just started going! the old man called. If we stop now, the wheels will sink again!

Grandfather, I have no desire to inconvenience you further. But I am lost and in need of assistance. I only ask that I may travel with you if it pleases you.

And where are you going, daughter?

To the Arak stronghold. To see the lord there.

Then there was a crash, as if someone had dropped a wine glass or a coffee cup, and Renzo said, "Great *gods*," and Arsenault realized they had come to the Arak stronghold, that Promethi had been tracking Adayze all along—using him to do it.

Promethi chuckled. "Enjoying my surprise, Renzo?"

"But you put him off the ship! Long ago! How is it that—great gods!" Renzo said again and his voice shook.

Arsenault tried to lift his head. Everything spun. By now the spinning had become a pleasant warm feeling that took him away from the gnawing pain in his foot. The day bled together—Renzo's shocked face, Promethi smiling his close-mouthed, secret smile, and Fariq standing beside him, dressed in a deep blue silk coat. The coat was the exact color of the ocean off the southern coast of Vençal. If he closed his eyes, maybe he could drift back to Orienne, stay there this time, forever.

"Where do you want me to take him, my lord?" Fariq said.

"To the holding cells, of course. I'll retrieve him after the simulacrum delivers Adayze to me."

⚛

*A*T SUNSET, *A*RSENAULT *WATCHED HIMSELF WALK INTO THE* D*AKKARAN camp, next to Jon. The camp was full of camouflaged shelters, built to blend into the forest. Cannons, all covered by artfully woven and Fixed canvas, crates of arquebuses and barrels of gunpowder. The Dakkaran soldiers themselves were dressed like servants and farmers.*

Adayze sat in a folding camp chair in the biggest shelter, staring broodily at a map spread before her. She had traded her old, torn dress for trousers and a brown abaganda. Lantern light flickered in the dim interior of the shelter, gilding her skin with gold.

Jon ducked inside the tent, Arsenault's false self right after him.

Adayze shot out of her seat.

Jon! Arsenault! You're alive! My guards sent me word, but I didn't want to believe it.

Barely, Jon said with a grin, grabbing his sister in a tight embrace. It's been a hard journey to get here.

Adayze sighed as Jon put her back down, and her gaze shifted over to the simulacrum. By the gods, he wished it were him there, with Adayze looking at him like that. The other Arsenault—damn him—took full advantage of it, stepping up closer to her, taking her hand in his, and bowing before her, lifting her hand to his lips.

Fear made Arsenault's heart pound. He struggled for a grip on his magic, and damn all the gods' proscriptions. But he didn't have the strength. It slid away from him, except for an instant when Jon's gaze flickered off to the side, as if he'd heard or seen something from the corner of his eye...

Jon, dammit!

Adayze pulled away from the simulacrum, still casting her eyes in his direction. Look here. She pointed at the map. We've sent scouts to place charges around the walls. Nobody suspects anything yet. They're set to blow the walls in the morning. We'll start in with the cannons then.

Jon nodded, leaning on the table to look at the map. You'll station soldiers here and here. Those will be weak points in the wall.

How do you know, Jon? his other self said.

I rolled cowries. Adayze, treachery also turned up. Promethi undoubtedly has plans. Neyane's pirates helped me and Arsenault off that ship, but it was too easy. I'm sure Promethi has something up his sleeve, but I don't think Etranée had anything to do with it.

Promethi arrived a seven-day ago, I'm told. Took his contingent straight into the stronghold.

You never know what quarter darkness may come from, Adayze. Be careful with your trust.

Was it Arsenault's imagination or did Jon shoot the other Arsenault a quick glance? He should have, dammit, if what he'd seen on their journey hadn't been his imagination. His darker self didn't have any trouble keeping himself satisfied. Surely Jon had seen through Promethi's illusion. Surely he wouldn't accept that Arsenault would do the things his simulacrum did. Then again, Arsenault knew he had done most of them in other lives.

Sometimes it seems darkness comes from every quarter, Adayze said.

The other Arsenault moved behind her. He was never sure if he could really feel what his double was feeling or if he simply imagined it. Adayze was so close that if his double moved a fraction of an inch, the whole line of her body would be pressed up against him.

Jon, she said. Why don't you check in with my captains? I'd appreciate your feedback on the state of our army. Whether we have a chance at all.

Come on, Arsenault, Jon said.

But Adayze shook her head. N-no. Jon. Leave Arsenault here.

"Dammit," Arsenault mumbled—wherever he was. He hardly knew. Too much kacin whirling around his system, fever pushing in at the edges. It gave the scene in Adayze's tent a strange, too-bright glow.

Jon pressed his mouth closed, but he cut his eyes toward the simulacrum. Find me as soon as you're done talking, he told the other Arsenault. Don't dawdle.

The simulacrum touched his fingers to his forehead and bowed slightly, giving Jon a half-mocking smile that reminded Arsenault so much of Tavi for a moment he thought he was looking at a replica of his brother, not himself.

Jon shot him another glance, this one hotter and more suspicious, which gave Arsenault hope. Jon must have a plan for dealing with this. He'd used his fila magic to see through Promethi's simulacrum. But he shoved the canvas aside with an angry gesture and left the tent anyway.

Adayze, the other Arsenault said, resting his hands on her shoulders.

I thought they'd killed you, Adayze said. I wondered if you would come back. You said it wasn't a guarantee. You said you wouldn't remember.

Fariq shot me in the foot. I didn't die.

He ran his hands down her arms. She shivered but didn't move away. Instead, she closed her eyes and leaned back against him.

His gods-cursed double bent his head and kissed his way down Adayze's neck. Adayze made a small noise and the other Arsenault pushed the fabric of her abaganda off her shoulder and pressed his lips against the tendons, the skin Arsenault had never seen but only imagined... The freckles sprinkled over the soft mahogany, the citrus smell of her soap...

He wanted to throttle his double for taking advantage of her like this. He wanted to escape the magic, so he didn't have to watch and burn. He wanted to knife Promethi. He wanted to give himself some relief by his own hand. A part of him thought, No, that would be too much, but in the state he was in, every-thing swirled together—the anger, the guilt, the desire. It was all a dream, as vicious and painful as the maelstrom spinning off Thunder Cape.

She turned toward him abruptly, putting her hand on his chest. I missed you. I had a long while to think when I was gone and—Adayze ran her hand inside his shirt, over his collarbone. For a moment, her gaze fell on the small section of shoulder she'd exposed. Her eyes narrowed in confusion, like she was looking for something... His scars! The clawmarks, the gunshot! But then the other Arsenault ran his fingers under her chin and tilted her face upward to kiss her.

It lasted an interminably long time. Arsenault thought it would never end. But when it did, the other Arsenault brushed his lips against the corner of her mouth and said, And Edo? I was worried about him, too.

Adayze sighed, her eyes closed. Edo is safe, in—

"Adayze!" Arsenault yelled. He must have shoved himself up off whatever he was lying on and moved his foot too fast. Pain immediately knifed him, carrying him away from the scene he was watching. When the pain receded, Adayze was trembling, but she was pushing the other Arsenault away.

I'm not ready for that yet, Arsenault. I...I'm sorry. Why don't you go find Jon? And I'll...I'll see you later.

Had she heard him then? Had she used her Sight and caught a glimpse of what lay beneath Promethi's glamour?

Thank the gods the one thing Arsenault had never seen himself do, not in the Ice or anywhere else, was force a woman. Even in his darkest moments, he had never come to that. His double stood silent and Arsenault wondered what had passed between him and Adayze when Arsenault hadn't been able to See them.

Then the other Arsenault bowed. As you wish, he said and left the tent.

Mere moments later, Arsenault watched himself walk the perimeter of the camp, dripping a line of gunpowder out of a bag with a hole in it. In a weird reversal of the last thing he remembered doing as a free man, his double placed charges beneath two of the big Dakkaran cannons. Then he twisted some fuses and bit them off with his teeth.

Flint and steel struck sparks that showered down to the ground. The catch of a flame in the darkness and the Arsenault he had always been afraid of ran for Adayze's tent.

CHAPTER 81

ARSENAULT

"Arsenault. Arsenault!"

Arsenault opened his eyes, thinking he was still on the boat or in a dream. But the air was cool and dark and water dripped on stone. A face leaned over him.

"Arsenault, dammit!"

"Renzo," he choked, struggling to maintain his awareness. He lay on a stone shelf, the ankle of his good leg shackled to the wall. He lifted a hand to touch Renzo's face, disbelieving, but his fingertips brushed the soft hair of Renzo's beard and Renzo caught his hand and pulled him upright. A slim teenage boy wearing a scarf around his head was in the process of securing his bad foot between two thin pieces of wood with a linen bandage.

Maybe it's real?

"Stay with us," Renzo said softly. "We don't have much time."

"What are we doing?" Arsenault asked thickly. "Why are you here?"

"What do you think I'm doing? I just seduced a couple of prison guards to get to you. But someone will find their bodies soon."

"Where?"

"Promethi's cellars. The Arak have launched an attack against Adayze's army. This is our only chance to get you out. We need to make the most of it."

"Renzo," he rasped. He tried to grab Renzo's shirt but his fingers didn't want to grasp. "The attack was me—Promethi's simulacrum."

"If it was the simulacrum, it wasn't you, Arsenault. It was Promethi. But come on. If the guards catch us in here, everything will be for naught."

Renzo stuck a key into the manacle lock. It popped open with a click. The boy who'd been wrapping his foot stood, his face illuminated by the torchlight spilling through the bars.

"Zim!" Arsenault exclaimed. He swung his legs off the bench angrily, but his bad foot shot a volley of pain through him and his good foot cramped with pins and needles.

Renzo caught him with a grunt as he collapsed.

"They had my father," Zim said quickly. "Fariq carried him off the ship to Promethi. The Qalfan legation in Mdembu would have sent a special force of Nezari at once for him. But you never went."

"Where is your father then?"

"Here," Renzo said. "We found him. Fariq never told Zim where he was, just kept threatening to hurt his father if Zim didn't cooperate."

"And Promethi told my father the same thing—that Fariq would hurt me if my father didn't cooperate. I'm *sorry*, Arsenault. I truly wished you no ill. You were so good to us when we were on ship, so courageous. You gave the rest of us hope. But I could not risk my father." He swallowed. "I hope you'll understand."

He looked...young. A shock of straight black hair fell into his eyes as he looked down at the stone floor, then up again hopefully.

Arsenault slumped in Renzo's arms. "No son should have to make that choice. You did what you had to."

"Lovely," Renzo replied, his voice strained. "Now. Try to stand, Arsenault, and we'll take you to see Miha."

Panic overtook him. He tried to pull away from Renzo, but he didn't have the strength. "But, Renzo, the attack! That's where Jon and Adayze are, and Promethi's creation will have tricked her. Are we in the Arak stronghold? Is Guin here? Does Promethi have him? What are they doing to him?"

Zim put his hand on Arsenault's arm. "Arsenault. I think you're going to want my father's help."

"But we need to catch that simulacrum. Adayze thinks he's me, but he's leading her right to Promethi. And Guin! What about Guin? I promised!"

Renzo pulled him forward. "That's why you need to see Miha."

Zim supported him under his other arm as much as he was able. "Baba said to forgive you for the difficulties with your memory, but that we were to knock you insensible if you didn't want to come."

"Your father knows I have memory problems?"

"Yes," Renzo said. "He's going to help you get the Lady Adayze back. But, by all the gods, Arsenault, don't make me knock you out. You're heavy enough as it is."

✺

THIS PART OF THE HOLD WAS REMARKABLY CALM FOR A BATTLE TO BE raging just outside its walls. But as Renzo and Zim walked him by the other cells, he could hear whispers and moaning.

"Who?" he asked.

"Your galleymen," Renzo said. "Or what's left of them."

Arsenault jerked to a stop. "Guin?"

"When I was here earlier," Renzo said carefully, as he nudged Arsenault into motion again, leading him to a back staircase, "Promethi had half the galleymen in the fields and half down here. He showed me some of his experiments, so I could write to my brother. When I told you I was taken by pirates and ransomed, I didn't tell you the whole story. I was taken by one of Fariq's compatriots and got myself ransomed by telling him about my brother's connection to Promethi. They've been conversing by bird for a while now. That's why Promethi had me brought here."

"Did he really betray you to the Ibuu?"

"Yes, the bastard. He did it to draw you out, though he didn't know *you* were you. Fariq let him know by bird that you and Miha were on the ship. Apparently, he had heard a few stories about you. What did you do before Fariq took you off that island? Get yourself outlawed somehow?"

"Somehow," he mumbled.

"All right, don't talk about it now. Just put one foot in front of the other. Maybe some day you'll tell us the stories, eh?"

"Don't know what there is to tell. I'm a good enough swordsman and...you know I'm a Fixer."

"Here, up. Last flight."

"But...Guin?" Arsenault asked, wheezing with the effort of climbing, even though Renzo and Zim were doing the heavy work.

"Guin isn't here now," Zim said quickly. "He *was* here, locked in one of those cells, but Promethi's men came for him. I don't know where they take the men."

"You're telling me I might have been locked up right next to him?"

Zim and Renzo traded glances, and Arsenault knew.

"So, it's true. And you didn't think—no one told me or him—"

"He knew it was you, Arsenault," Zim said. "When Promethi's men brought you in. He tried to let you know he was here, but you were in a dream."

Arsenault stopped moving, hit with the enormity of what Zim had just said. *I missed him. All this way and I just...missed him.*

"No," he whispered. It wasn't only an injustice, it was deeply, fundamentally wrong. Surely the fatespinners wouldn't be so cruel. Then, louder—"No! Where did he go? I'll find him!"

"I said, I don't know where they take the men. He volunteered to take your place. You were supposed to go when Promethi was done with you, but somehow Guin convinced the guards to take him instead so we could rescue you."

"But *why*," Arsenault said in frustration. "What does Promethi do with the men?"

"He's bleeding them," Renzo said grimly. "Uses them to store magic, then drains it away. He wanted to show me how he could seal it up with a rune in their flesh. It's like Qalfan binding, but...different. Experimental magic."

"Dear gods! That's what you meant by experiments? And Guin took my place?"

"Arsenault, this was the only way we could get you out. If your simulacrum is still making mischief, you need to break free of Promethi or he'll use you against Adayze, the way he's been doing, yes? That's what you said, isn't it?"

Arsenault felt like he couldn't breathe. "I'm supposed to choose between Guin and Adayze?"

"My father said you shouldn't diminish Guin's choice," Zim said. "He said it was a courageous act of charity and that we should allow it to be so."

"What if I don't want it to be so?" *I refuse to let it be so. I don't deserve it.*

But Adayze...

Adayze deserved it, and Dakkar deserved a ruler like Adayze on the Ibuu's Throne. Somehow, he and Guin had ended up soldiers in a war bigger than the two of them. Selfishly, Arsenault wished Guin had been a coward, but it would be wrong to deny him his chance to be a hero when Arsenault knew everything Renzo and Zim were telling him was true.

And he still hated it. Hated it with every fiber of his being.

Renzo and Zim tugged him gently up the next step and he allowed himself to go. "Were you lying to me about your magic, Renzo?" he asked roughly.

"If I have any, it's dim. My brother got most of it."

"What's his Talent then?"

Renzo took a big breath, as if he needed courage. "My brother manipulates the magical abilities of others. It's almost as if he feeds on them. Lately he's become obsessed with knowing how to alter life itself. Our women are becoming increasingly infertile, though no one knows why. The consensus is that maybe conjure magic itself has become poisoned. Geoffre began his studies trying to discover how to solve this problem, but his purview has expanded."

"What does that mean?"

"He wants to know how to cheat death."

"For himself?"

"Probably. But...he'd also like to bring back Attrasca, I think."

Arsenault stopped moving his feet. "I don't think I heard right."

Renzo and Zim dragged him along and he moved his good foot forward.

"My brother thinks we ought to have an empire again," Renzo said. "Like the Etereans. Hundreds of years of House feuds have weakened Liera, not to mention the wars with Amora and Onzarro, attacks by Kavol pirates, threats by Qalfa..."

"But bringing back Attrasca? He's been dead, what, a thousand years?"

"One thousand five hundred and seventy-six years. To be exact."

That was a large number. An uncomfortably exact number. Arsenault darted Renzo a sideways glance.

"Attrasca was born in the Lieran hills," Renzo said sheepishly. "We keep track of these things."

"Your House is descended from him?"

"Alas, no. That would be the Aliente, a fact which is like a splinter festering under Geoffre's skin."

"The Aliente... They make the silk. The burgundy. In the Ibuu's uniforms."

"He's starting to think again, Renzo," Zim said, in pride or relief, Arsenault couldn't tell.

"Yes," Renzo said. "They're silk growers. Pallo d'Aliente, who became Head of House a few years ago, married a woman Geoffre was in love with. He even wrote poetry to her. I poked fun at him ceaselessly for that and one day I stole the poem and showed it to our father and..."

He looked pale for a moment, then swallowed, his throat bobbing with the effort. "Let's say that was a mistake. Which I'm still paying for. These feuds are serious, Arsenault, and when Geoffre says he'd like to bring Attrasca back and wipe out all the divisions, I don't think he's joking."

"Why would Promethi ally with him, though? If your brother wants an Eterean emperor..."

"I've no idea, Arsenault. But Geoffre's found a new god to worship. Or should I say an old god who's been rediscovered, and I'm not sure Promethi has as much respect for his ancestors as he ought."

"Which old god? You mean Ires?"

It would fit, if the man who wanted to resurrect the old Empire had chosen the deposed god of war as his patron. But Renzo shook his head.

"No, not Ires. We've always acknowledged Ires. Geoffre has gone farther afield. He's chosen to put himself under the aegis of the exiled god of knowledge. The one we've always called the Nameless because he killed his brother, Adalus."

Arsenault's whole body went cold. "Your brother...worships... Erelf? And Promethi does, too?"

"Arsenault," Renzo laughed shakily. "You look like you've just seen a ghost."

"Your brother can feed on the Talents of others and he's put himself under Erelf's patronage? He wants to bring ghosts back to life?"

"Does it matter so much, the god he worships?"

"It—yes. It matters a great deal. I never realized... Oh gods. This is what Ekyra meant. The gods are losing control of the magic and they're afraid if that happens, they'll lose their power over the world and each other. Erelf has been suffering in the shadows, discarded into the darkness despite all he did for his father in the God's War and now, he's maneuvering for his revenge." It seemed clear to him now, but how the hells were they supposed to stand in the way of the gods? Especially if he died and forgot this epiphany. How many times had this happened already?

"You're saying the gods are actively taking a role in events? As in the old times?" Renzo said in disbelief.

"They aren't even our gods," Zim said. "We recognize only the Magnificent Sun. Why should they have power over anything?"

"If they had power over everything, they wouldn't have to fight about it," Arsenault said. "But they have more power than we do and less humanity. Our lives are small to them, minuscule in the vast scope of time. They couldn't care less about a single human."

Renzo and Zim stopped outside a nondescript door in a small hall that looked dusty and unused. Zim leaned forward and rapped on it.

"Baba," he said softly against the wood. "It's me."

A lock scraped on the inside. Arsenault hadn't heard footsteps, so whoever was in the room had been waiting beside the door for them to arrive.

In a moment, a man pulled the door slowly open and leaned out to look around it.

He was an ordinary looking Qalfan man, wearing an undyed linen allaq, belted at the waist with a crimson sash, and no urqa. He had thick, wavy black hair shot through with silver at the temples and wide, expressive black eyes. A nose that had clearly seen some breaks, which gave him an air of worldly wisdom or at least experience.

He gave a hook of a grin, tentatively, to Arsenault.

"Hello, Arsenault," he said. "Do you remember me now?"

Arsenault stopped dead in the hallway, though Renzo and Zim were trying to pull him forward.

"*Oji*," he said.

Then he pulled back his fist and punched him.

CHAPTER 82

ARSENAULT

"You stabbed me, godsdammit!" Arsenault shouted. "You put us all in this fucking mess! If you'd just let me go—"

Oji—Miha la Hallad, the genius everyone wanted—rubbed his jaw. Arsenault had split his knuckles on it. He had the feeling it wasn't the first time he'd thrown a punch at Oji; he didn't have all his memories clear, but at least now he knew why the name *Oji la Kaif* had bothered him so much. He just didn't know *how* Oji had come to be *here*.

"Arsenault, that mutiny was never going to work," Oji said. "I had to save you somehow. The only way I could think to do it was to kill you. I knew you'd come back without your binding and we were sailing a ship full of metal!"

"Could you not have just *told* me who you were?"

"No, because it was bad enough that I was Miha la Hallad and they had my son."

"Dammit. Oji."

"Sit, Arsenault. Renzo, Zim—go. I'll take care of him and catch up."

Renzo looked at them oddly, but Zim pulled him out the door.

Arsenault sat because he couldn't stand anymore. The chambers Promethi had allotted Oji weren't luxurious, but neither were they poor; the chair Arsenault fell into was upholstered in silk. His foot throbbed in distracting agony.

"You'd better damn well explain yourself. That was a long, painful death... But you died, too, didn't you? I thought I saw you take a blow."

"Not exactly," Oji hedged. He knelt to examine Arsenault's foot. "It should be amputated, you know."

"Don't cut my foot off, Oji."

"Call me Miha. It'll be less confusing if other people hear you. I know you're in the habit of throwing your lives away with abandon, Arsenault, but I can't save this one unless I leave you with one less appendage."

"You didn't seem to care when you killed me!"

"Can we move past that? It was a desperate situation."

"I'm afraid of losing limbs," Arsenault said tightly. "I don't know if they'll grow back."

"And then you'll be stuck without a foot for all eternity? All right." Oji sat back on his haunches, sighing. "But I'm warning you, it'll get worse, especially if you try to use it."

"I can't not use it. I have to find Adayze and then I'm going to find Guin, even if I can't explain how I'm twenty years younger. And no matter what stupid heroic bullshit he pulls. He's a fucking carpenter!"

"What *do* you remember about me, Arsenault?"

It was always strange running into people who knew him from a previous life. But even stranger to run into someone who knew him from so long ago.

"I know Oji la Kaif wrote an enormous number of travelogues on the Eterean Empire and should have been left for vultures to pick clean over a thousand years ago," he said.

"Almost like you, eh?"

He had so little control over his magic now that it swirled through him unbidden. But Oji remained a confusing shuffle of images. A weird double vision overpowered him as the simulacrum paused to take in what he was thinking.

With enormous effort, Arsenault dammed the stream of magic. Oji had pulled out a boot and was turning it over in his hands, but he glanced up at Arsenault sharply.

"You're a mess, my friend. And before you say anything—admit that I set you free to foil all these plans. Where should I start?"

Arsenault shut his mouth. Oji was right, but he didn't want to acknowledge it out loud. Finally, he sighed and let it go. "How about at the beginning?"

Oji put the boot down. "The beginning. That's a long time ago." He pulled a pot off the table beside him and slathered a foul-smelling poultice onto Arsenault's foot. It smelled like sulfur and onions.

"I can't sneak up on anyone smelling like that. You might as well paint a target on my back."

"Give me a little credit, Arsenault. I'm not sending you into battle like this. Besides, the poultice will burn if you leave it on too long."

He furrowed his brow in concentration. The poultice heated up in response until it became almost painfully hot.

Arsenault tried not to grit his teeth. "So...you weren't cursed?"

"No. Or—well, perhaps. But not like you. One of these days I'm going to write this down for you instead of explaining it over and over. Though it *has* been a while. Last time was in Orienne, wasn't it? You were refusing to leave again and I had to talk you out. I should have known you'd retreat even farther after that. But the Outer Islands, Arsenault? You really were homesick."

Arsenault frowned, trying to recall what had happened in Orienne and why he had chosen to build a cabin in the craggy isolation of the Outer Islands, so close to Tule. But he might as well be groping his way through a dark room.

Oji flipped over a small hourglass. "That's how long the poultice needs to stay on your foot. After that, I'll give you this boot I've Fixed and help you find your Lady Adayze. By now you've probably figured out it's about more than two families fighting each other for kingship. Forces more important than a woman—"

Arsenault leaned over, cutting him off. "Oji. There is nothing more important than a promise made to a woman. Now, are you going to tell me why you're here and not a pile of bones in some Qalfan ossuary?"

❦

"I HIRED YOU AS AN ARTIST, DO YOU REMEMBER? TO ACCOMPANY ME on my travels in the north. You were the only northerner I'd ever known and I thought it might be good to have you as a guide. You spoke a lot of languages, although your Qalfan was atrocious. And you were good with a sword. I have no idea why you showed up at the emperor's palace and I doubt I ever will. You'll probably never recover those memories.

"I showed you how to wear your urqa and allaq Nezar style to scare away bandits on the Spice Road, and, with practice, your Qalfan became serviceable. We made a long meandering trip through the western provinces of Qalfa and Kavo. There were, of course, adventures, but it wasn't until we reached the High Peaks of Rojornick that things began to go seriously wrong."

"For some reason, I doubt everything you're talking about was an 'adventure,'" Arsenault murmured, "but go on."

"Well, from my perspective—I was having a marvelous time. Back home in Qalfa I'd been the pampered son of a magistrate. Every day was predictable and safe. I drew plans for the Office of Artifice. No one ever let me build anything and my father ensured I had no access to magic, so I was never tempted to use it. When I was offered a post as chronicler on an expedition to Eterea, I jumped at it. I wanted to show everyone what I was capable of, back then. I wanted excitement, too. And, by the Sun, I got it.

"You were less eager for excitement, as I recall. Particularly after we were taken by bandits in the high peaks and sold to some Kavol merchants."

"A little excitement goes a long way," Arsenault agreed. He winced as the urge to wiggle his toes became unbearable. It felt like someone had squeezed them in a vice.

"If your body conquers this infection, you'll always be crippled in that foot," Oji said, noticing. "The bones have set wrong."

"Who knows how much longer I'll have in this life, Oji. I'll deal with it. Go on with your story. The hourglass is nearly half gone."

"The Kavol took us on a ship. I spent my nights scheming and fuming about escape, while you were more pragmatic. Then a storm blew up and gave us our chance. Except the ship wrecked on Medeas. You don't remember Medeas?"

Medeas... Arsenault thought hard. "Is that the island...with the governor...a man named Granthus?"

"A demon named Granthus. Not the best place in the known world to be shipwrecked. The soldiers saw our Kavol slave markings, assumed we were pirates, and threw us in the stockade. By all the gods, that was the foulest place I've ever had the bad luck to be trapped. Do you remember the dragons, Arsenault?"

Oji watched him intently. Arsenault closed his eyes to shut out the room and images of dragons swooped at him out of the dark, flashing bronze, copper, silver, gold—metallic, sharp—feathered. He opened his eyes again, startled.

Oji nodded slowly. "And you remember the games?"

"Dragon...games?" he said uncertainly.

Oji's mouth tightened with regret for a moment. "I always think you'll remember the games if your god hates you as you say he does.

But you never do. The most important thing that ever happened to me and you never remember it."

"Maybe the worst punishment isn't to remember the pain, but to forget the good that came from it," Arsenault said softly.

Oji's lips twisted upward into a bitter expression that masqueraded as a smile. "The thought gives me some comfort. Is that terrible of me?"

"I wish—"

Oji waved his hand. "I know how your curse torments you, Arsenault. It's no matter. We fought our way out of the main arena. You dragged me into the catacombs below the circus. Because you saved me, I thought you would survive. I don't know how you made it, bleeding like you were, but it was too much. You bled to death and I could do nothing about it.

"I got lost in the caves, trying to find a way out. Most of what I remember about them is the darkness and the water. All I could hear was water dripping, dripping, dripping. I was so thirsty, I licked the water off the walls. As I stumbled further into the caverns, the walls began to glow. Water poured out of the rock, but it was as bright as the metal of your sword. If I had been in my right mind, I would have questioned such a substance; since I was near death, I just kept drinking. It was so sweet. When I had drunk my fill, I fell into a deep sleep. Eight days later you woke me by asking me who I was and where you were."

The sand had almost run its entire course into the bottom of the hourglass now. Oji darted a glance at it.

"Sometimes I wonder why you dragged me down there. Did you know the properties of those caves? Or were you just trying to find a good place to hide while you were dead?"

Arsenault tried to remember. "I don't know, Oji. I doubt I would have tried to make you immortal on purpose. I doubt I would have known how, in any case. Or are you just extremely long-lived?"

"That's what you always say, and I don't know. I stopped aging at a certain point. Or maybe I'm aging very, very slowly. I've noticed a few gray hairs recently. But I don't die and return like you do. Instead, all my wounds simply...heal."

The poultice had dried into a crackly paste on Arsenault's foot. Oji turned his attention to scraping it off. "Your wounds don't heal, though, Arsenault. This one—"

"I know. Look, find me again, all right? Don't stab me this time. We'll catch up later."

Oji laid his hand on Arsenault's knee. "Old friend. It distresses me that you always look the same as you did when I met you. Because I know what that means."

Arsenault squeezed Oji's hand in his own. "Give me the boot, Oji, whatever it does. Etranée says you're a famous Artificer now."

Oji wiped Arsenault's foot with a wet cloth, then set the cloth aside and picked up the boot. "Yes, what I did in the Nefeth was very effective, and I regret it. This boot, Arsenault... It should support your foot enough to bear weight. I put numbing agents in that poultice to help with the pain, but if you can handle it, you should take some kacin. Your foot won't stand up to a real battle, even with the boot. It will give out eventually."

"Fine. Not too much kacin, though. You know, the more you let the magic move through you..."

Oji was wrapping his foot snugly with a linen bandage. The pressure, oddly, gave him some relief. "Zim and Renzo told me what happened. You don't have to explain. Take a drink from that bottle beside you, Arsenault. One draught."

Arsenault obeyed. It was brandy, hot and sweet, laced with a hint of orange and the bitterness of kacin. A slow heat spread through him. He pushed the bottle away before he was tempted to drink more. "You got rid of that seal blocking your magic, I assume, a long time ago?"

"I think the magic burned it out. There's a difference in using magic from a distance and drinking it straight. But yes. I mostly get by on Fixing now. And no thanks to you. You've never been generous with your knowledge."

Arsenault grunted as Oji tied off the bandage on his foot. The kacin must have been very pure; the pain was already easing, like shaving off the edges of a rough piece of wood.

"Is Zim really your son?" he asked.

Oji smiled. "He is. His mother was a beautiful woman from Joffra. Eyes the color of polished topaz and skin like silk. Mind like a puzzle box. I never could keep up with her."

"Pardon, Oji, but I seem to remember that you were an intellectual. At least everybody says you were."

"That doesn't mean anything, Arsenault, and you know it. She could keep me running. It was one of the things I liked best about her." He sobered. "She died of fever when we were in the Nefeth. The authors writing the histories seem to leave out the fact that a large portion of the population died after peace had been declared. Of water fevers and other plagues. Zim was tiny at the time. Suddenly, I was left alone with a small boy."

"How do you stand it? To be married? To commit to that relationship, when you know she'll die and you'll keep on living? How can you promise anything when you know you can't promise she'll be the only one?"

"I don't think about it. Tima wasn't my first wife and if I keep living, she probably won't be the last. But she knew that. She would want me to be happy. Better to take love when it comes than to bear the pain of constant loneliness."

"You keep their memory with you always, Oji. I don't."

"It doesn't help to forget the grief?"

"To lose all the good memories, too? Knowing there were people I loved and being completely unable to remember who they were, what promises I might have made to them, the love or friendship we shared? No one leaves me early. I always leave them. And then I go on. How is that fair?"

Oji let out a heavy breath. "I suppose it's not. But where are you, Arsenault, if you won't allow yourself even the short happiness of being in love?"

Arsenault closed his eyes. His limbs felt increasingly far away from his body. "Doesn't matter. It would be better if I could keep going, alone, but I'm not strong enough. And then I want women I can't have, and where's the good in that? I've given up hope of marriage, Oji."

"One day, Arsenault. It will take someone special in special circumstances to match you, but one day."

"And until then?"

"You do what you have to. But if you stop trying, I think it will take something human out of you."

CHAPTER 83

ARSENAULT

AFTER OJI FITTED THE BOOT, HE HELPED ARSENAULT OUT OF THE chair and gave him a purple tunic. As Arsenault settled it on his shoulders, Oji pulled a long bundle out from under his mattress.

"Here, Arsenault. This belongs to you."

Arsenault frowned as he took it. It felt like a weapon, but he couldn't tell what it was until he shed the fabric wrappings onto the floor.

"My sword!"

He raised it to examine the blade. The runes flared briefly white, then died and left him staring at his own reflection in the mirror-polished surface. He looked bad—gaunt, hair hanging down in dirty strings, beard in desperate need of trimming, matted and tangled in wiry twists.

Oji came up behind him in the reflection, his expression worried. He hid it as soon as Arsenault turned.

Damn, but it was always odd to be recognized, to have a relationship acknowledged, and him having no idea of the depth.

"Where did you find it?" he asked.

"Fariq threw it in with all his other booty. I went looking for it after I'd recovered from the blow I took in the mutiny. Wasn't too hard to steal with most of the crew recovering. A lot of metal went overboard; it was lucky your sword didn't, but you have some sort of bond to it, don't you? You must have, to still own it after all these years."

"Why didn't you use it to get yourself and Zim out of there?"

"What, against a whole pirate crew? I'm a better swordsman than I used to be, but a whole pirate crew was a little too much even for you, wasn't it? Not that I didn't think about it, but I wasn't in any shape to use it either. Then Fariq docked in Mdembu and got rid of all of you. I thought I'd sit tight and wait for a chance, but Fariq took me and left Zim on the ship, and after that I couldn't do anything. I made them show him to me in a mirror every night, but I had to cooperate."

"What did Promethi make you do?"

"You won't be happy with me. Promethi wants Eterean machines —true Eterean machines, the kind that live with magic and blood. He communicates with a group of scholars from all over the world. They're seeing the gods moving, asking questions, trying to build some sort of perfect society based entirely on scholarly principles. It's terrifying, if you ask me. I'm ashamed they're using my books to support their actions, but I never had any idea my notes home would be so godsdamned successful."

"Is that why he has Fariq collecting Fixers for him? He needs blood that calls to magic?"

"Doesn't have to be from a Fixer. Wild magic, battle magic, what-ever. The Etereans sealed magic up inside people with a mark, like putting a cork in a bottle. Magic would build up without the ability to exit in use. Then when they needed it, they'd bleed it out."

The real meaning of Oji's words dawned on him slowly, like poison leaching into the water of a well. He lowered his sword and turned to Oji.

"*You've* been bleeding the galleymen? To keep Zim alive."

Oji recoiled. "No! I've been making Promethi machines, that's all. Clockwork gears. Metal. What he does with them..."

"Did you make a sphinx, by chance?"

"I—Yes. Why?"

Arsenault slammed his sword into the scabbard at his side. "You're right. I'm not happy with you, Oji. First you try to kill me and now your godsdamned machines! You had to know Fariq's promise meant shit, that he wasn't about to keep Zim alive forever. That damn sphinx nearly destroyed the Ibuu's court. Promethi meant it to kill Adayze's son! You could have built in some kind of sabotage to keep people safe."

"I didn't know how he was going to use it, Arsenault. Would you have risked your own children?"

Arsenault flinched. "It doesn't mean you don't owe reparation to the people your machine hurt."

"Why do you think I ran away after the Nefeth?" Oji said in a low, anguished voice. "I couldn't bear to see what I'd done. My machines... Always used for killing. I wish I *could* die, Arsenault. I'd have done away with myself long ago."

They both fell silent. What did you say to that? He'd thought exactly the same thing.

Finally, he asked, "How do I get out of here?"

"Promethi will be commanding the walls. Take the west staircase. It should be lightly guarded. Promethi sent warning weeks ago to move all the women, children, the elderly. Everyone left is a soldier."

"What are you going to do?"

"I thought I might foul the cannons and the ballistae, with Renzo and Zim to help."

Arsenault nodded. He turned to leave, putting weight on his foot experimentally. The fact that it held swept away his anger. He was suddenly hit with the knowledge that he would die soon. Leaving everyone he knew and cared for to fend for themselves.

Again.

He grabbed Oji's arm. "Thank you. I wish we had time to speak longer. I feel like you're an old friend, but I barely know you."

Oji gripped Arsenault's forearm in return and smiled, but it was bittersweet. "Some day, Arsenault, may we encounter each other again in peace."

CHAPTER 84
MIKELO
PAUPERS' TOMBS, PRESENT

"So... The man on the cart... He's the cat?" Silva whispered at Mikelo's ear.

Oh, dear gods, what do we do?

What if that body was like the cat and not a *body* at all?

Ridiculous to even think it. They were in a graveyard, of course the man was dead. The men lifted the body and unwound the bandages slowly, revealing dirty brown hair and ivory pale skin with a green cast along the jaw. The man looked as dead as if he'd been carved for the lid of an Eterean sarcophagus. But something about the way he felt, amid the flow of life around the table...

The flow of *life.*

"His lips," Mikelo whispered. "They're not blue."

Are we really going to put him in the ground? Cassis had asked in his dream of Arsenault. And Lobardin had answered, *Don't worry; we'll dig him back up.*

"They've drugged him," Mikelo whispered. "But he's not dead."

The heartbeat reeled him in, like he was a fish on a hook. He barely realized he was moving until Silva and the heron both put hands on him. He shook them off to slide through the crowd. The carters continued to unwind the cloths on the "dead" man, leaving him limp and naked on the wooden table.

Mikelo stopped near a tightly veiled Qalfan man where he had an unobstructed view of the table. The man's chest was moving. He could feel it more than he could see it.

A reed-thin man in burnt orange silks and a dog mask held out his hand and a woman dressed as Cythia's white hind put a long, silver scalpel into it.

"If I may have your attention!" the dog called out. "Our demonstration in Eterean science begins! The Etereans knew the workings of a man. When his body parts failed, due to injury or age, the Etereans replaced them. They sewed prostheses directly into the body and made them live. Imagine if we had such capabilities now, mistiri. Would the Onzarrans think they could hold any part of the southern trade routes? Would the Amorans ever threaten us again? It's even said the Etereans could raise the dead."

A murmur ran through the crowd.

Silva tightened his grip on Mikelo's elbow. "Let's get out of here. I don't like where this is headed."

"Which body parts do you think he's talking about?" the heron murmured. "A liver or an arm?"

"They have no metal," Mikelo said without thinking. He cursed himself when the beak of the heron's mask swiveled in his direction.

"You think they used metal to make the prostheses? That's an interesting hypothesis. Wouldn't it be too heavy?"

"They're not going to cut anything off, are they?" Silva said in horror. "He's not missing any body parts!"

"Why would a dead man need a metal limb anyway?" the heron asked.

"That man's not dead and they know it," Mikelo replied. "Mestere!" he called in a loud voice. "If you want to perform a dissection, hadn't you better make sure your subject is dead first?"

All chatter ceased. The only sounds were the wind and the waves gnawing at the shore. The Qalfan man turned around and stared at him.

The dog lowered his scalpel. "Are you suggesting I don't know what I'm doing?"

"I think you know exactly what you're doing. Who is he, mestere? A kinless drunk you picked up off the street? Or someone you need to be rid of?"

"What business is it of yours? Why do you want to stand in the way of progress?"

"The Etereans didn't perform their magic as party tricks."

The dog laughed. "I assure you, mestere, this isn't a party trick. Our esteemed scholar Mestere Wolf unearthed this information for us. Once you see, so many of the old stories will become illuminated. The statues the Etereans built to guard their buildings, to travel with

their armies, the giants and monsters that helped them win battles...
All the impossibilities that turn up again and again in the stories of
Oji la Kaif, the mythical figures who move in and out of fairy stories...
All will be explained."

Mestere Wolf.

Lupa.

Dear gods. There *was* a link. Dammit. He'd probably lost his chance
to get Jon's information, but he couldn't let a man die. Not in this
horrible way. Not in *any* way.

"If you think it's all a party trick, mestere, why don't you assist
me?" the dog asked with fake politeness.

"That wasn't the point," Mikelo said. "The point was the man's
alive—"

"And how do you know that?"

"His lips still have color in them!"

"So much the better, mestere. He's kinless. Leave him in the
streets and tomorrow he'll be spreading fevers. You two, bring
Mestere Buck up here and let him help."

The two gavaros in their leather masks materialized out of the
darkness. With their clown-carved mouths they looked like giant
dolls. Both drew swords.

Silva's hand went immediately to his hilt. Arsenault—in a hugely
ironic gesture—had begun to teach Silva knifework, but Silva would
be no match for these gavaros. Mikelo clamped down on his arm.

"No. I'll do it. You don't have to force me. Convince me this is
worthwhile, Mestere Dog."

Silva stared at him, but the only way he could save the man on the
table now was with a stealthy use of magic. And for that, he needed to
be touching him.

The gavaros retreated. The robed Qalfan man stepped out of his
way but brushed Mikelo's sleeve with his fingers. Mikelo glanced at
him in surprise.

Something about his eyes seemed familiar. Mikelo thought furiously, trying to connect the lines of the sketch that seemed to be
forming around Driese di Caprine, the heron, and now--her Qalfan
gavaro? Was Driese di Caprine an actual Empirist or was she the
heron who proclaimed themself a "pawn," if not a prisoner? And if
Driese di Caprine/the heron really was a prisoner of the woman in the
swan mask and the man at his back was the same Qalfan gavaro from
The Lady and the Vine, did that make him her gavaro or her warden?

A gathering like this in a cemetery of all places would be an enormous affront to charity in Qalfan eyes. If the gavaro was a practicing Qalfan, getting rid of the impurities would take weeks, months—years even. So *why was he here?*

"Now that you've seen his condition, do you still think I should save him?" the dog-faced man asked.

Up close the man smelled overwhelmingly of liquor, vomit, and piss. *Just play the bored householder.* "Even drunks have a right to exist, mestere. If that wasn't the case, how many of us would be here now?"

A smattering of laughter moved through the crowd. Mikelo used the distraction to quickly examine the man's chest. A dark mark curved over his skin just below his collarbone. Mikelo's breath caught. *A rune*.

It wasn't one Arsenault had taught him. He doubted Qalfans bound magic using Tulan runes, so what in all the hells was this? The only Fixer Mikelo had ever met who used Tulan runes was Arsenault. If Lupa had taught the Empirists what he knew, where had *he* learned them?

"Mestere Dog. Where does this man come from?"

"My men picked him up off the streets."

"I think you're lying. This mark isn't Eterean. Only someone with knowledge of rune magic could create this binding. Is he a northerner?"

"He's a drunk, mestere."

Without another word, the dog-masked man plunged his scalpel into the unconscious man's chest.

It was the worst sound in the world. Worse than the swords and screams of the battle with Geoffre and Erelf. It made him think of the businesslike way Arsenault had dressed a deer he'd shot for supper. Mikelo lurched forward, but the gavaros behind him grabbed his arms and held him in place.

The man's eyelids fluttered as his head came up off the table. A thin, reedy scream leaked from his mouth. The scalpel flashed, cutting open a flap of skin. The dog pulled it back with his fingers, revealing glistening pink gore. He left the knife blade wedged into the man's chest at the corner of the incision like he'd been cutting a block of wood.

At least it was sealing all the blood vessels. *Dammit, if I move too quickly, I could kill him trying to save him...*

"Bring the machinery here and catch the blood!"

An assistant pulled a covering off a lump beside the table Mikelo hadn't noticed—a fantastical metal dragon. The metal limb Cassis had brought them belonged to a bigger sculpture, but it must have looked something like this dragon when it had been whole. Mikelo waited for the dog to take his hand off the knife, but he didn't move. The gavaros' grip on his arms felt like iron, but if he used his magic…

"This is how the Etereans made their moving statues. They animated their guardians with magic, taken from those they conquered. This is what Lupa discovered!"

The dog wrenched out the knife.

A stream of blood gushed from the man's chest into the dragon's open, begging mouth before Mikelo could move. When it hit the metal, the golden life glow of the blood went out and the liquid turned a sludgy, steaming black—just like the pits of antivita left by the destruction of the lodge.

The opposite of life is not death…

The man gasped as the dragon's cheeks began to glow like a brazier with a fire inside it. With a screech, it lowered its head, blood dripping over its jaws. Its front feet creaked as it took a step, then its hind feet. As more blood hit it, it unfurled its wings. This was a true Eterean machine, not just a piece of one like the dented dragon claw. A *new* Eterean machine.

It gleamed bright silver, like Kyrra's arm. Feathers shot out of its body, covered its wings, until it looked like a giant bird of prey with teeth like daggers. Where the man's blood dripped onto the ground smoking holes appeared, exposing piles of dirty yellow bones, which began to glow with a sick green light. A putrescent smell unfurled over the graveyard.

The dragon rose through the fog that had begun to roll in cold off the sea, testing its wings. The man's blood dripped from its teeth.

"Idiots," the man on the table breathed, closing his eyes and shaking with weak pained sobs. "Oh, you idiots."

The crowd, which had been staring in amazement, suddenly broke.

A woman screamed. A man shoved her and then people began to run for the boats.

Triggered by the movement, the dragon swooped upon them. It picked up a man in an eagle mask and bashed him into a ragged temple wall. The gavaros holding Mikelo let go of him as the dragon soared back toward them, its claws thrust out like knives. Mikelo ducked and lunged for the man on the table. Mestere Dog—scalpel still gripped in his hand—cowered behind it.

The chaos of multiple deaths tore at Mikelo's magic. He wanted to heal all of them, but he could only save this one man. The man had lost so much blood it felt as if nothing but magic swirled through his veins, like he was hovering on the threshold of turning from human to ghost. Mikelo tried to staunch the flow of blood with his fingers, a losing battle, and poured his Sight into the man's body, searching desperately for a memory, a thought, *anything* he could Fix to patch the hole.

"What are you doing?" the dog screamed at him. "We need his body to feed the dragon!"

"You've already lost control of the dragon, mestere, and I can save him!"

The scalpel flashed toward his face. Mikelo flinched backward, but his magic reacted by reflex. It grasped hold of the dog mask and fused it to the man's face.

He was always a dog, a vengeful voice said in his mind, *and now he will remain one forever.*

Horror washed over him as the dog's head elongated, blurring into the man's hair. Yellow canines, streaked with blood, cracked through the man's gums. His screams turned to yelps and whines and he fell to the platform, writhing in agony, beating at the pain in his head with fingers that fused to become useless paws.

The realization that he had lost control of his own magic threatened to tear Mikelo free of the flow he needed to save the man the dog had been trying to *dissect,* for the gods' sake—

Where are your feet? he heard Arsenault say in his mind. *Use your desire for a better world and throw it in the face of the darkness!*

But if the darkness was his own?

Dammit, this is not the time to doubt. He grabbed for the light like a man trapped in a cave. It infused him suddenly, like someone had struck a match.

The feeling of wood beneath his hands, the scent of shellac and sawdust, the sound of a man's laughter in a snug workshop, and the company of a good dog...

It was an old memory, but it was one of the man's truest. *Gods bless him for this,* Mikelo thought fervently as he grabbed hold of it and bound it into the magic.

He wished he could explain how healing other people helped heal his own wounds, but it wasn't something that could be spelled out in words. Somehow the memory turned to warm, living flesh under his hand. Mikelo smoothed it over the gaping square the dog had cut into the man's chest, sealing the severed blood vessels and erasing the open wound, like a sculptor working in clay. The man arced off the table with a wheeze, but Mikelo held him down. He wasn't done yet. He took the foul, writhing binding and seared it away, aided by the man's own magic, which wanted desperately to escape its imprisonment.

"You're free," Mikelo told him. "Do you understand? *You're free now.*"

The man blinked. In the torchlight, it was hard to see the color of his eyes—a mossy gray, like a murky forest. They lit with wonder. His fingers tightened on Mikelo's shoulders before Mikelo could draw back.

"After all these years! I had given up!" He hugged an astonished Mikelo to his bare, blood-smeared chest, then hissed with the pain of the still tender wound and pushed Mikelo backward, laughing and crying at the same time.

"Tell me, though, why did I think of Arsenault? Was it because I was dying? Was it part of the healing? He's been dead for so long!"

Mikelo stared at him, stunned. "In your memory... That was Arsenault?"

The man he'd healed stared at him in confusion. "Do you *know* Arsenault? You're so young! My name is Guin. If you're some relation to him—"

"If you have some relation to Arsenault," the Qalfan man said as he put his sword straight through the chest of the mewling dog-man still writhing on the platform, "I would like to know about it. But first, we need to escape a dragon."

CHAPTER 85

MIKELO

MIKELO WATCHED IN SHOCK AS THE QALFAN GAVARO PULLED HIS sword from the man's chest. "May the Magnificent Sun accept your spirit," the gavaro said to the dead man as he wiped his blade clean on the man's silks. "I release you from your misery." Then he turned to Mikelo.

Silva threw himself in front of Mikelo, thrusting his knife out in a threatening manner. Mikelo took a step back, bewildered; had Silva been so close to him the whole time?

"He has no argument with you!" Silva shouted. "Leave him alone and let us go!"

The Qalfan pulled his urqa down, revealing a battered nose and an ironic curve at the corner of his mouth. "Your mestere just brought a man back from the dead and turned another into a dog. You think he needs you to protect him with that knife?"

"He could still be in danger from you!"

The gavaro sheathed his sword and raised his hands in peace. "It would be wrong of me to disallow such courage. But you can put the knife away. I only kill when necessary these days, and we have more important things to attend to."

He made a sign in the air—a Qalfan who did *magic?*—and a strong barrier, a distance between themselves and the rest of the night, descended on them. Then he began tugging off his robes.

The heron, standing in front of the platform, threw off the wig and mask. It *was* Driese di Caprine. Her long brown hair cascaded free and she grabbed it, twisting it viciously back up into the bun that had hidden it inside the night heron disguise. "Miha, what are you doing? Explain!"

"The mestere here saved a man I was looking for," *Miha*—the Qalfan gavaro—said, his voice muffled by the allaq he lifted over his head. Underneath his robes he wore a dark blue shirt and trousers. *Sere blue.* "Guin, this never should have happened to you. Here," he added, handing the robes to Mikelo. "Take off that damn mask and help Guin put these on, I swear by the Magnificent Sun himself I'm not about to do you any harm."

Guin stood beside the table, shivering. Mutely, Mikelo grabbed his own mask by the antlers and dropped it to the platform, where it rolled and clattered to a stop next to the dead dog-man his magic had created. Taking off the mask made him feel more human, but he wasn't sure that was what he wanted. He dragged his attention away from his monstrous creation—yet more proof that the man in the mirror was always ready to break free—and took the robes from Miha.

Screaming split the darkness. The dragon was hunting in the ruins now. Or maybe that was the ghosts. Mikelo shivered as he held the robes out to Guin. Now that the magic had retreated, cold and fear invaded him.

"I'll help," Silva muttered, coming up beside him. "The braindead arseholes, what the hell did they think was going to happen when they bled someone with magic blood? The graveyard is full of ghosts! That's what the godsdamned murder markers were *for*."

Guin darted Silva a shaky glance as Silva settled the robes over his shoulders, then spoke to Miha. "I d-didn't have time or ability to s-send a message. By the time I realized, it was too late. They're s-selling corpses alongside vases, statues, like they're the same bloody thing. *B-b-burn it all to the ground*, they say. The kingdoms, the cities, what the new gods wrought. Bring in a more rational governing, use magic. S-sounds fine until you learn h-how they want it done."

"You can tell me more later," Miha said. "After we escape this island."

"We should make for the boats," Silva said.

"We can't just leave those people," Mikelo said, finding his voice at last. "They're *dying*. We need to kill the dragon."

"You're already a hero!" Silva told him. "You're not Kyrra or Arsenault, and even they—"

Silva stopped, realizing Guin, the gavaro, and Driese were all staring at him. He locked his gaze with Mikelo's. They were both out of their depth here. *I should have just faced Renzo and Jon*, Mikelo thought. *Now what else have I gotten us into?*

"I've said something wrong, haven't I?" Silva said softly.

"Arsenault?" Guin asked in an odd tone—not quite a question, more like a plea. *Oh gods, he really did know Arsenault. What now?* "It's not a common name, but there must be more than one man named Arsenault, surely?"

"Probably not more than one Arsenault who fights dragons," Miha said dryly. "Who are you, Mestere Buck?"

Mikelo traded glances with Silva before deciding there was no reason to lie. "Mikelo di Prinze."

Driese gasped. "Geoffre's nephew? The one Cassis said Geoffre was grooming to be his heir? I thought you looked familiar!"

Mikelo tried not to wince at the word *nephew*. "Geoffre's dead, lady, and I helped kill him. I meant it when I said I was trying to play my own cards now. Not the ones Geoffre forced on me."

She eyed him warily. "Well, you'll never make those boats. Don't even try."

They looked to the docks. More boats had arrived, but they weren't taking people off the island. Instead, they were bringing men *onto* it. A line of gavaros wearing Prinze blue cut people down as they tried to push past. A woman jumped into the water while they watched, but her voluminous skirts weighed her down and she sank below the surface.

Mikelo whirled on Driese. "Whose are they? Are they Cassis's? Did you set everyone up?"

"Would that I had that power," she said, "but no. They're Devid di Prinze's, and my sponsor did it to weed out the chaff, the ones who are only here because they think it makes them seem dangerous and intellectual. And because she's trying to take complete control of the organization. I...I suspected who you were, but I didn't know you had changed sides, I apologize."

"So, you *were* trying to kill me!"

"I said, I apologize! I didn't have much choice. My sister is bullying me into it. Except this time, she's holding more than a doll over my head to make me jump."

"Your...sister," Mikelo said. "The swan. The swan is Tonia di Sere?"

"Good gods," Silva said. "Isn't she the one who hired Kyrra to kill Cassis? And now she's done all *this*?"

"Do you know a man named Lupa?" Mikelo asked. "The one who wore a wolf mask to these meetings?"

"I've only heard stories of him. Until recently—just a few months ago—I was with Cassis. Our affair wasn't supposed to turn out like this. It was just a *stupid* thing you do, you know, because you're tired of everyone *telling* you what you can and can't do? Except then—" She stopped speaking as if tears choked her. "I found myself with child. And I thought, shall I be shunned and turned out of my family, or shall I end up like Kyrra d'Aliente, armless, childless, kinless, dead? I had nowhere else to go, so I went with Cassis. He's not so bad, you know. He could have turned me away, too, but he didn't. He sent me away somewhere safe to give birth. But it wasn't safe. Not from my sister. She's utterly relentless. I'm guessing whoever she hired to kill Cassis failed—wait! Did you say *Kyrra?*"

"It's a long story," Mikelo replied. "One I will gladly tell you later. But you're saying that your sister is holding your baby hostage?"

"She paid a group of childsnatchers. Men and women who steal babies to sell to infertile householder couples. The woman came to me as a nurse. I...I was so exhausted. I just needed some sleep—and she *took my daughter.*"

An inexplicable panic suddenly overwhelmed him, which had nothing to do with dragons or gavaros. Could that be how Carolla had switched him out for a stillborn son? Was his mother not only a kacin eater but also a *childsnatcher?*

"We'll get her back," Miha said softly in a strained voice. "But this Sanctuary won't stand forever. We need to get to the other side of the island. I'll wager a guess, Mestere Mikelo di Prinze, that you have connections to Jon Barra, who's probably keeping an eye on you, just waiting to move in. My son Zim has tied up a boat and will be waiting for us. No sudden movements to attract that dragon or anything else. And be quiet. There's too much magic in the air."

☙❧

FOG ROLLED OVER THE BROKEN STONE WALLS, SO THICK IT HID THE others, though they were only an arms-length away. Mikelo and Silva supported Guin, who stumbled along between them. All Mikelo could see of Silva were disjointed body parts moving surreally in and out of the mist.

Miha's quiet voice drifted out of the swirling whiteness in front of him. "As long as we keep following this wall, we'll come out at the water on the eastern side. I dislike walking through these ruins, but it's the only route."

A feeling of unease crawled over Mikelo, multiplied by the inhuman screech of the dragon still hunting among the kinless graves. The fog reminded him too much of the antivita mist in the mountains, but the need for quiet made it worse. Every sound seemed magnified, like an alarm that would call the dragon or Tonia di Sere's army—Guin's labored breathing, a silk sleeve snagging the stone wall. Sometimes an image appeared in breaks in the fog, paintings on the ruins left by the mysterious people who had lived here before the Etereans—strange creatures with the arms and legs of men, but the heads of animals. Stags, lions, wolves...a dragon in the form of a woman, scaled and full-breasted, wearing her feathers like a cloak...

Suddenly, a figure loomed out of the mist in front of him—half-man, half bird, one eye sliced by a long, jagged scar, arms covered in glossy black raven feathers—

Mikelo jerked backward with a cry. *It's just a painting, dammit.*

The image began peeling itself off the wall.

The *fog* was magic. Just like the antivita mist. That was what Miha had meant by *magic in the air*, what Silva had meant by *the island is full of ghosts, what do they think the murder markers are for?*

He promised himself emphatically that he would always listen more closely to Silva's superstitious stories in the future. "Look out!" he hissed.

The ghost snapped at Guin's newly healed chest with its strange tooth-filled beak. Mikelo snatched him backward, and Guin lurched; Silva stumbled and the ghost's wing caught him in the side.

Mikelo tried to haul them both backward, but his foot shot straight through a rotten board into nothingness.

Godsdammit, the door to a crypt!

He tried to scramble back, but Guin's movement as he tried to gain *his* footing knocked him further off balance. His other foot left the edge of the pavers and he fell, pulling Guin and Silva with him. The crypt door splintered beneath their weight and they tumbled into the darkness of the crypt.

A rush of panic and only air around them too long, and then the stone floor of the crypt slammed into them; Mikelo splashed into ice-cold water and his ankle folded with the impact. Pain speared him and Guin hit stone on the way down with a sick thud and fell on top of him.

Silva, where's Silva—

A splash, a muffled impact. Silva cried out and then all was still.

For a moment, pain overwhelmed him. "Silva?" he gasped, but Silva didn't answer.

He dragged himself out from under Guin. The crypt was flooded with freezing seawater at least two handspans deep. Mikelo pushed Guin upright against a crumbling pillar and splashed through the water on his hands and knees, feeling for Silva. He found him submerged face-first in the water.

"Oh no, oh gods..." He yanked Silva out of the water by his shirt. Silva's head lolled forward and water poured from his hair. Mikelo struggled onto his feet, then hefted Silva onto a sarcophagus and pounded his chest with his fist, trying to quiet the babble of panic in the back of his head. "Breathe, Silva! Damn you, come on!"

Finally, thankfully, Silva began to cough. Water spewed from his mouth, but when it was done, Silva didn't wake, just groaned. "Leg," he murmured, rolling his head on the stone of the tomb.

It hung at an odd angle. Mikelo put his hands on it, urgently feeling—

"Dammit, broken," he muttered. Below the knee. He'd used so much magic tonight, he was nearly worn thin. He hated to admit it but avoiding himself and all the mirrors had been irresponsible; he should have spent more time learning to control his magic. Now, when it counted, he needed something left and he had so little...

"Breathe, Mikelo," he ordered himself. His voice sounded eerie in the empty depths of the stone crypt, the only other sounds the rippling seawater and Silva's wheezing breath. Guin still hadn't moved, which worried him...

It was too quiet. Shouldn't Miha and Driese be calling down to them?

He looked around for the first time. They were in a small chamber made of fitted stone blocks. Water dripped from the walls and ceiling. A mist so thick it looked like a down blanket obscured the opening they'd fallen through. No faces leaned in to check on them.

He limped toward the edge of the room hoping to find some way out.

"Mikelo," a voice said softly behind him.

The familiarity of the voice crawled up his spine. He curled his hands into fists at his side. "No," he whispered. "You can't be here, too."

"Turn around, Mikelo."

He closed his eyes. "You're only in my head."

"No, Mikelo. If you turn around, you'll see."

The other voice that lived in his head and sounded like Kyrra cursed at him. Called him a fucking idiot. Wanted him to search for a staircase or a ladder because how else had they brought the dead down? He needed to get Guin and Silva out of the godsdamned tomb, any way possible.

But he couldn't help turning around. To see for himself.

Geoffre di Prinze stood illuminated by ghost light, the scar on his forehead livid and pink. He was dressed in resplendent sky-blue silks edged with silver gilt thread. Probably the clothes he'd been buried in. He looked more substantial than he had in the other visions. As if he was truly standing across from Mikelo.

This was not a vision.

This was Geoffre's ghost.

"Surely you must have been buried in the Prinze crypt in the cliffs," Mikelo whispered.

"No," Geoffre replied. "My eldest son held a fancy funeral, then had my body dumped in the Paupers' Tombs. He wanted to get back at me, but of course he'd never paid attention to his lessons and was too modern for the old stories. But it was all woven by the fatespinners. They designed my plans into the tapestry. And now here we are, Mikelo, poised to seize your destiny. To become the Heir I knew you could be."

"I'm weaving my own threads now, not yours."

"You've known the truth for a long time, Mikelo. You're my son—not only in body, but in mind, too."

"Your bastard," Mikelo said harshly. "Your cast-off. You only came for me when your other sons couldn't live up to your expectations. None of us were ever good enough."

"Their mother was my second choice. We all laid aside our happiness for the good of our House. For Liera. Eterea."

"And how is this good for our House? You've split it apart with your scheming. Cassis and Devid and even your missing brother Renzo are fighting each other. Devid's bringing in the Qalfan Empire. Everyone hates the Prinze."

"They fear us, Mikelo, and that's as it should be."

"Just because you turned your back on love doesn't mean—"

"I had love ripped away from me," Geoffre said viciously. "I didn't turn my back on it. I was determined to marry Carolla no matter what—run away from my responsibilities, hand the Chair to Renzo with all its trappings. My father locked me in a tower and Carolla thought I'd abandoned her. She blamed *me* and married Pallo out of anger, and I couldn't even tell her *why* I hadn't met her on the road out of Liera. But *you* need to hear the whole story, Mikelo. Someone should, after all these years."

Geoffre paced. His hair ruffled in the anemic breeze seeping into the tomb and his feet moved through the water as if he had an actual body. That was the most terrifying thing—that he seemed to be alive, as if nothing Kyrra had done mattered. And despite himself, Mikelo found he wanted to know *why* Geoffre had put them all on this road to ruin. He needed a reason, for something—anything—to make sense.

"I resigned myself to my place," Geoffre continued. "Threw myself into my work. Married Frieda and had children. Then I began to hear rumors about Carolla and her marriage. Pallo didn't give Carolla the attention she deserved. The daughter she'd borne him was difficult and she was sequestered on that silk plantation, a prisoner to a life she wouldn't have chosen for herself. Finally, I couldn't stand it anymore. I contrived a trip through Karansis so I could pay a visit to the Villa d'Aliente on the way back to Liera. I meant only to explain to her what had happened. I thought I'd buried all those old passions. But I was wrong.

"We had seven nights together. Then I went back to my life and she to hers. Both of us knew what happened could never happen again. But then she found herself with child. I told myself it must be Pallo's. But I knew, both of us knew, it couldn't be. Thank the gods Pallo didn't."

Geoffre paused and ran his hand over his jaw, as if he were a real man and not a ghost. He looked gaunt, haunted. Mikelo found himself watching, fascinated, wishing he could turn away—angry not just at Geoffre but also at himself for listening.

"Did you tell her to hide the baby?" Mikelo said. "Did you tell her to fake a stillbirth so no one would ever know?"

"I told her *nothing*. I would have been happy to have the child. She tricked me into believing the child they put in the ground was you —*my* son, the son who should have been my heir if only my father had seen the importance of magic in our family lines—"

"It always comes down to magic, doesn't it? That's all you've ever really wanted. I'm not a person to you, just a vessel for magic!"

Geoffre lifted his hand to Mikelo's cheek. His touch was colder than winter. Mikelo jerked, but Geoffre leaned in close. His lips were tinged blue, his flesh stiff, unmoving. No breath brushed Mikelo's skin. "You're my son. Not just the son of some agreement I made. You're the son I wanted."

Mikelo tried to pull backwards. "You never told me. You let me believe I was an unwanted bastard and that it was Renzo's fault!"

"Only to protect you. The Aliente and the Caprine would have killed you without a second thought. Pallo hanged Kyrra, the child of his own body! There is no room for love in the games the Houses play."

Mikelo stumbled away, flinging out his arms in anger. "Well, maybe there should be! Where has it gotten us, building on a foundation of cruelty and ambition? Graveyards full of ghosts, a city of plague and shattered buildings..."

"We own all the ocean trade routes to Dakkar. Guns and kacin—those are ours now, because of the framework I laid. The Prinze control the silk trade and the sea routes for spices. If we were united, we could take the Conseli, and how would Onzarro stand against us? Amora? Can you imagine what a united Eterea would do? We could stand against the Qalfans. Take back our colonies in the east, make it all the way to Saien!"

"It's not worth it. Not if we achieve it this way—on the backs of all the sick and suffering, throwing our own people away, our own *families*, as if lives mean nothing!"

Geoffre tilted his head like a hawk. "I thought I Saw a stronger steel in you, something that ran hard and true. A sword I could temper. Perhaps I was wrong."

"That's because all you want is a weapon," Mikelo spat. "Not a human being with a mind of his own."

Geoffre stepped up close to him again, watching him like a hawk eyeing a mouse. "I believe a mind would just get in the way, Mikelo. And it makes me sad to say so."

Mikelo looked around wildly, but he'd backed himself up to an open tomb. Geoffre grabbed him by the shoulder and yanked Mikelo's shirt open, exposing the sword slice that ached beneath his silks.

In Dakkar, they told stories about ghosts that ate people. And Geoffre's dead eyes looked hungry.

How did you kill someone who was already dead? He tried to pull away, but Geoffre's grip was as strong as the grave.

"Let him go!"

Silva toppled off the tomb to *almost* stand in front of it. He held a firesteel in his hand and began to drag himself slowly toward Geoffre.

Geoffre laughed. "What do you think you're going to do with that?"

"Light it inside you. Fire drives off ghosts."

"Those are fairy stories. All I need to do is push you down. You're nothing. A serf. A whore."

The echo of words he himself had spoken in his dream tightened Mikelo's chest. Silva kept working his way inexorably closer. *No*, Mikelo wanted to tell him, but Silva looked like a ghost himself with the blood trickling down his temple, skin pale with pain, and murder in his eyes.

"You were the one who ordered those troops at Kafrin. You let your soldiers do whatever they wanted and they took my sister."

Movement behind Silva caught Mikelo's eye. Guin waking. He felt Guin's magic moving, too, faintly. Guin had allowed himself to be bound and bled to fight against darkness and now he was going to potentially drain his life just to save Mikelo? Somehow, Mikelo had to get both Silva and Guin out of this. He had to protect them from Geoffre.

The mirror, Mikelo. Use the mirror.

He didn't know where this voice came from. It seemed to come from inside him—not Geoffre or Kyrra or Arsenault, but his own. *Use the mirror. Don't be afraid of it.*

"Silva," he said. "Don't. Stay."

"This isn't just about you, Mikelo. You don't have to take everything on yourself."

"I have to take this, Silva. He's my father."

Silva stopped. "*What?*"

"You've accepted it now?" Geoffre said. "That's good, Mikelo, that's everything we need."

Everything we need. Maybe it was. To accept that all these injustices had been done, to him and by him, in not questioning Geoffre's lies. To accept that it was all injustice and he couldn't Fix anything in the past. He couldn't Fix the things that had created the darkness cowering inside him.

A part of him unwound at the realization. He pulled his sword—the fake Prinze sword, with the hilt wrapped and hidden; the one he had brought to this meeting, thinking he'd parade it as bait. Now it had a better purpose. He pulled the wrapping off as quickly as he could, exposing the fake dragon with its real sapphire eyes. The blade wasn't tiaannamir, but it was polished, magic-forged steel with a mirror sheen. Arsenault had hidden a rune in it, because that's what Arsenault did.

Sanctuary. Hope in the face of darkness.

Mikelo stepped closer to Geoffre, holding the sword in front of him. "What's this?" Geoffre asked. "That's not my sword. What did you do to it?"

"Mikelo..." Silva said, and then in increasing alarm, "Mikelo!"

Geoffre's reflection in the blade was ghostly and insubstantial. Mikelo relaxed. For once magic didn't feel like a battle. For once he knew this was the right thing to do, and the magic knew this was the right way to do it.

He Saw himself reflected in the blade. A tall, bedraggled man with haunted blue-green eyes, a mess of disheveled dark blond curls, and more than a scruff of beard on his cheeks, making him seem years older. But he did look like Kyrra around the eyes.

My sister.

He hoped she was well.

He didn't See the reflections of darkness he'd been afraid of. He knew they were in there, shadow parts of his self that would die if he let the light in to battle them. But the light burned. It exposed, it illumined, it forced you to be brave. And it was easier and safer to hide, to pray the light would pass you by.

But not embracing the truth wouldn't make it any less true. He couldn't let anyone else face Geoffre for him, and to face Geoffre, first he had to face the fear that had kept him in denial for so long—his fear of being unwanted, unworthy, unloved. Hungry. His acceptance that such a place was both his deserved state as well as his victimhood. Because he was a bastard, the son of a whore.

Only, it didn't matter where he had come from. Silva had shown him that. So he was a bastard and the son of a whore. So he was the son of a villain and a woman who had traded him for a dead child instead of loving him as her own.

He was Mikelo di Prinze.

And he was everything he needed to be for this moment.

The sword blade began to glow. It glowed so brightly it lit the entire room. The light flashed out—a flood of magic pouring out a knife-edge gap into the magic that had torn open in the sword Arsenault had forged.

"You'll come with me now," he whispered to Geoffre.

He grabbed his father by the shirt and dragged him inside.

CHAPTER 86

ARSENAULT

IRONDEL MOUNTAINS, PRESENT

THEY DIDN'T CATCH UP WITH LUPA AND THE CART UNTIL THE morning of the third day.

The road had been all uphill to that point and they had pressed the horses hard. The air grew thinner and colder and Arsenault's dizziness grew worse. But the hallucinations had diminished after the first night, when he'd wrapped himself in his cloak and curled up in a hollow at the foot of a giant beech tree like a dog, only to see Kyrra lying beside him.

You're thinking too much. Brooding never helped anybody.

"Is this a vision or are you a product of the poison?"

Does it matter, as long as I'm right?

"I suppose not," he mumbled.

Then she reached out to him in that way she had, pushing her fingers through his beard, brushing the line of his jaw with her thumb. He closed his eyes and she drew him forward and kissed him. He swore he could taste her on his tongue—faint and sweet, like honey cakes, accompanied by the brief, lingering fragrance of lavender.

He had slept then, really slept, and awakened to a moon three-quarters of the way across the sky and Lobardin shaking him by the shoulder, his feet half-frozen because the godsdamned cloak wasn't near long enough to cover him. He'd stamped some feeling into his feet and they'd moved on.

Now they were sitting on a ledge, looking down at Lupa's campsite. They'd caught up a few hours before dawn, which had given them the advantage of some sleep and a chance to eat breakfast.

Down on the flat, the gavaro Tomas tended a small fire, over which hung an iron kettle. Smoke and steam drifted into the gray air in thin tendrils as he poked the coals. Lupa and Kyrra were still in the coach, which made Arsenault worry. He hadn't seen either of them since they'd stopped. His nervous stomach made it harder to drink the last dose of antidote, but he choked it down and wiped his mouth with his sleeve.

"The arm should be set soon. Sometime today."

"Why does everything to do with magic always take eight days?" Lobardin asked.

Arsenault squinted to see better. He wished he had a spyglass, but maybe it was safer not to have a mirror with them of any kind. "Gods only know. The way it was explained to me, there's a day for each of the eight major gods. You have to pay tribute when magic makes you over, and you do it with your suffering. But after everything we've just gone through, I'm not sure magic is as beholden to the gods as they make it seem."

"Why not just take Lupa now?" Cassis said impatiently. "We've the high ground here, don't we?"

"We do," Arsenault agreed, studying the campsite one more time. If only Lupa would let Kyrra out of the godsdamned wagon. "Pass me that gun, Cassis."

Cassis handed the arquebus propped against the tree next to him to Arsenault. Cassis had been remarkably agreeable since the night with the knife. He seemed to have decided they were on the same side for now, which was all Arsenault could ask. He hadn't wanted to feel sympathy for Cassis, but he couldn't help feeling sympathy for the child Cassis had been, growing up under those conditions. Geoffre had warped everything he'd touched. Arsenault worried about Mikelo, but Jon would see him straight.

Arsenault settled the gun against his shoulder and squinted down the barrel at Tomas. The gavaro sat on an overturned bucket, hunched toward the fire with the posture of a man who wished he were anywhere else.

"You aren't going to shoot Tomas, are you?" Lobardin said.

"Have you developed a consience, Lobardin? I'm doing it to get Kyrra back."

Lobardin fidgeted. "He helped me blow the lodge. He's not like Lupa. I don't think he's loyal to him. Lupa bound him."

Arsenault lowered the gun. "Are you saying you like him?"

"Look, when you escape certain death with a man, it bonds you.

Without him, I wouldn't have been able to save our men or the camp women. Vokavik would have overrun us."

"Lobardin made the right decision," Cassis said, not looking at Lobardin or at Arsenault. "Trusting Tomas, blowing the lodge. I think you should listen to him. It was good strategy."

It was strange watching the two of them ease out of their old, tight skins now that Lobardin had cleaned up and was handed some responsibility and when Cassis allowed himself to be a real leader, not a tyrant like his father. Arsenault would have said they deserved each other not long ago, but maybe they were good for each other, too.

"It was good strategy," he admitted. "I don't know if Lupa knew what would happen when it fell. But I don't know that I'd buy a conspiracy where Tomas was angling to make it happen. He seems too young and nervous."

Accuracy would be shit at this range anyway. Unless...

Arsenault picked up the gun again and skimmed the filigreed lock plate with his fingertips. He'd always wanted to Fix a gun, but he'd never handled one when he wasn't forbidden to use his magic.

"What are you doing?" Cassis asked.

He'd already sunk too far into the magic to answer. The gun's essence snarled through him, hot and powerful, as he fused it into the metal parts. It kicked back through him like recoil.

Lobardin hit him on the shoulder. "Arsenault! What are you doing?"

He cursed and dropped the gun, then shook out his hands, which had begun to burn.

"The gun was glowing blue. Do you want to give us away?"

"Will it glow when we use it? That's hardly an improvement!" Cassis looked disgusted.

"Should make the gun more accurate," Arsenault mumbled, still flexing his fingers. "Do more damage where we want it to, so there's less collateral damage. Although if it comes down to him or Kyrra, I'm taking the shot."

"Will the gun be more effective against Lupa?"

"I don't know. He unraveled all my runes. It was like he knew them. He couldn't get that out of my books, so I don't know where he picked it up."

It continued to worry him that Lupa thought he'd been rescued by a goddess. Which goddess would that be?

No time now. "Give me the shot and let me Fix it, too."

Cassis smacked the shot into his hand. Arsenault was more careful with his control and made it in and out without succumbing to the temptation to stay under. But after he finished, he was starving. He ate his flatbread and stared at the camp.

"Dammit. If Kyrra would just come out."

"It does seem strange..." Lobardin began, but then the door of the carriage flew open and Lupa stepped out. The rising sun glinted off his spectacles and his curls danced wildly in the breeze as he turned and lifted his hand to someone in the carriage.

A silver hand extended from the interior and curled around Lupa's. Then a boot appeared and a leg, briefly exposed as the owner hiked up her long wine-colored skirts so she wouldn't step on them.

Arsenault's heart stopped. *Skirts? What in the underworld...*

Kyrra's head appeared in the doorway, her blond hair caught up, not in a queue but in a feminine style pinned with combs, a few tamed curls framing her face. The rest of her followed, revealing the whole dress. *Burgundy.* It had to be Aliente silk, the way it caught the dawn light, but it was cut in the latest Lieran fashion—low and square in the bodice, with tight lacing in the chest to lift the breasts up above the neckline in tempting curves. The skirts swept out behind her as she jumped down from the carriage. Gold winked against the skin of her bare neck and shoulders.

Even from a distance, it took his breath.

"Where in the name of all the gods did he find that much burgundy?" Lobardin said.

"She wasn't wearing that when she left." Cassis sounded stunned.

"And she's free," Lobardin added. "Is Lupa that idiotic?"

"No," Arsenault breathed. "I don't think so."

She looked steadier than she had in months. That was good. But the dress shook him. Had the arm changed her? Even without the blood to truly make it part of her?

How would he know?

Cooperating with Lupa *must* have been beneficial to her somehow. That was the only explanation that made sense. The others were just phantom fears—they had to be.

Lupa held out his arm and she took it. He seemed strangely familiar, different than he had before... Less like the eccentric intellectual, more like the wolf from which he took his name.

Arsenault tried to push down more fears, imagining what a Smith might have done to her to ensure her cooperation, but they lodged in his gut and filled him with cold fear and fury.

"Arsenault," Lobardin said in a low voice. "If you're going to take a shot, you ought to take it now."

He grabbed the gun. Without taking his eyes off the scene below, he filled the flashpan with powder, rolled the now perfectly round shot into the barrels, and tamped the wadding down. "Get to the horses. I want you away before I shoot. If it looks like the shot went bad, don't break cover. We'll make him think I'm alone." He lay down on his stomach with his flint and steel, as close to the edge of the ledge as possible.

"Si, Captain," Lobardin answered tersely.

Arsenault waited until he heard the spill and crunch of gravel from the horses, then gripped his flint and steel and counted to thirty.

He couldn't get a clear line on Lupa without going through Kyrra. There was no way around it—the only target was Tomas's back or his head. More merciful to kill fast.

He lit the wadding, lifted the gun to his shoulder, and aimed at Tomas's head.

❧

THE GUN LET GO IN A FLASH OF FIRE AND NOISE. HE'D BRACED himself with his foot against the trunk of a scraggly pine, but the magic made the gun kick back harder than he expected. The force shoved him against the tree. He strained his calf muscles against it to hold the gun straight. Magic spiraled along with the shot, hurtling it through the air toward the man who jumped up, knocking over the bucket, looking wildly toward the trees.

Just making himself a worse target, Arsenault thought in the brief instant before everything went to hell.

Kyrra tore herself away from Lupa and tackled Tomas out of the way.

The ball slammed into her metal arm. It jerked backward with the muffled, hollow ringing of magicked metal striking magicked metal.

Arsenault's stomach dropped like he'd just fallen from a great height. His heart banged against his rib cage. Kyrra slung the young gavaro to the ground and turned her back to the woods, raising both arms as she faced Lupa.

Was she bleeding? He couldn't tell with that godsdamned burgundy dress.

He leaped to his feet, slinging the gun over his arm. "Dammit, Kyrra!" he seethed, unsure whether he was furious or if he was simply overwhelmed by fear. He grabbed his pack and pulled himself onto his horse, then smacked the horse's flank and sent them skidding down the path as fast as he dared.

He wasn't even to the bottom of the hill when Lobardin reined his horse around hard to face him. "*What is she doing?*"

Kyrra knelt at Lupa's feet, arms crossed over her chest.

Please, whatever gods will still listen to me, don't let her be bleeding.

Tomas scrambled to his feet and made for his horse, but Kyrra lunged out of her supplicant pose and grabbed his ankles, sending him crashing back to the ground.

Lupa looked straight at the trees where they were hiding. Arsenault could swear Lupa was smiling. A cold wind shivered down his spine. Then Lupa pulled Kyrra to her feet, waved at them, and led her back to the carriage. She didn't stumble or stagger. She darted one glance over her shoulder, but her hair had pulled free of its combs and the wind blew her curls wild into her face, hiding it from him.

Tomas gathered up all the equipment from the campfire, kicked out the ashes, and climbed up on the driver's seat.

"We're just going to let them go?" Lobardin said, his mount dancing under him. "Arsenault?"

The forest whirled as if the earth were spinning while he stood completely still in the center of it, divorced from everything around him. Nothing seemed real. He had to force himself to reason through the fog. To accept that it *was* real and start thinking instead of feeling like he was drowning and unable to breathe.

The shot hit the metal. She was walking on her own. Better than she has in months.

Everything she'd done, she'd done on purpose.

"Arsenault!" Lobardin said again.

Arsenault let his breath out as slowly as he could. "Wait."

Tomas picked up the reins. The young gavaro looked backward at the trees before snapping the reins against the horses. The coach creaked into motion as the horses leaned into their traces.

"Well, Captain?" Cassis said, and Arsenault couldn't decide if he sounded worried or smug.

Arsenault let out another breath and finally his heart began to slow.

"She's running something. I don't know what it is." He pushed his hat up so he could wipe his sleeve across his sweating brow. His arm was shaking now, violently. He took another breath.

Lobardin grimaced as he wrapped his reins tighter in his fists, trying to still his prancing, overeager horse. "So, we *are* going to let them leave?"

"Well, I'm not going to kill Kyrra trying to rescue her, am I?"

The carriage disappeared around a cliff that jutted up out of the meadow. They watched it go in silence.

Arsenault tightened his hands on his own reins. "We're going to follow them, as closely as we can. And tonight, we'll grab Tomas."

CHAPTER 87

ARSENAULT

HIGH PEAKS REGION, PRESENT

THE DAY WAS A HARD, TENSE RIDE, ALWAYS UPWARD, THROUGH rough country and into ever thinner, colder air. Snow and ice began to lie on the road, which narrowed as it cut its way into the High Peaks of the Irondels. Arsenault spent most of the time obsessively trying to reassure himself that his shot hadn't hit anything vital and trying to figure out why Kyrra had saved Tomas.

Thankfully, the road eventually grew too difficult to do anything but concentrate on it, and breathing took all his effort. Trees gave way to grasses, then to sedge and, finally, to moss and lichen. Nothing else grew at this altitude. The caravans sent out crews in the spring, once there was some melting, to dig out the pass and throw cinders and sand on the slush and ice that remained, which was what they had been riding through since mid-afternoon. The road was a filthy scar in an otherwise majestic landscape. When the sun dropped below the jagged white peaks, it fired them for a moment with golden sparks like a fizzing Saien sparkler and the moon rose slowly into a black sky spangled with a million stars.

Snow and moonlight made it easy to watch Lupa's camp...and easy for Lupa to see them if they caught his attention.

Lupa only let Kyrra out twice, to relieve herself. Arsenault watched her carefully as she walked to the back of the rock shelter where Lupa had made camp. She carried her right arm gingerly, but it wasn't supported by a sling. He prayed that meant the ball hadn't done much damage.

"I believe that's long enough," Lupa said.

"It takes as long as it takes," she answered back. "Half the effort goes to keeping all these godsdamned skirts out of the way."

"I hope you'll remember your ladylike manners by the time I present you."

Kyrra walked up beside Lupa. "I know my manners, ser. I just don't see why I should use them."

Lupa looked her up and down, something strange about his expression, then put a hand lightly to the small of her back.

Kyrra stiffened. For a moment, Arsenault thought she was going to hit Lupa. Failing that, *he* wanted to take Lupa apart.

"Wait," Lobardin breathed into his ear. "If I can see the runes, I know you can."

The rock shelter was covered in runes, glowing in the darkness like suspended jewels, all of them set to spring on him. But watching Kyrra disappear again into the carriage, hearing the snick of the lock as it caught... that was too hard.

Tomas remained outside in the frigid night, looking miserable. His breath leaked through his scarf in tendrils of white cloud as he paced to the entrance of the overhang and back again, gripping his sword as if it were death itself.

Arsenault had some sympathy for him; it had been a long time since he'd been this cold. He'd forgotten what it was like to have his breath freeze in his beard, how the ice crinkled against his lips and skin, while the wind sliced through him like a blade. They were wearing the same winter fighting gear as Tomas, padded coats under leather jerkins, thick cloaks, scarves and gloves, all of it scavenged from Miranda's house, but it wasn't quite warm enough for these conditions.

"You know it's a trap, Arsenault," Lobardin said.

Arsenault squinted up at the overhang, where runes dangled like icicles. "We need to get Tomas outside the runes, since we can't get inside them. Lobardin, would he talk to you without alerting Lupa?"

"Worth a try. Although he might think *I* shot at him, trying to take Kyrra back for Cassis."

"As long as he assumes I'm dead. Let him see you. Say Cassis wants to negotiate. Bring him to that crevice in the rock we passed. Kyrra saved that man for a reason and I want to know what it is. Cassis, you're with me."

Cassis and Lobardin traded glances, but both nodded tersely. "Si, Captain," Lobardin said with barely any sarcasm, then moved closer to the overhang at a crouch.

"Load your pistol," Arsenault told Cassis as they slunk quietly back to the rocks. "But keep it hidden."

He slid himself into the crevice. The angle at which it sliced into the mountainside made it hard to see the opening in the dark. It was a tight fit and in the small space his breath only created more ice in his beard. The silence grew loud, magnifying the sounds of Cassis winding the wheellock and—finally—the crunching of boots on gravel and snow.

"Mestere di Prinze just wants to join you. But he needs assurance Ser Lupa won't hurt him if he makes himself known. See?"

Cassis had sat himself facing the crevice. Lobardin maneuvered so Tomas had to stand with his back to the narrow, unseen crack in the rocks. Tomas had his hand on his sword hilt but hadn't drawn it. Arsenault waited while the gavaro checked his surroundings, then edged forward, knife in hand.

"You shot at us this morning," Tomas said. "How do you expect Lupa to believe you want to negotiate?"

Cassis stood, pointing his dikkarro at Tomas's chest. "Perhaps he won't. But I can't miss from this distance and Kyrra isn't here to save you."

Tomas stared at the gun for a moment, then shook his head. "You won't shoot me. The sound of a gun will alert Lupa. This is all a bluff. I came here in earnest but if you're going to bluster—"

He turned his back on Cassis. *The man has balls,* Arsenault thought in grudging admiration. But now Tomas was staring straight at him.

The gavaro's eyes went wide in shock. Arsenault lunged forward, hooked a leg around Tomas's, and sent him crashing to the ground before he could get his sword out of the scabbard. *Probably thinks he's seeing a ghost.* Arsenault brought his boot down hard on Tomas's sword arm, pinning it beneath his heel, and drew the sword he'd taken from one of Lupa's dead gavaros.

He rested the point in the hollow of Tomas's throat. "Make one sound and I will kill you faster than he can shoot. We just want to ask you some questions. Decide now if you want to answer them or if you want to die. You have till the count of three. One—"

Tomas swallowed hard enough to jostle the blade. Then he nodded.

"Good decision. Disarm him, Lobardin. Then tie him up."

THEY BROUGHT TOMAS TO A CLUTCH OF ROCKS FAR ENOUGH WAY from Lupa's camp that they could talk. Arsenault shoved him down onto a boulder, took the gun from Cassis, and pressed it against Tomas's forehead.

"Your skull will muffle the sound," he said, settling his thumb on the dog, which Cassis had already pulled.

Tomas still looked dazed as he stared up at Arsenault. "But you saw the messera push me out of the way. You could have shot again and you didn't. That was *you* shooting, wasn't it?"

"I like to give Kyrra the benefit of the doubt. But she's not here to save you now. I have no problem getting rid of you if you won't cooperate."

"You don't understand."

"Why don't you help me then? First of all, I'd like to know why Kyrra saved your life. You'd better hope that ball didn't do damage."

"It hit her metal arm but didn't dent it. There wasn't much blood. It all soaked into the metal."

Blood in the metal was the only thing the arm was missing. She ought to be able to use it as well as she ever had now, but the blade tainted with Sella's death was also now part of her for good. "Why did she push you out of the way?"

"She felt an obligation to save a life?"

Lobardin laughed like he was startled, too loudly in the cold night. "Oh, that's rich. Kyrra?"

Arsenault shot him a sour glance. "Don't get sentimental about Kyrra. Let's try this again. Why did she push you away? Remember, I have a gun to your head. You might not have believed Cassis would shoot you, but you know I'm serious."

Tomas went sullenly silent. His jaw tightened and he dropped his gaze to the snow-scarred ground. "I didn't believe her when she said you were still alive," he said quietly. "I saw them put you in the ground. But you were already supposed to be dead."

"Say that again?"

Tomas tilted his head up. His eyes gleamed hard in the snowlight. "Everyone said you were dead. My uncle. My mother. My foster parents. *Everyone.*"

An uneasy feeling slithered into the pit of Arsenault's stomach. "Who is your uncle? Your mother?"

Tomas took a deep breath. The gun slipped on his skin and Arsenault had to steady it.

"Jonawak dom B'ara is my uncle," he said. "And the Ibuu Adayze dom B'ara is my mother."

◈

ARSENAULT FLIPPED THE GUN UP AND AWAY AND PUT HIS FOOT down, taking as much of a step backward as he could on the steep, rocky slope.

"You're *Adayze's* child?" he said in amazement.

Cassis looked like he wanted to spit. "I told you, Arsenault, I thought Jon double-crossed you—"

"Shut up," Arsenault said, then studied Tomas's face. "You can't be Edo. Edo had darker skin, black hair...brown eyes." He frowned. "I'm sure that's true. I'm sure I remember Edo."

"I'm not Edo. Tomas is my given name."

"What is your birth order?" Arsenault asked.

Tomas looked straight at him. "Second."

Edo's Dagger. Gods.

Arsenault pointed the gun at the ground and pressed his thumb hard against the spring that held the dog back. It sprang forward, releasing the dog without discharging. He threw the gun back at Cassis, who caught it and looked at him in confusion.

"But, Arsenault..."

"You and Lobardin go back down and make sure nothing happens below. Let me know if Lupa stirs."

"How?"

"Make a...a wolf howl. Or an owl hoot. Something."

Lobardin shook his head and smacked Cassis on the shoulder. "And he kept your armies on the run. Come on. We'll keep an eye on Lupa."

By the glance Lobardin threw at him as they left, Arsenault knew his cooperation would be chalked up as a debt for later. But at least he went and maneuvered Cassis out of the way, too.

"Going to untie me now?" Tomas said.

"Did you tell Kyrra you had some relation to Jon or did she figure it out?"

Tomas looked away uncomfortably. "She has a way of prying information out of you."

"If you're not prepared for it, yes. *Why* are you working for Lupa?"

"You know my mother is in exile in Vençal?"

Arsenault dipped his head. He hadn't known where Adazye was, but he supposed it didn't matter.

"My brother is in Vençal, too. Living in Ris among the scholars and the intellectuals—talking in the cafés, studying at the university. So was I, until about two years ago. That's when Lupa showed up, rifling through the library, asking for all the stacks of old books, everything he could find about Eterean magic...all their copies of Oji la Kaif's books."

"Oji," Arsenault muttered. "Of course."

Tomas looked at him strangely. "He is the authority on the Eterean world. Lupa was looking for descriptions of magical rituals. The sketches were worth more, I think, in many cases. Oji's books include plans for machines and drawings of them in use. That was very helpful to the Empirists."

Sketches. Yes, of course.

Oji had wanted him to sketch everything. From mountain foxes to the metal sphinxes and other monsters the Etereans used to keep their populations in line, the ones they gave their guards to patrol the cities on the outer edges of the Empire. Oji had dragged him along to those rituals, peppered him with questions, made him explain everything to the best of his ability, then wrote it all down. Until somehow they had been separated, and Oji had gone on writing books, and he had stopped being an artist and instead picked up his role as killer again.

"Well," Arsenault said, feeling sick at his unremembered role in everything the Empirists were now trying to inflict upon the world. "I suppose Oji would know."

"That's a strange way to put it. Are you going to untie me or not? You still don't trust I am who I say I am?"

Arsenault pulled his knife and cut through the knot. Tomas sighed in relief as he brought his arms around and rubbed his wrists.

"So, what was Lupa looking for?"

Tomas rubbed his jaw thoughtfully. The wool of Tomas's fingerless gloves caught on a light coating of stubble. Arsenault scratched his own beard, distracted for the moment—trying to figure out how old Tomas was.

"I don't know, exactly. In the beginning, Lupa seemed harmless enough. A scholar obsessed with a bunch of dusty old books. The intellectuals in Ris used to invite him to parties to ridicule him, but he never seemed to notice. He just went on and on about Attrasca and the revelations he'd had in Tule and how the Etereans had brought everyone together and that they must have had a source of magic we don't have in the world today to keep people alive longer—how there were Old World legends alive today, if we just knew where to look... He had a lot of strange theories. The more wine he drank, the stranger they got. It was a form of entertainment."

"Edo goes to a lot of these parties?"

"The exiled prince of Dakkar is in high demand."

"Right. So, Lupa was putting a ruse over on you?"

Tomas looked troubled. "If he was, he was good at it. But then he began to change. At parties, when he drank, he began to get vicious. He stopped being the entertainment and instead became a maelstrom at the center of every party, sucking everyone into his mad schemes. He carried himself differently—*looked* different. My mother discovered that he'd struck up a relationship with the Prinze, so she had me get closer to him. Somehow, I ended up with a job as his secretary— I'm still not sure exactly how it came about. It just seemed to fall into my lap."

"And now you're a gavaro. Good thing you're handy with that sword."

"I always knew I'd have to serve Edo in this way. But I didn't expect all the magic. I didn't know magic would do those things."

If Arsenault hadn't been watching, he would have missed the shudder that passed through Tomas like the shiver of breath on water. "He twists things. Creates metal creatures that aren't like anything that should be alive."

Arsenault pushed aside the fear for Kyrra this information provoked. "Do you have your mother's Sight? Is that why he bound you?"

"I'm a Fixer," he said. Then, after a heartbeat pause, he added, "You know my mother has Sight?"

Arsenault shifted uncomfortably. "I know a few things about your mother."

Tomas's head snapped up. Anger flashed over his face.

Light eyes, a voice whispered in Arsenault's mind. *He has light eyes*.

Arsenault squashed the voice down, hard. "What is Lupa doing to Kyrra? Why did he give her that dress? Why has he let her go free?"

"Are you really married to her?" Tomas asked.

In the snow-reflected moonlight, it was easy to see the tense earnestness of Tomas's face—the features that had seemed only vaguely familiar to him not long before. Now that Arsenault knew what he was looking for, he could pick out the resemblance. Adayze's cheekbones. The shape of her eyes. But Tomas's hair was not black and the color of his skin edged more toward a light chestnut than Adayze's deep mahogany. If he'd done a better job of his beads, people would have assumed without doubt that he was Tiresian.

But his eyes... Arsenault had been ignoring the fact that they weren't just *light*. They were gray.

Like his.

He felt like throwing up. He wanted to walk away, but there was nowhere to go. He put his hand over his mouth and raked his thumb and fingers through his beard. He didn't trust himself to speak, but he had to.

"You're my son," he said. The words didn't make sense, so he had to say them again. "My *son*." His legs felt like they were going to go out from under him. He felt behind him and sat shakily on a boulder. "Dear gods. I was going to kill you."

If Kyrra hadn't saved Tomas, he'd be dead.

Kyrra knows he's my son.

"They all told me you were dead," Tomas said angrily. "They told me you sacrificed yourself, like a hero. My mother, my uncle, Renzo, Etranée. Every one of them told me the same thing."

"Renzo? Etranée?"

"My foster parents."

"G-gods. Renzo raised you? And *Etranée?*"

"She said—"

Arsenault put up his hand and closed his eyes. "No. Stop." He felt like he was suffocating again. He forced himself to take one long, slow breath, and then another, and finally he opened his eyes to see Tomas watching him belligerently. "It's a long, complicated story. I'll tell you when I can, but now isn't the time. I need to know about Kyrra."

"You didn't answer my question, though. Are you really married to Kyrra d'Aliente?"

Arsenault gave him a sharp glance. "That's not what you're asking. You're asking did I run out on your mother."

"They all made it sound like you were a hero. When I came to Eterea, I kept hearing your name and I thought—the Aliente general had to have been another Arsenault, he couldn't have been you. But when I found out the general was connected to Jon, I realized it *must* have been you—the same you who supposedly died before I was born. Maybe not the hero I had been led to believe, but still dead. Then I walked into the farmhouse and there you were. Not old enough to be my father, but *you*, and hiding Kyrra d'Aliente in a safe room. Lupa wanted me to kill you and... I didn't know what to do."

Tomas twined his hands together between his knees and stared at them, all the muscles in his face pulled downward as if he had been overcome by the tug of the earth.

What in all the hells was he supposed to say? Arsenault rubbed his head where Tomas had hit him with the sword hilt. The cut there was still rough and healing.

Finally, he sighed.

"All I can be is honest, Tomas; I don't have time to explain. I loved your mother, I never knew about you, I'm not a hero, and I would walk through the underworld to get Kyrra back. Is that enough?"

Tomas studied him for a moment. Then he said, "I met my uncle Jon in Liera when Lupa was still with the Empirists there. He said I might run into Kyrra d'Aliente, and I was to promise to look out for her. He said we were on the same side. Do you believe me?"

"Are we in a stalemate then?"

Tomas stood. "I guess so. Lupa freed Kyra because she agreed to his terms."

Arsenault frowned. "Terms of surrender? And he had this out of her while the magic was still remaking her arm?"

"He makes sure I'm outside when he wants to talk to her. From what I overheard, Kyrra was involved in some kind of negotiation in the past—not too long ago. An offer, her for you. Lupa gave her the chance to take it and she did. I tried to explain to her that I had... that I had killed you, but I guess she knew better."

What did *not too long ago* mean? *What the hell are you doing, Kyrra?*

"She had an offer from the Empirists?"

"I don't know. She said, *I'll give myself up to set him free*, and after that Lupa struck her bonds and made her put on that dress."

Arsenault growled in frustration. He shoved himself up off the rock and looked into the clear black, star-dusted sky toward Rojornick. If only the cold air knifing him in the lungs would help clear his thoughts.

"She's got a lot of damn nerve, calling me an idiot for doing the same godsforsaken thing she's doing right now."

"Lupa was expecting you. Told me to rouse him if I heard anything suspicious, not to rely on the runes. I thought he was talking about Lobardin and Mestere di Prinze. But it makes sense now."

"He doesn't think his runes are enough?"

"I wouldn't bet on them not being enough, but he sleeps a lot. Cries out sometimes. It's like he's fighting a battle in his dreams."

Arsenault rubbed the line of his jaw. "Does he wake easily?"

"He makes sure Kyrra is right next to him."

Arsenault tried to ignore the feelings that inspired in him. "She sleeps beside him...willingly?"

Tomas looked like he was going to speak, then stopped in frustration. "What do I call you anyway?"

As if I know.

"Arsenault will be easiest." The whole situation made him want to jump out of his skin, but he tried to soften his voice.

"Arsenault," Tomas said, like he was trying the word on for size. "I got the sense she was buying time. She was in and out of sleep and dreams while her arm healed."

"That sounds right. Did he take all her weapons?"

"He disarmed her as soon as he took her in the cottage."

Arsenault laughed guiltily. "I wouldn't say she's *disarmed*, Tomas. It's been eight days. Tell her... Those terms are unacceptable to me. I'm going to ruin all her plans. Again."

"What are you going to do?"

"I'll figure something out. Best I don't tell you anyway. Then you can't give anything away."

"That's the Dagger's life, isn't it? A tool in the hand to use, but never to know." A bitter note had entered Tomas's voice. It sounded strange coming from someone so young.

"Tomas." The word floated in the air as a frigid cloud. "Sometimes it's better not to know."

CHAPTER 88

ARSENAULT

ARAK STRONGHOLD, TWENTY YEARS AGO

OJI'S BOOT WORKED WELL. ARSENAULT COULD RUN, AFTER A fashion, though he still limped. He cast out his awareness for the copy Promethi had made of him and found him listening, huddled with Adayze against the stronghold wall.

I need to return to my people, Arsenault! Adayze said.

No, you need to stay alive, the false Arsenault replied. He pulled her suddenly against him so she couldn't run. *What use is it if you're killed?*

What respect will they have for me if I don't lead them? Arsenault, let me go!

She tugged against the simulacrum, but the simulacrum tightened his grip and sneered at her.

Right. Out the fucking wall. Now.

The staircase wound around and around in the dim light. Tallow candles guttered, filling the stagnant, smoke-filled air with the scent of rancid beef. By the time Arsenault reached the door, he felt like he was breathing through soup.

The lack of guards made him nervous.

When he shoved the door open, sword drawn, he realized he was right to be nervous. The door opened into the yard, inside the wall. The gate ahead of him was barred with iron and guarded by a company of men with pikes. The sky had turned an ominous orange. Explosions from the big guns echoed into the yard, punctuated by the boom of Dakkaran cannons hurling shot at the defenders and the low roar of fire eating through the forest like a monster.

There must be a different way in and out.

Arsenault shrank back into the stairwell, letting the magic flow through him again. The simulacrum was pulling Adayze down the wall. She battled him, but of course his darker self wouldn't take that into account. His false self was Promethi's creature, just like the metal automata Oji had created, and Promethi's directive was driving him now.

"You! What are you doing there?"

Arsenault jerked upright. An Arak soldier stood before him. He gave Arsenault a fierce look.

"Who are you? Who sent you down here?"

In Arsenault's mind's eye, he watched the fake him drag Adayze toward the corner of the wall. Arak soldiers came at them, and Dakkarans, seeing Adayze struggling, ran to her aid.

The false Arsenault cut them down.

Have you gone mad? Adayze shouted.

This madness began long ago, his other self said.

He'd waited too long before giving an account. The Arak guard narrowed his eyes suspiciously and reached out for him. By all the gods, he wished he had a knife for close-quarters fighting. Instead, he drew his sword left-handed and bashed the pommel into the guard's jaw.

The guard fell back, cursing, but raised his sword and shield and lunged at Arsenault. Arsenault stumbled out of the way as best he could with his hurt foot. Still gripping the hilt of his sword left-handed, he drove it toward the man's face again.

The man tried to block with his shield. The hilt of Arsenault's sword clipped the edge and lost some of its momentum, but still crashed into the guard's mouth. Bone crunched and blood immediately gushed from the wound. The man reeled backward, reflexively trying to staunch the flow of blood with his sword arm.

Arsenault drew his sword back over his shoulder to get more room to use the blade, then stabbed it toward the gap between the man's breastplate and his gorget.

The guard couldn't move fast enough. The blade slid through the unprotected opening, grinding into vertebrae as it pierced the flesh near his collarbone and continued out the back. Arsenault levered his sword free with his foot on the man's leg and the guard flopped to the dusty floor like a rag doll, blood gleaming burgundy on his armor.

Breathing hard, Arsenault stepped over him and ran into the yard to find the corner passage where his false self had shoved Adayze.

A SPRING ENTERED UNDER THE WALL TO PROVIDE THE FORTRESS A source of water in the event of a siege. A portcullis blocked the entrance, which was glutted with ferns and cycads and guarded by a handful of Arak guards with pikes.

Thinking quickly, Arsenault stepped into full view of the soldiers and unbuckled and dropped his sword belt. "Lord Promethi gave me orders," he said, stripping himself out of the Arak tunic and throwing it on the ground beside his sword belt, which he leaned down to pick up. "He said I'll have my freedom if I can crawl through this passage unseen and sabotage the remaining guns of the Dakkar."

"Like they won't notice a northerner walking into their camp?"

"Everybody knows Lady Adayze has a guard who looks like me. They'll just think I'm him. Look, I've a magic mark."

He finished buckling his sword belt back on and pulled his shirt open to reveal the scars left by the lion's claws.

The lead guard frowned. "Are you sure that's a magic mark?"

"It was left by magic." Arsenault shrugged his shirt back into place. "Look. I'm fucked. The lord's given me a suicide mission. I go and the Dakkar catch and kill me, or I stay here and Lord Promethi slices my neck open. Which would you choose?"

"Eh, he's right," one of the guards said, scratching his jaw.

"He might lead the Dakkar back to the passage."

"Then we'll be here to cut them down as soon as they come out, won't we? Get two more guards if you're worried."

The first guard grunted. "All right." He turned to Arsenault. "I'd like to see you crawl through the damn thing anyway. Don't cry for us if you get stuck in the middle."

Arsenault gave the guard a pained smile and a brief salute with his fist to his chest, then sloshed into the water and rattled the portcullis up. He hoped Oji's boot was waterproof.

The guards slammed the portcullis down once he was inside. The sound echoed off the dark, wet walls. Arsenault listened hard for the sound of human movement, but the only sounds were running water and his own heavy breathing.

It was a dark, close nightmare of a crawl. The ceiling grew lower and lower, just as the guard had warned him, and he had to drag himself through the water on his stomach. Then he heard voices.

"Adayze. I've sworn myself to protect you, haven't I? That's all I'm doing."

"Arsenault, you're not listening to me; what's wrong with you?"

"I know you thought there was no way for us to be together. But I think you're wrong."

Arsenault hauled himself through the tight passage as quickly as he could, scraping his back on the rough stone above him, and clambered to his knees and then to his feet as the passage opened.

His false self had pushed Adayze up against the wall. She hadn't yet gone for her knife, but she looked frightened and angry.

He drew his sword. It barely made a sound, but Adayze looked up all the same, and so did his other self, glancing back over his shoulder.

Adayze's eyes went wide. "What in all creation…"

Arsenault stabbed at the simulacrum, hoping to impale him through the back. But the false Arsenault whirled away at the last moment, drawing his own sword as he did so. Arsenault twisted his sword into a high cut and the other Arsenault brought his up to block. Sparks rained down on the wet stone floor. The sword, at least, was real.

"He's one of Promethi's creations," Arsenault tried to explain while also meeting his own snarling advance. "Promethi Fixed him from my thoughts." Another whirl, another blow that got caught up in a bind. Arsenault sent himself careening backward against the wall, but the other Arsenault knew exactly where his weaknesses were. He lashed out at Arsenault's bad leg. Arsenault jumped backward and his foot crumpled. He fell to one knee beside Adayze.

"One of us is a creation," the other Arsenault said smoothly, pressing his advantage with an overhead blow Arsenault barely parried. He shoved the other's blade back as he stood up, surging upward with a hilt blow aimed at the other Arsenault's jaw. But the simulacrum dodged. Arsenault made a noise of frustration through his teeth and the runes on his sword flared white.

"Adayze will have to decide which is which. I believe we're evenly matched," the other Arsenault said.

"Promethi knew I would trust you," Adayze said, looking between them.

"It's all my fault," Arsenault gasped. "Didn't have the strength to fight Promethi off." He met another of his own blows, shoved the other Arsenault off, then punched him in the face.

Blood erupted from the simulacrum's nose. Odd blood. Not blood. It leaked out over the simulacrum's lip and disappeared in a red mist in the air.

With a snarl, the simulacrum drove the hilt of his sword toward

Arsenault's jaw. Arsenault jerked out of the way, but the hilt clipped him, stunning him, and his foot twisted again. Pain flared, drowning out his awareness. When his vision returned, he was on his knees and his other self was swinging his sword down in a two-handed cut at the back of his neck.

This was it then, dammit. This was how he was going to die this time—murdered by himself in a much more physical way than ever before. But would the simulacrum continue if he was dead?

Finding out was a gamble he couldn't take. He hurled himself to the side in a desperate attempt to avoid the sword, knowing it was useless.

The blade caught him across the back and side. Pain bloomed, but... not the killing blow he'd expected.

What the hells?

The other Arsenault's boots scuffled on the stone. Calves nudged his side, then knees buckled. Hit him in the ribs.

Arsenault jerked out of the way and looked up.

Adayze's knife sprouted up from between his simulacrum's shoulder blades, buried to the hilt.

She had her other knife out, too. The simulacrum was down, but he wasn't dead. He swung his sword up toward Adayze, but she danced out of the way, luring him back toward her.

Fuck that.

Arsenault propelled himself forward in a scrambling lunge, swiping his sword up off the ground. He thrust it straight through his simulacrum's mid-section. The sword entered just above his hip. It encountered some resistance when the edge ground past his spine—whatever the hells the simulacrum's spine was made of—and then the tip of the sword emerged over the simulacrum's other hip. More of that weird blood poured out, steaming, onto the stones. The simulacrum turned, face transformed by hate and fury, and Arsenault jerked the sword upward to do more damage before he stood and yanked it out.

The simulacrum collapsed onto the floor. All the runes on Arsenault's sword flared and he rammed the blade straight down into his simulacrum's back.

He knew in his heart it wouldn't be the last time he battled himself. But at least this time, he'd won.

"Is he dead?" Adayze asked in a shaky voice.

Arsenault swiped his blade clean on the simulacrum's shirt. It didn't move. Arsenault took a deep breath and moved his good foot from his double's back.

It was damn eerie to see himself stretched out on the ground with that many gaping, bloody wounds, the hilt of a knife sticking out of his back.

"I think so," Arsenault answered. As he slid his sword into its scabbard, his hands began to tremble, then his legs, and he couldn't stand anymore. He put a hand out to catch himself on the wall, but Adayze grabbed his arm instead.

He turned toward her in surprise. Coming down off the fight still running through him, everything surprised him—his soaking wet clothes, stuck to his body and dripping onto the stones, the stiffening, changing body that lay on the floor, blurring around the edges as if the past weeks had been a dream—Adayze's eyes looking into his, her arm locked under his arm, her body pressed up warm and alive against him.

He raised his hands to her face and kissed her.

She made a noise in her throat. There was nothing gentle left in either of them. She tangled her fingers in his braid, yanking him down to her. Her mouth hard on his again, she shoved him into the wall of the cave, tugging on the laces of his shirt, sliding her hands over his bare chest as he fell against the stone.

The impact barely registered. He grabbed her hips and carried her with him. She fell into him, fitting her body to his. He kissed her again, pulled the knot of her sash free to run his hands under her shirt and feel her skin while she fumbled with his sword belt.

It thumped to the floor. She jerked the laces on his trousers free.

"Adayze," he breathed against her neck.

"Yes, Arsenault," she said. "*Yes*, just this once."

She wrapped her hand around him. He shivered and growled deep in his throat. Then he picked her up and turned her around to the wall, losing himself inside her until she cried out again and again, and he did, too, all the fear and guilt and loneliness and pain of the past weeks burned away for the moment in that sudden, violent feeling of release.

CHAPTER 89

ARSENAULT

In a moment, reason returned. Along with the pain in his foot.

He let her down, reluctantly moving his face away from the warmth of her cheek and the soft touch of her hair. Dank, clammy air replaced the scent and feel of her, along with the realization of where they were and what was probably going on above them.

"This isn't exactly how I would have planned things," he murmured, unsure whether he ought to apologize.

But she smiled in a shaky, shy way and touched his cheek. "I wouldn't have either. But I would have regretted not having at least *once*."

She pulled him down to kiss him. He closed his eyes and rested in the feeling.

Then she pulled away and bent to pick up her sash and his swordbelt.

"Adayze," he said when she handed it to him. "I'm going to die."

"I'm not sure that's what a woman wants to hear in this situation, Arsenault. What do you mean?"

"My foot. Fariq shot me. I don't know how much time has passed. But it's gone bad. Oji—" He stopped and corrected himself. "Miha la Hallad gave me some medicine and Fixed a boot, but neither will last forever."

"Arsenault. When we get out of here—"

"I'm unlikely to get out of here, Adayze."

Adayze's eyes gleamed with angry determination. "*When* we get out of here, you can explain everything. But please don't apologize now."

"I have to get Promethi and his brother. I still don't know how Dirik figures into things, since Promethi seems to be in charge. You can go back or stay here, in safety…"

"I'm not a coward!"

"Forgive me, Adayze, but I don't know how your people see your role. Should I protect you or let you go? You know I wish you would stay, but…"

Adayze laughed softly and shook her head. "That copy of you was excellent, but it didn't take long to know he wasn't *you*. Everything was too smooth. There wasn't enough resistance and guilt."

"I'm not sure how I feel about that characterization, Adayze."

"You should feel it's accurate. But there were no clawmarks on that copy. No scars on your collarbone. I thought maybe you *had* died and perhaps changed because of it. When *you* showed up with that sword… It was still quite a shock."

Arsenault glanced at the hilt of his sword. "I'm glad you were happy to see me. And, ah, my sword."

Adayze giggled and clapped her hand over her mouth. "You're a rogue. Where did you get the sword?"

For a moment, he felt much younger. "It's mine. Fariq stole it in the raid. Miha gave it back to me."

"And this Miha…"

"Is a famous Qalfan artificer who is hopefully sabotaging Promethi's cannons right now." Arsenault sobered. "But Adayze, if Promethi's creation knew Edo's location, that means Promethi knows where he is, too."

"I thought that might be the way of it." Adayze's face grew haggard. "These past few weeks, Arsenault… They've been so difficult. When you and Jon walked into my tent, I can't explain how relieved I was."

"Shall I take you back out to Jon or—"

"No. Jon and my captains will be doing what they can. The only reason they would need me is for morale. Neyane's pirate-hunters threw in their lot with us and are reinforcing us with more guns and ammunition. Promethi's surprise attack is a blow, but we can still turn him back. It's up to you and me to kill Promethi and his brother. Jon has sent word back to my father to arrest Neyane. She was using her privateers as real pirates, taking the loot and selling it for coin or passing it on to Promethi. I don't know why she would betray us like that, but it doesn't matter now. We just need to take care of it."

Adayze couldn't hide the grief in her voice. Arsenault swallowed harshly and bowed. "As you say, lady."

"Arsenault!"

"Adayze. I'm a soldier under your command."

She gave him a dark look. "Have you ever been under our command, Arsenault?"

He couldn't lie to her. "I have and I haven't. Guin was being held in the cellars, along with the other galleymen. Promethi is committing atrocities I thought died out long ago and Guin went in my place. I need to save him. I promised, Adayze."

She nodded shortly, finished tying her sash, then secured both knives against her hips. "Your duplicate pulled me out of the tent before I could grab my gun," she said ruefully.

Before his courage failed, he confessed, "My duplicate was the one who set the charges. Promethi had me spying on you for weeks. Adayze, I need to apologize before—"

Adayze pressed her hand against his mouth. "And *I* said, don't apologize to me now, Arsenault. It's not certain you're going to die, and if you do..."

He took her hand by the wrist and lowered it. "If I do, it's more than likely I'll forget everything about you. I'm taking a risk just admitting this. The gods will probably add to my sentence next time, but since you've seen..."

"I won't abandon you, Arsenault."

He didn't believe her—there were too many demands on her to make promises like that—but he nodded anyway, and they continued together through the passage.

❦

"Clasp your hands behind your back," Arsenault whispered when they emerged, dripping wet, on the other side of the narrow space. "And trust me."

He rattled the portcullis loudly. At the sound, the guards jumped into the stream and peered into the passage, waving a torch.

"Lion's ass. You made it back!" the guard exclaimed. "Who do you have with you?"

"The Lady Adayze. Are you bastards going to let me in or not?"

They hurried to winch the gate open. Arsenault slid his arm

through Adayze's as if she were bound and nudged her gently forward. She looked ahead in stony silence as they splashed underneath the gate and out into the yard of the stronghold.

"Where's the lord?" Arsenault asked.

"In the watchtower." One of the guards gestured with his chin at the tallest of the towers. There was a ring of windows at the top, a long tube sticking out of one of them. It looked almost like a cannon, except it was too small.

A spyglass. A big one.

He didn't want to admit it, but he was afraid of Promethi, and he didn't know how much time he had left on Oji's magic. He opened his mouth to speak, when an enormous explosion rocked the wall. Streaks of red and orange bloomed in a fountain of sparks and light. Men screamed. Shards and twisted pieces of metal pelted down out of the sky, pattering to the ground like some kind of demon rain.

Arsenault dragged Adayze away from the wall, sheltering her with his body.

"What in all the hells was that?"

He grinned. "Oji and Renzo."

By the time he reached the end of his sentence another explosion sprayed more metal into the air. A body hit the ground heavily near them, limbs twisting with the impact. The hole in his chest would have killed him before he fell.

"Fila preserve us," Adayze said, staring at the body as they skirted it.

"If the fila sent Oji, that's what they're doing," Arsenault answered. "Let's just hope he and Renzo don't get caught. Come on, run for the tower."

The yard had disintegrated into chaos as soldiers poured out to reinforce the wall. More explosions thundered as the sun rose in a red mist over the trees, but it was hard to tell their source. They seemed to be happening everywhere all at once.

As he and Adayze reached the tower, a tremendous splintering crack echoed behind them. The Dakkarans must have moved their remaining cannons to bombard the gate.

"Jon's still alive," Adayze gasped.

Arsenault was breathing hard, too. Running increased the pain in his foot. "If they can break down the gates, they've got a chance. But Promethi will send nightmares if he hasn't already. That's Promethi's Talent. He Fixes fear."

They ducked inside the tower. Arsenault ripped Adayze's knives out of his belt and handed them to her.

"The snake in the garden…"

"Your fears."

"Your duplicate?"

"Mine."

"What's at the top of the stairs, Arsenault?"

Arsenault looked up. The windowless stairwell was thick with dark; at the top, where there ought to be a landing, the air shimmered. A nameless feeling of dread settled in his gut.

He cursed as he fought against it. "Promethi has it runed, of course. That's what you're feeling now. The fear."

"Can you undo the runes?"

"Unwrite them, you mean? I told you, Adayze, my curse proscribes me from using magic. Sometimes I can trick the gods, but…"

Dammit.

He closed his eyes briefly, trying to shake off Promethi's magic. The pain in his foot was becoming a distraction, though; he probably wouldn't make it…

"Damn. It." He opened his eyes. "I'm going to die anyway."

"I wish you would stop saying that!" Adayze said with desperation. "I will have physicians! They will look at your foot! If you can't use your magic…"

"Adayze. Promethi's magic is trying to keep us at the bottom of the stairs. It's planting reasons in our minds to give up."

"When you said he Fixed fear, I thought there would be some *thing* to fight."

"I wouldn't be surprised if there was something more solid on the other side. But fear and despair are the first line of defense, aren't they?"

"Followed by dread and terror? Gods, I don't want to go up there. Is Promethi's brother the same? Will we have to face them both?"

"One step at a time, Adayze." He sought her hand with his. She gripped his fingers tightly.

"Right." She stepped onto the first step and pulled him with her. His foot had begun to ache and climbing the stairs made him hiss in pain.

"Do you think he's sent men to kill Edo, Arsenault?"

"I don't know." More pain. Gods. He wasn't going to be able to see this through, the magic wouldn't last long enough…

"Have I killed my son? I only wanted to keep him safe. But how many people have died because of my ruse?"

"No second guessing, Adayze," Arsenault said through gritted teeth.

"And you. You're in pain."

"I deserve it. I'm the one who caused all this trouble in the first place."

"This is the magic?"

"Yes. It eats into you. Gets into all the soft places."

"It's not all magic, though."

"Some of us have soft spots that are easy to prod..." His voice trailed away as he saw what was standing in the dark waiting for him.

"*Sella.*"

CHAPTER 90

ARSENAULT

SHE WAS JUST AS BEAUTIFUL AS SHE HAD BEEN IN LIFE.

Her dark auburn hair lay loose over her shoulders and her skin gleamed in the darkness, as if she were illuminated by the moon. She wore her bloody green dress, the hem of it sopping wet from the kiss of ocean waves, but she also wore her wings—great white wings like an egret's. She stretched out her arms, hands palm up in supplication.

Ari. Stay there.

He felt as if he were frozen to the riser anyway. "*Sella*. I have to go past."

"Arsenault?" Adayze asked in alarm. "What is it? What do you see?"

If you enter this room, you'll be set on a path. Go back, Ari. You don't need this knowledge. Go back before my father finds you out.

"Your father is always watching," Arsenault whispered. He tried to tell himself she was just an illusion, but the words rang hollow with her standing in front of him, half human, half goddess—the ghost he had always desperately hoped would haunt him.

Adayze took his hands in hers, trying to hold his gaze, but he couldn't stop looking at Sella. "Arsenault. Listen to me. Whoever you're speaking to, I can't see her. Do you hear me? This is Promethi's magic!"

He finally tore his gaze away from Sella to look at Adayze. "It's the ghost of my wife." He opened his hand and showed Adayze his palm. The scar was so faint, when Adayze had adopted him for the B'ara, she'd almost sliced through it. No one would notice unless he pointed it out. "See there? The vow? Bound to me forever. But I broke it."

Adayze laid her finger gently on his palm. "But this other line means you are B'ara, and the B'ara keep their own. The fila—our fila—will see you safe."

"Why would they want me?"

"Whatever you've done in the past doesn't matter, Arsenault. You are blood now. It's a pledge I've made to you that must be kept."

"But I made a pledge once, too. A pledge that was supposed to last forever. And I violated it in the worst way."

"Didn't you hear me, Arsenault? *That doesn't matter now*. All that matters is the next step. The magic is trying to stop you, isn't that what you told me?"

His eyes searched hers, desperately wanting to see truth in their liquid depths. "Do you mean that, Adayze? You're not... You won't abandon me?"

Adayze lifted her hand to his face. "Arsenault. I promise we won't abandon you."

He stood for a moment, catching her hand in his.

We, she had said. Not *I*.

Well, that was honesty. That was all he could ask for. She was the leader of her people. So why was he so disappointed? He was going to die and leave her, not the other way around.

He dipped his head. She took it for a nod and stepped onto the next riser. He followed, trying to ignore the way Sella put her hands up as he passed, calling out in anguish, *Ari Ari Ari*.

He and Adayze walked together through the darkness on the landing, toward the light spilling out from beneath a closed door. It creaked open when he pushed on it.

Promethi stood with his eye to the spyglass, in front of an enormous fourposter bed curtained with mosquito netting and draperies of blue and lavender silk. A long form lay there, propped up by pillows. The early morning sunlight glinted on metal among the blankets.

Promethi straightened as Arsenault and Adayze stepped into the room.

"I wondered when you would find your way up here. Of course, I expected a different version of you, Arsenault, but I appear to have been betrayed. Doubly betrayed, as I see my cannons have all been reduced to slag."

Adayze pulled her knives. "Speaking of betrayal, Promethi. You attempted the murder of a member of the Dakkaran royal family. You've been smuggling artillery. You attacked a Dakkaran army. You collaborate with pirates. All of those are hanging offenses."

"And how many times will you hang me then? Oh, but I don't have the benefit of the drugs you gave Arsenault, do I? You can probably only hang me once."

"I would hang you a thousand times if I could. I can't believe you thought I might *marry* you."

"I didn't, actually. But I did think you might marry my brother."

"The one who lets you do all his dirty work? How have you taken all this power from him, Promethi? He'll hang, too, for the things you've done."

Promethi turned to the figure in the bed. "I told you she'd say that, brother."

"That's because she doesn't understand," the man lying there said, his voice a low rumble in the shadows.

Adayze went stiff. Arsenault caught her arm, but she pulled away from him, trembling.

"Speak again. You sound like—"

"It does my heart good to see you, Adayze."

"*Isa,*" she cried and ran to the bedside.

Arsenault cast about desperately in his memory for a mention of the name, who it might be...

And then he remembered.

Adayze's husband.

Beside him, sitting on a gilt chair, half hidden by the curtains, was Guin.

❧

ARSENAULT HAD ENVISIONED A REUNION WITH GUIN MANY TIMES, as part of his struggle to remember Guin at all. In those future imaginings, he'd tried to focus on the details he recalled—the beard, the soft eyes, the gentle cast of his features. But now he realized the Guin in his mind had been his own invention, a totem to cling to so he could keep going.

The real Guin was emaciated and pale. His beard had been shaved. His eyes were not soft, his features not gentle. They looked as if they had been slashed into the world. It was like seeing the unfinished sketch when you had in mind the finished painting. Like the artist had decided to start over.

Guin started to rise. "Who are you?" Arsenault knew he looked like a wild man, but not the middle-aged wild man Guin had found in his stable. Then, slowly, Guin ventured, "Arsenault?"

Arsenault had thought that even without all his memories, the deep knowledge of their friendship would return. That it existed somewhere in his bones and would bubble up instantly when he saw Guin. But he felt like he was looking at a stranger.

The realization was worse than taking a blow.

It didn't matter. He could still fulfill his promise.

"Promethi. This thing you're doing is evil. Let him go."

"Adayze can tell you what she thinks before you accuse me of evil."

Adayze glared at Promethi. Then she yanked back the netting and the curtains on the bed, revealing a man Arsenault recognized.

The lion man from the ravine.

Arsenault had saved Adayze's husband. Which was just the sort of trick the gods liked to play. Maybe Promethi had Fixed a double of him from his fears, too, a shapeshifter to spy on Adayze.

Half of Isa seemed to be made of metal.

"Isa!" Adayze exclaimed. "Your arm, your leg...your foot! What is this?"

"I think Promethi had better explain, Adayze."

She whirled on Promethi. "What have you done to him? How long have you been keeping Isa prisoner?"

"He's not Isa, lady. Well, at least not entirely."

"You don't make *sense*."

"I'll explain if you'll listen. It's quite a tale." Promethi walked around the bed and put his hand on the back of Guin's chair. Arsenault's skin crawled. How many times had he felt Promethi at his back in just that way? The man never stood in front of you; he always attacked from behind.

"Your father's Dagger arranged a secret meeting between my brother Dirik and your husband Isa. It was supposed to be for peace. Instead, it was all treachery. Once the ship set sail and the meeting began, the Dagger's guards fell on my brother and his entourage. In desperation, he and his guards fought valiantly against them. Shots were discharged. Your husband was gravely injured, my brother even more so. To add insult to injury, Neyane ordered her own pirate crew to scuttle the ship so no evidence would ever be found."

Her own pirate crew... Arsenault didn't want to believe it, but it had to be true. "Etranée," he swore. "She said she didn't always agree with the targets Neyane gave her, that there were some she regretted hitting. She attacked your brother's ship, didn't she? But why not kill all who were left when Fariq attacked the riverboat?"

"You're jumping ahead in the story, Arsenault. Dirik had asked me to oversee the proceedings of his parley from the shore by Sight, because he was worried it might be a trap. I Saw *everything*. I took out my own boat, but it all happened so quickly, it was done before I could get there. Neyane's pirates were under orders to sink the unarmed ship with cannon, ensuring that even those who had carried out Neyane's orders would take their secrets to the bottom of the sea. But I wasn't content that my brother's murderers should merely be stranded on a sinking ship. In a fury of rage and terror, I killed all of them. I was going to kill your husband, too, when my brother stopped me. *No*, he said, *Isa was not party to this. Let him live*.

"But Isa's injuries were too serious. Lead shot had ripped through his arm and leg, leaving them broken and useless. Infection would kill him if the pain didn't. Fortunately, I'd been doing quite a bit of research into the old magical techniques of the Qalfans and Etereans. I thought I could help if my brother wanted me to."

Promethi paced as he spoke, back and forth behind the spyglass.

"Then my brother died. I had no way to bring his body back to Arak lands with me. I Saw the shade come out of his body and I knew it would be trapped on that ship forever, forced to haunt the wreck until justice was done.

"I had to make a decision quickly. It seemed like the best decision I could make in those horrible circumstances, one that would honor my brother's wishes to the best of my ability, while also saving my brother's soul from an eternity of agony.

"I told Isa I thought I could save him. I only had one request. First, he had to harbor my brother's ghost."

"You...*what?*" Adayze exclaimed.

Isa reached for her hand. "I did it for you, Adayze. For the child you were carrying. I couldn't leave you alone. And I was ashamed. Dirik had come to parley with us in good faith and Neyane's people murdered him. I wanted to make amends and I wanted to live. So, I opened myself to Dirik's ghost and harbor him within me now. He's not a bad man."

Adayze's eyes widened. Her aura crackled with rage. "His brother tried to murder your child!"

Isa pushed himself up off the pillows on his good elbow with a look of shocked surprise. "Promethi—brother—is this true?"

"Of course not. Arsenault has encouraged the lady to jump to conclusions." Promethi's voice was smooth. Soothing.

False.

Arsenault had experienced that voice before.

"You're blaming it all on Arsenault?" Adayze cried out incredulously. "My child was threatened by *monsters*! If you wanted to bring us here, why didn't you just say you were caring for Isa? Why did you have to Shape a nightmare and kill my people?"

"Perhaps a miscalculation on my part," Promethi said. "But I needed to get your attention."

"You're lying," she said. "Isa, he's *lying*. How could you have believed him in the first place?"

"Because his brother is not a bad man!" Isa said through his teeth. Sweat had formed on his brow, as if it was a great exertion just for Isa to speak. "Promethi, you promised me the child would live, you said—"

Promethi raised his head. The mask of politeness—*the veneer of nicety*—fell away and his eyes crackled with fury. "I had to promise you something, didn't I, to save my brother from Dakkaran treachery? Don't you think it's fitting for you to lose someone dear to you, too, Isa? I remain faithful to my family binding. We will put another child on the Throne, a child more of my brother's spirit than yours!." He whipped around to face Adayze. "But tell me. Why should I have tried to woo you here to your own husband?"

"If you had told me, Promethi—"

"If I had told you, would you have believed me? And if you had seen, would you have accepted? Look at him, Adayze. Would you want to be married to him like this?"

"I..." Her words died as if she'd suddenly been struck dumb. Emotions warred in her eyes as she stared at the metal revealed by the rumpled blankets. "You're like the sphinx now, aren't you?" she whispered.

"No," Isa said softly. "Tell her about the metal, Promethi."

"Very well. You shall now hear the second act of the story." He smiled contemptuously, an expression that made Arsenault want to punch him. Instead, he examined the room for weapons and exits. Guin remained still, too, watching him with gray-green eyes that seemed too large in his thin face.

"I transferred Isa onto the ship I'd commandeered," Promethi continued, "and sent his ship with all its corpses to the bottom of the sea. Then I hired a Qalfan surgeon to amputate Isa's ruined limbs. I blackmailed Neyane, threatening to reveal what I knew about her attempts to derail the peace and kill the Heir's husband."

Promethi screwed his face up as if he'd eaten something distasteful. "No, that's not exactly true. It wasn't blackmail. In my grief, I thought, *if the B'ara cast us as villains, as descendants of the Nightmare Man, then I will become the Nightmare Man.* I entered Neyane's nightmares and turned them against her. I promised I would find a way to include her in the new kingdom we would build if she helped me. If she chose not to... Her deepest fear was that she would never be acknowledged publicly for who she was, the wrongs committed against her, and what she'd accomplished in spite of them, so I vowed that if she didn't help me, I would ensure that she died in obscurity, erased from history forever. Did you know she was firstborn, Adayze?"

Adayze crossed her arms over her chest. "You are building your case on lies. Why not tell me more of them?" But she looked uncertain. They didn't *all* sound like lies.

That was the problem with men like Promethi. Some of what they told you would always be true. It was just truth that was twisted, a small speck of dirt suddenly magnified to appear monstrous.

"You know Neyane and the Ibuu are twins, though," Promethi said. "Their father reversed their positions. Since the political climate was precarious at the time, he made the Dagger the public target as his "Heir" and kept his real Heir safe, raised as Dagger. He was afraid of *my* grandfather, and with good cause. My grandfather refused to stand for his unjust laws. *Your* grandfather's ruse nearly worked. Your father was at the country house for the massacre, but the real Heir was secreted away, safe.

"Somehow, though, both twins survived and without their father to steer the course, things got mixed up. Perhaps your grandfather took his secrets to the grave with him. Perhaps your grandmother had never been aware of his plans, though surely she would have known which of the two was born first? The girl had been hidden as the child of a scullery maid. The boy had become a symbol of B'ara victory, and he needed a regent.

"Whatever the reason, your grandmother kept things as they were, and no one was ever the wiser. Except for the Ibuu and Neyane, of course, who wondered if it was all a dream they'd had as children. It wasn't until Neyane began digging that she realized what lies she'd been told. By then, why would the Ibuu step down when he'd already had a lifetime of rule?"

"No," Adayze said. "No, that can't be true. That's just a storyline from a cheap drama you've stolen to make me doubt my family."

"Why would I care about your succession? One B'ara is the same as another. And you must realize there was only one way Fariq could know what you were doing on that riverboat, and that was because he was also working with Neyane. *She* cares very much about the succession. She wants her rightful place back."

"Why not assassinate my father then?" Adayze asked. "She's the Dagger. She has the means to do it."

"Assassination isn't enough for her, though. She wants him to be ridiculed. Disliked, discredited, dismissed. To publicly fail so she can step in. She couldn't let me stop her."

"Why didn't she assassinate you then?"

Promethi smiled his cold smile. "Fear has its uses. If I alone knew about Isa, she couldn't kill me until she found out where he was and killed him. I told her I'd been experimenting with Eterean metal, that I'd be willing to give her the results of those experiments in exchange for supply—as a peace offering of sorts. Without knowing it, Neyane supplied the means of Isa's survival. I brought Isa back here and set about looking for a man who could replace his limbs."

Arsenault let his breath out. *Dammit—Oji.* Out loud he said, "Miha la Hallad."

Promethi inclined his head. "Very good, Arsenault. When Fariq lost you to Adayze, he thought you'd probably die. At the time, we just thought you were a particularly strong Fixer. I didn't know about your Talent, or I would have put more effort into recapturing you and bringing you here to help Miha. But Miha had to go about it on his own. The limbs aren't perfect. There's something missing."

Gods. How much breath could he let in and out to keep calm, to not feel like he was going to pace the room like the lion in the ravine?

"Blood," he said. "From someone with magic. Are you doing this voluntarily, Guin?"

"He was using up the other men," Guin said. "I volunteered to take their place, to be permanent—to take your place, too, Arsenault, dammit. Why didn't you go on with your life? Why did you have to come back to this?"

"How could you think I would just let you go? What kind of man do you think I am?"

And yet, how many times had he been tempted to walk away? How many people had he left behind when he'd built his cabin in the mountains? Guin's words felt like a stab in the heart because they came so close to being true.

"Sometimes you just get a gift. I won't have much more blood to give and then I'll be through with this suffering. Lord Promethi said what I was doing would promote peace—"

"Peace?" Arsenault exploded. "Bleeding you almost to death, stealing your free will, and forcing your magic to go against everything it should be—that's not a gift, Guin! Not to me!"

"Arsenault." Adayze put her hand on his shoulder and Arsenault closed his mouth angrily. "Let Promethi finish."

He didn't like the uncertain glimmer in her eyes—like she might be considering something Guin or Promethi had said.

"Any sort of magical blood can fuel a machine," Promethi said. "Because it only works for a little while. But to make metal live... we need a Talent for metal. Miha was able to attach the prostheses, but they're just pretty sculptures. In fact, I believe they may kill him... unless we're able to find a suitable trigger. As it were."

"So, all of that and he's going to die after all?" Adayze said. "Is this your idea of torture?"

"Oh, no, my lady," Promethi said. "The blood of anyone with magic will keep him alive for a short time. That's what I've been using the other Fixers for. But the process is so unwieldy."

Arsenault wasn't quite sure he'd heard right. "The galleymen and all the others Fariq's been taking... You're killing *all* of them to keep your brother alive? It's not machines, it's *just* for your brother?"

Adayze stared at him, then at her husband, the horror growing on her face. "Isa. You would let this happen? All those people?"

"Adayze..." he rasped, the fingers of his flesh hand twitching toward her. "I have been too weak even to kill myself. And what would have happened to you and Edo if I had? I thought I was protecting you, I thought Promethi was honoring his promises..."

"We can stop it, you know," Promethi said.

"What? How? Whatever it takes, we will do it! You can't take the lives of other people to prolong the life of the one you love! That's not what a leader does!"

"Perhaps not. Perhaps it's only what a man does to ensure the survival of his family. It's unsustainable, anyway. We need a Smith. People notice when someone as important as one of *our* Smiths is killed. We need one who doesn't matter."

His gaze fell on Arsenault.

Arsenault's shoulders sagged. "Why did you frame me for the sphinx's crimes, then? If you needed me so badly?"

"I didn't know you were a Smith until you Fixed the metal to defeat it. Then it was too late. The Ibuu was going to kill one of us and I didn't want it to be me. But I must confess, I didn't expect justice to be so swift and sure. Or that you would be convicted on a story clearly spun from thin air. I thought I'd at least be able to use your dying body, but the Guard got rid of you much too quickly."

"I would ask if you'd let the rest of the men in your cellars and Guin go free, but I don't trust you. You'll lie to get me to bleed. Adayze—"

"Arsenault."

He turned to face her. And he knew. By the look in her eyes, he knew. He had always known, she was a leader first.

"We will end this violent rivalry between our bindings," she said, speaking to Promethi but looking at him until finally she turned. "I had hoped to do it by crushing the seat of your power, Promethi, but I didn't have all the information. Now I think I do." She took a deep breath. "And because we maintain the authority of the Ibuu's Throne and I am the Heir, I will bear the responsibility of the decision.

"I will put Neyane to justice, but you will go to justice, too, Promethi. You *are* going to let all those men in your cellars go, along with this man here, this *Guin*. In return, we will save my husband and your brother, and together, we will ensure that the B'ara and Arak seal this peace."

Promethi was silent for a moment. Then he bowed stiffly. "This is acceptable to me. As long as you ensure my brother lives."

Adayze took a deep breath. "Arsenault. You told me you were my soldier. But when I cut your hand, I made you B'ara. You have the choice to renounce the binding. I will cut you again and you will forever bear the scar of renunciation. I would never force you to give your life, but I am *asking* you to do it—for something bigger than we are as individuals."

Please, her eyes said. *Please don't turn away from me when I need you the most.*

"You don't know what you're asking," he whispered.

"I do," she said. "Believe me. I do."

She put her hand to his face. In front of her husband and Guin and Promethi. The gesture said everything. He could have been a second husband or a concubine. She could have let him die of the wound in his foot in secret and no one would have questioned that he had healed, and they could have built their relationship over again. There were other Smiths she could give to Isa if she spent more time looking, that would feed the metal that formed Isa's body the same as Arsenault's blood would. But she wouldn't callously throw away life like that without meaning. She knew Arsenault *would* come back, but he could see that she also knew if he died like this in front of other people, she wouldn't be able to bring him back to her.

She was asking him to say good-bye.

Forever.

"The fila blessed our lives with you," she said. "But this is the decision I must make as Heir."

Guin pushed himself up out of the chair. "I offered myself so Arsenault could go free. So he could live!"

"I told you, Guin, I can't accept that gift. Especially since what they need is blood with metal in it, or more people will die. Just... promise me one thing. What Promethi was doing... More people are involved and there will be many more consequences. Promise me you'll root them out."

"Yes—of course—Arsenault!"

Good. It didn't really matter what Guin did, but maybe now he had something to live for—a purpose. The thing Guin had provided him. It seemed like the least he could do.

Arsenault pulled his belt knife with his right hand. Bared his left wrist.

"No graveclothes," he said. "No coffins."

He lifted the knife.

Adayze grabbed his hand. He stared at her in surprise as she took the knife from him.

"No, Arsenault. The responsibility rests on my shoulders. That means I bear both good and evil."

"Adayze! No—I—"

She slashed the knife deep into his vein.

Blood pumped out in time to the beat of his heart, splashing down onto the metal of Isa's arm along with Adayze's tears. He tried to turn and hug her, to let her know it would all be over soon, but the world began spinning too fast and it was all he could do to shower Isa's leg in his blood, leaving a bright red stream that flowed over Isa's metal shin onto his foot.

The last thing Arsenault saw before he collapsed was his blood gleaming burgundy on the silver muscles of Isa's arm.

Just like Aliente silk.

CHAPTER 91

ARSENAULT

HIGH PEAKS REGION, PRESENT

THE PASS WHERE THEIR ROAD JOINED THE SPICE ROAD WAS SO HIGH, Arsenault's nose started bleeding. He staunched it with his scarf, but it left his beard stiff with blood and he had to rub his face with snow to clean it off.

The rocks loomed over the road like the towers of a fortress. The landscape was eerily empty, the morning air heavy with unnatural silence. Gray clouds hung low and oppressive, muffling everything with their claustrophobic blanket. He sat on an icy ledge jutting out of a rock shelter, gripping the sketch of the marriage bed he wanted to build for Kyrra in his numb, gloved fingers.

Cassis and Lobardin huddled inside in their cloaks, smashed together for warmth as they dozed. They'd built a small fire, burned it just long enough to create a few coals. No fire at all would have meant freezing to death, but the weather had warmed overnight—a bad sign, because it meant a storm was moving in. He knew he ought to retreat into the cave, sleep a little, and share some body heat with the other two instead of sitting out here brooding over all that there was to lose, but every time he closed his eyes, more memories assaulted him and he was tired of fighting them off.

Renzo.
Promethi.
Oji.
Guin.
Isa.
Adayze.

Jon.

His anger kept him hotter than the cooling coals did anyway.

He was angry at Adayze for having the mercy to allow him to forget her so well—so well he'd never seen her once since that morning in the tower. Instead, he'd woken days later in the back of a wagon driven by a strange Qalfan man and his son, with Jon leaning over him, asking, *Do you know who I am, ghost?*

And he was angry at Jon for keeping all Adayze's secrets. That anger went deeper, because he understood why Adayze had sent him away, but he didn't understand why Jon couldn't have told him, just once, that he had a *son*.

Then again, he understood completely. Because telling him would have led him back to Adayze and from there to Promethi. It would have put the child Tomas in danger, would have destroyed everything Adayze had built as a failsafe for her precarious peace, which had ultimately proved too fragile to hold. He remembered getting the news that Isa had inexplicably walked into a forge one day and set himself alight. It had baffled him at the time, but now he understood.

Promethi had convinced his brother Dirik to use Geoffre di Prinze to help the Arak onto the Ibuu's Throne; as long as Dirik lived in Isa, Adayze and Edo were in danger. So, Isa had done the only thing he could do to defeat Dirik: he destroyed his body, both flesh and metal, and ensured that Adayze and Edo were safely outside Mdembu when the attack came. And *he* must have been the one who'd saved the Ibuu's library from burning, because he'd been in charge of it. He'd scattered all Jon's manuscripts to the winds so Promethi wouldn't find them. What else had he done to protect his family, his people?

In the face of Isa's sacrifice, Arsenault didn't know what to call his anger. Maybe he was angry at Isa, too, for being so fucking noble. Maybe he was even angry at himself for wanting more. Jon's continued presence in his life meant that Adayze had kept the promise she'd made to him all those years ago. She hadn't abandoned him. She'd gifted him with Jon's loyalty and friendship. A gift that Jon kept giving, with his lies that spoke of a far greater, underlying truth.

It was no wonder Jon was ambivalent about Kyrra. The peace Adayze and Isa had maintained for over a decade had saved innumerable lives, but it was only a bandage temporarily staunching the wounds of multiple betrayals. Jon must have seen their reflection every time he'd looked into Kyrra's arm, but Arsenault still couldn't forgive him for withholding her presence from him, especially when he'd been drowning as Andris.

"I hope you're thinking up some foolproof plan," Lobardin said, coming to sit next to him. "With that look on your face."

Arsenault slid the sketch of the bed back into his tunic and sniffed. His nose was running again, and he tasted the copper and salt of blood in the back of his throat. "There are no foolproof plans."

"Optimist." Lobardin reached into his pack and handed Arsenault a hard biscuit, then pulled out a wedge of cheese, cut a slice off it, and handed that to Arsenault, too. Arsenault nodded his thanks and Lobardin made his own meager breakfast. "What were you thinking about then?"

Arsenault took a big bite of biscuit and cheese. He didn't want to talk to Lobardin. And yet, he found himself grateful, in a way, for Lobardin's presence. He'd been inside his own head for too long. Lobardin was a different man without kacin, and the warmth of another human being was something. They sat shoulder to shoulder in the small opening and looked down on the Spice Road.

"Tomas," he lied—or at least, that was only partial truth. "And Kyrra."

"Have you tried to See her again?"

"No. Too risky. This is where she told me to make a move, so we'll handle it as if we were bandits." Arsenault looked toward the summit of the mountain, where blue ice poured out of a giant snowfield in a great frozen river. It dammed the chasms between the peaks, then ended in a frozen waterfall that spilled into an unfrozen lake the color of a tourmaline. The road squeezed through the tight, rocky space, then escaped it only to immediately cross a flimsy bridge spanning the lake.

Arsenault gestured with the remaining crescent of his cheese. "The easiest thing to do will be to trap the carriage on the bridge. Cassis will hide in the rocks at the other end, then he'll come out to block the road and encourage Tomas to step down at gunpoint if he's driving. If it's Lupa..."

"If it's Lupa, I'm going to shoot first and ask questions later," Lobardin said.

"I doubt we'll be that lucky. Tomas will probably be driving."

"It would be nice if you'd part with a little more information about him, Arsenault. I know he must have told you more than you told us last night."

Arsenault pushed the rest of the cheese into his mouth while he wondered how much he could really tell Lobardin. He'd already explained Tomas's connection to Adayze and Jon, just not his own role in the situation.

He rooted around in his pack for the bottle of brandy he'd brought from the farmhouse. He fumbled with the cork in his big leather gloves but finally managed to pull it. The brandy made a lovely warm fire down his gullet. He hoped it would settle his nerves, but that would take more than brandy.

He passed Lobardin the bottle.

"I think we can count on Tomas in a fight. Kyrra trusts him and Tomas knows what Lupa can do because he's seen it, so...five of us against Lupa, why won't that work?"

"I don't know, Arsenault. Why won't it? You still sound worried."

Five against one were decent odds, even considering Lupa's considerable ability. So why was his gut churning, telling him cheese and brandy had been a bad idea?

Lobardin squinted at him. "You are worried. Not just about Kyrra."

"Tomas said Kyrra made Lupa a deal—her for me. If he's using her as bait to get me, that does worry me. But why would Lupa want me instead of her in the first place?"

The real question was, *had she really made the deal with Lupa?*

And if she hadn't...

Who was Lupa actually in league with?

Lobardin twirled the brandy bottle in his hands like he was thinking, then suddenly stopped. "Your god. That's who you think is behind this. You think Kyrra's trying to free you from him and Lupa's working as a tool of the god the same way Geoffre did, so when we attack that carriage, we're really going to be facing a *god* not a man. Son of an ass, Arsenault, were you planning to tell us before or after we made it down there?"

"That was going to depend on whether I could figure out anything to do about it," Arsenault replied.

❧

THE SUN WAS HIGH BEFORE THE RATTLE OF LUPA'S CARRIAGE echoed through the narrow canyon of the pass, but it shone only weakly through the thick blanket of low clouds. A few spits of moisture fell, water or ice, it was hard to tell.

"Storm moving in soon," Arsenault muttered, testing his gloves and greaves. They'd roused Cassis, and Arsenault had Fixed a sword and a knife for each of them. Now they were hidden in a cleft in the rock with the horses, just off the road.

Cassis's horse danced under him as he squinted up at the sky. "What kind of storm are we talking about?"

Arsenault swung himself up on his own mount. A breath of wind kissed his face with cold and he pulled his hat down to block it. His axe formed a comforting weight against his back.

"Snow probably, and a lot of it. If Lupa gets away from me, use the magicked metal to kill him. If you feel any irrational fear, fight through it; it's probably the magic. Cassis, if you're the one who lets him escape this time, I'll hunt you down and kill you too, understand?"

"Your faith warms my heart, Arsenault."

"I don't care. I just want to be done with Lupa. We'll need to head for shelter immediately afterward. Back to the cave up there, all right? Take any blankets and supplies you can find in the carriage and get under cover as quickly as you can."

"You think it's going to be that bad, Arsenault? That fast?" Cassis said in disbelief.

"It's likely a sanval that blew in from the south."

Lobardin watched the sky, looking more and more worried as Arsenault talked. "What if the fight goes bad on that bridge, Arsenault? There isn't a lot of space to maneuver."

Arsenault took a deep breath. "Come here, both of you."

Lobardin and Cassis traded glances, but they both urged their mounts closer. He caught their horses by the bridles and drew the Sanctuary rune in the air before them. It glimmered blue in the cold, thick air, as if diffused by moisture. Lobardin blinked, but Cassis didn't see it at all.

That all of them might be safe, Arsenault thought fervently. *That all of us but Lupa come out of this alive. Especially Kyrra and Tomas. That they live long lives, and Mikelo, too, safe and full of love and peace and happiness.*

A life of love and peace and happiness was mostly beyond the influence of magic, but Arsenault added it to his intention anyway, in the hopes that some god might receive it as a prayer and find it within their power to grant.

Lobardin and Cassis leaned back in their saddles, looking slightly dazed. Then Arsenault gave Cassis's horse a pat on the neck. "Get in place now."

Cassis touched the brim of his hat, then wheeled his horse and set out down the path to the road. The sound of the carriage rattled closer.

Arsenault threw Lobardin the gun he'd Fixed. Lobardin slung it over his shoulder.

"Let the battle magic take you if it comes to it. I tried to explain to Kyrra it's magic not madness, but I don't know if she ever believed me."

"If you'd been taken by Ires, you'd understand," Lobardin said. "You'd best mount, Arsenault."

Arsenault put his foot in the stirrup and levered himself up onto his horse's back. He would need to run this horse like a demon to catch Lupa after he passed. There was a chance the horse would slip on the steep slope in the loose gravel, but he couldn't think about that. He tucked in tight to the horse's back. Their breath mingled in white clouds in the cold.

And then the carriage clattered by on the road below.

Tomas was driving, wrapped up in his thick cloak and hunched over the reins. The shutters of the carriage were tightly closed and the horses stepped nervously in a quick trot.

Arsenault let it run past him into the curve the rocks made, then squeezed his mount with his knees and touched his heels to her flanks. The mare leaped down the path, skidding on the loose stone, but soon got her back legs under her and jumped for the level road leading through the rocks. Wind with ice in it whipped past Arsenault's face, stinging his cheeks and making his eyes stream, and behind him he heard Lobardin urge his horse on, then curse as it hit the same patch of gravel.

In a moment, Arsenault emerged from the pinch in the rocks. Cassis stood at the other end of the bridge, gun drawn. The carriage creaked and banged to a stop, rattling the boards of the bridge as Tomas hauled up hard on the reins. It would be a tight squeeze getting his own horse in beside the carriage. He'd known that, but it was one thing to think it through and another to try it with a live horse.

He urged the horse onto the bridge anyway, but the horse didn't like it. The boards weren't nailed to a frame, but rather to rope and thick steel wire—the thickest he'd ever seen, Eterean and Fixed with magic. It shook and swung, and Arsenault caught a glimpse of the green surface of the lake below winking white with waves. Vertigo assaulted him and he gripped the horse's mane too hard. The horse shied sideways, bumping the webbed side of the bridge, and the whole thing shuddered beneath him.

Cursing, Arsenault hurled himself off the horse's back, hit the bridge running, and pulled his axe while he ran. Lupa shoved open the carriage doors just as Arsenault ran up beside him. Cassis lowered the dikkarro and took aim at Lupa's back.

It should have been easy. Pull the trigger, take the shot, and Arsenault would finish him off with an axe blow as soon as the ball hit him, to make sure he died. But Lupa lunged back into the carriage just as Cassis fired the gun.

The ball went wide and high, hurtling over Lupa's shoulder—tearing through the fabric of his shirt but doing no real damage. Arsenault lurched to the side, narrowly avoiding being shot himself. Lupa jerked Kyrra out in front of him.

"Want to take that risk again?" Lupa asked.

There was something strange about him. Something that caught Arsenault and stopped him, for an instant that seemed to take forever.

He did look different. And there was something different in his voice, too. Something...familiar.

It didn't seem possible, and yet... The wild cinnamon curls had darkened to the color of charred wood, falling from a widow's peak; the boyish cheeks were carved now with strong shadows, the mouth a long, mobile but cruel line amid the black stubble of a beard he was just starting...

And the eyes. The stormy green sea eyes.

"*Tavi*," Arsenault breathed. "By all the gods, how is it you?"

CHAPTER 92

KYRRA

IRONDEL MOUNTAINS, PRESENT

LUPA HAD BEGUN TO LOOK LIKE ARSENAULT ALMOST AS SOON AS he'd put me in the carriage. At first, I thought it a trick of my eyes— my mind casting wishes into the universe like throwing coins into a fountain. I had been in and out of magic for so long, I'd begun to question everything I saw, everything I thought, even on good days. But after Arsenault Fixed my arm with the Prinze sword, filled the holes and dents, and chased away the antivita, I'd begun to feel stronger. The strange metal seeped into me slowly, touched by gods, legends, time—the wrongful and righteous deaths of so many. Thank the gods I couldn't feel the Shape of all of them. But the old guardians that had formed my original arm began to stir, feeling a purpose again.

And there was a woman.

I felt her in the metal the same way I felt Arsenault in it, though not as strong. Her signature was buried beneath his touch, the runes he'd etched into the molten surface of my bicep and forearm two layers deep now, as central to the structure as if they formed a skeleton. Trapped inside that framework was a history—tragedy, treachery, Truth.

I had never expected to find any kind of truth forged into the Prinze sword, but Ires had been right. That's where it was. Where *she* was. Hiding.

When I'd asked Arsenault about Sella—*how do you know she's dead?* —I'd been thinking in human terms, like what happened to Arsenault when he died. Maybe she got back up with the same body and kept going. But she was a goddess. Her truth was far stranger than Arsenault's.

Somehow, on the edge of the blade that should have killed her, she'd thrust her death into the magic which held it—and her—in suspension. The way Ires had stored his own death inside the magic so he could fight the new gods who had killed the old gods and forced *their* deaths into the magic first.

None of the gods were immortal. That was their dirty little secret, which the magic was forced to keep. Magic was keeping them alive, the way it had long, long ago, when the stories spoke of elixirs the gods drank to remain gods. But instead of drinking magic, the gods had forced the magic to swallow *their* mortality.

Sella had taken it one step further. Magic was her closest ally. She had convinced it to let her hide inside it—*all* of her.

But the magic was cracking. A force that existed to create and bring into being was now forced to harbor death; a force all about *truth* was being asked to *lie*. The contradictions were tearing it apart.

I could see now why Ires thought the magic needed a guardian and why my arm had been slowly—or not so slowly—driving me mad. Sella's presence paced uneasily at the edge of my mind, just as I uneasily felt her out.

I had to force myself to bide my time. Eight fucking days. I knew Lupa wouldn't kill me, and I knew Lobardin had hidden Arsenault so Lupa would give up on him. When Arsenault finally stepped into the magic, I knew he hadn't died or forgotten about me. I didn't like taking the time to heal, but now I knew I had time to do it.

I made myself sit through all eight days of swirling magic dreams, chasing ancient Fixers down the hallways of my visions.

I say that as if my dreams formed a house. There *was* a house in my dreams, but it was nothing like I expected. Magic in the old legends always seems as if it's done in castles and strongholds, directed by kings and queens and emperors.

But the magic that went into the metal of my arm was made in a tidy stone house overlooking a gray sea. The house's garden was wild with berry bushes and flowers and children, two dark-haired boys and a girl with flaming red hair who tumbled about like a litter of puppies around a small shed in the back corner of the yard.

The shed was full of metal. Sculpted silver pieces and parts, strange animal heads and legs, claws and paws and teeth. Swords, knives, and thin little stiletto daggers made for assassinations in the dark. The sound of a hammer at the forge inside the shed rang out incessantly in the cold sea air.

Don't bother Da, one of the boys told the little girl. *It's dangerous in there and he's busy.*

But I want to show him my flowers, the little girl said.

The boys stopped the girl from going into the shed. The hammer rang out and I watched as a dark-haired man bent over the anvil, sweat running down his temples, his shirt damp under his leather apron, sleeves rolled up past his elbows. The muscles of his forearms corded taut with every blow of the hammer. With his bare finger, he traced a series of runes into the flat of the blade. Then, when he was finished, he plunged the blade into a bucket, and steam boiled up in clouds that glowed white with magic.

Arsenault's sword. He was forging it, there, in my vision. This was his house and his family.

He looked impossibly young. Perhaps someone who had met him as Andris in Liera wouldn't have thought so. But with no scar and no metal streak in his hair, without the pain of his past in his eyes, he seemed too young to have a child the age of his oldest boy.

The boy—gray-eyed like Arsenault—led his sister into the house and solemnly placed her flowers in a pottery cup before dipping her a drink from the milk bucket. The other boy followed, dipping his own cup, but the little girl was walking backwards all around the room and bumped into him, making him spill his drink. They squabbled for a moment about who should clean it up. The oldest boy wiped up the spilled milk with a rag and then Arsenault came out of the shed, cleaning the black grime off his hands and face with a towel.

Where's your mother? he asked.

Out. The boy poured some water into a washbasin and rinsed out the dirty rag. He seemed horribly responsible for a child his age.

Out where?

Look at my flowers, Da, the little girl said. *Aren't they pretty?*

Arsenault looked down at the flowers and a smile broke over his face. I had never seen him smile like that, without hesitation. He sat at the table and took the girl on his lap. *They are beautiful flowers, love, but I'd really like to know where your mama is. Do you know, Pippa?*

She's with Uncle Tavi. He came and got her. She said good-bye. Didn't you hear her?

Arsenault frowned. Unease filtered into the scene like a cold breath of wind. *The hammer must have been too loud. Well, love, what do you think we can find to eat? Shall we scrounge for ourselves?*

There's the sorr and stockfish, the younger boy said. The two boys looked almost like twins. I could see only Arsenault in them, not their mother. All her traits must have been passed on to her daughter, with her wild, flaming hair.

Ah, well. Another meal of sorr today won't hurt us. He looked troubled as he spooned a smooth, thick white substance out of a crock into four bowls—yogurt, it looked like, or something like our soft, curdy sheep cheese—and sat to eat with his children.

As they bent to their meal, mumbling a prayer of thanks over it, the magic swept me away from that kitchen to a small hidden room in an attic, where a candle guttered and a man and a woman knelt beside each other on the floor, a heavy blanket covering their shoulders. A metal sculpture gleamed in the light before them.

Sella, the man said. *I don't know why you're hesitating.*

Making these machines isn't as simple as you think. You're asking me to animate a corpse. Ari says if people find out I've used my Talents this way—

Ari worries too much what people will think. He's so bound up in being respected he spends all his time at it. You don't owe Ari anything, Sella. I know you married him to get away from your father. If I had been the oldest son...

Tavi, don't.

Well, isn't it true? If I had been eldest, you would have picked me. Wouldn't you? Sella?

He lifted her long, auburn curls off her shoulder and nuzzled against her neck as he spoke, pressing his lips to her skin. I didn't want to watch Sella with Arsenault's brother. I didn't want to realize how *alike* they looked—the same knife-edge nose, the sharp cut of the jaw beneath the dark stubble of beard, the dark hair, the widow's peak. But Tavi's mouth was different, his lips thinner, his expression more cynical, his eyes...

There was something about his eyes. They were green, a forest color, edged with the gray of stone. When he looked at Sella, his pupils grew large and dark and the green burned hot. But when he turned away from her, his eyes cooled as if they were metal taken off a fire. Then the green turned sly and dangerous, the color of water in a mossy well, the kind that waited to drown unsuspecting travelers.

Sella didn't seem to notice. Or perhaps she was drawn to the darkness, to the mystery of what might exist in its depths. I understood the attraction of risk. But Tavi seemed like a risk too dangerous to take. You got the idea, looking at him, that he would be the sort of man to whom violence came easy and careless, as long as it served his ends. I had known men like him. I steered clear of them or put them in their places quick. Otherwise, you could be sure they'd take your wage and trod on you to advance in the ranks, leaving you alone on the battlefield when it counted.

It was hard to believe he and Arsenault shared the same parents. But damn everything if they didn't look as alike as Arsenault's own boys did. It felt strange watching him seduce Sella.

Arsenault's wife.

It felt strange to be watching her, too, after catching glimpses of her in dreams and visions. I felt like a kacin addict, hating the kacin I was smoking but doing it anyway. I knew it was poison to make comparisons, but I couldn't help it. I drank my jealousy down like a drug.

Perhaps if she hadn't been a goddess...

Her thick auburn mane fell to her waist, curling in waves around her face like sparking embers from a fire. So different from my own cropped-off straw-yellow curls, frizzy with inattention. Her long, dark lashes swept over cat-green eyes and lay against the pale skin of her cheek, so smooth it might have been polished marble, making me only too aware of every freckle the sun had kissed onto my face, that nick at the corner of my eye, and probably more scars since I'd fought Erelf. The thin chemise she wore showed off the shape of her, the shadows of her breasts, the enticing curve of her hip as she tucked her legs beneath her and leaned into Tavi. The way he kissed his way down the graceful line of her neck made my mouth dry.

Gods. It was like when I'd been fighting in Kavo and the men in my company had dragged me along with them to the whorehouse. I think they had bets on whether I'd choose a man or a woman. I hadn't known what to do, but I worried that if I did nothing, it would make me seem weak in the eyes of the men. So, to put them all off, I threw coins at the girls and told them I just wanted to watch.

Later, I lay awake on my cot—drunk and burning—and I missed Arsenault with an ache so fierce it felt like it would devour me from the inside out.

I knew how this story ended, knew Arsenault would play the villain. Yet the fury that boiled up in me at both Sella and Tavi felt like it would blind me. Maybe Tavi had instigated the trouble, but Sella had condemned Arsenault to an eternity of torture simply so she could *hide*. I longed for a sword in my hand, to save Arsenault from the curse that had been laid on his life. Even if it meant I would never meet him.

But there was nothing I could do, and the magic was not kind. It trapped me there, watching, as Tavi pushed Sella's chemise up over her hips and ran his hands all over her body. Then, as they sat like that, pressed together, his lips on her skin, he said, *Ari will never know, Sella. And neither will your father. Your secret is safe with me.*

My secret was supposed to be safe with Ari. But somehow you found out.

I know a lot of secrets about you, Tavi said. *I know you like to be touched here...and here...and here..."*

Dear gods, I thought at the magic. Why are you showing me this? Why can't I close my eyes and stop seeing it? I want to go back to that stinking carriage rattling over the road to Rojornick, with that bastard Lupa and his gavaro with the gray eyes that remind me of Arsenault's...

The only thing worse would have been to be stuck watching her with Arsenault.

On that thought, Sella touched the metal that lay before them. A stream of white light wrapped around the silver metal like a shroud. The metal was cast in the shape of an arm...but not an arm. It had scales and feathers and talons, like a cross between a lizard's leg and a bird's foot and the arm of a woman. When the magic went into it, I could see the phantom shape of the thing it had been cut away from, the sleek, ghostly form of a large animal with a mouthful of dagger-like teeth.

Both sculpture and image were too damn familiar.

There, she said, sighing. *I don't know how you found that old piece of me, but it will live again if you want it to. You can't keep abusing the magic like this, Tavi. I know you're only trying to keep Tule safe now that the guardians are gone, but Ari's right—*

All I ever hear about is godsdamned Ari. The magic only gave him his Talents because of you. I was always a better Smith, until the magic decided you needed better. Ari doesn't believe we're in danger. But you know war is coming here, too.

Knowing and practicing necromancy are two different things! The magic doesn't like having anything to do with death. We need to worry more about the antivita. It will swallow everything if we let it. And if we keep playing with death, it will.

And Ari's not listening to you about that either, is he? What does he have? Some plan to take you and the children and run away? He's so fucking honorable in his protector role, he'll get you all killed. Tavi ran his hands up into Sella's hair and his voice broke. *You know he doesn't love you like I do. Can't you pretend to follow our rules? Just for a little while?*

If I followed your rules, I'd be with Ari and my children right now. And you wouldn't have that dragon to use for a guardian, would you?

The dragon Lupa had brought to Cassis. It wasn't just a machine, it was—

⚜

"She's a dragon!" I gasped, coming out of the dream so suddenly I felt like I'd just clawed my way out of a wave. "That's what Arsenault meant about the gods being shiftier! Sella was a dragon! That limb was a piece of *her* and you knew it!"

Lupa was sitting beside me, Arsenault's broken sword across his knees, and I was still bound in metal. Lupa jumped, getting the sword out in front of him, though the antivita had continued to eat through the blade until it was only a handful of needle-like shards held together by the hilt.

Lupa stared at me, breathing almost as hard as I was. Behind his spectacles, his eyes were large and frightened. His hair... I was sure it was darker now than it had been when I'd first seen him at the farm-house. Over the past few days, he'd seemed to maintain his wolfish-ness, but there had also been times when he acted more like a frightened dog.

"Messera. What are you talking about?"

"Stop calling me that!" I shouted at him. "I'm only allowed titles because of your fake papers! You know good and well what I'm talking about. Son of a *bitch*. You were trying to trap him!"

"I don't know who Sella is, I don't know why she would be part of a dragon—I don't know why you won't cooperate! Don't you want to save your city? Devid di Prinze will destroy it. He's not strong enough to hold the Houses together. But you have a chance! I shouldn't have to force you! Who put you in those bonds?"

"You did, you idiot! You're taking me *away* from Cassis! Don't you remember?"

His brow furrowed and he tilted his head down so his spectacles slid toward the tip of his nose. He pushed them back with one finger, then settled them on the bridge of his nose with a false calm. The sword in his other hand dipped toward the floor.

I thought about making a move for it, but my bonds were made from the same metal as my arm, too strong to break.

I stilled my frustration and watched him. Really watched him. Taking my concentration back left me feeling more drained than any physical struggle, but I hung onto it. A strange battle moved over his face. His eyes sharpened and the muscles in his jaw stood out as if he were clenching his teeth. Then he took in a big breath through his nose. He pulled off his glasses. Set them down on the bench, as if he didn't need them anymore. The muscles of his jaw relaxed and his mouth settled into a more confident line. A crueler line.

He grabbed my metal bonds and shoved me against the back of the coach, then leaned in close to me—close enough to see his eyes.

I could have sworn that in the farmhouse his eyes had been mostly golden brown. But the colors had traded places and now the green swirled over the brown like rising water.

His hair—with big dark streaks in it, like the reverse of having it colored by the sun—brushed my cheeks as it fell forward.

I wasn't imagining it. He *did* look more like Arsenault. And those green eyes...

"How is that possible?" I murmured, unable to stop searching his face.

He leaned back against the cushioned seat, his lips hooked upward in a mockery of Arsenault's smile. "Figured it out, have you? I thought you'd stay down in the magic a little longer, but you surprise me."

"How did you do it? Are you like Arsenault? Cursed to come back, not to remember?"

He chuckled and put the sword down beside me. My fingers itched, wanting to take it even in its ruined state, but I couldn't move. He lifted his hand to my hair and pushed it back behind my ear. I tried not to flinch.

"No, love, I am actually dead. Or my body is, in any case. Why do you think your people set up all those disturbing black stone markers all over the place? They don't do it for fun."

"The stories about vengeful ghosts..."

"All true. Some ghosts do wander the landscape, looking for vengeance, but they're useless. The markers are less to warn you of vengeful ghosts who will let you go if you run away and more to warn you about ghosts who might want to steal your nice warm body so they can extend their time under the sun."

"You stole Bruzzia's body. And the goddess who saved him..."

"My first indication Sella wasn't as dead as I thought she was," Tavi confirmed. "I'd been searching for her for—well, if I say *years*, you'll know that's a vast understatement, yes? Bruzzia was only a nominal Empirist when he came to Tule. A small-time antiquities dealer and con man who'd lucked into a stash of treasures he'd at least had the good sense to recognize, though he had no understanding of how the pirate market worked. He'd discovered a stash hidden in a warehouse and swindled some ignorant gavaros out of it. But when he began selling the pieces, he ran afoul of the network and ended up in Geoffre di Prinze's study. Geoffre provided the funds for him to sail to Tule, where he discovered that metal limb and my bones. And then —*finally*—I was free."

"You're leaving out the part where Erelf maneuvered people like he was playing chess, aren't you?"

Tavi shrugged. "He's a god, he makes things happen. I warned Ari, you know. I told him the magic was moving and the gods were getting nervous and to be careful because they were choosing sides. When the magic threatens to slip away from them... Well, they can't ignore that. But Ari didn't listen to me."

"How many times has he died since you told him? It's not fair to expect him to remember when he's doomed to forget."

"And whose fault is that? He thought he was so righteous. Taking his children down to our parents' house, then coming to look for me. Finding Sella and I together in that room and fooling himself into thinking he was doing justice by attacking me. He tries to say Sella's death was an accident, but it was his temper and his pride that did it."

"You're a snake. Arsenault's never pretended it was anything other than his fault. But how can you blame him for everything when you're the one who betrayed the bond of brothers?"

"As if Sella had no say in any of this?"

"She can bear her part of the burden then. Especially for saving Bruzzia. She still couldn't just let you die, could she?"

"She loves me," Tavi said simply. "I thought my brother's problem with jealousy would worry you at least a little. What happens when you do something he doesn't like?"

"If Arsenault was going to murder me because I made him angry, I'd have been dead long ago. You'll have to try harder."

Tavi watched me for a long moment, as if trying to decide whether I was telling the truth or just handing him a large measure of bravado.

To be honest, I wasn't feeling very brave. But it wasn't because I was worried about Arsenault's anger or his jealousy. I'd Seen enough to know Arsenault's anger had been directed against his brother—who hadn't learned a damn thing after being dead all these years. He still wanted what his brother had, was still using people—literally, in the case of poor Bruzzia—to get what he wanted. I could deal with him. He had no hooks in me. He was just a bastard.

What worried me was Sella. The two promises Arsenault had made.

Now that a piece of her existed in my arm, would she try to blot me out the way Tavi had blotted out Bruzzia? I could fight against that. But not against the harder choice, which was to admit we might be on the same side, with Ires and against Erelf. To choose to keep her secret—or to expose her, if that would free Arsenault from his curse. Even if I *was* afraid Arsenault would want her over me. Because she was a goddess. And she was first.

I was tired of letting fear and anger run my life. It was time to take a chance on trust. And a fool's promise that was the least foolish decision I had ever made.

"In for a cato, in for an astra," I said brightly.

Tavi gave me a strange look. "I wouldn't have chosen anyone vowed to Ari if I'd had a choice, but he gave you that fucking arm *and* put a piece of Sella in it. If he didn't do it on purpose, it smacks of fate. I don't like that."

"Oh. Fate's not under Erelf's jurisdiction, is it? That's Ekyra's province."

He glared at me. Then the anger changed to appraisal.

"You *are* different from Sella. I wondered if Ari had chosen you because you reminded him of her."

I balled my right hand into a fist unconsciously. When I realized what I had done, I barely caught myself before I flushed in triumph. Being able to move my fingers was a damn good sign.

I flexed my fingers again to prove to myself it hadn't been a fluke. "I doubt it. Men often like to tell me I'm a demon, not a goddess. Arsenault knew what he was getting into."

"Well, the arm will be set soon and then there will be a connection. Eventually it will obliterate everything."

"What makes you think she doesn't want to stay dead?"

He looked startled, as if he'd never contemplated that possibility.

I laughed. "So, you'll only give her a choice if she picks the answer you like?"

"She'll have the choice," he growled, "because you'll give it to her. Or if she wants to, she'll just take you."

Not fucking likely. Goddess or not.

I'd help her hide, keep her away from Tavi, but I wasn't about to let her take me over. There was a line.

I put on a grin. "So I've got a piece of a goddess grafted onto my body. The boys in my old company would have been glad of that. Probably would have taken more coin at arm wrestling."

Tavi stared at me like most men did—as if he'd just dragged up some strange and incomprehensible creature from the depths of the sea.

"Erelf would like to remind you of the offer he made you. To take you in exchange for Ari. He'll agree to make Ari's reprieve permanent if you give yourself to him. Think how complete Ari's happiness will be when he learns Sella is back, too."

"You expect me to believe you care about Arsenault's happiness? I already told Erelf I don't believe he wouldn't cheat."

Tavi shrugged. "Let's just say there are larger forces at work and I'm willing to bend a little on some things. Besides, Ari's the kind of man who can convince himself he ought to be happy even if he's being beaten with a stick. It's ridiculous. Surely, you've seen this about him?"

I narrowed my eyes at him, trying to fill in the sketch he was drawing for me—and refusing to be baited about his description of Arsenault, which was annoyingly true. It left him open to all sorts of mistreatment. Before, Erelf had wanted me as a bride because he missed his daughter and wanted more children. Sella had hidden herself so effectively in plain sight, in the one place her father would never look—in the Prinze sword. Maybe Erelf had begun to suspect and that was why he had wanted Geoffre in the first place, but he didn't have his sister Ekyra's foresight or her hindsight...

The answer hit me like a flash. Erelf didn't know *because the gods weren't all-knowing*.

And they weren't immortal either. They'd just hidden their deaths inside the magic, like Sella had.

I needed to buy myself and Arsenault some time.

"And Erelf will let go of Arsenault? For good?" I asked, as if I were considering the offer.

"I've been told you could work something out."

"And you'd get Sella back, of course."

"I loved her much more than my brother did. He could never satisfy her. Not like I could."

He looked at me.

I'm not sure if he liked what he saw or if he was just trying to weigh in his head what it would be like to have Sella in my body, while he was Tavi in Lupa-Bruzzia's body. How we would fit together. Maybe he was trying to decide what Arsenault saw in me or he was thinking about stealing something—someone—his brother loved away from him. Again.

I was wearing women's clothes and his gaze willed me to be weak —weaker than him anyway. Instead, I gave him my best smile.

"I've never had any complaints with Arsenault."

For a moment, Tavi looked surprised. Then he laughed. "I suppose with enough practice...maybe for *you*. Not for her."

"I wouldn't insult me like that, Tavi. If you want me to *be* her."

"You're not in the least bit curious what it would be like?"

I looked him up and down. "Honestly? No. And having watched the old you in action... I'll take your brother, thank you."

Tavi snorted. "Your loss, I'm afraid."

"But..." I said, and he looked at me again.

I chose my next words carefully. "I'll give myself up to set Arsenault free to live the life he chooses. Not one he's condemned to."

CHAPTER 93

KYRRA

WHEN I SAW THE BURGUNDY SILK DRESS FOR THE FIRST TIME, I could only stare. I had tried so hard to convince myself that the vision of my wedding was only an invention of Erelf's, but here was Tavi holding a dress practically the twin of the one I had seen in my dream. I wondered where he had found that much Aliente silk. People killed to possess it as often as they were executed for possessing it, but I knew of only one new source, in Conseli territory, and it wasn't producing yet.

Being dressed like an Aliente doll made me grind my teeth, but I forced myself to stand still. The coach had stopped for the night. Tavi lit the interior with a glowing piece of magicked metal he set in a holder like a candle. I hoped Arsenault was using his Sight to keep track of me, but at the same time, I didn't want him to See me shivering in this see-through silk chemise and these silk stockings with Tavi at my back. He laced me up quick and businesslike with Bruzzia's smooth fingertips, so unlike Arsenault's workworn and calloused hands.

Tavi turned me around and examined his handiwork. I faced him the way I'd face an enemy soldier. His gaze lingered on my breasts until I wanted to punch him. Then it dropped to the exaggerated curves the stays made of my waist and hips. The shadow of my thighs showed through the thin fabric of the chemise, so I was sure it didn't leave anything else to the imagination.

"Perhaps I begin to understand what my brother sees in you," he murmured.

"Am I supposed to be flattered?"

"If you're giving yourself up for my brother's life, you're doing a poor job of it. You have to be willing, you know."

I'd show him *willing*.

I grabbed him by the shirt with my left hand and yanked him close, crushing my mouth against his and forcing his lips open with my tongue. I had the satisfaction of surprising him. But then he leaned into it, gripping me by the shoulders, trying to swallow my mouth with his.

I shoved him backwards. His hands slid off my arms and he bounced on the bench seat. His head knocked against the coach wall with a hard thunk.

"I'll be willing when I see that my conditions are met," I said. "Not till then."

He wiped my kiss off his mouth with his sleeve and watched me with glowering green eyes that flickered, suddenly uncertain. The effort of pushing him had taken a lot of strength out of me. If he pressed his advantage, I would be in trouble. I braced myself, but a shadow of doubt crossed his face as he rose and gathered the dress in his arms.

"Will you put this on, messera?" he asked in a conciliatory tone that made me wonder who had the upper hand now. Was Tavi still fighting for precedence over Bruzzia? If they were battling each other for supremacy of the body, could I bring the scholar back on purpose?

Tomas opened the door. "Ser? Messera? Is everything all right? I heard a thump."

It was impossible, after I'd spent hours locked in the carriage with Tomas, to notice the familiar line of his jaw and those storm-gray eyes, and not remember the way Arsenault had looked at Adayze in the visions the magic had shown me.

Magic didn't care about feelings. Or at least it didn't care about mine. It showed me things I'd rather not see, told me things I never should have known and would have refused to hear if I'd had the choice. The magic had been only too eager to expose the secrets it kept, so now I knew more about everyone than I would have liked.

"Everything's fine, Tomas," Tavi said. "Just make sure no one approaches us unaware. And let me know if those runes fire."

Tomas's eyes darted over me in my underclothes, then he quickly looked away. "Pardon, ser, but won't you know?"

Tavi looked startled. Or maybe it was Bruzzia. The combination of the two of them had been *Lupa*, but I needed to make finer distinctions if I wanted to get out of here. Whoever he was, he groped on the bench for his glasses and settled them on his nose. "Yes, of course. But you'll double-check, won't you, Tomas? I expect we'll be followed."

"You don't think Mestere di Prinze will take the marriage papers back to Liera? That...that captain... He's, I mean, I killed him. Didn't I?"

I knew then if I hadn't known before: Arsenault was surely his father. If Adayze and Jon had placed him here on purpose, they had put him in an impossible situation. But I didn't think Jon would have lied to Arsenault when Arsenault had asked him directly. He could have lied about who Tomas was while still acknowledging he knew Tomas, which would have been the safer course.

Tavi—no, Bruzzia—frowned in a distracted way. "Yes," he said. "I thought so. I mean, he must have been dead. I gave it a few days, but...oh. Oh."

He stared at the bundle of burgundy fabric in his hands and a brick-red flush crept slowly above the stubble of his beard. He looked at me in my lacy silk stays and his eyes widened. He thrust the dress at Tomas.

"Tomas," he pled. "Please help the messera put on this dress."

Then he pushed past him and went out into the night.

⚜

TOMAS FUMBLED WITH THE LACES OF THE GOWN, AWKWARD WITH embarrassment. "I'm sorry. I've never really done this before."

I eyed him over my shoulder. "I find that hard to believe. You're handsome enough. You don't have to be so proper with me."

"No, I'm telling the truth. And not...not simply because I'm unfamiliar with Lieran dresses. I don't... Forgive me, messera."

The gown was hard not to admire, but it emphasized my female form in a way I'd never seen. The last time I'd worn a comparably elaborate silk gown, I'd been sixteen years old. My mother would never have allowed me to wear anything as scandalous as this dress then.

"I suppose you should call me Kyrra," I sighed.

I had no idea who I was supposed to be or what I was supposed to want anymore. The only thing I knew for damn sure was that I didn't want Tavi or Bruzzia or whoever Lupa happened to be at the moment admiring me in it.

The only way out was through. I turned to face Tomas. "You're Arsenault's son, aren't you?"

Startled, he lifted his gaze to mine. "Messera?"

"*Kyrra*," I told him firmly. "Or Kyris, I don't care which. You have a lot to learn about your father if you don't know it already."

Tomas stepped backward. "But—how—"

I tapped the corner of my eye. "You share his eyes. And I have Sight. It comes and goes. I don't know if you knew that about me?"

"My magic is bound, so I can't See anything myself. It's like walking around blindfolded. It's hard to tell what's what about you, messera."

I let the *messera* go. I didn't know if I should try to stop people using it or not, but it still felt odd. "Look. Arsenault can tell you what you'll need to know. When he comes."

"But mess—*Kyrra*. He's dead. I-I killed him. I'm *sorry*, I didn't know what to do. I thought he'd died long ago. My mother sent me here to spy on Lupa..."

"That explains why your uncle didn't know it was you, but perhaps it's all the same. Arsenault's not dead."

"But—"

"It was a trick. To make him seem dead, so Lupa would leave him alone. It's too much to explain right now." I cast a quick glance at the door and dumped the rest of the information in a rush, like a mad dash for cover on the battlefield. "When we get to the intersection with the Spice Road, we'll be able to make our move. Bandits always hide in the rocks and it's easy to cut off the bridge. Illichnaya sends out patrols, too. Maybe even staffed by some of the gavaros I used to work with."

Which would be a gift of the gods. I took a breath and went on.

"Illichnaya will grant you haven if you give them the name *Kyris di Nada*. So, if things don't work out and you can get away, run like all hells for Illichnaya and get help. You must have a map?"

"Yes, of course. But—"

"Tomas, remember." I tapped my temple. "*Sight*. Lupa's coming back; quick, knot those laces."

He dropped his head and finished his knots.

The next day, Arsenault shot me. And the blood that dripped down onto my arm finished waking the dragon.

CHAPTER 94

KYRRA

THE MORNING OF THE NINTH DAY AFTER ARSENAULT FIXED MY arm, I woke on the floor of the carriage with Tavi at my side. For once I didn't begrudge him; it was cold this high in the mountains and body heat was body heat. The space between the benches was cramped and we slept pressed together under a pile of blankets stolen from Miranda's house. Sella's presence stirred inside me, ghostlike, not overpowering. I was still trying to map her, pacing off the limits restlessly, like a wolf meeting another wolf in new territory.

My upper right arm, where the ball from Arsenault's gun had carved a shallow groove, was sore. But the arm itself felt strong and new. It didn't creak or pain me in the cold as much as it used to, and the precision of my fingers was finer than it had ever been.

It was still a metal arm. I had been sleeping with it outside the blankets. The metal was so cold it burned. I tucked it under the blanket again, resting it unavoidably against Tavi's chest. He hissed in a breath and opened his eyes.

For a moment, he looked disoriented and wild, as if he didn't know who or where he was. He always woke like this. He would sometimes doze with no warning as we clattered down the road. But if I moved, he came instantly awake, and the muddle in his eyes usually resolved in favor of Tavi, not Bruzzia. I got the feeling that the process of Tavi taking over Bruzzia's body was nearing its end, as Bruzzia simply grew too weary to battle Tavi's will. Every now and then Bruzzia still triumphed, especially when he was embarrassed. Bruzzia's inexperience with women was a powerful thing.

It had given me an idea, if I could gather enough courage.

The carriage was already moving. Tomas had spent most of the night outside. I'd thought, early in the dark, that I heard a scuffle. The runes had flared bright blue for an instant, then subsided. Tavi peered at the window, but then acted as if it were nothing, gesturing for me to lie down.

I was tired of lying down. But what else was there to do? I'd dozed to kill the time, but now we were close enough to the pass I could put my plan in motion.

The man facing me looked as if half of him was drowning and wanted me to rescue him and the other half would rather drag me under and drown me, too.

I wanted to take a deep breath for courage, but I dared not. I wasn't used to this kind of ruse, but if I could bring Bruzzia out instead of Tavi...

Everything would be easier.

I put my flesh hand on his shoulder and his eyes cut sideways at it. Tavi's green, skeptical gaze won out. Waking, with his hair rumpled and the muscles of his face relaxed, he bore more resemblance to Arsenault. But that only made me miss Arsenault more.

I traced my thumb down the rounded outline of the muscles of his arm. Bruzzia was a scholar, not a warrior like Arsenault; his muscles weren't as defined, but if he knew how to use a sword, he'd have reach. I wasn't sure Bruzzia *could* use a sword. The key would be to force a physical confrontation, not a magical one. If I could just keep him off guard...

When I brought my gaze back up to his, Tavi was watching me, questioning. His mouth curved up into that cold smile so unlike Arsenault's.

"Good morning?" he said.

I had two problems. One was to put Bruzzia off guard. The other to make Tavi believe I was sincere.

"Good morning," I answered. "I believe my arm feels better."

"And your other injuries?"

I'd be winded if I tried to run a distance or swing a sword for any length of time, but I answered truthfully. "Better."

"Good." He touched my hair. His gaze continued to track over my face—searching for an indication Sella had taken over, I supposed. I wasn't sure how to fake that, but I did know how to embarrass Bruzzia.

When I didn't pull back, his touch on my hair became less hesitant. His fingers threaded through my curls and his gaze drifted away from my face. He pushed the blanket down and pulled the neck of my dress off my shoulder to examine the bandage on my right arm.

The metal had crept almost up to my shoulder. The bullet had cut right at the edge of skin and metal. The wound had scabbed up right away.

"I'll put more honey on that wound today," Tavi said. "Wouldn't want to go to this much trouble only to have you die of fever."

"I've survived worse."

The neck of my dress remained off my shoulder. He finally noticed I hadn't pulled away from him and narrowed his eyes suspiciously.

I smiled and jerked my arm back. Then I flipped the blankets off and stood up.

The swaying of the carriage almost knocked me off my feet, but I caught myself on the looped rope handle hanging from the roof. Then I put my leg up on the bench, hiked my skirts up to my thigh, and bent to adjust my stocking.

Tavi—or whoever he was now—pushed himself up on his elbow to watch. A flush rose on his neck. I didn't think I could show Tavi anything that would make him blush, so maybe Bruzzia had begun to surface.

I continued to straighten the seam, skimming my fingers down my calf. I made sure I leaned over far enough to give him a good look down the bodice of my dress.

The flush spread from his neck to his cheeks.

"Messera," he murmured. He attempted to scramble to his feet despite the sway of the carriage. "Are you sure—"

I grabbed my stays, which I'd asked him to unlace last night to sleep. Sleeping with them on was like sleeping in armor. "Here." I put my foot back on the floor. "Help me put these on."

I slid into them, then presented my backside to him, pressing much too close for him to tie the stays.

The carriage hit a bump and knocked me backward. His hands had nowhere to go but my hips. If he'd had a knife, I would have had it off him in an instant and buried it in his ribs. Instead, he clutched me against him and nuzzled his lips and nose into my hair.

Shit.

Was this Tavi or Bruzzia? Maybe I had miscalculated.

I whirled around—too fast. He stepped back against the bench seat, but then leaned forward and crushed his mouth against mine.

Dammit, who was I dealing with? I didn't think it was Tavi, but I hadn't expected this kind of passion from Bruzzia. He pushed the stays off my arms. They hit the floor of the carriage with a thump and my breasts rubbed loose against the silk and his chest. He kept kissing me—on the lips, the corner of my mouth, my neck, behind my ear— apparently unaware of my surprise.

"Messera," he breathed in between kisses, "it's been so *difficult*... I thought he would help us... I thought... I've wanted you...dear *gods*, I didn't want you to be hurt..."

Fucking hells. What do I do now?

I didn't have to do much to encourage him. He planted fumbling, impassioned kisses down my chest to my neckline. His hands edged upward until they brushed my breasts.

I gave up the ruse and bashed him in the side of the head with my metal fist.

Our awkward position didn't give me a lot of leverage. My blow didn't have the power behind it to knock him unconscious, but he let go of me with a muffled curse and staggered to the side, and I lunged for the carriage door.

It was locked. I pulled it open just as Bruzzia—Tavi now—caught me around the middle and yanked me backward. The slushy gravel of the road passed by quickly underneath the gap between the door and the bottom of the carriage. It had begun to rain or sleet and the wheels kicked up a fine mist of water through the gap. If Tomas noticed what was happening, he didn't slow down. I grabbed the top edge of the doorframe and braced myself in the doorway with my foot.

"Do you love Ari so little?" Tavi shouted at me. "You gave me your word! You said you'd give yourself to set him free!"

"I said I'd give myself if my conditions were met. Did you or Erelf have any intention of setting him free? To the life he wants to live?"

"Did you give us a chance?"

"The life he wants to live involves *me*, dammit! I've not violated any promises! When you steal a man's wife..."

Tavi bellowed and ripped me out of the doorway. I fell backward on top of him, got caught up in my skirts, and floundered onto the bench. Tavi grabbed me by the hair and jerked me back down, then drove his hand into my nose.

Blood erupted over both of us. Through its haze, I gripped his throat with my metal hand and squeezed as hard as I could, pressing my thumb down into his windpipe.

His eyes bulged. He clawed at my arm, wheezing and gasping. My vision threatened to go black—from effort or the blood leaking out of my nose or Ires or all three, who knew—and I tightened my grip.

Suddenly my arm felt like it was on fire, the way it had when Arsenault had Fixed it. I cried out and let go of Tavi. Tavi swayed above me, his eyes dark and hot with hate.

"Ari shouldn't have wasted the metal on you," he spat. "You've got a death wish."

The carriage creaked to a stop. Tavi brought his head up like a spooked horse and I hurriedly wiped the blood from my face with the sleeve of my dress. My right arm cooled, calming the pain, and I clambered upright.

"Why are we stopping?" Tavi muttered. "The horses shouldn't need rest so soon..."

Something clattered behind us—the sound of thumping, clicking as if on wood, and then...running.

The bridge.

I stood as fast as I could, but Tavi was already shoving open the door that had swung shut when we'd stopped. He leaned out ahead of me, but the sharp crack of a gunshot chased him back inside. He reached up into a slot above the doorway and took down a gun. Then, he grabbed me and jerked me out the doorway with him.

Arsenault.

He was wearing a hat and holding his axe like he'd stepped out of an old Dagmari epic, and dear gods, it was good to see him again. His gaze swept over me with fear and concern, then snapped back to Tavi.

Who had fired the gun?

"Want to take that risk again?" Tavi growled at him.

Arsenault's eyes widened as he stared at the man he knew as Lupa. The axe sagged in surprise as recognition dawned on his face.

"*Tavi,*" he said. "By all the gods, how is it you?"

Then, before I could move, Tavi pulled out the godsdamned gun.

CHAPTER 95

ARSENAULT

THE BRIDGE

I T ALL HAPPENED SO FAST . S EEING HIS BROTHER STARING BACK AT him from Lupa's body stunned him so much, Tavi had a gun to Kyrra's head before his frozen mind knew what was happening.

Arsenault tore his gaze away from Lupa's—*Tavi's*—face and studied Kyrra. Streaks of blood marred her upper lip and cheek. Her dress was rumpled, the neck pulled off her right shoulder, allowing a glimpse of a white bandage just above the gleam of her metal arm. She wasn't wearing stays and the cream-colored chemise that peeked out beneath the gown was pulled very low on her breasts. He lifted his eyes to hers and instead of cool gray-blue, he saw fright.

He swung his head back to Lupa.

Lupa—*his brother*—was wearing an unlaced, untucked shirt.

It's not the same, a voice in his head screamed at him. *It's not the same!*

It wasn't the outward form of this situation that made Arsenault's blood a roaring in his ears. It was the memory of the last time he had seen Tavi in the flesh. Tavi's hands all over Sella, Sella in bed beneath him, the waves of her hair spilling around her, dangling over the side of the mattress...

Arsenault stared up at Kyrra again, at the black mouth of the gun hidden in her golden hair, the red smears of blood beneath her nose, her rumpled dress.

"You've destroyed everyone I've ever loved, Tavi." He felt like the words had to be forced through his chest, through his teeth. "I won't let you take Kyrra, too. What do you want me to do?"

Tavi's lips curled upward in a victorious, knife-slice of a smile. "Hello to you, too, brother. I want what I've always wanted. Leave me alone. How many lives have you lived since your first? This is only my second chance and I mean to make the most of it."

"Not with her."

Tavi laughed. "Oh, yes, with her. Have you grown so dense you couldn't feel the metal even when you worked it?"

"You didn't know where Sella was. You were dead, latched onto Erelf like a dog trying to stay in favor with his master, and you had no idea where Sella was. You're just trying to humiliate me like you always did, by making yourself look smart at my expense."

"Does it matter? I'm going to bring her back, Ari. This time, she'll choose me *first*."

"Tavi, you fucking *bastard*. All that time you had to think and still, all you can think about is yourself?" His voice froze in his throat as a thought occurred to him. "Kyrra, is that you?"

Kyrra looked at him level. She no longer seemed as frightened. Instead, that blue spark was back in her eyes, the stubborn fire that had fascinated him so long ago, when she was just a water girl covered in dirt and he was only a gavaro riding borders and fixing roofs. She settled back on her heels and her chin came up in defiance...

It was *her*. All Kyrra. Not Sella at all.

Everything knotted up inside him let go in a rush of... There wasn't a word for the kind of relief he felt.

"He won't shoot me," Kyrra said quietly. "He needs me alive."

Of course he does. But I need you more.

For the first time, he became aware that Cassis, Lobardin, and Tomas had all moved carefully around him in a wary semicircle. Lobardin and Cassis had their guns out. In the slushy mix falling from the clouds, Lobardin's arquebus was smoking—primed and ready to shoot.

Arsenault caught Kyrra's gaze.

"Lobardin," he said.

Guns fired simultaneously.

৩৵৩

SOMETIMES YOU COULD SEE IT COMING WHEN EVERYTHING WAS going to go to shit.

You knew the rotting wound in your foot was going to kill you. You knew the fever in your gut was insurmountable and you'd best give into it. You didn't have any reason to fight against it and it was easier to die and forget.

Easier on everyone around you, too. Then they could move on.

Tell your son you were a hero.

Settle down with a husband. Raise a family.

Put the grief in a box and get over it.

But sometimes death came out of nowhere. Before you were ready for it. Before you wanted it.

Something heavy and hard slammed into Arsenault's chest, followed by a burst of excruciating pain. When he came to his senses, the hand he'd placed over his ribs was covered in blood. Tavi held his gun outstretched, still smoking.

Leveled directly at him.

Kyrra cried out and whirled on Tavi. She smashed her metal arm into his face and he fell into the carriage. Arsenault staggered backward against the rope railing. He grabbed the top rope to keep from falling to his knees. Lobardin and Cassis were shouting—swearing—he couldn't tell—running forward...

Cassis yanked Tavi off the steps and hit him in the face with the stock of his pistol. Blood flew in the air, mixing with the sleet. Kyrra drew her fist back to hit Tavi again, but Tavi gripped her arm instead. A wave of magic ripped through it.

Her arm seethed red with heat and the outline of feathers crested on her forearm. She cried out in pain and fell onto the bridge. A powerful presence, called up from deep within the magic itself, moved inside her as it woke from its slumber. Arsenault could *See* it, a brilliant light too intense to be confined to the metal, and at the same time, a presence that had once seemed to him bright and true—a lantern in a night wood, a hearth fire when the storm raged outside. He had spent so many lives wishing, *praying* for this—the evidence that Sella was immortal after all.

But she'd had her time. He'd betrayed her trust far more thoroughly than she'd betrayed his, and he was sorry for it. He'd paid for his actions every day of his very long life. And by all the gods, if he was going to die now, finally and forever, he was not going to let his shattered vow cut Kyrra's life short, too.

He slung off his cloak, picked up his axe, and swung it in a hard, desperate slice through the railing of the bridge. It was hard to breathe, but the blood wasn't flowing fast. He thought he'd have time.

Hoped he'd have time.

Had to have time.

He lurched forward and grabbed Kyrra by her metal hand. She stared up at him, startled, afraid. Tavi's magic faltered for an instant.

"Don't let go," Arsenault whispered.

He cast himself backward off the bridge and brought her with him.

CHAPTER 96

KYRRA

THE BRIDGE

THE WATER WAS SO COLD AND THE SHOCK SO GREAT MY HEART stopped beating when we hit it, but Tavi's magic let go of me, too. My arm screamed as we plunged deep into the freezing water. I opened my mouth to gasp for air and water rushed in.

It filled my lungs and my body still tried to breathe it. Terror gripped me so tightly nothing made sense. I felt like I had escaped somewhere outside my body to watch the whole thing unfolding: Arsenault hanging on to me and shoving off the bottom, clawing his way toward the surface; the clear, green water, tainted by a great cloud of burgundy blood flowering up from Arsenault's side.

Gods damn it all, I couldn't swim. And my arm kept dragging me down.

I kicked and thrashed with my other arm. Arsenault made a noise at me. I saw his wide, panicked eyes, his waxy, pale face, the way his dark hair floated around us...

And then I blacked out.

✦

I AWOKE TUCKED INTO A TIGHT ROCK CREVICE, COUGHING UP water with the brief memory of Arsenault's fist pounding my back, the rough touch of his magic, and his lips brushing my forehead. But when I sat up, expecting to see him, he wasn't there. Instead, a trail of blood splatters led to the opening of the crevice and out into the snow.

It was snowing heavily now, mixed with icy bullets of sleet. The wind screamed off the glacier, shoved me backward, and froze my wet dress to my body. I had to find Arsenault. But the falling, blowing snow soon covered the blood trail and I was lost in a swirl of blinding, stinging whiteness.

There was no up and no down in a storm like this. In the High Peaks, any step might send me plunging to my death, but I could barely see my own feet. I forced myself to think because if I didn't neither of us would have a chance at survival. I thought we would be on the southeast shore of the lake, which meant if I looped around to my right, I would find the road again, before it tracked onto the bridge. Because I was on the lake shore, it ought to be fairly level, so there was less chance of falling into a ravine or off a cliff.

My fear for Arsenault threatened to overwhelm me. Tavi's shot had blown a hole in his chest, just below his heart. At the very least he would have broken ribs. And unless he stopped bleeding soon, he'd die. Or freeze in the storm.

What in all the hells had he been thinking?

"Dammit," I said, then louder, "Arsenault! ARSENAULT!"

There was no answer.

And then, a faint jangling.

I ran in the direction of the sound, stumbling, tripping on the godsdamned dress, clawing my way uphill. By the time I made it, I was out of strength and shivering so badly I could barely walk. I kept falling onto my knees and my vision began to gray.

The jangling sound was louder now. I hurled myself up the last bit of slope, onto the road.

Two horses materialized like wraiths out of the whiteness. I didn't have the strength to get out of the way and instead threw my arms over my head and curled up in a ball, hoping they would leap over me.

"Ho!" a voice called. Horses squealed as their riders pulled them up fast. Their hooves skidded to a stop not far from my body. I hoped to all the gods it was Lobardin and Cassis. I'd never expected to want to see Cassis as much as I did now. I hoped Arsenault had made it back to them, but a cold feeling was growing in the pit of my stomach —far colder than the ice trying to burrow its way into my flesh.

Gunshot wounds like that killed.

Would he really die since he was on a reprieve from his sentence? Or would the gods lock him into his shackles again, so that when he awoke, he would forget me and all that I meant to him, the scar on his hand erased to a nearly invisible line like the other two he'd shown me?

Snow and rocks crunched as one of the riders threw himself off his horse. I lowered my arms. All I could see were the rider's boots. I looked up, expecting to see trousers shoved into the uppers. Instead, a Qalfan man squatted before me, dressed in heavy Nezari robes and a thick black coat trimmed in silver and belted with a sash. He wore his urqa wrapped tightly around his head and a hood lined with sheep's wool over it.

His eyes widened in surprise when he saw me. He shot back to his feet and rapidly shed his coat. With his right hand, he pulled down his left sleeve and I got a shock. Instead of a hand, he had a hook.

He dropped back to his knee and wrapped me in the coat, using the hook to keep his balance. He rose again and pulled his urqa down over his mouth.

"Nibas!" he shouted over the gale. "It's a woman! Maybe from that carriage on the bridge!"

My thoughts moved slowly. *Nibas*, I thought. *I know a Nibas, too...*

The other rider dismounted and bent to peer at me. He was similarly bundled up, the lower half of his face wrapped in a black scarf, the hood of his coat hiding what was surely a mass of Tiresian beaded braids tied off at the nape of his neck. I jerked in surprise. The coat slid off my shoulders and I reached up with my right hand to pull it back up.

He stared at my hand. His dark brown eyes grew round and wide.

Nibas. Dear gods, is it...

"By the Magnificent Sun!" the Qalfan man exclaimed. "*Kyris*? Is that you?"

"Razi?" I said in wonder.

So they *had* been headed north, just like Nibas had been threatening for months. Nibas had taken Razi out of Lieran territory back to somewhere he knew the lay of the land and could make some money. I'd gambled that the visions I'd Seen were true, hoped they'd end up at Illichnaya, which wasn't far. I'd directed Arsenault to the first pass on purpose. But this *had* to be Ekyra's work.

Joy and gratitude surged within me, but they were emotions provoked by desperation and fear. I struggled to climb to my feet, and almost fell. Nibas caught me. "Thank the gods," I said. "I'm looking for a man. He's hurt, lost—"

I realized I didn't know where Tavi was either. Had Arsenault gone back to take care of him for good?

That was likely, the bastard. He probably thought he needed to keep Tavi away from me, damn him.

Razi and Nibas were still staring at me, dumbfounded. In another situation, I would have been worried that Razi and Nibas—whom I had fought with and drank with and trusted, but who only knew me as the male gavaro *Kyris*—were seeing me dressed as a woman. But not now. My teeth began to chatter again.

"L-l-look, I need to get out of these r-r-ridiculous c-clothes. I'll explain later. But I'm looking for a man. He's b-been sh-sh-shot."

"Shot?" Razi said. "Was it bandits? We found a carriage on the bridge. Looked like a fight, but there wasn't anybody—" He stopped and stared at me. "Did you go over the bridge, Kyris?"

"Y-yes. And Ar-Arsenault, too. I have to find him, dammit. Have you seen him?"

Nibas frowned. "Arsenault. The Aliente captain you were looking for?"

"I f-found him. And lost him. Dammit, Nibas!"

"We've been all over here, Kyris. We found only you. A broken bridge, a carriage, no horses. If he was here, he's gone now."

"He's probably down by the lake—"

"Going down there in this storm would be suicide, Kyris."

"But—"

"You'll freeze to death in that fucking dress if we stay out here much longer," Razi said, sweeping his gaze over me again. "And if we stay out here talking, we won't make it back either. Come *on*, Kyris. Maybe your captain found a horse and made for the hold."

I wanted to argue, to put up a fight. But I was so, so cold. And maybe Razi was right. Maybe Arsenault had found a horse. Maybe Lobardin and Cassis had found him. Or Tomas. Maybe Tomas had found Arsenault and run for Illichnaya like I'd told him to.

Razi put his arm around my shoulders and pulled me, not ungently, toward his horse.

I went with him, wracked with huge shivers and a pain in my heart that was much, much worse.

CHAPTER 97

ARSENAULT

He wasn't going to make it.

Should have stayed with Kyrra. Died beside her. Holding her.

But all he had been thinking about was making sure Tavi didn't find her again.

He wove through the snow, gasping for breath like a drowning man, blood still leaking through his shirt. His clothes had frozen into stiff folds that crackled like icicles when he stumbled and fell. He'd gotten turned around somewhere, but maybe if he headed to his left...

His legs had stopped working. He couldn't get up. He panicked, wheezing with the effort of breathing, feeling like he had the lake in his lungs, suffocating him, though it was probably blood.

He managed to open his right hand. He gazed at the newest scar that stretched, still pink, across his palm.

His heart sped up, but he had nowhere to go.

Just down. Into the soft, soft snow.

EPILOGUE

"Mikelo."

Mikelo, wake up.

Mikelo opened his eyes. He lay in a bed with sunlight streaming in the window. A man with curly hair the color of fine brandy leaned over him, his dark blue eyes shadowed with concern, handsome features pulled tight with worry.

Silva.

"Take some water, Mikelo, please."

Mikelo tried to sit up against the pillows but barely managed to lift his head. His body ached all over. He felt hot and cold at the same time. He was wrapped in bandages and drenched with sweat and someone had splinted his ankle.

Silva wasn't the only person in the room. There were many more people.

Jon Barra stood behind Silva, wearing a traditional Dakkaran tunic of crimson silk shot through with burgundy threads, the rosewood hilt of his curved knife sticking up through the sash at his waist.

Driese di Caprine wasn't wearing any disguises now. Instead, she wore a gown of dark Caprine green silk and her head was bare, her brassy brown hair pinned with two golden combs at the back of her head. Her gavaro was here, too, the Qalfan man with the heavy black brows and the sparkle of silver at his temples.

And, congregated at the door, Guin, the man he'd saved, the pirate captain Etranée, Renzo di Prinze, and a Dakkaran man and woman he didn't know, both wearing crimson B'ara tunics and a lot of gold.

"Is he awake now?" the Dakkaran woman asked. "In his right mind?"

"I don't know, Adayze," Jon said. "Why don't you ask him?"

Now that he saw her up close, she bore some resemblance to Jon. The few silver threads that twisted through her black locs were the only sign that hinted at her age. The tall, broad man who stood next to her was younger, his skin a deeper walnut color, and the way he rubbed his short, sparse beard gave him a marked resemblance to Jon.

"Well?" Adayze said. "Are you awake?"

"I don't know you," Mikelo croaked.

Silva sighed and sat back in his seat. "He is awake. Finally."

She smiled. "I am the Lady Adayze dom B'ara, the rightful Ibuu of the Dakkar. And this is my son, Edo. I am pleased to meet you, Mikelo di Prinze. I hear you are a very powerful Fixer."

He tried to shrug. The bindings around his chest and the healing wound beneath pulled tight, and he winced instead. He vaguely remembered healing Guin. Then they had fallen into a tomb, and...

And.

He didn't remember anything after that.

"What happened?" he asked.

"You saved me, is what happened," Silva said. "We were in the tomb with Geoffre's ghost, and then there was a bright light and you dragged Geoffre's ghost into it. Oji and Driese pulled Guin and me out of the tomb—Oji healed my leg—but you were just—Mikelo, you were *gone*. No one could find you anywhere. Then suddenly, you *appeared* again—fell onto the floor inside Jon's house. Oji healed you, too."

"You've been wandering around Liera, haven't you?" the Qalfan man said. Was his name Oji? That didn't sound right, but he couldn't remember...

Mikelo nodded, although those memories were murky, too. Wandering around Liera... The canals with their trash... The dirty lagoon...

"That cut on your chest was infected. And the gods only know what other fevers you contracted. But hopefully you're on the mend now."

"How many days?" he asked.

"Eight," Silva said.

"Why are you all in my room?"

"Because," Jon said with a troubled frown, "your cousin Cassis has apparently disappeared without a trace, the Empirists say they have papers showing Kyrra d'Aliente is alive and Cassis pardoned her and married her, and Devid di Prinze is claiming Cassis's disappearance a victory and signing accords to bring in Qalfan soldiers as we speak. Most of the Houses are ready to rebel. More householders are standing outside."

"Why?"

"To declare you the official Householder of House di Prinze, of course. Silva neglected to mention that you fell into a room full of diplomats wearing the Prinze sword."

Sit up, Mikelo, a voice in his head said. *This is your chance. No one needs to know that sword is a fake.*

The voice made him uncomfortable. He wasn't sure he ought to do what it said. He had wanted to be Householder once, but...

No, don't do it. Go back down into your fevers, Mikelo. Anything but this. Wait for Kyrra and Arsenault.

He was confused. Why were there two voices in his head? He frowned, looking around at the faces in the room—faces that all seemed to be concerned for him, faces he was sure he should know...

Who was that man with the dark blue eyes again?

"Mikelo, are you sure you're feeling well enough for this?" the man murmured, leaning over him. "I'll kick everyone out for you, no problem. You deserve to take your time."

Silva, Silva, Silva, the other voice in Mikelo's head all but shouted. *SILVA!*

Mikelo pushed it aside. "No," he said. "I feel fine. Let them all in. I'll take the Seat."

Silva gave him a troubled glance but went to open the door. When he did, Mikelo glanced to the side and noticed a mirror sitting on the nightstand.

Funny.

His eyes seemed much bluer than they ever had before.

⁂

THE TRIBUNAL OF THE GODS WAS IN AN UPROAR.

Arsenault knelt on one knee in the center of the circle, in his usual stance, while the gods argued about him. He felt like his muscles were made from wires, wound so tightly they would snap if the gods didn't come to a decision soon. They were arguing about whether to let him die, finally. Whether his reprieve meant his sentence no longer applied at this moment.

Some of the gods voted to let him die, others said he hadn't served out his sentence. Erelf surprised everyone by voting for death and the wires inside Arsenault felt like they were crushing his bones.

So, this was it? He'd finally gotten what he wanted and it meant he'd failed Kyrra.

But then Ekyra stood. "Ari," she said. "What do you want?"

Arsenault raised his head. His heart had stopped its hammering only to burn. He felt like he was being roasted alive. The taste of ashes and dirt filled his mouth. The taste of death, despair—defeat.

"Will it matter what I answer? Or is Fortune asking?"

"I would grant him a boon," Ekyra said—not to him, but to her fellow gods. "Because he pleases me. One favor."

Tekus shifted on his throne. He looked troubled, though he'd propped his head on his fist and rested his elbow on the broad, curving bones that formed the arm of his chair. Like he was trying to maintain a façade of boredom. "And what favor would that be, daughter?"

"To choose his fate, this once."

Her words were like lighting a fuse. All the gods fell silent, stunned. Tekus straightened in his chair, his black-kelp hair slipping back over his shoulder. Erelf gripped his hat so tightly it looked as if he would rip it in two.

"A choice?" he seethed. "He's a criminal, he doesn't deserve a *choice*—"

Tekus waved his hand for silence. Erelf gritted his teeth.

"No," Tekus said. "This is fair. Ari has been released from your vengeance for the time being and such a favor is within Fortune's power to grant. Go on, daughter."

Erelf looked murder at Tekus, like he wanted to run him through with the sword that hung at his side. But he'd existed in his role as the exiled son long enough to know he was only one step away from Ires's fate if he pushed too hard. His knuckles went white, but all he could do was fume.

Ekyra let a small, enigmatic smile play across her lips as she turned back to Arsenault. "Choose well, Ari, because your choice will be permanent. Do you choose death and freedom from your sentence, or will you return and submit again to your fetters?"

Arsenault looked over the circle of gods' faces, each of them terrible and beautiful. His gaze snagged for a moment on Erelf with his scar, glaring at him, and then at Adalus, whose antlers had grown longer, almost to the point at which Erelf would kill him again.

Adalus, the god of sacrifices, stared back at him with calm gray eyes.

He could choose death. Go down to the underworld. Be reunited with everyone he loved who had gone before him. His parents. His children. Rie, the woman who had been so kind to him in Orienne. All the other friends and lovers he had encountered over the years.

He could finally lay down the burden of being Sella's failed protector. Truly and for all eternity let go.

He was so tired. For an instant, he was tempted. Then he opened his palm and looked at the scar.

"Send me back," he said.

Ekyra's smile grew. She inclined her head.

"So shall it be done. Good-bye, Ari. Until next time. And may that time be long."

He touched his forehead in salute and closed his eyes.

When he opened them, he was lying on the cold rock floor of a cave, covered in blankets, and two men he didn't know were sitting beside him.

He sat up fast, gasping for breath. The blankets pooled in his lap.

"Arsenault!" one of the men said. He had blue-black hair and reminded Arsenault of a raven. The other man was wearing a hat, but his handsome features seemed familiar... Arsenault got the feeling he hadn't liked him.

Whoever he was.

"Dear gods. Is that the way it happens every time?" the man with the black hair said. "That's damned unnerving. I thought for sure your corpse would begin to stink soon."

"Who are you?" Arsenault asked.

"You don't remember us?" the other man asked warily.

Arsenault concentrated. Vague images flitted across his mind—the black-haired man on a horse beside him, guarding silkhouses and fighting off bandits on a country estate; the other man in a city conservatory, in bathhouses, in a mountain cottage, on a bridge holding a gun...

And on the tails of those memories, a woman with long gold curls, eyes the color of blue silk, a wicked grin, and a defiant, determined tilt to her chin—loved so much the feeling escaped every word he could use to confine it.

Arsenault reached into his charred and torn tunic and pulled out a water-smeared sketch of a marriage bed. "If I knew you, I've forgotten your names," he said. "But if you know where Kyrra is, you'd better tell me now."

THANK YOU FOR READING!

I hope you enjoyed *Fool's Promise*. If you have a minute, please consider leaving a rating or short review. You may not think your review matters, but indie authors (like me) depend on readers like you to spread the word and help other readers discover our books. And I would love to know what you thought about this second book in the Eterean Empire series!

If you'd like more Eterean Empire content—including the free short story, "Roses in Winter", which follows Kyrra on her mission to avenge Markus Seroditch—you can sign up for my newsletter at angelaboord.com, where you'll also get book news, sneak peeks, and progress reports!

Kyrra and Arsenault's story will continue in Book 3, tentatively titled *Fool's Guard*. You can also read more about Kyrra's history as a gavaro in *Smuggler's Fortune,* in which she meets Razi and has a run-in with a ferret belonging to Nibas. And if you're curious about the island of Medeas and its dragons, you might like my novella *Dragonmeat,* about a woman trying to keep her disabled father alive under the repressive Eterean regime starving out her city to rid it of dragons.

AFTERWORD AND ACKNOWLEDGMENTS

"If you want to work on your art, work on your life."
—Anton Chekhov

This is my pandemic book.

It wasn't supposed to be. I sent it off for its initial editing in February of 2020. In March, the world ended. And thus began a rocky road to publication which would end up taking far, far longer than I expected.

We had a rough pandemic at my house. Much of the journey was reflected in the seemingly impossible problems I ran into while trying to revise the plot of this book. I had a vision of writing a book that didn't skip over the struggles of recovering from Fantasy Novel Trauma, but anyone who's had to deal with a serious health problem or chronic mental health issues knows that recovery can mostly be a slog. It doesn't happen dramatically, all at once, but in little daily pieces, and that's hard to convey in fiction. As I grappled with the book, my husband and I were navigating our own medical maze, trying to find answers to the serious and baffling symptoms of regression my youngest daughter with Down Syndrome was suffering. The bottom came when a speech therapist handed me an evaluation that put her receptive and expressive speech levels at around the age of a 1 month old. This was a far cry from the pre-pandemic four year old who liked to draw and sing to her stuffed animals and pretended to read books and shoot webs like Spiderman.

The stress at times was unbearable. Four hours of sleep a night became our average as the mystery disorder disrupted her sleep patterns and locked her in her body, unable to interact with us, to use her fingers to grip, to do almost anything she had done before. The pandemic meant that we waited for close to a year to make appointments with specialists only to be told that they wouldn't see her anyway. For a long time Arsenault felt stuck and so did I. It was hard to write a book about recovering from trauma and starting anew when every day seemed to bring another impossible struggle, with no end in sight.

By the time we began to see glimmers of hope, our lives had been turned upside down. Fortunately, in those darkest moments, we were finally able to find a few heroes who *did* listen to us and *were* able to help. Little by little, as we began to climb the mountain of recovery with my daughter (which we're still climbing), I also began to climb the mountain of recovery with Arsenault and Kyrra. In the summer of 2023, the problem with the plot that had kept me screeching to a halt finally broke free. I rewrote most of the middle of the book, in addition to Part 1 *again*, which I felt like I had been writing over and over again for eternity. I found myself writing forward with more and more excitement as the vision I'd had for the book *finally* started to come together.

So my first thank you goes to my friend Diane and the doctors and therapists who have been working so hard to bring Abby back. You give us all hope and I can't thank you enough for caring so much about my little girl.

If it weren't for Brandon Sanderson's creative writing lectures generously available for free on Youtube, you probably wouldn't be holding this book in your hands right now. So thank you, Mr. Sanderson, for helping me fix that plot problem and for reigniting my love of epic fantasy with your Stormlight Archive books, which I also read while I was feverishly revising *Fool's Promise*.

To all my early readers—thank you for braving a book that still had a lot of growing pains ahead of it. In particular, thank you to Nancy and Fiona for letting me know that Kyrra needed more to do; to Beth Hindmarch for her early editing which opened the door for Guin; to Krystle and Bjorn for reading all the way to the end of that first draft. To Salt and Sage for their excellent feedback on the past narrative in Dakkar.

To Connor, who read one of the middle, cyborg drafts—thank you for helping me regain some of my confidence in Arsenault.

For later draft help—thanks to Noah Sky for copy editing a book that needed a lot of line editing and still being invested in the narrative; to Isabelle Wagner for her enthusiasm while editing out about a million em-dashes and also for the comments about Kyrra/Ires fan-fic, which made me laugh; and to Adam for beta-reading the Part I that finally made it into the book.

To the DNF Crew—I feel privileged to have been able to weather the pandemic with y'all. It always helps to know you're just a whale emoji away.

Most importantly—to my family. Thank you to my kids for being enthusiastic supporters of my writing, even when dinner is late and the laundry isn't done, for passing my books along to your friends, and most of all, for being you. And to Andy—thank you for being my partner, in sickness and in health, in good times and bad, for the past thirty years.

Finally, to all of YOU reading this now—thank you for accompanying me on this journey, for all your comments and support, for being willing to spend your time with these characters in this world that has lived in my brain for so long. It means a lot.

—Angela

EXTRAS

FOR FURTHER READING

Confession: I love worldbuilding. I also love bibliographies, and I will happily sit and read them the way I read actual books. (I'm a cookbook reader, too, as if that's not completely evident by this point.) Since I'm often asked about the research that goes into building my stories, I thought I would share some of the sources that provided me with ideas for *Fool's Promise*.

A critic once famously called Guy Gavriel Kay's stories "history with a quarter turn to the fantastic". Mine are more like history making a sharp left turn, but I do take a lot of inspiration from the real world. My goal in building the universe of the Eterean Empire has always been to make it *feel* like a Mediterranean Renaissance world rather than to disguise actual historical events. That often means that the sources that inspire the story get thrown into the pot and eventually cook down in almost unrecognizable form to story soup. But for the most part, the sources I'm including are ones that have had a direct, traceable effect.

Mercenaries and Their Masters by Michael Mallett is the classic work on Italian condottieri. I actually didn't own a copy of this book when I wrote *Fortune's Fool*, for better or worse, but it was quite helpful in revising *Fool's Promise* and I will definitely come back to it in the future. It's an invaluable source for details of mercenary life, from how much mercenaries were paid to the problems caused by unemployed mercenaries free to move around both city and countryside (like Geoffre's).

The Renaissance was an interesting transition period between medieval and modern in a lot of ways, but one of the most applicable to my books is the area of warfare. The Italian Wars (1494-1559) were the first wars to use arquebusiers and mobile field artillery in an extensive way, and they forever changed the nature of warfare. I have a bunch of books I dip in and out of for inspiration in this area, including: *The Art of Renaissance Warfare* by Stephen Turnbull, *The Italian Wars 1494-1559* by Michael Mallett and Christine Shaw, *Firearms and Fortifications: Military Architecture and Siege Warfare in Sixteenth Century Siena* by Simon Pepper and Nicholas Adams, and *History and Warfare in Renaissance Epic* by Michael Murrin.

For galleys, *Galleons & Galleys* by John F. Guilmartin, Jr contains many excellent drawings, and for pirate raiding of humans—*Pirates of Barbary: Corsairs, Conquests, and Captivity in the Sixteenth Century Mediterranean* by Adrian Tinniswood helped me craft Arsenault's experience. I have to admit that the pirate battles probably owe most of their imagery to the many (many) times I've watched the (1998) Horatio Hornblower A&E miniseries, which was one of my oldest's favorite videos when he was young.

I did some reading on the medieval West African kingdoms of Ghana, Mali, and Songhai in order to write Arsenault's story in Dakkar. *African Dominion: A New History of Empire in Early and Medieval West Africa* by Michael A. Gomez was the most comprehensive, if a bit dry. *The Golden Rhinoceros: Histories of the African Middle Ages* by François-Xavier Fauvelle is another excellent (less dry) book with chapters you can dip in and out of. An excellent and concise introduction is *A Glorious Age in Africa: The Story of Three Great African Empires* by Daniel Chu and Elliott Skinner. *Sundiata: An Epic of Old Mali,* an oral epic written down in French by Djibril Tamsir Niane and translated into English by GD Pickett, is also, I think, essential. (Sorcery, shapeshifting, a disabled child who becomes king basically through an enormous effort of his own determination...and he was a real, historical person.) *The Ocean of Churn: How the Indian Ocean Shaped Human History* by Sanjeev Sanyal was a whirlwind description of the ancient Indian Ocean trade and it helped inspire the vibrant feeling I wanted to give Mdembu.

Adayze's situation with her suitors owes its inspiration to the *Odyssey*, and as I wrote Kyrra's new sections into the revision I found myself thinking quite a lot about Helen of Troy. I read two books by Natalie Haynes: *Divine Might: Goddesses in Greek Myth* and *Pandora's Jar: Women in Greek Myth* which helped me think about Kyrra and Sella's place in my Greco-Roman inspired mythos. For more on women's place and family life as having evolved from the Eterean Empire, an informative source was *Family and Marriage in the Middle Ages* by Frances and Joseph Gies, one of their classic medieval life books I'd somehow avoided reading in my Western Civ classes in college. I read a great paper online about the anthropology of gender and sexuality primarily focusing on the classical world—but alas, the Internet seems to have swallowed it.

The Eterean Empire itself is based somewhat more on the Etruscans than on ancient Rome, but the Etruscans unhelpfully left only a few tiny scraps of writing (literally, as the Etruscans wrote on linen and the most extensive piece of Etruscan was found wrapping a mummy in Egypt.) I did a lot of scrolling through dubious Internet sources to research Etruscan gods and goddesses, but if you search for "vanth", you'll turn up an Etruscan female figure with wings who is theorized to have guided souls to the underworld. I found some suggestions that seemed to indicate the figures can also be androgynous, so that's how I imagine Ires's vanth guards. Automata really are part of the ancient world, though; the Romans built machines using hydraulics, and if you don't mind an extremely interesting subject being unfairly dried out, the book *Gods and Robots: Myths, Machines, and Ancient Dreams of Technology* by Adrienne Mayor is a treasure trove.

Details about the books and antiquities trade came from two books: *The Swerve: How the World Became Modern* by Stephen Greenblatt which doesn't really spend much time telling how finding Lucretius's poem *On the Nature of Things* made the world modern, but does spin a fascinating account of the world of late medieval/Renaissance book hunters/collectors, who apparently had quite vicious rivalries (some things I just tuck away in my brain for later use). *The Medici Conspiracy: The Illicit Journey of Looted Antiquities* by Peter Watson and Cecilia Todeschini is a fascinating story of the modern black market in antiquities which moved millions of dollars in priceless artifacts from countries like Greece, Italy, Egypt and Iraq to collectors and Western museums.

Finally, Oji la Kaif owes his existence to the medieval Muslim explorers who wrote so many accounts of their travels—Ibn Battuta most famously, but also many, many more (See *Ibn Fadlān and the Land of Darkness* for a collection of accounts by "Arab Travellers in the Far North"). I was stuck figuring Oji out and then somehow I was led to read about Al-Khidr, an immortal traveler from Islamic legend, and everything suddenly clicked together.

Finally, the leaky roof of the farmhouse owes its existence to the hours of Youtube videos from Martjin Doolard and Raising Voyagers which my husband watched during the summer of 2023. There's just something soothing about watching other people do backbreaking labor to rescue stone houses in the Italian Alps...

DRAMATIS PERSONAE

- **Adayze dom B'ara**—de facto Ibuu in exile after the destruction of the royal family of Dakkar
- **Aleya**—chirurgeon wife of murdered gun smuggler Vadz
- **Alozh Vokavik**—Kavol general for hire, once a major figure in the wars between Rojornick and Kavo, now fighting for Devid di Prinze
- **Arsenault/Ari Gunnarsson**—Tulan gavaro, Fixer, spy with a cursed past
- **Banye**—member of the Ibuu's Palace Guard
- **Boucher**—Fariq's first mate on the Gannet
- **Cassis di Prinze**—Geoffre di Prinze's younger son, father to Kyrra's lost child
- **Chayma**—Adayze's healer, a powerful conjure woman
- **Devid di Prinze**—Geoffre di Prinze's older son, de facto heir to the House di Prinze
- **Dirik dom Arak**—heir to the Arak binding in Dakkar
- **Driese di Caprine**—mistress of Cassis di Prinze and sister to Tonia di Sere
- **Ekyra**—Goddess of fortune
- **Erelf**—God of magic/God of knowledge
- **Etranée Bizet**—notorious pirate of the Dakkaran coast, captain of the Good Fortune
- **Fillipo**—Miranda's older son
- **Geoffre di Prinze**—Former Householder of the House di Prinze

- **Guin**—Fixer, carpenter from the Outer Isles
- **Hani**—Miranda's younger son
- **Haq**—member of the Ibuu's Palace Guard
- **Ires**—insane God of War, imprisoned beneath the volcano Mount Kosemi
- **Isa dom Arak-B'ara**—Adayze's husband and diplomat for the B'ara
- **Jemma**—Jon Barra's wife, killed in the burning of Mdembu
- **Jon Barra/Jonawak dom B'ara**—member of the destroyed royal house of Dakkar, brother and Dagger to the current Ibuu in exile, Adayze dom Barra,
- **Junei**—Jon Barra's main contact in Cassis di Prinze's camp, liaison with Lobardin
- **Koji**—Etranée's bodyguard and first mate on the Good Fortune
- **Kyrra d'Aliente/Kyris di Nada**—deposed and disowned heir of the fallen House d'Aliente
- **Lobardin di Cozin**—banished youngest son of the powerful Amoran House di Cozin
- **Lupa**—Empirist scholar of ancient Eterean lore
- **Markus Seroditch**—Murdered Rojornicki lord of Illichnaya, whom Kyrra fought for as a gavaro during her years of exile
- **Miha la Hallad**—doctor aboard Fariq's galley *the Gannet*, father to Zim, famous Qalfan artificier
- **Mikelo di Prinze**—bastard Prinze son, Fixer, groomed by Geoffre as his choice for heir
- **Miranda**—conjure woman, owner of the house where Arsenault and Kyrra recover, Jon Barra's contact in the north country
- **Neyane dom B'ara**—the Ibuu's sister and Dagger, aunt to Adayze and Jon
- **Nibas**—Tiresian archer, friend, and former comrade-in-arms of Kyrra in Rojornick
- **Niki**—bartender of the Pepperpot Inn
- **Oji la Kaif**—famous writer, explorer, and scholar of the Eterean Empire
- **Omalade dom B'ara**—Jon and Adayze's mother, one of the Ibuu's wives

- **Promethi dom Arak**—brother to the heir of the Arak binding in Dakkar
- **Razi**—Qalfan gavaro, member of the elite Nezari sect of warriors, and friend of Kyrra
- **Renzo di Prinze**—Geoffre di Prinze's younger brother, supposedly lost in Dakkaran waters
- **Sandro**—Etranée's Qalfan-Lieran navigator on the Good Fortune
- **Seely**—Etranée's quartermaster on the Good Fortune
- **Sella**—Arsenault's murdered wife/Goddess of Sight
- **Silva**—former shepherd and courtesan whose family lived on Aliente lands
- **Tavi**—Arsenault's murdered brother
- **The Ibuu**—the old ruler of Dakkar, father of Jon and Adayze
- **Tomas**—Lupa's secretary
- **Tonia di Sere**—wife of murdered heir to the House di Sere, sister to Driese di Caprine
- **Trefan di Cozin**—one of Lobardin's older brothers sent to negotiate with Devid di Prinze
- **Yasi la Fariq**—Qalfan pirate captain dealing in the kidnapping and sale of galleymen
- **Yeo**—the Good Fortune's de facto chirurgeon
- **Zim la Hallad**—cabin boy aboard Fariq's galley the *Gannet*, son of Miha

MAJOR LIERAN HOUSES

Note: The final "e" is pronounced in all Eterean names, usually as /ay/, "r" is rolled, and "i" is generally pronounced /ee/.

- Aliente
- Caprine
- Forza
- Garonze
- Imisi
- Prinze
- Sere

ETEREAN GODS

- **Tekus**—Father God and god of the sea
- **Ahra**—wife to Tekus
- **Adalus**—son of Tekus, the Dying God; god of springtime, sacrifices, and harvest
- **Erelf**—exiled son of Tekus and brother to Adalus; god of knowledge, secrets, and magic
- **Ekyra**—daughter of Tekus; goddess of fortune, also called the Huntress
- **Ires**—insane god of war; shackled deep within the volcano Kosemi
- **Cythia**—daughter of Tekus; goddess of love
- **Pana**—daughter of Tekus; name means "willing".
- **Lusa**—daughter of Tekus; goddess of the moon
- **Sella**—Erelf's daughter; goddess of Sight

GLOSSARY

- **allaq**—Qalfan body robes falling to mid-calf, usually worn with trousers beneath.
- **arquebus**—long matchlock gun, comparable to a rifle.
- **astra**—gold coin minted by the Lieran Circle.
- **cato**—copper coin minted by the Lieran Circle, of lesser value than the astra.
- **conjure woman**—a woman experienced in the use of **conjure magic**, a variety of magic used specifically by women and having to do primarily with the body and fertility.
- **dikkarro**—a hand-held wheellock pistol, named for Dakkar, its country of invention.
- **dog**—the spring-loaded arm on a wheellock pistol that holds the pyrite. The dog rests on the cover of the pan that holds the powder. When the trigger is pulled, it opens the pan cover, the wheel rotates, and the pyrite comes into contact with the powder, igniting it.
- **Eter**—the language spoken and written by the ancient Etereans, who unified the peninsula and ruled an empire many hundreds of years before the story takes place.
- **eyi**—strategy game played in Dakkar based on dropping and collecting stones or seeds.
- **fila**—supernatural, godlike beings native to Dakkar.
- **Fixer**—a magic user who can use magic to **Shape** (or **Fix**) objects according to their will. Depending on the material a

Fixer operates upon, a Fixer may also be called an **Artisan** or a **Smith**.

- **galleyman**—a criminal sentenced to row Qalfan galleys for his crimes. In practice, galleymen were often innocent men kidnapped by pirates and sold to galleys using forged sentences to prove their "crimes".
- **gavaro**—a mercenary or sword-for-hire. Gavaros form the bulk of the fighting forces among the city-states of the Eterean peninsula. They are also hired as guards, assassins, bounty hunters, and debt collectors.
- **guarnello**—the common dress of peasant women in the Eterean peninsula. A long jumper worn over a lighter underdress. The bodice laces up to provide support in lieu of stays.
- **Head of House**—the lead householder of a House, who makes decisions and rules everyone of that House name.
- **High Peaks**—the highest peaks in the Irondels, on the border of Rojornick and Liera.
- **householder**—any member of the noble Houses of the Eterean peninsula. When capitalized (**Householder**) this refers to the Head of House.
- **Ibuu**—the ruler of Dakkar, male or female.
- **imya**—clear liquor imported from Rojornick.
- **indij**—card game favored by gavaros in which the jester is the strongest card.
- **kacin**—powdery, white drug formed by drying and grinding berries from a plant grown in Dakkar. Can be smoked or taken orally. Induces sleepiness, functions as a pain killer. Addictive. The leaves of the plant can be chewed for a milder effect.
- **kai dahn**—dice game imported from Saien and favored by sailors.
- **Messera/messera**—In its capitalized form, the title for the first wife of the Head of House. Uncapitalized, it functions as an honorific for any married female householder. (Equivalent of "mistress")
- **Mestere/mestere**—In its capitalized form, the title for the Head of House. Uncapitalized, it functions as an honorific for any male householder. (Equivalent of "master")

- **Mistiri/mistiri**—the plural form for the man and woman who are Head of House, or, uncapitalized, householders in general. (Equivalent of "masters").
- **Nezar/Nezari**—member or members of an elite Qalfan fighting order who often hire out as mercenaries.
- **sanval**—the spring wind from the south that often brings violent storms; also the storms the wind brings.
- **See/Sight**—the magical ability to see the truth or underlying nature of people or things. Not always able to be controlled.
- **ser**—honorific for male members of the free merchant class, who are neither nobles or serfs.
- **sera**—honorific for female members of the free merchant class, who are neither nobles or serfs.
- **Spice Road**—northern overland trade route to Saien, Qalfa, and Dakkar.
- **sontana**—afternoon nap.
- **sweetweed**—mild drug imported by Qalfans, usually smoked.
- **Thunder Cape**—a vicious whirlpool of magic blocking the northern sea route to Dakkar, rumored to be caused by a giant sea serpent.
- **urqa**—the headcloths used by Qalfans, especially men, to cover their heads and faces.
- **vota**—religious artifact, usually carved of wood and imbued with life-like attributes by conjure magic. Used in religious ceremonies in place of live sacrifices or to satisfy different needs of the owner – luck, health, love, etc.

ABOUT THE AUTHOR

Angela Boord is a hopeless romantic, a nerdy introvert, and the author of SPFBO5 Finalist FORTUNE'S FOOL. She can usually be found with her nose in a book when she's not writing her own dark fantasy epics of hope, redemption, and relationships in all their messy glory. Angela and her husband live in northern Mississippi in a house full of children, books, and innumerable quantities of Legos.

Subscribe to Angela's mailing list at Angelaboord.com for free short stories and a peek into her writing process!

ALSO BY ANGELA BOORD

ETEREAN EMPIRE

Fortune's Fool, Eterean Empire #1

Smuggler's Fortune

Dragonmeat

RAI ASCENDANT

Through Dreams So Dark

INCLUDED IN

The Alchemy of Sorrow